The
WarCraft®
Archive

THE
WARCRAFT®
ARCHIVE

RICHARD A. KNAAK
CHRISTIE GOLDEN
JEFF GRUBB
CHRIS METZEN

POCKET BOOKS

NEW YORK LONDON TORONTO SYDNEY

POCKET BOOKS, a division of Simon & Schuster, Inc.
1230 Avenue of the Americas, New York, NY 10020

ISBN-13: 978-1-4165-2582-0
ISBN-10:   1-4165-2582-3

This Pocket Books trade paperback edition November 2006

10 9 8

POCKET and colophon are registered trademarks of Simon & Schuster, Inc.

Cover art by Glenn Rane

Manufactured in the United States of America

For information regarding special discounts for bulk
purchases, please contact Simon & Schuster Special Sales
at 1-800-456-6798 or business@simonandschuster.com.

CONTENTS

INTRODUCTION

It all started one quiet afternoon, a little over six years ago. I was sitting at my desk, slogging through the campaign script for a little game called *Warcraft 3: Reign of Chaos*—when the phone rang. Common enough, right?

"*What up*, this is Metzen."

"Hello, Chris—this is Richard Knaak calling. I wanted to talk with you about possibly writing a novel based on Warcraft."

. . .

"*Chris, are you there?*"

Yeah, I was there all right—flat on the floor. Dumbstruck. Mind-blown. Geek-factor redlining. This couldn't possibly be THE Richard Knaak, right? *Mr.* Dragonlance? The creator of Huma, Magus, and Kaz? The writer that I'd been reading since I was in the eight grade? *Indeed it was.* And as I came to my senses and started jamming with the man, I had what most geeks can only refer to as a *nerd-epiphany*. I knew then—that fateful phone call wasn't just the spark of a single licensed novel—but the genesis of a series of imaginative collaborations that would redefine the scope and spirit of the Warcraft setting.

After about twenty minutes of me shouting things like "*I'm not worthy! I'm not worthy!*" into the phone, Richard and I finally began to jam on the concept that would become *Day of the Dragon*. Given his mastery of dragon-related tales, we agreed that expanding the role of dragons in the Warcraft setting would be a great direction. Between us, we fleshed out the idea of the five dragon Aspects and the history of the dragon flights. Richard found a way to weave the dragons' lore into the fabric of Azeroth's war-torn history while making it feel as if it had always been there from the start.

Day of the Dragon was the first in Pocket Books' line of novels based upon Blizzard's keystone game universes—Warcraft, StarCraft, and Diablo—and it quickly set the high watermark for every book that would follow. Needless to say, Richard hit it out of the park—and I was curious to see how he'd handle stories set in our other game worlds. As of this writing, Richard has penned eight Blizzard novels—including the Warcraft: War of the Ancients trilogy— as well as a Warcraft Manga series published through Tokyopop. He claims he's just getting started.

For the second Warcraft book, I suggested novelizing the plotline of the ill-fated Warcraft Adventure Game that had been cancelled some years before. The rough plotline of *Lord of the Clans* focused on the young orc, Thrall, and his quest to redeem his people from the bonds of corruption. Thrall's tale was very close to my heart and I knew we needed someone *mighty* to bring the story to life. With the clock ticking, Pocket editor Marco Palmieri brought in ace-writer Christie Golden to take a crack at the book. Given that Christie was best known for her *Star Trek* novels, I had to ask:

"Marco, c'mon—what does a *Star Trek* writer know about orcs anyway?"

"Chris, trust me on this."

Well, it turns out that Christie is both fast and brilliant, my friends. She took my loose plot notes for the game and transformed them into a smart, heartfelt tale of honor, loss and redemption. She seemed to have an immediate affinity for the orcs—and knew how to balance their brutal warrior exteriors with the noble hearts beating within. I knew it would be difficult to turn orcs into heroes. Christie made it look easy.

As a encore to *Lord of the Clans*, Christie recently finished the manuscript for *Rise of the Horde*—the tale of how the orcs first fell victim to their terrible curse. Believe me when I say, it's totally epic. I can't wait to see what else Christie has to say about our wayward orcs and their expanding role within the Warcraft setting.

Following *Lord of the Clans*, I wanted to give fans a look into the events surrounding the first Warcraft game—and show how the orcs and humans first came into conflict. While we had a rough idea for the tale, *The Last Guardian* didn't really take shape until uber-genius Jeff Grubb came aboard. As a fan of *Dungeons & Dragons* and the various TSR worlds that had popped up over the years, I was pretty familiar with Jeff's work as both a writer and an RPG designer. Needless to say, it was a huge honor to jam with Jeff and watch as he turned Medivh's fall from grace into a stirring tragedy that perfectly captured the terror and destruction that marked the orcs' arrival on Azeroth.

While all this was going on, Marco had a crazy idea to publish a series of eBooks based on Blizzard's game properties. Being young and stupid, I jumped at the chance to churn out some Warcraft fiction of my own. The intent was to create a Warcraft story that spoke to the very essence of what orcs and humans *are*—and how each race has equal capacity to behave like *monsters*. In deference to those readers who actually downloaded *Of Blood and Honor* from the internet (I LOVE you guys, whoever you are!), I can't express how excited I am to see this story in real print.

In fact, it's pretty amazing to see all these books bound as a single archive edition. It's wild to see how far we've come in six short years—and to see how huge the Warcraft setting has become around the world. If you haven't read these tales before, I hope you enjoy them as much as I have. Each of them is a unique window into an ever-evolving world—and the imaginative collaborations that gave it form.

Chris Metzen
Vice President, Creative Development
Blizzard Entertainment
June, 2006

Day of
the Dragon

RICHARD A. KNAAK

About the Author

RICHARD A. KNAAK is the *New York Times* bestselling author of more than thirty fantasy novels and over a dozen short pieces, including *The Legend of Huma* for the Dragonlance series and the epic *War of the Ancients* saga for *Warcraft*. Aside from his extensive work in *Warcraft*, *Diablo*, and *Dragonlance*, he is also known for his popular *Dragonrealm* series, which includes ten novels and six online novellas, and the *Sunwell Trilogy*, a *Warcraft* manga published by Tokyopop. His *Aquilonia* trilogy, based on the world of Robert E. Howard's *Conan*, is now coming out in print from Penguin/Ace. Currently, he is at work on the second and third volumes of the epic *Diablo: The Sin War*, the first novel in his *Ogre Titans* saga—the followup to his *Minotaur Wars*—plus other projects.

Those interested in learning more about his work should join his e-mail list by contact him at his website www.sff.net/people/knaak.

ONE

War.

It had once seemed to some of the Kirin Tor, the magical conclave that ruled the small nation of Dalaran, that the world of Azeroth had never known anything but constant bloodshed. There had been the trolls, before the forming of the Alliance of Lordaeron, and when at last humanity had dealt with that foul menace, the first wave of orcs had descended upon the lands, appearing out of a horrific rip in the very fabric of the universe. At first, nothing had seemed able to stop these grotesque invaders, but gradually what had looked to be a horrible slaughter had turned instead into an agonizing stalemate. Battles had been won by attrition. Hundreds had died on both sides, all seemingly for no good reason. For years, the Kirin Tor had foreseen no end.

But that had finally changed. The Alliance had at last managed to push back the Horde, eventually routing them entirely. Even the orcs' great chieftain, the legendary Orgrim Doomhammer, had been unable to stem the advancing armies and had finally capitulated. With the exception of a few renegade clans, the surviving invaders had been rounded up into enclaves and kept under secure watch by military units led personally by members of the Knights of the Silver Hand. For the first time in many, many years, lasting peace looked to be a promise, not a faint wish.

And yet . . . a sense of unease still touched the senior council of the Kirin Tor. Thus it was that the highest of the high met in the Chamber of the Air, so-called because it seemed a room without walls, only a vast, ever-changing sky with clouds, light, and darkness, racing past the master wizards as if the time of the world had sped up. Only the gray, stone floor with its gleaming diamond symbol, representing the four elements, gave any solidity to the scene.

Certainly the wizards themselves did nothing in that regard, for they, clad in their dark cloaks that covered not only face but form, seemed to waver with the movements of the sky, almost as if they, too, were but illusion. Although their numbers included both men and women, the only sign of that was whenever one of them spoke, at which point a face would become partially visible, if somewhat indistinct in detail.

There were six this meeting, the six most senior, although not necessarily the most gifted. The leaders of the Kirin Tor were chosen by several means, magic but one of them.

"Something is happening in Khaz Modan," announced the first in a stentorian voice, the vague image of a bearded face briefly visible. A myriad pattern of stars floated through his body. "Near or in the caverns held by the Dragonmaw clan."

"Tell us something we don't already know," rasped the second, a woman likely of elder years but still strong of will. A moon briefly shone through her cowl. "The orcs there remain one of the few holdouts, now that Doomhammer's warriors have surrendered and the chieftain's gone missing."

The first mage clearly took some umbrage, but he kept himself calm as he replied. "Very well! Perhaps this will interest you more. . . . I believe Deathwing is on the move again."

This startled the rest, the elder woman included. Night suddenly changed into day, but the wizards ignored what, for them, was a common thing in this chamber. Clouds drifted past the head of the third of their number, who clearly did not believe this statement.

"Deathwing is dead!" the third declared, his form the only one hinting at corpulence. "He plunged into the sea months ago after this very council and a gathering of our strongest struck the mortal blow! No dragon, even him, could withstand such might!"

Some of the others nodded, but the first went on. "And where was the corpse? Deathwing was like no other dragon. Even before the goblins sealed the adamantium plates to his scaly hide, he offered a threat with the potential to dwarf that of the Horde. . . ."

"But what proof do you have of his continued existence?" This from a young woman clearly in the bloom of youth. Not as experienced as the others, but still powerful enough to be one of the council. "What?"

"The death of two red dragons, two of Alexstrasza's get. Torn asunder in a manner only one of their own kind—one of gargantuan proportions—could have managed."

"There are other large dragons."

A storm began to rage, the lightning and rain falling upon the wizards and yet touching neither them nor the floor. The storm passed in the blink of an eye, a blazing sun once more appearing overhead. The first of the Kirin Tor gave this latest display not even the least of his interest. "You have obviously never seen the work of Deathwing, or you'd never make that statement."

"It may be as you say," interjected the fifth, the outline of a vaguely elven visage appearing and disappearing faster than the storm. "And, if so, a matter of import. But we hardly can concern ourselves with it for now. If Deathwing lives and now strikes out at his greatest rival's kind, then it only benefits us. After all, Alexstrasza is still the captive of Dragonmaw clan, and it is her off-spring that those orcs have used for years to wreak bloodshed and havoc all over the Alliance. Have we all so soon forgotten the tragedy of the Third Fleet of Kul Tiras? I suspect that Lord Admiral Daelin Proudmoore never will. After all, he lost his eldest son and everyone else aboard those six great ships when the monstrous red leviathans fell upon them. Proudmoore would likely honor Deathwing with a medal if it proved true that the black beast was responsible for these two deaths."

No one argued that point, not even the first mage. Of the mighty vessels, only splinters of wood and a few torn corpses had been left to mark the utter destruction. It had been to Lord Admiral Proudmoore's credit that he had not faltered in his resolve, immediately ordering the building of new warships to replace those destroyed and pushing on with the war.

"And, as I stated earlier, we can hardly concern ourselves with that situa-tion now, not with so many more immediate issues with which to deal."

"You're referring to the Alterac crisis, aren't you?" rumbled the bearded mage. "Why should the continued sniping of Lordaeron and Stromgarde worry us more than Deathwing's possible return?"

"Because now Gilneas has thrown its weight into the situation."

Again the other mages stirred, even the unspeaking sixth. The slightly cor-pulent shade moved a step toward the elven form. "Of what interest is the bickering of the other two kingdoms over that sorry piece of land to Genn Greymane? Gilneas is at the tip of the southern peninsula, as far away in the Alliance as any other kingdom is from Alterac!"

"You have to ask? Greymane has always sought the leadership of the Alliance, even though he held back his armies until the orcs finally attacked his own borders. The only reason he ever encouraged King Terenas of Lor-daeron to action was to weaken Lordaeron's military might. Now Terenas maintains his hold on the Alliance leadership mostly because of our work and Admiral Proudmoore's open support."

Alterac and Stromgarde were neighboring kingdoms that had been at odds since the first days of the war. Thoras Trollbane had thrown the full might of Stromgarde behind the Lordaeron Alliance. With Khaz Modan as its neighbor, it had only made sense for the mountainous kingdom to support a united action. None could argue with the determination of Trollbane's war-riors, either. If not for them, the orcs would have overrun much of the Alliance during the first weeks of the war, certainly promising a different and highly grim outcome overall.

Alterac, on the other hand, while speaking much of the courage and right-eousness of the cause, had not been so forthcoming with its own troops. Like

Gilneas, it had provided only token support; but, where Genn Greymane had held back out of ambition, Lord Perenolde, so it had been rumored, had done so because of fear. Even among the Kirin Tor it had early on been asked whether Perenolde had thought to perhaps make a deal with Doomhammer, should the Alliance crumble under the Horde's unceasing onslaught.

That fear had proven to have merit. Perenolde had indeed betrayed the Alliance, but his dastardly act had, fortunately, been short-lived. Terenas, hearing of it, had quickly moved Lordaeron troops in and declared martial law in Alterac. With the war in progress, no one had, at the time, seen fit to complain over such an action, especially Stromgarde. Now that peace had come, Thoras Trollbane had begun to demand that, for its sacrifices, Stromgarde should receive as just due the entire eastern portion of its treacherous former neighbor.

Terenas did not see it so. He still debated the merits of either annexing Alterac to his own kingdom or setting upon its throne a new and more reasonable monarch . . . presumably with a sympathetic ear for Lordaeron causes. Still, Stromgarde had been a loyal, steadfast ally in the struggle, and all knew of Thoras Trollbane's and Terenas's admiration for one another. It made the political situation that had come between the pair all the more sad.

Gilneas, meanwhile, had no such ties to any of the lands involved; it had always remained separate from the other nations of the western world. Both the Kirin Tor and King Terenas knew that Genn Greymane sought to intervene not only to raise his own prestige, but to perhaps further his dreams of expansion. One of Lord Perenolde's nephews had fled to that land after the treachery, and rumor had it that Greymane supported his claim as successor. A base in Alterac would give Gilneas access to resources the southern kingdom did not have, and the excuse to send its mighty ships across the Great Sea. That, in turn, would draw Kul Tiras into the equation, the maritime nation being very protective of its naval sovereignty.

"This will tear the Alliance apart. . . ." muttered the young mage with the accent.

"It has not come to that point yet," pointed out the elven wizard, "but it may soon. And so we have no time to deal with dragons. If Deathwing lives and has chosen to renew his vendetta against Alexstrasza, I, for one, will not oppose him. The fewer dragons in this world the better. Their day is done, after all."

"I have heard," came a voice with no inflection, no identifiable gender, "that once the elves and dragons were allies, even respected friends."

The elven form turned to the last of the mages, a slim, lanky shape little more than shadow. "Tales only, I can assure you. We would not deign to traffic with such monstrous beasts."

Clouds and sun gave way to stars and moon. The sixth mage bowed slightly, as if in apology. "I appear to have heard wrong. My mistake."

"You're right about the importance of calming this political situation down," the bearded wizard rumbled to the fifth. "And I agree it must take priority. Still, we can't afford to ignore what is happening around Khaz Modan! Whether or not I'm wrong about Deathwing, so long as the orcs there hold the Dragonqueen captive, they're a threat to the stability of the land!"

"We need an observer, then," interjected the elder female. "Someone to maintain watch on matters and only alert us if the situation there becomes critical."

"But who? We can spare no one now!"

"There is one." The sixth mage glided a step forward. The face remained in shadow even when the figure spoke. "There is Rhonin. . . ."

"Rhonin?!?" burst out the bearded mage. "Rhonin! After his last debacle? He isn't even fit to wear the robes of a wizard! He's more of a danger than a hope!"

"He's unstable," agreed the elder woman.

"A maverick," muttered the corpulent one.

"Untrustworthy . . ."

"Criminal!"

The sixth waited until all had spoken, then slowly nodded. "And the only skilled wizard we can afford to be without at this juncture. Besides, this is simply a mission of observance. He will be nowhere near any potential crisis. His duty will be to monitor matters and report back, that is all." When no more protests arose, the dark mage added, "I am certain that he has learned his lesson."

"Let us hope so," muttered the older of the women. "He may have accomplished his last mission, but it cost most of his companions their lives!"

"This time, he will go alone, with only a guide to bring him to the edge of Alliance-controlled lands. He shall not even enter Khaz Modan. A sphere of seeing will enable him to watch from a distance."

"It seems simple enough," the younger female responded. "Even for Rhonin."

The elven figure nodded brusquely. "Then let us agree on this and be done with the topic. Perhaps if we are fortunate, Deathwing will swallow Rhonin, then choke to death, thus finishing forever the matters of both." He surveyed the others, then added, "And now I must demand that we finally concentrate on Gilneas's entry into the Alterac situation and what role we may play to diffuse it. . . ."

He stood as he had for the past two hours, head down, eyes closed in concentration. Around him, only a dim light with no source gave any illumination to the chamber, not that there was much to see. A chair he had left unused stood to the side, and behind him on the thick, stone wall hung a tapestry upon which had been sewn an intricate, knowing eye of gold on a field of violet. Below the eye, three daggers, also gold, darted earthward. The flag and symbols of Dalaran had stood tall in their guardianship of the Alliance during the war, even if not every member of the Kirin Tor had performed their duties with complete honor.

"Rhonin . . ." came a voice without inflection, from everywhere and nowhere in the chamber.

From under thick, fiery hair, he looked up into the darkness with eyes a startling green. His nose had been broken once by a fellow apprentice, but despite his skills, Rhonin had never bothered to have it fixed. Still, he was not unhandsome, with a strong, clean jaw and angular features. One permanently arched brow ever gave him a sardonic, questioning look that had more than once gotten him in trouble with his masters, and matters were not helped by his attitude, which matched his expression.

Tall, slim, and clad in an elegant robe of midnight blue, he made for quite a sight, even to other wizards. Rhonin hardly appeared recalcitrant, even though his last mission had cost the lives of five good men. He stood straight and eyed the murk, waiting to see from which direction the other wizard would speak to him.

"You summoned. I've waited," the crimson-tressed spellcaster whispered, not without some impatience.

"It could not be helped. I myself had to wait until the matter was brought up by someone else." A tall cloaked and hooded figure half-emerged from the gloom—the sixth member of the Kirin Tor inner council. "It was."

For the first time, some eagerness shone in the eyes of Rhonin. "And my penance? Is my probation over?"

"Yes. You have been granted your return to our ranks . . . under the provision that you accede to taking on a task of import immediately."

"They've that much faith left in me?" Bitterness returned to the young mage's voice. "After the others died?"

"You are the only one they have left."

"That sounds more realistic. I should've known."

"Take these." The shadowy wizard held out a slim, gloved hand, palm up. Above the hand there suddenly flashed into existence two glittering objects—a tiny sphere of emerald and a ring of gold with a single black jewel.

Rhonin held out his own hand in the same manner . . . and the two items appeared above it. He seized both and inspected them. "I recognize the sphere of seeing, but not this other. It feels powerful, but not, I'm guessing, in an aggressive manner."

"You are astute, which is why I took up your cause in the first place, Rhonin. The sphere's purpose you know; the ring will serve as protection. You go into a realm where orc warlocks still exist. This ring will help shield you from their own devices of detection. Regrettably, it will also make it difficult for us to monitor you."

"So I'll be on my own." Rhonin gave his sponsor a sardonic smile. "Less chance of me causing any extra deaths, anyway. . . ."

"In that regard, you will not be alone, at least as far as the journey to the port. A ranger will escort you."

Rhonin nodded, although he clearly did not care for any escort, especially a ranger. Rhonin and elves did not get along well together. "You've not told me my mission."

The shadowed wizard propped back, as if sitting in an immense chair the younger spellcaster could not see. Gloved hands steepled as the figure seemed to consider the proper choice of words. "They have not been easy on you, Rhonin. Some in the council even considered forever dismissing you from our ranks. You must earn your way back, and to do that, you will have to fulfill this mission to the letter."

"You make it sound like no easy task."

"It involves dragons . . . and something they believe only one of your *aptitude* can manage to accomplish."

"Dragons . . ." Rhonin's eyes had widened at first mention of the leviathans and, despite his tendency toward arrogance at most times, he knew he sounded more like an apprentice at the moment.

Dragons . . . Simply the mention of them instilled awe in most younger mages.

"Yes, dragons." His sponsor leaned forward. "Make no mistake about this, Rhonin. No one else must know of this mission outside of the council and yourself. Not even the ranger who guides you nor the captain of the Alliance ship who drops you on the shores of Khaz Modan. If word got out what we hope from you, it could set all the plans in jeopardy."

"But what is it?" Rhonin's green eyes flared bright. This would be a quest of tremendous danger, but the rewards were clear enough. A return to the ranks and obvious added prestige to his reputation. Nothing advanced a wizard in the Kirin Tor quicker than reputation, although none of the senior council would have ever admitted to that base fact.

"You are to go to Khaz Modan," the other said with some hesitation, "and, once there, set into motion the steps necessary to free from her orc captors the Dragonqueen, *Alexstrasza*. . . ."

TWO

Vereesa did not like waiting. Most people thought that elves had the patience of glaciers, but younger ones such as herself, just a year out of her apprenticeship in the rangers, were very much like humans in that one regard. She had been waiting three days for this wizard she was supposed to escort to one of the eastern ports serving the Great Sea. For the most part, she respected wizards as much as any elf respected a human, but this one had earned nothing but her ire. Vereesa wanted to join her sisters and brothers, help hunt down each and every remaining orc still fighting, and send the murderous beasts to their well-deserved deaths. The ranger had not expected her first major assignment to be playing nursemaid to some doddering and clearly forgetful old mage.

"One more hour," she muttered. "One more hour, and then I leave."

Her sleek, chestnut-brown, elven mare snorted ever so slightly. Generations of breeding had created an animal far superior to its mundane cousins, or so Vereesa's people believed. The mare was in tune with her rider, and what would have seemed to most nothing more than a simple grunt from the horse immediately sent the ranger to her feet, a long shaft already notched in her bow.

Yet the woods around her spoke only of quiet, not treachery, and this deep within the Lordaeron Alliance she could hardly expect an attack by either orcs or trolls. She glanced in the direction of the small inn that had been designated the meeting place, but other than a stable boy carrying hay, Vereesa saw no one. Still, the elf did not lower her bow. Her mount rarely made a sound unless some trouble lurked nearby. Bandits, perhaps?

Slowly the ranger turned in a circle. The wind whipped some of the long, silver-white hair across her face, but not enough to obscure her sharp sight. Almond-shaped eyes the color of purest sky blue drank in even the most minute shift of foliage, and the lengthy, pointed ears that rose from her thick hair could pick up even the sound of a butterfly landing on a nearby flower.

And still she could find no reason for the mare's warning.

Perhaps she had frightened away whatever supposed menace had been nearby. Like all elves, Vereesa knew she made an impressive appearance.

Taller than most humans, the ranger stood clad in knee-high leather boots, forest-green pants and blouse, and an oak-brown travel cloak. Gloves that stretched nearly to her elbows protected her hands while yet enabling her to use her bow or the sword hanging at her side with ease. Over her blouse she wore a sturdy breastplate fashioned to her slim but still curved form. One of the locals in the inn had made the mistake of admiring the feminine aspects of her appearance while entirely ignoring the military ones. Because he had been drunk and possibly would have held back his rude suggestions otherwise, Vereesa had only left him with a few broken fingers.

The mare snorted again. The ranger glared at her mount, words of reprimand forming on her lips.

"You would be Vereesa Windrunner, I presume," a low, arresting voice on her blind side suddenly commented.

She had the tip of the shaft directly at his throat before he could say more. Had Vereesa let the arrow loose, it would have shot completely through the newcomer's neck, exiting through the other side.

Curiously, he seemed unimpressed by this deadly fact. The elf stared him up and down—not an entirely unpleasant task, she had to admit—and realized that her sudden intruder could only be the wizard for whom she had been waiting. Certainly that would explain her mount's peculiar actions and her own inability to sense his presence before this.

"You are Rhonin?" the ranger finally asked.

"Not what you're expecting?" he returned with just the hint of a sardonic smile.

She lowered the bow, relaxing slightly. "They said a wizard; that was all, human."

"And they told me an elven ranger, nothing more." He gave her a glance that almost made Vereesa raise the bow again. "So we find ourselves even in this matter."

"Not quite. I have waited here for three days! Three valuable days wasted!"

"It couldn't be helped. Preparations needed to be made." The wizard said nothing more.

Vereesa gave up. Like most humans, this one cared nothing for anyone but himself. She considered herself fortunate that she had not had to wait longer. It amazed her that the Alliance could have ever triumphed against the Horde with so many like this Rhonin in their ranks.

"Well, if you wish to make your passage to Khaz Modan, then it would be best if we left immediately." The elf peered behind him. "Where is your mount?"

She half-expected him to tell her that he had none, that he had used his formidable powers to transport himself all the way here . . . but if that had been the case, Rhonin would not have needed her to guide him to the ship. As a wizard, he no doubt had impressive abilities, but he also had his limits. Besides, from what little she knew of his mission, she suspected that Rhonin would need everything he had just to survive. Khaz Modan was not a land welcoming to outsiders. The skulls of many brave warriors decorated the orc tents there, so she had heard, and dragons constantly patrolled the skies. No, not a place even Vereesa would have gone without an army at her side. She was no coward, but she was also no fool.

"Tied near a trough by the inn, so that he can get some water. I've already ridden long today, milady."

His use of the title for her might have flattered Vereesa, if not for the slight touch of sarcasm she thought she noted in his tone. Fighting down her irritation with the human, she turned to her own horse, replaced the bow and shaft, then proceeded to ready her animal for the ride.

"My horse could do with a few more minutes' rest," the wizard suggested, "and so could I."

"You will learn to sleep in the saddle quickly enough . . . and the pace I set at first will enable your steed to recoup. We have waited far too long. Few ships, even those of Kul Tiras, are endeared to the thought of sailing to Khaz Modan simply for a wizard on observation duty. If you do not reach port soon, they may decide that they have more worthy and less suicidal matters with which to deal."

To her relief, Rhonin did not argue. Instead, with a frown, he turned and headed back toward the inn. Vereesa watched him depart, hoping that she would not find herself tempted to run him through before they managed to part company.

She wondered about his mission. True, Khaz Modan remained a threat because of the dragons and their orc masters there, but the Alliance already had other, more well-trained observers in and around the land. Vereesa suspected that Rhonin's mission concerned a very serious matter, or else the Kirin Tor would have never risked so much for this arrogant mage. Still, had they considered the matter well enough when they had chosen him? Surely there had to have been someone more able—and trustworthy? This wizard had a look to him, one that spoke of a streak of unpredictability that might lead to disaster.

The elf tried to shrug off her doubts. The Kirin Tor had made up their minds in this matter, and Alliance command had clearly agreed with them or else she would not have been sent along to guide him. Best she put aside any concerns. All she had to do was deliver her charge to his vessel, and then Vereesa could be on her way. What Rhonin might or might not do after their separation did not concern her in the least.

For four days they journeyed, never once threatened by anything more dangerous than a few annoying insects. Had circumstances been different, the trek might have seemed almost idyllic, if not for the fact that Rhonin and his guide had barely spoken with one another all that time. For the most part, the wizard had not been bothered much by that fact, his thoughts focused on the dangerous task ahead. Once the Alliance ship brought him to the shores of Khaz Modan, he would be on his own in a realm still overrun not only with orcs but patrolled from the sky by their captive dragons. While no coward, Rhonin had little desire to face torture and slow, agonizing death. For that alone, his benefactor in the council had provided him with the latest known movements of the Dragonmaw clan. Dragonmaw would be most on the watch now, especially if, as Rhonin had been told, the black leviathan Deathwing did indeed live.

Yet, as dangerous as the mage's quest appeared, Rhonin would not have turned back. He had been given an opportunity to not only redeem himself but to advance among the Kirin Tor. For that he would forever be most grateful to his patron, whom he only knew by the name *Krasus*. The title was surely a false one, not an uncommon practice among those in the ruling council. The masters of Dalaron were chosen in secret, their ascension known only to their fellows, not even their loved ones. The voice of Rhonin's benefactor could be nothing like his true voice . . . if male was even the correct gender.

It was possible to guess the identities of some of the inner circle, but Krasus remained an enigma even to his clever agent. In truth, though, Rhonin barely even cared about Krasus's identity anymore, only that through him the younger wizard could achieve his own dreams.

But those dreams would remain distant ones if he never made his ship. Leaning forward in the saddle, he asked, "How much farther to Hasic?"

Without turning, Vereesa blandly replied, "Three more days at least. Do not worry; our pace will now get us to the port on time."

Rhonin leaned back again. So much for their latest conversation, only the second of today. The only thing possibly worse than riding with an elf would have been traveling with one of the dour Knights of the Silver Hand. Despite their ever-present courtesy, the paladins generally made it clear that they considered magic an occasional, necessary evil, one with which they would do without at all other times. The last one that Rhonin had encountered had quite clearly indicated that he believed that, after death, the mage's soul would be condemned to the same pit of darkness shared by the mythical demons of old. This no matter how pure Rhonin's soul might have been otherwise.

The late afternoon sun began to sink among the treetops, creating contrasting areas of brightness and dark shadow among the trees. Rhonin had hoped to reach the edge of the woods before dark, but clearly they would not do so. Not for the first time, he ran through his mental maps, trying not only to place their present location but verify what his companion had said about still making the ship. His delay in meeting with Vereesa had been unavoidable, the product of trying to find necessary supplies and components. He only hoped it would still not prove to jeopardize his entire mission.

To free the Dragonqueen . . .

An impossible, improbable quest to some, certain death to most. Yet, even during the war, Rhonin had proposed such. Clearly, if the Dragonqueen were freed, it would at the very least strip from the remaining orcs one of their greatest weapons. However, circumstance had never enabled such a monumental quest to come to fruition.

Rhonin knew most of the council hoped he would fail. To be rid of him would be to erase what they considered a black mark from the history of their order. This mission had a double edge to it; they would be astounded if he succeeded, but relieved if he failed.

At least he could trust in Krasus. The wizard had first come to him, asking if his younger counterpart still believed he could do the impossible. Dragonmaw clan would forever retain its hold on Khaz Modan unless Alexstrasza was freed, and so long as the orcs there continued the work of the Horde, they remained a possible rallying point for those in the guarded enclaves. No one wanted the war renewed. The Alliance had enough strife within its own ranks to keep it busy.

A brief rumble of thunder disturbed Rhonin's contemplations. He looked up but saw only a few cottony clouds. Frowning, the fiery-haired spellcaster turned his gaze toward the elf, intending to ask her if she, too, had heard the thunder.

A second, more menacing rumble set every muscle taut.

At the same time, Vereesa *leapt* at him, the ranger somehow having managed to turn in the saddle and push herself in his direction.

A massive shadow covered their surroundings.

The ranger and the wizard collided, the elf's armored weight shoving both off the back of Rhonin's own mount.

An ear-shattering roar shook the vicinity, and a force akin to a tornado ripped at the landscape. As the wizard struck the hard ground, through the shock of pain he heard the brief whinny of his mount—a sound cut off the next moment.

"Keep down!" Vereesa called above the wind and roaring. "Keep down!"

Rhonin, though, twisted around so as to see the heavens—and saw instead a hellish sight.

A dragon the color of raging fire filled the sky above. In its forepaws it held what remained of his horse and his costly and carefully chosen supplies. The crimson leviathan consumed in one gulp the rest of the carcass, eyes already fixed on the tiny, pathetic figures below.

And seated atop the shoulders of the beast, a grotesque, greenish figure with tusks and a battle-ax that looked nearly as large as the mage barked orders in some harsh tongue and pointed directly at Rhonin.

Maw gaping and talons bared, the dragon dove toward him.

"I thank you again for your time, Your Majesty," the tall, black-haired noble said in a voice full of strength and understanding. "Perhaps we can yet keep this crisis from tearing your good work asunder."

"If so," returned the older, bearded figure clad in the elegant white and gold robes of state, "Lordaeron and the Alliance will have much to thank you for, Lord Prestor. It's only because of your work that I feel Gilneas and Stromgarde might yet see reason." Although no slight man himself, King Terenas felt a little overwhelmed by his larger companion.

The younger man smiled, revealing perfect teeth. If Terenas could have found a more regal-looking man than Lord Prestor, he would have been surprised. With his short, well-groomed black hair, clean-shaven hawklike features that had set many of the women of the court atwitter, quick mind, and a bearing more princely than any prince in the Alliance, it was not at all surprising that everyone involved in the Alterac situation had taken to him, Genn Greymane included. Prestor had an engaging manner that had actually made the ruler of Gilneas smile on a rare occasion, so Terenas's marveling diplomats had informed him.

For a young noble whom no one had even heard of prior to five years before, the king's guest had made quite a reputation for himself. Prestor came from the most mountainous, most obscure region of Lordaeron, but could claim bloodlines in the royal house of Alterac as well. His tiny domain had been destroyed during the war by a dragon attack and he had come to the capital on foot, without even one servant to dress him. His plight and what he had made of himself since his arrival had become the thing of storybook tales. More important, his advice had aided the king many times, including during the dark days when the graying monarch had debated on what to do about Lord Perenolde. Prestor had, in fact, been the swaying factor. He had given Terenas the encouragement needed to seize power in Alterac, then solidify martial law there. Stromgarde and the other kingdoms had understood the need for action against the traitorous Perenolde, but not Lordaeron's continued holding of that kingdom for its own purposes after the war had ended. Now at last, Prestor appeared to be the one who could explain it all to them and make them accept any final decision.

Which had, of late, made the aging, broad-featured monarch mull over a possible solution that would stun even the clever man before him. Terenas refused to turn over Alterac to Perenolde's nephew, whom Gilneas had tried to support. Nor did he think it wise to divide the kingdom in question between Lordaeron and Stromgarde. That would surely earn the wrath of not only Gilneas, but Kul Tiras even. Annexing Alterac completely was also out of the question.

What if, though, he placed the region in the capable hands of one admired by all, one who had shown he wanted nothing but peace and unity? An able administrator, too, if King Terenas were any judge, not to mention someone certain to remain a true ally and friend to Lordaeron. . . .

"No, indeed, Prestor!" The king reached up to pat the much taller lord on the shoulder. Prestor had to be nearly seven feet in height, but while slim, he could hardly be called lanky. Prestor well fit his blue and black dress uniform, looking every inch the martial hero. "You've much to be proud about . . . and much to be rewarded for! I'll not soon forget your part in this, believe me!"

Prestor fairly beamed, likely believing he would soon have his tiny realm restored to him. Terenas decided to let the boy keep that little dream; when the ruler of Lordaeron proposed him as new monarch of Alterac, the expression on Prestor's face would be that much more entertaining. It was not every day that someone became king . . . unless they inherited the position, of course.

Terenas's honored guest saluted him, then, bowing gracefully, retreated from the imperial chamber. The elder man frowned after Prestor left, thinking that the silken curtains, the golden chandeliers, and even the pure white marble floor could not brighten the room enough now that the young noble had departed. Truly Lord Prestor stood out among the many odious courtiers flocking to the palace. Here was a man anyone could believe in, a man worthy of trust and respect in all matters. Terenas wished his own son could have been more like Prestor.

The king rubbed his bearded chin. Yes, the perfect man to rebuild the honor of a land and at the same time restore harmony between the members of the Alliance. New and strong blood.

Considering the matter further, Terenas thought of his daughter, Calia. Still a child, but certainly soon to be a beauty. Perhaps one day, if matters went well, he and Prestor could strengthen their friendship and alliance with a royal marriage, too.

Yes, he would go talk to his advisors now, relate to them his royal opinion. Terenas felt certain that they would agree with him on this decision. He had met no one yet who disliked the young noble.

King Prestor of Alterac. Terenas could just imagine the look on his friend's face when he learned the extent of his reward. . . .

"You've the shadow of a smile on your face—did someone die a horrible, grisly, bloody death, o venomous one?"

"Spare me your witticisms, Kryll," Lord Prestor replied as he shut the great iron door behind him. Above, in the old chalet given over to him by his host, King Terenas, servants specifically chosen by Prestor stood guard to see that no unwarranted visitors dropped in. Their master had work to do, and even if none of the servants truly knew what went on in the chambers belowground, they had been made to know that it would be their lives if he was disturbed.

Prestor expected no interruptions and trusted that those lackeys would obey to the death. The spell upon them, a variation of the one that caused the king and his court to so admire the dashing refugee, allowed no room for second thoughts. He had honed its effectiveness quite well over time.

"Most humble apologies, o prince of duplicity!" rasped the smaller, wiry figure before him. The tone in the other's voice held hints of mischief and madness and an inhuman quality—not surprising, as Prestor's companion was a goblin.

His head barely reaching above the noble's belt buckle, some might have taken the slight, emerald-green creature for weak and simple. The madcap grin, however, revealed long teeth so very sharp and a tongue blood-red and almost forked. Narrow, yellow eyes with no visible pupils sparkled with merriment, but the sort of merriment that came from pulling the wings off flies or the arms off experimental subjects. A ridge of dull brown fur rose up from behind the goblin's neck, finishing as a wild crest above the hideous creature's squat forehead.

"Still, there is reason to celebrate." The lower chamber had once been used to house supplies. In those days, the coolness of the earth had kept wine rack after wine rack at just the right temperature. Now, however, thanks to a little engineering on the part of Kryll, the vast room felt as if it sat in the middle of a raging volcano.

For Lord Prestor, it felt just like home.

"Celebrate, o master of deceit?" Kryll giggled. Kryll giggled a lot, especially when foul work was afoot. The emerald creature's two chief passions were experimentation and mayhem, and whenever possible he combined the two. The back half of the chamber was, in fact, filled with benches, flasks, powders, curious mechanisms, and macabre collections all gathered by the goblin.

"Yesss, celebrate, Kryll." Prestor's penetrating, ebony eyes fixed unblinkingly on the goblin, who suddenly lost his smile and all semblance of mockery. "You would like to be around to join in that celebration, wouldn't you?"

"Yes . . . Master."

The uniformed noble took a moment to breathe in the stifling air. An expression of relief crossed his angular features. "Aaah, how I miss it . . ." His face hardened. "But I must wait. Go only when necessary, eh, Kryll?"

"As you say, Master."

The smile, now so very sinister, returned to Prestor's expression. "You are likely looking at the next king of Alterac, you know."

The goblin bent his narrow but muscular body nearly to the ground. "All hail his royal majesty, King D—"

A clatter made both glance to the right. From a metal grate leading to an old ventilation shaft emerged a smaller goblin. Nimbly, the tiny figure pulled itself through the opening and rushed over to Kryll. The newcomer wore a fiendishly amused look on his ugly face, a look that quickly faded under Prestor's intense gaze.

The second goblin whispered something into Kryll's large, pointed ear. Kryll hissed, then dismissed the other creature with a negligent wave of the hand. The newcomer vanished back through the open grate.

"What is it?" Although the words came calmly and smoothly from the lips of the aristocrat, they also clearly demanded no hesitation on the part of the goblin to answer.

"Aaah, gracious one," Kryll began, the madcap smile once more upon his bestial face. "Luck is with you this day, it seems! Perhaps you should consider making a wager somewhere? The stars must truly favor—"

"*What is it?*"

"Someone . . . someone is attempting to free Alexstrasza. . . ."

Prestor stared. He stared so long and with such intensity that Kryll fairly shriveled up before him. Surely now, the goblin imagined, surely now death would come. A pity that. There had been so many more experiments he had wanted to try, so many more explosives to test . . .

At that moment, the tall, black figure before him broke out laughing, a laugh deep, dark, and not entirely natural.

"Perfect . . ." Lord Prestor managed to utter between bouts of mirth. He stretched his arms out as if seeking to capture the very air. His fingers seemed impossibly long and almost clawed. "So perfect!"

He continued to laugh and, as he did, the goblin Kryll settled back, marveling at the odd sight and shaking his head ever so slightly.

"And they call *me* mad," he muttered under his breath.

THREE

The world became fire.

Vereesa cursed as she and the wizard scattered under the inferno suddenly exhaled by the crimson behemoth as it descended. If Rhonin had not delayed the start of their journey, this would have never happened. They would have arrived in Hasic by now, and she would have parted from his company. Now, it seemed very likely both of them would be parting with their lives. . . .

She had known that the orcs of Khaz Modan still sent out occasional dragon flights to wreak terror on the otherwise peaceful lands of their enemies, but why had she and her companion had the misfortune to be found by one? Dragons were fewer these days, and the realms of Lordaeron immense.

She glanced at Rhonin, who had thrown himself deeper into the woods. Of course. Somehow it had to do with the fact that her companion was a wizard. Dragons had senses far above those of even elves; some said they could, within limitations, even smell magic. Somehow this disastrous turn of events had to be the wizard's fault. The orc and his dragon had to have come for him.

Rhonin evidently thought something similar, for he hurried from her sight as quickly as he could, darting into the woods in the opposite direction from her. The ranger snorted. Wizards were never good in the front line; it was easy to attack someone from a distance or behind his back, but when they had to actually face a foe . . .

Of course, it *was* a dragon.

The dragon veered toward the vanishing human. Despite what she might personally think of him, Vereesa did not want to see the spellcaster dead. Yet, peering around, the silver-haired ranger saw no manner by which she could aid him. Her mount had been taken along with his, and with it had gone her favored bow. All that remained with her was her sword, hardly a weapon to be used against such a rampaging titan. Vereesa looked around for something else she could use, but nothing suited.

That left her with little choice. As a ranger, she could not let even the wizard fall to harm if she could help it. Vereesa had to do the only thing she could think of in order to possibly save his life.

The elf leapt up from her hiding place, waved her hands in the air, and shouted, "Here! Over here, spawn of a lizard! Here!"

However, the dragon did not hear her, his—Vereesa had finally managed to identify it as a male—attention on the burning woods below him. Somewhere in that inferno Rhonin struggled to survive. The dragon sought to make certain that he did not.

Cursing, the elven warrior looked around and found a heavy rock. For a human, what she sought to do would have been nigh unto impossible, but for her it still remained in the realm of probability. Vereesa only hoped her arm was as good as it had been a few short years back.

Stretching back, she threw the rock directly at the head of the crimson leviathan.

She had the distance, but the dragon suddenly moved, and for a moment Vereesa expected her rock to miss. However, although it did not hit the head, the projectile did bounce off the tip of the nearest of the webbed wings. Vereesa did not even expect to injure the beast—a mere rock against hard dragonscale a laughable weapon—but what she had hoped for was to attract the behemoth's attention.

And so she did.

The massive head immediately swerved her way, the dragon roaring in annoyance at this interruption. The orc shouted something unintelligible at his mount.

The great winged form abruptly banked, steering toward her. She had succeeded in taking his attention from the hapless mage.

And now what? the ranger chided herself.

The elf turned and ran, already knowing she had no chance of outpacing her monstrous pursuer.

The treetops above her burst into flames as the dragon coated the landscape. Burning foliage dropped before her, cutting off Vereesa's intended route. Without hesitation, the ranger shifted to the left, diving among trees that had not yet become a part of the inferno.

You are going to die! she informed herself. *All for that useless wizard!*

An ear-splitting roar made her look over her shoulder. The red dragon had reached her, and even now one taloned paw stretched down to seize the fleeing ranger. Vereesa imagined that paw crushing her or, worse fate, dragging her into the behemoth's horrific maw, where she would be chewed up or swallowed whole.

Yet, just as death came within inches of her, the dragon suddenly pulled back his claws and began squirming in midair. The claws raked against his own torso. In fact, every set of claws was trying to scratch somewhere, anywhere, as if—as if the leviathan suffered an incredibly painful itch. Atop him, the orc struggled for control, but he might as well have been the very flea that seemed to trouble the dragon for all the beast obeyed him now.

Vereesa stopped and stared, never having witnessed so startling a sight. The dragon twisted and turned as he tried to relieve his agony, his actions growing more and more frantic. His orc handler could barely hold on. What, the elf wondered, could have caused the monster so much—

The answer came out as a whisper. "Rhonin?"

And, as if by saying his name she had summoned him like some ghost, the mage stood before her. His fiery hair hung disheveled and his dark robe had become muddy and torn, but he looked undeterred by what he had so far suffered.

"I think it'd be better if we left while we could, eh, elf?"

She did not need him to offer again. This time, Rhonin led the way, using some skill, some magical ability, to guide them through the blazing forest. As a ranger, Vereesa could not have done better herself. Rhonin led her along paths the elf could not even see until they were upon them.

All the while, the dragon soared overhead, tearing at its hide. Once Vereesa glanced up and saw that he had even managed to draw blood, his own claws one of the few things capable of ripping through his armored skin. Of the orc she saw no more sign; at some point the tusked warrior must have lost his grip and fallen. Vereesa felt no remorse for him.

"What did you do to the dragon?" she finally managed to gasp.

Rhonin, intent on finding the end of the blaze, did not even look back at her. "Something that didn't turn out the way I planned! He should've suffered more than an intense irritation!"

He actually sounded annoyed with himself, but the ranger, for once, found herself impressed by him. He had turned certain death into possible safety—provided they found their way out.

Behind them, the dragon roared his frustration at the world.

"How long will it last?"

Now he finally paused to eye her, and what she saw in that gaze unsettled her greatly. "Not nearly long enough. . . ."

They redoubled their efforts. Fire surrounded them wherever they turned, but at last they reached its very edge, racing past the flames and out into a region where only deadly smoke assailed them. Both choking, the pair stumbled on, searching for a path that would keep the wind blowing at them from the front and, consequently, help to slow the fire and smoke behind.

And then another roar shook them, for it did not speak of agony, but rather fury and revenge. Wizard and ranger turned about, glanced at the crimson form in the distance.

"The spell's worn off," Rhonin muttered unnecessarily.

It had indeed worn off, and Vereesa could see that the dragon knew exactly who had been responsible for his pain. With an almost unerring aim, the dragon pushed toward them with his massive, leathery wings, clearly intent on making them pay.

"Do you have another spell for this?" Vereesa called as they ran.

"Perhaps! But I'd rather not use it here! It could take us with it!"

As if the dragon would not do that anyway. The elf hoped that Rhonin would see his way to unleashing this deadly spell before they both ended up as fare for the behemoth.

"How far—" The wizard had to catch his breath. "How far to Hasic?"

"Too far."

"Any other settlement between here and there?"

She tried to think. One place came to mind, but she could not recall either its name or its purpose. Only that it lay about a day's journey from here. "There is something, but—"

The dragon's roar shook them both again. A shadow passed overhead.

"If you do have another spell that might work, I would suggest using it now." Vereesa wished again for her bow. With it she could have at least tried for the eyes with some hope of success. The shock and agony might have been enough to send the monster flying off.

They nearly collided as Rhonin came to an unexpected halt and turned to face the dire threat. He took hold of her arms with surprisingly strong hands, for a wizard, then shifted the ranger aside. His eyes literally glowed, something Vereesa had heard could happen with powerful mages but had never in her life seen.

"Pray that this doesn't backfire on us," he muttered.

His arms went up straight, hands pointed in the direction of the red dragon.

He started to mutter words in a language that Vereesa did not recognize, but which somehow sent shivers up and down her spine.

Rhonin brought his hands together, started to speak again—

Through the clouds came three more winged forms.

Vereesa gasped and the tall wizard held his tongue, stalling the spell. He looked ready to curse the heavens, but then the elf recognized what had emerged just above their horrific foe.

Gryphons . . . massive, eagle-headed, leonine-bodied, winged gryphons . . . with riders.

She tugged at Rhonin's arm. "Do not do anything!"

He glared at her, but nodded. They both looked up as the dragon filled their view.

The three gryphons suddenly darted around the dragon, catching him by surprise. Now Vereesa could identify the riders, not that she had really needed to do so. Only the dwarves of the distant Aerie Peaks, a foreboding, mountainous region beyond even the elven realm of Quel'thalas, rode the wild gryphons . . . and only these skilled warriors and their mounts could face dragons in the air.

Although much smaller than the crimson giant, the gryphons made up for the size difference with huge, razor-sharp talons that could tear off dragonscale and beaks that could rip into the flesh beneath. In addition, they could move more swiftly and abruptly through the sky, turning at angles a dragon could never match.

The dwarves themselves did not simply manage their mounts, either. Slightly taller and leaner than their earthier cousins, the mountain dwarves were no less muscled. Although their favored weapons when patrolling the skies were the legendary Stormhammers, this trio carried great double-edged battle-axes with lengthy handles that the warriors manipulated with ease. Made of a metal akin to adamantium, the blades could cut through even the bony, scaled heads of the behemoths. Rumor had it that the great gryphon-rider Kurdran had struck down a dragon more immense than this one with just one well-aimed blow from an ax like these.

The winged animals circled their foe, forcing him to constantly turn from side to side to see which one threatened most. The orcs had early on learned to be wary of the gryphons, but without his own rider, this particular monster appeared somewhat lost as to what to do. The dwarves immediately took advantage of that fact, making their mounts dart in and out, much to the dragon's growing frustration. The long beards and ponytails of the wild dwarves fluttered in the wind as they literally laughed in the face of the giant menace. The bellowing laughter only served to antagonize the dragon more, and he slashed about madly, accompanying his futile attacks with spurts of flame.

"They are completely disorienting him," Vereesa commented, impressed by the tactics. "They know he is young and that his temper will keep him from attacking with strategy!"

"Which makes it a good time for us to leave," Rhonin replied.

"They might need our help!"

"I've a mission to fulfill," he said ominously. "And they've got matters well in hand."

True enough. The battle seemed to belong to the gryphon-riders, even though they had yet to strike a blow. The trio kept flying around and around the red dragon, so much so that he nearly looked dizzy. He tried his best to keep his eyes on one, but ever the others would distract him. Only once did flame come close to touching one of his winged opponents.

One of the dwarves suddenly began hefting his mighty ax, the head of it gleaming in the late-day sun. He and his mount flew once more about the dragon, then, as they neared the back of the behemoth's skull, the gryphon suddenly darted in.

Claws sank into the neck, ripping away scale. Even as the pain registered in the dragon's mind, the dwarf brought the mighty ax around and swung hard.

The blade sank deep. Not enough to kill, but more than enough to make the dragon shriek in agony.

Out of sheer reflex, he turned. His wing caught the dwarf and the gryphon by surprise, sending them spiraling out of control. The rider managed to hold on, but his ax flew out of his grip, falling earthward.

Vereesa instinctively started in the direction of the weapon, but Rhonin blocked her path with his arm. "I said that we need to leave!"

She would have argued, but one more glance at the combatants revealed that the ranger could be of no use. The wounded dragon had flown higher into the air, still harassed by the gryphon-riders. Even with the ax, all Vereesa could have done was wave it futilely.

"All right," the elf finally muttered.

Together they hurried from the struggle, relying now on Vereesa's knowledge of where their ultimate destination lay. Behind them, the dragon and the gryphons shrank to tiny specks in the heavens, in part because the battle itself had moved in the opposite direction of the elf and her companion.

"Curious . . ." she heard the wizard whisper.

"What is?"

He started. "Those ears aren't just for show, then, are they?"

Vereesa bristled at the insult, even though she had heard far worse. Humans and dwarves, quite jealous of the natural superiority of the elven race, often chose the long, tapering ears as the focus of their ridicule. At times, her ears had been compared to those of donkeys, swine, and, worst of all, *goblins*. While Vereesa had never drawn a weapon on anyone because of such comments, more often than not she had still left them much regretting their choice of words.

The emerald eyes of the mage narrowed. "I'm sorry; you took that as an insult. Didn't mean it that way."

She doubted the veracity of his statement, but knew she had to accept his weak attempt at an apology. Forcing down her anger, she asked again, "What do you find so curious?"

"That this dragon should appear in so timely a fashion."

"If you think like that, you might as well ask where the gryphons came from. After all, they chased it off."

He shook his head. "Someone saw him and reported the situation. The riders merely did their duties." He considered. "I know Dragonmaw clan's supposed to be desperate, supposed to be trying to rally both the other rebel clans and the ones in the enclaves, but this wouldn't be the way to go about it."

"Who can say what an orc thinks? This was clearly a random marauder. This was not the first such attack in the Alliance, human."

"No, but I wonder if—" Rhonin got no further, for suddenly they both became aware of movement in the forest . . . movement from every direction.

With practiced ease, the ranger slid her blade free from its sheath. Beside her, Rhonin's hands disappeared into the deep folds of his wizard's robes, no doubt in preparation for a spell. Vereesa said nothing, but she wondered how much aid he would be in close combat. Better he stand back and let her take on the first attackers.

Too late. Six massive figures on horseback suddenly broke through the woods, surrounding them. Even in the dimming sunlight their silver armor gleamed sharp. The elf found a lance pointing at her chest. Rhonin not only had one touching his breast, but another between his shoulder blades.

Helmed visors with a leonine head for a crest hid the features of their captors. As a ranger, Vereesa wondered how anyone could move in such suits, let alone wage war, but the six maneuvered in the saddle as if completely unencumbered. Their huge, gray warhorses, also armored on top, seemed unperturbed by the extra weight foisted upon them.

The newcomers carried no banner, and the only sign of their identities appeared to be the image of a stylized hand reaching to the heavens embossed on the breastplate. Vereesa thought she knew who they were from this alone, but did not relax. The last time the elf had met such men, they had worn different armor, with horns atop the helm and the lettered symbol of Lordaeron on both their breastplate and shield.

And then a seventh rider slowly emerged from the forest, this one in the more traditional armor that Vereesa had first been expecting. Within the shadowy, visorless helm, she could see a strong and—for a human—older and wiser face with a trim, graying beard. The symbols of both Lordaeron and his own religious order marked not only his shield and breastplate, but also his helm. A silver lion's-head buckle linked together the belt in which hung one of the mighty, pointed warhammers used by such as him.

"An elf," he murmured as he inspected her. "Your strong arm is welcome." The apparent leader then eyed Rhonin, finally commenting with open disdain, "And a *damned soul*. Keep your hands where we can see them and we won't be tempted to cut them off."

As Rhonin clearly fought to keep his fury down, Vereesa found herself caught between relief and uncertainty. They had been captured by paladins of Lordaeron—the fabled Knights of the Silver Hand.

The two met in a place of shadow, a place reachable only by a few, even among their own kind. It was a place where dreams of the past played over and over, murky forms moving about in the fog of the mind's history. Not even the two who met here knew how much of this realm existed in reality and how much of it existed only in their thoughts, but they knew that here no one would be able to eavesdrop.

Supposedly.

Both were tall and slim, their faces covered by cowls. One could be identified as the wizard Rhonin knew as Krasus; the other, but for the greenish tinge of the otherwise gray robes, might as well have been the wizard's twin. Only when words were spoken did it become clear that, unlike the councilor of the Kirin Tor, this figure was definitely male.

"I do not know why I've even come," he commented to Krasus.

"Because you had to. You needed to."

The other let loose with an audible hiss. "True, but now that I'm here, I can choose to leave any time I desire."

Krasus raised a slim, gloved hand. "At least hear me out."

"For what reason? So that you can repeat what you have repeated so many times before?"

"So that for once what I am saying might actually register!" Krasus's unexpected vehemence startled both.

His companion shook his head. "You've been around them much too long. Your shields, both magical and personal, are beginning to break down. It's time you abandoned this hopeless task . . . just as we did."

"I do not believe it hopeless." For the first time, a hint of gender, a voice far deeper than any of the other members of the Kirin Tor's inner circle would have believed possible. "I cannot, so long as she is held."

"What she means to you is understandable, Korialstrasz; what she means to us is that of the memory of a time past."

"If that time is past, then why do you and yours still stand your posts?" Krasus calmly retorted, his emotions once more under control.

"Because we would see our final years calm ones, peaceful ones. . . ."

"All the more reason to join with me in this."

Again the other hissed. "Korialstrasz, will you never give in to the inevitable? Your plan does not surprise us, who know you so well! We've seen your little puppet on his fruitless quest—do you think he can possibly accomplish his task?"

Krasus paused for a moment before replying. "He has the potential . . . but he is not all I have. No, I think he will fail. In doing so, however, I hope that his sacrifice will aid in my final success . . . and if you would join with me, that success would be more likely."

"I was right." Krasus's companion sounded immensely disappointed. "The same rhetoric. The same pleading. I only came because of the alliance, once strong, between our two factions, but clearly I should not have even bothered because of that. You are without backing, without force. There is only you now, and you must hide in the shadows—" he gestured at the mists surrounding them "—in places such as this, rather than show your true nature."

"I do what I must. . . . What is it that you do, anymore?" An edge once more arose in Krasus's voice. "What purpose do you exist for, my old friend?"

The other figure started at this penetrating question, then abruptly turned away. He took a few steps toward the embracing mists, then paused and looked back at the wizard. Krasus's companion sounded resigned. "I wish you the very best on this, Korialstrasz; I really do. I—*we*—just don't believe that there can be any return to the past. Those days are done, and we with them."

"That is your choice, then." They almost parted company, but Krasus suddenly called out. "One request, though, before you return to the others."

"And what is that?"

The mage's entire form seemed to darken, and a hiss escaped him. "Do not ever call me by that name again. *Ever.* It must not be spoken, even here."

"No one could possibly—"

"*Even here.*"

Something in Krasus's tone made his companion nod. The second figure then hurriedly departed, vanishing into the emptiness.

The wizard stared at the place where the other had stood, thinking of the repercussions of this futile conversation. If only they could have seen sense! Together, they had hope. Divided, they could do little . . . and that would play into their foe's hands.

"Fools . . ." Krasus muttered. *"Abysmal fools . . ."*

FOUR

The paladins brought them back to a keep that had to have been the unnamed settlement of which Vereesa had earlier spoken. Rhonin was unimpressed by it. Its high stone walls surrounded a functional, unadorned establishment where the holy knights, squires, and a small population of common folk attempted to live in relative frugality. The banners of the brotherhood flew side-by-side with those of the Lordaeron Alliance, of which the Knights of the Silver Hand were the most staunch supporters. If not for the townsfolk, Rhonin would have taken the settlement for a completely military operation, for the rule of the holy order clearly had control over all matters here.

The paladins had treated the elf with courtesy, some of the younger knights adding extra charm whenever Vereesa spoke with them, but with the wizard they would not traffic any more than necessity demanded, not even when, at one point, he asked how far they still had to go to reach Hasic. Vereesa had to repeat the question in order for him to find out. Despite initial impressions, the pair were not, of course, prisoners, but Rhonin certainly felt like an outcast among them. They treated him with minimal civility only because their oath to King Terenas demanded it of them, but otherwise he remained a pariah.

"We saw both the dragon and the gryphons," their leader, one Duncan Senturus, boomed. "Our duty and honor demanded we ride out immediately to see what aid we might be."

The fact that the combat had been entirely aerial and, therefore, far out of their reach apparently had not dampened their holy enthusiasm nor struck a chord with their common sense, Rhonin thought wryly. They and the ranger made for good company in that. Curiously, though, the wizard felt a twinge of possessiveness now that he did not have to deal with Vereesa on his own. *After all, she was appointed my guide. She should remain true to her duty until Hasic.*

Unfortunately, as for Hasic, Duncan Senturus had intentions for that, too. As they dismounted, the broad-shouldered senior knight offered his arm to the elf, saying, "Of course, it would be remiss of us to not see you along the safest and quickest route to the port. I know it's a task you've been given, milady, but clearly it was chosen by a higher power that your paths would lead you to us. We know well the way to Hasic, and so a small party, led by myself, will journey with you come the morrow."

This seemed to please the ranger, but hardly encouraged Rhonin any. Everyone in the keep eyed him as if he had been transformed into a goblin or orc. He had suffered enough disdain around his fellow spellcasters and felt no need to have the paladins add further to his troubles.

"It's very kind of you," Rhonin interjected from behind them. "But Vereesa is a capable ranger. We'll reach Hasic in time."

Senturus's nostrils flared as if he had just smelled something noxious. Keeping his smile fixed, the senior paladin said to the elf, "Allow me to personally escort you to your quarters." He glanced at one of his subordinates. "Meric! Find a place to put the wizard. . . ."

"This way," grumbled a hulking young knight with a full mustache. He looked ready to take Rhonin by the arm even if it meant breaking the limb in question. Rhonin could have taught him the folly of doing that, but for the sake of his mission and peace between the various elements of the Alliance, he simply took a quick step forward, coming up beside his guide and not saying a word through the entire journey.

He had expected to be led to the most dank, most foul place in which they could honestly let him bed down for the night, but instead Rhonin found himself with a room likely no more austere than those used by the dour warriors themselves. Dry, clean, and with stone walls that surrounded him on all sides save where the wooden door stood, it certainly served Rhonin better than some of the places he had stayed in the past. A single, neatly kept wooden bed and a tiny table made up the decor. A well-used oil lamp appeared to be the only means of illumination, not even the tiniest of windows evident. Rhonin thought of at least requesting a window, but suspected the knights had nothing better to offer. Besides, this would better serve to keep curious eyes from him.

"This will do," he finally said, but the young warrior who had brought Rhonin here had already begun to depart, closing the door as he left. The wizard tried to recall if the outside handle had a bolt or some sort of lock, but the paladins would surely not go that far. Damned soul Rhonin might be to them, but he was still one of their allies. The thought of the mental discomfort that last put the knights through cheered him a bit. He had always found the Knights of the Silver Hand a sanctimonious lot.

His reluctant hosts left him alone until evening meal. He found himself seated far from Vereesa, who seemed to have the commander's ear whether she wanted it or not. No one but the elf spoke more than a few words to the wizard throughout the entire repast, and Rhonin would have left shortly after that if the subject of dragons had not been brought up by none other than Senturus.

"The flights have grown more common the last few weeks," the bearded knight informed them. "More common and more desperate. The orcs know that their time is short, and so they seek to wreak what havoc they can before the day of their final judgment." He took a sip of wine. "The settlement of Juroon was set aflame by two dragons just three days ago, more than half its population dead in the ungodly incident. That time, the beasts and their masters fled before the gryphon riders could reach the site."

"Horrible," Vereesa murmured.

Duncan nodded, a glint of almost fanatical determination in his deep brown eyes. "But soon a thing past! Soon we shall march on the interior of Khaz Modan, on Grim Batol itself, and end the threat of the last fragments of the Horde! Orc blood will flow!"

"And good men'll die," Rhonin added under his breath.

Apparently the commander had hearing as good as that of the elf, for his gaze immediately shifted to the mage. "Good men will die, aye! But we have sworn to see Lordaeron and all other lands free of the orc menace and so we shall, no matter what the cost!"

Unimpressed, the wizard returned, "But first you need to do something about the dragons, don't you?"

"They will be vanquished, spellcaster; sent to the underworld where they belong. If your devilish kind—"

Vereesa softly touched the commander's hand, giving him a smile that made even Rhonin a bit jealous. "How long have you been a paladin, Lord Senturus?"

Rhonin watched with some amazement as the ranger transformed into an enchanted and enchanting young woman, akin to those he had met in the royal court of Lordaeron. Her transformation in turn changed Duncan Senturus. She teased and toyed with the graying knight, seeming to hang on his every word. Her personality had altered so much that the observing wizard could scarce believe this was the same female who had ridden as his guide and his guard for the past several days.

Duncan went into great detail about his not-so-humble humble beginnings, as the son of a wealthy lord who chose the order to make his name. Although surely the other knights had heard the story before, they listened with rapt attention, no doubt seeing their leader as a shining example to their own careers. Rhonin studied each briefly, noticing with some unease that these other paladins barely blinked, barely even breathed, as they drank in the tale.

Vereesa commented on various parts of his story, making even the most mundane accomplishments of the elder man seem wondrous and brave. She downplayed her own deeds when Lord Senturus asked her of her past training, although the mage felt certain that, in many skills, his ranger readily surpassed their host.

The paladin seemed enamored by her act and went on at tremendous length, but Rhonin finally had enough. He excused himself—an announcement that drew the attention of no one—and hurried outside, seeking air and solitude.

Night had settled over the keep, a moonless dark that enveloped the tall wizard like a comforting blanket. He looked forward to reaching Hasic and setting forth on his voyage to Khaz Modan. Only then would he be done with paladins, rangers, and other useless fools who did nothing but interfere with his true quest. Rhonin worked best alone, a point he had tried to make before the last debacle. No one had listened to him then, and he had been forced to do what he had to in order to succeed. The others on that mission had not heeded his warnings, nor understood the necessity of his dangerous work. With the typical contempt of the nontalented, they had gone charging directly into the path of his grand spell . . . and thus most had perished along with the true targets—a band of orc warlocks intent on raising from the dead what some believed had been one of the demons of legend.

Rhonin regretted each and every one of those deaths more than he had ever let on to his masters in the Kirin Tor. They haunted him, urged him on to more risky feats . . . and what could be more risky than attempting, all by himself, to free the Dragonqueen from her captors? He had to do it all by himself, not only for the glory it would bring him, but also, Rhonin hoped, to appease the spirits of his former comrades, spirits who never left him even a moment's rest. Even Krasus did not know about those troubling specters— likely a good thing, as it might have made him question Rhonin's sanity *and* worth.

The wind picked up as he made his way to the top of the keep's surrounding wall. A few knights stood sentry duty, but word of his presence in the settlement had evidently traveled swiftly, and after the first guard identified him by way of inspection by lantern, Rhonin once again became shunned. That suited him well; he cared as little for the warriors as they did for him.

Beyond the keep, the vague shapes of trees turned the murky landscape into something magical. Rhonin found himself half-tempted to leave the questionable hospitality of his hosts and find a place to sleep under an oak. At least then he would not have to listen to the pious words of Duncan Senturus, who, in the mage's mind, seemed far more interested in Vereesa than a knight of the holy order should have been. True, she had arresting eyes and her garments suited her form well—

Rhonin snorted, eradicating the image of the ranger from his thoughts. His forced seclusion during his penance had clearly had more of an effect on him than he had realized. Magic was his mistress, first and foremost, and if Rhonin *did* decide to seek the company of a female, he much preferred a more malleable type, such as the well-pampered young ladies of the courts, or even the impressionable serving girls he found occasionally during his travels. Certainly not an arrogant, elven ranger . . .

Best to turn his attention to more important matters. Along with his unfortunate mount, Rhonin had also lost the items Krasus had given him. He had to do his best to make contact with the other wizard, inform him as to what had happened. The young mage regretted the necessity of doing so, but he owed too much to Krasus to not try. By no means did Rhonin consider turning back; that would have ended his hopes of ever regaining face not only among his peers but also with himself.

He surveyed his present surroundings. Eyes that saw slightly better than average in the night detected no sentries in the near vicinity. A watchtower wall shielded him from the sight of the last man he had passed. What better place than here to begin? His room might have served, too, but Rhonin favored the open, the better to clear the cobwebs from his thoughts.

From a pocket deep within his robe he removed a small, dark crystal. Not the best choice for trying to create communication across miles, but the only one left to him.

Rhonin held the crystal up to the brightest of the faint stars overhead and began to mutter words of power. A faint glimmer arose within the heart of the stone, a glimmer that increased slowly in intensity as he continued to speak. The mystical words rolled from his tongue—

And at that moment, the stars abruptly *vanished*. . . .

Cutting off the spell in mid-sentence, Rhonin stared. No, the stars he had fixed on had not vanished; he could see them now. Yet . . . yet for a brief moment, no more than the blink of an eye, the mage could have sworn . . .

A trick of the imagination and his own weariness. Considering the trials of the day, Rhonin should have gone to bed immediately after dining, but he had first wanted to attempt this spell. The sooner he finished, then, the better. He wanted to be fully rejuvenated come the morrow, for Lord Senturus would certainly set an arduous pace.

Once more Rhonin raised the crystal high and once more he began muttering the words of power. This time, no trick of the eye would—

"What do you do there, spellcaster?" a deep voice demanded.

Rhonin swore, furious at this second delay. He turned to the knight who had come across him and snapped, "Nothing to—"

An explosion rocked the wall.

The crystal slipped from Rhonin's hand. He had no time to reach for it, more concerned with keeping himself from tumbling over the wall to his death.

The sentry had no such hope. As the wall shook, he fell backward, first collapsing against the battlements, then toppling over. His cry shook Rhonin until its very abrupt end.

The explosion subsided, but not the damage caused by it. No sooner had the desperate wizard regained his footing when a portion of the wall itself began to collapse inward. Rhonin leapt toward the watchtower, thinking it more secure. He landed near the doorway and started inside—just as the tower itself began to teeter dangerously.

Rhonin tried to exit, but the doorway crumbled, trapping him within.

He started a spell, certain that it was already too late. The ceiling fell upon him—

And with it came something akin to a gigantic hand that seized the wizard in such a smothering grip Rhonin completely lost his breath . . . and all consciousness.

Nekros Skullcrusher brooded over the fate that the bones had rolled for him long, long ago. The grizzled orc toyed with one yellowed tusk as he studied the golden disk in the meaty palm of his other hand, wondering how one who had learned to wield such power could have been sentenced to playing nursemaid and jailer to a brooding female whose only purpose was to produce progeny after progeny. Of course, the fact that she was the greatest of dragons might have had something to do with that role—that and the fact that with but one good leg Nekros could never hope to achieve and hold on to the role of clan chieftain.

The golden disk seemed to mock him. It always seemed to mock him, but the crippled orc never once considered throwing it away. With it he had achieved a position that still kept him respected among his fellow warriors . . . even if he had lost all respect for himself the day the human knight had hacked off the bottom half of his left leg. Nekros had slain the human, but could not bring himself to do the honorable thing. Instead, he had let others drag him from the field, cauterize the wound, and help build for Nekros the support he needed for his maimed appendage.

His eyes flickered to what remained of the knee and the wooden peg attached there. No more glorious combat, no more legacy of blood and death. Other warriors had slain themselves for less grievous injuries, but Nekros *could* not. The very thought of bringing the blade to his own throat or chest filled him with a chill he dared not mention to any of the others. Nekros Skullcrusher very much wanted to live, no matter what the cost.

There were those in Dragonmaw clan who might have already sent him on his way to the glorious battlefields of the afterlife if not for his skills as a warlock. Early on, his talent for the arts had been noticed, and he had received training from some of the greatest. However, the way of the warlock had demanded from him other choices that Nekros had not wanted to make, dark choices that he felt did not serve the Horde, but rather worked to undermine it. He had fled their ranks, returned to his warrior ways, but from time to time his chieftain, the great Shaman, Zuluhed, had demanded the use of his other talents—especially in what even most orcs had believed impossible, the capturing of the Dragonqueen, Alexstrasza.

Zuluhed wielded the ritualistic magicks of the ancient shaman belief as few had done since first the Horde had been formed, but for this task, he had also needed to call upon the more sinister powers in which Nekros had been trained. Through resources the wizened orc had never revealed to his crippled companion, Zuluhed had uncovered an ancient talisman said to be capable of tremendous wonders. The only trouble had been that it had not responded to shamanistic spellwork no matter how great the effort put in by the chieftain. That had led Zuluhed to turn to the only warlock he felt he could trust, a warrior loyal to Dragonmaw clan.

And so Nekros had inherited the *Demon Soul*.

Zuluhed had so named the featureless gold disk, although at first the other orc had not known why. Nekros turned it over and over, not for the first time marveling at its impressive yet simplistic appearance. Pure gold, yes, and shaped like a huge coin with a rounded edge. It gleamed in even the lowest light, and nothing could tarnish its look. Oil, mud, blood . . . everything slipped off.

"This is older than either shaman or warlock magic, Nekros," Zuluhed had told him. *"I can do nothing with it, but perhaps you can. . . ."*

Trained though he was, the peg-legged orc had doubted that he, who had sworn off the dark arts, could do better than his legendary chieftain. Still, he had taken the talisman and tried to sense its purpose, its use.

Two days later, thanks to his astonishing success and Zuluhed's firm guidance, they had done what no one would have imagined possible, especially the Dragonqueen herself.

Nekros grunted, slowly raising himself to a standing position. His leg ached where the knee met the peg, an ache intensified by the great girth of the orc. Nekros had no illusions about his ability to lead. He could scarcely get around the caves as it was.

Time to visit her highness. Make certain that she knew she had a schedule to maintain. Zuluhed and the few other clan leaders left free still had dreams of revitalizing the Horde, stirring those abandoned by the weakling Doomhammer into a revolt. Nekros doubted these dreams, but he was a loyal orc, and as a loyal orc he would obey his chieftain's commands to the letter.

The *Demon Soul* clutched in one hand, the orc trundled through the dank cavern corridors. Dragonmaw clan had worked hard to lengthen the system already running through these mountains. The complex series of corridors enabled the orcs to deal more readily with the burdensome task of raising and training dragons for the glory of the Horde. Dragons filled up a lot of space and so needed separate facilities, each of which had to be dug out.

Of course, there were fewer dragons these days, a point Zuluhed and others had made with Nekros quite often lately. They needed dragons if their desperate campaign had any hope of succeeding.

"And how'm I supposed to make her breed faster?" Nekros grunted to himself.

A pair of younger, massive warriors strode by. Nearly seven feet tall, each as wide as two of their human adversaries, the tusked fighters dipped their heads briefly in recognition of his rank. Huge battle-axes hung from harnesses on their backs. Both were dragon-riders, new ones. Riders had a death ratio about twice that of their mounts, generally due to an unfortunate loss of grip. There had been times when Nekros had wondered whether the clan would run out of able warriors before it ran out of dragons, but he never broached the subject with Zuluhed.

Hobbling along, the aging orc soon began to hear the telltale signs of the Dragonqueen's presence. He noted labored breathing that echoed through the immediate area as if some steam vent from the depths of the earth had worked its way up. Nekros knew what that labored breathing meant. He had arrived just in time.

No guards stood at the carved-out entrance to the dragon's great chamber, but still Nekros paused. Attempts had been made in the past to free or slay the gargantuan red dragon within, but all those attempts had ended in grisly death. Not from the dragon, of course, for she would have embraced such assassins with relief, but rather from an unexpected aspect of the talisman Nekros held.

The orc squinted at what seemed nothing but an open passage. "Come!"

Instantly, the very air around the entrance flared. Tiny balls of flame burst into being, then immediately merged. A humanoid form began to fill, then overflow, the entrance.

Something vaguely resembling a burning skull formed where the head should have been. Armor that appeared to be flaming bone shaped itself into the body of a monstrous warrior that dwarfed even the enormous orcs. Nekros felt no heat from the hellish flames, but he knew that if the creature before him touched the orc even lightly, pain such as even a seasoned fighter could not imagine would rake him.

Among the other orcs it had been whispered that Nekros Skullcrusher had summoned one of the demons of lore. He did not discourage that rumor, although Zuluhed knew better. The monstrous creature guarding the dragon had no sense of independent thought. In attempting to harness the abilities of the mysterious artifact, Nekros had unleashed something else. Zuluhed called it a golem of fire—perhaps of the essence of demon power, but certainly not one of the supposedly mythical beings.

Whatever its origins or its previous use, the golem served as the perfect sentry. Even the fiercest warriors steered clear of it. Only Nekros could command it. Zuluhed had tried, but the artifact from which the golem had emerged seemed now tied to the one-legged orc.

"I enter," he told the fiery creature.

The golem stiffened . . . then shattered in a wild shower of dying sparks. Despite having witnessed this departure time and time again, Nekros still backed up some, not daring to move forward until the last of the sparks had faded away.

The moment the orc stepped inside, a voice remarked, "I . . . knew . . . you would be . . . here soon. . . ."

The disdain with which the shackled dragon spoke affected her jailer not in the least. He had heard far worse from her over the years. Clutching the artifact, he made his way toward her head, which, by necessity, had been clamped down. They had lost one handler to her mighty jaws; they would not lose another.

By rights the iron chains and clamps should not have been sufficient to hold such a magnificent leviathan, but they had been enhanced by the power of the disk. Struggle all she might, Alexstrasza would never be able to free herself. That, of course, did not mean that she did not try.

"Do you need anything?" Nekros did not ask out of any concern for her. He only wanted to keep her alive for the Horde's desires.

Once the crimson dragon's scales had gleamed like metal. She still filled the vast cavern tail to head, yet these days her rib bones showed slightly underneath the skin and her words came out more beleaguered. Despite her dire condition, though, the hatred in those vast, golden eyes had not faded, and the orc knew that if the Dragonqueen ever *did* escape, he would be the first one down her gullet or fried to a crisp. Of course, since the odds of that were so very minor, even one-legged Nekros did not worry.

"Death would be nice. . . ."

He grunted, turning away from this useless conversation. At one point during her lengthy incarceration, she had tried to starve herself, but the simple tactic of taking her next clutch of eggs and breaking one of them before her horrified eyes had been enough to end that threat. Despite knowing that each hatchling would be trained to terrorize the Horde's enemies and likely die because of that, Alexstrasza clearly held out hope that someday they would be free. Shattering the egg had been like shattering a part of that hope. One less dragon with the potential to be his own master.

As he always did, Nekros inspected her latest clutch. Five eggs this time. A fair number, but most were a bit smaller than usual. That bothered him. His chieftain had already remarked on the runts produced in the last batch, although even a runt of a dragon stood several times higher than an orc.

Dropping the disk into a secure pouch at his waist, Nekros bent to lift up one of the eggs. The loss of his leg had not yet weakened his arms, and so the massive orc had little trouble hefting the object in question. A good weight, he noted. If the other eggs were this heavy, then at least they would produce healthy young. Best to get them down to the incubator chamber as soon as possible. The volcanic heat there would keep them at just the right temperature for hatching.

As Nekros lowered the egg, the dragon muttered, "This is all useless, mortal. Your little war is all but over."

"You may be right," he grunted, no doubt surprising her with his candor. The grizzled orc turned back to his gargantuan captive. "But we'll fight to the end, lizard."

"Then you shall do so without us. My last consort is dying, you know that. Without him, there will be no more eggs." Her voice, already low, became barely audible. The Dragonqueen exhaled with effort, as if the conversation had taxed her already weakening strength too much.

He squinted at her, studying those reptilian orbs. Nekros knew that Alexstrasza's last consort was indeed dying. They'd started out with three, but one had perished trying to escape over the sea and another had died of injuries when the rogue dragon Deathwing had caught him by surprise. The third, the eldest of the lot, had remained by his queen's side, but he had been centuries older than even Alexstrasza, and now those centuries, coupled with past near-mortal injuries, had taken their toll.

"We'll find another, then."

She managed to snort. Her words barely came out as a whisper. "And how . . . would you go about doing that?"

"We'll find one . . ." He had no other answer for her, but Nekros would be damned if he would give the lizard that satisfaction. Frustration and anger long held in began to boil over. He hobbled toward her. "And as for you, lizard—"

Nekros had dared come within a few yards of the Dragonqueen's head, aware that, thanks to the enchanted bonds, she would be unable to flame or eat him. Thus it was to his tremendous dismay that suddenly Alexstrasza's head, brace and all, suddenly twisted toward him, filling his gaze. The dragon's maw opened wide, and the orc had the distinctive displeasure of gazing deep into the gullet of the creature who was about to make a snack of him.

Or would have, if not for Nekros's quick reaction. Clutching the pouch in which he carried the *Demon Soul,* the warlock muttered a single word, thought a single command.

A pained roar shook the chamber, sending chunks of rock falling from the ceiling. The crimson behemoth pulled back her head as best she could. The brace around her throat glowed with such power that the orc had to shield his eyes.

Near him, the fiery servant of the disk materialized in a flash, dark eye sockets looking to Nekros for command. The warlock, however, had no need for the creature, the artifact itself having dealt with the nearly disastrous situation.

"Leave," he commanded the fire golem. As the creature departed in an explosive display, the crippled orc dared walk before the dragon. A scowl spread across his ugly features, and the frustration of knowing that he served a cause lost urged Nekros to greater anger at the leviathan's latest attempt on his life.

"Still full of tricks, eh, lizard?" He glared at the brace, which Alexstrasza had clearly worked long to loosen from the wall. The enchantment affecting her bonds did not extend to the stone upon which they were fastened, Nekros realized. That mistake had nearly cost him.

But failing to achieve his death would now cost her. Nekros fixed his heavily browed gaze on the now truly injured dragon.

"A daring trick . . ." he snarled. "A daring trick, but a foolish one." He held up the golden disk for her widening eyes to see. "Zuluhed commanded I keep you as healthy as possible, but my chieftain also commanded me to punish whenever I thought necessary." Nekros tightened his grip on the artifact, which now glowed bright. "Now is—"

"Excuse this pitiful one's interruption, o gracious master," came a jarring voice from within the cavern. "But word's come you must hear, oh, you must!"

Nekros nearly dropped the artifact. Whirling about as best he could with one good leg, the huge orc stared down at a pitifully tiny figure with batlike ears and a vast set of sharp teeth set in a mad grin. Nekros did not know what bothered him more, the creature himself or the fact that the goblin had somehow managed to infiltrate the dragon's cavern without being stopped by the golem.

"You! How'd you get in here?" Reaching down, he grasped the tiny form by the throat and lifted him upward. All thought of punishing the dragon vanished. "How?"

Even though he spoke words half-choked, the foul little creature still smiled. "J-just walked in, o gracious m-master! Just w-walked in!"

Nekros considered. The goblin must have entered when the fire golem had come to its master's aid. Goblins were tricky and often found their way into places thought secure, but even this clever rogue could not have worked his way inside otherwise.

He let the beast drop to the ground. "All right! Why come? What news do you bring?"

The goblin rubbed his throat. "Only the most important, only the most important, I assure you!" The toothy smile broadened. "Have I ever let you down, wondrous master?"

Despite the fact that, deep down, Nekros felt that goblins had less of a sense of honor than a ground slug, the orc had to admit that this one had never steered him wrong. Questionable allies at best, the goblins played many games of their own, but always fulfilled the missions set upon them by Doomhammer and, before him, the great Blackhand. "Speak, then, and be quick about it!"

The devilish imp nodded several times. "Yes, Nekros, yes! I come to tell you that there is a plan under way, more than one, actually, to free—" He hesitated, then cocked his head toward weary Alexstrasza, "—that is, to cause great disaster to Dragonmaw clan's dreams!"

An uncomfortable sensation coursed down the orc's spine. "What do you mean?"

Again the goblin cocked his head toward the dragon. "Perhaps elsewhere, gracious master?"

The creature had the right of it. Nekros glanced at his captive, who appeared to be unconscious from pain and exhaustion. Still, better to be wary around her for now. If his spy brought him the news he suspected, the orc warlock hardly wanted the Dragonqueen to hear the details.

"Very well," he grunted. Nekros hobbled toward the cavern entrance, already mulling over the likely news. The goblin hopped beside him, grinning from ear to ear. Nekros felt tempted to wipe that annoying smile off the other's face, but needed the creature for now. Still, for the slightest excuse . . . "This'd better be good, Kryll! You understand?"

Kryll nodded as he hurried to keep up, his head bobbing up and down like a broken toy. "Trust me, Master Nekros! Just *trust* me. . . ."

FIVE

e had nothing to do with the explosion," Vereesa insisted. "Why would he do something like that?"

"He is a wizard," Duncan returned flatly, as if that answered any and all questions. "They care nothing about the lives and livelihoods of others."

Well aware of the prejudices of the holy order toward magic, Vereesa did not try to argue that point. As an elf, she had grown up around magic, even could perform some slight bit herself, and so did not see Rhonin in the terrible light that the paladin did. While Rhonin struck her as reckless, he did not seem to her so monstrous as to not care about the lives of others. Had he not helped her during their flight from the dragon? Why bother to risk himself? He could still have gotten to Hasic on his own.

"And if he is not to blame," Lord Senturus continued, "then where has he gone? Why is there no trace of him in the rubble? If he is innocent of this, his body should be there along with the two of our brothers who perished during his spell. . . ." The man stroked his beard slightly. "No, this foul work is the fault of his, mark me."

And so you would hunt him down like an animal, she thought. Why else had Duncan summoned ten of his best to ride with them in search of the missing spellcaster? What Vereesa had originally seen as a rescue mission had quickly revealed itself as otherwise. When she and the rest had heard the explosion, discovered the ruin, the elf had felt a twinge inside her heart. Not only had she failed to keep her companion alive, but he and two other men had perished for no good reason. However, Duncan had clearly from the first seen it otherwise, especially when a search had revealed no trace of Rhonin's corpse among the rubble.

Her first thought had been of goblin sappers, well-versed in sneaking up to a fortress and setting off deadly charges, but the senior paladin had insisted that his region had been swept clean of any trace of the elements of the Horde, goblins especially. While the foul little creatures did possess a few fantastic and utterly improbable flying machines, none had been reported. Besides, such an airship would have had to move with lightning speed to avoid detection, something not possible for the cumbersome devices.

Which, of course, left Rhonin as the most likely source of the destruction.

Vereesa did not believe it possible of him, especially since he had been so dedicated to fulfilling his mission. She only hoped that if they found the young wizard she would be able to keep Duncan and the others from running him through before they had a chance to find out the truth.

They had scoured the nearby countryside and were now headed toward the actual direction of Hasic. Although it had been suggested by more than one of the younger knights that Rhonin had likely used his magic to spirit himself away to his destination, Duncan Senturus had evidently not thought enough of the wizard's abilities in that respect to take it to heart. He fervently believed that they would be able to track down the rogue mage and bring him to justice.

And as the day aged and the sun began its downward climb, even Vereesa began to question Rhonin's innocence. *Had* he caused the disaster, then fled the murderous scene?

"We shall have to make camp soon," Lord Senturus announced some time later. He studied the thickening woods. "While I do not expect trouble, it would serve us little good to go wandering through the dark, possibly missing our quarry at our very feet."

Her own eyesight superior to that of her companions, Vereesa considered continuing on by herself, but thought better of it. If the Knights of the

Silver Hand discovered Rhonin without her, the wizard stood little chance of surviving.

They rode on a bit farther, but spotted nothing. The sun slipped below the horizon, leaving only a faint glow of light to illuminate their way. As he had promised, Duncan called a reluctant halt to the search, ordering his knights to immediately set up camp. Vereesa dismounted, but her eyes continued to sweep over the surrounding territory, hoping against hope that the fiery wizard would make himself known.

"He is nowhere about, Lady Vereesa."

She turned to look up at the lead paladin, the only man among the searchers tall enough to force her to such an action. "I cannot help looking, my lord."

"We will find the scoundrel soon enough."

"We should hear his story first, Lord Senturus. Surely that is fair enough."

The armored figure shrugged as if it did not make a difference either way to him. "He will be given his chance to make his penance, of course."

After which they would either take Rhonin back in chains or execute him on the spot. The Knights of the Silver Hand might be a holy order, but they were also known for their expedience in meting out justice.

Vereesa excused herself from the senior paladin, not trusting her tongue to keep her from infuriating him at this point. She led her horse to a tree at the edge of the campsite, then slipped in among the trees. Behind her, the sounds of the camp muted as the elf moved farther into her own element.

Again she felt the temptation to continue with the search on her own. So very easy for her to move lithely through the forest, seek out those crevices and areas of thick foliage that might hide a corpse.

"Always so eager to go rushing off, handling matters in your own inimitable style, eh, Vereesa?" her first tutor had asked one day shortly after her induction into the select training program of the rangers. Only the best were chosen for their ranks. *"With such impatience, you might as well have been born a human. Keep this up and you will not be among the rangers for very long. . . ."*

Yet despite the skepticism of more than one of her tutors, Vereesa had prevailed and risen to among the best of her select group. She could not now fail that training by turning reckless.

Promising herself that she would return to the others after a few minutes' relaxation in the forest, the silver-haired ranger leaned against one of the trees and exhaled. Such a simple assignment, and already it had nearly fallen apart not once but twice. If they never found Rhonin, she would have to think of something to say to her masters, not to mention even the Kirin Tor of Dalaran. None of the fault in this lay with her, but—

A sudden gust of wind nearly threw Vereesa from the tree. The elf managed to cling to it at the last moment, but in the distance she could hear the frustrated calls of the knights and the wild clattering of loose objects tossed about.

As quickly as the wind struck, it suddenly died away. Vereesa pushed her disheveled hair from her face and hurried back to camp, fearful that Duncan and the others had been attacked by some terrible force akin to the dragon earlier that day. Fortunately, even as she approached, the ranger heard the paladins already discussing the repair of their camp, and as she entered the area, Vereesa saw that, other than bedrolls and other objects lying strewn about, no one seemed much out of sorts.

Lord Senturus strode toward her, eyes filled with concern. "You are well, milady? No harm has come to you?"

"Nothing. The wind surprised me, that is all."

"Surprised everyone." He rubbed his bearded jaw, gazing into the darkened forest. "It strikes me that no normal wind blows in such a manner. . . ." He turned to one of his men. "Roland! Double the guard! This may not be the end of this particular storm!"

"Aye, milord!" a slim, pale knight called back. "Christoff! Jakob! Get—"

His voice cut off with such abruptness that both Duncan, who had turned back to the elf, and Vereesa looked to see if the man had suddenly been struck down by an arrow or crossbow bolt. Instead, they found him staring at a dark bundle lying amidst the bedrolls, a dark bundle with legs stretched together and arms crossed over the chest, almost as if in deathly repose.

A dark bundle gradually recognizable as Rhonin.

Vereesa and the knights gathered around him, one of the men holding a torch near. The elf bent down to investigate the body. In the flickering light of the torch, Rhonin looked pale and still, and at first she could not tell whether he breathed or not. Vereesa reached for his cheek—

And the eyes of the mage opened wide, startling everyone.

"Ranger . . . how nice . . . to see you again. . . ."

With that, his eyes closed once more and Rhonin fell asleep.

"Fool of a wizard!" Duncan Senturus snapped. "You'll not up and vanish after good men have died, then think you can simply reappear in our midst and go to sleep!" He reached for the spellcaster's arm, intending to shake Rhonin awake, but let out a startled cry the moment his fingers touched the dark garments. The paladin gazed at his gauntleted hand as if he had been bitten, snarling, "Some sort of devilish, unseen fire surrounds him! Even through the glove it felt like seizing hold of a burning ember!"

Despite his warning, Vereesa had to see for herself. Sure enough, she felt some discomfort when her fingers touched Rhonin's clothes, but nothing of the intensity that Lord Senturus had described. Nevertheless, the ranger pulled back her hand and nodded agreement. She saw no reason at the moment why she should inform the senior paladin of the difference.

Behind her Vereesa heard the scrape of steel as it slid from its sheath. She quickly glanced up at Duncan, who had already begun shaking his head at the knight in question. "No, Wexford, a Knight of the Silver Hand cannot slay any foe who cannot defend himself. The stain would be too great to our oaths. I think we must post guards for the evening, then see what happens with our spellcaster here in the morning." Lord Senturus's weathered visage took on a grim aspect. "And, one way or another, justice *will* be served once he awakes."

"I will stand by him," Vereesa interjected. "No one else need do so."

"Forgive me, milady, but your association with—"

She straightened, staring the senior paladin in the eye as best she could. "You question the word of a ranger, Lord Senturus? You question my word? Do you assume that I will help him flee again?"

"Of course not!" Duncan finally shrugged. "If that is what you want, then that is what you want. You have my permission. Yet to do so all night with no relief—"

"That is my choice. Would you do any less with one left in your charge?"

Vereesa had him there. Lord Senturus finally shook his head, then turned to the other warriors and began giving orders. In seconds, the ranger and the wizard were alone in the center of camp. Rhonin had been left atop two of the bedrolls, the knights not certain as to how to remove them without getting burned.

She examined the sleeping form as best she could without touching him again. Rhonin's robes appeared torn in places and the face of the wizard bore tiny scars and bruises, but otherwise he seemed to be unharmed. His expression looked drained, however, as if he had suffered great exhaustion.

Perhaps it was the near darkness through which she inspected him, but Vereesa thought that the human looked so much more vulnerable now, even sympathetic. She also had to admit that he had fair looks, although the elf quickly eliminated any other thoughts along that line. Vereesa tried to see if there was any method by which she could make the unconscious mage's position more comfortable, but the only way to do so would have meant revealing that she could tolerate touching him. That, in turn, might have encouraged Lord Senturus to try to use her to better secure Rhonin, which went against the elf's bond to the mage.

With no other recourse, Vereesa settled near the prone body and looked around, eyeing the area for any possible threat. She still found Rhonin's sudden reappearance very questionable and, although he had said little about it, clearly so did Duncan. Rhonin hardly seemed capable of having transported himself to the midst of their camp. True, such an effort would explain why he now lay almost comatose, but it still did not ring true. Rather, Vereesa felt as if she looked at a man who had been kidnapped, then tossed back after the kidnapper had done with him what he would.

The only question that remained—who could have done such a fantastic thing . . . and why?

He woke knowing that they were all against him.

Well, not all of them, perhaps. Rhonin did not know exactly where he stood—providing he could stand at all—with the elven ranger. By rights, her oath to see him safely to Hasic should have meant she would defend him even against the pious knights, but one never knew. There had been an elf in the party from his last mission, an older ranger much like Vereesa. That ranger, however, had treated the wizard much the same way as Duncan Senturus did, and without the elder paladin's level of tact.

Rhonin exhaled lightly so as not to alert anyone just yet to his consciousness. He had only one way of finding out where he stood with everyone, but he needed a few more moments to collect his thoughts. Among the initial questions he would be asked would be his part in the disaster and what had happened to him afterward. Some bit of the first half the weary wizard could answer. As for the second, they likely knew as much as he.

He could delay no longer. Rhonin took another breath, then purposely stretched, as if waking.

Beside him, he heard slight movement.

With planned casualness, the mage opened his eyes and looked about. To his relief and—surprisingly—some pleasure, Vereesa's concerned countenance filled his immediate field of vision. The ranger leaned forward, striking sky-blue eyes studying him close. Those eyes suited her well, he thought for a moment . . . then quickly dismissed the thought as the sound of clanking metal warned him that the others knew he had awakened.

"Back among the living, is he?" Lord Senturus rumbled. "We shall see how that lasts—"

The slim elf immediately leapt to her feet, blocking the paladin's path. "He has only just opened his eyes! Give him time to recoup and eat at least before you question him!"

"I will deny him no basic right, milady, but he shall answer questions *while* he has his breakfast, not after."

Rhonin had propped himself up by his elbows just enough to be able to see Duncan's scowling visage, and knew that the Knights of the Silver Hand believed him to be some sort of traitor, possibly even a murderer. The weakened mage recalled the one unfortunate sentry who had plummeted to his death and suspected that there might have been more such victims. Someone had no doubt reported Rhonin's presence on the wall, and the natural prejudices of the holy order had added up the facts and gotten the wrong answer, as usual.

He did not want to fight them, doubted that at this point he could even cast more than one or two light spells, but if they tried to condemn him for what had happened at the keep, Rhonin would not hold back to defend himself.

"I'll answer as best I can," the wizard replied, declining any aid from Vereesa as he struggled to his feet. "But, yes, only with some food and water in my stomach."

The normally bland rations of the knights tasted sweet and delicious to Rhonin from the moment of the first bite. Even the tepid water from one of the flasks seemed more like wine. Rhonin suddenly realized that his body felt as if it had been forcibly starved for nearly a week. He ate with gusto, with passion, with little care for manners. Some of the knights watched him with amusement, others, especially Duncan, with distaste.

Just as his hunger and thirst at last began to level off, the questioning began. Lord Senturus sat down before him, eyes already judging the spell-caster, and growled, "The time for confession is at hand, Rhonin Redhair! You have filled your belly, now empty the burden of sin from your soul! Tell us the truth about your misdeed on the keep wall. . . ."

Vereesa stood beside the recuperating mage, her hand by the hilt of her sword. She clearly had positioned herself so as to act as his defender in this informal court, and not, Rhonin liked to think, simply because of her oath. Certainly, after their experience with the dragon, she knew him better than these oafs.

"I'll tell you what I know, which is to say not much at all, my lord. I stood atop the keep wall, but the fault of the destruction isn't mine. I heard an explosion, the wall shook, and one of your tin warriors had the misfortune to fall over the side, for which you've my sympathy—"

Duncan had not yet put on his helmet, and so now ran a hand through his graying, thinning hair. He looked as if he fought the valiant struggle to maintain control of his temper. "Your story already has holes as wide as the chasm in your heart, wizard, and you have barely even started! There are those who live, despite your efforts, who saw you casting magic just before the devastation! Your lies condemn you!"

"No, *you* condemn me, just as you condemn all my kind for merely existing," Rhonin quietly returned. He took another bite of hard biscuit, then added, "Yes, my lord, I cast a spell, but one only designed to communicate along the distances. I sought advice from one of my seniors on how to proceed on a mission that has been sanctioned by the highest powers in the Alliance . . . as the honorable ranger here'll vouch, I'd say."

Vereesa spoke even as the knight's eyes shifted to her. "His words bear truth, Duncan. I see no reason why he would cause such damage—" She held up a hand as the elder warrior started to protest, no doubt again pressing the point that all wizards became damned souls the moment they took up the art. "—and I will meet any man, including you, in combat, if that is what it takes to restore his rights and freedom."

Lord Senturus looked disgruntled at the thought of having to face the elf in battle. He glared at Rhonin, but finally nodded slowly. "Very well. You have a staunch defender, wizard, and on her word and bond I will accept that you are not responsible for what happened." Yet the moment he finished the statement, the paladin thrust a finger at the mage. "But I would hear more about your own experience during that time and, if you can dredge it from your memories, how you come to be dropped in our midst like a leaf fallen from a high tree. . . ."

Rhonin sighed, knowing he could not escape the telling. "As you wish. I'll try to tell you all I know."

It was not much more than he had related prior. Once more the weary mage spoke to them of his trek to the wall, his decision to try to contact his patron, and the sudden explosion that had rocked the entire section.

"You are certain of what you heard?" Duncan Senturus immediately asked him.

"Yes. While I can't prove it beyond doubt, it sounded like a charge being set off."

The explosion did not mean that goblins were responsible, but of course, years of war had ingrained such thoughts into even the head of the wizard. No one had reported goblins in this part of Lordaeron, but Vereesa came up with a suggestion. "Duncan, perhaps the dragon that pursued us earlier also carried with it one or two goblins. They are small, wiry, and certainly capable of hiding at least for a day or two. That would explain much."

"It would indeed," he agreed with reluctance. "And if so, we must be doubly vigilant. Goblins know no other pastimes than mischief and destruction. They would certainly strike again."

Rhonin went on with his story, telling next how he fled to the dubious safety of the tower, only to have it collapse about him. Here, though, he hesitated, knowing for certain that Senturus would find his next words questionable, at the very least.

"And then—*something*—seized me, my lord. I don't know what it was, but it took me up as if I was a toy and whisked me away from the devastation. Unfortunately, I couldn't breathe because I was held so tight, and when I next opened my eyes—" The wizard looked at Vereesa. "It was to see her face."

Duncan waited for more, but when it became clear that his wait would be fruitless, he slapped one hand against his armored knee and shouted, "And that is it? That is all you know?"

"That's all."

"By the spirit of Alonsus Faol!" the paladin snapped, calling upon the name of the archbishop whose legacy had led, through his apprentice, Uther Lightbringer, to the creation of the holy order. "You have told us nothing, *nothing* of worth! If I thought for one moment—" A slight shift by Vereesa made him pause. "But I have given my word and taken that of another. I will abide by my previous decision." He rose, clearly no longer interested in remaining in the company of the wizard. "I also make another decision here and now. We are already on route to Hasic. I see no reason why we should not move on as quickly as possible and get you to your ship. Let them deal with your situation as they see fit! We leave in one hour. Be prepared, wizard!"

With that, Lord Duncan Senturus turned and marched off, his loyal knights following immediately thereafter. Rhonin found himself alone save for the ranger, who walked to a spot before him and sat down. Her eyes settled on his. "Will you be well enough to ride?"

"Other than exhaustion and a few bruises, I seem in one piece, elf." Rhonin realized that his words had come out a little sharper than he had intended. "I'm sorry. Yes, I'll be able to ride. Anything to get me to the port on time."

She rose again. "I will prepare the animals. Duncan brought an extra mount, just in case we did find you. I will see to it that it is waiting when you finish."

As the ranger turned, an unfamiliar emotion rose within the tired spellcaster. "Thank you, Vereesa Windrunner."

Vereesa looked over her shoulder. "Taking care of the horses is part of my duty as your guide."

"I meant about standing with me during what might have turned into an inquisition."

"*That,* too, was part of my duty. I took an oath to my masters that I would see you to your destination." Despite her words, however, the corners of her mouth twitched upward for a moment in what might have been a smile. "Better ready yourself, Master Rhonin. This will be no canter. We have much time to make up."

She left him to his own devices. Rhonin stared at the dying campfire, thinking about all that had happened. Vereesa did not know how close to the truth she had been with her simple statements. The journey to Hasic would be no easy gallop, but not just for the sake of time.

He had not been entirely truthful with them, not even the elf. True,

Rhonin had not left out any part of his story, but he had left out some of his conclusions. He felt no guilt where the paladins were concerned, but Vereesa's dedication to their journey and his safety stirred some feelings of remorse.

Rhonin did not know who had set the charge. Goblins likely. He really did not care. What did concern him was what he had quickly passed over, even misdirected. When he had talked of being seized from the crumbling tower, he had not told them about having felt as if a giant hand had done so. They probably would not have believed him or, in the case of Senturus, pointed at it as proof of his communing with demons.

A giant hand *had* saved Rhonin, but no human one. Even his brief moment of consciousness had been enough to recognize the scaly skin, the wicked, curved talons greater in length than his entire body.

A *dragon* had rescued the wizard from certain death . . . and Rhonin had no idea why.

SIX

So where is he? I've little time to waste pacing around in these decadent halls!"

For what seemed the thousandth time, King Terenas silently counted to ten before responding to Genn Greymane's latest outburst. "Lord Prestor will be here before long, Genn. You know he wants to bring us all together on this matter."

"I don't know anything of the sort," the huge man in black and gray armor grumbled. Genn Greymane reminded the king of nothing less than a bear who had learned to clothe himself, albeit somewhat crudely. He seemed fairly ready to burst through his armor, and if the ruler of Gilneas downed one more flagon of good ale or devoured one more of the thick Lordaeron pastries Terenas's chefs had prepared, surely that would happen.

Despite Greymane's ursine appearance and his arrogant, outspoken manner, the king did not underestimate the warrior from the south. Greymane's political manipulations had been legendary, this latest no less so. How he had managed to give Gilneas a voice in a situation that should not have even concerned the faraway kingdom still amazed Terenas.

"You might as well tell the wind to stop howling," came a more cultured voice from the opposite end of the great hall. "You'll have more success there than getting that creature to quiet even for a moment!"

They had all agreed to meet in the imperial hall, a place where, in times past, the most significant treaties in all Lordaeron had been agreed to and signed. With its rich history and ancient but stately decor, the hall cast an aura of tremendous significance upon any discussion taking place here . . . and certainly the matter of Alterac was of significance to the continued life of the Alliance.

"If you don't like the sound of my voice, Lord Admiral," Greymane snarled, "good steel can always make certain you never hear it—or anything else—again."

Lord Admiral Daelin Proudmoore rose to his feet in one smooth, practiced sweep. The slim, weathered seaman reached for the sword generally hanging at the side of his green naval uniform, but the sheath there rattled empty. So, too, did the sheath of Genn Greymane. The one thing reluctantly agreed upon from the first had been that none of the heads of state could carry arms into the discussions. They had even agreed—even *Genn Greymane*—to having themselves searched by selected sentries from the Knights of the Silver Hand, the only military unit they all trusted despite its outward allegiance to Terenas.

Prestor, of course, was the reason that this incredible summit had managed to reach even this point. Rarely did the monarchs of the major realms come together. Generally, they spoke through couriers and diplomats, with the occasional state visit thrown in as well. Only the amazing Prestor could have convinced Terenas's uneasy allies to abandon their staffs and personal guard outside and join together to discuss matters face-to-face.

Now, if only the young noble would himself arrive. . . .

"My lords! Gentlemen!" Desperate for assistance, the king looked to a stern figure standing near the window, a figure clad in leather and fur despite the relative warmth of the region. A fierce beard and jagged nose were all Terenas could make out of Thoras Trollbane's gruff visage, but he knew that, despite Thoras's intense interest in whatever view lay outside, the lord of Stromgarde had digested every word and tone of his counterparts. That he did nothing to aid Terenas in this present crisis only served to remind the latter of the gulf that had opened up between them since the start of this maddening situation.

Damn Lord Perenolde! the king of Lordaeron thought. *If only he had not forced us into all of this!*

Although knights from the holy order stood by in case any of the monarchs came to actual blows, Terenas did not fear physical violence so much as he did the shattering of any hope of keeping the human kingdoms allied. Not for a moment did he feel that the orc menace had been forever eradicated. The humans had to remain allied at this crucial moment. He wished Anduin Lothar, regent lord of the refugees from the lost kingdom of Azeroth, could have been here, but that was not possible, and without Lothar, that left only—

"My lords! Come, come! Surely this isn't seemly behavior for any of us!"

"Prestor!" Terenas gasped. "Praise be!"

The others turned as the tall, immaculate figure entered the great hall. *Amazing the effect the man had on his elders,* so the king thought. *He walks into a room and quarrels cease! Bitter rivals lay down their weapons and talk of peace!*

Yes, definitely the choice to replace Perenolde.

Terenas watched as his friend went about the chamber, greeting each monarch in turn and treating all as if they were his best friends. Perhaps they were, for Prestor seemed not to have an arrogant bone in his body. Whether dealing with the rough-edged Thoras or the conniving Greymane, Prestor seemed to know how best to speak with each of them. The only ones who had never seemed to fully appreciate him had been the wizards from Dalaran, but then, they were wizards.

"Forgive my belated arrival," the young aristocrat began. "I'd ridden out into the countryside this morning and not realized just how long it would take me to get back."

"No need for apologies," Thoras Trollbane kindly returned.

Yet another example of Prestor's almost magical manner. While a friend and respected ally, Thoras Trollbane never spoke kindly to anyone without much effort. He tended to speak in short, precise sentences, then lapse into silence. The silences were not intended as insults, as Terenas had gradually learned. Instead, the truth was that Thoras simply did not feel comfortable with long conversations. A native of cold, mountainous Stromgarde, he much preferred action over talk.

Which made the king of Lordaeron even more pleased that Prestor had finally arrived.

Prestor surveyed the room, meeting each gaze for a moment before saying, "How good it is to see all of you again! I hope that this time we can resolve our differences so that our future meetings will be as good friends and sword-mates. . . ."

Greymane nodded almost enthusiastically. Proudmoore wore a satisfied expression, as if the noble's coming had been the answer to his prayers. Terenas said nothing, allowing his talented friend to take control of the meeting. The more the others saw of Prestor, the easier it would be for the king to present his proposal.

They gathered around the elaborately decorated ivory table that Terenas's grandfather had received as a gift from his northern vassals, after his successful negotiations with the elves of Quel'Thalas over the borders there. As he always did, the king planted both hands firmly on the tabletop, seeking to draw guidance from his predecessor. Across the table, Prestor's eyes met his for a moment. Looking into those strong, ebony orbs, the robed monarch relaxed. Prestor would handle any matters of dispute.

And so the talks began, first with stiff opening words, then more heated, blunt ones. Yet, under the guidance of Prestor, never did any threat of violence arise. More than once he had to take one or another of the participants in hand and engage in private conversation with them, but each time those intimate dialogues ended with a smile on Prestor's hawklike visage and great advancement toward the mending of Alliance ties.

As the summit tapered to a close, Terenas himself held such an exchange. While Greymane, Thoras, and Lord Admiral Proudmoore drank from the finest of the king's brandy, Prestor and the monarch huddled near the window overlooking the city. Terenas had always enjoyed this view, for from it he could see the health of his people. Even now, even with the summit going on, his subjects went about their duties, pushed on with their lives. Their faith in him bolstered his weary mind, and he knew that they would understand the decision he would make this day.

"I don't know how you did it, my boy," he whispered to his companion. "You've made the others see the truth, the need! They're actually sitting in this chamber, acting civilly with not only each other, but me! I thought Genn and Thoras would demand my hide at one point!"

"I merely did what I could to assuage them, my lord, but thank you for your kind words."

Terenas shook his head. "Kind words? Hardly! Prestor, my lad, you've single-handedly kept the Alliance from crumbling to bits! What did you tell them all?"

A conspiratorial look crossed his companion's handsome features. He leaned close to the monarch, eyes fixed on Terenas's. "A little of this, a little of that. Promises to the admiral about his continued sovereignty of the seas, even if it meant sending in a force to take control of Gilneas; to Greymane about future naval colonies near the coastal edge of Alterac; and Thoras Trollbane thinks that he'll be ceded the eastern half of that region . . . all when I become its legitimate ruler."

For a moment, the king simply gaped, not certain that he had heard right. He stared into Prestor's mesmerizing eyes, waiting for the punch line to the awful joke. When it did not come, though, Terenas finally blurted in a quiet voice, "Have you taken leave of your senses, my boy? Even jesting about such matters is highly outrageous and—"

"And you will not remember a thing about it, regardless, you know."

Lord Prestor leaned forward, his eyes seizing Terenas's own gaze and refusing to release it. "Just as none of them will remember what I truly told them. All you need to recall, my pompous little puppet, is that I have guaranteed a political advantage for you, but one that demands for its culmination and success my appointment as ruler of Alterac. Do you understand that?"

Terenas understood nothing else. Prestor had to be chosen new monarch of the battered realm. The security of Lordaeron and the stability of the Alliance demanded it.

"I see that you do. Good. Now you will go back and, just as the conference comes to an end, you will make your bold decision. Greymane already knows he will act the most reticent, but in a few days, he will agree. Proudmoore will follow your lead and, after mulling the situation a bit, Thoras Trollbane will also acquiesce to my ascension."

Something nudged at the robed king's memory, a notion he felt compelled to express. "No . . . no ruler may be chosen without . . . without the agreement of Dalaran and the Kirin Tor. . . ." He struggled to complete his thought. "They are members of the Alliance, too. . . ."

"But who can trust a wizard?" Prestor reminded him. "Who can know their agenda? That's why I had you leave them out of this situation in the first place, is it not? Wizards cannot be trusted . . . and eventually they must be dealt with."

"Dealt with . . . you're right, of course."

Prestor's smile widened, revealing what seemed far more teeth than normal. "I always am." He put a companionable arm around Terenas. "Now, it is time we returned to the others. You are very satisfied with my progress. In a few minutes, you will make your suggestion . . . and we shall move on from there."

"Yes . . ."

The slim figure steered the king back to the other monarchs, and as he did, Terenas's thoughts returned to the business at hand. Prestor's more dire statements now lay buried deep in the king's subconscious, where the ebony-clad noble desired them.

"Enjoying the brandy, my friends?" Terenas asked the others. After they nodded, he smiled and said, "A case will go back with each of you, my gift for your visit."

"A splendid show of friendship, wouldn't you say?" Prestor urged Terenas's counterparts.

They nodded, Proudmoore even toasting the monarch of Lordaeron.

Terenas clasped his hands together. "And thanks to our young associate here, I think we'll all leave even closer in heart than we were before."

"We've not signed any agreement yet," Genn Greymane reminded him. "We've not even agreed what to do about the situation."

Terenas blinked. The perfect opening. Why wait any longer to make his grand suggestion?

"As to that, my friends," the king said, taking Lord Prestor's arm and guiding him toward the head of the table. "I think I've hit upon the solution that will appeal to us all. . . ."

King Terenas of Lordaeron smiled briefly at his young companion, who could not possibly have any idea of the great reward he was about to receive. Yes, the perfect man for the role. With Prestor in charge of Alterac, the future of the Alliance would be assured.

And then they could begin to deal with those treacherous wizards in Dalaran. . . .

"This is not right!" the heavyset mage burst out. "They've no cause to leave us out of this!"

"No, they don't," returned the elder woman. "But they have."

The mages who had met earlier in the Chamber of the Air now met there again, only this time there were five. The one that Rhonin would have known as Krasus had not taken his position in this magical place, but the others were too concerned with the events of the outside world to wait. The lords of the untalented had met in seclusion, discussing a major situation without the general guidance of the Kirin Tor. While most among this council respected King Terenas and some of the other monarchs, it disturbed them that the ruler of Lordaeron would put together such an unprecedented summit. One of the inner council of the Kirin Tor had ever been present at such past events. It had only been fair, as Dalaran had always stood at the forefront of the Alliance's defense.

Times, though, appeared to be changing.

"The Alterac dilemma could have been resolved long ago," pointed out the elven mage. "We should have insisted on our proper part in the proceedings."

"And started another incident?" retorted the bearded man in stentorian tones. "Haven't you noticed of late how the other realms have been pulling back from us? It's almost as if they fear us now that the orcs've been pushed to Grim Batol!"

"Absurd! The untalented have always been suspicious of magic, but our faith to the cause is without question!"

The elder woman shook her head. "When has that mattered to those who fear our abilities? Now that the orcs have been battered, the people begin to notice that we're not like them; that we are superior in every way. . . ."

"A dangerous way to think, even for us," came the calm voice of Krasus. The faceless wizard stood in his chosen spot.

"About time you got here!" The bearded wizard turned toward the newcomer. "Did you find out anything?"

"Very little. The meeting was unshielded . . . yet all we could read were surface thoughts. Those told us nothing we did not know before. I finally had to resort to other methods to garner even some success."

The younger female dared speak. "Have they made a decision?"

Krasus hesitated, then raised a gloved hand. "Behold . . ."

In the center of the chamber, directly over the symbol etched in the floor, materialized a tall, human figure. In every way, he looked as real, if not more so, than the gathered wizards. Majestic of frame, clad in elegant, dark clothing and with features avian and handsome, he brought a moment of silence to the six.

"Who is he?" the same woman asked.

Krasus surveyed his companions before answering, "All hail the new ruler of Alterac, *King Prestor the First.*"

"*What?*"

"This is outrageous!"

"They can't do this without us—can they?"

"Who is this Prestor?"

Rhonin's patron shrugged. "A minor noble from the north, dispossessed, without backing. Yet, he seems to have ingratiated himself not only to Terenas, but even the rest, Genn Greymane included."

"But to make him *king?*" snapped the bearded spellcaster.

"On the surface, not a terrible choice. It places Alterac as once more an independent kingdom. The other monarchs find much about him they respect, so I gather. He seems to have single-handedly kept the Alliance from falling apart."

"So you approve of him?" the elder female asked.

In reply, Krasus added, "He also seems to have no history, apparently is the reason we have not been included in these talks, and—most curious of all— appears as a void when touched by magic."

The others muttered among themselves about this strange news. Then the elven wizard, clearly as puzzled as the rest, inquired, "What do you mean by the last?"

"I mean that any attempt to study him through magic reveals *nothing.* Absolutely *nothing.* It is as if Lord Prestor does not exist . . . and yet he must. Approve of him? I think I fear him."

Coming from this eldest of the wizards assembled, the words sank deep. For a time the clouds flew overhead, the storms raged, and the day turned into night, but the masters of the Kirin Tor simply stood in silence, each digesting the facts in his or her own way.

The youthful male broke the silence first. "He's a wizard then, is he?"

"That would seem most logical." Krasus returned, dipping his head slightly to accent his agreement.

"A powerful one," muttered the elf.

"Also logical."

"Then, if so," continued the elven mage, "who? One among us? A renegade? Surely a wizard of this ability would be known to us!"

The younger woman leaned toward the image. "I don't recognize his face."

"Hardly surprising," retorted her elder counterpart. "When each of us could wear a thousand masks ourselves . . ."

Lightning flashed through Krasus, going unnoticed by him. "A formal announcement will take place in two weeks. After that, unless one of the other monarchs changes his mind, this Lord Prestor will be crowned king a month later."

"We should lodge a protest."

"A start. However, what we really need to do, I think, is to find out the truth about this Lord Prestor, search into every crevice and tomb and discover his past, his true calling. We dare not confront him openly until then, for he surely has the backing of every member of the Alliance but us."

The elder woman nodded. "And even we cannot face the combined might of the other kingdoms, should they find us too much of a nuisance."

"No, we cannot."

Krasus dismissed the image of Prestor with a wave of his hand, but the young noble's countenance had already been burned into the minds of each of the Kirin Tor. Through silence, they agreed on the importance of this quest.

"I must depart again," Krasus said. "I suggest all of you do as I and think hard on this dire matter. Follow all trails, no matter how obscure and impossible, but follow them swiftly. If the throne of Alterac is filled by this enigma, I suspect that the Alliance will not long stand firm, however of one mind its rulers presently are." He took a breath. "And I fear that Dalaran may fall with the rest if that happens."

"Because of this one man?" the bearded wizard spouted.

"Because of him, yes."

And as the rest pondered his words, Krasus vanished again—

—to rematerialize in his sanctum, still shaken by what he had discovered. Guilt wracked him, for Krasus had not been entirely truthful with his counterparts. He knew—or rather *suspected*—far more about this mysterious Lord Prestor than he had let on to the others. He wished that he could have told them everything, yet not only would they have questioned his sanity, but even if they had believed him, it might only have served to reveal too much about himself and his methods.

He could ill afford to do that at this desperate juncture.

May they act as I hope they will. Alone in his darkened sanctum, Krasus dared at last pull back his hood. A single dim light with no visible source offered the only illumination in the chamber, and in its soft glow stood revealed a handsome, graying man with angular features treading near the cadaverous. Black, glittering eyes hinted of even more age and weariness than the rest of the visage. Three long scars traveled side by side down the right cheek, scars that, despite their age, still throbbed with some pain.

The master wizard turned his left hand over, revealing the gloved palm. Atop that palm suddenly materialized a sphere of light blue. Krasus passed his other hand over the sphere and immediately images formed within. He leaned back to observe those images, a high stone chair sliding into place behind him.

Once more Krasus observed the palace of King Terenas. The regal stone structure had served the monarchs of the realm for generations. Twin turrets rising several stories flanked the main edifice, a gray, stately structure like a miniature fortress. The banners of Lordaeron flew prominently not only from the turrets, but the gated entrance as well. Soldiers clad in the uniforms of the King's Guard stood station outside the gates, with several members of the Knights of the Silver Hand on duty within. Under normal conditions, the paladins would not have been a part of the defense of the palace, but with some minor matters still to be discussed by the various monarchs visiting, clearly the trustworthy warriors were needed now.

Again the wizard passed his other hand over the sphere. To the left of the vision of the palace emerged the picture of an inner chamber. Staring at it, the wizard brought the chamber into better view.

Terenas and his youthful protégé. So, despite the end of the summit and the other rulers' imminent departures, Lord Prestor still remained with the king. Krasus felt a great temptation to try to probe the mind of the ebony-clad aristocrat, but thought better of it. Let the others attempt that likely impossible feat. One such as Prestor would no doubt expect such incursions and deal with them promptly. Krasus did not want to reveal his hand just yet.

However, if he dared not probe the thoughts of the man, at least he could research his background . . . and where better to start that than at the chateau where the regal refugee had taken up residence under the king's protection?

Krasus waved one hand over the sphere and a new image formed, that of the building in question, as viewed from far away. The wizard studied it for a moment, seeing and detecting nothing of consequence, then sent his magical probe closer.

As his probe neared the high wall surrounding the building, a minor spell, much more minor than he had expected, briefly prevented his entry. Krasus readily sidestepped the spell without setting it off. Now his view revealed the very exterior of the chateau, a rather morbid place despite its elegant facade. Prestor evidently believed in keeping a neat house, but not necessarily a pleasant one. Not at all a surprise to the mage.

A quick search revealed yet another defensive spell, this one more elaborate yet still nothing Krasus could not circumnavigate. With one deft gesture, the angular figure once more bypassed Prestor's handiwork. Another moment and Krasus would be inside, where he could—

His sphere blackened.

The blackness spread beyond the edges of the sphere.

The blackness *reached* for the wizard.

Krasus threw himself from the chair. Tentacles of purest night enveloped the stone seat, pouring over it as they would have the mage himself. As Krasus came to his feet, he watched the tentacles pull away—leaving no trace of the chair behind.

Even as the first tentacles reached for him, more sprouted from what remained of the magical orb. The mage stumbled back, for one of the few times in his life momentarily startled into inaction. Then, recalling himself, Krasus muttered words not heard by another living soul in several lifetimes, words he himself had never uttered, only read with fascination.

A cloud sparkled into life before him, a cloud that thickened like cotton. It immediately flowed toward the seeking tentacles, meeting them in midair.

The first tentacles to touch the soft cloud crumbled, turning to ash that faded even as it touched the floor. Krasus let out an exhalation of relief—then watched in horror as the second set of tentacles enshrouded his counterspell.

"It cannot be . . ." he muttered, eyes wide. "It cannot be!"

As the others had done to the chair, these ebony limbs now took in the cloud, absorbed it, *devoured* it.

Krasus knew what he faced. Only the *Endless Hunger,* a spell forbidden, acted so. He had never witnessed its casting before, but any who had studied the arts as long as he had would have recognized its foul presence. Yet, something had been changed, for the counterspell he had chosen should have been the one to end the threat. For a minute it had seemed to . . . and then a sinister transformation had occurred, a shifting in the dark spell's essence. Now the second set of tentacles came at him, and Krasus did not immediately know how to stop them from adding him to their meal.

He considered fleeing the chamber, but knew that the monstrous thing would simply continue after him no matter where in the world Krasus might hide. That had been part of the *Endless Hunger*'s special horror; its relentless pursuit generally wore the victim down until he simply gave up.

No, Krasus had to put a stop to it here and now.

One incantation remained that might do the work. It would drain him, leave him useless for days, but it did have the potential to rid Krasus of this dire threat.

Of course, it also could kill him as readily as Lord Prestor's trap would.

He threw himself aside as one tentacle reached out. No more time to weigh matters. Krasus had only seconds to formulate the spell. Even now the *Hunger* moved to cut him off, to envelop him whole.

The words which the elder mage whispered would have sounded to the ordinary person like the language of Lordaeron spoken backwards, with the wrong syllables emphasized. Krasus carefully pronounced each, knowing that even one slip due to his predicament meant utter oblivion for him. He thrust out his left hand toward the reaching blackness, trying to focus on the very midst of the expanding horror.

The shadows moved swifter than he had thought possible. As the last few words fell from his tongue, the *Hunger* caught him. A single, slim tentacle wrapped itself around the third and fourth fingers of his outstretched hand. Krasus felt no pain at first, but before his eyes those fingers simply faded, leaving open, bleeding wounds.

He spat out the last syllable just as agony suddenly coursed through his body.

The sun exploded within his tiny sanctum.

Tentacles melted away like ice caught in a furnace. Light so brilliant it blinded Krasus even with his eyes shut tight filled every corner and crack. The wizard gasped and fell to the floor clutching his maimed hand.

A hissing sound assailed his ears, sending his already heightened pulse racing more. Heat, incredible heat, seared his skin. Krasus found himself praying for a swift end.

The hiss became a roar that rose and rose in intensity, almost as if a volcanic eruption were about to take place in the very midst of the chamber. Krasus tried to look, but the light remained too overwhelming. He pulled himself into a fetal position and prepared for the inevitable.

And then . . . the light simply ceased, plunging the chamber into a still darkness.

The master mage could not at first move. If the *Hunger* had come for him now, it would have found him without the ability to resist. He lay there for several minutes, trying to regain his sense of reality and, when he finally recalled it, stem the flow of blood from his terrible wound.

Krasus passed his good hand over the injured one, sealing the bloody gap. He would not be able to repair the damage. Nothing touched by the dark spell could ever be regenerated.

He finally dared open his eyes. Even the unlit room initially appeared too bright, but, gradually, his eyes adjusted. Krasus made out a couple of shadowed forms—furniture, he believed—but nothing more.

"*Light . . .*" the battered spellcaster muttered.

A small emerald sphere burst into being near the ceiling, shedding dim illumination across the chamber. Krasus scanned his surroundings. Sure enough, the shapes he had seen were his remaining bits of furniture. Only the chair had not survived. As for the *Hunger,* it had been completely eradicated. The cost had been great, but Krasus had triumphed.

Or perhaps not. So much catastrophe in the space of a few seconds, and he did not even have anything to show for it. His attempt to probe the chateau of Lord Prestor had ended in defeat.

And yet . . . and yet . . .

Krasus dragged himself to his feet, summoned a new chair identical to the first. He fell into the chair gasping. After a momentary glance at his ruined appendages to assure himself that the bleeding had indeed stopped, the wizard summoned a blue crystal with which to once more view the noble's abode. A horrific notion had just occurred to him, one that, after all that had happened, he believed he could now verify with but a short, safe glimpse.

There! The traces of magic were evident. Krasus followed the traces further, watched their intertwining. He had to be careful, lest he reawaken the foulness he had just escaped.

Verification came. The skill with which the *Endless Hunger* had been cast, the complexity with which its essence had been altered so as to make his first counterattack unsuccessful—both pointed to knowledge and technique beyond even that of the Kirin Tor, the best mages humanity and even the elves could offer.

But there was another race whose trafficking in magic went farther back than the elves.

"I know you now. . . ." Krasus gasped, summoning a view of Prestor's proud visage. "I know you now, despite the form you wear!" He coughed, had to catch his breath. The ordeal had taken much out of Krasus, but the realization of just whose power he had confronted in many ways struck him deeper than any spell could have. "I know you—*Deathwing!*"

SEVEN

Duncan reined his horse to a halt. "Something is wrong here."

Rhonin, too, had that feeling, and coupled with his suspicions over what had happened to him at the keep, he could not help wondering if what they observed now somehow related to his journey.

Hasic lay in the distance, but a subdued, silent Hasic. The wizard could hear nothing, no sound of activity. A port such as this should have been bustling with noise loud enough to reach even their party. Yet, other than a few birds, he could make out no sound of life.

"We received no word of trouble," the senior paladin informed Vereesa. "If we had, we would have ridden here immediately."

"Maybe we are just overanxious because of the trek." Yet even the ranger spoke in low, cautious tones.

They sat there for so long that Rhonin finally had to take matters into his own hands. To the surprise of the others, he urged his mount forward, determined to reach Hasic with or without the rest.

Vereesa quickly followed, and Lord Senturus naturally hurried after her. Rhonin held back any expression of amusement as the Knights of the Silver Hand pushed forward to take the lead from him. He could tolerate their arrogance and pomposity for a little longer. One way or another, the wizard and his undesired companions would depart company in the port.

That is . . . if anything was left of the port.

Even their mounts reacted to the silence, growing more and more tentative. At one point, Rhonin had to prod his animal to move on. None of the knights made jests over his difficulty, though.

To their relief, as the party drew nearer, they did begin to hear some sounds of life from the direction of the port. Hammering. A few voices raised. Wagon movement. Not much, but at least proof that Hasic had not become a place of ghosts.

Still, they approached cautiously, aware that something did not sit well. Vereesa and the knights kept one hand by their sword hilts, while Rhonin began running through his spells in his mind. No one knew what to expect, but they all clearly expected it soon.

And just as they rode within sight of the town gate, Rhonin spotted three ominous forms rising into the sky.

The wizard's horse shied. Vereesa grabbed hold of the reins for Rhonin and brought the animal under control. Some of the knights began to draw their swords, but Duncan immediately signaled them to return the weapons to their sheaths.

Moments later, a trio of gigantic gryphons descended before the group, two alighting onto the tops of the mightiest trees, the third landing directly in their path.

"Who rides toward Hasic?" demanded its rider, a bronze-skinned, bearded warrior who, despite likely not even coming up to the mage's shoulder, looked capable of lifting not only him, but his horse as well.

Duncan immediately rode forward. "Hail to you, gryphon-rider! I am Lord Duncan Senturus of the order of the Knights of the Silver Hand, and I lead this party to the port! If you will permit a question, has some misfortune befallen Hasic?"

The dwarf gave a harsh laugh. He had none of the stout look of his more earthbound cousins, instead seeming more like a barbarian warrior who had been taken by a dragon and crushed to half-size. This one had shoulders even wider than those of the strongest knight and muscles that rippled of their own accord. A wild mane of hair fluttered behind the stocky, unyielding face.

"If you can call a pair of dragons just a misfortune, then, yes, Hasic suffered one! They came three days ago, tearing apart and burning anything they could! If not for my flight here having arrived that very morning, you'd find none of your precious port intact, human! They had barely begun when we took them in the sky! A glorious battle it was, though we lost Glodin that day!" The dwarves slapped a fist over their hearts. "May his spirit fight proud through eternity!"

"We saw a dragon," Rhonin interjected, fearful for a moment that the trio would break into one of the epic mourning songs he had heard about. "About that time. With an orc handler. Three of you came and fought it—"

The lead rider had scowled at him as soon as his mouth had opened, but at mention of the other struggle, the dwarf's eyes had lit up and a wide smile had returned to his face. "Aye, that was us as well, human! Tracked down the cowardly reptile and took him in the sky! A good and dangerous fight that was, too! Molok up there—" He indicated a fuller, slightly bald dwarf atop the tree to Rhonin's right. "—lost a fine ax, but at least he still has his hammer, eh, Molok?"

"Would rather shave off my beard than lose my hammer, Falstad!"

"Aye, 'tis the hammer that impresses the ladies most, 'tisn't it?" Falstad replied with a chuckle. The dwarf seemed to notice Vereesa for the first time. Brown eyes glittered bright. "And here's a fine elven lady now!" He made a bad attempt at a bow while still atop the gryphon. "Falstad Dragonreaver at your service, elven lady!"

Rhonin belatedly recalled that the elves of Quel-'Thalas had been the only other people whom the wild dwarves of the Aeries truly trusted. That, of course, did not look to be the entire reason why Falstad now focused on Vereesa; like Senturus, the gryphon-rider clearly found her very attractive.

"My greetings, Falstad," the silver-haired ranger solemnly returned. "And my congratulations on a victory well fought. Two dragons are much for any flight group to claim."

"All a day's task for mine, all a day's task!" He leaned as near as he could. "We've not been graced with any of your folk in this area, though, especially not so fine a lady as yourself! In what way can this poor warrior serve you best?"

Rhonin felt the hair on the nape of his neck bristle. The dwarf's tone, if not his words, offered more than simple assistance. Such things should not have disturbed the wizard, yet for some reason they did at this moment.

Perhaps Duncan Senturus felt the same way, for he answered before anyone else could. "Your offer of aid is appreciated, but likely not necessary. We have but to reach the ship that awaits this wizard so that he may be on his way from our shores."

The paladin's response made it sound as if Rhonin had been exiled from Lordaeron. Gritting his teeth, the frustrated mage added, "I am on an observation mission for the Alliance."

Falstad appeared unimpressed. "We've no cause to stop you from entering Hasic and searching for your vessel, human, but you'll find that not so many remain after the dragons attacked. Likely yours is flotsam on the sea!"

The thought had already occurred to Rhonin, but hearing it from the dwarf made the point sink home. However, he could not be defeated this early in his quest. "I have to find out."

"Then we'll be out of your way." Falstad urged his mount forward. He took one last long glance at Vereesa and grinned. "A definite pleasure, my elven lady!"

As the ranger nodded, the dwarf and his mount rose up into the air. The massive wings created a wind that blew dust into the eyes of the party, and the sudden nearness of the gryphon as it left the ground made even the most hardened of the horses step back. The other riders joined Falstad, the three gryphons quickly dwindling in the heavens. Rhonin watched the already faint forms bank toward Hasic, then fly off at an incredible rate of speed.

Duncan spat dust from his mouth; from his expression, his opinion of the dwarves was clearly not that much higher than what he thought of wizards. "Let us ride. We may still find fortune on our side."

Without another word they rode toward the port. It did not take long for them to see that Hasic had suffered even more than Falstad had let on. The first buildings they came across stood more or less intact, but with each passing moment the visible damage intensified. Crop fields in the outer lands had been scorched, the landowners' domiciles reduced to splinters. Stronger structures with stone bases had withstood the onslaught much better, but now and then they saw one that had been completely demolished, as if one of the dragons had chosen that place to alight.

The stench of burnt matter especially touched the wizard's heightened senses. Not everything the two leviathans had charred had been made of wood. How many of Hasic's inhabitants had perished in this desperate raid? On the one hand, Rhonin could actually appreciate the desperation of the orcs, who certainly had to know by now that their chances of winning the war had dropped to nil, but on the other hand . . . deaths such as these demanded justice.

Curiously, several areas near the very harbor itself looked entirely intact. Rhonin would have expected these to be in the worst condition, but other than a sullenness among the workers they saw, everything here looked as if Hasic had never been attacked.

"Perhaps the ship survived after all," he muttered to Vereesa.

"I do not think so. Not if that is any sign."

He looked out into the harbor itself, to the place at which the ranger pointed. The wizard squinted, trying to identify what exactly he saw.

"The mast of a ship, spellcaster," Duncan gruffly informed him. "The rest of the vessel and her valiant crew no doubt reside in the water below."

Rhonin bit back a curse. Surveying the harbor, he now saw that bits and pieces of wood and other material dotted the surface, flotsam from more than a dozen ships, the mage suspected. Now he realized in part why the port itself had survived; the orcs must have directed their mounts to attack the Alliance vessels first, not wanting them to escape. It did not explain why the outer reaches of Hasic had suffered worse than the interior, but perhaps most of that damage had taken place after the coming of the gryphon-riders. Not the first time that a settlement had found itself caught in the midst of a violent struggle and suffered for it. Still, the devastation would have been a lot worse if the dwarves had not come along. The orcs would have had their dragons level the port and try to slay everyone within sight.

Speculation, however, did not help with the problem at hand, namely the fact that now he had no ship on which to travel to Khaz Modan.

"Your quest is ended, wizard," Lord Senturus announced for no good reason that Rhonin could see. "You have failed."

"There may yet be a boat. I've the funds to hire one—"

"And who here will sail to Khaz Modan for your silver? These poor wretches have suffered through enough trials. Do you expect some of them to sail willingly to a land still held by the very orcs who did this?"

"I can only try to find out. I thank you for your time, my lord, and wish you well." Turning to the elf, Rhonin added, "And you as well, rang—Vereesa. You're a credit to your calling."

She looked startled. "I'm not leaving you yet."

"But your task—"

"Is incomplete. I cannot in good conscience leave you here with nowhere to go. If you still seek a way to Khaz Modan, I shall do what I can to help you—Rhonin."

Duncan suddenly straightened in the saddle. "And certainly we cannot leave matters so, either! By our honor, if you believe this task still worthy of continuation, then I and my fellows will also do what we can to seek transport for you!"

Vereesa's decision to remain for the time being had pleased Rhonin, but he could have done without the Knights of the Silver Hand. "I thank you, my lord, but there're many in need here. Wouldn't it be best if your order helped the good people of Hasic to recover?"

For the space of a breath, he actually thought that he had rid himself of the elder warrior, but after some clear deliberation with himself, Duncan finally announced, "Your words have some merit for once, wizard, yet I think we can arrange that both your mission and Hasic can benefit from our presence. My men will aid the citizens in recovery efforts while I take a personal hand in seeing if we can find a craft for you! That should settle the matter rightly, eh?"

Defeated, Rhonin simply nodded. At his side, Vereesa reacted with more grace. "Your assistance will no doubt prove invaluable, Duncan. Thank you."

After the senior paladin had sent the other knights on their way, he, Rhonin, and the ranger briefly discussed how best to go about their search. They soon agreed that separate paths would cover more ground, with all three returning at evening meal to discuss any possibilities. Lord Senturus clearly doubted that any of them would have success, but his duty to Lordaeron and the Alliance—and possibly his infatuation with Vereesa—demanded he do his part.

Rhonin scoured the northern area of the port, seeking out any craft larger than a dinghy. The dragons had been thorough, however, and as the day waned, he found himself with nothing yet to report. It gradually got to the point where he remained uncertain as to which bothered him more—being unable to find transport, or fearing that the so-grand lord knight would be the one to present them with the answer to Rhonin's predicament.

There were methods by which a wizard could span such long distances, but only those like the both legendary and cursed Medivh had ever used them with confidence. Even if Rhonin did successfully cast the spell, he risked not only possible detection by any orc warlock in the area, but also unexpected changes in his destination due to the emanations from the region where the Dark Portal lay. Rhonin did not want to find himself materializing over an active volcano. Yet, by what other method could he make his journey?

While he struggled to find an answer, the recovery of Hasic took place around him. Women and children gathered what wreckage they found floating in from the harbor, scavenging whatever still seemed of use and piling the rest to one side for later disposal. A special unit of the town guard went along the shoreline, searching for the waterlogged corpses of any of the mariners who had gone down with their ships. A few of the people stared at the somber, dark-clad mage as he walked among them, some of the parents pulling their children to them as he passed. Now and then Rhonin read expressions that hinted of blame, as if somehow he had been responsible for this terrible assault. Even under such dire conditions the common folk could not forget their prejudices and fears concerning his kind.

Above him, a pair of the gryphons flew past, the dwarves maintaining watch for any new attack. Rhonin doubted the region would be seeing any dragon strikes soon, the last one having cost the orcs far too much. Falstad and his companions would have better served the port by landing and helping those left, but the wary spellcaster suspected that the dwarves, not the most friendly of Lordaeron's allies, preferred to stay aloft and aloof. Given any good reason, they no doubt would have even abandoned Hasic entirely rather than—

Another reason?

"Of course . . ." Rhonin muttered. He watched the two creatures and their riders descend to the southwest. Who else but the dwarves might find his offer tempting? Who else was insane enough?

Disregarding the spectacle he might be making of himself, Rhonin ran after the dwindling figures.

Vereesa left the southernmost edge of the docks in total disgust. Not only had she met with no success, but of all the human settlements she had visited, Hasic ranked among the highest in stench. It had little to do with the disaster or even the smell of fish. Hasic just stank. Most humans had little enough sense of smell; the people here clearly had none.

The ranger wanted to be rid of this place, to return to her own kind so that she could be appointed to a more critical role, but until Vereesa could satisfy herself that she had done all she could for Rhonin, the ranger could not, in good conscience, depart. Yet there seemed no method by which the wizard might continue with his journey, one she now remained positive had to do with more than simply observation. Rhonin had revealed himself far too determined to be simply going on such a minor mission. No, he had something else in mind.

If only she knew what it might be . . .

The time for evening meal fast approached. With no sign of hope, the ranger headed inland, utilizing the most direct streets and alleys available despite the sometimes overwhelming scents. Hasic also maintained land routes to its neighbors, especially the major realms of Hillsbrad and Southshore. Although it would take more than a week to reach either one, perhaps that remained the only chance.

"Well . . . my beautiful elven lady!"

She looked the wrong way at first, thinking one of the humans spoke so with her, but then Vereesa recalled who had last used such terms. The ranger turned to her right and shifted her gaze more earthward . . . there to see Falstad in all his half-sized glory, the wild dwarf's eyes bright and his mouth open in a wide, knowing grin. He carried a sack over one shoulder and had his great hammer slung over the other. The weight of either would have left many an elf or human slumping from effort, but Falstad carried both with the ease of his kind.

"Master Falstad. Greetings to you."

"Please! I am Falstad to my friends! I am master of nothing save my own wondrous fate!"

"And I am simply Vereesa to my friends." Although the dwarf seemed to have a high opinion of himself, something in his manner made it hard not to like him, albeit not as much as Falstad possibly hoped. He did little to hide his interest in her, even allowing his eyes now and then to wander below her face. The ranger decided she had to deal with that situation immediately. "And they remain my friends only so long as they treat me with the respect with which I in turn treat them."

The dark orbs shot back up to meet her own, but otherwise Falstad pretended innocence. "How goes your quest to set the wizard on the water, my elven lady? Not good, I'd say, not good at all!"

"No, not good. It seems that the only vessels not damaged took to the sea as soon as they could for safer climes. Hasic is a port without function. . . ."

"A pity, a pity! We should discuss this further over a good flagon of spirits! What say you?"

She held back the slight smile his jovial persistence stirred. "Another time, perhaps. I still have a task to fulfill and you—" Vereesa indicated the sack "—seem to have one of your own."

"This little pouch?" He swung the heavy sack around with ease. "Some small bit of supplies, enough to last us until we leave this human place. All I need do is give them to Molok and you and I can be on our way to—"

The polite yet more blunt refusal forming on the ranger's lips died away as the angry squawk of a gryphon some short distance away—followed by voices rising in argument—set both her and Falstad to full alertness. Without a word the dwarf turned from her, sack dropped to the ground and stormhammer already unslung. He moved with such incredible swiftness for one of his build and size that even though Vereesa immediately followed after, Falstad had already vanished halfway down the street.

Vereesa unsheathed her own weapon, picking up her pace. The voices grew stronger, more strident, and she had the uncomfortable feeling that one of them belonged to Rhonin.

The street quickly gave way to one of the open areas caused by the devastation. Here some of the gryphon-riders awaited their leader, and here the wizard had apparently decided to accost them for some inexplicable reason. Wizards had often been called mad, but surely Rhonin had to be one of the most insane if he thought himself safe in arguing with wild dwarves.

And, in fact, one of them already had the mage by the clasp of his robe and had lifted the human up more than a foot off the ground.

"I said leave us be, foul one! If your ears don't be working, then I might as well tear them off!"

"Molok!" Falstad shouted. "What's this spellcaster done that's so enraged you?"

Still holding Rhonin in the air, the other dwarf, who could have been Falstad's twin save for a scar across his nose and a less humorous cast to his features, turned to his leader. "This one's followed Tupan and the others, first to the base camp, then, even after Tupan turned him away and flew off, here to where we all agreed to meet! Told him thrice to clear off, but the human just won't see good sense! Thought maybe he'd see clearer if I gave him a higher point from which to think about things!"

"Spellcasters . . ." the flight leader muttered. "You've my lasting sympathy, my elven lady!"

"Tell your companion to put him down, or I shall be forced to show him the superiority of a good elven sword over his hammer."

Falstad turned, blinking. He stared at the ranger as if seeing her for the first time. His gaze briefly shifted to the sleek, gleaming blade, then back to the narrowed, determined eyes.

"You'd do that, wouldn't you? You'd defend this creature from those who've been the good friends of your people since before these humans even existed!"

"She has no need to defend me," came Rhonin's voice. The dangling mage seemed more annoyed by his predicament than rightfully fearful. Perhaps he did not realize that Molok could easily break his back in two. "Thus far, I've held my temper in check, but—"

Anything he said from this point on would only ensure that a struggle would develop. Vereesa moved swiftly, cutting off Rhonin with a wave of her hand and setting herself between Falstad and Molok. "This is utterly reprehensible! The Horde has not even been completely destroyed, and already we are at each other's throat. Is this how allies are to act? Have your warrior release him, Falstad, and we shall see if we cannot resolve this with reason, not fury."

"'Tis only a spellcaster . . ." the lead gryphon rider muttered, but he nonetheless nodded, signaling Molok to release Rhonin.

With some reluctance, the other dwarf did just that. Rhonin straightened his robe and pushed his hair back in place, his expression guarded. Vereesa prayed that he would maintain his calm.

"What happened here?" she demanded of him.

"I came to them with a simple proposal, that was all. That they chose to react the way they did shows their barbaric—"

"He wanted us to fly him to Khaz Modan!" snapped Molok.

"The gryphon-riders?" Vereesa could not help but admire Rhonin's audacity, if not his recklessness. Fly across the sea on the back of one of the beasts—and not even as the principal rider, but someone forced to hold on to the dwarf in control? Truly Rhonin's mission had to be of more importance than he had let on for the wizard to attempt to convince Molok and the others to do this! Small wonder they thought him mad.

"I thought them capable and daring enough . . . but evidently I was wrong about that."

Falstad took umbrage. "If there's a hint at all in your words that we're cowards, human, I'll do to you what I kept Molok from doing! There's no more bold people, no mightier warriors, than the dwarves of the Aerie Peaks! 'Tisn't that we fear the orcs or dragons of Grim Batol; 'tis more that we care not to suffer the touch of your kind any more than necessary!"

Vereesa expected fury from her charge, but Rhonin only pursed his lips, as if he had expected Falstad's response to be so. Thinking of her own past thoughts and comments concerning wizards, the ranger realized that Rhonin must have lived most his life with such condemnations.

"I am on a mission for Lordaeron," the mage replied. "That's all that should matter . . . but I see it doesn't." He turned his back on the dwarves and started off.

Sword still gripped tight, Vereesa came to a swift and desperate decision, born from her suspicions concerning Rhonin's so-called observation mission. "Wait, mage!" He paused, no doubt somewhat surprised by her abrupt call. The ranger, however, did not speak to him, but rather faced the lead gryphon-rider again. "Falstad, is there no hope at all that you might take us as close as possible to Grim Batol? If not, then Rhonin and I are surely defeated!"

The dwarf's expression grew troubled. "I thought the wizard was traveling alone."

She gave him a knowing look, hoping that Rhonin, who watched her carefully, would not misunderstand. "And what would his chances be the first time he faced a strong orc ax? He might handle one or two with his spells, but if they came close, he would need a good sword arm."

Falstad watched her brandish the blade, the troubled look fading. "Aye, and a good arm it is, with or without the sword!" The dwarf glanced at Rhonin, then his men. He tugged on his lengthy beard, his gaze returning to Vereesa. "For him, I'd do very little, but for you—and the Lordaeron Alliance, of course—I'd be more than willing. Molok!"

"Falstad! You can't be serious—"

The lead dwarf went to his friend's side, putting a companionable arm around the shoulder of a dismayed Molok. "'Tis for the good of the war, brother! Think of the daring you can boast about! We may even slay a dragon or two along the way to add to our glorious annals, eh?"

Only slightly mollified, Molok finally nodded, muttering, "And I suppose you'll be carrying the lady behind you?"

"As the elves are our eldest allies and I'm flight leader, aye! My rank demands it, doesn't it, brother?"

This time Molok only nodded. His glowering expression said all else.

"Wonderful!" roared Falstad. He turned back to Vereesa. "Once more the dwarves of the Aerie Peaks come to the rescue! This calls for a drink, a flagon of ale or two, eh?"

The other dwarves, even Molok, lit up at this suggestion. The ranger saw that Rhonin would have preferred to take his leave at this point, but chose not to say such. Vereesa had given him his transport to the shores of Khaz Modan, and possibly even near to Grim Batol, and so it behooved him to show his gratitude to all involved. True, Falstad and his fellows would also have been glad to be rid of Rhonin, but Vereesa gave silent thanks that she would have someone other than the gryphon-riders with whom to talk.

"We shall be happy to join you," she finally replied. "Is that not so, Rhonin?"

"Very much so." His words came out with all the enthusiasm of one who had just discovered something odorous in the shoe he had just put on.

"Excellent!" Falstad's gaze never once shifted to the wizard. To Vereesa he said, "The Sea Boar is still intact and much appreciative of our fine business in the past! They should be able to scrounge up a few more casks of ale! Come!"

He would have insisted on escorting her himself, but the ranger expertly maneuvered away from his reach. Falstad, perhaps more eager for ale than elves at the moment, seemed not to take any notice of her slight. Waving to his men, he led them off in the direction of their favored inn.

Rhonin joined her, but as she attempted to follow after the dwarves, he suddenly pulled her aside, his expression dark.

"What were you thinking?" the flame-haired mage whispered. "Only *I* am heading to Khaz Modan!"

"And you would never have the chance to get there if I had not mentioned my going with you. You saw how the dwarves reacted earlier."

"You don't know what you're trying to get yourself into, Vereesa!"

She pushed her face within scant inches of his own, daring him. "And what is it? More than simply observation of Grim Batol. You plan something, do you not?"

Rhonin almost seemed ready to answer her, but at that moment another figure called out. They both looked back to see Duncan Senturus coming toward them.

Something struck the elf. She had not thought of the paladin when she had been trying to convince Falstad to carry Rhonin and her across the sea. Knowing the knight as she already did, Vereesa had the horrible feeling that he would insist on going with them, too.

That thought had not likely occurred yet to the wizard, whose fury still centered around the ranger. "We'll talk of this when we've more privacy, Vereesa, but know this already—when we reach the shores of Khaz Modan, I and *only* I will continue on! You'll be returning with our good friend Falstad . . . and if you think of going any farther—"

His eyes flared. Literally flared. Even the stalwart elf could not help but lean back in astonishment.

"—I'll send you back here myself!"

EIGHT

They were closing in on Grim Batol.

Nekros had known this day would come. Since the catastrophic defeat of Doomhammer and the bulk of the Horde, he had begun counting the days until the triumphant humans and their allies would come marching toward what remained of the orcs' domain in Khaz Modan. True, the Lordaeron Alliance had had to fight tooth and nail every inch of the way, but they had finally made it. Nekros could almost envision the armies amassing on the borders.

But before those armies struck, they hoped to weaken the orcs much further. If he could trust the word of Kryll, who had no reason to lie this time, then a plot was afoot to either release or destroy the Dragonqueen. Exactly how many had been sent, the goblin had not been able to say, but Nekros envisioned an operation as significant as this, combined with reports of increased military activity to the northwest, to require at least a regiment of handpicked knights and rangers. There would also certainly be wizards, powerful ones.

The orc hefted his talisman. Not even the *Demon Soul* would enable him to defend the lair sufficiently, and he could expect no help from his chieftain at this point. Zuluhed had his followers preparing for the expected onslaught to the north. A few lesser acolytes watched the southern and western borders, but Nekros had as much faith in them as he did the mental stability of Kryll. No, as usual, everything hinged on the maimed orc himself and the decisions he made.

He hobbled through the stone passage until he came to where the dragon-riders berthed. Few remained of the veterans, but one Nekros trusted well still rode at the forefront of every battle.

Most of the massive warriors were huddled around the central table in the room, the place where they discussed battle, ate, drank, and played the bones. By the rattling coming from within the gathered throng, someone had a good game going on even now. The riders would not appreciate his interruption, but Nekros had no other choice.

"Torgus! Where's Torgus?"

Some of the warriors looked his way, angry grunts warning him that his intrusion had better be of some import. The peg-legged orc bared his teeth, his heavy brow furrowing. Despite his loss of limb, he had been chosen leader here and no one, not even dragon-riders, would treat him as less.

"Well? One of you lot say something, or I'll start feeding body parts to the Dragonqueen!"

"Here, Nekros . . ." A great form emerged from within the group, rising until it stood a head taller than any of the other orcs. A countenance ugly even by the standards of his own race glared back at Nekros. One tusk had been broken off and scars graced both sides of the squat, ursine face. Shoulders half again as wide as that of the elder warrior connected to muscular arms as thick as Nekros's one good leg. "I'm here . . ."

Torgus moved toward his superior, the other riders making a quick, respectful retreat from his path. Torgus walked with all the bristling confidence of an orc champion, and with every right, for under his guidance his dragon had wreaked more havoc, sent to death more gryphon-riders, and caused more routing of human forces than any of his brethren. Markers and medallions from Doomhammer and Blackhand, not to mention various clan leaders such as Zuluhed, dangled from the ax harness around his chest.

"What do you want, old one? Another seven and I'd have cleaned out everyone! This better be good!"

"It's what you've been trained for!" Nekros snapped, determined not to be humiliated by even this one. "Unless you only fight the battles of wagering now?"

Some of the other riders muttered, but Torgus looked intrigued. "A special mission? Something better than scorching a few worthless human peasants?"

"Something maybe including soldiers and a wizard or two! Is that more your game?"

Brutish red orbs narrowed. "Tell me more, old one. . . ."

Rhonin had his transport to Khaz Modan. The thought should have pleased him much, but the cost that transport demanded seemed far too high to the wizard. Bad enough that he had to deal with the dwarves, who clearly disliked him as much as he did them, but Vereesa's claim that she needed to come along, too—granted, a necessary subterfuge in order to actually gain Falstad's permission—had turned his plans upside down. It had been paramount that he journey to Grim Batol alone—no useless comrades, no risk of a second catastrophe.

No more deaths.

And, as if to make matters worse, he had just discovered that Lord Duncan Senturus had somehow convinced the unconvincible Falstad to take the paladin along as well.

"This is insanity!" Rhonin repeated, not for the first time. "There's no need for anyone else!"

Yet, even now, even as the gryphon-riders prepared to fly them to the other side of the sea, no one listened. No one cared to hear his words. He even suspected that, if he protested much more, Rhonin might actually find himself the only one *not* going, as nonsensical as that seemed. The way Falstad had been looking at him of late . . .

Duncan had met with his men, giving Roland command and passing on his orders. The bearded knight turned over to his younger second what seemed a medallion or something similar. Rhonin almost thought nothing of it—the Knights of the Silver Hand seeming to have a thousand different rites for every minor occasion—but Vereesa, who had come up to his side, chose then to whisper, "Duncan has handed Roland the seal of his command. If something happens to the elder paladin, Roland will permanently ascend to his place in the rolls. The Knights of the Silver Hand take no chances."

He turned to ask her a question, but she had already stepped away again. Her mood had been much more formal since his whispered threat to her. Rhonin did not want to be forced to do something to make the ranger return, but he also did not want anything to befall her because of his mission. He even did not want anything dire to happen to Duncan Senturus, although likely the paladin had far more chance of surviving in the interior of Khaz Modan than Rhonin himself.

"'Tis time for flight!" Falstad shouted. "The sun's already up and even old ones have risen and begun their day's chores! Are we all ready at last?"

"I am prepared," Duncan replied with practiced solemnity.

"So am I," the anxious spellcaster quickly answered after, not wanting anyone to think that he might be the reason for any delay. Had he had his way, he and one of the riders would have departed the night before, but Falstad had insisted that the animals needed their full night's rest after the activities of the day . . . and what Falstad said was law among the dwarves.

"Then let us mount!" The jovial elf smiled at Vereesa, then extended his hand. "My elven lady?"

Smiling, she joined him by his gryphon. Rhonin fought to maintain an expression of indifference. He would have rather she had ridden with any of the dwarves other than Falstad, but to comment so would only make him look like an absolute fool. Besides, what did it matter to him with whom the ranger rode?

"Hurry up, wizard!" grumbled Molok. "I'd just as soon get this journey over with!"

Clad more lightly, Duncan mounted behind one of the remaining riders. As a fellow warrior, the dwarves respected, if not liked the paladin. They knew the prowess of the holy order in battle, which had apparently been why it had been easier for Lord Senturus to convince them of the necessity of bringing him along.

"Hold tight!" Molok commanded Rhonin. "Or you may end up as fish bait along the way!"

With that, the dwarf urged the gryphon forward . . . and into the air. The wizard held on as best he could, the unnatural sensation of feeling his heart jump into his throat giving him no assurance as to the safety of the journey. Rhonin had never ridden a gryphon, and as the vast wings of the animal beat up and down, up and down, he decided quickly that, should he survive, he would never do so again. With each heavy flap of the part avian, part leonine creature's wings, the wizard's stomach went up and down with it. Had there been *any* other way, Rhonin would have eagerly chosen it.

He had to admit, though, that the creatures flew with incredible swiftness. In minutes, the group had flown out of sight of not only Hasic, but the entire coast. Surely even dragons could not match their speed, although the race would have been close. Rhonin recalled how three of the smaller beasts had darted around the head of the red leviathan. A dangerous feat, even for the gryphons, and likely capable by few other animals alive.

Below, the sea shifted violently, waves rising threateningly high, then sinking so very, very low. The wind tore at Rhonin's face, wet spray forcing him to pull the hood of his robe tight in order to at least partially protect himself. Molok seemed unaffected by the harsh elements and, in fact, appeared to revel in them.

"How—how long do you think before we reach Khaz Modan?"

The dwarf shrugged. "Several hours, human! Couldn't say better than that!"

Keeping his darkening thoughts to himself, the wizard huddled closer and tried to ignore the journey as much as possible. The thought of so much water underneath him bothered Rhonin more than he had thought. Between Hasic and the shores of Khaz Modan only the ravaged island kingdom of Tol Barad brought any change to the endless waves, and Falstad had previously indicated that the party would not be landing there. Overwhelmed early in the war by the orcs, no life more complex than a few hardy weeds and insects had survived the Horde's bloody victory. An aura of death seemed to radiate from the island, one so intense that even the wizard did not argue with the dwarf's decision.

On and on they flew. Rhonin dared an occasional glimpse at his companions. Duncan, of course, faced the elements with a typically stalwart pose, evidently oblivious to the moisture splattering his bearded countenance. Vereesa, at least, showed some effects of having to travel in this insane manner. Like the mage, she kept her head low for the most part, her lengthy silver hair tucked under the hood of her travel cloak. She leaned close to Falstad, who seemed, to Rhonin, to be enjoying her discomfort.

His stomach eventually settled to something near tolerable. Rhonin peered at the sun, calculated that they had now been in the air some five hours or more. At the rate of speed with which the gryphon traveled the skies, surely they had to be past the midway point. He finally broke the silence between Molok and himself, asking if this would be so.

"Midway?" The dwarf laughed. "Two more hours and I think we'll see the crags of western Khaz Modan in the distance! Midway? Ha!"

The news more than his companion's sudden good humor made Rhonin smile. He had survived nearly three-fourths of the journey already. Just a little over a couple of hours and his feet would at last be planted firmly on the ground again. For once, he had made progress without some dire calamity to slow him down.

"Do you know a place to land once we get there?"

"Plenty of places, wizard! Have no fear! We'll be rid of you soon enough! Just hope that it doesn't pour before we get to them!"

Peering up, Rhonin inspected the clouds that had formed over the period of the last half-hour. Possible rain clouds, but he suspected that, if so, they would hold off more than long enough for the party to reach their destination. All he need worry about now was how best to make his way to Grim Batol once the others returned to Lordaeron.

Rhonin well knew how audacious his plan might look to the rest should they discover the truth. Again he thought of the ghosts that haunted him, the specters of the past. They were his true companions on this mad quest, the furies that drove him on. They would watch him succeed or die trying.

Die trying. Not for the first time since the deaths of his previous companions did he wonder if perhaps that would be the best conclusion to all of this. Perhaps then Rhonin would truly redeem himself in his own eyes, much less the ghosts of his imagination.

But first he had to reach Grim Batol.

"Look there, wizard!"

He started, not realizing that, at some point, he had drifted off. Rhonin stared past Molok's shoulder in the direction the dwarf now pointed. At first the wizard could see nothing, the ocean mists still splattering his eyes. After clearing his gaze, however, he saw two dark specks on the horizon. Two stationary specks. "Is that land?"

"Aye, wizard! The first signs of Khaz Modan!"

So near! New life and enthusiasm arose within Rhonin as he realized that he had managed to sleep through the remainder of the flight. Khaz Modan! No matter how dangerous the trek from here on, he had at least made it this far. At the rate at which the gryphons soared, it would only be a short time before they touched down on—

Two new specks caught his attention, two specks in the sky that *moved*, growing larger and larger, as if they closed in on the party.

"What are those? What's coming toward us?"

Molok leaned forward, squinting. "By the jagged ice cliffs of Northeron! Dragons! Two of them!"

Dragons . . .

"Red?"

"Does the color of the sky matter, wizard? A dragon is a dragon and, by my beard, they're coming fast for us!"

Glancing in the direction of the other gryphon-riders, Rhonin saw that Falstad and the rest had also spotted the dragons. The dwarves immediately began adjusting their formation, spreading out so as to present smaller, more difficult targets. The wizard noted Falstad steering more to the rear, likely due to the fact that Vereesa rode with him. On the other hand, the gryphon upon which Duncan Senturus traveled raced ahead, nearly outpacing the rest of the group.

The dragons, too, moved with strategy in mind. The larger of the pair rose to a higher altitude, then broke away from its companion. Rhonin instantly recognized that the two leviathans intended to force the gryphons into an area between them, where they could better pick off the smaller creatures and their riders.

Hulking forms atop each dragon coalesced into two of the largest, most brutish orcs the wary mage had ever seen. The one atop the greater behemoth looked to be the leader. He waved his ax toward the other orc, whose beast instantly veered farther to the opposite direction.

"Well-skilled riders, these!" shouted Molok with much too much eagerness. "The one on the right most of all! This will be a glorious battle!"

And one in which Rhonin might very well lose his life, just as it seemed he might have a chance to go on with his mission. "We can't fight them! I need to get to the shore!"

He heard Molok grunt in frustration. "My place is in the battle, wizard!"

"My mission must come first!"

For a moment he thought that the dwarf might actually throw him off their mount. Then, with much reluctance, Molok nodded his head, calling, "I'll do what I can, wizard! If an opening presents itself, we'll try for the shore! I'll drop you off and that'll be the end of it between us!"

"Agreed!"

They spoke no more, for at that point, the two opposing forces reached one another.

The swifter, much more agile gryphons darted about the dragons, quickly frustrating the lesser one. However, burdened as they were by extra weight, the animals ridden by Rhonin and the others could not maneuver quite so fast as usual. A massive paw with razor talons nearly swiped Falstad and Vereesa, and a wing barely missed clipping Duncan and the dwarf with him. The paladin and his companion continued to fly much too close, as if they sought to take on the one dragon in some bizarre sort of hand-to-hand combat.

With some effort, Molok removed his stormhammer, waving it about and shouting like someone who had just had his hair set on fire. Rhonin hoped that the dwarf would not forget his promise in the heat of battle.

The second dragon came down, unfortunately choosing Falstad and Vereesa for his main target. Falstad urged his gryphon on, but the wings could not beat fast enough with the elf in tow. The huge orc urged his reptilian partner on with murderous cries and mad swings of his monstrous battle-ax.

Rhonin gritted his teeth. He could not just let them perish, especially the ranger.

"Molok! Go after that larger one! We've got to help them!"

Eager as he was to obey, the scarred dwarf recalled Rhonin's earlier demand. "What about your precious mission?"

"Just go!"

A huge grin spread over Molok's visage. He gave a yell that sent every nerve in the mage's body into shock, then steered the gryphon toward the dragon.

Behind him, Rhonin readied a spell. They had only moments before the crimson leviathan would reach Vereesa. . . .

Falstad brought his mount around in a sudden arc that startled the dragon rider. The great behemoth soared past, unable to match the maneuverability of its smaller rival.

"Hold tight, wizard!"

Molok's gryphon dove almost straight down. Trying not to let base fears overwhelm him, Rhonin went over the last segment of his spell. Now if he could manage enough breath to cast it—

The dwarf let out a war cry that brought the attention of the orc. Brow furrowing, the grotesque figure twisted around so as to meet his new foe.

Stormhammer briefly met battle-ax.

A shower of sparks nearly caused the wizard to lose his grip. The gryphon squawked in surprise and pain. Molok nearly toppled from his seat.

Their mount reacted quickest, racing higher into the sky, nearly into the thickening clouds above. Molok readjusted his seating. "By the Aerie! Did you see that? Few weapons or their wielders can stand against a stormhammer! This'll be a fascinating match!"

"Let me try something first!"

The dwarf's expression darkened. "Magic? Where's the honor and courage in that?"

"How can you battle the orc if the dragon won't let you near again? We got lucky once!"

"All right! So long as you don't steal the battle!"

Rhonin made no promises, mostly because he hoped to do just that. He stared at the dragon, which had quickly followed them up, muttering the words of power. At the last moment, the wizard glanced at the clouds above.

A single bolt of lightning shot down, striking at the pursuing giant.

It hit the dragon full on, but the effects were not what Rhonin had hoped. The creature's entire form shimmered from wing tip to wing tip and the beast let out a furious shriek, but the beast did not plummet from the heavens. In fact, even the orc, who no doubt suffered great, did nothing more than slump forward momentarily in his seat.

Disappointed, the wizard had to console himself that at least he had stunned the massive creature. It also occurred to him that now neither he nor Vereesa were in any immediate danger. The dragon struggled just to keep itself aloft.

Rhonin put a hand on Molok's shoulder. "To the shore! Quickly now!"

"Are you daft, wizard? What about the battle that you just told me to—"

"Now!"

More likely because he wanted to be rid of his exasperating cargo than because he believed in any authority on the mage's part, Molok reluctantly steered his gryphon away again.

Searching around, the anxious spellcaster sought any sign of Vereesa. Neither she nor Falstad were to be found. Rhonin thought of countermanding his order again, but he knew he *had* to reach Khaz Modan. Surely the dwarves could handle this pair of monsters. . . .

Surely they could.

Molok's gryphon had already begun to pull them away from their former adversary. Rhonin again contemplated sending them back.

A vast shadow covered them.

Both man and dwarf looked up in astonishment and consternation.

The second dragon had come up on them while they had been preoccupied.

The gryphon tried to dive out of reach. The brave beast almost made it, but talons ripped through the right wing. The leonine beast roared out its agony and tried desperately to stay aloft. Rhonin looked up to see the maw of the dragon opening. The gargantuan horror intended to swallow them whole.

From behind the dragon soared a second gryphon, Duncan and his dwarf companion. The paladin had positioned himself in an awkward manner and seemed to be trying to direct the dwarf to do something. Rhonin had no idea what the knight intended, only that the dragon would be upon the wizard and Molok before he could cast a suitable spell.

Duncan Senturus leapt.

"Gods and demons!" Molok shouted, for once even the wild dwarf astounded by the courage and insanity of another being.

Only belatedly did Rhonin understand what the paladin sought to do. In a move that would have left anyone else falling to their doom, the skilled knight landed with astonishing accuracy on the neck of the dragon. He clutched the thick neck and adjusted his position even as both the beast and its orc handler finally registered exactly what had happened.

The orc raised his ax and tried to catch Lord Senturus in the back, just barely missing. Duncan took one look at him, then seemed to forget his barbaric opponent from there on. Instead he inched himself forward, avoiding the awkward attempts by the dragon to snap at him.

"He must be mad!" Rhonin shouted.

"No, wizard—he's a *warrior.*"

Rhonin did not understand the dwarf's subdued, respectful tone until he saw Duncan, legs and one arm wrapped tight around the reptilian neck, draw his gleaming blade. Behind the paladin, the orc slowly crawled forward, a murderous red glare in his eyes.

"We've got to do something! Get me nearer!" Rhonin demanded.

"Too late, human! There are some epic songs meant to be. . . ."

The dragon did not try to shake Duncan free, no doubt in order to avoid doing the same to its handler. The orc moved with more assurance than the knight, quickly coming within range of a strike.

Duncan sat nearly at the back of the beast's head. He raised his long sword up, clearly intending to plunge it in at the base, where the spine met the skull.

The orc swung first.

The ax bit into Lord Senturus's back, cutting through the thinner chain mail the man had chosen for the journey. Duncan did not cry out, but he fell forward, nearly losing his sword. Only at the last did he retain his hold. The knight managed to press the point against the spot intended, but his strength clearly began to give out.

The orc raised his ax again.

Rhonin cast the first spell to come to mind.

A flash of light as intense as the sun burst before the eyes of the orc. With a startled cry, he fell back, losing both his grip on his weapon and his seating. The desperate warrior fumbled for some sort of hold, failed, and dropped over the side of the dragon's neck, screaming.

The wizard immediately turned his worried gaze back to the paladin—who stared back at him with what Rhonin almost thought a mixture of gratitude and respect. His back a spreading stain of deep red, Duncan yet managed to straighten, lifting his sword hilt up as high as he could.

The dragon, realizing at last that he had no reason to remain still any longer, began to dip.

Lord Duncan Senturus rammed the blade deep into the soft area between the neck and skull, burying his blade halfway into the leviathan.

The red beast twitched uncontrollably. Ichor shot forth from the wound, so hot it scalded the paladin. He slipped back, lost hold.

"To him, damn it!" Rhonin demanded of Molok. "To him!"

The dwarf obeyed, but Rhonin knew they would never reach Duncan in time. From across the way he saw another gryphon soar near. Falstad and Vereesa. Even with so much weight already upon his mount, the lead rider hoped to somehow rescue the paladin.

For a moment, it seemed as if they would. Falstad's gryphon neared the teetering warrior. Duncan looked up, first at Rhonin, then at Falstad and Vereesa.

He shook his head . . . and slumped forward, rolling off the shrieking dragon.

"No!" Rhonin stretched a hand toward the distant figure. He knew that Lord Senturus had already died, that only a corpse had fallen, but the sight stirred up all the misgivings and failures of the wizard's last mission. His fear had come to pass; now he had already lost one of those with him, even if Duncan had invited himself along.

"Look out!"

Molok's sudden warning stirred him from his reverie. He looked up to see the dragon, still aloft despite its death throes, spinning wildly about. The gargantuan wings fluttered everywhere, moving almost at random. Falstad barely got his own beast out of range of one, and too late Rhonin realized that this time he and Molok would not escape a blow by the other.

"Pull up, you blasted beast!" roared Molok. "Pull—"

The wing struck them full force, ripping the mage from his seat. He heard the dwarf scream and the gryphon squawk. Stunned, Rhonin barely realized that, for a moment at least, he flew higher into the sky. Then, gravity took over and the half-conscious wizard began to descend . . . rapidly.

He needed to cast a spell. *Some* spell. Try as he might, however, Rhonin could not concentrate enough to even recall the first words. A part of him knew that this time he would surely die.

Darkness overwhelmed him, but an unnatural darkness. Rhonin wondered if perhaps he was blacking out. However, from the darkness suddenly came a booming voice, one that struck a distant chord in his memory.

"I have you again, little one! Never fear, never fear!"

A reptilian paw so great that Rhonin did not even fill the palm enveloped the wizard.

NINE

D uncan!"

"'Tis too late, my elven lady!" Falstad called. "Your man's already dead—but what a glorious tale to leave behind!"

Vereesa cared nothing about glorious tales nor the incorrect assumption that she had admired Lord Senturus more than she actually did. All that mattered to her was that a brave man whom she had come to know all too briefly had perished. True, like Falstad, the elf had immediately realized that it had only been Duncan's shell that had fallen earthward, but the horror of his tragic death had still struck her deep.

Yet, Vereesa took some comfort in the knowledge that Duncan had managed the near-impossible. The dragon had been struck a mortal blow, one that caused it to continue to thrash about madly. The dying leviathan sought to pull the blade from the base of its skull, but its efforts grew weaker and weaker. It was only a matter of time before the giant joined its slayer in the depths of the sea.

However, even in dying the dragon remained a threat. A wing nearly caught the dwarf and her. Falstad had the gryphon dive in order to avoid the wild movements of the behemoth. Vereesa held on for dear life, no longer able to concern herself with Duncan's fate.

As for the second dragon, it, too, still menaced the gryphons. Falstad brought his mount up again, rising above the other monster in order to prevent them being seized by the horrific talons. Another rider narrowly escaped the snapping jaws.

They could no longer remain here. The orc guiding this second beast clearly had vast experience in aerial combat with gryphons. Sooner or later his mount would catch one of the dwarves. Vereesa wanted no more deaths. "Falstad! We have to get away!"

"For you I would do that, my elven lady, but the scaly beast and its handler seem to have other ideas!"

True enough, the dragon now appeared fixated on Vereesa and her companion, most likely at the orc's behest. Perhaps he had noted the second rider, and possibly thought her of some importance. In fact, the very presence of the two crimson behemoths brought many questions to the ranger's mind—

specifically whether or not they had come because of Rhonin's mission. If so, then he more than she should have been the likely target. . . .

And where was Rhonin? As Falstad urged the gryphon to greater speed and the dragon closed behind them, the elf quickly glanced around, but again found no sign of him. Disturbed, she took a second look. Not only did Vereesa not see the mage, but she could not even locate the gryphon he had been riding.

"Falstad! I do not see Rhonin—"

"A worry for another time! 'Tis more important that you hold tight!"

She obeyed . . . and just in time. Suddenly the gryphon arced at such a severe angle that, had Vereesa hesitated, she might have been tossed off.

Talons slashed at the spot she and the dwarf had most recently occupied. The dragon roared its frustration and banked.

"Prepare for battle, my elven lady! It appears we are not to have any other choice!"

As he unslung his stormhammer, Vereesa cursed again the loss of her bow. True, she had a sword, but unlike Duncan, the ranger could not yet bring herself to commit such a sacrifice. Besides, she still needed to find out what had happened to Rhonin, who remained her first priority.

The orc had his own long battle-ax out, and now waved it around his head, shouting some barbaric war cry. Falstad responded with a guttural cry of his own, clearly eager for combat despite his earlier concern for Vereesa. With nothing left for her to do, the ranger held on, hoping that the dwarf's aim would be true.

A titanic form the color of night dropped in among the combatants, falling upon the crimson dragon and sending both beast and handler into a state of confusion.

"What in the name of—" was all Falstad managed.

The elf found herself speechless.

Black wings twice the span of those of the red filled Vereesa's vision, metallic glints from those wings almost blinding her. A tremendous roar shook the sky like thunder, sending the gryphons scattering.

A dragon of immense proportions snapped at the smaller red one. Dark, narrow orbs eyed the lesser leviathan with contempt. The orc's dragon roared back, but clearly it did not find this new foe to its liking.

"We may be done for now, my elven lady! 'Tis none other than the dark one himself!"

The black goliath spread his wings wide, and the sound that escaped his mighty jaws reminded Vereesa of harsh, mocking laughter. Again she caught sight of metal—*plates* of metal—spread across much of the newcomer's vast body. The natural armor of a dragon proved difficult enough to pierce; what metal would a creature such as this wear to protect its hard scales?

The answer came quick. *Adamantium.* Only it truly outshone the nearly impenetrable scale . . . and only one great leviathan had ever put himself through such agony in the name of power and ego.

"*Deathwing . . .*" she whispered. "*Deathwing . . .*"

Among the elves, it had been said long ago that there were five great dragons, five leviathans who represented arcane and natural forces. Some claimed that Alexstrasza the red represented the essence of life itself. Of the others, little was known, for even before the coming of humans the dragons had lived sheltered, hermitic existences. The elves had felt their influence, had even dealt with them on various occasions, but never had the elder creatures truly revealed their secrets.

Yet, among the dragons, there *had* been one who had made himself known to all, who ever reminded the world that, before all other races, *his* kind had ruled. Although originally bearing another name, he himself had long ago chosen *Deathwing* as his title, the better to show his contempt and intentions for the lesser creatures around him. Even the elders of Vereesa's race could not claim to know what drove the ebony giant, but throughout the years he had done what he could to destroy the world built by the elves, dwarves, and humans.

The elves had another name for him, spoken only in whispers and only in the elder tongue almost forgotten. *Xaxas.* A short title with many meanings, all dire. Chaos. Fury. The embodiment of elemental rage, such as found in erupting volcanoes or shattering earthquakes. If Alexstrasza represented the elements of life that bound the world together, then Deathwing exemplified the destructive forces that constantly sought to rip it apart.

Yet now he hovered before them, attempting, it seemed, to defend them from one of his own kind. Of course, Deathwing likely did not see it that way. This was a foe with scale of crimson, the color of his greatest rival. Deathwing hated dragons of all other colors and did his best to see that each he confronted perished, but those bearing the mantle of Alexstrasza the ebony behemoth despised most.

" 'Tis an impossible sight, eh?" murmured Falstad, for once subdued. "And yet I thought the foul monster dead!"

So had the ranger. The Kirin Tor had combined the might of the best of their human wizards with those of their elven counterparts to finally, so they had claimed, bring an end to the threat of the black fury. Even the metallic plates that Deathwing had long ago convinced the mad goblins to literally weld to his body had not protected him from those sorcerous strikes. He had fallen, fallen . . .

But now, apparently, flew triumphant again.

The war against the orcs had suddenly become a very minute thing. What were all the remnants of the Horde in Khaz Modan compared to this single, sinister giant?

The lesser dragon, also evidently a male, snapped angrily at Deathwing. The snout came near enough that the black beast could have swatted it with his left forepaw, but for some reason Deathwing held that paw closed and near to his body. Instead, he whipped his tail at his adversary, sending the red reeling back. As the black dragon moved, under the shifting metal plates what seemed to be a vast series of veins filled with molten fire radiated along both his throat and torso, flaring with each roar from the titan. Legend had it that to touch those veins of fire was to risk truly being burned. Some said this was due to an acidic secretion by the dragon, but other tales took it as literal flame.

Either way, it meant death.

"The orc is either brave beyond compare, a fool, or without any control over his beast!" Falstad shook his head. "Even I would not remain in such a fray if it could be helped!"

The other gryphons neared. Tearing her gaze away from the posturing dragons, Vereesa inspected the newcomers, but saw no sign of either Molok or Rhonin. In fact, their little group now numbered only her and four dwarves.

"Where is the wizard?" she called to the others. "Where is he?"

"Molok is dead," one of them proclaimed to Falstad. "His mount lies drifting in the sea!"

For their small stature, dwarves had incredibly muscular, dense bodies and so did not float well. Falstad and the others chose to take the discovery of the dead gryphon as proof enough of the warrior's fate.

But Rhonin was human and, therefore, whether dead or alive, stood a better chance of floating for a time. Vereesa seized on that slight hope. "And the wizard? Did you see the wizard?"

"I think 'tis obvious, my elven lady," Falstad returned, glancing back at her.

She clamped her mouth shut, knowing he spoke truth. At least with the incident at the keep, there had been enough question. Here, however, matters seemed final. Even Rhonin's magic certainly could not have saved him up here and from this height, striking the water below would have been like striking solid rock. . . .

Unable to keep from glancing down, Vereesa made out the half-sunken form of the other red dragon. Death must have come to Rhonin and Molok from one of the creature's mad turns during its final fit. She only hoped the end had been swift for both.

"What should we do, Falstad?" called out one of the other dwarves.

He rubbed his chin. "Deathwing is no warrior's friend! He'll no doubt come after us after he deals with this lesser beast! Facing him is no proper battle! Would take a hundred stormhammers just to dent his hide! Best if we return and let others know what we've seen!"

The other dwarves looked to be in agreement with this, but Vereesa found she could not give up so readily despite the obvious. "Falstad! Rhonin is a wizard! He is likely dead, but if he still lives—if he still floats down there—he could still need our help!"

"You're daft, if you'll pardon me for saying so, my elven lady! No one could've survived a fall like that, even a wizard!"

"Please! Just one sweep of the surface—and then we can depart!" Certainly if they found nothing then, her duty to the mage and his never-to-be-fulfilled mission would be at an end. That her sense of guilt would linger much, much longer was something the ranger could do nothing about.

Falstad frowned. His warriors looked at him as if he would have to be mad to spend any more time in the vicinity of Deathwing.

"Very well!" he growled. "But only for you, only for you!" To the others, Falstad commanded, "Go on back already without us! We should be behind you before long, but if for some reason we don't return, make certain that someone knows of the dark one's reappearance! Go!"

As the other dwarves urged their own mounts west, Falstad had his animal dive. However, as they swiftly headed down to the sea, a pair of savage roars made both elf and dwarf look up in concern.

Deathwing and the red bellowed at one another over and over, each cry louder and harsher than the previous. Both beasts had their talons out and their tails whipping about in a frenzy. Deathwing's crimson streaks gave him a frightening and almost supernatural appearance, as if he were one of the demons of legend.

"The posturing's over," Vereesa's companion explained. "They're about to fight! Wonder what the orc must be thinking?"

Vereesa had no concern for the orc. She again focused her concentration toward the search for Rhonin. As the gryphon soared just a few yards over the water, she surveyed the area in vain for the human. Surely there had to be some trace of him! The desperate ranger could even make out the twisted form of the dead mount not too far from them. Whether dead or alive, the wizard had to be somewhere near—unless he had actually managed after all to magick himself away from the danger?

Falstad grunted, clearly having decided that they were wasting their time. "There's nothing here!"

"Just a little longer!"

Again savage cries drew their attention skyward. The battle had begun in earnest. The red dragon tried to cut around Deathwing, but the larger beast presented too great an obstacle. The membraned wings alone acted as walls that the lesser dragon could not get past. He tried flaming one of them, but Deathwing flapped out of the way, not that the fire would have likely done more than slightly singe him.

In the process of trying to scorch his opponent, Deathwing's foe left himself open. The ebony giant could have easily raked the nearest wing of the red beast, but again the left forepaw remained shut and near to the chest. Instead, he whipped his tail at the other leviathan, sending the crimson dragon scurrying away again.

Deathwing did not look injured, so why would he hold back?

"That's it! We search no longer!" Falstad shouted. "Your wizard's at the bottom of the sea, I'm sorry to say! We've got to leave now before we join him!"

The elf ignored him at first, watching the black dragon and trying to make sense of his peculiar fighting technique. Deathwing utilized tail, wings, and other limbs, everything but the left forepaw. Now and then he moved it enough to reveal its obvious health, but always it returned to the nearness of his body.

"Why?" she murmured. "Why do that?"

Falstad thought that she spoke with him. "Because we gain nothing here but the possibility of death, and while Falstad never fears death, he prefers it on his own terms, not those of that armored abomination!"

At that moment, Deathwing, even with one paw incapacitated, caught hold of his adversary. The vast wings hemmed in the smaller red dragon, and the lengthy tail wrapped around the lower limbs. With his remaining three paws, the black leviathan tore a series of bloody gaps across the torso of his foe, including one set near the base of the throat.

"Up, blast you!" Falstad demanded of his flagging gryphon. "You'll have to wait a little longer to rest! Get us out of here first!"

As the furred beast pushed skyward as best it could, Vereesa watched as Deathwing cut yet another deep series of wounds across his counterpart's chest. A tiny rain began underneath the crimson dragon, the monster's life fluids showering the sea beneath.

With tremendous effort, the lesser beast managed to free himself. Tottering, he pushed off from Deathwing, then hesitated, as if distracted by something else.

To Vereesa's surprise, the red dragon suddenly turned and flew, in rather haphazard fashion, in the direction of Khaz Modan.

The battle had not lasted more than a minute, perhaps two, but in that short space of time Deathwing had nearly slaughtered his foe.

Curiously, the gargantuan black did not pursue. Instead, he peered at the paw held close to his chest, as if looking over something within the folded digits.

Something . . . or *someone*?

What had Rhonin told Duncan and her about his astonishing rescue from the crumbling tower? *I don't know what it was, but it took me up as if I was a toy and whisked me away from the devastation.* What other creature could so easily take a full grown man and carry him off as if he were no more than a toy? Only the fact that such an astounding act had been unheard of until this time had kept the ranger from seeing the obvious. A dragon had carried the wizard off to safety!

But . . . Deathwing?

The black dragon suddenly flew toward Khaz Modan, but not quite in the direction his crimson counterpart had fled. As he headed away from them, Vereesa noted that he continued to keep the one palm close, as if doing what he could to protect a precious cargo.

"Falstad! We need to follow him!"

The dwarf glanced at her as if she had just asked him to ride into the very maw of the behemoth. "I'm the bravest of warriors, my elven lady, but your suggestion hints at madness!"

"Deathwing has Rhonin! Rhonin is the reason that the dragon did not use his one forepaw!"

"Then clearly the wizard is as good as dead, for what would the dark one want with him other than as a snack?"

"If that was the case, Deathwing would have eaten him before. No. He clearly has some need of Rhonin."

Falstad grimaced. "You ask much! The gryphon's weary and will need to land soon!"

"Please! Just as far as you can! I cannot leave him like this! I have sworn an oath!"

"No oath would take you this far," the gryphon rider muttered, but he nonetheless steered his mount back toward Khaz Modan. The animal made noises of protest, but obeyed.

Vereesa said nothing more, knowing that Falstad had the right of it. Yet, for reasons unclear to her, she could not even now abandon Rhonin to what seemed an obvious fate.

Rather than try to fathom her own mind, the ranger pondered the dwindling form of Deathwing. He had to have Rhonin. It made too much sense in her mind.

But what would Deathwing—who hated all other creatures, who sought the destruction of orc, elf, dwarf, and human—possibly want with the mage?

She remembered Duncan Senturus's opinion of wizards, one shared not only by the other members of the Knights of the Silver Hand, but most other folk as well. *A damned soul,* Duncan had called him. Someone who would just as readily turn to evil as good. Someone who might—make a *pact* with the most sinister of all creatures?

Had the paladin spoken greater truth than even he had realized? Could Vereesa now be attempting to rescue a man who had, in actuality, sold his soul to Deathwing?

"What does he want of you, Rhonin?" she murmured. "What does he want of you?"

Krasus's bones still ached and pain occasionally shot through his system, but he had at least managed to heal himself sufficiently to return to the troubles at hand. However, he dared not tell the rest of the council what had occurred, even though the information would have been relevant to their own tasks. For now, among the Kirin Tor, the knowledge of Deathwing's human guise had to be his and his alone. The success of Krasus's other plans quite possibly depended on it.

The dragon sought to be king of Alterac! On the surface, an absurd, impossible notion; but what Krasus knew of the black dragon indicated that Deathwing had something more complex, more cunning, in mind. Lord Prestor might be pushing to create peace among the members of the Alliance, but Deathwing desired only blood and chaos . . . and that meant that this peace created by his ascension to that minor throne would only be the first step toward formulating even worse disharmony later on. Yes, peace today would mean *war* tomorrow.

If he could not tell the Kirin Tor, there were others to whom Krasus could speak. He had been rejected by them over and over, but perhaps this time one would listen. Perhaps the wizard's mistake had been asking their agents to come to him. Perhaps they would listen if he brought the terror to their very sanctums.

Yes . . . then they might listen.

Standing in the midst of his dark sanctum, his hood pulled forward to the point where his face completely vanished within, Krasus uttered the words to take him to one of those whose aid he most sought. The ill-lit chamber grew hazy, faded. . . .

And suddenly the mage stood in a cavern of ice and snow.

Krasus gazed around him, overawed by the sight despite previous visits here long, long ago. He knew in whose domain he now stood, and knew that of all those whose aid he sought this one might take the greatest umbrage at such a brazen intrusion. Even Deathwing respected the master of this chilling cavern. Few ever came to this sanctum in the heart of cold, inhospitable Northrend, and fewer still departed from it alive.

Great spires that almost appeared to be made of pure crystal hung from the icy ceiling, some twice, even three times, the height of the wizard. Other, rockier formations jutted up through the thick snow that not only blanketed much of the cavern floor, but the walls as well. From some inner passage light entered the chamber, casting glittering ghosts all about. Rainbows danced with each brush of the spires by a slight wind that somehow had managed to find its way inside from the cold, bleak land above this magical place.

Yet, behind the beauty of this winter spectacle lay other, more macabre sights. Within the enchanting blanket of snow, Krasus made out frozen shapes, even the occasional limb. Many, he knew, belonged to the few great animals who thrived in the region, while a couple, especially one marked by a hand curled in grisly death, revealed the fate of those who had dared to trespass.

More unnerving evidence of the finality of any intruder's fate could even be found in the wondrous ice formations, for in several dangled the frozen corpses of past uninvited visitors. Krasus marked among the most common a number of ice trolls—massive, barbaric creatures of pale skin and more than twice the girth of their southern counterparts. Death had not come kind to them, each bearing expressions of agony.

Farther on, the mage noted two of the ferocious beastmen known as wendigos. They, too, had been frozen in death, but where the trolls had revealed their terror at their horrible deaths, the wendigos wore masks of outrage, as if neither could believe they had come to such straits.

Krasus walked through the icy chamber, peering at others in the macabre collection. He discovered an elf and two orcs that had been added since his last sojourn here, signs that the war had spread even to this lonely abode. One of the orcs looked as if he had been frozen without ever having realized what fate had befallen him.

Beyond the orcs Krasus discovered one corpse that startled even him. Upon first glance, it seemed but a giant serpent, a peculiar enough monster to find in such a frozen hell, but the coiled body suddenly altered at the top, shifting from a cylindrical form to a nearly human torso—albeit a human torso covered with a smattering of scales. Two broad arms reached out as if trying to invite the wizard to join the creature's grisly doom.

A face seemingly elven but with a flatter nose, a slit of a mouth, and teeth as sharp as a dragon greeted the newcomer. Shadowy eyes with no pupils glared in outrage. In the dark and with the bottom half of his form hidden, this being would have passed for either elf or man, but Krasus knew him for what he was—or rather, had been. The name began to form on the wizard's tongue unbidden, as if the sinister, icy victim before him somehow drew it forth.

"Na—" Krasus started.

"You are nothing, nothing, nothing, if not audaciousss," interjected a whispering voice that seemed to trail on the very wind.

The faceless wizard turned to see a bit of the ice on one wall pull away—and transform into something nearly akin to a man. Yet the legs were too thin, bent at too awkward an angle, and the body resembled more that of an insect. The head, too, had only a cursory resemblance to that of a human, for although there were eyes, nose, and mouth, they looked as if some artisan had started on a snow sculpture, then abandoned the idea as fruitless once the first marks for the features had been traced.

A shimmering cloak encircled the bizarre figure, one that had no hood, but a collar that rose into great spikes at the back.

"Malygos . . ." Krasus murmured. "How fare you?"

"I am comfortable, comfortable, comfortable—when my privacy isss left to me."

"I would not be here if I had any other choice."

"There isss always one other choice—you can leave, leave, leave! I would be *alone!*"

The wizard, though, would not be daunted by the cavern's master. "And have you forgotten why you dwell so silently, so alone, in this place, Malygos? Have you forgotten so soon? It is, after all, only a few centuries since—"

The icy creature stalked around the perimeter of the cavern, ever keeping what passed for his eyes locked on the newcomer. "I forget nothing, nothing, nothing!" came the harsh wind. "I forget the days of darkness least of all. . . ."

Krasus rotated slowly so as to keep Malygos in front of him at all times. He knew no reason why the other should attack, but at least one of the others had hinted that perhaps Malygos, being eldest of those who still lived, might be more than a bit mad.

The stick-thin legs worked well on the snow and ice, the claws at the ends digging deep. Krasus was reminded of the poles men in the cold climes used to push themselves along on their skis.

Malygos had not always looked so, nor did he even now have to retain such a shape. Malygos wore what he wore because in some deep recess of his mind he preferred this over even the shape to which he had been born.

"Then you remember what he who calls himself *Deathwing* did to you and yours."

The outlandish face twisted, the claws flexed. Something akin to a hiss escaped Malygos.

"I *remember*. . . ."

The cavern suddenly felt much more cramped. Krasus held his ground, knowing that to give in to Malygos's tortured world might very well condemn him.

"I remember!"

The ice spires shivered, creating a sound at first like a tiny bell, then quickly rising to a near ear-piercing cry. Malygos poked his way toward the wizard, scratch of a mouth wide and bitter. Pits deepened beneath the pale imitation of a brow.

Snow and ice spread, grew, filling the chamber more and more. Around Krasus, some of the snow swirled, rose, became a spectral giant of mythic proportions, a dragon of winter, a dragon of ghosts.

"I remember the promise," the macabre figure hissed. "I recall the covenant we made! Never death to another! The world guarded forever!"

The wizard nodded, even though not even Malygos could see within the confines of his hood. "Until the betrayal."

The snow dragon now stretched wings. Less than real, more than a phantasm, it moved in reaction to the emotions of the cavern's lord. Even the mighty jaws opened and closed, as if the spectral puppet spoke instead.

"Until the betrayal, the betrayal, the betrayal . . ." A blast of ice burst forth from the snow dragon, ice so harsh and deadly that it tore into the rocky walls. *"Until Deathwing!"*

Krasus kept one hand from Malygos's sight, knowing that at any moment he might have to use it for swift spellcasting.

Yet, the monstrous creature held himself in check. He shook his head—the snow dragon repeating his gesture—and added, in a more reasonable voice, "But the day of the dragon had already passed, and none of us, none of us, *none of us,* saw anything to fear from him! He was but one aspect of the world, its most base and chaotic reflection! Of all, his day had come and gone with the most permanence!"

Krasus leapt back as the ground before him shuddered. He thought at first that Malygos had tried to catch him unaware, but instead of an attack, the ground simply rose up and formed yet another dragon, this one of earth and rock.

"For the *future,* he said," Malygos went on. "For when the world would have only humans, elves, and dwarves to watch over its life, he said! Let all the factions, all the flights, all the *great dragons*—the *aspects*—come together and re-create, reshape the foul piece, and we would have the key to forever protecting the world even after the last of us had faded away!" He looked up at the two phantasms he had created. "And I, I, I . . . I, Malygos, stood with him and convinced the rest!"

The two dragons swirled around one another, became one another, intertwining over and over. Krasus tore his eyes from them, reminding himself that although the one before him clearly despised Deathwing over all other creatures, it did not mean that Malygos would aid him . . . or even let him leave the chill cavern.

"And so," interjected the faceless wizard. "Each dragon, especially the *aspects,* imbued it with a bit of themselves, bound themselves, in a sense, to it—"

"Forever put themselves at its mercy!"

Krasus nodded. "Forever ensured that it would be the one thing that could have power over them, although they did not know it then." He held up one gloved hand and created an illusion of his own, an illusion of the object of which they spoke. "You remember how deceiving it looked? You remember what a simple-looking object it was?"

And at the summoning of the image, Malygos gasped and cringed. The twin dragons collapsed, snow and rock spilling everywhere but not at all touching either the wizard or his host. The rumble echoed through the empty passages, no doubt even out into the vast, empty wilderness above.

"Take it away, take it away, take it away!" Malygos demanded, nearly whimpered. Clawed hands tried to cover the indistinct eyes. "Show it to me no more!"

But Krasus would not be stopped. "Look at it, my friend! Look at the downfall of the eldest of races! Look at what has become known to all as the *Demon Soul!*"

The simple, shining disk spun over the mage's gloved palm. A golden prize so unassuming that it had passed into and out of the possession of many without any of them ever realizing its potential. Only an illusion appeared here now, yet it still put such fear in the heart of Malygos that it took him more than a minute to force his gaze upon it.

"Forged by the magic that was the essence of every dragon, created to first fight the demons of the Burning Legion, then to trap their own magical forces within!" The hooded spellcaster stepped toward Malygos. "And used by Deathwing to betray all other dragons just when the battle was done! Used by him against his very allies—"

"Cease this! The *Demon Soul* is lost, lost, *lost,* and the dark one is dead, slain by human and elven wizards!"

"Is he?" Stepping over what remained of the two phantasms, Krasus dismissed the image of the artifact and instead brought forth another. A human, a man clad in black. A confident young noble with eyes much older than his appearance indicated.

Lord Prestor.

"This man, this mortal, would be the new king of Alterac, Alterac in the heart of the Lordaeron Alliance, Malygos. Do you not find anything familiar about him? You, especially?"

The icy creature moved closer, peering at the rotating image of the false noble. Malygos inspected Prestor carefully, cautiously . . . and with growing horror.

"This is *no* man!"

"Say it, Malygos. Say who you see."

The inhuman eyes met Krasus's own. "You know *very* well! It *is* Deathwing!" A bestial hiss escaped the grotesque being that had once worn the majestic form of a dragon. *"Deathwing . . ."*

"Deathwing, yes," Krasus returned, his own tone almost emotionless. "Deathwing, who has been twice thought dead. Deathwing, who wielded the *Demon Soul* and forever ended any hope of a return to the Age of the Dragon. Deathwing . . . who now seeks to manipulate the younger races into doing his treacherous bidding."

"He will have them at war with one another. . . ."

"Yes, Malygos. He will have them at war with one another until only a few survive . . . at which point Deathwing will finish those. You know what a world he desires. One in which there is only he and his selected followers. Deathwing's *purified* realm . . . with no room even for those dragons not of his ilk."

"Nooo . . ."

Malygos's form suddenly expanded in all directions, and his skin took on a reptilian cast. The coloring of that skin changed, too, from an icy white to a dark and frosty silver-blue. His limbs thickened and his visage grew longer, more draconic. Malygos did not complete the transformation, though, stopping at a point that left him resembling a horrific parody of dragon and insect, a creature of nightmare. "I allied myself with him, and for this my flight saw ruin. I am all that is left of mine! The *Demon Soul* took my *children,* my *mates.* I lived only with the knowledge that he who had betrayed all had perished, and that the cursed disk had been forever expunged—"

"So did we all, Malygos."

"But he lives! He lives!"

The dragon's sudden rage left the cavern quivering. Icy spears lanced the snowy floor, creating further tremors that rocked Krasus.

"Yes, he lives, Malygos, he lives despite your sacrifices. . . ."

The macabre leviathan eyed him closely. "I lost much—too much! But you, you who call yourself Krasus, you who once also wore the form of *dragon,* you lost all, too!"

Visions of his beloved queen passed quickly through Krasus's mind. Visions of the days when the red flight of Alexstrasza had been ascendant washed over him. . . .

He had been the second of her consorts—but the first in loyalty and love.

The wizard shook his head, clearing away painful memories. The yearn-ing to patrol the skies once more had to be quelled. Until things changed, he had to remain human, remain Krasus—not the red dragon *Korialstrasz*.

"Yes . . . I lost much," Krasus finally replied, his control returned to him. "But I hope to regain something . . . something for all of us."

"How?"

"I would free Alexstrasza."

Malygos roared with mad laughter. He roared long and hard, far longer than even his madness warranted. He roared in mockery of all the wizard hoped to achieve. "*That* would serve you well—provided you could achieve such an impossible goal! But what good does that do me? What do you offer *me*, little one?"

"You know what Aspect she is. You know what she may do for you."

The laughter ceased. Malygos hesitated, clearly not wanting to believe, yet desperate to do so. "She could not—*could* she?"

"I believe it may be possible. I believe enough of a chance exists that it would be worth your efforts. Besides, what other future do you have?"

The draconic features intensified, and the wizard's host swelled incredibly. Now at last a beast five, ten, twenty times the size of Krasus stood before him, nearly all vestiges of the macabre creature Malygos had first been, gone. A dragon stood before Krasus, a dragon not seen since the days before humankind.

And with his return to his original form, so, apparently, returned some of Malygos's misgivings, for he asked the one question that Krasus had both dreaded and waited for. "The orcs. How is it that the orcs can hold her? That I have always wondered, wondered, wondered . . ."

"You know the only way they could keep her as prisoner, my friend."

The dragon reared his gleaming silver head back and hissed. "The *Demon Soul*? Those insignificant creatures have the *Demon Soul*? That is why you flashed that foul image before me?"

"Yes, Malygos, they have the *Demon Soul* and although I do not think that they know fully what they wield, they know enough to keep Alexstrasza at bay . . . but that is not the worst of it."

"And what could be worse?"

Krasus knew that he had nearly pulled the elder leviathan close enough to sanity to agree to help in rescuing the Dragonqueen, but that what he told Malygos next might put to ruination those accomplishments. Nonetheless, for the sake of more than simply his beloved mistress, the dragon who masqueraded as one of the wizards of the Kirin Tor had to tell his one possible ally the truth. "I believe Deathwing now knows what I do . . . and will also not stop until the cursed disk—and Alexstrasza—are both *his*."

TEN

For the second time in the past few days, Rhonin awoke among the trees. This time, however, the face of Vereesa did not greet him, which proved something of a disappointment. Instead, he awoke to a darkening sky and complete silence. No birds sang in the forest, no animals moved among the foliage.

A sense of foreboding touched the wizard. Slowly, cautiously, he lifted his head, glanced around. Rhonin saw trees and bushes, but nothing much more. No dragon, certainly, especially one so imposing and treacherous as—

"Aaah, you are awake at last. . . ."

Deathwing?

Rhonin looked to his left—a place he had already surveyed earlier—and watched with trepidation as a piece of the growing shadows around him detached, then coalesced into a hooded form reminiscent of someone he knew.

"Krasus?" he muttered, a moment later realizing this could not be his faceless patron. What moved before him wore the shadows with pride, lived as part of them.

No, he had been correct the first time. *Deathwing.* The shape might *seem* human, but, if dragons could possibly wear such forms, this could only be the black beast himself.

A face appeared under the hood, a man of dark, handsome, avian features. A noble face . . . at least on the surface. "You are well?"

"I'm in one piece, thank you."

The thin mouth jutted upward slightly at the edges in what almost would have been a smile. "You know me, then, human?"

"You're . . . you're Deathwing the Destroyer."

The shadows around the figure moved, faded a little. The face that almost passed for human, almost passed for elf, grew slightly more distinct. The edges of the mouth jutted up a bit more. "One among many of my titles, mage, and as accurate and inaccurate as any other." He cocked his head to one side. "I knew I chose well; you do not even seem surprised that I appear to you thus."

"Your voice is the same. I could never forget it."

"More astute than some you are, then, my mortal friend. There are those who would not know me even if I transformed before their very eyes!" The figure chuckled. "If you would like proof, I could do that even now!"

"Thank you—but, no." The last vestiges of day began to fade behind the wizard's ominous rescuer. Rhonin wondered how long he had been unconscious—and where Deathwing had brought him. Most of all, he wondered why he still lived.

"What do you want of me?"

"I want nothing of you, Wizard Rhonin. Rather, I wish to help *you* in your quest."

"My quest?" No one but Krasus and the Kirin Tor inner council knew of his true mission, and Rhonin had already begun to wonder if even all of the latter knew. Master wizards could be secretive, with their own hidden agendas set ahead of all others. Certainly, though, his present companion should have been in the dark about such matters.

"Oh, yes, Rhonin, your quest." Deathwing's smile suddenly stretched to a length not at all human, and the teeth revealed in that smile were sharp, pointed. "To free the great Dragonqueen, the wondrous Alexstrasza!"

Rhonin reacted instinctively, uncertain as to how the leviathan had learned of his true mission but still confident that Deathwing had not been meant to discover it. Deathwing despised all beings, and that included those dragons not of his ilk. No past tale in history had ever spoken of any love between this great beast and the crimson queen.

The spell the wary mage suddenly utilized had served him well during the war. It had crushed the life out of a charging orc with the blood of six knights and a fellow wizard on his meaty hands, and in a lesser form had held one of the orc warlocks at bay while Rhonin had cast his ultimate spell. Against dragons, however, Rhonin had no experience. The scrolls had insisted that it worked especially well at binding the ancient behemoths. . . .

Rings of gold formed around Deathwing—

—and the shadowy figure walked right through them.

"Now, was that *really* necessary?" An arm emerged from the cloak. Deathwing pointed.

A rock next to where Rhonin lay *sizzled* madly . . . then melted before his very eyes. The molten stone dribbled into the ground, seeped into every crack, disappearing without a trace as rapidly as it had melted in the first place. All in only scant seconds.

"This is what I could have done to you, wizard, if such had been my choice. Twice now your life is owed to me; must I make it a third and final time?"

Rhonin wisely shook his head.

"Reason at last." Deathwing approached, becoming more solid as he neared. He pointed again, this time at the mage's other side. "Drink. You will find it most refreshing."

Looking down, Rhonin discovered a wine sack sitting in the grass. Despite the fact that it had not been there a few seconds before, he did not hesitate to pick it up, then sip from the spout. Not only had his incredible thirst demanded it of him by this point, but the dragon might take his refusal as yet another act of defiance. For the moment, Rhonin could do nothing but cooperate . . . and hope.

His ebony-clad companion moved again, briefly growing indistinct, almost insubstantial. That Deathwing, let alone *any* dragon, could take on human form distressed the wizard. Who could say what a creature such as this could do among Rhonin's people? For that matter, how did the wizard know that Deathwing had not *already* spread his darkness through this very method?

And, if so, why would he now reveal such a secret to Rhonin—unless he intended to eventually silence the mage?

"You know so little of us."

Rhonin's eyes widened. Did Deathwing's powers include the ability to read another's thoughts?

The dragon settled near the human's left, seeming to sit upon some chair or massive rock that Rhonin could not see behind the flowing robe. Under a widow's peak of pure night, unblinking sable eyes met and defeated Rhonin's own gaze.

As the wizard looked away, Deathwing repeated his previous statement. "You know so little of us."

"There's—there's not much documentation on dragons. Most of the researchers get eaten."

Weak as the wizard's attempt at humor might have seemed to Rhonin, Deathwing found it quite amusing. He laughed. Laughed hard. Laughed with what, in others, would have been an insane edge.

"I had forgotten how amusing your kind can be, my little friend! How amusing!" The too-wide, too-toothsome smile returned in all its sinister glory. "Yes, there might be some truth to that."

No longer complacent in simply lying down before the menacing form, Rhonin sat straight up. He might have continued on to a standing position, but a simple glance from Deathwing seemed to warn that this might not be wise at such a juncture.

"What do you want of me?" Rhonin asked again. "What am I to you?"

"You are a means to an end, a way of achieving a goal long out of reach—a desperate act by a desperate creature. . . ."

At first Rhonin did not comprehend. Then he saw the frustration in the dragon's expression. "You—are *desperate*?"

Deathwing rose again, spreading his arms almost as if he intended to fly off. "What do you see, human?"

"A figure in shadowy black. The dragon Deathwing in another guise."

"The obvious answer, but do you not see more, my little friend? Do you not see the loyal legions of my kind? Do you see the many black dragons—or, for that matter, the crimson ones, who once filled the sky, long before the coming of humans, of even elves?"

Not exactly certain where Deathwing sought to lead him, Rhonin only shook his head. Of one thing he had already become convinced. Sanity had no stable home in the mind of this creature.

"You see them not," the dragon began, growing slightly more reptilian in skin and form. The eyes narrowed and the teeth grew longer, sharper. Even the hooded figure himself grew larger, and it seemed that wings sought to escape the confines of his robe. Deathwing became more shadow than substance, a magical being caught midway in transformation.

"You see them not," he began again, eyes closing briefly. The wings, the eyes, the teeth—all reverted to what they had seemed a moment before. Deathwing regained both substance and humanity, the latter if only on the surface. ". . . because they no longer *exist*."

He seated himself, then held out a hand, palm up. Above that hand, images suddenly leapt into being. Tiny draconic figures flew about a world of green glory. The dragons themselves fluttered about in every color of the rainbow. A sense of overwhelming joy filled the air, touching even Rhonin.

"The world was ours and we kept it well. The magic was ours and we guarded it well. Life was ours . . . and we reveled in it well."

But something new came into the picture. It took a few seconds for the suspicious mage to identify the tiny figures as elves, but not elves like Vereesa. These elves were beautiful in their own way, too, but it was a cold, haughty beauty, one that, in the end, repelled him.

"But others came, lesser forms, minute life spans. Quick to rashness, they plunged into what we knew was too great a risk." Deathwing's voice grew almost as chill as the beauty of the dark elves. "And, in their folly, they brought the *demons* to us."

Rhonin leaned forward without thinking. Every wizard studied the legends of the demon horde, what some called the *Burning Legion*, but if such monstrous beings had ever existed, he himself had found no proof. Most of those who had claimed dealings with them had generally turned out to be of questionable states of mind.

Yet, as the wizard tried to catch even a glimpse of one of the demons, Deathwing abruptly closed his hand, dismissing the images.

"If not for the dragons, this world would no longer be. Even a thousand orc hordes cannot compare to what we faced, to what we sacrificed ourselves against! In that time, we fought as one! Our blood mingled on the battlefield as we drove the demons from our world. . . ." The dark figure closed his eyes for a moment. ". . . and in the process, we lost control of the very thing we sought to save. The age of our kind passed. The elves, then the dwarves, and finally the humans each laid their claims to the future. Our numbers dwindled and, worse, we fought among ourselves. *Slew* one another."

That much, Rhonin knew. *Everyone* knew of the animosity between the five existing dragon flights, especially between the black and crimson. The origins of that animosity lay lost in antiquity, but perhaps now the wizard could learn the awful truth. "But why fight one another after sacrificing so much together?"

"Misguided ideas, miscommunication . . . so many factors that you would not understand them all even if I had the time to explain them." Deathwing sighed. "And because of those factors, we are reduced to so few." His gaze shifted, became more intense again. The eyes seemed to bore into Rhonin's own. "But that is the past! I would make amends for what had to be done . . . for what *I* had to do, human. I would help you free the Dragonqueen *Alexstrasza*."

Rhonin bit back his first response. Despite the easy manner, despite the guise, he still sat before the most dire of dragons. Deathwing might pretend friendship, camaraderie, but one wrong word could still condemn Rhonin to a grisly end.

"But—" he tried to choose his words carefully, "—you and she are enemies."

"For the same insipid reasons our kind has so long fought. Mistakes were made, human, but I would rectify them now." The eyes pulled the wizard toward them, *into* them. "Alexstrasza and I should not be foes."

Rhonin had to agree with that. "Of course not."

"Once we were the greatest of allies, of friends, and that can happen again, do you not agree?"

The mage could see nothing but those penetrating orbs. "I do."

"And you are on a quest to rescue her yourself."

A sensation stirred within Rhonin, and he suddenly felt uncomfortable under Deathwing's gaze. "How did you—how did you find out about that?"

"That is of no consequence, is it?" The eyes snared the human's again.

The discomfort faded. Everything faded under the intense stare of the dragon. "No, I suppose not."

"On your own, you would fail. There is no doubt of that. Why you continued as long as you did, even I cannot fathom! Now, though, now, with my aid, you *can* do the impossible, my friend. You *will* rescue the Dragonqueen!"

With that, Deathwing stretched forth a hand, in which lay a small silver medallion. Rhonin's fingers reached out seemingly of their own accord, taking that medallion and bringing it close. He looked down at it, studying the runes etched around the edge, the black crystal in the middle. Some of the runes he knew the meaning of, others he had never seen in his life, though the mage could sense their power.

"You *will* be able to rescue Alexstrasza, my fine little puppet," the too-wide grin stretched to its fullest. "Because with this, I will be there to guide you the entire *way.* . . ."

How did one lose a dragon?

That question had reared its ugly head time and time again, and neither Vereesa nor her companion had a satisfactory answer. Worse, night had begun to settle over Khaz Modan, and the gryphon, already long exhausted, clearly could not go on much farther.

Deathwing had been in sight nearly the entire trek, if only from a great distance. Even the eyes of Falstad, not so nearly as sharp as the elf's, had been able to make out the massive form flying toward the interior. Only whenever Deathwing had flown through the occasional cloud had he vanished, and that for no more than a breath or two.

Until an hour past.

The gargantuan beast and his burden had entered into the latest cloud, just as they had so many others previous. Falstad had kept the gryphon on target and both Vereesa and the dwarf had watched for the reappearance of the leviathan on the other side. The cloud had been alone, the next nearest some miles to the south. The ranger and her companion could see it almost in its entirety. They could not possibly miss when Deathwing exited.

No dragon had emerged.

They had watched and waited, and when they could wait no longer, Falstad had urged his animal to the cloud, clearly risking all if Deathwing hid within. The dark one, however, had been nowhere to be found. The largest and most sinister of dragons had utterly vanished.

" 'Tis no use, my elven lady," the gryphon rider finally called. "We'll have to land! Neither we nor my poor mount can go any farther!"

She had to agree, although a part of her still wanted to continue the hunt. "All right!" The ranger eyed the landscape below. The coast and forests had long given way to a much rockier, less hospitable region that, she knew, eventually built up into the crags of Grim Batol. There were still wooded areas, but overall the coverage looked very sparse. They would have to hide in the hills in order to achieve sufficient cover to avoid detection by orcs atop dragons. "What about that area over there?"

Falstad followed her pointing finger. "Those rough-hewn hills that look like my grandmother, beard and all? Aye, 'tis a good choice! We'll descend toward those!"

The fatigued gryphon gratefully obeyed the signal to descend. Falstad guided him toward the greatest congregation of hills, specifically, what looked like a tiny valley between several. Vereesa held on tight as the animal landed, her eyes already searching for any possible threat. This deep into Khaz Modan, the orcs surely had outposts in the vicinity.

"The Aerie be praised!" the dwarf rumbled as they dismounted. "As much as I enjoy the freedom of the sky, that's far too long to sit on anything!" He rubbed the gryphon's leonine mane. "But a good beast you are, and deserving of water and food!"

"I saw a stream nearby," Vereesa offered. "It may have fish in it, too."

"Then he'll find it if he wants it." Falstad removed the bridle and other gear from his mount. "And find it on his own." He patted the gryphon on the rump and the beast leapt into the air, suddenly once more energetic now that his burdens had been taken from him.

"Is that wise?"

"My dear elven lady, fish don't necessarily make a meal for one like him! Best to let him hunt on his own for something proper. He'll come back when he's satiated, and if anyone sees him . . . well, even Khaz Modan has some wild gryphons left." When she did not look reassured, Falstad added, "He'll only be gone for a short time. Just long enough for us to put together a meal for ourselves."

They carried with them a few provisions, which the dwarf immediately divided. With a stream nearby, both took their fill of what remained in the water sacks. A fire was out of the question this deep into orc-held territory, but fortunately the night did not look to be a cool one.

Sure enough, the gryphon did return promptly, belly full. The animal settled down by Falstad, who dropped one hand lightly on the creature's head as he finished eating.

"I saw nothing from the air," he finally said. "But we can't assume that the orcs aren't near."

"Shall we take turns at watch?"

" 'Tis the best thing to do. Shall I go first or you?"

Too wound up to sleep, Vereesa volunteered. Falstad did not argue and, despite their present circumstances, immediately settled down, falling asleep but a few seconds later. Vereesa admired the dwarf's ability to do so, wishing that she could be like him in that one respect.

The night struck her as too silent compared to the forests of her childhood, but the ranger reminded herself that these rocky lands had been despoiled by the orcs for many years now. True, wildlife still lived here—as evidenced by the gryphon's full stomach—but most creatures in Khaz Modan were much more wary than those back in Quel'Thalas. Both the orcs and their dragons thrived heavily on fresh meat.

A few stars dotted the sky, but if not for her race's exceptional night vision, Vereesa would have nearly been blind. She wondered how Rhonin would have fared in this darkness, assuming that he still lived. Did he also wander the wastelands between here and Grim Batol, or had Deathwing brought him far beyond even there, perhaps to some realm entirely unknown to the ranger?

She refused to believe that he had somehow allied himself with the dark one, but, if not, what did Deathwing do with him? For that matter, could it be that she had sent Falstad and herself on a wild dragon-chase, and that Rhonin had not been the precious cargo the armored leviathan had been carrying?

So many questions and no answers. Frustrated, the ranger stepped away from the dwarf and his mount, daring to survey some of the enshrouded hills and trees. Even with her superior eyesight, most resembled little more than black shapes. That only served to make her surroundings feel more oppressive and dangerous, even though there might not be an orc for miles.

Her sword still sheathed, Vereesa ventured farther. She came upon a pair of gnarled trees, still alive but just barely. Touching each in turn, the elf could feel their weariness, their readiness to die. She could also sense some of their history, going far back before the terror of the Horde. Once, Khaz Modan had been a healthy land, one where, Vereesa knew, the hill dwarves and others had made their homes. The dwarves, however, had fled under the relentless onslaught of the orcs, vowing someday to return.

The trees, of course, could not flee.

For the hill dwarves, the day of return would come soon, the elf felt, but by then it would probably be too late for these trees and many like them. Khaz Modan was a land needing many, many decades to recoup—if it ever could.

"Courage," she whispered to the pair. "A new Spring will come, I promise you." In the language of the trees, of all plants, Spring meant not only a season, but also hope in general, a renewal of life.

As the elf stepped back, both trees looked a little straighter, a little taller. The effect of her words on them made Vereesa smile. The greater plants had methods beyond even the ken of elves through which they communicated with one another. Perhaps her encouragement would be passed on. Perhaps some of them would survive after all. She could only hope.

Her brief rapport with the trees lightened the burden on both her mind and heart. The rocky hills no longer felt so foreboding. The elf moved along more readily now, certain that matters would yet turn out for the best, even in regards to Rhonin.

The end of her watch came far more quickly than she had assumed it would. Vereesa almost thought of letting Falstad sleep longer—his snoring indicated that he had sunken deep—but she also knew that she would only be a liability if her lack of rest later caused her to falter in battle. With some reluctance, the elf headed back to her companion—

—and stopped as the nearly inaudible sound of a dried branch cracking warned that something or someone drew near.

Not daring to wake Falstad for fear of losing the element of surprise, Vereesa walked straight past the slumbering gryphon-rider and his mount, pretending interest in the dark landscape beyond. She heard more slight movement, again from the same direction. Only one intruder, perhaps? Maybe, maybe not. The sound could have been meant to draw her in that very direction, the better to prevent Vereesa from discovering other foes waiting in silence.

Again came the slight sound of movement—followed by a savage squawk and a huge form leaping from nearby her.

Vereesa had her weapon ready even as she realized that it had been Falstad's gryphon who had reacted, not some monstrous creature in the woods. Like her, the animal had heard the faint noise, but, unlike the elf, the gryphon had not needed to weigh options. He had reacted with the honed instincts of his kind.

"What is it?" snarled Falstad, leaping to his feet quite effortlessly for a dwarf. Already he had his stormhammer drawn and ready for combat.

"Something among those old trees! Something your mount went after!"

"Well, he'd better not eat it until we've the chance to see what it is!"

In the dark, Vereesa could just make out the shadowy form of the gryphon, but not yet its adversary. The ranger could, however, hear another cry over those of the winged beast, a cry that did not sound at all like a challenge.

"No! No! Away! Away! Get off of me! No tidbit am I!"

The pair hurried toward the frantic call. Whatever the gryphon had cornered certainly sounded like no threat. The voice reminded the elf of someone, but who, she could not say.

"Back!" Falstad called to his mount. "Back, I say! Obey!"

The leonine avian seemed disinclined at first to listen, as if what he had captured he felt either belonged to him or could not be trusted free. From the darkness just beyond the beaked head came whimpering. *Much* whimpering.

Had some child managed to wander alone out here in the midst of Khaz Modan? Surely not. The orcs had held this territory for years! Where would such a child have come from?

"Please, oh, please, oh, please! Save this insignificant wretch from this monster— *Pfaugh!* What breath it has!"

The elf froze. No child spoke like that.

"Back, blast you!" Falstad swatted his mount on the rump. The animal stretched his wings once, let out a throaty squawk, then finally backed away from his prey.

A short, wiry figure leapt up and immediately began heading in the opposite direction. However, the ranger moved more swiftly, racing forward and snagging the intruder by what Vereesa realized was one lengthy ear.

"Ow! Please don't hurt! Please don't hurt!"

"What've you got there?" the gryphon-rider muttered, joining her. "Never have I heard something that squealed so! Shut it up or I'll have to run it through! It'll bring every orc in hearing running!"

"You heard what he said," the frustrated elf told the squirming form. "Be silent!"

Their undesired companion quieted.

Falstad reached into a pouch. "I've something here that'll help us bring a little light onto matters, my elven lady, although I'm thinking I already know what sort of scavenger we've caught!"

He pulled out a small object, which, after setting his hammer aside, he rubbed between his thick palms. As he did this, the object began to glow rather faintly. A few more seconds' action, and the glow increased, finally revealing the object to be some sort of crystal.

"A gift from a dead comrade," Falstad explained. He brought the glowing crystal toward their captive. "Now let's see if I was correct—aye, I *thought* so!"

So had Vereesa. She and the dwarf had captured themselves one of the most untrustworthy creatures in existence. A goblin.

"Spying, were you?" the ranger's companion rumbled. "Maybe we should run you through now and be done with it!"

"No! No! Please! This disgraceful one is no spy! No orc-friend am I! I just obeyed orders!"

"Then what are you doing out here?"

"Hiding! Hiding! Saw a dragon like the night! Dragons try to eat goblins, you know!" The ugly, greenish creature stated the last as if anyone should understand that.

A dragon like the night? "A black dragon, you mean?" Vereesa held the goblin nearer. "You saw this? When?"

"Not long! Just before dark!"

"In the sky or on the ground?"

"The ground! He—"

Falstad looked at her. "You can't trust the word of a goblin, my elven lady! They don't know the meaning of truth!"

"I will believe him if he can answer one question. Goblin, was this dragon alone, and, if not, who was with him?"

"Don't want to talk about goblin-eating dragons!" he began, but one prod by Vereesa's blade opened a reservoir of words. "Not alone! Not alone! He had another with him! Maybe to eat, but first to talk! Didn't listen! Just wanted to get away! Don't like dragons and don't like wizards—"

"Wizards?" both the elf and Falstad blurted. Vereesa tried to keep her hopes in check. "He looked well, this wizard? Unharmed?"

"Yes—"

"Describe him."

The goblin squirmed, waving his thin little arms and legs. The ranger did not find herself fooled by the spindly looking limbs. Goblins could be deadly fighters, with strength and cunning their puny forms belied.

"Red-maned and full of arrogance! Tall and clad in dark blue! Know no name! Heard no name!"

Not much of a description, but certainly enough. How many tall, red-haired wizards dressed in dark blue robes could there be, especially in the company of Deathwing?

"That sounds like your friend," Falstad replied with a grunt. "Looks like you were right after all."

"We need to go after him."

"In the dark? First, my elven lady, you've not slept at all, and second, even though the dark gives us cover, it also makes it damn hard to see anything else—even a dragon!"

As much as she desired to go on with the hunt right now, Vereesa knew that the dwarf had a point. Still, she could not wait until morning. Precious time would slip away. "I only need a couple of hours, Falstad. Give me that and then we can be on our way."

"It'll still be dark . . . and, in case you've forgotten, big as he is, Death-wing's as black as—as night!"

"We do not have to go searching for him, though." She smiled. "We already at least know where he landed—or rather, one of us here does."

They both looked at the goblin, who clearly desired to be elsewhere.

"How do we know we can trust him? 'Tis no tall tale that these little green thieves are notorious liars!"

The ranger turned the sharp tip of her sword toward the goblin's throat. "Because he will have two options. Either he shows us where Deathwing and Rhonin landed, or I cut him up for dragon bait."

Falstad chuckled. "You think even Deathwing could stomach the likes of him?"

Their short captive quivered and his unsettling yellow eyes, completely lacking in pupils, widened in outright fear. Despite the close proximity of the sword tip, the goblin began hopping up and down in wild fashion. "Will gladly show you! Gladly indeed! No fear of dragons here! Will guide you and lead you to your friend!"

"Keep it down, you!" The ranger tightened her hold on the devilish creature. "Or will I have to cut out your tongue?"

"Sorry, sorry, sorry . . ." murmured their new companion. The goblin quieted down. "Don't hurt this miserable one. . . ."

"*Pfah!* 'Tis a poor excuse of even a goblin we've got here!"

"So long as he shows us the way."

"This wretch will guide you well, mistress! Very well!"

Vereesa considered. "We will have to bind him for now—"

"I'll tie him to my mount. That'll keep the foul rodent under control."

The goblin looked even more ill at this latest suggestion, so much so that the silver-haired ranger actually felt some sympathy for the emerald creature. "All right, but make certain that your animal will not do him any harm."

"So long as he behaves himself." Falstad eyed the prisoner.

"This poor excuse will behave himself, honest and truly. . . ."

Withdrawing the tip of her blade from his throat, Vereesa tried to mollify the goblin a little. Perhaps with a little courtesy, they could get more out of the hapless being. "Lead us to where we want to go, and we will let you loose before there is any danger of the dragon eating you. You have my word on that." She paused. "You have a name, goblin?"

"Yes, mistress, yes!" The oversized head bobbed up and down. "My name is *Kryll,* mistress, *Kryll!*"

"Well, Kryll, do as I ask and all will go well, understand?"

The goblin fairly bounced up and down. "Oh, yes, yes, I do, mistress! I assure you, this miserable one'll lead you exactly where you need to go!" He gave her a madcap grin. "I promise you. . . ."

ELEVEN

Nekros fingered the *Demon Soul,* trying to decide his next move. The orc commander had been unable to sleep most of the night, Torgus's failure to return from his mission eating at the thoughts of the elder warrior. Had he failed? Had both dragons perished? If so, what sort of force did that mean the humans had sent to rescue Alexstrasza? An army of gryphon-riders with wizards in tow? Surely even the Alliance could not afford to send such might, not with the war to the north and their own internal squabbles. . . .

He had tried to contact Zuluhed with his concerns, but the shaman had not responded to his magical missive. The orc knew what that meant; with matters already so dire elsewhere, Zuluhed had no time for what likely seemed to him his subordinate's fanciful fears. The shaman expected Nekros to act as any orc warrior should, with decisiveness and assurance . . . which left the maimed officer back at square one.

The *Demon Soul* gave him great power to command, but Nekros knew that he did not understand even a fraction of its potential. In fact, understanding the depths of his ignorance made the orc uncertain as to whether he dared even *try* to use the artifact for more than he already had. Zuluhed still did not realize what he had passed to his subordinate. From what little Nekros had discovered on his own, the *Demon Soul* contained such relentless power that, wielded with skill, it could likely wipe out the entire Alliance force the orc officer knew to be massing near the northern regions of Khaz Modan.

The trouble was, if wielded carelessly, the disk could also obliterate all of Grim Batol.

"Give me a good ax and two working legs and I'd throw you into the nearest volcano. . . ." he muttered at the golden artifact.

At that moment, a harried-looking warrior barged into his quarters, ignoring his commander's sudden glare. "Torgus returns!"

Good news at last! The commander exhaled in relief. If Torgus had returned, then at least one threat had been eradicated after all. Nekros fairly leapt from his bench. Hopefully Torgus had been able to take at least one prisoner; Zuluhed would expect it. A little torture and the whining human would no doubt tell them everything they needed to know about the upcoming invasion to the north. "At last! How far?"

"A few minutes. No more." The other orc had an anxious expression on his ugly face, but Nekros ignored it for the moment, eager to welcome back the mighty dragon-rider. At least Torgus had not let him down.

He put away the *Demon Soul* and hurried as fast as he could to the vast cavern the dragon-riders used for landings and takeoffs. The warrior who had brought word followed close behind, curiously silent. Nekros, however, welcomed the silence this time. The only voice he wanted to hear was that of Torgus, relating his great victory over the outsiders.

Several other orcs, including most of the surviving riders, already awaited Torgus at the wide mouth of the cavern. Nekros frowned at the lack of order, but knew that, like him, they eagerly awaited the champion's triumphant arrival.

"Make way! Make way!" Pushing past the rest, he stared out into the faint light of predawn. At first, he could not spot either leviathan; the sentry who had noted their imminent arrival surely had to have the sharpest eyes of any orc. Then . . . then, gradually, Nekros noted a dark form in the distance, one that swelled in size as it neared.

Only one? The peg-legged orc grunted. Another great loss, but one he could live with now that the threat had been vanquished. Nekros could not tell which dragon returned, but, like the others, he expected it to be Torgus's mount. No one could defeat Grim Batol's greatest champion.

And yet . . . and yet . . . as the dragon coalesced into a defined shape, Nekros noticed that it flew in ragged fashion, that its wings looked torn and the tail hung practically limp. Squinting, he saw that a rider did indeed guide the beast, but that rider sat half-slumped in the saddle, as if barely conscious.

An uncomfortable tingle ran up and down the commander's spine.

"Clear away!" he shouted. "Clear away! He'll need lots of room to land!"

In truth, as Nekros stumped away, he realized that Torgus's mount would need nearly all the free room in the vast chamber. The closer the dragon got, the more his erratic flight pattern revealed itself. For one brief moment, Nekros even thought that the leviathan might crash into the side of the mountain, so badly did he maneuver. Only at the last, perhaps urged on by his handler, did the crimson monster manage to enter.

With a crash, the dragon landed amongst them.

Orcs shouted in surprise and consternation as the wounded beast slid forward, unable to halt his momentum. One warrior went flying as a wing clipped him. The tail swung to and fro, battering the walls and bringing down chunks of rock from the ceiling. Nekros planted himself against one wall and gritted his teeth. Dust rose everywhere.

A silence suddenly filled the chamber, a silence during which the maimed officer and those who had managed to get out of the dragon's path began to realize that the gargantuan creature before them had made it back to the roost . . . only to die.

Not so, however, the rider. A figure arose in the dust, a teetering yet still impressive form that unlashed itself from the giant corpse and slid down the side, nearly falling to his knees when he touched the floor. He spat blood and dirt from his mouth, then peered around as best he could, searching . . . searching . . .

For Nekros.

"We're lost!" bellowed the bravest, the strongest of the dragon-riders. "We're lost, Nekros!"

Torgus's arrogance had now been tempered by something else, something that his commander belatedly recognized as resignation. Torgus, who had always sworn to go down fighting, now looked so very defeated.

No! Not him! The older orc hobbled over to his champion as quickly as he could, his expression darkening. "Silence! I'll have none of that talk! You shame the clans! You shame yourself!"

Torgus leaned as best he could against the remains of his mount. "Shame? I've no shame, old one! I've only seen the truth—and the truth is that we've no hope now! Not here!"

Ignoring the fact that the other orc stood taller and outweighed him, Nekros took hold of the rider by the shoulders and shook him. "Speak! What makes you spout such treason?"

"Look at me, Nekros! Look at my mount! You know what did this? You know what we fought?"

"An armada of gryphons? A legion of wizards?"

Bloodstains covered the once magnificent honors still pinned to Torgus's chest. The dragon-rider tried to laugh, but got caught in a coughing fit. Nekros impatiently waited.

"Would—would've been a fairer fight, if I say so! No, we saw only a handful of gryphons—probably bait! Have to be! Too small for any useful force—"

"Never mind that! What did this to you?"

"What did this?" Torgus looked past his commander, eyeing his fellow warriors. "Death itself——death in the form of a black dragon!"

Consternation broke out among the orcs. Nekros himself stiffened at the words. "Deathwing?"

"And fighting for the humans! Came from the clouds just as I tried for one of the gryphons! We barely escaped!"

It could not be . . . and yet . . . it *had* to be. Torgus would not have made up such a bald lie. If he said that Deathwing had done this—and certainly the rips and tears that decorated the giant corpse added much credence to his words—then Deathwing *had* done this.

"Tell me more! Leave out no detail!"

Despite his own condition, the rider did just that, telling how he and the other orc had come upon the seemingly insignificant band. Scouts, perhaps. Torgus had seen several dwarves, an elf, and at least one wizard. Simple pickings, save for the unexpected sacrifice of a human warrior who had somehow single-handedly slain the other dragon.

Even then, Torgus had expected little more trouble. The wizard had proved some annoyance, but had vanished in the midst of combat, likely having fallen to his death. The orc had moved in on the party, ready to finish them.

That had been when Deathwing had attacked. He had made simple work of Torgus's own beast, who had initially refused his handler's instructions and had sought battle. No coward, Torgus had nonetheless immediately known the futility of battling the armored behemoth. Over and over during the struggle he had shouted for his mount to turn away. Only when the red dragon's wounds had proven too much had the beast finally obeyed and fled.

As the story unfolded, Nekros saw all his worst nightmares coming true. The goblin Kryll had been correct in informing him that the Alliance sought to wrest the Dragonqueen from orc control, but the foul little creature had either not known or had not bothered to tell his master about the forces amassed for that quest. Somehow the humans had managed the unthinkable—a pact with the only creature both sides respected and feared.

"Deathwing . . ." he muttered.

Yet, why would they would waste the armored behemoth on such a mission? Surely Torgus had it right when he said that the band he had discovered had to be scouts or bait. Surely a much vaster force followed close behind.

And suddenly it came to Nekros what was unfolding.

He turned to face the other orcs, fighting to keep his voice from cracking. "The invasion's begun, but the north's not it! The humans and their allies're coming for us first!"

His warriors glanced at one another in dismay, clearly realizing that they faced more threat than any in the Horde could have imagined. It was one thing to die valiantly in battle, another to know one faced certain slaughter.

His conclusions made perfect sense to Nekros. Move in unexpectedly from the west, seize the southern portion of Khaz Modan, free or slay the Dragonqueen—leaving the remnants of the Horde in the north, near Dun Algaz, bereft of their chief support—then move up from Grim Batol. Caught between the attackers from the south and those coming from Dun Modr, the last hopes of the orc race would be crushed, the survivors sent to the guarded enclaves set up by the humans.

Zuluhed had left him in charge of all matters concerning the mountain and the captive dragons. The shaman had not seen fit to respond, therefore he assumed he could trust Nekros to do what he must. Very well, then, Nekros would do just *that*.

"Torgus! Get yourself patched up and get some sleep! I'll be needing you later!"

"Nekros—"

"Obey!"

The fury in his eyes made even the champion back down. Torgus nodded and, with the aid of a comrade, moved off. Nekros turned his attention back to the others. "Gather whatever's most important and get it into the wagons! Move all the eggs in crates padded with hay—and keep them warm!" He paused, going down a mental list. "Be prepared to slay any dragon whelps still too wild to train properly!"

This made Torgus pause. He and the other riders eyed their commander with horror. "*Slay* the whelps? We need—"

"We need whatever can be moved quickly—just in case!"

The taller orc eyed him. "In case of what?"

"In case I don't manage to take care of Deathwing. . . ."

Now he had everyone staring at him as if he had sprouted a second head and turned into an ogre.

"Take care of Deathwing?" growled one of the other riders.

Nekros searched for his chief wrangler, the orc who aided him most in dealing with the Dragonqueen. "You! Come with me! We need to figure out how to move the mother!"

Torgus finally thought he knew what was going on. "You're abandoning Grim Batol! You're taking everything north to the lines!"

"Yes . . ."

"They'll just follow! Deathwing'll follow!"

The peg-legged orc snorted. "You've your orders . . . or am I surrounded now by whining peons instead of mighty warriors?"

The barb struck. Torgus and the others straightened. Nekros might be maimed, but he still commanded. They could do nothing but obey, regardless of how mad they thought his plans.

He pushed past the injured champion, pushed past all in his path, mind already racing. Yes, it would be essential to have the Dragonqueen out in the open, if only at the mouth of this very cavern. That would serve him best.

He would do as the humans had done. Set the bait—although, just in case he failed, the eggs, at least, had to reach Zuluhed. Even if only *they* survived, it would aid the Horde . . . and if Nekros could achieve victory, no matter if it cost him his life, then the orcs still had a chance.

One beefy hand slipped to the pouch where the *Demon Soul* rested. Nekros Skullcrusher had wondered about the limitations of the mysterious talisman—now he would have a chance to find out.

The dim light of dawn stirred Rhonin from what seemed one of the deepest slumbers he had ever experienced. With effort, the wizard pushed himself up and looked around, trying to get his bearings. A wooded area, not the inn of which he had been dreaming. Not the inn where he and Vereesa had been sitting, speaking of—

You are awake . . . good . . .

The words arose within his mind without any warning, nearly sending him into shock. Rhonin leapt to his feet, spinning around in a circle before finally realizing the source.

He clutched at the small medallion dangling around his throat, the one that had been given to him the night before by Deathwing.

A faint glow emanated from the smoky black crystal in the center, and as Rhonin stared at it, he recalled the entire night's events, including the promise the great leviathan had made. *I will be there to guide you the entire way,* the dragon had said.

"Where are you?" the mage finally asked.

Elsewhere, replied Deathwing. *But I am also with you. . . .*

The thought made Rhonin shudder, and he wondered why he had finally agreed to the dragon's offer. Likely because he really had not had any choice.

"What happens now?"

The sun rises. You must be on your way. . . .

Peering around, the wary mage eyed the landscape toward the east. The woods gave way to a rocky, inhospitable area that he knew from maps would eventually guide him to Grim Batol and the mountain where the orcs kept the Dragonqueen. Rhonin estimated that Deathwing had saved him several days' journey by bringing him this far. Grim Batol had to be only two or three days away, providing Rhonin pushed hard.

He started off in the obvious direction—only to have Deathwing immediately interrupt him.

That is not the way you should go.

"Why not? It leads directly to the mountain."

And into the claws of the orcs, human. Are you such a fool?

Rhonin bridled at the insult, but kept silent his retort. Instead, he asked, "Then where?"

See . . .

And in the human's mind flashed the image of his present surroundings. Rhonin barely had time to digest this astonishing vision before it began *moving.* First slowly, then with greater and greater swiftness, the vision moved along a particular path, racing through the woods and into the rocky regions. From there it twisted and turned, the images continuing to speed up at a dizzying rate. Cliffs and gullies darted by, trees passed in a blur. Rhonin had to hold on to the nearest trunk in order not to become too swept up by the sights within his mind.

Hills grew higher, more menacing, at last becoming the first mountains. Even then, the vision did not slow, not until it suddenly fixed on one peak in particular, one which drew the wizard despite his hesitations.

At the base of that peak, Rhonin's view shifted skyward with such abruptness that he nearly lost all sense of equilibrium. The vision climbed the great peak, always showing areas that the wizard realized contained ledges or handholds. Up and up it went, until at last it reached a narrow cave mouth—

—and ended as abruptly as it had begun, leaving a shaken Rhonin once more standing amidst the foliage.

There is the path, the only path that will enable you to achieve our goal. . . .

"But that route will take longer, and go through more precarious regions!" He did not even want to think of climbing that mountainside. What seemed a simple route for a dragon looked most treacherous to a human, even one gifted with the power of magic.

You will be aided. I did not say you would have to walk the entire way. . . .

"But—"

It is time for you to begin, the voice insisted.

Rhonin started walking . . . or rather, Rhonin's *legs* started walking.

The effect lasted only seconds, but it proved sufficient to urge the wizard on. As his limbs returned to his own use, Rhonin pressed forward, unwilling to suffer through a second lesson. Deathwing had shown him quite easily how powerful the link between them was.

The dragon did not speak again, but Rhonin knew that Deathwing lurked somewhere in the recesses of his mind. Yet for all the black leviathan's power, he seemed not to have total control over Rhonin. At the very least, Rhonin's thoughts appeared to be hidden from his draconic ally's inspection. Otherwise, Deathwing would not have been pleased with the wizard at this very moment, for Rhonin already worked to find a way to extricate himself from the dragon's influence.

Curious. Last night he had been more than willing to believe most of what Deathwing had told him, even the part concerning the black's desire to rescue Alexstrasza. Now, however, a sense of reality had set in. Surely of all creatures Deathwing least desired to see his greatest rival free. Had he not sought the destruction of her kind throughout the war?

Yet he recalled also that Deathwing had answered that question, too, very late in their conversation.

"The children of Alexstrasza have been raised by the orcs, human. They have been turned against all other creatures. Her freedom would not change what they have become. They would still serve their masters. I slay them because there is no other choice—you understand?"

And Rhonin *had* understood at the time. Everything the dragon had told him the night before had rung so true—but in the light of day the wizard now questioned the depths of those truths. Deathwing might have meant all he said, yet that did not mean that he did not have other, darker reasons for what he did.

Rhonin contemplated removing the medallion and simply throwing it away. However, to do so would certainly draw his unwanted ally's attention, and it would be so very simple for Deathwing to locate him. The dragon had already proven just how swift he could be. Rhonin also doubted that, if Deathwing had to come for him again, the armored behemoth would do so as comrade.

For now, all he could do was continue on along the selected path. It occurred to Rhonin that he carried no supplies, not even a water sack, those items now in the sea along with the hapless Molok and their gryphon. Deathwing had not even seen fit to provide him with anything, the food and drink the dragon had given him last night apparently all the sustenance the wizard would receive.

Unperturbed, Rhonin pushed on. Deathwing wanted him to reach the mountain, and with this the mage agreed. Somehow, Rhonin would make it there.

As he climbed along the ever more treacherous terrain, his thoughts could not help but return to Vereesa. The elf had shown a tenacious dedication to her duty, but surely now she had turned back . . . providing that she, too, had survived the attack. The notion that the ranger might not have survived formed a sudden lump in Rhonin's throat and caused him to stumble. No, surely she had survived, and common sense had dictated that she return to Lordaeron and her own kind.

Surely so . . .

Rhonin paused, suddenly filled with the urge to turn around. He had the great suspicion that Vereesa had not followed common sense, but rather had insisted on going on, possibly even convincing the unconvincible Falstad into flying her toward Grim Batol. Even now, assuming nothing else had befallen her, Vereesa might well be on his trail, slowly closing in on him.

The wizard took a step toward the west—

Human . . .

Rhonin bit back a curse as Deathwing's voice filled his head. How had the dragon known so quickly? Could he read the mage's thoughts after all?

Human . . . it is time you refreshed yourself and ate. . . .

"What—what do you mean?"

You paused. You were looking for water and food, were you not?

"Yes." No sense telling the dragon the truth.

You are but a short distance from such. Turn east again and journey a few minutes more. I will guide you.

His opportunity lost, Rhonin obeyed. Stumbling along the jagged path, he gradually came to a small patch of trees in the middle of nowhere. Amazing how even in the worst stretches of Khaz Modan life thrust forth. For the shade alone Rhonin actually gave thanks to his undesired ally.

In the center of the copse will you find what you desire. . . .

Not *all* he desired, although the wizard could not tell Deathwing that. Nonetheless, he moved with some eagerness. More and more, food and water appealed to him. A few minutes' rest would certainly help, too.

The trees were short for their kind, only twelve feet in height, but they offered good shade. Rhonin entered the copse and immediately looked around. Surely there had to be a brook here and possibly some fruit. What other repast could Deathwing offer from a distance?

A *feast,* apparently. There, in the very center of the wooded area, sat a small display of food and drink such as Rhonin could not have imagined finding. Roasted rabbit, fresh bread, cut fruit, and—he touched the flask with some awe—chilled water.

Eat, murmured the voice of the dragon.

Rhonin obeyed with gusto, digging into the meal. The rabbit had been freshly cooked and seasoned to perfection; the bread retained the pleasant scent of the oven. Forgoing manners, he drank directly from the flask . . . and discovered that, although the container should have been half-empty after that, it remained full. Thereafter, Rhonin drank his fill without concern, knowing that Deathwing wanted him well . . . if only until the wizard reached the mountain.

With his magic he could have conjured something of his own, but that would have drawn strength from him that he might need for more drastic times. In addition, Rhonin doubted that even he could have created such a repast, at least not without much effort.

Sooner than he hoped, Deathwing's voice came again. *You are satiated?*

"Yes . . . yes, I am. Thank you."

It is time to move on. You know the way.

Rhonin did know the way. In fact, he could picture the entire route the dragon had shown him. Deathwing had apparently wanted to make certain that his pawn did not wander off in the wrong direction.

With no other choice, the wizard obeyed. He paused only long enough to take one more glance behind him, hoping against hope that he might see the familiar silver hair even in the distance, and yet also wanting neither Vereesa nor even Falstad to follow him. Duncan and Molok had already perished because of his quest; too many deaths weighed now on Rhonin's shoulders.

The day aged. With the sun having descended nearly to the horizon, Rhonin began questioning Deathwing's path. Not once had he seen, much less confronted, an orc sentry, and surely Grim Batol still had those. In fact, he had not even seen a single dragon. Either they no longer patrolled the skies here or the wizard had wandered so far afield that he had gone outside their range.

The sun sank lower. Even a second meal, apparently magicked into being by Deathwing, did not assuage Rhonin. As the last light of day disappeared, he paused and tried to make out the landscape ahead. So far, the only mountains he could see stood much too far away in the distance. It would take him several days just to reach them, much less the peak where the orcs kept the dragons.

Well, Deathwing had brought him to this point; Deathwing could explain now how he thought the human could possibly reach his destination.

Clutching the medallion, Rhonin, his eyes still on the distant mountains, spoke to the empty air. "I need to talk with you."

Speak . . .

He had not entirely expected the method to work. So far, it had always been the dragon who had contacted him, not the other way around. "You said this path would take me to the mountain, but if so, it'll take far longer than I've time. I don't know how you expected me to reach the peak so quickly on foot."

As I said earlier, you were not meant to travel the entire way by so primitive a method. The vision I sent of the path was so that you would ever remain secure in the knowledge that you had not become lost.

"Then how am I supposed to reach it?"

Patience. They should be with you soon.

They?

Remain where you are. That would be the best.

"But—" Rhonin realized that Deathwing no longer spoke with him. The wizard once again contemplated tearing the medallion from his throat and tossing it among the rocks, but where would that leave him? Rhonin still had to get to the orcs' domain.

Who did Deathwing mean?

And then he heard the sound, a sound like no other he had ever encountered. His initial thought was that it might be a dragon, but, if so, a dragon with a terrible case of indigestion. Rhonin gazed into the darkening sky, initially seeing nothing.

A brief flash of light caught his attention, a flash of light from above.

Rhonin swore, thinking that Deathwing had set him up to be captured by the orcs. Surely the light had been some sort of torch or crystal in the hand of a dragon-rider. The wizard summoned up a spell; he would not go without a fight, however futile it might prove.

Then the light flashed again, this time longer. Rhonin briefly found himself illuminated, a perfect target for whatever belching monster lurked in the dark heavens.

"Told you he was here!"

"I knew it all the time! I just wanted to see if you really did!"

"Liar! I knew and you didn't! I knew and you didn't!"

A frown formed on the young spellcaster's lips. What sort of dragon argued with itself in such inane, high-pitched tones?

"Watch that lamp!" cursed one of the voices.

The light suddenly flipped away from Rhonin and darted up. The beam briefly shone on a huge oval form—a point at the front—before flickering on to the rear, where the wizard made out a smoking, belching device that turned a propeller at the end of the oval.

A balloon! Rhonin realized. *A zeppelin!*

He had actually seen one of the remarkable creations before, during the height of the war. Astonishing, gas-filled sacks so massive in size that they could actually lift an open carriage containing two or three riders. In the war, they had been utilized for observation of enemy forces on both land and sea, yet what amazed Rhonin most about them had not been their existence, but that they had been powered by resources other than magic—by oil and water. A machine neither built by nor requiring spells drove the balloon, a remarkable device that turned the propeller without the aid of manpower.

The light returned to him, this time fixing on Rhonin with what seemed determination. The riders in the flying balloon had him in sight now, and clearly had no intention of losing him again. Only then did the fascinated mage recall exactly which race had proven to have both the ingenuity and touch of madness necessary to dream of such a concept.

Goblins—and goblins served the Horde.

He darted toward the largest rocks, hoping to lose himself long enough to at least come up with a spell appropriate for flying balloons, but then a familiar voice echoed in his head.

Stay!

"I can't! There're goblins above! I've been spotted by their airship! They'll summon the orcs!"

You will not move!

Rhonin's feet refused to obey him any longer. Instead, they turned him back to face the unnerving balloon and its even more unnerving pilots. The zeppelin descended to a point just above the hapless wizard's head. A rope ladder dropped over the side of the observation carriage, barely missing Rhonin.

Your transport has arrived, Deathwing informed him.

TWELVE

Lord Prestor's ascension seems almost inevitable," the shadowy form in the emerald sphere informed Krasus. "He has an almost amazing gift of persuasion. You are correct; he *must* be a wizard."

Seated in the midst of his sanctum, Krasus eyed the globe. "Convincing the monarchs will require much evidence. Their mistrust of the Kirin Tor grows with each day . . . and that can only also be the work of this would-be king."

The other speaker, the elder woman from the inner council, nodded back. "We've begun watching. The only trouble is, this Prestor proves very elusive. He seems able to enter and leave his abode without us knowing."

Krasus pretended slight surprise. "How is that possible?"

"We don't know. Worse, his chateau is surrounded by some very nasty spellwork. We almost lost Drenden to one of those surprises."

That Drenden, the baritoned and bearded mage, had nearly fallen victim to one of Deathwing's traps momentarily dismayed Krasus. Despite the man's bluster, the dragon respected the other mage's abilities. Losing Drenden at a time like this could have proven costly.

"We must move with caution," he urged. "I will speak with you again soon."

"What are you planning, Krasus?"

"A search into this young noble's past."

"You think you'll find anything?"

The hooded wizard shrugged. "We can only hope."

He dismissed her image, then leaned back to consider. Krasus regretted that he had to lead his associates astray, if only for their own good. At least their intrusions into Deathwing's "mortal" affairs would have the result of distracting the black. That would give Krasus a bit more time. He only prayed that no one else would risk themselves as Drenden had done. The Kirin Tor would need their strength intact if the other kingdoms turned on them.

His own excursion to visit Malygos had ended with little sense of satisfaction. Malygos had promised only to consider his request. Krasus suspected that the great dragon believed he could deal with Deathwing in his own sweet time. Little did the silver-blue leviathan realize that time no longer remained for any of the dragons. If Deathwing could not be stopped now, he might never be.

Which left Krasus with one much undesired choice now.

"I must do it. . . ." He had to seek out the other great ones, the other Aspects. Convince one of them, and he might still gain Malygos's sworn aid.

Yet, She of the Dreaming ever proved a most elusive figure . . . which meant that Krasus's best bet lay in contacting the Lord of Time—whose servants had already rejected the wizard's requests more than once.

Still, what else could he do but try again?

Krasus rose, hurrying to a bench upon which many of the items of his calling stood arranged in vials and flasks. He scanned row upon row of jars, eyes quickly passing chemicals and magical items that would have left his counterparts in the Kirin Tor greatly envious, and more than a little curious as to how he could have obtained many of the articles in question. If they ever realized just how long he had been practicing the arts . . .

There! A small flask containing a single withered flower caused him to pause.

The Eon Rose. Found only in one place in all the world. Plucked by Krasus himself to give to his mistress, his love. Saved by Krasus when the orcs stormed the lair and, to his disbelief, took her and the others prisoner.

The Eon Rose. Five petals of astonishingly different hues surrounding a golden sphere in the center. As Krasus lifted the top of the flask, a faint scent that suddenly recalled his adolescence wafted under his nose. With some hesitation, he reached in, took hold of the faded bloom—

—and marveled as it suddenly returned to its legendary brilliance the moment his tapering fingers touched it.

Fiery red. Emerald green. Snowy silver. Deep-sea blue. Midnight black. Each petal radiated such beauty as artists only dreamed of. No other object could surpass its inherent beauty, no other flower could match its wondrous scent.

Holding his breath for a moment, Krasus *crushed* the wondrous bloom.

He let the fragments fall into his other hand. A tingle spread from his palms to his fingers, but the dragon mage ignored it. Holding the remnants up high over his head, the wizard muttered words of power—then threw what was left of the fabled rose to the floor.

But as the crushed pieces touched the stone, they turned suddenly to sand, sand that spread across the chamber floor, overwhelmed the chamber itself, *washed* across the chamber, covering everything, eating away everything . . .

. . . and leaving Krasus abruptly standing in the midst of an endless, swirling desert.

Yet, no desert such as this had any mortal—or even Krasus himself, for that matter—ever witnessed, for here lay scattered, as far as the eye could see, fragments of walls, cracked and scoured statues, rusted weapons, and—the mage gaped—even the half-buried bones of some gargantuan beast that, in life, had dwarfed even dragons. There were buildings, too, and although at first one might have thought they and the relics around them all part of one vast civilization, a closer look revealed that no one structure truly belonged with another. A teetering tower such as might have been built by humans in Lordaeron overshadowed a domed building that surely had come from the dwarves. Some distance farther, an arched temple, its roof caved in, hinted of the lost kingdom of Azeroth. Nearer to Krasus himself stood a more dour domicile, the quarters of some orc chieftain.

A ship large enough to carry a dozen men stood propped on a dune, the latter half of it buried under sand. Armor from the reign of the first king of Stromgarde littered another smaller dune. The leaning statue of an elven cleric seemed to say final prayers over both vessel and armor.

An astonishing, improbable display that gave even Krasus pause. In truth, the sights before the wizard resembled nothing more than some gargantuan deity's macabre collection of antiquities . . . a point not far from fact.

None of these artifacts were native to this realm; in fact, no race, no civilization, had ever been spawned here. All the wonders that stood before the wizard had been gathered quite meticulously and over a period of countless centuries from other points all over the world. Krasus could scarcely believe what he saw, for the effort alone staggered even his imagination. To bring such relics, so many of them so massive or so delicate, to this place . . .

Yet, despite all of it, despite the spectacle before his eyes, an impatience began to build up as Krasus waited. And waited. And waited more, with not even the slightest hint that anyone acknowledged his presence.

His patience, already left ragged by the events of the past weeks, finally snapped.

He fixed his gaze on the stony features of a massive statue part man, part bull, whose left arm thrust forth as if demanding that the newcomer leave, and called out, "I know you are here, Nozdormu! I know it! I would speak with you!"

The moment the dragon mage finished, the wind whipped up, tossing sand all about and obscuring his vision. Krasus stayed his ground as a full-fledged sandstorm suddenly buffeted him. The wind howled around him, so loud that he had to cover his ears. The storm seemed determined to lift him up and throw him far away, but the wizard fought it, using magic as well as physical effort to remain. He would not be turned away, not without the opportunity to speak!

At last, even the sandstorm appeared to realize that he would not be deterred. It swept away from him, now focusing on a dune a short distance away. A funnel of dust arose, pushing higher and higher into the sky.

The funnel took on a shape . . . a dragon's shape. As large as, if not larger than, Malygos, this sandy creation moved, stretched dusty brown wings. Sand continued to add to the dimension of the behemoth, but sand seemingly mixed with gold, for more and more the leviathan forming before Krasus glittered in the blazing light of the desert sun.

The wind died, yet not one grain of sand or gold broke from the draconic giant. The wings flapped hard, the neck stretched. Eyelids opened, revealing gleaming gemstones the color of the sun.

"Korialstraszzzz . . ." the sandy behemoth practically spat. "You dare disturb my ressst? You dare disssturb my *peace?"*

"I dare because I must, o great Lord of Time!"

"Titles will not appeassse my wrath . . . would be best if you went . . ." The gemstones flared. ". . . and went now!"

"No! Not until I speak to you of a danger to all dragons! To all creatures!"

Nozdormu snorted. A cloud of sand bathed Krasus, but his spells kept it from affecting him. One could never tell what magic might dwell within each and every grain in the domain of Nozdormu. One bit of sand might be enough to ensure that the history of a dragon named Korialstrasz turned out never to have happened. Krasus might simply cease to exist, unremembered even by his beloved mistress.

"Dragonssss, you say? Of what concern isss that to you? I see only one dragon here, and it isss certainly not the mortal wizard Krasusss—not anymore! Away with you! I would return to my collection! You wassste too much of my precious time already!" One wing swept protectively over the statue of the man-bull. "Ssso much to gather, ssso much to catalog . . ."

It suddenly infuriated Krasus that this, one of the greatest of the five Aspects, he through whom Time itself coursed, this dragon cared not a whit what went on in the present or the future. Only his precious collection of the world's past meant anything to the leviathan. He sent out his servants, his people, to gather whatever they could find—all so that their master could surround himself with what had once been and ignore both what was and what might be.

All so that he, in his own way, could ignore the passing of their kind just as Malygos did.

"Nozdormu!" he shouted, demanding the glittering sand dragon's attention again. "Deathwing lives!"

To his horror, Nozdormu took in this terrible news with little change. The gold and brown behemoth snorted once more, sending a second cloud assailing the tinier figure. "Yesss . . . and ssso?"

Taken aback, Krasus managed to blurt, "You—know?"

"A question not at all worth anssswering. Now, if you've nothing more with which to further bother me, it isss time for you to depart." The dragon reared his head, bejeweled eyes flaring.

"Wait!" Forgoing any sense of dignity, the wizard waved his arms back and forth. To his relief, Nozdormu paused, negating the spell he had been about to use to rid himself of this bothersome mite. "If you know that the dark one lives, you know what he intends! How can you ignore that?"

"Becaussse, asss with all things, even Deathwing will pass into time . . . even he will eventually be part . . . of my collection. . . ."

"But if you joined—"

"You've had your sssay." The glittering sand dragon rose higher and as he did, the desert flew up, adding further to his girth and form. Torn free by the winds, some of the smaller objects in Nozdormu's bizarre collection joined with that sand, becoming, for the moment, a very part of the dragon. "Now leave me be. . . ."

The winds now whipped up around Krasus—and *only* Krasus. Try as he might, this time the dragon wizard could not hold his ground. He stumbled back, shoved hard time and time again by the ferocious gusts.

"I came here for the sake of *all* of us!" Krasus managed to shout.

"You should not have disssturbed my ressst. You should not have come at all. . . ." The glittering gemstones flared. "In fact, that would have been bessst of all. . . ."

A column of sand shot up from the ground, engulfing the helpless wizard. Krasus could see nothing else. It grew stifling, impossible to breathe. He tried to cast a spell in order to save himself, but against the might of one of the Aspects, against the Master of Time, even his substantial powers proved minuscule.

Bereft of air, Krasus finally succumbed. Consciousness fading, he slumped forward—

—and watched, in startlement, as the petals of the Eon Rose dropped to the stone floor of his sanctum without any effect.

The spell should have worked. He should have been transported to the realm of Nozdormu, Lord of the Centuries. Just as Malygos embodied magic itself, so, too, did Nozdormu represent time and timelessness. One of the most powerful of the five Aspects, he would have proven a powerful ally, especially should Malygos suddenly choose to retreat into his madness. Without Nozdormu, Krasus's hopes of success dwindled much.

Kneeling, the mage picked up the petals and repeated the spell. For his troubles, Krasus was rewarded only with a horrendous headache. How could that be, though? He had done everything right! The spell should have worked—unless somehow Nozdormu had caught wind of the wizard's intention to plead with him and had cast a spell preventing Krasus from entering the sandy realm.

He swore. Without a chance to visit Nozdormu, he had no hope, however slight it might have been in the first place, of convincing the powerful dragon to join his plan. That left only She of the Dreaming . . . the most elusive of the Aspects, and the only one he had never, ever, spoken with in all his lengthy life. Krasus did not even know how to contact her, for it had oft been said that Ysera lived not wholly in the real world—that, to her, the dreams were the reality.

The dreams were the reality? A desperate plan occurred to the wizard, one that, had it been suggested to him by any of his counterparts, would have made Krasus break from his accustomed form and laugh loud. How utterly ridiculous! How utterly hopeless!

But, as with Nozdormu, what other choice did he have?

Turning back to his array of potions, artifacts, and powders, Krasus searched for a black vial. He found it quickly, despite not having touched it in more than a century. The last time he had made use of it—it had been to slay what had seemed unslayable. Now, however, he sought to only borrow one of its most vicious traits, and hope that he did not measure wrong.

Three drops on the tip of a single bolt had killed the Manta, the Behemoth of the Deep. Three drops had slain a creature ten times the size and strength of a dragon. Like Deathwing, nearly all had believed the Manta unstoppable.

Now Krasus intended to take some of the poison for himself.

"The deepest sleep, the deepest dreams . . ." he muttered to himself as he took the vial down. "That is where she must be, where she *has* to be."

From another shelf he removed a cup and a small flask of pure water. Measuring out a single swallow in the cup, the dragon mage then opened the vial. With the greatest caution, he brought the open bottle to the cup of water.

Three drops to slay, in seconds, the Manta. How many drops to assist Krasus on the most treacherous of journeys?

Sleep and death . . . they were so very close in nature, more so than most realized. Surely he would find Ysera there.

The tiniest drop he could measure fell silently into the water. Krasus replaced the top on the vial, then took up the cup.

"A bench," he murmured. "Best to use a bench."

One immediately formed behind him, a well-cushioned bench upon which the king of Lordaeron would have happily slept. Krasus, too, intended to sleep well on it . . . perhaps forever.

He sat upon it, then raised the cup to his lips. Yet, before he could bring himself to drink what might be his last, the dragon in human guise made one last toast.

"To you, my Alexstrasza, *always* to you."

"There was someone here, all right," Vereesa muttered, studying the ground. "One of them was human . . . the other I can't be certain about."

"Pray tell, how do you know the difference?" asked Falstad, squinting. He could not tell one sign from another. In fact, he could not even *see* half of what the elf saw.

"Look here. This boot print." She indicated a curved mark in the dirt. "These are human-style boots, tight-fitting and uncomfortable."

"I'll take your word. And the other—the one you can't identify?"

The ranger straightened. "Well, clearly there are no signs of a dragon being around, but there are tracks over here that match nothing I know."

She knew that, once again, Falstad could not see what to her sharp eyes screamed out their curious presence. The dwarf did his best, though, studying the peculiar striations in the earth. "You mean these, my elven lady?"

The marks appeared to flow toward where the human—surely *Rhonin*—had at one time or another stood. Yet, they were not footprints, not even pawprints. To her eyes, it looked as if something had floated, dragging something else behind it.

"This gets us no closer than the first spot this little green beast brought us to!" Falstad seized Kryll by the scruff of his neck. The goblin had both hands tied behind him and a rope around his waist, the other end of which had been tied around the neck of the gryphon. Despite that, neither Vereesa nor the wild dwarf trusted that their unwilling companion might not somehow escape. Falstad especially kept his eye on Kryll. "Well? Now what? 'Tis becoming clear to me that you're leading us around! I doubt you've even seen the wizard!"

"I have, I have, yes, I have!" Kryll smiled wide, possibly in the hope of swaying his captors, but a goblin's toothy grin did little to impress those outside of their race. "Described him, didn't I? You know I saw him, don't you?"

Vereesa noticed the gryphon sniffing at something hidden behind a bit of foliage. Using her sword, she prodded at the spot, then dragged out the object in question.

On the tip of her sword hung a small, empty wine sack. The elf brought it to her nose. A heavenly bouquet wafted past. The elf briefly closed her eyes.

Falstad misread her expression. "As bad as all that? Must be dwarven ale!"

"On the contrary, I have not come across such a fabulous aroma even at the table of my lord back in Quel'Thalas! Whatever wine filled this sack far outshone even the best of his stock."

"Which means to my feeble mind—?"

Dropping the sack, Vereesa shook her head. "I do not know, but somehow I cannot help thinking that it means that Rhonin *was* here, if only for a time."

Her companion gave her a skeptical look. "My elven lady, is it possible that you simply wish it to be true?"

"Can you answer me who else might have been in this region, drinking wine fit for kings?"

"Aye! The dark one, after he'd sucked the marrow from the bones of your wizard!"

His words made her shiver, but she remained steadfast in her belief. "No. If Deathwing brought him this far, he had some other reason than as a repast!"

"Possible, I suppose." Still holding on to the goblin, Falstad glanced up at the darkening sky. "If we hope to get much farther before night, we'd best be getting on our way."

Vereesa touched the tip of her blade against Kryll's throat. "We need to deal with this one first."

"What's to deal with? Either we take him with us, or do the world a favor and leave it with one less goblin to worry about!"

"No. I promised I would release him."

The dwarf's heavy brow furrowed. "I don't think that's wise."

"Nevertheless, I made that promise." She stared hard at him, knowing that if he understood elves as much as he should, Falstad would see the sense in not pursuing this argument.

Sure enough, the gryphon-rider nodded—albeit with much reluctance. "Aye, 'tis as you say. You made a promise and I'll not be the one to try to sway you." Not quite under his breath, he added, "Not with only one lifetime to me . . ."

Satisfied, Vereesa expertly cut the bonds around Kryll's wrists, then removed the loop from his waist. The goblin fairly bounced around, so overjoyed did he seem by his release.

"Thank you, my benevolent mistress, thank you!"

The ranger turned the tip of the sword back toward the creature's throat. "Before you go, though, a few last questions. Do you know the path to Grim Batol?"

Falstad did not take this question well. Brow arched, he muttered, "What're you thinking?"

She purposely ignored his question. "Well?"

Kryll's eyes had gone wide the moment she asked. The goblin looked ashen—or at least a paler shade of green. "No one goes to Grim Batol, benevolent mistress! Orcs there and dragons, too! Dragons eat goblins!"

"Answer my question."

He swallowed, then finally bobbed his oversized head up and down. "Yes, mistress, I know the way—do you think the wizard is there?"

"You can't be serious, Vereesa," Falstad rumbled, so upset he had for once called her by name. "If your Rhonin is in Grim Batol, then he's lost to us!"

"Perhaps . . . perhaps not. Falstad, I think he always *wanted* to reach that place, and not simply to observe the orcs. I think he has some other reason . . . although what it could have to do with Deathwing, I cannot say."

"Maybe he plans on releasing the Dragonqueen single-handedly!" the gryphon-rider returned with a snort of derision. "He's a mage, after all, and everyone knows that they're all *mad!*"

An absolutely absurd notion—but for a moment it gave Vereesa pause. "No . . . it could not be that."

Kryll, meanwhile, seemed to be trying to think really hard about something, something that did not at all look to please him. At last, his face screwed up in an expression of distaste, he muttered, "Mistress wants to go to Grim Batol?"

The ranger considered it. It went even beyond her oath, but she had to push forward. "Yes. Yes, I do."

"Now see here, my—"

"You do not have to come with me if you do not want to, Falstad. I thank you for your aid thus far, but I can proceed from here alone."

The dwarf shook his head vehemently. "And leave you alone in the middle of orc territory with only this untrustworthy little wretch? Nay, my elven lady! Falstad will not leave a fair damsel, however capable a warrior she might also be, on her own! We go together!"

In truth, she appreciated his company here. "You may turn back at any time, though; remember that."

"Only if you're with me."

She glanced again at Kryll. "Well? Can you tell me the way?"

"Cannot tell you, mistress." More and more the spindly creature's expression soured. "Best . . . best if I show you, instead."

This surprised her. "I granted you your freedom, Kryll—"

"For which this poor wretch is so eternally grateful, mistress . . . but only one path to Grim Batol offers certainty, and without me," he dared look slightly egotistical, "neither elf nor dwarf will find it."

"We've got my mount, you little rodent! We'll simply fly over—"

"In a land of dragons?" The goblin chuckled, a hint of madness there. "Best to fly right into their mouths and be done with it, then. . . . No, to enter

Grim Batol—if that is truly what mistress desires—you'll have to follow me."

Falstad would not hear of that and immediately protested, but Vereesa saw no choice but to do as the goblin suggested. Kryll had led them true so far, and although she did not, of course, trust him entirely, she felt certain that she would recognize if he tried to lead them astray. Besides, clearly the goblin wanted nothing to do with Grim Batol himself, or else why would he have been where they had found him? Any of his kind who served the orcs would have been in the mountain fortress, not wandering the dangerous wilds of Khaz Modan.

And if he could lead her yet to Rhonin . . .

Having convinced herself that she chose correctly, Vereesa faced the dwarf. "I will go with him, Falstad. It is the best—the only—choice I have."

His broad shoulders slumping, Falstad sighed. " 'Tis against my better judgment, but, aye, I'll go with you—if only to keep an eye on this one, so I can lop off his traitorous head if I prove right!"

"Kryll, must we go on foot the entire way?"

The misshapen little creature mused for a moment, then replied, "No. Can travel some distance with gryphon." He gave her a smile full of teeth. "Know just where beast should land!"

Despite his apparent misgivings, Falstad started for the gryphon. "Just tell us where to go, you little rodent. The sooner we're there, the sooner you can be on your way. . . ."

The goblin's weight added little to the powerful animal's burden, and soon the gryphon was on its way. Falstad, of course, sat in front, the better to control his mount. Kryll sat behind him with Vereesa taking up the rear. The elf had resheathed her sword and now held a dagger ready just in case their undesired companion attempted something.

Yet, although the goblin's directions were not always the clearest, Vereesa saw nothing that hinted of duplicity. He kept them near to the ground and always guided them along paths that steered them from the open areas. In the distance, the mountains of Grim Batol grew nearer. A sense of anxiety spread through the ranger as she realized that she approached her goal, but that anxiousness was tempered by the fact that, even now, she had come across no sign of either Rhonin or the black dragon. Surely this close to the mountain fortress the orcs would have been able to sight such a leviathan.

And as if thinking of dragons allowed one to conjure them up, Falstad suddenly pointed east, where a massive form rose into the sky.

"Big!" he called. "Big and red as fresh blood! Scout from Grim Batol!"

Kryll immediately acted. "Down there!" the goblin pointed at a ravine. "Many places to hide—even for a gryphon!"

With little other choice, the dwarf obeyed, guiding his mount earthward.

The dragon's form grew larger and larger, but Vereesa noted that the crimson beast also headed in a more northerly direction, possibly to the very northern border of Khaz Modan, where the last desperate forces of the Horde sought to hold back the Alliance. That made her wonder about the situation there. Had the humans begun their advance at last? Could the Alliance itself even now be halfway to Grim Batol?

If so, it would still be too late for her purposes. Yet, the nearing presence of the Alliance might aid in one way, if it made the orcs here concentrate on matters other than their own immediate defenses.

The gryphon alighted in the ravine, the animal instinctively seeking the shadows. No coward, the gryphon had the sense to know when to choose a battle.

Vereesa and the others leapt off, finding their own places to hide. Kryll pressed himself against one rocky wall, his expression that of open terror. The ranger actually found herself feeling some sympathy for him.

They waited for several minutes, but the dragon did not fly by. After what seemed far too long a time, the impatient ranger decided to see for herself if the beast had changed direction. Getting a proper grip on the rock, she climbed up.

The elf saw nothing in the darkening sky, not even a speck. In fact, Vereesa suspected that they could have departed this ravine long before, if only one of them had dared look.

"No sign?" whispered Falstad, climbing up beside her. For a dwarf, he proved himself quite nimble crawling up the side.

"We are clear. Very much so."

"Good! Unlike my hill cousins, I've no taste for holes in the ground!" He started down. "All right, Kryll! The danger's done! You can peel yourself—"

The moment his voice cut off, Vereesa jerked her head around. "What is it?"

"That damned spawn of a frog's gone!" He scrambled down the rest of the way. "Vanished like a will-o'-the-wisp!"

Dropping down as safely as she could, the ranger joined Falstad in scanning the immediate area. Sure enough, despite the fact that they should have been able to see the goblin's retreating figure in either direction, not one sign of Kryll existed. Even the gryphon acted baffled, as if it, too, had not even noticed that the spindly creature had run off.

"How could he have just disappeared?"

"Wish I knew that myself, my dear elven lady! A neat trick!"

"Can your gryphon hunt him down?"

"Why not just let him go? We're better off without him!"

"Because I—"

The ground underneath her feet suddenly softened, broke apart. The elf's boots sank deep within seconds.

Thinking that she had walked into mud, she tried to pull free. Instead, Vereesa only sank deeper, and at an alarming rate. It almost felt as if she were being *pulled* down.

"What in the name of the Aerie—?" Falstad, too, had sunk deep, but in the dwarf's case that meant he suddenly stood up to his knees in dirt. Like the ranger, he attempted to extricate himself, only to completely fail.

Vereesa grabbed for the nearest rock face, trying to seize hold. For a moment, she succeeded, managing to slow her progress downward. Then, something powerful seemed to take hold of her ankles, pulling with such force that the ranger could no longer keep her grip.

Above them she heard a panicked squawk. Unlike Vereesa and the dwarf, the gryphon had managed to pull up in time to avoid being dragged under. The animal fluttered above Falstad's head, trying, it seemed, to get a grip on its master. However, as the beast dropped lower, columns of dirt suddenly shot up, trying, Vereesa realized in horror, to seize the mount. The gryphon narrowly escaped, forced now to fly up so high that the animal could not possibly aid either warrior.

Which left Vereesa with no notion as to how to escape.

Already the earth came up to her waist. The thought of being buried alive set even the elf on edge, yet, in comparison to Falstad's predicament, hers seemed slightly less immediate. The dwarf's shorter stature meant that he already had trouble keeping his head above ground. Try as he might, even the mighty strength of the gryphon-rider could not help him. He grabbed furiously at the soft earth, ripping up handfuls that did him no good whatsoever.

In desperation, the ranger reached out. "Falstad! My hand! Reach for it!"

He tried. They both tried. The gap between them had grown too great, however. In growing horror, Vereesa watched as her struggling companion was inevitably pulled under.

"My—" was all he managed before disappearing from sight.

Now buried up to her chest, she froze for a moment, staring at the slight mound of dirt that was all that remained to mark his passage. The ground there did not even stir. No last thrust of a hand, no wild movement underneath.

"Falstad . . ." she murmured.

Renewed force at her ankles tugged her deeper. As the dwarf had done, Vereesa snatched at the earth around her, digging deep valleys with her fingers but doing herself no good. Her shoulders sank in. She lifted her head skyward. Of the gryphon she saw no sign, but another figure, so very familiar, now leaned out from a small crevice that the elf had missed earlier.

Even in the waning light, she could see Kryll's toothy smile.

"Forgive me, my mistress, but the dark one insists that no one interfere, and so he left me the task of seeing to your deaths! A menial bit of work and one undeserving of a clever mind such as mine, but my master does, after all, have very large teeth and so sharp claws! I certainly couldn't refuse him, could I?" His grin stretched wider. "I hope you understand. . . ."

"Damn you—"

The ground swallowed her up. Dirt filled the elf's mouth, then, seemingly, her hungry lungs.

She blacked out.

THIRTEEN

The goblin airship floated among the clouds, now surprisingly silent as it neared its destination.

At the bow of the vessel, Rhonin kept a watchful eye on the two figures guiding him toward his destiny. The goblins darted back and forth, adjusting gauges and muttering among themselves. How such a mad race could have created this wonder had been beyond him. Each moment, the airship seemed destined to destroy itself, yet the goblins ever managed to right matters.

Deathwing had not spoken to Rhonin since telling him to board. Knowing that the dragon would have made him do so whether he desired to or not, the wizard had reluctantly obeyed, climbing up into the airship and trying not to think what would happen if it all came tumbling down.

The goblins were Voyd and Nullyn, and they had built this vessel themselves. They were great inventors, so *they* said, and had offered their services to the wondrous Deathwing. Of course, they had said the last with just a hint of sarcasm in their tones. Sarcasm and fear.

"Where are you taking me?" he had asked.

This question had caused his two pilots to eye him as if he had lost all sense. "To Grim Batol, of course!" spouted one, who seemed to have twice the teeth of any goblin Rhonin had ever had the misfortune to come across. "To Grim Batol!"

The wizard had known that, of course, but he had wanted the exact location where they intended to drop him. Rhonin did not at all trust the pair not to leave him in the middle of an orc encampment. Unfortunately, before Rhonin could ask, Voyd and his partner had been forced to respond to an emergency, in this case a spout of steam erupting from the main tank. The goblins' airship utilized both oil and water in order to run, and if some component involving one was not breaking down at a critical moment, then something involving the other *was*.

It had made for a fairly sleepless night, even for one such as Rhonin.

The clouds through which they flew had grown so thick that it felt as if the mage journeyed through a dense fog. Had he not known at what altitude he sailed, Rhonin might have imagined that this vessel traversed not the sky, but rather the open sea. In truth, both journeys had much in common, including the danger of crashing on the rocks. More than once, Rhonin had watched as mountains had suddenly materialized on either side of the tiny ship, a few coming perilously close. Yet, while he had prepared for the worst, the goblins had kept on with their tinkering—and even occasionally napping—without so much as a glimpse at the near-disasters around them.

Daylight had long come, but the deeply overcast weather kept it nearly as dark as late dusk. Voyd seemed to be using some sort of magnetic compass to guide them along, but the one time Rhonin had studied it, he had noticed that it had a tendency to shift without warning. In the end, the wizard had concluded that the goblins flew by sheer luck more than any sense of direction.

Early on, he had estimated the length of the trip, but for some reason, even though Rhonin felt that they should have reached the fortress by now, his two companions kept assuring him that they still had quite some time left before arrival. Gradually he came to the suspicion that the airship flew about in circles, either due to the faulty compass or some intention on the goblins' parts.

Although he sought to remain focused on his quest, Rhonin found Vereesa slipping into his thoughts more and more. If she lived, she followed him. He knew her well enough. The knowledge dismayed him as much as it pleased. How could the elf possibly learn about the airship? She might end up wandering Khaz Modan or, even worse, assume rightly and head straight to Grim Batol.

His hand tightened on the rail. "No . . ." he muttered to himself. "No . . . she wouldn't do that . . . she *can't* . . ."

Duncan's ghost already haunted him, just as those of the men from his previous mission did. Even Molok stood with the dead, the wild dwarf glowering in condemnation. Rhonin could already imagine Vereesa and even Falstad joining their ranks, empty eyes demanding to know why the wizard lived after their sacrifices.

It was a question that Rhonin often asked of himself.

"Human?"

He looked up to see Nullyn, the more squat of the pair, standing just beyond arm's length from him. "What?"

"Time to prepare to disembark." The goblin gave him a wide, cheerful smile.

"We're here?" Rhonin dredged himself up from his dark thoughts and peered into the mist. He saw nothing but more mist, even below. "I don't see anything."

Beyond Nullyn, Voyd, also grinning merrily, took the rope ladder and tossed the unattached end over the side. The slapping of the rope against the hull represented the only sound the wizard heard. Clearly the ladder had not touched bottom anywhere.

"This is it. This is the place, honest and truly, master wizard!" Voyd pointed toward the rail. "Look for yourself!"

Rhonin did . . . with care. It would not have struck him as unlikely that the goblins might use their combined strength to toss him over the side despite Deathwing's desires. "I see nothing."

Nullyn looked apologetic. "It is the clouds, master wizard! They obscure things to your human eyes! We goblins have much sharper vision. Below us is a very soft, very safe ledge! Climb down the ladder and we'll gently drop you off, you'll see!"

The mage hesitated. He wanted nothing more than to be rid of the zeppelin and its crew, but to simply take the goblins' word about whether any land actually lay close below—

Without warning, Rhonin's left hand suddenly reached out, catching Nullyn by surprise. The mage's fingers closed around the goblin's throat, squeezing hard despite Rhonin's attempt to pull back.

A voice not his own, but exceedingly familiar to the human, hissed, *"I gave the command that no tricksss were to be played, no acts of treachery performed, worm."*

"M-mercy, grand and g-glorious m-master!" choked Nullyn. "Only a game! Only a g—" He managed no more, Rhonin's grip having tightened more.

Forcing his gaze down as much as he could, the helpless wizard saw the black stone in the medallion giving off a faint glow. Once more Deathwing had used it to seize control of his human "ally."

"Game?" murmured Rhonin's lips. *"You like games? I have a game for you to play, worm. . . ."*

With little effort, the human's arm shifted, dragging a struggling Nullyn toward the rail.

Voyd let out a squeak and scurried back toward the engine. Rhonin struggled against Deathwing's control, certain that the black leviathan intended to drop Nullyn to his doom. While the wizard had no love for the goblin, neither did he want the creature's blood on his hands—even if the dragon presently made use of them.

"Deathwing!" he snapped, belatedly surprised that his lips were his own for the moment. "Deathwing! Don't do this!"

Would you rather they had led you into their little ploy, human? came the voice in his head. *The drop would not have been at all pleasant for one who cannot fly. . . .*

"I'm not that much of a fool! I'd no intention of climbing over the rail, not on a goblin's word! You wouldn't have bothered saving me in the first place if you thought me that addled!"

True . . .

"And I'm not without power of my own." Rhonin raised his other hand, which Deathwing had not deemed necessary to use. Muttering a few words, the wizard produced a flame above his index finger, a flame which he then directed toward the already panicked face of Nullyn. "There are other ways to teach a goblin lessons in trust."

Barely able to breathe and unable to flee, Nullyn's eyes widened and the spindly creature tried to shake his head. "B-be good! Only meant to t-tease! Never meant h-harm!"

"But you'll drop me off on a proper place, right? One of which both Deathwing and I would approve?"

Nullyn could only manage a squeak.

"This flame I can make larger." The magical fire sprouted to twice its previous length. "Enough to burn a hull even from below, maybe set off flammable oil . . ."

"N-no tricks! N-no tricks! Promise!"

"You see?" the crimson-tressed mage asked his unseen companion. "No need to drop him over the side. Besides, you might want to make use of him again."

In reply, Rhonin's possessed hand abruptly released its hold on Nullyn, who dropped to the deck with a thud. The goblin lay there for several seconds, trying desperately to gain his breath back.

Your choice . . . wizard.

The human exhaled, then, glancing at Voyd—who still cowered by the engine—called out, "Well? Get us to the mountain!"

Voyd immediately obeyed, frantically turning levers and checking gauges. Nullyn finally recovered enough to join his partner, the beaten goblin not once glancing back.

Extinguishing the magical flame, Rhonin peered over the rail again. Now at last he could make out some sort of formation, hopefully the crags of Grim Batol. He assumed from Deathwing's earlier words and images that the dragon still wanted him set down directly on the peak, preferably somewhere near a gap leading inside. Surely the goblins knew this. Any other choice they made at this point would mean that they had still not learned the folly of crossing either their distant master or the wizard. Rhonin prayed that it would not be so. He doubted that Deathwing would allow the goblins to escape punishment twice.

They began to draw near to one peak in particular, one that Rhonin had vague memories of, even though he had never been to Grim Batol before. With growing eagerness he leaned forward for a better look. Surely this had to be the mountain from the vision that Deathwing had forced upon him. He searched for telltale signs—a recognizable outcropping or a familiar crevice.

There! The very same narrow cave mouth from his dizzying journey of the mind. Barely large enough for a man to stand in, provided he managed the terrifying climb up several hundred feet of sheer rock. Yet, still it would serve. Rhonin could scarcely wait, more than happy to be rid of the mischievous goblins and their outrageous flying machine.

The rope ladder still dangled free, ready for his use. The wary mage waited while Voyd and his partner maneuvered their ship nearer and nearer. Whatever his previous thoughts about the zeppelin, Rhonin had to admit that now the goblins controlled it with a measure of accuracy he found admirable.

The ladder clattered slightly against the rock wall just to the left of the cave.

"Can you keep it steady here?" he called to Nullyn.

A nod was all he received from the still fearful pilot, but it satisfied Rhonin. No more tricks. Even if they did not fear him, they certainly feared the long reach of Deathwing.

Taking a deep breath, Rhonin crawled over the side. The ladder wobbled dangerously, slapping him more than once against the side of the mountain. Ignoring the shock of each strike, the wizard hurried as best he could to the bottom rung.

The slim ledge of the cave stood just a little under him, but although the goblins had the zeppelin positioned as precisely as they could, the high mountain winds kept twisting Rhonin away from safety. Three times he tried to get his footing, and three times the wind dragged him away, leaving his foot dangling hundreds of feet in the air.

Worse, as the current grew stronger, the airship, too, began to shift, sometimes drawing away a few critical inches. The voices of the two goblins rose in frantic argument, although the actual words were lost to the struggling mage.

He would have to risk jumping. With conditions as they were, casting a spell would be too chancy. Rhonin would have to rely on physical skill alone—not his first choice.

The airship veered without warning, slapping him hard against the rock.

Rhonin let out a gasp, barely managing to hang on. If he did not abandon the ladder soon, the next collision might just be enough to stun him and cause a fatal loss of grip.

Taking a deep breath, the battered wizard studied the distance between himself and the ledge. The ladder rocked to and fro, threatening again to toss him hard against the rock.

Rhonin waited until it brought him near the ledge—then threw himself toward the cave.

With a painful grunt, he came down on the slim ledge. His feet momentarily slipped, one finding no purchase whatsoever. The wizard scrambled to pull himself forward, finally making progress.

When at last he felt secure enough, Rhonin dropped to the ground, panting. It took him a few seconds to regain his breath, at which point he rolled onto his back.

Beyond, Voyd and Nullyn had apparently just realized that they had finally rid themselves of their unwanted passenger. The goblin airship began to pull away, the rope ladder still dangling from the side.

Rhonin's hand suddenly shot up, his index finger pointing toward the fleeing vessel.

He opened his mouth to scream, knowing what would happen next. *"Nooo!"*

The same words he had spoken earlier to create the flickering flame over his hand now erupted from his mouth, but this time they were not spoken by the wizard himself.

A stream of pure fire greater than any the horrified spellcaster had ever summoned shot forth—directly toward the airship and the unsuspecting goblins.

The flames engulfed the zeppelin. Rhonin heard screams.

The airship exploded as its stockpile of oil ignited.

As the few remaining fragments plunged from the sky, Rhonin's arm dropped to his side.

Drawing in what breath he had, the mage snapped, "You shouldn't have done that!"

The winds will keep the explosion from being heard, replied the cold voice. *And the pieces will fall to a deep valley little used. Besides, the orcs are used to the goblins destroying themselves in the midst of their experiments. You need not fear discovery . . . my friend.*

Rhonin had not been concerned about his own safety at that moment, only the lives of the two goblins. Death in combat was one thing; punishment such as the black dragon had meted out to his two rebellious servants was another.

You would do yourself better to continue on into the cave, Deathwing continued. *The elements outside are hardly fit for you.*

Not at all mollified by the leviathan's attempt at concern, Rhonin yet obeyed. He had no desire to be swept off the ledge by the ever-increasing winds. For better or worse, the dragon had brought him this close to his goal—one that he could now admit to himself he had suspected he might never reach on his own. Deep down, the wizard had believed all along he would perish—hopefully, at least, *after* he had made amends. Now, perhaps he had a chance. . . .

At that moment a monstrous sound greeted Rhonin, a sound he recognized instantly. A dragon, of course, and one young and fit. Dragons and orcs. They awaited him in the depths of the mountain, awaited the lone mage.

Reminded him that he might yet die, just as he had originally imagined. . . .

The human was strong. Stronger than imagined.

Clad once more in the guise of Lord Prestor, Deathwing considered the pawn he had chosen. Usurping the wizard that the Kirin Tor had sent on this absurdly impossible quest had seemed the simplest thing. He would turn their folly into victory—but *his* victory. This Rhonin would do that for him, although not in the way the mortal expected.

Yet the wizard showed much more defiance than Deathwing had assumed possible. Strong of will, this one. A good thing that he would perish in the course of matters; such strong will bred strong wizards—like Medivh. Only one name among humans had the black leviathan ever respected, and that had been Medivh's. Mad as a goblin—not to mention as unpredictable as one—he had wielded power unbelievable. Not even Deathwing would have faced him willingly.

But Medivh was dead—and the ebony leviathan believed that to be the case despite the recent rumors to the contrary. No other wizard came anywhere near to having the mad one's skills, and never would, if Deathwing had his way.

Yet if Rhonin would not obey him blindly—as the monarchs of the Alliance did—he would obey out of the knowledge that the dragon watched his every move. The two insipid goblins had made for an object lesson. Perhaps they had only planned to put terror into the heart of their passenger, but Deathwing had not had time for such foolishness. He had warned Kryll to choose a pair who would fulfill their mission without any nonsense. When the chief goblin had completed his own tasks, Deathwing would speak to him about his choices. The black dragon was not at all pleased.

"You had better not fail, little toad," he hissed. "Or your brethren on board the airship will have considered themselves fortunate compared to the fate I will deal you. . . ."

He dropped all thought of the goblin. Lord Prestor had an important meeting with King Terenas . . . about the Princess Calia.

Clad in the finest suit to be found among any of the nobles of the land, Deathwing admired himself in the lengthy mirror in the front corridor of his chateau. Yes, every inch a future king. Had humans carried within them even a shred of the dignity and power that he possessed, the dragon might have thought to spare them. However, what stared back at him represented to Deathwing the perfection that the mortals could never even hope to attain. He did them a favor by ending their miserable existences.

"Ssssoon," he whispered in promise to himself. "Ssssoon."

His carriage took him directly to the palace, where the guards saluted and immediately bid him enter. A servant met Deathwing inside the front hall, begging his pardon for the king not being there personally to greet him. Now fully into his role as the young noble who sought only peace between all parties, the dragon pretended no annoyance, smiling as he asked the human to lead him to where Terenas desired him to wait. He had expected the king not to be ready for him, especially if Terenas still had to explain to his young daughter her chosen future.

With all opposition to his ascension swept aside and the throne only days from his grasp, Deathwing had hit upon what he felt the perfect addition to his plans. How much better to strengthen his hold than to wed the daughter of one of the most powerful of the kingdoms in the Alliance? Of course, not all of the reigning monarchs had had viable choices. In fact, at this moment in time, only Terenas and Daelin Proudmoore had daughters either single or beyond infancy. Jaina Proudmoore, however, was much too young and, from what the dragon had so far researched, possibly already too difficult to control, or else he might have waited for her. No, Terenas's daughter would do just fine.

Calia still remained at least two years away from marriage, but two years hardly mattered to the ageless dragon. By that time not only would the others of his kind be either under his domination or dead, but Deathwing would have maneuvered himself into a political position in which he could truly begin undermining the foundation of the Alliance. What the brutish orcs had failed to do from without—he would do from within.

The servant opened a door. "If you'll wait within, my lord, I'm sure His Majesty will be with you shortly."

"Thank you." Caught up in his reverie, Deathwing did not notice that he had two new companions awaiting him until just after the door had shut behind him.

The cloaked and hooded figures bowed their shadowed heads slightly in his direction.

"Our greetings, Lord Prestor," rumbled the bearded one.

Deathwing fought back the frown nearly descending upon his mouth. He had expected to confront the Kirin Tor, but not in the palace of Terenas. The enmity the dragon had magically built up among the various rulers toward the wizards of Dalaran should have prevented the latter from daring to visit.

"My greetings to you, sir and madam."

The second mage, old for a female of the race, returned, "We had hoped to meet you sooner than this, my lord. Your reputation has spread throughout the kingdoms of the Alliance . . . especially in Dalaran."

The magic wielded by these wizards kept their features obscured for the most part, and although with but a single action Deathwing could have pierced their veils, the dragon chose not to do so. He already knew this pair, albeit not by name. The bearded one had a familiar feel to his aura, as if Deathwing and the wizard had recently come into contact. The false noble suspected that this mage had been responsible for at least one of the two major attempts to break through the protective spells around the chateau. Considering the potency of those spells, it surprised Deathwing a little that the man still lived, much less confronted him now.

"And the reputation of the Kirin Tor is known to all as well," he replied.

"And becoming more known with each day . . . but not in the way we wish, I must say."

She hinted of his handiwork. Deathwing found no threat there. By this time, they suspected him a rogue wizard—powerful but not nearly the threat he truly presented.

"I had expected to meet His Majesty here alone," he said, turning the conversation to his advantage. "Has Dalaran some business with Lordaeron?"

"Dalaran seeks to keep abreast of situations important to all kingdoms of the Alliance," the woman replied. "Something a bit more difficult of late, due to our not being notified of major summits between members."

Deathwing calmly walked over to the side table, where Terenas always kept a few bottles of his best on hand for waiting guests. Lordaeron wine represented in his mind the only worthwhile export the kingdom offered. He poured a small amount in one of the jeweled goblets nearby. "Yes, I spoke with His Majesty, urging him to request you join in the deliberations over Alterac, but he seemed adamant about leaving you out of them."

"We know the outcome, regardless," huffed the bearded man. "Congratulations are in order for you, Lord Prestor."

Not once had they offered their names, nor had he offered his. Yes, they truly kept an eye on him—as much as Deathwing allowed, that is.

"It came as a surprise to me, I must tell you. All I ever hoped was to help keep the Alliance from falling apart after Lord Perenolde's unfortunate behavior."

"Yes, a terrible thing that. One would've never thought it of the man. I knew him when he was younger. A bit timid, but didn't seem the traitorous type."

The elder female suddenly spoke up. "Your former homeland is somewhere not too distant from Alterac, is it not, Lord Prestor?"

For the first time, Deathwing felt a twinge of annoyance. This game no longer pleased him. Did she know?

Before he could answer, the grandly decorated door on the opposite side of the entrance opened and King Terenas, his mood clearly not at all pleasant, barged inside. A blond, cherubic boy barely more than a toddler followed behind, clearly trying to get his father's attention. However, Terenas took one look at the two shadowy wizards and the frown on his face deepened further.

He turned to the child. "Run along back to your sister, Arthas, and try to calm her. I'll be with you as soon as I can, I promise."

Arthas nodded and, with a curious glance at his father's visitors, headed back through the door.

Terenas shut the door behind his son, then instantly whirled on the mages. "I thought I told the major-domo to inform you that I've no time for you today! If Dalaran has any claims or protests to make concerning my handling of Alliance matters, they can send a formal writ through our ambassador there! Now, *good day!*"

The pair seemed unmoved. Deathwing held back a triumphant smile. His hold on the king remained strong even when the dragon had to deal with other matters, such as Rhonin.

Thinking of his newest pawn, Deathwing hoped that the wizards would take Terenas's forceful dismissal to heart and leave. The sooner they were gone, the sooner he could get back to checking on their younger counterpart.

"We'll be going, Your Majesty," rumbled the male spellcaster. "But we've been empowered to tell you that the council hopes you'll see reason on this before long. Dalaran has always been a steadfast, loyal ally."

"When it chooses to be."

Both mages ignored the monarch's harsh statement. Turning to Deathwing, the female said, "Lord Prestor, it has been an honor to meet you face-to-face at last. I trust it will not be the final time."

"We shall see." She made no attempt to extend her hand and he did not encourage it. So. They had warned him that they would continue to watch him. No doubt the Kirin Tor believed this would make him more cautious, even uncertain, but the black dragon only found their threats laughable. Let them waste their time crouching over scrying spheres or trying to convince the rulers of the Alliance to see reason. All they would gain by their efforts would be the further enmity of the other humans—which would work just perfectly for Deathwing.

Bowing, the two mages retreated from the chamber. Out of respect for the king, they did not simply vanish, as he knew they could. No, they would wait until back in their own embassy, out of sight of untrusting eyes. Even now, the Kirin Tor took care with appearances around others.

Not that it would matter in the long run.

When the wizards had at last gone, King Terenas began speaking. "My most humble apologies for that scene, Prestor! The very nerve of them! They barge into the palace as if Dalaran and not Lordaeron ruled here! This time they go too far—"

He froze in mid-sentence as Deathwing raised a hand toward him. After glancing at both doors in order to assure himself that no one would come running in and find the king bewitched, the false noble stepped to a window overlooking the palace grounds and the kingdom beyond. Deathwing waited patiently, watching the gates through which all visitors passed in and out of Terenas's royal residence.

The two wizards stepped into sight, heading away. Their heads leaned toward one another as they engaged in urgent yet clearly private conversation with one another.

The dragon touched the expensive glass plate on the window with his index finger, drawing two circles there, circles that glowed deep red. He muttered a single word.

The glass in one of the circles shifted, puckered, shaped itself into a parody of a mouth.

"—nothing at all! He's a blank, Modera! Couldn't sense a thing about him!"

In the other circle, a second, somewhat more delicate, mouth formed. "Perhaps you're still not recovered enough, Drenden. After all, that shock you suffered—"

"I'm over it! Take more than that to kill me! Besides, I know you were probing him, too! Did *you* sense anything?"

A frown formed on the feminine mouth. "No . . . which means he's very, very powerful—possibly almost as powerful as Medivh."

"He must be using some powerful talisman! No one's that powerful, not even Krasus!"

Modera's tone changed. "Do we really know how powerful Krasus is? He's older than the rest of us. That surely means something."

"It means he's cautious . . . but he is the best of us, even if he isn't master of the council."

"That was his choice—more than once."

Deathwing leaned forward, his once mild curiosity now growing stronger. "What's he doing, anyway? Why's he keeping so secret?"

"He says he wants to try to find out about Prestor's past, but I think there's more. There's always more with Krasus."

"Well, I hope he finds out something soon, because this situation is—what is it?"

"I feel a tingling on my neck! I wonder if—"

Up in the palace, the dragon quickly waved his hand across the two glass mouths. The pane instantly flattened, leaving no trace. Deathwing backed away.

The female had finally sensed his spellwork, but she would not be able to trace it back to him. He did not fear them, however skilled for humans they were, but Deathwing had no desire at the moment to drag out his confrontation with the pair. A new element had been added to the game, one that, for the first time, made the dragon just a little pensive.

He turned back to Terenas. The king still stood where Deathwing had left him, mouth open and hand out.

The dragon snapped his fingers.

"—and I won't stand for it! I've a mind to cut off all diplomatic relations with them immediately! Who rules in Lordaeron? Not the Kirin Tor, whatever they might think!"

"Yes, probably a wise move, Your Majesty, but draw it out. Let them lodge their protest, then begin closing the gates on them. I'm very certain that the other kingdoms will follow suit."

Terenas gave him a weary smile. "You're a very patient young man, Prestor! Here I've been ranting and you simply stand there, accepting it all! We're supposed to be discussing a future marriage! True, we've more than two years before it can take place, but the betrothal will require extensive planning!" He shrugged. "Such is the way of royalty!"

Deathwing gave him a slight bow. "I understand completely, Your Majesty."

The king of Lordaeron began telling him about the various functions his future son-in-law would need to attend over the next several months. In addition to taking charge of Alterac, young Prestor would have to be present for each occasion in order to strengthen the ties between him and Calia in the eyes of the people and his fellow monarchs. The world would need to see that this match would be the beginning of a great future for the Alliance.

"And once we take Khaz Modan and Grim Batol back from those infernal orcs, we can begin plans for a ceremonial return of the lands to the hill dwarves! A ceremony you shall lead, my dear boy, as you are possibly one of those most responsible for holding this Alliance together long enough for victory. . . ."

Deathwing's attention slipped further and further away from the babblings of Terenas. He knew most of what the old man would say—having placed it into the human's mind earlier. Lord Prestor, the hero—imagined or otherwise—would reap his rewards and slowly, methodically, begin the destruction of the lesser races.

However, what interested the dragon more at the moment was the conversation between the two wizards, and especially their mention of another of the Kirin Tor, one Krasus. Deathwing found him of interest. He knew that there had been earlier attempts to circumnavigate the spells surrounding the chateau, and that one of those attempts had triggered the *Endless Hunger,* one of the oldest and most thorough traps ever devised by a wielder of magic. The dragon also knew that the *Hunger* had failed in its function.

Krasus . . . was this the name of the wizard who had evaded a spell as ancient as Deathwing himself?

I may have to learn more about you, the dragon thought as he absently nodded in response to Terenas's continued babble. *Yes, I may have to learn more. . . .*

FOURTEEN

K rasus slept, slept deeper than he ever had, even as a small hatchling. He slept the sleep halfway between dreaming and something else, that eternal slumber from which not even the mightiest conqueror could awake. He slept knowing that each hour that passed slid him nearer and nearer to that sweet oblivion.

And while he slept, the dragon mage dreamed.

The first visions were murky ones, simple images from the sleeper's subconscious. However, they were soon followed by more distinct and much starker apparitions. Winged figures both draconic and otherwise fluttered about, seeming to scatter in panic. A looming man in black mocked him from a distance. A child raced along a winding, sun-drenched hill . . . a child who suddenly transformed into a twisted, undead thing of evil.

Troubled by the meanings of these dreams even in the depths of his slum-

ber, the wizard shifted uneasily. As he did, he dropped deeper yet, entering a
realm of pure darkness that both smothered and comforted him.

And in that realm, a voice, a soft yet commanding voice, spoke to the desperate dragon mage.

You would sacrifice anything for her, would you not, Korialstrasz?

In his sanctum, Krasus's lips moved as he mouthed a reply. *I would give
myself if that is what it takes to free her. . . .*

Poor, loyal Korialstrasz . . . A shape formed in the darkness, a shape that fluc-
tuated with each breath of the sleeping figure. In his dreams, a drifting Krasus
tried to reach for that shape, but it vanished just as he almost caught it.

In his mind, it had been Alexstrasza.

*You slip quicker and quicker toward the final rest, brave one. Is there something
you would ask of me before that happens?*

Again his lips moved. *Only that you help her . . .*

*Nothing for yourself? Your fading life, perhaps? Those who have the audacity to
drink to death should be rewarded with a full goblet of his finest vintage. . . .*

The darkness seemed to be pulling him in. Krasus found it hard to
breathe, hard to think. The temptation to simply turn over and accept the
comforting blanket of oblivion grew stronger.

Yet he forced himself to reply. *Her. All I ask is for her.*

Suddenly he felt himself dragged upward, dragged to a place of color and
light, a place where it became possible to breathe again, to think again.

Images assailed him, images not from his own dreams—but from the
dreams of others. He saw the wishes and wants of humans, dwarves, elves, and
even orcs and goblins. He suffered their nightmares and savored their sweet sensations. The images were legion, yet as each passed him by, Krasus immediately
found it impossible to recall them, just as he found it so hard to recall even his
own dreams.

In the midst of this flowing landscape, another vision formed. However,
while all around it moved as mist, this one retained a shape—more or less—
that grew to overwhelm the small figure of the wizard.

A graceful draconic form, half substance, half imagination, spread its
wings as if waking. Hints of faded green, such as seen in a forest before the
setting of night, spread across the torso of the leviathan. Krasus looked up,
prepared to meet the dragon's eyes—and saw that they were closed as if in
sleep. However, he had no doubt that the Mistress of Dreams perceived him
all too well.

*Such a sacrifice will I not demand from you, Korialstrasz, you who have always
been a most interesting dreamer. . . .* The edges of the dragon's mouth curled up
slightly. *A most intriguing dreamer . . .*

Krasus sought to find stable footing, to find *any* footing, but the ground around him remained malleable, almost liquid. He was forced to float, a position that left him feeling wanting. *I thank you, Ysera....*

Ever polite, ever diplomatic, even to my consorts, who have, in my name, rejected your desires more than once.

They did not understand the situation fully, he countered.

You mean I did not understand the situation fully. Ysera drifted back, her neck and wings rippling as if reflected in a suddenly disturbed pool. Ever her eyelids remained shut, but her great visage focused quite distinctly on the intruder to her realm. *It is not so simple a matter to free your beloved Alexstrasza, and even I cannot say if the cost is worth it. Is it not better to let the world run its course, to do as it will? If the Giver of Life is to be freed, will it not happen of its own accord?*

Her apathy—the apathy of *all* three of the Aspects he had visited—set the dragon mage's mind afire with anger. *And is Deathwing truly to be the culmination of the world's course, then? He certainly will be if none of you do anything but sit back and dream!*

The wings folded in. *Mention not that one!*

Krasus pushed. *Why, Lady of Dreams? Does he give you nightmares?*

Although the lids stayed tight, Ysera's eyes surely held some dire emotion. *He is one whose dreams I will never enter—again. He is one who is quite possibly more terrible in his sleep than even waking.*

The beleaguered wizard did not pretend to understand the last. All that concerned him was the fact that none of these great powers could summon up the wherewithal to make a stand. True, thanks to the *Demon Soul* they were not what they once had been, but still they wielded terrible power. Yet, it appeared that all three felt that the Age of the Dragon had passed, and that even if they *could* alter the future, it would not be worth dragging themselves out of their self-imposed stupors.

I know that you and yours still circulate among the younger races, Ysera. I know that you still influence the dreams of the humans, elves, and—

To a point, Korialstrasz! There are limits to even my *domain!*

But you have not given up entirely on the world then, have you? Unlike Malygos and Nozdormu, you do not hide in madness or the relics of times past! After all, are not dreams also of the future?

As much as they are the past; you would do well to remember that!

The faint image of a human woman holding up a new baby drifted by. The brief glimpse of a young boy doing epic battle with childish monsters of his own imagining flickered into and out of existence. Krasus momentarily surveyed the various dreams forming and dissipating around him. As many dark as there were those of a lighter nature, but that was how it had always been. A balance.

Yet, in his mind, his queen's continued captivity and Deathwing's determination to wrest the world from the younger races upset that balance. There would be no more dreams, no more hopes, if both situations were not rectified.

With or without your help, Ysera, I will go on. I must!

You are certainly welcome to do so. . . . The dream dragon's form wavered.

Krasus turned away from her, ignoring the intangible images that scattered in his wake. *Then either send me back to my sanctum or drop me into the abyss! Perhaps it would be best if I do not live to see the fate of the world—and what becomes of my queen!*

He expected Ysera to send him back to the arms of oblivion, so that he would no longer be able to harp on the subject of his Alexstrasza to either her or any of the other Aspects. Instead, the dragon mage felt a gentle touch on his shoulder, an almost tentative touch.

Turning, Krasus found himself facing a slim, pale woman, beautiful but ethereal. She stood clad in a flowing gown of pale green gossamer, a veil partially obscuring her lower features. In some ways she reminded him of his queen—and yet not.

The eyes of the woman were closed.

Poor, struggling Korialstrasz. Her mouth did not move, but Krasus knew the voice for hers. Ysera's voice. A pensive expression formed on the pale face. *You* would *do anything for her.*

He did not understand why she bothered to repeat what they both knew already. Krasus again turned from the Lady of Dreams, searching for some path by which he could escape this unreal domain.

Do not go yet, Korialstrasz.

And why not? he demanded, turning back—

Ysera stared at him, eyes fully open. Krasus froze, unable not to stare back at those eyes. They were the eyes of everyone he had ever known, ever loved. They were eyes that knew him, knew every bit about him. They were blue, green, red, black, golden—every color that eyes could be.

They were even his own.

I will consider what you have said.

He could scarcely believe her. *You will—*

She raised a hand, silencing him. *I will consider what you have said. No more, no less, for now.*

And—and if you find you agree with me?

Then I will endeavor to convince Malygos and Nozdormu of your quest . . . and from them I can promise nothing, even then.

It was more than Krasus had come with, even more than he had hoped for at this point. Perhaps it would come to nothing, but it at least gave him hope to carry into battle.

I—I thank you.

I have done nothing for you yet . . . except kept your dreams alive. The brief smile that crossed Ysera's lips had a regretful tinge to it.

He started to thank her again, wanting her to understand that even this much would give him the strength he needed to go on, but suddenly Ysera seemed to drift away from him. Krasus reached for her, but the distance already proved too great, and when he sought to step forward, she only moved away more swiftly.

Then it occurred to him that She of the Dreaming had not moved; he had. *Sleep well and good, poor Korialstrasz,* came her voice. The slim, pale figure wavered, then dissipated completely. *Sleep well, for in the battle you seek to fight you will need all your strength and more. . . .*

He tried to speak, but even his dream voice would not work. Darkness descended upon the dragon mage, the comforting darkness of slumber.

And do not undervalue those you think only pawns. . . .

The mountain fortress of the orcs proved not only to be more immense than even Rhonin had supposed, but more confusing. Tunnels that he expected would bring him toward his goal would suddenly turn off in different directions, even often rising instead of descending. Some ended, for no good reason that he could decipher. One such tunnel forced him to backtrack for more than an hour, not only stealing precious time but depleting his already flagging strength.

It did not help at all that Deathwing had not spoken to him once in all that time. While Rhonin in no way trusted the black dragon, at least he knew that Deathwing would have guided him to the captive leviathan. What could have drawn the attention of the dark one away?

In an unlit corridor, the weary mage finally sat down to rest. He had with him a small water sack given to him by the hapless goblins, and from this Rhonin took a sip. After that, Rhonin leaned back, believing that a few minutes' relaxation would enable him to clear his mind and allow him to better traverse the passages again.

Did he really imagine that he could free the Dragonqueen? The doubts had increased more and more as he tried to wend his way through the mountain. Had he come here just to commit some grand suicide? His life would not bring back those who had died and, in truth, they had all made choices of their own.

How had he ever dreamt of such an insane quest? Thinking back, Rhonin recalled the first time the subject had come up. Forbidden to take part in the activities of the Kirin Tor after the debacle of his last mission, the young wizard had spent his days brooding, seeing no one and eating little. Under the conditions of his probation, no one had been allowed to see him, either, which had made it more surprising when Krasus had materialized before him, offering his support in Rhonin's efforts to return to the ranks.

Rhonin had always thought that he needed no one, but Krasus had convinced him otherwise. The master wizard had discussed his younger counterpart's dire situation in great detail, to the point where Rhonin had openly asked for his aid. Somehow the topic of dragons had arisen, and from there the story of Alexstrasza, the crimson behemoth held captive by the orcs, forced to breed savage beasts for the glory of the Horde. Even though the main element of the Horde itself had been shattered, so long as she remained a prisoner, the orcs in Khaz Modan would continue to wreak havoc on the Alliance, killing countless innocents.

It had been at that juncture that the notion to free the dragon had occurred to Rhonin, a notion so fantastic that he felt only he could have devised it. It had made perfect sense at the time. Redeem himself or die trying in a scheme that would be forever spoken of among his brethren.

Krasus had been so very impressed. In fact, Rhonin now recalled that the elder mage had spent much time with him, working out details and encouraging the red-haired spellcaster. Rhonin freely admitted to himself now that perhaps he would have dropped the idea if not for his patron's urging. In some ways, it seemed as if the quest had been more Krasus's than his own. Of course, what would the faceless councilor achieve by sending his protégé off on such a mission? If Rhonin succeeded, some credit might go to the one who had believed in him, but if he failed . . . what good would that do Krasus?

Rhonin shook his head. If he kept asking himself questions such as these, soon he would come to believe that his patron had actually been the force behind this quest, that he had somehow used his influence to make the younger wizard *want* to journey to these hostile lands.

Absurd . . .

A sudden noise nearly brought Rhonin to his feet, and he realized that somewhere in the course of his thinking he had drifted off to sleep. The wizard pressed himself against the wall, waiting to see who passed in the darkened corridor. Surely the orcs knew that the tunnel ended. Could they have come here specifically in search of him?

Yet the noise—barely discernible as muttered conversation—slowly faded away. The wizard realized that he had been the victim of the complex acoustics of the cavern system. The orcs he had heard likely were several levels away from him.

Could he follow those sounds, though? With growing hope, Rhonin moved cautiously in the direction from which he believed the conversation had come.

Even if it had not exactly originated from that location, at least the echoes might eventually lead him to where he hoped to go.

How long he had slept, Rhonin could not say, but as he journeyed along, he heard more and more sounds, almost as if Grim Batol had just awakened. The orcs seemed to be in the midst of a flurry of activity, which presented the mage with something of a problem. Now there came too many noises from too many directions. Rhonin did not want to accidentally step into the practice quarters of the warriors, or even their mess hall. All he wanted was the chamber where the Dragonqueen lay prisoner.

Then, a draconic roar cut through the sounds, a high roar that died quickly. Rhonin had already heard such cries before, but had not thought about them. Now he cursed himself for a fool; would not all the dragons be kept in the same general region? At the very worst, following the cries would at least get him nearer to *some* beast, and then perhaps he could find the trail to the queen's chamber from there.

For a time he wended his way through the tunnels with little problem, most of the orcs seemingly far away, at work on some great project. Briefly the wizard wondered if Grim Batol planned for battle. By now the Alliance had to be pressing the orc forces in northern Khaz Modan. Grim Batol would need to support their brethren up there if the Horde hoped to drive the humans and their allies back.

If so, the activity would work to Rhonin's advantage. Not only would the orcs' minds be occupied by this, but there would be less of them. Surely every handler with a trained mount would be in the sky soon, on the way to the north.

Encouraged, Rhonin set a more daring pace, a more certain one—which but seconds later nearly sent him stumbling into the very arms of a pair of huge orc warriors.

They were, fortunately, even more stunned to see him than he was them. Rhonin immediately raised his left hand, muttering a spell that he had hoped to save for more dire circumstances.

The nearest of the orcs, his ugly, tusked face twisting into a berserker rage, reached for the ax slung on his back. Rhonin's spell caught him directly in the chest, throwing the massive warrior hard against the nearest rock wall.

As the orc struck the wall, he *melded* into the very rock. Briefly the outline of his form remained behind, mouth still open in rage, but then even that faded into the wall . . . leaving no trace of the creature's savage end.

"Human scum!" roared the second, his ax now in hand. He took a heavy swing at Rhonin, chipping off bits of stone as the wizard managed to duck out of the way. The orc lumbered forward, bulky, dull green form filling the narrow corridor. A necklace of dried, wrinkled fingers—human, elven, and otherwise—dangled before Rhonin's eyes, a collection to which his foe no doubt wished to add him. The orc swung again, this time coming perilously near to severing the mage in two lengthwise.

Rhonin stared at the necklace again, a grim idea in mind. He pointed at the necklace and gestured.

His spell briefly made the orc pause, but when the savage warrior saw no visible effect, he laughed scornfully at the pitiful little human. "Come! I make it quick for you, wizard!"

But as he raised his ax, a scratching sensation forced the orc to look down at his chest.

The fingers on his necklace, more than two dozen strong, had moved to his throat.

He dropped the ax and tried to pull them away, but they had already dug in tight. The orc began to cough as the fingers formed a macabre hand of sorts, a hand cutting off his air.

Rhonin scrambled back as the orc began to swing about wildly, trying to peel away the avenging digits. The wizard had intended the spell only as a diversion while he came up with something more final, but the severed fingers seemed to have taken the opportunity to heart. Vengeance? Even as a mage, Rhonin could not believe that the spirits of the warriors slain by this orc had somehow urged the fingers to this grand effort. It had to be the potency of the spell itself.

Surely it had to be. . . .

Whether vengeful ghosts or simply magic, the enchanted fingers did their terrible work with seeming eagerness. Blood covered much of the orc's upper chest as nails tore into the softer throat. The monstrous warrior collapsed to his knees, eyes so desperate that Rhonin finally had to look away.

A few seconds later, he heard the orc gasp—then a heavy weight fell to the tunnel floor.

The massive berserker lay in a bloody heap, the fingers still dug deep into his neck. Daring to touch one of the severed digits, Rhonin found no movement, no life. The fingers had performed their task and now had returned to their previous state, just as his spell had intended.

And yet . . .

Shaking off such thoughts, Rhonin hurried past the corpse. He had nowhere to put the body and no time to think about it. Before long someone would discover the truth, but the wizard could not help that. Rhonin had to concern himself only with the Dragonqueen. If he did manage to free her, perhaps she would at least carry him off to safety. In that, truly, lay his only possibility of escape.

He managed to traverse the next few tunnels without interruption, but then found himself heading toward a brightly lit corridor from which the babble of voices grew loud and strong. Moving with more caution, Rhonin edged up to the intersection, peering around the corner.

What he had taken for a corridor had proven to actually be the mouth of a vast cavern that opened up to the right, a cavern in which scores of orcs worked hard at loading up wagons and preparing draft animals, all as if they intended some long journey from which they would not likely soon return.

Had he been correct about the battle north? If so, why did it seem *every* orc intended to depart? Why not simply the dragons and their handlers? It would take far too long for these wagons to reach Dun Algaz.

Two orcs came into sight, the pair carrying some great weight between them. Clearly they would have preferred to put down whatever it was they carried, but for some reason dared not do so. In fact, Rhonin thought that they took special care with their burden, almost as if it were made of gold.

Seeing that no one looked in his direction, the wizard took a step forward in order to better study what the orcs so valued. It was round—no, *oval*—and a bit rough in outer appearance, almost scaly. In fact, it reminded Rhonin of nothing more than an—

An *egg*.

A *dragon's* egg, to be precise.

Quickly his gaze shifted to some of the other wagons. Sure enough, he now realized that several of them bore eggs in some stage of development, from smoother, nearly round ones to others even more scaled than the first, eggs clearly near to hatching.

With the dragons so essential to the orcs' fading hopes, why would they be risking such precious cargo on such a journey?

Human.

The voice in his head nearly made Rhonin shout. He flattened against the wall, then quickly slipped back into the tunnel. Finally certain that none of the orcs could see him, Rhonin seized the medallion around his neck and gazed at the black crystal in the center.

Sure enough, it now glowed slightly.

Human . . . Rhonin . . . where are you?

Did Deathwing not know? "I'm in the very midst of the orc fortress," he whispered. "I was looking for the Dragonqueen's chamber."

You found something else, though. There was a glimpse of it. What was it?

For some reason, Rhonin did not want to tell Deathwing. "It was only the orcs at battle practice. I nearly walked in on them without realizing it."

His response was followed by a lengthy silence, so lengthy, in fact, that he nearly thought Deathwing had broken the link. Then, in a very even tone, the dragon returned, *I wish to see it.*

"It's nothing—"

Before Rhonin could say another word, his body suddenly rebelled against him, turning back toward the cavern and the many, many orcs. The outraged spellcaster tried to protest, but this time even his mouth would not work for him.

Deathwing brought him to the spot where he had last stood, then made the wizard's right hand hold up the medallion. Rhonin guessed that Deathwing observed all through the ebony crystal.

At battle practice . . . I see. . . . And is this how they practice their retreating?

He could not reply to the leviathan's mocking retort, nor did he think that Deathwing really cared if he did. The dragon forced him to stay in the open while the medallion surveyed everything.

Yes, I see. . . . You may return to the tunnel now.

His body suddenly his own again, Rhonin slipped out of sight, thankful that the orcs had been so busy with their task that no one had chanced to look up. He leaned against a wall, breathing heavily and realizing that he had been far more frightened of discovery than he would have thought possible. So, evidently, Rhonin was not as suicidal as he had once imagined.

You follow the wrong path. You must go back to the previous intersection.

Deathwing made no comment about Rhonin's attempt at subterfuge, which worried the wizard more than if the dragon had. Surely Deathwing, too, pondered the orcs' moving of the eggs—unless he knew something about it already? How could that be possible, though? Certainly no one here would relay that information to him. The orcs feared and despised the black dragon at least as much as—if not more than—they did the entire Lordaeron Alliance.

Despite those concerns, he immediately followed Deathwing's instructions, backtracking along the corridor until he came to the intersection in question. Rhonin had ignored it earlier, thinking its narrow appearance and lack of lighting meant it was of little significance. Surely the orcs would have kept any tunnel of importance better lit.

"This way?" he whispered.

Yes.

How the dragon knew so much about the cavern system continued to bother Rhonin. Surely Deathwing had not gone wandering through the tunnels, not even in his human guise. Could he have done so in the form of an orc? Possibly so, and yet that, too, did not seem the answer.

The second tunnel on your left. You will take that one next.

Deathwing's directions appeared flawless. Rhonin waited for one mistake, one error, that would indicate the dragon guessed, at least in part. No such mistake occurred. Deathwing knew his way around the orcs' sanctum as good as, if not better than, the bestial warriors themselves.

Finally, after what felt like hours more of traveling, the voice abruptly commanded, *Cease.*

Rhonin paused, although he had no clue as to what concerned Deathwing enough to demand this stop.

Wait.

A few moments later, voices from down the tunnel carried to the wizard.

"—where you were! I've questions for you, questions!"

"Most sorry, my grand commander, most sorry! It could not be helped! I—"

The voices faded away just as Rhonin strained to hear more. He knew one to be that of an orc, evidently even that of the one in charge of the fortress, but the other speaker had been of quite a different race. A goblin.

Deathwing made use of goblins. Could that be how he knew so much about this vast lair? Had one of the goblins here also been serving the dark one?

He would have liked to have followed and heard more of the conversation, but the dragon suddenly ordered him on again. Rhonin knew that if he did not obey, Deathwing might very well make him march. At least while Rhonin had control of his limbs, he could still feel as if he had some choice in matters.

Crossing the tunnel down which the orc commander and the goblin had gone, Rhonin descended through a deep tunnel toward what seemed the very bowels of the mountain. Surely now he had to be near the Dragonqueen. In fact, he almost swore that he could hear the breathing of a giant, and since there were no true giants in Grim Batol, that left only dragons.

Two corridors ahead. Turn right. Follow until you see the opening to your left.

Deathwing said no more. Rhonin again obeyed his instructions, quickening the pace as much as possible. His nerves were on edge. How much longer would he have to wander through this mountain?

He turned right, followed the next passage on and on. From the dragon's simplistic instructions, Rhonin had expected to come across the opening mentioned in fairly quick time, but even after what had to be half an hour he had seen nothing, not even another intersection. Twice he had asked Deathwing if he would soon arrive, but his unseen guide remained silent.

Then, just as the wizard felt ready to give up—he saw a light. A dim one, to be sure, but definitely a light . . . and on the left side of the corridor.

Hopes renewed, Rhonin hurried toward it as quickly as he could without making much noise. For all he knew, a dozen orcs stood guard around the Dragonqueen. He had spells ready, but hoped they could be preserved for other, more desperate moments.

Halt!

Deathwing's voice reverberated through his head, nearly causing Rhonin to collide with the nearest wall. He flattened against it instead, certain that some sentinel had discovered him.

Nothing. The passage remained empty of any but himself.

"Why did you call out?" he whispered to the medallion.

Your destination lies before you . . . but the way may be guarded by more than flesh.

"Magic?" He had thought of that already, but the dragon had not given him any chance to carefully check for himself.

And sentries of magical origin. There is a quick way to discover the truth. Hold out the medallion before you as you move toward the entrance.

"What about guards of flesh and blood? I still have to worry about them."

He could hear the dark one's growing irritation. *All will be known, human. . . .*

Certain that, at the very least, Deathwing wanted him to reach Alexstrasza, Rhonin held the medallion before him and slowly edged forward.

I detect only minor spells—minor to one such as I, that is, the dragon informed him as he neared. *I will deal with them.*

The black crystal suddenly flared, almost causing the startled mage to lose his hold.

The protective spells have been eradicated. A pause. *There are no sentries inside. They would not need them, even without magical spells. Alexstrasza is thoroughly chained and bolted to her surroundings. The orcs have been quite efficient. She is completely secure.*

"I should go in?"

I would be disappointed if you did not.

Rhonin found Deathwing's phrasing slightly curious, but did not think long on it, more concerned with the hope of at last facing the Dragonqueen. He wished Vereesa could have been here now, then wondered why that would so please him. Perhaps—

Even thoughts of the silvery-tressed elf faded as he stepped into the entranceway and beheld for the first time the gargantuan red behemoth *Alexstrasza.*

And found her staring back, an emotion in her reptilian eyes that seemed to him akin to fear—but not for herself.

"No!" she rumbled as best as the brace around her throat enabled her. *"Step back!"*

At the same time, Deathwing's voice, its tone triumphant, uttered, *Perfect!*

A flash of light surrounded the wizard. Every fiber of his being shook as some monstrous force ripped through him. The medallion slipped from his suddenly limp fingers.

As he collapsed, he heard Deathwing repeat the single word, laughing afterward.

Perfect. . . .

FIFTEEN

Vereesa gasped as breathing once more became an option for her. The nightmare of being buried alive slowly receded as she gulped in great lungfuls of air. Gradually, full calm returned to her and she finally opened her eyes—to see that she had traded one nightmare for another.

Three figures hunched about a tiny fire in the midst of what appeared to be a small cave. The flames gave their grotesque forms an additional element of horror, for because of it she could make out the ribs beneath the skin and the mottled, scaly flesh that hung loosely. Worse, she could clearly see the long, cadaverous faces with beaklike noses and elongated chins. The ranger could especially make out the narrow, insidious eyes and the sharp, sharp, teeth.

The three were clad in little more than ragged kilts. Throwing axes sat beside each figure, weapons that Vereesa understood these creatures used with enviable skill.

Despite her attempts to keep silent, some minor movement on her part must have reached the long, pointed ears that so reminded the ranger of goblins, for one of her captors immediately looked her way.

"Supper's awake," he hissed, a patch covering what remained of his left eye.

"Looks more like dessert to me," returned a second, bald where the other two wore long, shaggy mohawks.

"Definitely dessert," grinned the third, who wore a tattered scarf that had once belonged to one of Vereesa's own kind. He seemed lankier than the other two, and spoke as if no one would dare contradict him. The leader, then.

The leader of a trio of hungry-looking trolls.

"Slim pickings lately," the scarf-wearer went on. "But time now for a feast, yes."

Something to the ranger's right suddenly let out what would have been quite a telling epithet if not for the gag that smothered the words. Twisting her head as best as the carefully tied ropes allowed her, Vereesa saw that Falstad, too, still lived, albeit for how long she could not say. Rumors had long persisted, even before the days of the Troll Wars, that these hideous creatures saw anything other than themselves as fair game for food. Even the orcs, who had accepted them as allies, had been said to ever keep one eye on the nimble, cunning fiends.

Fortunately, due to both the Troll Wars and the battle against the Horde, their foul race had dwindled in numbers greatly. Vereesa herself had never seen a troll before, only knew them from drawings and legends. She found she would have much preferred to keep it that way.

"Patience, patience," murmured the scarf-wearer in a mock sympathetic voice. "You'll be first, dwarf! You'll be first!"

"Can't we do it now, Gree?" begged the one-eyed troll. "Why can't we do it now?"

"Because I said so, Shnel!" With one hard fist, Gree suddenly struck Shnel in the jaw, sending the second creature rolling.

The third troll hopped to his feet, encouraging both of his companions to more blows. Gree glared at him, literally staring the bald troll down. Meanwhile, Shnel crawled back to his place by the tiny fire, looking completely subdued.

"*I* am leader!" Gree slapped a bony, taloned hand against his chest. "Yes, Shnel?"

"Yes, Gree! Yes!"

"Yes, Vorsh?"

The hairless monstrosity bobbed his head over and over. "Yes, oh, yes, Gree! Leader you are! Leader you are!"

As with elves, dwarves, and especially humans, there had existed different types of trolls. Some few spoke with the sophistication of elves—even while they tried to take one's head. Others ranged toward the more savage, especially those who most frequented the barrows and other underground realms. Yet Vereesa doubted that there could be any lower form of troll than the three base creatures who had captured her and Falstad—and clearly had still darker designs for them.

The trio went back to some muffled conversation around the tiny fire. Vereesa again looked to the dwarf, who stared back at her. A raised eyebrow by her was answered by a shake of his head. No, despite his prodigious strength, he could not escape the tight bonds. She shook her head in turn. However barbaric the trolls might be, they were true experts in knot-tying.

Trying to remain undaunted, the ranger peered around at her surroundings—what little there was to see of them. They seemed to be in the midst of a long, crudely hewn tunnel, likely of the trolls' own making. Vereesa recalled the long, taloned fingers, just perfect for digging through the rock and earth. These trolls had adapted well to their environment.

Despite already knowing the results in advance, the elf nonetheless tried to find some looseness in her ropes. She twisted around as cautiously as she could, rubbed her wrists nearly raw, but to no avail.

A horrific chuckle warned her that the trolls had seen at least her final attempts.

"Dessert's lively," commented Gree. "Should make for good sport!"

"Where's the others?" groused Shnel. "Should've been here by now!"

The leader nodded, adding, "Hulg knows what'll happen if he doesn't obey! Maybe he—" The troll suddenly seized his throwing ax. *"Dwarves!"*

The ax went spinning through the tunnel, passing just a few inches from Vereesa's head.

A guttural cry followed but a moment later.

The walls of the tunnel erupted with short, sturdy forms letting out battle calls and waving short axes and swords.

Gree pulled out another, slightly longer ax, this one evidently for hand-to-hand combat. Shnel and Vorsh, the latter crouched, let loose with throwing axes. The elf saw one squat attacker fall to Shnel's weapon, but Vorsh's went wide. The trolls then followed the example of their leader and readied stronger, bulkier axes as the newcomers surrounded them.

Vereesa counted more than half a dozen dwarves, each clad in ragged furs and rusting breastplates. Their helmets were rounded, form-fitting, and lacking any horns or other unnecessary adornments. As with Falstad, most had beards, although they seemed shorter and better trimmed.

The dwarves wielded their axes and swords with practiced precision. The trolls found themselves pressed closer and closer to one another. Shnel it was who fell first, the one-eyed beast not seeing the warrior who came in on his blind side. Vorsh barked a warning, but it came too late. Shnel took a wild swing at his new foe, missing completely.

The dwarf drove his sword into the lanky troll's gut.

Gree fought the most savagely. He landed one good blow that sent a dwarf tumbling back, then nearly beheaded another. Unfortunately, his ax broke as it collided with the longer, well-built one wielded by his latest opponent. In desperation, he seized the dwarf's weapon by the upper handle and struggled to take it out of the shorter fighter's grip.

The well-honed blade of another ax caught the troll leader in the back.

The elf almost felt some sympathy for the last of her captors. Vorsh, eyes wide with the knowledge of his impending doom, looked ready to whimper. Nonetheless, he continued waving his ax at the nearest of the dwarves, almost landing a bloody strike by sheer luck. However, he could do nothing to stem the tide of foes who now advanced in an ever-tightening circle, swords and axes ready.

In the end, Vorsh's death approached butchery.

Vereesa turned her gaze away. She did not face forward again until a steady voice with a hint of gravel in it commented, "Well, no wonder the trolls fought so hard! Gimmel! Ye see this?"

"Aye, Rom! Much better sight than what I've found over here!"

Thick hands pulled her to a sitting position. "Let's see if we can get these ropes off ye without too much damage to that fine form!"

She looked up into the face of a ruddy dwarf at least six inches shorter than Falstad and built much stockier. Despite first appearances, however, his expert handling of the ropes quickly informed the ranger that she should not take him or any of his companions for clumsy, especially after the manner in which they had dispatched the trolls.

Up close, the garments of the dwarves took on an even more ragged appearance, not surprising if they had been subsisting, as Vereesa suspected, on whatever they could steal from the orcs. A distinctive odor also prevailed, indicating that bathing had also long been at a premium.

"Here ye go!"

Her ropes fell away. Vereesa immediately pulled free the gag, with which the dwarf had not bothered. At the same time, a long string of swearwords from her side indicated that Falstad, too, had now been completely released.

"Shut ye mouth or I'll stuff that gag back in permanent!" Gimmel snarled back.

"It'd take a hand's worth of you hill dwarves to bring one from the Aerie down!"

A rumble of discord indicated that their rescuers could readily become new captors if the gryphon-rider did not quiet. Stumbling to her feet—and recalling at the last moment that the tunnel did not quite match her height in this area—the anxious ranger snapped, "Falstad! Be polite with our companions! They have, after all, saved us from a horrid fate!"

"Aye, ye have the right of it," Rom replied. "The damn trolls, they eat anything of flesh—dead or alive!"

"They mentioned some companions," she suddenly recalled. "Perhaps we had better leave this place before they come—"

Rom raised his hand. His crinkled features reminded Vereesa of a tough old dog. "No need to worry about them. That's how we found this trio." He mused a moment longer. "But ye may be right, nonetheless! It's not the only band of trolls in this region. The orcs, they use 'em almost like hunting hounds! Anything other than an orc that crosses these ruined lands is fair game—and they've even taken one of their own allies from the mountain when they've thought they could!"

Images of the fates that had been planned for them coursed through Vereesa's head. "Disgusting! I thank you wholeheartedly for your timeliness!"

"Had I known it would've been ye we were rescuing, I'd have made this sorry bunch move faster!"

Gimmel, eyes shifting much too often to the elf, joined his leader. "Joj's dead. Still stickin' halfway out the hole. Narn's bad; he'll need fixin' up. The rest of the wounded can travel well enough!"

"Then let's be moving on! That means ye, too, butterfly!" The last referred to Falstad, who bristled at what apparently had to be a harsh insult to one of the Aerie dwarves.

Vereesa managed to calm him down with a soft touch on his shoulder, but her friend continued to glower as the party started off. The elf noticed that the hill dwarves stripped not only the trolls of any useful items, but also their dead companion. They made no move to try to bring the body with them, and when Rom noticed her glance, he shrugged in mild shame.

"The war demands some proprieties be left behind, lady elf. Joj would've understood. We'll see that his stuff is divided up to his nearest kin and that they also get an extra share of the trolls' items . . . not that there was much, sorry to say."

"I had no idea that there were any of you left in Khaz Modan. It was said that all the dwarves left when it became clear that they could not hold the land against the Horde."

Rom's canine face turned grim. "Aye, all that *could* leave did! Wasn't possible for all of us, ye know! The Horde, it came like the proverbial plague, cutting off much of us from any route! We were forced to go deeper underground than we'd ever gone before! Many's that died at that time, and many more's that died since!"

She looked over his ragtag band. "How many are you?"

"My clan? Seven and forty, where once we counted hundreds! We've talked with three others, two larger than ourselves. Put that total number at three hundred and a little over, and ye still only got a small fraction of what we once were in this land!"

"Three hundred and more's still quite a number," rumbled Falstad. "Aye, with that many, I'd have gone to take Grim Batol back!"

"And perhaps if we fluttered about in the sky like dizzy bugs, we might confuse them enough to make that seem possible, but on the ground or under it, we're still at a disadvantage! Takes only one dragon to scorch a forest and bake the earth below!"

Old enmities between the Aerie and the hills threatened to explode again. Vereesa quickly tried to breach the gap between the two. "Enough of this! It is the orcs and theirs who are the enemies, am I not correct? If you fight with one another, does that not serve their purpose alone?"

Falstad mumbled an apology to her, as did Rom. However, the elf would not let matters settle at only that. "Not good enough. Turn and face one another, then swear you will fight only for the good of all of us! Swear that you will always remember that it is the orcs who slew your brothers, the orcs who killed what you loved."

She knew no specifics about either of the dwarves' pasts, but could draw upon the common understanding that everyone who fought in the war had lost someone or something dear. Rom had no doubt lost many loved ones, and Falstad, who belonged to a reckless yet daring aerial band, surely had suffered the same.

To his credit, the gryphon-rider held his hand out first. "Aye, 'tis the right of it. I'll shake."

"If ye be doing it, I'll be doing it."

Murmurs arose briefly from the other hill dwarves as the two clasped hands. Likely this sort of quick compromise would have been impossible under any circumstances other than the immediate ones.

The party moved on. This time it was Rom who asked the questions. "Now that the danger of trolls is behind us, lady elf, ye should tell us what brings ye and that one to our wounded land. Is it as we hope—that the war turns back on the orcs, that Khaz Modan will soon be free again?"

"The war is moving against the Horde, that much is true." This brought some gasps and quiet cheers from the dwarves. "The bulk of the Horde was broken a few months back, and Doomhammer has disappeared."

Rom paused in his tracks. "Then why are the orcs still in command of Grim Batol?"

"You've to ask on that?" interjected Falstad. "First of all, the orcs still hold out in the north around Dun Algaz. 'Tis said they're beginning to cave in, but they won't go down without a fight."

"And the second, cousin?"

"You've not noticed that they've dragons?" Falstad asked with mock innocence on his face.

Gimmel snorted. Rom gave his second-in-command a glare, but then nodded in resignation. "Aye, the dragons. The one foe we, earthbound, cannot battle. Caught a young one on the ground once and made short work of it—with the loss of one or two good warriors, sad to say—but for the most part, they stay up there and we're forced to hide down here."

"You've fought the trolls, though," Vereesa pointed out. "And surely the orcs as well."

"The occasional patrol, aye. And the trolls, we've done them some damage, too—but it all means nothing if our home's still under the orc ax!" He stared her in the eye. "Now, I ask again. Tell me who ye are and what ye doing here! If Khaz Modan's still orcish, then ye would have to be suicidal to come to Grim Batol!"

"My name is Vereesa Windrunner, ranger, and this is Falstad of the Aeries. We are here because I search for a human, a wizard, tall of height and young. He has hair of fire, and when last I saw him, he was headed this direction." She decided to omit the black dragon's presence for the moment, and was grateful that Falstad did not choose to add that information himself.

"And as daft as wizards are, especially human ones, what would he be thinking of doing near Grim Batol?" Rom studied the pair with some growing suspicion, Vereesa's tale no doubt just a bit too far-fetched for his tastes.

"I do not know," she admitted, "but I think it has something to do with the dragons."

At this, the dwarven leader let out a bellowing laugh. "The dragons? What's he plan to do? Rescue the red queen from bondage? She'll be so grateful she'll gobble him right up out of excitement!"

The hill dwarves all found this terribly amusing, but the elf did not. To his credit, Falstad did not join in the merriment, although he, of course, knew about Deathwing, and most likely assumed that Rhonin had already long ago been "gobbled up."

"I swore an oath, and because of it I will go on. I must reach Grim Batol and see if I can find him."

The merriment changed to a mixture of astonishment and disbelief. Gimmel shook his head as if not certain that he had heard right.

"Lady Vereesa, I respect ye calling, but surely ye can see how outrageous such a quest is!"

She carefully studied the hardened band. Even in the near dark, she could see the weariness, the fatalism. They fought and they dreamed of their homeland free, but most likely thought that it would never happen in their lifetime. They admired bravery, as all dwarves did, but even to them the elf's quest bordered on the insane.

"You and your people have saved us, Rom, and for that I thank you all. But if I can ask one boon, it is to show me the nearest tunnel leading to the mountain fortress. I will take it alone from there."

"You'll not be journeying alone, my elven lady," objected Falstad. "I've come too far to turn back now . . . and I'm of a mind to find a certain goblin and skin his hide for boots!"

"Ye both be daft!" Rom saw that neither would be swayed. Shrugging, he added, "But if it's a way to Grim Batol ye want, then I'll not set that task to another. I'll take ye there myself!"

"Ye cannot go alone, Rom!" snapped Gimmel. "Not with the trolls on the move and the orcs near there! I'll go with ye to watch ye back!"

Suddenly, the rest of the band decided that they, too, needed to go along in order to watch the backs of their leaders. Both Rom and Gimmel tried to argue them down, but as one dwarf was generally as stubborn as another, the leader finally came up with a better notion.

"The wounded must return home, and they need some to watch them, too—and no arguments from ye, Narn, ye can barely stand! The best thing to do is roll the bones; the half with the high numbers comes with! Now, who has a set?"

Vereesa hardly wanted to wait for the band to gamble in order to find out who would be traveling with them, but saw no other choice. She and Falstad watched as various dwarves—Narn and the other wounded excluded—set dice rolls against one another. Most of the hill dwarves used their own sets, Rom's question having been responded to by a veritable sea of raised arms.

The last had made Falstad chuckle. "The Aerie and the hills might have their differences, but you'll find few dwarves of any kind who don't carry the dice!" He patted a pouch on his belt. "Can see what heathens the trolls were; they left mine on me! 'Tis said that even the orcs like to roll the bones, which makes 'em a step up from our late captors, eh?"

After much too long a time for Vereesa's taste, Rom and Gimmel returned with seven other dwarves, each with determined expressions on their faces. Looking at them, the elf could have sworn that they were all brothers—although, in fact, at least two hinted at being sisters. Even female dwarves sported strong beards, a sign of beauty among members of the race.

"Here's ye volunteers, Lady Vereesa! All strong and ready to fight! We'll lead ye to one of the cave mouths in the base of the mountain, then ye are on ye own after that."

"I thank you—but, do you mean that you actually have a path that lets you journey into the mountain itself?"

"Aye, but it's no easy one . . . and the orcs don't patrol it alone."

"What do you mean by that?" burst Falstad.

Rom gave the other dwarf the same innocent smile that Falstad had given him earlier. "Have ye not heard they've dragons?"

The sanctum of Krasus had been built over an ancient grove, one older than even the dragons themselves. It had been built by an elf, later usurped by a human mage, then seized long after its abandonment by Krasus himself. He had sensed the powers lingering underneath it and had managed to draw from them on rare occasions, but even the draconic wizard had been surprised to one day discover the concealed entrance in the most remote part of his citadel, the entrance that led to the glittering pool and the single, golden gemstone set in the midst of the bottom.

Each time he entered the chamber, he felt a sense of awe so rare for one of his kind. The magic here made him feel like a human novice just shown his first incantation. Krasus knew that he had only touched a bare trace of the pool's potential, but that was enough to make him leery of trying to seize more. Those who grew greedy in their need for magical power tended to eventually become consumed by it—literally.

Of course, Deathwing had somehow managed to avoid that fate so far.

Despite being so deep underground, the water was not devoid of life—or something approaching it. Even though no clearer liquid existed in all the world, try as he might, Krasus could never completely focus on the tiny, slim forms that darted around, especially in the vicinity of the gemstone. At times, he had sworn they were nothing but shimmering, silver fish, yet now and then the dragon mage swore that he saw arms, a human torso, even on a rare occasion—legs.

Today, he ignored the inhabitants of the pool. His confrontation with She of the Dreaming had given him some hope of aid, but Krasus knew that he could not plan for it. Time swiftly approached when he would have to commit himself.

And that had been why he had come here now, for among its properties, the pool seemed able to rejuvenate those who drank from it, at least for a time. His use of the poison in order to reach the hidden realms of Ysera had left Krasus drained, and if matters demanded he act quickly, then he wanted to be able to respond.

Bending down, the wizard cupped a hand and gathered a small bit of water. He had tried a mug the first time he had dared sip, only to discover that the pool rejected anything crafted. Krasus leaned over the edge, wanting any drops that escaped his palm to return from whence they had come. His respect for the power within had become that great over the years.

Yet as he drank, a rippling in the surface caught his eye. Krasus glanced down at what should have been the perfect reflection of his human form— but, instead, turned out to be something much different.

Rhonin's youthful visage gazed up at him . . . or so the wizard first thought. Then he realized that his pawn's eyes were closed and the head lolled slightly to the side as if . . . as if dead.

Across Rhonin's face appeared the thick, green hand of an orc.

Krasus reacted instinctively, reaching into the water to pull the foul hand away. Instead, he scattered the image and, when the ripples had finally subsided, saw only his own reflection again.

"By the Great Mother . . ." The pool had never shown this ability before. Why now?

Only then did Krasus recall the parting words of Ysera. *And do not undervalue those you think only pawns . . .*

What had she meant by that, and why had he now seen Rhonin's face? Judging by the glimpse the senior wizard had just had, his young counterpart had either been captured or killed by the orcs. If so, it was too late for Rhonin to be of any more value to Krasus—although having apparently reached the mountain fortress, he had fulfilled the true mission on which his patron had sent him.

Combined with other bits of evidence that Krasus had let the orcs in Grim Batol discover over the past several months, the dragon mage had hoped to stir up the commanders there, make them think that a second invasion, a more subtle one, would be slipping in from the west. While quite a force still remained based in the mountain fortress, its true power lay in the dragons bred and trained there . . . and those grew fewer with each passing week. Worse for the orcs in the mountain, the few they had were more and more being sent north to help the bulk of the Horde, leaving Grim Batol bereft of almost all its defenses. Against a determined army comparable in size to that now fighting in the vicinity of Dun Algaz, even the well-positioned orcs in the mountain would eventually succumb, thereby losing the chance to raise any more dragons for the war effort.

And without more dragons to harry the Alliance forces in the north, the remnants of the Horde would at last crumble under the continual onslaught.

Such a force could have been raised and sent in from the west if not for the general lack of cooperation on the part of the leaders of the Alliance. Most felt that Khaz Modan would fall in its own time; why risk more on such a mission? Krasus could not believe that they would not use a two-pronged assault to finally rid the world of the orc threat, but that proved once again the shortsighted thinking of the younger races. Originally, he had tried to persuade the Kirin Tor to push the course of action to Dalaran's neighbors, but as their influence over King Terenas had begun to slip, his own comrades on the council had turned instead to salvaging what remained of their position in the Alliance.

And so Krasus had decided to play a desperate bluff, counting on the devious thinking and paranoia inherent in the orc command. Let them believe the invasion *was* on its way. Let them even have physical proof to go along with the rumors he and his agents had spread. Surely then they would do the unthinkable.

Surely then they would abandon their mountain fortress and, with Alexstrasza under careful watch, move the dragon breeding operation north.

The plan had started as a wild hope, but to even Krasus's surprise, he noted astonishing results. The orc in command of Grim Batol, one Nekros Skullcrusher, had, of late, grown more and more certain that the mountain's days of use were numbered, and numbered low. The wizard's wild rumors had even taken on a life of their own, growing beyond his expectations.

And now . . . and now the orcs had proof in the person of Rhonin. The young spellcaster had played his part. He had shown Nekros that the seemingly impervious fortress could readily be infiltrated, especially through magic. Surely now the orc commander would give the word to abandon Grim Batol.

Yes, Rhonin had played his part well . . . and Krasus knew that he would never forgive himself for using the human so.

What would his beloved queen even think of him when she found out the truth? Of all the dragons, Alexstrasza most cared for the lesser races. They were the children of the future, she had once said.

"It had to be done," he hissed.

Yet, if the vision in the pool had been meant to remind him of the fate of his pawn, it had also served to incite the wizard. He had to know more.

Bowing before the pool, Krasus closed his eyes and concentrated. It had been quite some time since he had contacted one of his most useful agents. If that one still lived, then surely he had some knowledge of the activities presently going on in the mountain. The dragon mage pictured the one with whom he sought to speak, then reached out with his thoughts, with all his strength, to open the link the two shared.

"Hear me now . . . hear my voice . . . it is urgent that we talk . . . the day may be on us at last, my patient friend, the day of freedom and redemption . . . hear me . . . Rom . . ."

SIXTEEN

L ift him up," grunted the bestial voice.

Sturdy hands harshly seized a dazed Rhonin by the upper arms and dragged him to his feet. Cold water suddenly splashed all over his face, stirring him to consciousness.

"His hand. That one." One of those holding the wizard up lifted Rhonin's left arm. Someone grabbed his hand, took hold of his little finger—

Rhonin screamed as the bone cracked. His eyes flew wide open, and he found himself staring at the brutal visage of an older orc much scarred by years of fighting. The orc's expression showed no sign of pleasure at the human's pain, but rather a slight hint of impatience, as if Rhonin's captor would have preferred to be elsewhere dealing with matters of greater import.

"Human." The word came out sounding like a curse. "You've one chance for life; where's the rest of your party?"

"I don't—" Rhonin coughed. The pain from his broken finger still coursed through him. "I'm alone."

"You take me for a fool?" grunted the leader. "You take Nekros for a fool? How many fingers left, eh?" He tugged on the one next to the broken finger. "Many bones in the body. Many bones to be cracked!"

Rhonin thought as quickly as the pain would allow him. He had already informed his captor that he had come alone and that had not satisfied the orc. What did this Nekros want to hear? That his mountain had been invaded by an army? Would that actually please him?

Of course, it might also help to keep Rhonin alive until he could find some means of escape.

He still did not know what had happened, only that, despite his precautions, he had been fooled by Deathwing. Evidently the dragon had *wanted* the mage discovered. But why? It made as much sense as Nekros's seeming desire to have enemy soldiers wandering through his very fortress!

Rhonin could worry about Deathwing's murky plans later. For now, the ragged wizard's life came first.

"No! No . . . please . . . the others . . . I'm not certain where they are . . . got separated . . ."

"Separated? Don't think so! You came for her, didn't you? You came for the Dragonqueen! That's your mission, wizard! I know it!" Nekros leaned close, his breath threatening to smother Rhonin back into unconsciousness. "My spies heard! You heard, didn't you, Kryll?"

"Oh, yes, oh, yes, Master Nekros! I heard it all!"

Rhonin tried to glance past the orc, but Nekros would not let him see who spoke. Still, the voice itself said much about the spy's identity, especially that this Kryll had to be the goblin he had heard earlier.

"I say again to you, human, that you came for the dragon, isn't that so?"

"I got sep—"

Nekros slapped him across the face, leaving a trail of blood at the edge of Rhonin's mouth. "Another finger'll be next! You came to free the dragon before your armies reached Grim Batol! You figured the chaos would work for you, didn't you?"

This time, Rhonin learned. "Yes . . . yes, we did."

"You said 'we'! That's twice now!" The lead orc leaned back in triumph.

For the first time, the injured mage noticed Nekros's maimed leg. Small wonder this brutal orc commanded the dragon-breeding program instead of a savage war party.

"You see, great Nekros? Grim Batol is no longer safe, my glorious commander!" pitched in the high voice of the goblin. "Who knows how many more enemies still lurk in its countless tunnels? Who knows how long before the Alliance marches on you—with the dark one leading the way? A pity nearly all your remaining dragons are already up near Dun Algaz! You can't possibly defend the mountain with so few! Best if the enemy did not find us here at all rather than waste so much precious—"

"Tell me something I *don't* know, little wretch!" He poked a meaty finger into Rhonin's chest. "Well, this one and his comrades've come too late! You'll not get the dragon or her young, human! Nekros's thought ahead of you all!"

"I don't—"

Another slap. The only benefit of the stinging pain in the beaten wizard's face was that it took away from the agony of his broken finger. "You can have Grim Batol, human, for all the good it's worth! May the whole thing fall down on you!"

"Nekros—you must . . . must stop this insanity!"

Rhonin's head jerked up. He knew that voice, even though he had heard it but once before.

His guards also reacted to the voice, turning enough to enable him to see the gargantuan, scaled form so wickedly bound by chains and clamps. Alexstrasza, the great Dragonqueen, could scarcely move. Her limbs, tail, wings and throat were held firmly in place. She could clearly open her tremendous jaws, but only enough to eat and speak with effort.

Captivity had not treated her well. Rhonin had seen dragons before, crimson ones especially, and those had all had scales that bore a certain metallic sheen. Alexstrasza's, on the other hand, had become dull, faded, and in many places looked loose. She did not seem at all well when he studied her reptilian countenance, either. The eyes had a washed-out look to them, not to mention an incredible weariness.

He could only imagine what her imprisonment had been like. Forced to bear young who would be trained by her captors to serve their murderous cause. Never likely seeing them once the eggs were taken from her. Perhaps she even regretted the lives lost because of her deadly progeny. . . .

"You've no permission to speak, reptile," snarled Nekros. He reached into a pouch at his side and clutched something.

Rhonin's skin tingled as a magical force of astonishing proportions awoke. He did not know what the orc did, yet it made the Dragonqueen cry out with such pain that everyone but Nekros seemed affected by it.

Despite her agony, though, Alexstrasza continued. "You—you waste both energy and—and time, Nekros! You fight for what is—is already—lost!"

With a groan, she finally closed her eyes. Her breathing, so rapid the moment before, briefly grew shallow before returning to a somewhat more normal rate.

"Only Zuluhed commands me, reptile," the one-legged orc muttered. "And he's far from here." His hand slipped free from the pouch. At the same time the magical force that Rhonin had felt abruptly faded away.

The wizard had heard many rumors as to how the Horde could possibly keep such a magnificent creature under their control, but none matched what he had just witnessed. Clearly some artifact or device of tremendous strength lay in that pouch. Did Nekros even truly understand the power he wielded? With such at his beck and call, he could have ruled the Horde himself!

"We need to hunt down the others," the elder warrior turned to a guard standing by the entranceway. "Where'd you find the guard's body?"

"Fifth level, third tunnel."

Nekros's brow furrowed. "Above us?" He studied Rhonin as if looking over a prime piece of beef. "Wizard's work! Start searching everything from fifth level up, then—leave no tunnel alone! Somehow they've come from above!" A slow grin spread across his outlandish, tusked features. "Maybe not magic after all! Torgus saw the gryphons! That's it! The rest of 'em came after Deathwing drove Torgus off!"

"Deathwing—Deathwing s-serves no one—but himself!" Alexstrasza suddenly pronounced, eyes opening wide. She sounded almost fearful, for which Rhonin could not blame her. Who did not fear the black demon?

"But he works now with the humans," insisted her captor. "Torgus saw him!" His hand slapped the pouch. "Well, maybe we'll be ready for him, too!"

Now Rhonin could not help but stare at the pouch and its contents, which, judging by the vague shape, seemed to be a medallion or disk. What power could it have that Nekros believed would even work against the armored behemoth?

"It's dragons you all want. . . ." Once more Nekros faced the wizard. "And it's dragons you'll get . . . but you and the dark one won't be happy long, human!" He waved toward the exit. "Take him away!"

"Kill him?" grunted one of the guards in what seemed hopeful tones.

"Not yet! More questions later for this one . . . maybe! You know where to put him! I'll come right after to make certain that even his magic won't help him!"

The two massive orcs holding on to Rhonin pulled him forward with such vigorous force that he thought that they would wrench his arms from the shoulder sockets. Through somewhat blurred vision, he caught a glimpse of Nekros turning to another orc.

"Double the work! Get the wagons ready! I'll deal with the queen! I want everything prepared!"

Nekros passed from Rhonin's field of vision—and another figure entered.

The goblin that the orc had called Kryll winked at Rhonin, as if both shared a secret. When the wizard opened his mouth, the malevolent little figure shook his oversized head and smiled. In his hands, the goblin clutched something tight, something that drew the human's attention.

Kryll slid one hand back just long enough for Rhonin to see what he carried. *Deathwing's medallion.*

And as the guards dragged him out of the commander's chamber, it came to the worn mage that he now knew how Deathwing had garnered so much information about Grim Batol. He also knew that, whatever Nekros planned, the orc, like Rhonin, did exactly as the black dragon *wanted*.

Although at home in the forests and hills, Vereesa had to admit that, when it came to the underworld, she could not tell one tunnel from another. Her innate sense of direction seemed to fail her—either that or the fact that she had to continually duck distracted her too much. Even though trolls used these tunnels from time to time, most had been hewed out by dwarves in the days when the region around Grim Batol had served as part of a complex mining community. That meant that Rom, Gimmel, and even Falstad had little difficulty navigating them, but the tall elf had to walk bent over much of the time. Her back and legs ached, but she gritted her teeth, unwilling to show any sign of weakness among these hardy warriors. After all, Vereesa had been the one who had insisted on coming here in the first place.

Yet she finally had to ask, "Are we almost near?"

"Soon, very soon," replied Rom. Unfortunately, he had been saying that for some time now.

"This entrance," Falstad mused. "Where's it again?"

"The tunnel comes out in what used to be a transport point for the gold we mined. Ye may even see a few old tracks, if the orcs haven't melted them all down for weaponry."

"And in this way we can get inside?"

"Aye, ye can follow back along the old path even if the tracks're gone. They've some guards there, though, so it won't be easy."

Vereesa thought this over. "You mentioned dragons, too. How far above?"

"Not dragons in the sky, Lady Vereesa, but ones on the ground. That's where it gets tricky, ye might say."

"On the ground?" snorted Falstad.

"Aye, ones with damaged wings or too untrusted to let fly. Should be two on this side of the mountain."

"On the ground . . ." the dwarf from the Aerie muttered. "Be a different sort of battle . . ."

Rom suddenly paused, pointing ahead. "There 'tis, Lady Vereesa! The opening!"

The ranger squinted but even with her exceptional night vision, she could not make out the supposed opening.

Falstad apparently did. "Awful small. Be a tight fit."

"Aye, too tight for orcs and they think too tight for us, but there's a trick to it."

Still unable to see anything, Vereesa had to satisfy herself with following the dwarves. Only when they had nearly reached what seemed a dead end did she begin to notice a little bit of light filtering in from above. Stepping closer, the frustrated elf noticed a slit barely big enough to fit her sword through, much less her body.

She glanced down at the leader of the hill dwarves. "A trick to it, you say?"

"Aye! The trick is that ye must move these rocks here, carefully set by us, in order to open the gap big enough, but ye can't reach them from the outside! From there it looks to be all one rock, and it'd take the orcs powerful more time than they'd like to do the job!"

"They know you are underground, though, do they not?"

Rom's expression grew dour. "Aye, but with the dragons about, they fear little from us. The way ye must go to get inside is a dangerous one. That must be evident to ye. It frustrates us to be so close and yet be unable to rid ourselves of these cursed invaders. . . ."

For some reason she could not fathom, Vereesa sensed that the dwarven leader had not told her everything. What he had said might be true to some extent, but for some other reason his people had not made much use of this route. Had something happened in the past to make them shy away from it, or was it truly that dangerous out there?

If the latter, did the elf really want to take the risk?

She had already committed herself. If not for Rhonin, then for whatever she might do to help end this interminable war—although Vereesa still held out hope that somehow she might find the wizard alive.

"We should get started. Is there a certain pattern needed when removing the rocks from their positions?"

Rom blinked. "Lady elf, ye must wait until dark! Any sooner and ye will be sighted, sure as I stand before ye!"

"But we cannot wait that long!" Vereesa had no idea how many hours had passed since she and Falstad had been captured by the trolls, but surely only a few hours at most.

" 'Tis only an hour and a little more, Lady Vereesa! Surely that's worth ye life!"

That little of a wait? The ranger eyed Falstad.

"You were out for a very long time," he replied to her unspoken question. "For a while, I thought you dead."

The elf tried to calm herself down. "Very well. We can wait until then."

"Good!" The leader of the hill dwarves clapped his hands together. "That'll give us time to eat and rest!"

Although at first Vereesa felt too tense to even consider food, she accepted the simple fare that Gimmel offered her a few minutes later. That these struggling souls would share what little they had spoke of the depths of their compassion and camaraderie. Had the dwarves wanted to, they could have very well slain Falstad and her after having dealt with the trolls. No one outside of their group would have ever been the wiser.

Gimmel took charge of seeing to it that everyone shared equally in the provisions. Rom, after taking his portion, slowly wandered off, saying that he wished to inspect some of the side tunnels they had passed earlier for any sign of troll activity.

Falstad ate with gusto, seemingly enthused by the taste of the dried meat and fruit. Vereesa ate with less enthusiasm, dwarven fare not famous for its succulent taste in either the elven or human realms. She understood that they cured the meat in order to better preserve it, and even marveled that someone had found or grown fruit in this dismal land, but her more sensitive taste buds even now complained to her. However, the food was filling, and the ranger knew that she would need the energy.

After finishing her fare, Vereesa rose and looked around. Falstad and the other dwarves had settled in to relax, but the impatient elf needed to walk. She grimaced, thinking again how her instructor would have called her so human right now. Most elves early on outgrew their tendencies toward impatience, but some retained that trait for the rest of their lives. Those generally ended up either living beyond the homeland or taking on tasks that let them travel extensively in the name of their people. Perhaps, if she lived through this, she might choose one of those paths, maybe even visit Dalaran.

Fortunately for Vereesa, the tunnels here had been carved out somewhat higher than many of those through which she had earlier passed. For the most part, the elf managed to traverse the rocky corridors with minimal bending, even occasionally standing unhindered.

A muffled voice some distance ahead suddenly made her halt. The ranger had journeyed farther than she had intended, enough so that she might have very well dropped herself right into troll territory. With tremendous care so as not to make a sound, Vereesa drew her blade, then inched forward.

The voice did not sound like that of a troll. In fact, the nearer she moved, the more it seemed to her that she knew the speaker—but how?

"—couldn't be helped, great one! Didn't think ye wanted them to know about ye!" A pause. "Aye, an elf ranger fair of face and form, that's her." Another pause. "The other? A wild one from the Aerie. Said his mount escaped when the trolls took 'em."

Try as she might, Vereesa could not hear the other half of the conversation, but she at least knew who presently spoke. A hill dwarf, and one very much familiar to her.

Rom. So his comment about searching the tunnels had not entirely been truth. But who did he speak with and why did the elf not hear that one? Had the dwarf gone mad? Did he talk with himself?

Rom did not speak now save to acknowledge that he understood what his silent companion said. Risking discovery, Vereesa edged toward the corridor from which the dwarf's voice came. She leaned around just enough in order to observe him with one eye.

The dwarf sat on a rock, staring down into his cupped palms, from which a faint, vermilion glow radiated. Vereesa squinted, trying to see what he held.

With some difficulty, she made out a small medallion with what appeared to be a jewel in the center. Vereesa did not have to be a wizard like Rhonin to recognize an object of power, an enchanted talisman created by magic. The great elven lords utilized similar devices in order to communicate with either their counterparts or their servants.

What wizard, though, now spoke with Rom? Dwarves were not known for their fondness for magic nor, for that matter, for their fondness for the ones who wielded it.

If Rom had links to a wizard, one whom the dwarf apparently even served, why did he and his band still wander the tunnels, hoping for the day when they might be free to walk under the heavens? Surely this great spellcaster could have done something for them.

"*What?*" Rom suddenly blurted. "Where?"

With startling swiftness, he looked up, his gaze focusing directly on her.

Vereesa backed out of sight, but she knew her reaction had been too late. The dwarven leader had spotted her, even despite the darkness.

"Come out where I can see ye!" he called. When she hesitated, Rom added, "I know 'tis ye, Lady Vereesa. . . ."

Seeing no more reason for subterfuge, the ranger stepped into the open. She made no attempt to sheathe her sword, not at all certain that Rom might not be a traitor to his own people, much less her.

She found him eyeing her in disappointment. "Here I thought I'd gone far away enough to avoid them sharp, elven ears! Why did ye have to come here?"

"My intent was innocent, Rom. I only needed to walk. Your intent, how-ever, leaves many questions. . . ."

"This business is none of ye concern—eh?"

The gemstone in the medallion briefly flared, startling both of them. Rom tipped his head slightly to the side, as if again listening to the unheard speaker. If so, then he clearly did not like what he heard.

"Do ye think it wise—aye, as ye say. . . ."

Vereesa tightened her grip on her sword. "Who do you speak with?"

To her surprise, Rom held out the medallion. "He'll tell ye himself." When she did not take the proffered medallion, he added, "He's a friend, not a foe."

Still wielding the sword, the elf reached out with her free hand and gin-gerly took hold of the talisman. She waited for a jolt or searing heat, but the medallion actually felt cool, harmless.

My greetings to you, Vereesa Windrunner.

The words echoed in her skull. Vereesa nearly dropped the medallion, not because of the voice, but rather that the speaker knew her name. She glanced at Rom, who seemed to encourage her to converse.

Who are you? the ranger demanded, sending her own thoughts toward the unseen speaker.

Nothing happened. She glanced again at the dwarf.

"Did he say anything to ye?"

"In my mind he did. I replied the same way, but he does not answer back."

"Ye have to talk to the talisman! He'll hear ye voice as thought on his end. The same when he speaks to ye." The canine features looked apologetic. "I've no reason why 'tis so, but that's the way it works. . . ."

Returning her gaze to the medallion, Vereesa tried again. "Who are you?"

You know me through my missives to your superiors. I am Krasus of the Kirin Tor.

Krasus? That had been the name of the wizard who had arranged with the elves for Vereesa to guide Rhonin to the sea in the first place. She knew lit-tle more about him than that her masters had reacted with respect when pre-sented with his request. Vereesa knew of few other humans who could command such from any elven lord.

"I know your name. You are also Rhonin's patron."

A pause. An *uneasy* pause if the ranger were any judge.

I am responsible for his journey.

"You know that he may be a prisoner of the orcs?"

I do. It was not intended.

Not intended? Vereesa felt an unreasonable fury arise within her. Not intended?

His mission was to observe, after all. Nothing more.

The elf had long ago ceased believing that. "Observe from where? The dungeons of Grim Batol? Or was he to meet with the hill dwarves for some reason you have not stated?"

Another pause. Then, *The situation is far more complex than that, young one, and growing more so by the moment. Your presence, for instance, was not part of the plan. You should have turned around at the seaport.*

"I swore an oath. I felt that it extended beyond the shores of Lordaeron."

Near her, Rom wore a befuddled look. Bereft of the means by which to speak to the wizard, he could only guess at Krasus's end of the conversation and to what Vereesa's responses might refer.

Rhonin is . . . fortunate, Krasus finally replied.

"If he still lives," she nearly snapped.

Yet again, the wizard hesitated before answering. Why did he act as he did? Surely he did not care what befell Rhonin. Vereesa knew enough about the ways of the spellcasters, both human and elf, to understand that their kind ever used each other if given the opportunity. It only surprised her that Rhonin, who had seemed more clever, had fallen for this Krasus's trickery.

Yes . . . if he still lives. . . . More hesitation. *. . . then it is up to us to see what can be done to free him.*

His reply completely startled her. She had hardly expected it of him.

Vereesa Windrunner, hear me out. I have made some lapses in judgment—for great concerns—and the fate of Rhonin is one of those lapses. You intend to try to find him, do you not?

"I do."

Even in the mountain fortress of the orcs? A place of dragons, too?

"Yes."

Rhonin is fortunate to have you as a comrade . . . and I hope to be as fortunate now. I will do what I can to aid you in this formidable quest, although the physical danger will be yours, of course.

"Of *course,*" the elf wryly returned.

Please return the talisman to Rom. I would speak with him for a moment.

More than willing to part with the wizard's tool, Vereesa handed the medallion back to the dwarf. Rom took it and stared into the jewel. Occasionally he nodded his head, although clearly whatever Krasus said bothered him much.

Finally, he looked up at Vereesa. "If ye really think it necessary . . ."

She realized his words were for the wizard. A moment later, the glow from the jewel dimmed. Rom, looking not at all happy, extended the talisman to the elf.

"What is this?"

"He wants ye to have it for the journey. Here! He'll tell ye himself!"

Vereesa took the object back. Immediately Krasus's voice filled her head again. *Rom told you that I wished you to carry this?*

"Yes, but I do not want—"

Do you wish to find Rhonin? Do you wish to save him?

"Yes, but—"

I am your only hope.

She would have argued with him, but, in truth, the ranger knew that she needed aid. With only Falstad and herself, the odds already stood stacked against her.

"All right. What do we do?"

Place the talisman around your neck, then return with Rom to the others. I will guide you and your dwarven companion into the mountain . . . and to the most likely place where you might find Rhonin.

He did not offer all she needed, but enough to make her agree. Slipping the chain over her head, Vereesa let the medallion rest upon her chest.

You will be able to hear me whenever I wish it, Vereesa Windrunner.

Rom walked past her, already heading back. "Come! We're wasting time, lady elf."

As she followed, Krasus continued to talk to her. *Make no mention of what this medallion does. Do not even speak around others unless I give permission. Only Rom and Gimmel presently know my role.*

"And what is that?" she could not help muttering.

Trying to preserve a future for us all.

The elf wondered about that, but said nothing. She still did not trust the wizard, but had little other choice.

Perhaps Krasus knew that, for he added, *Hear me now, Vereesa Windrunner. I may tell you to do things you might not think in the best interests of you or those you care about. Trust that they are. There are dangers ahead you do not understand, dangers that alone you cannot face.*

And you understand them all? Vereesa thought, knowing that Krasus would not hear the question.

There is still a short period of time before the sun sets. I must attend to a matter of import. Do not depart from the tunnels until I give you the word. Farewell for now, Vereesa Windrunner.

Before she could protest, his voice had faded away. The ranger cursed under her breath. She had accepted the spellcaster's questionable aid, now she had to obey his commands. Vereesa did not like at all putting her life—not to mention Falstad's—in the hands of a wizard who commanded from the safety of his far-off tower.

Worse, the elf had just put their lives in the hands of the same wizard who had sent Rhonin on this insane journey in the *first* place . . . and seemingly left him to die.

SEVENTEEN

At some point on the journey to where the orcs intended to keep him prisoner, Rhonin had collapsed back into unconsciousness. Admittedly, he had been aided in great part by his guards, who had used every excuse to hit him or twist his arms agonizingly. The pain of his broken finger had seemed little compared to what they had done to him by the time he blacked out.

Yet now, at last, the wizard woke—and woke to the nightmare of a fiery skull with black eye sockets smiling malevolently at him.

Sheer reflex made the startled wizard attempt to pull away from the monstrous visage, but doing so only rewarded Rhonin with more agony and the discovery that his wrists and ankles had been shackled tight. Try as he might, he could not escape the near presence of the demonic horror looming above him.

The fiend, though, did not move. Gradually, Rhonin fought down his horror and studied the motionless creature closer. Far taller and broader than the human, it wore what seemed flaming bone for armor. What he had taken for a sinister smile had actually simply been due to the fact that the demonic sentinel had no flesh covering its visage. Fire surrounded it, but the mage felt no heat. Still, he suspected that if those blazing skeletal hands touched him, the results would be very, very painful indeed.

For lack of any better thought, Rhonin tried to speak to the creature. "What—who are you?"

No reply. Other than the flickering flames, the macabre figure remained motionless.

"Can you hear me?"

Nothing again.

Less fearful and more curious now, the wizard leaned forward as best his chains would let him. Suspicious, he moved one leg back and forth as best he could. Still he received no response, not even a shifting of the head toward his moving limb.

As horrific as the creature looked, it seemed less of a living thing than a statue. Although demonic in appearance, it could be no demon. Rhonin had studied golems, but had never seen one before, certainly not one constantly ablaze. Still, he could think of it as nothing else.

The wizard frowned, wondering at the golem's capabilities. In truth, he had only one way to find out . . . and, after all, the wizard needed to escape.

Trying to ignore his pain, Rhonin started to move his remaining fingers ever so slightly for a spell that would, he prayed, rid himself of the monstrous guard—

With astonishing swiftness, the fiery golem reached forward, seizing Rhonin's already maimed appendage in a grip that completely enveloped it.

A searing fire engulfed the human, but a fire within, one that burned at his very *soul*. Rhonin screamed, then screamed again. He screamed long and hard until he could scream no more.

Barely conscious, his head slumped over, he prayed for the inner fire to either end or consume him utterly.

The golem removed its hand from his.

The flames within dwindled away. Gasping, Rhonin managed to lift his head enough to look at the horrific sentinel. The golem's grotesque mockery of a face stared right back, completely indifferent to the tortures through which it had put its victim.

"Damn—damn you . . ."

Beyond the golem, a familiar chuckle made the hairs on the back of the mage's head stand on end.

"Naughty, naughty!" piped the high voice. "Play with fire, you get burned! Play with fire, you get burned!"

Rhonin tipped his head to the side—cautiously at first, then more when he saw that his monstrous companion did not react. Near the entrance stood the wiry goblin Nekros had called Kryll, the same goblin that Rhonin knew also worked for Deathwing.

In fact, Kryll even now carried the medallion with the black crystal. The wizard marveled at the goblin's arrogance. Surely Nekros would wonder why his minion still held on to Rhonin's talisman.

Kryll noticed the direction of his gaze. "Master Nekros never saw you with it, human—and we goblins are always picking up trinkets!"

There had to be more to it, though. "He's also too busy to notice, isn't he?"

"Clever, human, clever! And if you told him, he wouldn't listen! Poor, poor Master Nekros has much on his mind! Moving dragons and eggs is quite a chore, you know!"

The golem did not react at all to Kryll's presence, which did not surprise Rhonin. Unless the goblin attempted to free the prisoner, it would leave Kryll alone.

"So you serve Deathwing . . ."

A frown momentarily escaped the creature. "His bidding I've done . . . yes. For very, very long . . ."

"Why've you come here? I've served your master's purpose, haven't I? I played his fool well, didn't I?"

This, for some reason, cheered Kryll up again. His toothy smile wider than ever, he replied, "No greater fool could there have been, for you played one for more than the dark lord. Played you one for me, too, human!"

Rhonin could scarce believe him. "How did I do that? In what way did I serve *you*, goblin?"

"In much the same, much the same, as you did the dark lord—who thinks a goblin so low as to serve any master without reason of his own!" A hint of what had to be bitterness escaped Kryll. "But I've served enough, I have!"

Rhonin frowned. Could the mad little creature mean what the wizard thought he meant? "You plan to betray even the dragon? How?"

The grotesque goblin fairly hopped in glee. "Poor, poor Master Nekros is in such a state! Dragons to move, eggs to move, and stinking orcs to march around! Little time to think if that's what others actually want him to do! Might've thought more, but now that the Alliance surely invades from the west, can't be bothered! Has to act! Has to be an orc, you know!"

"You're not making any sense. . . ."

"Fool!" More laughter from the goblin. "You brought me this!" He held up the medallion, then gave Rhonin a false frown. "Broken in fall—so Lord Deathwing thinks!"

As the prisoner watched, Kryll began peeling away at the stone in the center. After a few moments of effort, the gem popped out into the wiry goblin's hand. He held it up for Rhonin to see. "And with it—no more Deathwing. . . ."

Rhonin could scarcely believe him. "No more *Deathwing*? You hope to use that stone to bring him down?"

"Or make him serve Kryll! Yes, perhaps he shall serve me." An exhalation of pure hatred escaped Kryll. ". . . and no more toadying for the reptile! No more being his lackey! I planned long and hard for this, I did, waiting and waiting and watching for when he'll be most vulnerable, yes!"

Fascinated despite himself, the captured spellcaster blurted, "But how?"

Kryll backed toward the entrance. "Nekros will provide the way, not that he knows . . . and this?" He tossed the stone into the air, then caught it again. "It is a *part* of the dark lord, human! A scale turned to stone by his own magic! It must be so for the medallion to work! You know what it means to hold a part of a dragon?"

Rhonin's thoughts raced. What had he once heard? "'To bear some bit of the greatest of the leviathans is to have a hold on their power.' But that's never been done! You need tremendous magic yourself to make it work! Where—"

The golem reacted to his sudden agitation. The ghoulish jaws opened and the skeletal hand started to reach for Rhonin. The wizard immediately froze, not even breathing.

The fiery form paused, but did not withdraw. Rhonin continued to hold his breath, praying that the monstrosity would back away.

Kryll chuckled at his predicament. "But you're busy now, human! So sorry to overstay! Wanted to tell *someone* of my glory—someone who'll be dead soon enough, eh?" The goblin hopped away. "Must go! Nekros will need my guidance again, yes, he will!"

Rhonin could hold his breath no longer. He exhaled, hoping that his hesitation had been enough.

A mistake.

The golem reached for him—and all thought of the traitorous little Kryll vanished as the fires once more consumed Rhonin from within.

Darkness came all too slowly and yet in some ways too quickly for Vereesa. As Krasus had directed, she had told no one about the medallion's purpose and, at further urging from Rom, had secreted it as best she could within her garments. Her travel cloak, well-worn by this point, had managed to obscure it for the most part, although anyone who looked closely would have at least been able to make out the chain.

Shortly after their return to the party, Rom had taken Gimmel aside and spoken with him. The elf had noticed both briefly look her way. Rom evidently wanted his second to also know of Krasus's decision and, judging by the other dwarf's falling expression, Gimmel had not liked it any more than his chieftain.

The moment the light through the hole vanished, the dwarves began to methodically remove the stones. Vereesa saw no reason why this rock or that one had to be taken away before another, but Rom's people were adamant. She finally settled back, trying not to think of all the time wasted.

As the last of the stones were removed, the wizard's voice, sounding oddly haggard at first, echoed in her head.

The way out . . . is it open, Vereesa Windrunner?

She had to turn away and pretend to cough in order to mumble, "Just finished."

Then you may proceed. Once outside, remove the talisman from wherever it is you have hidden it. That will enable me to see what lies ahead. I will speak no more until you and the Aerie dwarf are out of the tunnels.

As she turned back, Falstad came up to her. "You ready, my elven lady? The hill dwarves want to be rid of us quickly, seems to me."

In fact, Rom stood by the entrance even now, his dimly seen form impatiently gesturing for the pair to climb out into the open. Vereesa and Falstad hurried past him, picking their way up to the widened hole as best they could. The ranger's foot slipped once, but she managed to regain her ground. Above her, the wind beckoned her on. She had no love for the underworld and hoped that circumstances would not send her back there soon.

Falstad, who had reached the top first, now extended a strong hand to help her up. With easy effort, he lifted her high, then set her standing next to him.

The instant the two exited, the dwarves began filling up the hole. It dwindled rapidly inside even as Vereesa got her bearings.

"So what do we do now?" asked Falstad. "Climb up that?"

He indicated the base of the mountain, even in the dark of night clearly a sheer rock face for the first several hundred feet up. Try as she might, the elf could not see any immediate opening, which puzzled her. Rom had led her to believe that they would see it almost immediately.

She turned to call down to him, only to discover that barely any sign of the hole remained. Vereesa knelt, then put an ear by the small gap. She could hear nothing at all.

"Forget them, my elven lady. They've gone back into hiding." Falstad's tone revealed a hint of contempt for his hill cousins.

Nodding, the elf finally recalled Krasus's instructions. Pulling her cloak aside, she removed the medallion from hiding, placing it squarely on her chest. Vereesa assumed that the wizard would be able to see in the dark, else he would be of little aid to them now.

"What's that?"

"Help . . . I hope." Krasus might have warned her not to tell anyone, but surely he did not expect her to leave Falstad guessing. The dwarf might think her mad if she started talking to herself.

Everything is quite visible, the wizard announced, causing her to start. *Thank you.*

"What's wrong? Why did you jump?"

"Falstad, you know that the Kirin Tor sent Rhonin on a mission?"

"Aye, and not the foolish one he mentioned, either. Why?"

"This medallion is from the wizard who chose him, who sent him on his true quest—part of which, I think, required Rhonin to enter the mountain."

"For what reason?" He did not sound at all surprised.

"That has not been made completely clear to me so far. As for this medallion, it enables one of those wizards, Krasus, to speak with me."

"But I can't hear anything."

"That, unfortunately, is how it works."

"Typical wizardry," the dwarf remarked, using the same tone of voice he had used when commenting on his hill cousins' deficiencies.

You had best move on, suggested Krasus. *Time is, as they say, of the essence.*

"Did something just happen to you? You jumped again!"

"As I said, you cannot hear him, but I can. He wants us to move on. He says he can guide us!"

"He can see?"

"Through the crystal."

Falstad walked up to the medallion, thrusting a finger at the stone. "I swear by the Aerie that if you play us false, my ghost'll hunt you down, spellcaster! I swear it!"

Tell the dwarf our goals are similar.

Vereesa repeated the statement to Falstad, who grudgingly accepted it. The elf, too, had reservations, ones she kept to herself. Krasus had said that their goals were "similar." That did not mean that they were one and the same.

Despite those thoughts, she passed on Krasus's first instructions to the letter, assuming that he would at least get them inside. His directions seemed peculiar at first, for they forced the pair to circumnavigate part of the mountain in a manner that seemed far too time-consuming. However, the wizard then led them along an easier path that quickly brought them to a tall but narrow cave mouth that Vereesa assumed *had* to be their way in. If not, then she would certainly have a word with their dubious guide.

An old dwarven mine, Krasus said. *The orcs think it leads nowhere.*

Vereesa studied it as best she could in the dark. "Why have Rom and his people not used it if it leads inside?"

Because they have been patiently waiting.

She wanted to ask what they waited for, but suddenly Falstad grabbed at her arm.

"Hear that!" the gryphon-rider whispered. "Something coming!"

They backed behind an outcropping—just in time. A fearsome shape strode purposefully toward the area of the cave, hissing as it came. Vereesa noted a draconic head peering around, red orbs faintly glowing in the night.

"And there's an even better reason why they've not used that way before," Falstad muttered. "Knew it was too good to be true!"

The dragon's head stiffened. The beast turned toward the general direction of the two.

You must remain silent. A dragon's ears can be very sharp.

The elf did not bother to relay that unnecessary knowledge. Gripping her sword, she watched as the behemoth took a few steps toward where they hid. Not nearly so great in size as Deathwing, but nonetheless large enough to dispatch her and Falstad with ease.

Wings suddenly stretched behind the head—wings that, with her night vision, the ranger could see had developed malformed. Small wonder this dragon acted as guard dog for the orcs.

And where was its handler, for that matter? The orcs never left a dragon alone, even one cursed never to fly.

A barked command quickly answered that question. From far behind the beast came a floating torch that gradually revealed itself to be in the hand of a hulking orc. In his other hand he carried a sword nearly as long as Vereesa. The guard yelled something to the dragon, who hissed furiously. The orc repeated his order.

Slowly, the beast began to turn from where the pair hid. Vereesa held her breath, hoping that the warrior and his hound would hurry off.

At that moment, the gem in the medallion suddenly flared so bright it lit up the entire area around the outcropping.

"Smother that!" Falstad whispered.

The ranger tried, but it was already too late. Not only did the dragon turn back, but this time the orc reacted, too. Torch and blade before him, he started toward their hiding place. The crimson leviathan stalked behind him, ready to move at his command.

Remove the medallion from around your neck, Krasus commanded. *Be prepared to throw it in the direction of the dragon.*

"But—"

Do it.

Quickly removing the talisman, Vereesa readied it in her hand. Falstad glanced at his companion, but held his tongue.

The orc drew nearer. Alone, he represented enough of a challenge, but with the dragon at his side, the ranger and her companion had little hope.

Tell the dwarf to step out, reveal himself.

"He wants you to go out there, Falstad," she muttered, not sure why she even bothered to tell the dwarf such folly.

"Would he prefer I walk into the mouth of the dragon or just lie down in front of the beast and let it gnaw on me at its leisure?"

There is little time.

Again she repeated the wizard's words. Falstad blinked, took a deep breath, and nodded. Stormhammer ready, he slipped around Vereesa and past the protection of the rocks.

The dragon roared. The orc grunted, tusked mouth widening in an anticipatory grin.

"Dwarf!" he growled. "Good! Was gettin' bored out here! You'll make good sport before you're fed to Zarasz here! He's been feelin' hungry!"

" 'Tis you and yours who'll make for good sport, pigface! I was getting a little cool out here! Crushing in your thick skull will warm my bones up, all right!"

Both orc and beast advanced.

Throw the talisman at the dragon now. Be certain it lands near the vicinity of his mouth.

The command sounded so absurd that at first Vereesa doubted that she had heard correctly. Then it occurred to her that perhaps Krasus could cast a spell through the medallion, one that would at least incapacitate the savage creature.

Throw it now, before your friend loses his life.

Falstad! The ranger leapt out, surprising both sentries. She took one fast glance at the orc—then, with expert aim, threw the medallion at the mouth of the dragon.

The dragon stretched forward with equally amazing accuracy, catching the talisman in his jaws.

Vereesa swore. Surely Krasus had not expected that.

However, a peculiar thing happened, one that caused all three warriors to pause. Instead of either swallowing or tossing aside the medallion, the leviathan stood still, cocking his head. In his mouth, a red aura erupted, but one that seemed to have no ill effect on the dragon.

To everyone's bewilderment, the behemoth *sat down.*

Not at all pleased by this turn, the orc shouted a command. The dragon, however, did not seem to hear him, instead looking as if he listened to another voice far away.

"Your hound's found a toy to play with, orc!" mocked Falstad. "Looks like you'll have to fight your own battles for once!"

In response, the tusked warrior thrust his torch forward, nearly setting the dwarf's beard ablaze. Cursing, Falstad brought his stormhammer into play, coming close to crushing the orc's outstretched arm. That, in turn, enabled the guard to make a jab with his sword.

Vereesa stood undecided. She wanted to help Falstad, but did not know if at any moment the dragon might suddenly break out of his peculiar trance and rejoin his handler. If that happened, someone had to be ready to face the beast.

The dwarf and his adversary traded blows, the torch and sword evening matters against the hammer. The orc tried to drive Falstad back, no doubt hoping that his foe would trip on the highly uneven ground.

The elf took one more look at the dragon. He still had his head cocked to the side. The eyes were open, but they seemed to be staring off.

Steeling herself, Vereesa turned from the leviathan and headed to Falstad's rescue. If the dragon attacked them, so be it. She could not risk letting her comrade die.

The orc sensed her coming, for as she thrust at him, he swung the torch around. Vereesa gasped as the flames came within scant inches of her face.

Yet her coming forced the guard to fight on two fronts, and because of this, his attempt to burn her had left him open. Falstad needed no urging to take advantage of it. The hammer came down.

A guttural cry from the orc nearly smothered the sound of bone cracking. The sword slipped from the tusked warrior's quivering hand. The hammer had shattered the arm at the elbow, leaving the entire arm useless.

Fueled by both pain and fury, the crippled guard shoved the torch into Falstad's chest. The dwarf stumbled back, trying to beat out the fires smoldering on both his beard and chest. His brutish foe tried to advance, but the elf cut him off.

"Little elf!" he snarled. "Burn you, too!"

Between the torch and his own lengthy arm, his reach far exceeded her own. Vereesa ducked twice as the fire came at her. She had to end this quickly, before the orc managed to catch her off guard.

When he swung at her next, she aimed not for him, but rather for the torch. That meant letting the flames come perilously near. The orc's savage face twisted into an expression of anticipation as he thrust.

The tip of her sword dug into the wood, ripping it from the startled sentry's fingers. Her success far better than expected, Vereesa fell forward, pushing the torch with her.

The fire caught the orc full in the face. He roared in pain, brushing the torch away. The damage had been done, though. His eyes, nose, and most of his upper countenance had been seared by the heat. He could no longer see.

Acting with some guilt, but knowing she had to silence him, Vereesa ran the blind orc through, cutting off his pained cries.

"By the Aerie!" snapped Falstad. "Thought I'd never put myself out!"

Still gasping, the elf managed, "Are—are you—all right?"

"Saddened at the loss of so many good years' beard growth, but I'll get over it! What's the matter with our overgrown hound there?"

The dragon had dropped down on all fours now, as if preparing to sleep. The medallion still lay in his mouth, but, as they watched, he gently dropped it to the ground before him—then looked at the pair as if expecting one of them to retrieve it.

"Does he want us to do what I think he wants us to do, my elven lady?"

"I am afraid so . . . and I know by whose suggestion, too." She started toward the expectant behemoth.

"You're not seriously going to try to pick it up, are you?"

"I have no choice."

As the ranger neared, the dragon peered down at her. Dragons were rumored to see very well in the dark, and had an even greater sense of smell. This close, Vereesa would surely not escape.

Using the edge of her cloak, she gingerly picked up the talisman. Left so long in the dragon's mouth, it dripped with saliva. With some disgust, the elf wiped it off as best she could on the ground.

The gem suddenly glowed.

The way is clear, came Krasus's monotone voice. *Best you hurry before others come.*

"What did you do to this monster?" she muttered.

I spoke with him. He understands now. Hurry. Others will eventually come.

The dragon understood? Vereesa wanted to ask the wizard more, but knew by now that he would give her no satisfactory answer. Still, he had somehow done the impossible, and for that she had to thank him.

She replaced the chain around her neck, letting the talisman once more dangle free. To Falstad, the ranger simply said, "We are to move on."

Still shaking his head at the sight of the dragon, the dwarf followed after her.

Krasus remained true to his word. He guided them through the abandoned mine, leading them at last down a passage that Vereesa would have never thought led the way into the mountain fortress. It forced the pair to climb a tight and quite precarious side passage, but at last they entered the upper level of a fairly spacious underground cavern.

A cavern filled with scurrying orcs.

From the ledge on which they crouched, they could see the fearsome warriors packing away material and filling wagons. On one side, a handler put a young dragon through the paces, while a second handler looked to be preparing for imminent departure.

"Looks as if they're all planning to leave!"

It seemed so to her as well. She leaned over for a better look.

It worked . . .

Krasus had spoken, but Vereesa knew immediately from his tone that his words had only been meant for himself. Likely he did not even know that he had said anything out loud. Had he planned somehow to make the orcs depart Grim Batol? Despite her surprise at the wizard's handling of the dragon, the elf doubted that he could have *this* much influence.

The one dragon readied for flight suddenly moved toward the main mouth of the cavern. His handler finished strapping himself in and readied for flight. Unlike in combat, this dragon was laden with supplies.

She leaned back again, thinking. While in many ways the abandoning of Grim Batol meant great things to the Alliance, it left too many questions and more than a few worries. What need would the orcs have for Rhonin if they departed here? Surely they would not bother to bring an enemy wizard along.

And did they really intend to move *all* the dragons?

She had waited for Krasus to give them their next steps, but the wizard remained eerily silent. Vereesa looked around, trying to decide by which path they might quickest find where Rhonin was being held . . . assuming all along that he had not already been slain.

Falstad put a hand on her shoulder. "Down there! See him?"

She followed his gaze—and saw the goblin. He scurried along another cavern ledge, heading for an opening far to their left.

" 'Tis Kryll! Can be no other!"

The elf, too, felt certain of it. "He knows his way around here well, it seems!"

"Aye! That's why he led us to their allies, the trolls!"

But why had the goblin not let them be captured by the orcs? Why turn them over instead to the murderous trolls? Surely the orcs would have been interested in questioning the pair.

Enough wondering. She had an idea. "Krasus! Can you show us how to get down to where that goblin is heading?"

No voice echoed in her head.

"Krasus?"

"What's wrong?"

"The wizard seems not to be responding."

Falstad snorted. "So we're on our own?"

"For now, it seems." She straightened. "The ledge over there. It should take us where we want to go. The orcs would want the tunnels to be fairly consistent."

"So we go on without the wizard. Good. I like that better."

Vereesa nodded grimly. "Yes, we go on without the wizard—but not our little friend Kryll."

EIGHTEEN

Too slow. They were much too slow.

Nekros shoved a peon forward with an angry grunt, urging the worthless, lower-caste orc to quicker work. The other orc cringed, then scurried off with his burden.

The lower-caste orcs were useless for anything but menial labor, and right now Nekros found them wanting even in that one skill. As it was, he had been forced to make the warriors work alongside them in order to get everything accomplished by dawn. Nekros had actually considered leaving in the dead of night, but that had no longer been possible and he certainly had not wanted to wait another day. Each day no doubt brought invasion nearer, although his scouts, clearly blind to reality, insisted that they so far had found no more traces of an advance force, much less an army. Never mind that Alliance warriors on gryphons had already been sighted, a wizard had found his way into the mountain, and the most dire of all dragons now served the enemy. Simply because the scouts could not see them did not mean that the humans and their allies were not already nearing Grim Batol.

Still in the midst of trying to get the menials to understand the urgency of their packing, the maimed orc did not at first notice his chief handler come up. Only when he heard an uncomfortable clearing of the throat did Nekros turn.

"Speak, Brogas! Why do you skulk like one of these wretches?"

The slightly stout younger orc grimaced. His tusks tended to turn down at the sides, giving his already frowning face an even more dour look. "The male . . . Nekros, I think he dies soon!"

More bad news and some of the worst possible! "Let's see this!"

They hurried as fast as they could, Brogas carefully maintaining a pace that would not make his superior's handicap more evident. Nekros, however, had greater concerns on his mind. In order to continue the breeding program, he needed a female *and* a male. Without one or the other, he had nothing . . . and Zuluhed would not like that.

They came at last to the cavern in which had been housed the eldest and only surviving consort of Alexstrasza. Tyranastrasz had surely been a most impressive sight when compared to other dragons. Nekros gathered that at one point the old crimson male had even rivaled Deathwing in size and power, although perhaps that had simply been legend. Nonetheless, the consort still filled the massive chamber quite ably, so much so that at first the orc leader could not believe that such a giant could possibly be ill.

Yet the moment he heard the dragon's unsteady breathing, he knew the truth. Tyran, as all called him, had suffered several seizures in the past year. The orc had once assumed that dragons were immortal, only dying when slain in battle; but he had discovered over time that they had other limitations, such as disease. Something within this venerable behemoth had stricken Tyran with a slow but fatal ailment.

"How long's the beast been like that?"

Brogas swallowed. "Since last night, on and off . . . but he looked better a few hours ago!"

Nekros whirled on his handler. "Fool! Should've told me sooner!"

He almost struck the other orc, then considered how useless it would have been to have had the knowledge. He had suspected for some time he would lose the elder dragon, but had just not wanted to admit it.

"What do we do, Nekros? Zuluhed'll be furious! Our skulls'll sit atop poles!"

Nekros frowned. He, too, had conjured up that image in his mind . . . and not liked it one bit, of course. "We've no choice! Get him prepared for moving! He comes, dead or alive! Let Zuluhed do what he will!"

"But, Nekros—"

Now the one-legged orc *did* strike his subordinate. "Simpering fool! Obey orders!"

Subdued, Brogas nodded and rushed off, no doubt to beat the lesser handlers while they worked to fulfill Nekros's commands. Yes, Tyran would be coming with the rest, whether or not he still breathed. At the very least he would serve as a decoy. . . .

Taking a step nearer, Nekros studied the great male in detail. The mottled scales, the inconsistent breathing, the lack of movement . . . no, Alexstrasza's consort did not have long left in the world—

"Nekros . . ." rumbled the Dragonqueen's voice suddenly. "Nekros . . . I smell you near. . . ."

Willing to use any excuse to not think of what Tyran's passing might mean to his own skin, the heavyset orc made his way to the female's chamber. As his usual precaution, he reached into his belt pouch and kept one hand on the *Demon Soul*.

Through slitted eyes, Alexstrasza watched him enter. She, too, had seemed somewhat ill of late, but Nekros refused to believe that he would lose her, too. More likely she knew that her last consort might soon be dead. Nekros wished one of the other two had survived; they had been much younger, more virile, than Tyran.

"What now, o queen?"

"Nekros, why do you persist in this madness?"

He grunted. "Is that all you wanted of me, female? I've more important things to do than answer your silly questions!"

The dragon snorted. "All your efforts will only lead to your death. You have the chance to save yourself and your men, but you will not take it!"

"We're not craven, backstabbing scum like Orgrim Doomhammer! Dragonmaw clan fights to the bloody end, even if it be our own!"

"Trying to flee to the north? That is how you fight?"

Nekros Skullcrusher brought out the *Demon Soul*. "There're things you don't even know, ancient one! There're times when flight leads to fight!"

Alexstrasza sighed. "There is no getting through to you, is there, Nekros?"

"At last you learn."

"Tell me this, then. What were you doing in Tyran's chamber? What ails him now?" Both the dragon's eyes and tone of voice were filled with her concern for her consort.

"Nothing for you to worry your head about, o queen! Better to think of yourself. We'll be moving you soon. Behave, and it'll be much more painless. . . ."

With that said, he pocketed the *Demon Soul* and left her. The Dragonqueen called his name once, no doubt to again implore him to tell her about the health of her mate, but Nekros could no longer spend time worrying about dragons—at least not *red* ones.

Even though the column would likely leave Grim Batol before the Alliance invaders reached it, the orc commander knew with absolute certainty that one creature would still arrive in time to wreak havoc. Deathwing would come. The black leviathan would be there come the morning—if only because of one thing.

Alexstrasza . . . The black dragon would come for his rival.

"Let them all come!" snarled the orc to himself. *"All* of them! All I need is for the dark one to be first. . . ." He patted the pouch where he kept the *Demon Soul.* ". . . and then Deathwing will do the rest!"

Consciousness returned to Rhonin, albeit barely at first. Yet, even as weakened as he felt, the wizard immediately remained still, recalling what had happened to him the last time. He did not want the golem sending him back to oblivion—especially since Rhonin feared that this time he would not come back.

As his strength returned, the imprisoned spellcaster cautiously opened his eyes.

The fiery golem was nowhere to be seen.

Stunned, Rhonin lifted his head, eyes opening wide.

No sooner had he done this when suddenly the very air before him flared and hundreds of minute balls of fire exploded into being. The fiery orbs swirled around, quickly combining, forming a vaguely humanoid shape that sharpened in the space of a breath.

The massive golem re-formed in all its grotesque glory.

Expecting the worst, Rhonin lowered his head, shutting his eyes at the same time. He waited for the magical creature's horrific touch . . . and waited and waited. At last, when curiosity finally got the better of his fear, the wary mage slowly, carefully, opened one eye just enough to see.

The golem had vanished again.

So. Rhonin remained under its watchful gaze even if now he could not see it. Nekros clearly played games with him, although perhaps Kryll had somehow arranged this latest trickery. The wizard's hopes faded.

Perhaps it would be better this way. After all, had he not thought that his death might better serve those who had died because of him? Would that not at last satisfy his own feelings of guilt?

Unable to do anything else, Rhonin hung there, paying no attention to the passage of minutes nor the continual sounds of the orcs finishing their preparations for departure. When he chose to, Nekros would return and either take the wizard with him or, more likely, question Rhonin one last time before executing him.

And Rhonin could do nothing.

At some point after he closed his eyes again, weariness took hold and led him into a more gentle slumber. Rhonin dreamed of many things—dragons, ghouls, dwarves . . . and Vereesa. Dreaming of the elf soothed some of his troubled thoughts. He had known her only a short time, but more and more he found her face popping up in his thoughts. In another time and place, perhaps he could have gotten to know her better.

The elf became the center point of his dreaming, so much so that Rhonin could even hear her voice. She called his name over and over, at first longingly, then, when he did not reply, with more urgency—

"*Rhonin!*" Her voice grew distant, just a whisper now, yet somehow it also seemed to have more substance to it.

"*Rhonin!*"

This time her call actually stirred him from his dreams, pulled him from his slumber. Rhonin fought at first, having no desire at all to return to the reality of his cell and his imminent death.

"*He doesn't answer. . . .*" muttered another voice, not at all as soft and musical as Vereesa's. The wizard vaguely recognized it, and the knowledge brought him further toward a waking state.

"*Perhaps that is how they can keep him secure with only chains and no bars,*" the elf replied. "*It looks as if you told the truth. . . .*"

"*I would not lie to you, kind mistress! I would not lie to you!*"

And that last, shrill voice did what the other two could not. Rhonin threw aside the last vestiges of sleep . . . and just barely kept himself from shouting out.

"*Let's get this done, then,*" Falstad the dwarf muttered. The footsteps that followed indicated immediately to the wizard that the dwarf and others headed toward him.

He opened his eyes.

Vereesa and Falstad did indeed enter the chamber, the elf's arresting visage full of concern. The ranger had her sword drawn, and around her neck she wore what almost looked like the medallion Deathwing had given Rhonin, save that this one had a stone of crimson where the other had been as black as the soul of the sinister leviathan.

Beside her, the dwarf had his hammer sheathed on his back. For a weapon, he carried a long dagger—the tip of which presently touched the throat of a snarling *Kryll*.

The sight of the first two, especially Vereesa, filled Rhonin with hope—

Behind the tiny rescue party, the fire golem re-formed in complete silence.

"Look out!" the dismayed wizard shouted, his voice raspy from so many previous screams.

Vereesa and Falstad dropped to opposing sides as the monstrous skeletal figure reached for them. Tossed by the dwarf, Kryll slid toward the very wall where Rhonin had been chained. The goblin swore as he bounced hard against the rock.

Falstad rose first, throwing his dagger at the golem—who completely ignored the blade that clattered against the bony armor—then pulling free his stormhammer. He swung at the inhuman sentinel even as Vereesa leapt to her feet to join in the attack.

Still weak, Rhonin could not do anything at the moment but watch. The ranger and the dwarf came at their fiendish adversary from opposing directions, trying to force the golem into a fatal mistake.

Unfortunately, Rhonin doubted that they could even slay the creature by mortal means.

Falstad's first swing pushed the monster back a step, but on the second one, the golem seized hold of the upper handle. The gryphon-rider became embroiled in a horrible tug-of-war as the golem tried to pull him toward it.

"The *hands!*" the mage gasped. "Watch the hands!"

Burning, fleshless fingers grabbed for Falstad as he came within range. The desperate dwarf let go of his precious hammer, tumbling out of immediate reach of his foe.

Vereesa darted forward, thrusting. Her elven blade did little against the macabre armor, which easily deflected it. The golem turned toward her, then threw the stormhammer in her direction.

The ranger nimbly leapt aside, but now she found herself the only one with any sort of defense against the inhuman guard. Vereesa thrust twice more, nearly losing her blade the second time. The golem, apparently impervious to edged weapons, attempted with each attack to seize the sword by the blade.

His friends were losing . . . and Rhonin had done nothing to help.

It only grew worse. Having regained his balance, Falstad started for his hammer.

The mouth of the ghoulish warrior opened incredibly wide—

A fearsome spout of black fire nearly engulfed Falstad. Only at the last did he manage to roll away, but not before his clothing had been singed.

That left Vereesa alone and in the direct path of the golem.

Frustration tore at Rhonin. She would die if he did nothing. They *all* would die if he did nothing.

He had to free himself. Summoning his strength as best he could, the battered spellcaster called up a spell. With the golem occupied, Rhonin had the chance to concentrate on his efforts. All he needed was a moment more. . . .

Success! The shackles holding his limbs burst open, clattering against the rocky wall. Gasping, Rhonin stretched his arms once, then focused on the golem—

A heavy weight struck him on the upper back. An intense pressure on Rhonin's throat cut off all air.

"Naughty, naughty wizard! Don't you know you're supposed to *die*?"

Kryll had a hold around Rhonin's throat that stunned the wizard completely. He had known that goblins were far stronger than they appeared, but Kryll's might bordered on the fantastic.

"That's it, human . . . give in . . . fall to your knees. . . ."

Rhonin almost wanted to do just that. The lack of air had his mind spinning, and that, coupled with the tortures he had suffered at the hands of the golem, nearly did him in. Yet, if he fell, so, too, would Vereesa and Falstad. . . .

Concentrating, he reached a hand back to the murderous goblin.

With a high shriek, Kryll released his hold and dropped to the floor. Rhonin fell against the wall, trying to get his breath back and hoping that Kryll would not take advantage of his weakness.

He need not have worried. Burned on his arm, the goblin hopped away from Rhonin, cursing. "Foul, foul wizard! Damn your magic ways! Will leave you to my friend here, leave you to feel his tender touch!"

Kryll hopped toward the exit, laughing darkly at the intruders' fate.

The golem paused in his struggle with Vereesa and the dwarf, his deathly gaze shifting to the escaping Kryll. His jaws opened—

A burst of ebony fire shot forth from the skeletal maw, completely enveloping the unsuspecting goblin.

With a mercifully short cry, Kryll perished in a ball of flame, so quickly incinerated by the magical fire that only ash drifted to the floor . . . ash and the ruined medallion the goblin had carried in his belt pouch.

"He slew the little wretch!" Falstad marveled.

"And we are certain to be next!" reminded the elf. "Even though I feel no heat, my blade has half turned to slag from the flames surrounding his body, and I doubt I can dodge him much longer!"

"Aye, if I could get my hammer I might be able to do something, but— look out!"

Again the golem unleashed a blast, but this time at the ceiling. The furious column of flame did more than heat the rock, though. As it struck, the flames *shattered* the ceiling, sending massive chunks down on the trio.

One caught Vereesa on the arm, hitting with such violence that the ranger dropped to the floor. The torrent forced Falstad away from her and prevented Rhonin from even trying to make any move in her direction.

The fiery golem focused on the fallen elf. The jaws opened again—

"No!" Utilizing raw will, Rhonin countered, throwing up a shield as powerful as any he had ever created.

The dark flames struck the invisible barrier with their full fury . . . and rebounded back at the golem.

Rhonin would not have expected the creature's own weapon to have any effect on it, but the flames not only took hold of their wielder, they coursed over him with hunger. A roar erupted from the golem's fleshless throat, an ungodly, inhuman roar.

The monstrous creature quivered—then exploded, unleashing magical forces of hurricane proportion into the tiny mountain chamber.

Unable to withstand those forces, what remained of the ceiling collapsed atop the defenders.

In the dark of night, the dragon Deathwing flew east across the sea. Swifter than the wind, he headed toward Khaz Modan and, more significantly, Grim Batol. The dragon actually smiled to himself, a sight that any other creature would have turned from in mortal terror. All went as intended in every venture. His plans for the humans had moved along so very smoothly. Why, just hours ago, he had received a missive from Terenas, outlining how just a week after "Lord Prestor's" coronation, word would go out that the new monarch of Alterac would be wedding the king of Lordaeron's young daughter the day she turned of age. Just a few scant years—the blink of an eye in the life of a dragon—and he would be in place to set about the annihilation of the humans. After them, the elves and dwarves, older and without the vigor of humanity, would fall like the leaves on a dying tree.

He would savor those days well, come the future. Now, however, Deathwing attended to a more immediate and even more gratifying situation. The orcs prepared to abandon their mountain fortress. By dawn, they would be moving the wagons out, heading for the Horde's last stronghold in Dun Algaz.

With them would go the dragons.

The orcs expected an Alliance invasion from the west. At the very least, they expected gryphon-riders and wizards . . . and one black giant. Deathwing had no intention of disappointing Nekros Skullcrusher on that account. From Kryll, he knew that the one-legged orc had something in mind. The dragon looked forward to seeing what folly the puny creature planned. He suspected he knew, but it would be interesting to find out if an orc could have an original thought for a change.

The dim outline of Khaz Modan's shore came up on the horizon. Better equipped to see in the dark, Deathwing banked slightly, heading more to the north. Only a couple of hours remained until sunrise. He would have plenty of time to reach his chosen perch. From there, the dragon would be able to watch and wait, choose just the right moment.

Alter the course of the future.

Another dragon flew, too, a dragon who had not flown in many years. The sensations of unfettered flight thrilled him, yet they also served to remind just how out of practice he had become. What should have been completely natural, what should have been an inherent part of his very being, seemed out of place.

Korialstrasz the dragon had been Krasus the wizard for far too long.

Had it been daylight already, those who would have witnessed his passing would have noted a dragon of great, if not gargantuan, proportions, larger than most, but certainly not one of the five Aspects. A brilliant blood-red and sleek of form, in his youth Korialstrasz had been considered quite handsome for his kind. Certainly he had caught the eye of his queen. Swift, deadly, and quick of thought in battle, the crimson giant had also been among her greatest defenders, protecting the honor of the flight and becoming her foremost servant when it came to dealing with the new, upcoming races.

Even before the capture of his beloved Alexstrasza, he had spent most of his later years in the form of the wizard Krasus, generally only reverting to his true self when secretly visiting her. As one of her younger consorts, he had not held the position of authority that Tyranastrasz had, but Korialstrasz had known that he had yet held a special place in the heart of his queen. That had been why he had volunteered in the first place to be her primary agent among the most promising and diverse of the new races—humanity—helping to guide it to maturity whenever possible.

Alexstrasza no doubt thought him dead. After her capture and the subjugation of the rest of the dragonflight, he had seen his own subterfuge as the only way to continue the struggle. Return fully to the guise of Krasus and aid the Alliance in its war against the orcs. It had disheartened him to have to assist in the death of his own blood, but the young drakes raised by the Horde knew little of their kind's past glory, rarely ever living long enough to grow

out of their bloodlust and begin to learn the wisdom that had ever truly been
a dragon's legacy. In aiding the elf and dwarf in their bid for entry into the
mountain, he had been fortunate enough to speak into the mind of one of
those youngsters, calming the drake and explaining what had to be done.
That the other dragon had listened had been heartening. Some hope
remained for at least one.

But so much still had to be done, enough so that, once more, Korialstrasz
had turned his back on the mortals and left them to their own devices. The
moment he had viewed the wagons through the medallion, heard the barked
order from the orc officers, he had realized that all for which he had struggled
was about to come to fruition. The orcs had taken the bait and were departing from Grim Batol. They would be moving his beloved Alexstrasza into the
open—where he could at last rescue her.

Even then, it would not be simple. It would require guile, timing, and, of
course, pure luck.

That Deathwing lived and clearly plotted the downfall of the Lordaeron
Alliance had presented itself as a new and terrible concern, one that had, for a
time, threatened the upheaval of everything for which Korialstrasz had
planned. Yet, from what he had discovered as Krasus, it seemed that Deathwing had become too immersed in the politics of the Alliance to even concern himself with the distant orcs and what remained of the once proud red
flight of dragons. No, Deathwing played his own game of chess, with the various kingdoms as pieces. Left to his own devices, he would surely cause war
and devastation among them. Fortunately, such a game required years, and so
Korialstrasz felt little concern for the humans back in Lordaeron and beyond.
Their situation could wait until he had freed his beloved.

However, if the fleet dragon could ignore the growing threat to the very
lands he had taken under his wing, one other matter still gnawed at his
thoughts until he could ignore it no longer. Rhonin—and the two who had
gone in search of him—had trusted in Krasus the wizard, not knowing that to
Korialstrasz the dragon, the rescue of his queen meant more than life itself.
The lives of three mortals had seemed of very little consequence in comparison to that—or so he had thought until recently.

Guilt wracked the dragon. Guilt not only for his betrayal of Rhonin, but
also his neglect of the elf and the dwarf after promising to guide them inside.

Rhonin had likely been slain some time ago, but perhaps it was not too
late to save the other two. The crimson leviathan knew that he would not be
able to concentrate on his quest until he had at least satisfied himself with
doing what he could for them.

On the very tip of southwestern Khaz Modan, only a few hours from
Ironforge, Korialstrasz picked out a secluded peak in the midst of the moun-

tain chain there and alighted. He took a few moments to orient himself, then shut his eyes and focused on the medallion that he had made Rom give to the ranger, Vereesa.

Although she likely thought the stone in the center only a gem, it was, in fact, a very part of the dragon. Fashioned through magic into its present form, it had begun its existence as one of his scales. The ensorcelled scale bore properties that would have astounded any mage—if they had known how to cast dragon magic. Fortunately for Korialstrasz, few did, else he would not have risked creating the medallion in the first place. Both Rom and the elf clearly believed the gem only useful for communication purposes, and the dragon had no intention of correcting their misconceptions.

As the wind howled and snow buffeted the great behemoth, Korialstrasz folded his wings near his head, the better to shield it while he concentrated. He pictured the elf as he had seen her through the talisman. Pleasant to look at for one of her kind, and clearly concerned for Rhonin. A very capable warrior, too. Yes, perhaps she still lived, her and the dwarf from the Aeries.

"Vereesa Windrunner . . ." he quietly called. "Vereesa Windrunner!" Korialstrasz closed his eyes, trying to focus his inner sight. Curiously, he could see nothing. The medallion should have enabled him to see whatever the elf pointed it toward. Had she hidden it from view?

"Vereesa Windrunner . . . make some sound, however slight, to acknowledge that you hear me."

Still nothing.

"Elf!" For the first time, the dragon nearly lost his composure. "Elf!"

And still no reply, no image. Korialstrasz focused his full concentration on the medallion, trying to listen for any sound, even the snarls of an orc.

Nothing.

Too late . . . his sudden act of conscience had come too late to save Rhonin's rescuers, and now they, too, had perished because of the dragon's lack of thought.

As Krasus, he had played on Rhonin's guilt, played on the memories of those companions that the wizard had lost during his previous mission. It had made Rhonin quite malleable. Now, however, he began to understand just how the human had felt. Alexstrasza had always talked of the younger races in tones of caring, of nurturing, as if they, too, were her children. That care she had infected her consort with, and as Krasus he had worked hard to see to it that the humans matured properly. However, his queen's capture by the orcs had shaken his thinking to its very foundations and caused Korialstrasz to forget her teachings . . . until now.

Yet, it had still come much too late for these three.

"But it is not too late for you, my queen," the dragon rumbled. Should he survive this, he would dedicate his life to making up for his failure to Rhonin and the others. For now, though, all that mattered was the rescue of his mate. She would understand . . . he hoped.

Spreading his wings wide, the majestic red dragon took to the air, heading north.

To Grim Batol.

NINETEEN

Nekros Skullcrusher turned from the devastation, grim but determined not to let it lead him astray from his intentions.

"So much for the wizard . . ." he muttered, trying not to think of what spell the human could have possibly cast that had, in the process, also destroyed the seemingly invincible golem. Clearly very powerful, so much so that it had not only cost the wizard his life, but had brought down the mountain on an entire section of tunnels.

"Dig the body out?" asked one of the warriors.

"No. Waste of time." Nekros clutched the pouch with the *Demon Soul*, thinking ahead to the culmination of his desperate plans. "We leave Grim Batol *now.*"

The other orcs followed him, most still uneasy about this sudden decision to depart the fortress but not at all enamored with the idea of staying behind—especially if the wizard's spell had weakened the remaining tunnel systems.

An incredible pressure pushed down on Rhonin's head, a pressure so immense he felt as if at any moment his skull would burst open. With some effort, he forced his eyes open, trying to see if he could find out what pressed on him and how he could quickly remove it.

Turning his blurry gaze upward, he gasped.

An avalanche of rock—literally a ton and more—floated just a foot or so above his head. A dim radiance, the only visible sign of the shield he had cast earlier, revealed the one reason why he had not been crushed to pulp.

The pressure in his head, he realized, had been some part of his mind that had managed to keep the spell intact and, thereby, saved his life. The increasing pain, however, served to tell the trapped mage that with each passing second the spell weakened.

He shifted, trying to make himself more comfortable in the hope that it would relieve some of the pressure—and felt something pressing against the bottom of his head. Rhonin carefully reached down to remove it, assuming it to be some pebble. However, the moment his fingers touched it, he felt a slight hint of magic.

Curiosity momentarily shifting his attention from the horror above him, Rhonin pulled the object near enough to see.

A black gemstone. Surely the same stone that had once been set in the center of Deathwing's medallion.

Rhonin frowned. The last time he had seen the medallion had been after Kryll's death. At the time, he had not paid any attention to the stone, his mind more concerned with the danger to Vereesa and—

Vereesa! The elf's face blossomed full into his thoughts. She and the dwarf had been farther away, protected by the initial spell, but—

He shifted, trying to see. However, as he moved, the pressure in his head multiplied and the stones above dropped a few precious inches more.

At the same time, he heard a deep-voiced curse.

"F-Falstad?" Rhonin gasped.

"Aye . . ." came the somewhat distant reply. "I knew you lived, wizard, since we'd not been flattened, but I was beginnin' to think you'd never wake! About time!"

"Have you—is Vereesa alive?"

" 'Tis hard to say. The light from this spell of yours lets me see her a little, but she's too distant for me to check! Not heard anything out of her since I woke!"

Rhonin gritted his teeth. She *had* to be alive. "Falstad! How far above you are the rocks?"

A sardonic laugh escaped his companion. "Near enough to tickle my nose, human, else I'd have slid over to check her sooner! Never thought I'd be alive at my own burial!"

The mage ignored the last, thinking about what the dwarf had said about the nearness of the avalanche. Clearly the farther the spell extended from Rhonin, the less it covered. Both Vereesa and Falstad had been protected from being crushed, but the ranger might possibly have been struck hard on the head—perhaps even slain by the deadly blow.

Yet Rhonin had to hope otherwise.

"Human—if 'tis not too much to ask—can you do *anything* for us?"

Could he rescue them? Did he have either the power or the strength remaining? He pocketed the black stone, now wholly concerned with the more desperate matter. "Give me a few moments. . . ."

"And what else would I be doing, eh?"

The pressure in the wizard's head continued to increase at a frightening pace. Rhonin doubted his shield could last much longer, and yet he had to maintain it while attempting this second, perhaps even more complex spell.

He had to not only transport all three of them from this precarious position, but send them to a safe place. All this while his battered form cried out for recuperation.

How did the spell go? It pained him to think, but at last Rhonin summoned the words. Attempting this would draw away his concentration from the shield, though. If he took too long . . .

What choice do I have?

"Falstad, I'm going to try now. . . ."

"That would please me to no end, human! I think the rocks're already pressing against my chest!"

Yes, Rhonin, too, had noticed the shift. He definitely had to hurry.

He muttered the words, drew the power. . . .

The rocks above him shifted ominously.

Utilizing his good hand, Rhonin drew a sign.

The shield spell *failed*. Tons of stone dropped upon the trio—

—And suddenly he found himself lying on his back, staring into the cloud-covered heavens.

"Dagath's Hammer!" Falstad roared from his side. "Did you have to cut it so close?"

Despite the pain, Rhonin pushed himself up to a sitting position. The chill wind actually aided, snapping him out of his disoriented state. He looked in the dwarf's direction.

Falstad, too, sat up. The gryphon-rider had a wild look in his eyes that for once had nothing to do with battle. His visage had turned absolutely pale, something Rhonin would never have imagined of the stalwart warrior.

"Never, never, never will I crawl into another tunnel! From now on, 'tis only the sky for me! Dagath's Hammer!"

The wizard might have replied, but a groan from farther on caught his attention. Rising on unsteady feet, he struggled his way toward Vereesa's prone form. At first Rhonin wondered if he had imagined the groan—the ranger looked completely lifeless—but then Vereesa repeated it.

"She's—she's alive, Falstad!"

"Aye, you can tell that from her moaning, I'll bet! Of course she's alive! Quick, though! How does she fare?"

"Hold on . . ." Rhonin cautiously turned the elf over, studying her face, her head, and her body. She had been bruised in some places and her arm bore stains of blood, but otherwise she seemed in as good a shape as either of her companions.

While he cautiously held her head up to study a bruise at the top, Vereesa's eyes fluttered open. "R-Rhon—"

"Yes, it's me. Take it easy. I think you got struck hard on the head."

"Remember . . . remember that—" The ranger closed her eyes for a moment—then suddenly sat up, eyes flaring wide, mouth open in horror. *"The ceiling! The ceiling! It is falling in on us!"*

"No!" He took hold of her. "No, Vereesa! We're safe! We're safe. . . ."

"But the cavern ceiling . . ." The elf's expression relaxed. "No, we are not in the cave any longer . . . but where *are* we, Rhonin? How did we get here? How did we survive in the first place?"

"You remember the shield that saved us from the golem? After the monster destroyed itself, the shield held up, even when the ceiling collapsed. Its sphere of protection shrank, but it still held up enough to keep us from being crushed to death."

"Falstad! Is he—"

The dwarf came up on her other side. "'Tis all of us he's saved, my elven lady. Saved but dropped us off in the middle of nowhere!"

Rhonin blinked. Middle of nowhere? He looked around. The snowy ridge, the chill winds—growing chillier by the moment—and the incredible cloud cover all about them . . . the wizard knew exactly where they were, even despite the darkness surrounding them. "Not nowhere, Falstad. I think I sent us to the very top of the mountain. I think that everything, including the orcs, lies far below us."

"The top of the mountain?" Vereesa repeated.

"Aye, that would make sense."

"And judging by the fact that I can see both of you better and better, I fear that it's nearing dawn." Rhonin grew grim again. "Which means, if Nekros Skullcrusher is an orc of his word, that they'll be leaving the fortress at any moment, eggs and all."

Both Vereesa and the dwarf looked at him. "Now why would they do anything so daft?" asked Falstad. "Why abandon a place so secure?"

"Because of an impending invasion from the west, wizards and dwarves all riding swift, cunning gryphons. Hundreds, perhaps thousands of dwarves and wizards. Maybe even some elves. Against so much, especially magic, Nekros and his men would have no chance even of defending from within the mountain. . . ." The wizard shook his head. The situation might have been different if the commander had realized the true potential of the artifact he carried, but apparently either Nekros did not or his loyalties to his master in Dun Algaz were stronger. The orc had chosen to go north, and north he would go.

Falstad still could not believe it. "An invasion? Where would even an orc get a mad idea like that?"

"From us. From our being here. Especially me. Deathwing wanted me here just to serve as evidence of some forthcoming attack! This Nekros is mad! He already apparently believed that an assault was imminent, and when I showed up in his very midst, he felt certain of it." Rhonin eyed his broken finger, which had grown numb. He would have to deal with it when he could, but for now, so much more was at stake than a single finger.

"But why would the black beast want the orcs to leave?" the ranger asked. "What would he gain?"

"I think I know. . . ." Standing, Rhonin went to the edge of the mountain and peered down, bracing himself so that the wind would not blow him off the edge. He could still see nothing below, but imagined that he heard some sort of noise . . . perhaps of a military column with wagons moving out? "I think that instead of rescuing the red Dragonqueen—as he tried to convince me—he wants to slay her! It was too much of a risk while she was inside, but in the open he can swoop down and kill her with a single blow!"

"Are you sure?" the elf asked, joining him.

"It has to be." He looked up. Even the thick cloud cover up here could not obscure the fact that dawn fast approached. "Nekros wanted to leave by dawn. . . ."

"Is he daft?" muttered Falstad. "Would've made more sense if the blasted orc had tried to leave during the cover of darkness!"

Rhonin shook his head at Falstad. "Deathwing can see fairly well in the night, maybe even better than any of us! Nekros indicated at one point in the questioning that he was prepared for anything, even Deathwing! In fact, he even seemed eager for the dark one to appear!"

"But that would make the least sense of all!" the ranger returned. "How could a single orc defeat him?"

"How could he keep control of the Dragonqueen—and where did he summon a creature like the golem?" The questions disturbed him more than he let on. Clearly the object that the orc carried had significant abilities, but was it *that* powerful?

Falstad suddenly waved for silence, then pointed northwest, well beyond the mountain.

A vast, dark shape broke momentarily through the higher clouds, then disappeared from sight again as it descended.

"'Tis Deathwing . . ." the gryphon-rider whispered.

Rhonin nodded. The time for conjecture was over. If Deathwing had come, it meant only one thing. "Whatever is to happen, it's begun."

The lengthy orc caravan moved out as the first light of dawn touched Grim Batol. The wagons were flanked at beginning and end by armed warriors wielding freshly honed axes, swords, or pikes. Escorts rode with the peon drivers, especially on the wagons bearing the precious dragon eggs. Each orc traveled as if prepared to face the enemy at any given second, for word of the supposed invasion from the west had reached even the lowest of the low.

On one of the few horses available to the orcs, Nekros Skullcrusher watched the departure with impatience. He had sent the dragon-riders and their mounts on ahead to Dun Algaz, in order that, even if he failed in what he attempted, a few dragons would still be available to the Horde. A pity that he had dared not use them to transport the eggs, but from one previous attempt the commander had learned the folly of trying that.

Erecting a wagon capable of bearing a dragon would have been impossible, and so it had fallen to Nekros himself to take control of the two senior beasts. Both Alexstrasza and, remarkably, Tyran, followed at the rear of the column, ever aware of the power the *Demon Soul* had over them. For the ill consort, this had to be a harsh situation; Nekros doubted that the male would survive the journey, yet the orc knew there had been no other choice.

They still made for an impressive sight, the two great leviathans. The female more than the male, since she remained in better health. Nekros once caught her glaring at him, her hatred radiating in her eyes. The orc cared not a whit. She would obey him in all things so long as he wielded the one artifact capable of managing *any* dragon.

Thinking of dragons, he looked skyward. The overcast heavens presented any behemoth with ample places to hide, but eventually something had to happen. Even if the Alliance forces were too far away, Deathwing would surely come. Nekros counted on that.

The humans would learn the folly of entrusting victory to the dark one. What ruled one dragon certainly ruled another. With the *Demon Soul,* the orc commander would seize control of the most savage of all beasts. He, Nekros, would be master of Deathwing ... but only if the damned reptile ever appeared.

"Where're you, you blasted creature?" he muttered. "Where?"

The last row of warriors exited the cavern mouth. Nekros watched them march by. Proud, wild, they hearkened back to the day when the Horde knew no defeat, knew no enemy it could not slaughter. With Deathwing at his command, he would restore that glory to his people. The Horde would rise anew, even those who had surrendered. The orcs would sweep over the Alliance lands, cutting down the humans and the others.

And perhaps there would be a new chieftain of the Horde. For the first time, Nekros dared imagine himself in such a role, with even Zuluhed bowing before him. Yes, he who would bring victory to his people would surely be acclaimed ruler.

War Chief Nekros Skullcrusher . . .

He urged his mount forward, rejoining the column. It would look suspicious if he did not ride with them. Besides, where he positioned himself did not truly matter; the *Demon Soul* gave him control from a distance. No dragon could be released by it unless he willed it—and certainly the grizzled orc had no intention of doing that.

Where was that blasted black beast?

And, as if in answer, an ear-splitting howl arose. However, the howl did not come from the sky, as Nekros had initially believed, but rather from the very earth surrounding the orcs. It caused consternation among the warriors as they turned about, trying to find the enemy.

A breath later—the ground erupted with *dwarves.*

They seemed everywhere, more dwarves than even Nekros could have imagined still remained in all of Khaz Modan. They burst from the earth, swinging axes and waving swords, charging the column from every side.

Yet, although momentarily stunned, the orcs quickly recovered. Shouting out their own war cries, they turned to meet the attackers. The guards stayed with the wagons, but they, too, readied themselves, and even the peons, pathetic for most things, pulled out clubs. It took little training for an orc to be able to crush something with a piece of wood.

Nekros kicked at a dwarf who tried to pull him down. One of the commander's aides quickly stepped in, and a pitched battle began between the two. Nekros steered the horse nearer to the wagons, needing a moment himself to adjust to the situation. Instead of an invasion, he had been attacked by scavengers, for these looked to be the ragged mob that he had always known existed in the tunnels around the mountains. Judging by the numbers now, the trolls had apparently not done their work well.

But where was Deathwing? He had planned for the dragon. There had to be a dragon!

A thundering roar shook the combatants. A vast form darted half-seen through the thick clouds, then broke free, diving toward the orcs.

"At last! At last you've come, you black—" Nekros Skullcrusher froze, utterly baffled. He clutched the *Demon Soul,* but, at the moment, did not even think about using it as he had planned.

The dragon diving toward him had scales the color of fire, not darkness.

"We need to get down there," muttered Rhonin. "I need to see what's happening!"

"Can't you just do as you did in the chamber?" asked Falstad.

"If I do, I won't have any strength to help us once we land . . . besides, I don't know where to put us. Would you like to end up right in front of an orc swinging an ax?"

Vereesa glanced over the edge. "It does not appear too likely that we can climb down, either."

"Well, we can't stay up here forever!" The dwarf paced for a moment, then suddenly looked as if he had just stepped in something terrible. "Hestra's wings! What a fool! Maybe he's still around!"

Rhonin eyed the dwarf as if he had lost his wits. "What're you talking about? Who?"

Instead of answering, Falstad reached into a pouch. "Those blasted trolls took it earlier, but Gimmel handed it back . . . aah! Here 'tis!"

He pulled out what looked to be a tiny whistle. Both Rhonin and Vereesa watched as the dwarf put the whistle to his lips and blew as hard as he could.

"I don't hear anything," the wizard remarked.

"I'd have wondered about you if you had. Just wait. He's well-trained. Best mount I ever had. Mind you, we weren't taken by the trolls that far from this region. He would've stayed for a while. . . ." Falstad looked a little less certain. "'Tis not that long since we were separated. . . ."

"You are trying to summon your gryphon?" the ranger asked, her skepticism clear.

"Better trying that than trying to sprout wings, eh?"

They waited. Waited for what seemed like an eternity to Rhonin. He felt his own strength returning—despite the chill conditions—but feared still to drop the trio into a location that might mean their immediate death.

Yet, it appeared he would have to try. The wizard straightened. "I'll do what I can. I recall an area not far from the mountain. I think Deathwing showed it to me in my mind. I may be able to send us there."

Vereesa took him by the arm. "Are you certain? You do not look ready yet." Her eyes filled with concern. "I know what that must have cost you back in the chamber, Rhonin. That was no minor spell you cast, then managed to maintain even for Falstad and myself. . . ."

He very much appreciated her words, but they had no other choice. "If I don't—"

A large winged form suddenly materialized through the clouds. Both Rhonin and the elf reacted, certain that Deathwing attacked.

Only Falstad, who had been watching closely, did not act as if their doom had come. He laughed and raised his hands toward the oncoming shape.

"Knew he'd hear! You see! Knew that he'd hear!"

The gryphon squawked in what the mage could have sworn were tones of glee. The massive beast flew swiftly toward them—or rather, his rider in particular. The animal fairly leapt atop Falstad, only the beating wings keeping the full weight of the gryphon from nearly crushing the dwarf.

"Ha! Good lad! Good lad! Down now!"

Tail wagging back and forth in a fashion more akin to a dog than a part-leonine beast, the gryphon landed before Falstad.

"Well?" the short warrior asked his companions. "Is it not time to go?"

They mounted as quickly as they could. Rhonin, still the weakest, sat between the dwarf and Vereesa. He had doubts about the gryphon's ability to carry them all, but the animal did just fine. On an extended journey, Falstad readily admitted, they would have had more trouble, but for a short trip, the gryphon would have no difficulties.

Moments later, they broke through the clouds—and into a sight they had not at all expected.

Rhonin had supposed that the sounds of battle would be the hill dwarves trying to take advantage of the orcs' cumbersome wagon train, but what he had not thought to see was a dragon other than Deathwing soaring above the battle.

"A red one!" the ranger called. "An older male, too! Not one raised in the mountain, either!"

He recognized that, too. The orcs had not held the queen long enough for such a behemoth to mature. Besides, the Horde also had a habit of slaying the dragons before they grew too old and independent. Only the young could be managed well enough by their orc handlers.

So where had this crimson leviathan come from, and what did he do here now?

"Where do you want us landing?" Falstad shouted, reminding him of a more immediate situation.

Rhonin quickly scanned the area. The battle seemed mostly contained around the column. He caught sight of Nekros Skullcrusher on horseback, the orc holding something in one hand that gleamed bright despite the clouds. The wizard forgot Falstad's question as he tried to make out the object. Nekros appeared to be pointing it toward the new dragon. . . .

"Well?" demanded the dwarf.

Tearing his eyes from the orc, Rhonin concentrated hard. "There!" He pointed at a ridge a short distance from the rear of the orc column. "That'll be best, I think!"

"Looks as good as any!"

Under the gryphon-rider's expert handling, the animal quickly brought them to their destination. Rhonin immediately slipped off, hurrying to the edge of the ridge in order to survey the situation.

What he saw made no sense whatsoever.

The dragon, which had looked ready to attack Nekros, now hovered as best he could in the air, roaring as if in some titanic struggle with an invisible foe. The wizard studied the orc commander again, noting how the glittering shape in Nekros's hand seemed to become brighter with each passing second.

An artifact of some sort, and so powerful that now even he could sense the emanations from it. Rhonin looked from the relic to the crimson giant.

How did the orcs maintain control over the Dragonqueen? It had been a question he had asked himself more than once in the past—and now Rhonin truly saw for himself.

The crimson dragon fought back, fought harder than the human could have imagined any creature doing. The trio could hear his painful roars, know that he suffered as few beings ever had.

And then, with one last rasping cry, the behemoth abruptly grew limp. He seemed to hover for a moment—then plummeted toward the earth some distance from the battle.

"Is he dead?" Vereesa asked.

"I don't know." If the artifact had not slain the dragon, certainly the high fall threatened to do that. He turned from the sight, not wishing to see so determined a creature perish—and suddenly saw yet another massive form dive from the clouds, this one a nightmare in *black*.

"Deathwing!" Rhonin warned the others.

The dark dragon soared toward the column, but not in the direction of either Nekros or the two enslaved dragons. Instead, he flew directly toward an unexpected target—the egg-laden carts.

The orc leader saw him at last. Turning, Nekros raised the artifact in Deathwing's direction, shouting out something at the same time.

Rhonin and the others expected to see even the black fall to this powerful talisman, but, curiously, Deathwing acted as if untouched. He continued his foray toward the wagons—and, clearly, the eggs they carried.

The wizard could not believe his eyes. "He doesn't care about Alexstrasza, dead or alive! He wants her eggs!"

Deathwing seized two of the wagons with surprising gentleness, lifting them up even as the orcs atop leapt away. The animals pulling the wagons shrieked, dangling helplessly as the dragon turned and immediately flew away.

Deathwing wanted the eggs intact, but why? What use were they to the lone dragon?

Then it occurred to Rhonin that he had just answered his own question. Deathwing wanted the eggs for his own. Red the dragons would be that hatched, but, under the dark one's fostering, they would become as sinister a force as he.

Perhaps Nekros realized this, or perhaps he simply reacted to the theft in general, but the orc suddenly turned and shouted toward the rear of the column. He continued to hold the artifact high, but now he pointed with his other hand at the vanishing giant.

One of the two red leviathans, the male, spread his wings rather ponderously and took off in pursuit. Rhonin had never seen a dragon who looked so deathly, so sick. He found himself amazed that the creature had managed to fly as high as he had. Surely Nekros did not think this ailing dragon any match for the younger, more virile Deathwing?

Meanwhile, the orcs and dwarves still fought, but the latter now battled with what seemed desperation, disappointment. It almost seemed as if they had put their hopes in the first red male. If so, Rhonin could understand their loss of hope now.

"I do not understand it," Vereesa said from beside him. "Why does Krasus not help? Surely the wizard should be here! Surely he is the reason the hill dwarves are finally attacking!"

"Krasus!" In all the excitement, Rhonin had forgotten about his patron. In truth, he had some questions for the faceless wizard. "What does he have to do with this?"

She told him. Rhonin listened, first in disbelief, then in growing fury. Yes, as he had begun to suspect, he had been used by the councilor. Not only him, though, but Vereesa, Falstad, and apparently the desperate dwarves below.

"After dealing with the dragon, he led us inside the mountain," she concluded. "Shortly thereafter, he would not speak to me again." The elf removed the medallion, showing it to him.

It looked remarkably like the one that Deathwing had given to Rhonin earlier, even down to the patterns. The bitter mage recalled noticing it when the elf and Falstad had tried rescuing him from the orcs. Had Krasus learned how to make it from the dragons?

At some point, the stone had become misaligned. Rhonin pushed it back into place with one finger, then glared at the gem, imagining that his patron could hear him. "Well, Krasus? Are you there? Anything else you'd like us to do for you? Should we die for you, maybe?"

Useless. Whatever power it had contained had evidently dissipated. Certainly Krasus would not bother to answer even if that had still been possible. Rhonin raised the relic high, ready to throw it off the ridge.

A faint voice in his head gasped, *Rhonin?*

The enraged wizard paused, startled to actually hear a reply.

Rhonin . . . praise . . . praise be . . . there may . . . there may still be . . . hope.

His companions watched him, not at all certain what he did. Rhonin said nothing, trying to think. Krasus sounded ill, almost dying.

"Krasus! Are you—"

Listen! I must conserve . . . energy! I see . . . I see you . . . you may be able to salvage something—

Despite misgivings, Rhonin asked, "What do you want?"

First . . . first I must bring you to me.

The medallion suddenly flared, spreading a vermilion light over the astonished spellcaster.

Vereesa reached for him. "Rhonin!"

Her hand went through his arm. He watched in horror as both she and Falstad—and the entire ridge—vanished.

Almost immediately, a different, rocky landscape materialized around him, a barren place that had seen too many battles and now, in the distance, witnessed another. Krasus had transported him west of the mountains, not far from where the orc column fought with the dwarves. He had not realized that the wizard had been so near after all.

Thinking of his traitorous patron, Rhonin turned about. "Krasus! Damn you, show yourself—"

He found himself staring into the eye of a fallen giant, the same red, draconic giant the human had seen plummet from the skies but minutes earlier. The dragon lay on his side, one wing thrust up, his head flat along the ground.

"You have my . . . my deepest apologies, Rhonin," the gargantuan creature rumbled with some effort. "For . . . for *everything* painful I have caused you and the others . . ."

TWENTY

So simple. So very simple.

As Deathwing turned to retrieve the next eggs, he wondered if he had overestimated the difficulties of his plan in the first place. He had always assumed that to have entered the mountain either as himself or in disguise would have been more risky, especially if Alexstrasza had noticed his presence. True, there would have been little chance of him being injured, but the eggs he had coveted might have been destroyed. He had feared that happening, especially if one of those eggs proved to be a viable female. Having long decided that Alexstrasza would never be his to control, Deathwing needed every egg he could get his talons on, so as to better his chances. That, in fact, had made him hesitate more than anything else. Now, though, it seemed that he had wasted time waiting, that nothing could have stood in his way then, just as nothing did now.

He corrected himself. Nothing but a sickly, doddering beast well past his prime who even now flew toward his doom.

"Tyran . . ." Deathwing would not dignify the other dragon by calling him by his full name. "You are not dead yet?"

"Give back the eggs!" the crimson behemoth rasped.

"So that they may be raised as dogs for those orcs? I will at least make them true masters of the world! Once more dragon flights will rule the skies and earth!"

His ailing adversary snorted. "And where is your flight, Deathwing? Aah, my pain makes me forget! They all *died* for your glory!"

The black leviathan hissed, spreading his wings wide. "Come to me, Tyran! I will be happy to send you on your way to oblivion!"

"Whether by the orc's command or not, I would still hunt you down until my last breath!" Tyran snarled. He snapped at the black's throat, barely missing.

"I shall send you back to your masters in bloody little pieces, old fool!"

The two dragons roared at one another, Tyran's cry a pale comparison to Deathwing's own.

They closed for combat.

Rhonin stared. *"Krasus?"*

The crimson dragon raised his head enough to nod once. "That is the name . . . I wear when . . . when human. . . ."

"Krasus . . ." Astonishment turned to bitterness. "You betrayed me and my friends! You arranged all this! Made me your puppet!"

"For which I will always have . . . regrets. . . ."

"You're no better than Deathwing!"

This made the leviathan cringe, but once more he nodded. "I deserve that. Perhaps that is the path . . . the path he took long ago. S-so easy to not see what . . . what one does to others . . ."

The distant sounds of battle reverberated even here, reminding Rhonin of other, more important matters than his pride. "Vereesa and Falstad are still back there—and those dwarves! They could all die because of you! Why did you summon me here, Krasus?"

"B-because there is still hope of seizing v-victory out of the chaos . . . the chaos I have helped to create. . . ." The dragon tried to rise, but managed only a sitting position. "You and I, Rhonin . . . there is a chance. . . ."

The wizard frowned, but said nothing. His only concern now lay in seeing to it that Vereesa, Falstad, and the hill dwarves survived this debacle.

"You . . . you do not reject me out of hand . . . good. I thank you for th-that."

"Just tell me what you intend."

"The orc commander w-wields an artifact . . . the *Demon Soul*. It has p-power over all dragons . . . save Deathwing."

Rhonin recalled how Nekros had tried to use it on the black leviathan with no visible effect. "Why not Deathwing?"

"Because he created it," responded a quiet, feminine voice.

The mage whirled about. He heard a gasp from the dragon.

A beautiful yet ethereal woman wearing a flowing emerald gown stood behind the wizard, a slight smile on her pale lips. Rhonin belatedly realized that her eyes were closed, yet she seemed to have no trouble knowing how best to face either him or the dragon.

"Ysera . . ." the crimson giant whispered reverently.

She did not acknowledge him immediately, though, instead continuing to answer Rhonin's question. "Deathwing it was who created the *Demon Soul*, and for a good cause at the time, so we believed." She strode toward the wizard. "Believed so much that we did as he asked, imparted to it some measure of our power."

"But he didn't impart his own, didn't impart his own!" snapped a male voice, strident and not completely sane. "Tell him, Ysera! Tell him how, after the demons were defeated, he turned on us! Used our own power on us!"

Atop a massive rock perched a skeletal, not-quite-human figure with jagged, blue hair and silver skin. Clad in a high-collared robe of the same two colors as his form, he looked like some mad jester. His eyes gleamed. Dagger-like fingers scratched at the rock upon which the figure squatted, gouging chasms into it.

"He will hear what he needs to hear, Malygos. No more, no less." She smiled slightly again. The longer Rhonin looked at her, the more she reminded him of Vereesa—but of Vereesa as he had once dreamt of her. "Yes, Deathwing neglected to tell us that part, and certainly pretended that he had sacrificed as we had. Only when he decided that he represented the future of our kind did we discover the horrible truth."

It finally occurred to Rhonin that Ysera and Malygos spoke of the black dragon as one of them. He turned his head back to the red leviathan, silently asking the creature he had known as Krasus if his suspicions were true.

"Yes . . ." the injured dragon replied. "They are what you believe them to be. They are two of the five great dragons, known in legend as the Aspects of the world." The red giant seemed to draw strength from their arrival. "Ysera . . . She of the Dreaming. Malygos . . . the Hand of Magic . . ."

"We are wasssting time here," muttered yet a third voice, another male. "Precioussss time . . ."

"And Nozdormu . . . Master of Time, too!" marveled the red dragon. "You have all come!"

A shrouded figure seemingly made of sand stood near Ysera. Under the hood appeared a face so desiccated it barely had enough dry flesh to cover the bone. Gemstone eyes glared at both the dragon and the wizard in growing impatience. "Yesss, we have come! And if thisss party takesss much longer, perhapsss I shall go, too! I've much to gather, much to catalog—"

"Much to babble about, much to babble about!" mocked Malygos from high up.

Nozdormu raised a withered yet strong hand toward the jester, who flashed his daggerlike nails at the hooded figure. The two looked ready to come to blows, both physical and otherwise, but the ghostly woman came between them.

"And this is why Deathwing has nearly triumphed," she murmured.

The two reluctantly backed down. Ysera turned to face everyone, her eyes still closed.

"Deathwing almost had us once, but we joined ranks again and made it so that at least he himself could never wield the *Demon Soul* again. We forced it from his hand and into the bowels of the earth—"

"But someone found it for him," interjected the red dragon, pulling himself together as best he could, now that hope had evidently returned. "I believe that he may even have led the orcs to it, knowing what they would do once they had it. If he cannot use it himself, he can certainly manipulate others into wielding it for his purposes—even if they do not realize it. I—I believe that it suited his plans for Alexstrasza to be captured, for she not only remained the lone power he feared, but it helped the Horde to wreak further havoc in the world without the dark one raising a paw in effort. Now . . . now that it is clear that the Horde has failed him, it better serves his purpose for the orcs to move her."

"Not her," corrected Ysera. "Her eggs."

"Her *eggs?*" the former Krasus blurted. "Not my queen herself?"

"Yes, the eggs. You know that the last of his mates perished in the first days of the war," she replied. "Slain by his own recklessness . . . so now he would raise our sister's get as his own."

"To create a new Age of Dragonsss . . ." spat Nozdormu. "The Age of Deathwing'sss Dragonsss!"

Suddenly Rhonin noticed that the four now stared at him, even Ysera with her closed eyes.

"We cannot touch the *Demon Soul,* human, and out of distrust, we have never tried to make another creature wield it for us. I believe I know what poor Korialstrasz here desired so much of you that he had to drag you from your friends, but while it seems the best way, he will not now be the one who keeps Deathwing occupied."

"It is my duty!" roared the red. "It is my penance!"

"It would be a waste. You are too susceptible to the disk. Besides, you are needed for other reasons. Tyran, who fights now for both his queen and his captor, will not survive. Alexstrasza will have need of you, dear Korial."

"Besides, Deathwing is our *brother,*" mocked Malygos. The talons dug deeper into the rock. "It's only right that *we* should play with him, we should play with him!"

"What do you want me to do?" Rhonin asked, eager yet also anxious. What *he* wanted most was to return to Vereesa.

Ysera faced him—and her eyes opened. For a brief moment, vertigo seized control of the human. The dreamlike eyes that stared back reminded him of everyone he had ever known, hated, or loved. "You, mortal, must take the *Demon Soul* from the orc. Without it, he cannot possibly do to us what he did to our sister and, by taking it, you might be able to free her from his control."

"But that will not deal with Deathwing," Korialstrasz insisted. "And because of the cursed disk, he is stronger than all of you together—"

"A point of fact we know," hissed Nozdormu. "And ssso did you when you came to usss! Well, you have usss now! Be sssatissfied with that!" He looked at his two companions. "Enough babble! Let usss be done with thisss!"

Ysera, her eyes closed again, turned to the dragon. "There is one thing you must do, Korialstrasz, and it does entail risk. This human cannot simply be magicked into the orcs' midst. The *Demon Soul* makes that risky, and there is also always the chance that he will find himself under the ax when he appears. You must instead bear him there—and pray that for the few seconds you are so near, the orc does not bind you to the foul disk this time." She walked up to the stricken dragon, touching the tip of his muzzle. "You are not one of us even if you are her consort, Korialstrasz, yet you fought the *Demon Soul*'s hungry grasp and escaped—"

"I worked hard to build myself up for that, Ysera. I thought I had cast my protective spells better, but in the end I failed."

"We can do this for you." Suddenly, both Malygos and Nozdormu stood beside her. All three had their left hands touching Korialstrasz's muzzle. "So much power the *Demon Soul* took from us, a little more will not matter. . . ."

Auras formed around the raised hands of the trio, the colors reminiscent of each of those contributing. The three auras combined, rapidly spreading from the Aspects to the dragon's muzzle and beyond. In seconds, Korialstrasz's entire immense form lay bathed in magic.

Ysera and the others finally backed away. The crimson behemoth blinked, then rose to his feet. "I feel—renewed!"

"You will need all of it," she remarked. To her two companions, she said, "We must see to our errant brother."

"About *time,* I would sssay!" snapped Nozdormu.

Without another word to either Rhonin or the red dragon, they turned away, facing the distant form of Deathwing. As one, the trio spread their arms wide—and those arms became wings that expanded and expanded. At the same time, their bodies widened, grew greater. Away went the garments, replaced by scale. Their faces lengthened, hardened, all vestiges of humanity shaping into draconic majesty.

The three gargantuan dragons rose high in the air, a sight so impressive that the wizard could only watch.

"I pray that they will be enough," muttered Korialstrasz. "But I fear it will not be so." He looked down at the tiny figure next to him. "What say you, Rhonin? Will you do as they bid?"

For Vereesa alone, he would have agreed. "All right."

The fight had early gone out of Tyran, and now so had the life. Deathwing roared his triumph as he clutched the limp form of the other dragon high. Blood still seeped from a score of deep wounds—most of them in the red's chest—and Tyran's paws were covered with burns, the cost of touching the acidic venom that dripped from the fiery veins coursing along the black's body. No one who touched Deathwing did not suffer in the end.

The dark one roared again, then let the lifeless form drop. In truth, he had done the ill red a favor; would not the other dragon have suffered worse if he had been forced to continue to live with his sickness? At least Deathwing had granted him a warrior's demise, however easy the battle had truly been.

Yet a third time he roared, wanting all to hear of his supremacy—

—and found instead answering roars coming from the west.

"What fool now dares?" he hissed.

Not one fool, Deathwing immediately saw, but *three.* Not *any* three, either.

"Ysssera . . ." he greeted coldly. "And Nozdormu, and my dear friend Malygosss, too . . ."

"It is time to end your madness, brother," the sleek green dragon calmly said.

"I am not your brother in anything, Ysera. Open your eyes to that fact, and also that nothing will prevent me from creating this new age of our kind!"

"You plan only an age in which you rule, nothing more."

The black dipped his head. "Much the same thing, as I see it. Best you go back to sleep. And you, Nozdormu? Pulled your head out of the sand at last? Do you not recall who is most powerful here? Even the three of you will not be enough!"

"Your time isss over!" spat the glittering brown behemoth. Gemstone eyes flared. "Come! Take your place in my collection of thingsss passst. . . ."

Deathwing snorted. "And you, Malygos? Have you nothing to say to your old comrade?"

In response, the chill-looking, silver-blue beast opened wide his maw. A torrent of ice shot forth, washing over Deathwing with incredible accuracy. However, as soon as the ice touched the fearsome dragon, it *transformed,* turning into a thousand thousand tiny crablike vermin that sought to tear at the scales and flesh of their host.

Deathwing hissed, and from the crimson veins acid poured forth. Malygos's creatures died by the hundreds, until only a few remained.

Expertly using two talons, the black dragon picked one of these off, then swallowed it whole. He smiled at his counterparts, revealing sharp, tearing teeth. "So that is how it is to be, then. . . ."

With an earth-shattering roar, he leapt at them.

"They will not defeat him!" Korialstrasz muttered as Rhonin and he neared the besieged orc column. "They cannot!"

"Then why bother?"

"Because they know that it is time to make a stand, regardless of the outcome! Rather would they pass from this world than watch it writhe and die in Deathwing's terrible grip!"

"Is there no way we can help them?"

The dragon's silence answered that.

Rhonin eyed the orcs ahead, thinking of his own mortality. Even if he managed to seize this artifact from Nekros, how long would he maintain hold of it? For that matter, what good would it do him? Could he wield it?

"Kras— Korialstrasz, the disk contains the power of the great dragons?"

"All save Deathwing, which is why he cannot be bound by its power!"

"But he can't wield it himself because of some spell the others cast?"

"So it seems . . ." The dragon banked.

"Do you know what the disk can do?"

"Many things, but none of them able to directly or indirectly affect the dark one."

Rhonin frowned. "How is that possible?"

"How long have you trained in magic, my friend?"

The wizard grimaced. Of all the arts, magic truly had to be one of the most contradictory, guided by laws all its own, laws quite changeable at the worst of times. "Point taken."

"The great ones have made up their minds, Rhonin! By being granted the chance to take the *Demon Soul*, you will not only free my queen—who will, I do not doubt, rise to their aid—but also have the wherewithal for finally crushing the remnants of the Horde! The *Demon Soul* can do that, if you learn to wield it properly, you know!"

He had not even considered that, but of course a relic like this would serve well against the orcs. "But it would take too long to learn how to use it!"

"The orcs did not have willing teachers! I am not one of the Five, Rhonin, but I can show you enough, I think!"

"Providing we both survive . . ." the mage whispered to himself.

"Yes, there is that." Apparently dragons had exceptional hearing. "Aah, there is the orc in question! Be ready!"

Rhonin prepared himself. Korialstrasz dared not get too near Nekros for fear of falling victim to the *Demon Soul*, which meant that, despite the talisman, the wizard had to use magic to reach the orc commander. He had cast many spells in the heat of battle before, but nothing had quite prepared Rhonin for this effort. The dragon might have tried, but around the vicinity of the relic, his magic would have fared worse than the wizard's.

"Get ready . . ."

Korialstrasz dropped lower.

"Now!"

The words came out of Rhonin in a gasp—and suddenly he floated in the air, directly over one of the wagons.

An orc driver looked up, gaped when he saw the wizard.

Rhonin dropped on top of him.

The collision softened his fall, but did nothing good for the orc. Rhonin scrambled to push the unconscious driver to the side, then searched the area for Nekros.

The one-legged commander remained on horseback, eyes fixed on the turning form of Korialstrasz. He raised the gleaming *Demon Soul* high—

"Nekros!" Rhonin shouted.

The orc looked his way, which had been just as the wizard wanted it. Now the dragon remained out of Nekros's reach.

"Human! Wizard! You're dead!" His heavy brow furrowed and a dark look crossed his hideous features. "Well . . . you will be soon!"

He pointed the artifact toward Rhonin.

The wizard quickly cast a shield, hoping that whatever Nekros threw at him would not be as terrible as the golem's flames. The great dragons had not seen fit to grant him some of the extra strength they had given to Korialstrasz, but then, the red behemoth had been near to total collapse, and they had needed the rest of their power for Deathwing. Rhonin's own hopes all lay in his own flagging capabilities.

A gigantic hand—a hand of flame—reached for him, trying to encircle the mage. However, Rhonin's spell held true, and the hand, rebounding off the faintly visible shield, instead engulfed an orc warrior about to behead his dwarven adversary. The orc let out one short scream before collapsing into a burning heap.

"Your tricks'll not hold you long from death!" growled Nekros.

The ground beneath the wagon began to shake, then crumble. Rhonin threw himself from the sinkhole that formed just as the wagon and the animals pulling it were dragged under. The shield spell dissipated, leaving the desperate mage undefended as he clung to what remained of the path.

Nekros urged his mount nearer. "Whatever happens this day, human, I'll at least be rid of you!"

Rhonin uttered a short, simple spell. A single clump of dirt flew up into the orc's face, lodging there despite his attempts to peel it away. Swearing, Nekros struggled to see.

The wizard pulled himself up, then leapt at the orc.

He came up a bit short, catching the arm that held the *Demon Soul* but unable to pull himself higher. Although still blinded, Nekros seized Rhonin by the collar, trying to get one heavy hand on the mage's throat.

"I'll kill you, human scum!"

Fingers closed around Rhonin's neck. Caught between attempting to pry the talisman free and saving his own life, Rhonin managed to accomplish neither. Nekros began to crush the life out of him, the incredible strength of the orc too much for the mage. Rhonin started a spell—

A winged shape suddenly darted past Nekros. Something landed on the back of the orc, throwing both him and the wizard off the horse and onto the rough ground.

They landed hard. The murderous grip on Rhonin's throat vanished as the two bounced in opposite directions.

Someone seized the dazed mage by the shoulders. "Up, Rhonin, before he recovers!"

"V-Vereesa?" He stared into her striking face, both astonished and pleased to see her.

"We saw the dragon drop you from the sky, then watched as you mag-icked yourself to safety! Falstad and I came as soon as we could, thinking you might need help!"

"Falstad?" Rhonin looked up, saw the gryphon-rider and his mount cir-cling back. Falstad had no weapon, yet he howled as if daring every orc in the column to come face him.

"Hurry!" the ranger cried. "We must get out of here!"

"No!" Reluctantly he pulled back. "Not until—look out!"

He pushed her aside just before a massive war-ax would have cut her in two. A beefy orc with ritual scars cut down each cheek raised the ax again, once more focusing on Vereesa, who had fallen to the side.

Rhonin gestured . . . and the ax handle suddenly stretched, weaving about as if some writhing serpent. The orc struggled to control it, only to find his weapon now twisting around him. Suddenly fearful, the warrior released his grip and, after managing to pull free of the living ax, ran off.

The wizard reached out a hand to his companion—

—and fell to the ground as a fist caught him in the back.

"Where is it?" roared Nekros Skullcrusher. "Where's the *Demon Soul?*"

Momentarily stunned, Rhonin did not quite understand the orc. Surely Nekros had the talisman. . . .

A piercing weight pressed down on him from the back. He heard Nekros say, "Stay where you're at, elf! All I need to do is lean a little harder and I'll crush your friend like a piece of fruit!" Rhonin felt cold metal against his cheek. "No tricks, mage! Give me the disk back and I may let you live!"

Nekros gave him just enough movement so that Rhonin could see the orc out of the corner of his eye. The commander had his wooden leg squarely on the wizard's spine, and Rhonin had no doubt that just a bit more pressure would snap the spine completely. "I d-don't have it!" The near-full weight of Nekros's massive body made it nearly impossible to breathe, much less speak. "I don't even know w-where it is!"

"I've no patience for your lies, human!" Nekros pushed a little harder. A hint of desperation colored his otherwise arrogant tone. "I need it now!"

"Nekrosss . . ." interrupted a thundering, hate-filled voice. "You had them ssslay my *children*! My *children!*"

Rhonin felt the orc suddenly shift, as if turning. Nekros let out a gasp, then, "No—!"

A shadow overwhelmed both Rhonin and his adversary. A hot, almost searing wind washed over the mage. He heard Nekros Skullcrusher scream—

—and suddenly the orc's weight vanished from his back.

Rhonin immediately rolled onto his back, certain that whatever had taken his enemy would now take him. Vereesa came to his aid, dragging him to her just as the mage registered what had created the vast shadow and why the voice accompanying it had been familiar.

Scales hanging loose in some areas, her wings bent awkwardly, the Dragonqueen Alexstrasza still presented a most astounding sight. She towered over all else, her head high in the sky as she roared in defiance. Of Nekros, Rhonin saw no sign; the great dragon had either swallowed the orc whole or tossed his body far away.

Alexstrasza roared again, then dipped her head down toward the wizard and elf. Vereesa looked ready to defend them both, but Rhonin signaled her to lower her blade.

"Human, elf, you have my gratitude for finally enabling me to avenge my children! Now, though, there are others who need my aid, however minuscule it might prove!"

She cast her eyes skyward, where four titans fought. Rhonin followed her gaze, watched for a moment as Ysera, Nozdormu, and Malygos battled Deathwing seemingly without result. Again and again the trio dove in, and each time the black monster repelled them easily.

"Three against one and they still can't do anything?"

Alexstrasza, already testing her wings for departure, paused to reply, "Because of the *Demon Soul,* we are more than halved! Only Deathwing remains whole! Would that it could be wielded against him or that we could regain the power lost to it, but neither of those options exists! We can only fight and hope for the best!" A roar from above shook the earth. "I must go now! Forgive me for leaving you thus! Thank you again!"

With that, the Dragonqueen rose into the air, her tail casually sweeping nearby orcs away yet ever avoiding the valiant dwarven attackers.

"There must be something we can do!" Rhonin looked around for the *Demon Soul.* It had to be somewhere.

"Never mind it!" Vereesa called. She deflected the ax of an orc, then ran the warrior through. "We still need to save ourselves!"

Rhonin, however, continued to search despite the pitched battle around him. Suddenly, his gaze alighted on a glittering object half-covered by the arm of a dead dwarf. The wizard raced over to it, hoping against hope.

Sure enough, it proved to be the draconic artifact. Rhonin studied it in open admiration. So simple and elegant, yet containing forces beyond the ability of any wizard, save perhaps the infamous Medivh. So much power. With it, Nekros could have become War Chief of the Horde. With it, Rhonin could become master of Dalaran, emperor of all the Lordaeron kingdoms. . . .

What was he thinking? Rhonin shook his head, scattering such thoughts. The *Demon Soul* had a seductive touch to it, one of which he had to beware.

Falstad, atop the gryphon, dropped down to join them. Somewhere along the way, he had managed to gain an orc battle-ax, which he had already clearly used well.

"Wizard! What ails you? Rom and his band may have the orcs on the run at last, but here 'tis not the place to stand and gawk at baubles!"

Rhonin ignored him, just as he had Vereesa. Somehow the key to defeating Deathwing had to be in using the *Demon Soul!* What *other* force could possibly do that? Even the four great dragons seemed not enough.

He held up the artifact, sensing its tremendous power and knowing that none of that power would help, at least not in its present form.

Which meant that perhaps nothing, *nothing,* would be able to stop Deathwing from achieving his goals. . . .

TWENTY-ONE

T hey threw their full might at him—or at least what remained of it. They threw both physical and magical assaults at Deathwing, and he shrugged all off. No matter how hard they fought against him, the fact remained that, diminished by their long-ago contributions to the *Demon Soul,* the other great Aspects might as well have been infants in comparison to the black leviathan.

Nozdormu cast the sand of ages at him, threatening, at least for a moment, to steal Deathwing's very youth. Deathwing felt the weakness spread through him, felt his bones grow stiff and his thoughts slower. Yet, before the change could become permanent, the raw power within the chaotic dragon surged high, burning away the sand, overwhelming the cunning spell.

From Malygos came a more frontal assault, the mad creature's fury almost enabling him to match Deathwing's power, if but for a moment. Icicles of lightning assailed Malygos's hated foe from all directions, intense heat and numbing cold simultaneously beating at Deathwing. Yet the enchanted iron plates embedded in the black's hide deflected nearly all of the raging storm away, readily enabling Deathwing to suffer what little made it through.

Of all of them, though, his most cunning and dangerous foe proved to be

Ysera. Initially, she stayed back, seeming content to let her comrades waste their efforts on him. Then Deathwing noticed a complacency in himself, a satisfaction that grew to distraction. Almost too late he realized that he had begun to daydream. Shaking his head, he quickly dislodged the cobwebs that she had cast within his mind—just as all three of his adversaries tried to seize him in their talons.

With several beats of his expansive wings, he pulled out of their grasp, then counterattacked. Between his forepaws formed a vast sphere of pure energy, primal power, that he threw into their very midst.

The sphere exploded as it reached the trio, sending Ysera and the others spiraling backward.

Deathwing roared his defiance. "Fools! Throw what you can at me! The outcome will be no different! I am power incarnate! You are nothing but shadows of the past!"

"Never underestimate what you may learn from the past, dark one. . . ."

A crimson shadow Deathwing had thought never to see aloft again filled his vision, surprising even him for once. "Alexstrasza . . . come to avenge your consort?"

"Come to avenge my consort and my children, Deathwing, for I know all too well that this is all because of you!"

"I?" The black behemoth gave her a toothy grin. "But even I cannot touch the *Demon Soul;* you and yours saw to that!"

"But something led the orcs to a place of which only dragons knew . . . and something hinted to them of the power of the disk!"

"Does it matter, anyway? Your day is past, Alexstrasza, while mine is about to come!"

The red dragon spread her wings wide and flashed her claws. Despite the deprivations of her captivity, she did not look at all weak at the moment. "It is your day that is over, dark one!"

"I have faced the ravages of time, the curse of nightmares, and the mists of sorcery, thanks to the others! What weapons do you bring?"

Alexstrasza met his sinister gaze with her own determined, unblinking orbs. "Life . . . hope . . . and what they bring with them . . ."

Deathwing took in her words—and laughed loud. "Then you are as good as dead already!"

The two giants charged one another.

"She cannot hope to beat him," Rhonin muttered. "None of them can, because they're all lacking what this damned artifact took from them!"

"If there is nothing we can do, then we should leave, Rhonin."

"I can't, Vereesa! I've got to do something for her—for all of us, actually! If they can't stop Deathwing, who will?"

Falstad eyed the *Demon Soul*. "Can you do nothing with that thing?"

"No. It won't work against Deathwing in any way."

The dwarf rubbed his hairy chin. "Pity 'tis not possible to give back the magic that thing stole! At least then they could fight with him on even terms. . . ."

The wizard shook his head. "That can't be—" He paused, trying to think. With the broken finger, his throbbing head, and the bruises all over his body, it took effort just to keep on his feet. Rhonin concentrated, focusing on what the gryphon-rider had just said. "But, then again, maybe it *can!*"

His companions looked at him in bewilderment. Rhonin quickly glanced around to assure himself that they were safe from orcs for the moment, then located the hardest rock he could find.

"What are you doing?" Vereesa asked, sounding as if she wondered whether he had lost his mind.

"Returning their power to them!" He put the *Demon Soul* on top of another stone, then raised the first high.

"What in blazes do you think—" was as far as Falstad managed.

Rhonin brought the rock down as hard as he could on the disk.

The rock in his hand cracked in two.

The *Demon Soul* glistened, not even blemished by the assault.

"Damn! I should've known!" He looked up at the dwarf. "Can you swing that thing with great accuracy?"

Falstad looked insulted. "It may be inferior orc work, but 'tis still a usable weapon and, as such, I can swing it as good as any!"

"Use it on the disk! Now!"

The ranger put a concerned hand on the wizard's shoulder. "Rhonin, do you really think this will work?"

"I know the spellwork that will return it to them, a variation used by those of my order when trying to draw from other relics, but it demands that the artifact in question be shattered, so that the forces binding the magic within won't exist any longer! I can give back to the dragons what they lost—but only if I can get the *Demon Soul* open!"

"Is that why, then?" Falstad hefted the war-ax. "Stand back, wizard! Would you like it in two neat halves or chopped into little fragments?"

"Just destroy it in whatever way you can!"

"Simple enough . . ." Raising the ax high, the dwarf took a deep breath— then swung so hard that Rhonin could see the intense strain in his companion's arm muscles.

The ax struck true—

Fragments of metal went flying.

"By the Aerie! The head! 'Tis completely ruined!"

A great gap in the blade gave proof of the *Demon Soul*'s hard surface. Falstad threw down the ax in disgust, cursing shoddy orc workmanship.

Rhonin, however, knew that the ax had not been at fault. "This is worse than I would've imagined!"

"Magic must protect it," Vereesa murmured. "Cannot magic also destroy it?"

"It would have to be something powerful. My magic alone wouldn't do it, but if I had another talisman—" He recalled the medallion Krasus—or, rather, Korialstrasz—had given Vereesa, but that had been left behind after the wizard and the red dragon had headed back to the battle. Besides, Rhonin doubted that it would serve well enough. Better if he had something from Deathwing himself, but that medallion had been lost in the mountain—

But he still had the stone! The stone created from one of the black dragon's own scales!

"It has to work!" he cried, reaching into his pouch.

"What've you got?" Falstad asked.

"This!" He pulled out the tiny stone, an object which in no manner impressed the other two. "Deathwing created this from his very being, just as he created the *Demon Soul* through his magic! It may be able to do what nothing else could!"

As they watched, he brought the stone to the disk. Rhonin debated how best to use it, then decided to follow the teachings of his craft—try the simple way first.

The black gem seemed to gleam in his grip. The wizard turned it on the sharpest edge he could find. Rhonin knew very well that his plan might not work, but he had nothing else to try.

With great caution, he ran the stone along the center of the foul talisman.

Deathwing's scale cut into the *Demon Soul*'s hardened gold exterior like a knife through butter.

"Look out!" Vereesa pulled him back just in time, as a plume of sheer light burst from the cut.

Rhonin sensed the intense magical energy escaping from the damaged talisman and knew he had to act fast, lest it be lost forever to those to whom it truly belonged.

He muttered the spell, adjusting it as he thought needed. The weary mage concentrated hard, not wanting to risk failure at so critical a juncture. It *had* to work.

A fantastic, glittering rainbow rose higher and higher, flying up into the heavens. Rhonin repeated his spell, emphasizing as best he could what he wanted as results. . . .

The nearly blinding plume, now hundreds of feet in height, twisted around—heading in the direction of the battling dragons.

"Did you do it?" the ranger breathlessly asked.

Rhonin stared at the distant forms of Alexstrasza, Deathwing, and the others. "I think so—I *hope* so. . . ."

"Have you not been through enough? Will you continue to fight what you cannot defeat?" Deathwing eyed his foes with utter contempt. What little respect had remained for them had long ago died away. The fools continued to bang their heads against the proverbial wall, even though they knew that, together, their power still lacked.

"You have caused too much misery, too much horror, Deathwing," Alexstrasza retorted. "Not just to us, but to the mortal creatures of this world!"

"What are they to me—or, for that matter, even you? I will never understand that!"

She shook her head in what he realized could be pity—for *him*? "No . . . you never will. . . ."

"I have toyed enough with you—all of you! I should have destroyed you four years ago!"

"But you could not! Creating the *Demon Soul* weakened even you for quite some time. . . ."

He snorted. "But now I have recovered my full strength! My plans for this world advance rapidly . . . and after I have slain all of you, I shall take *your* eggs, Alexstrasza, and create my perfect world!"

In response, the crimson dragon attacked again. Deathwing laughed, knowing that her spells would affect him no better than they had before. Between his own power and the enchanted plates grafted to his skin, *nothing* could hurt him—

"Aaargh!!" The fury of her magical attack tore at him with a force he could not have imagined. His adamantium plates did little to lessen the horrific impact. Deathwing immediately countered with a powerful shield, but the damage had been done. His entire body ached from pain such as he had not known in many centuries.

"What—have you—done to *me*?"

At first Alexstrasza looked surprised herself, but then a knowing—and triumphant—smile crossed her draconic features. "The bare beginnings of what I have these past years dreamed of doing, foul one!"

She looked larger, stronger. In fact, all four of them looked that way. A sensation coursed through the black dragon, the feeling that something had gone terribly wrong with his perfect plan.

"Can you feel it? Can you feel it?" Malygos babbled. "I am me again! What a glorious thing!"

"And it'sss about time!" returned Nozdormu, gemstone eyes uncommonly bright and gleaming. "Yesss, ssso very much about time!"

Ysera opened her arresting eyes, this time *so* arresting that it was all Deathwing could do to pull his gaze from them. "It is the end of the nightmare," she whispered. "Our dream has become truth!"

Alexstrasza nodded. "What was lost has been returned to us. The *Demon Soul* . . . the *Demon Soul* is *no more.*"

"Impossible!" the metallic behemoth roared. "Lies! Lies!"

"No," corrected the crimson figure. "The only lie left to disprove now is that you are invincible."

"Yesss," snapped Nozdormu. "I look forward to disssproving that ridiculousss fallacy. . . ."

And Deathwing found himself under attack by four elemental forces the likes of which he had never faced. No longer did he fight mere shadows of his rivals, but a quartet, each his equal—and he no match for all together.

Malygos brought the very clouds to him, clouds with suffocating holds around the black dragon's jaw and nostrils. Nozdormu turned time forward for Deathwing alone, sapping his adversary of strength by forcing Deathwing to suffer weeks, months, then years without rest. His defenses already crippled by these assaults, Ysera had no trouble invading his mind, turning the armored behemoth's thoughts to his worst nightmares.

Only then did Alexstrasza rise before him, the terrible nemesis. She gazed at Deathwing, still in part with pity, and said, "Life is my Aspect, dark one, and I, like all mothers, know both the pain and wonder that entails! For the past several years, I have watched my children be raised as instruments of war, slaughtered if they proved insufficient or too willful! I have lived knowing that so many died that I could do nothing for!"

"Your words mean nothing to me," Deathwing roared as he futilely struggled to shrug off the others' horrific assaults. *"Nothing!"*

"No, they likely do not . . . which is why I shall let you experience firsthand all that I have suffered. . . ."

And she did just that.

Against any other attack, even the nightmares of Ysera, Deathwing could summon some defense, but against Alexstrasza's he had no weapon upon which to draw. She attacked with pain, but *her* pain. She dealt not with agony as he knew it, but with that of a loving mother who suffered with each child torn from her, with each child turned into something terrible.

With each child who perished.

"You will go through all I have gone through, dark one. Let us see if you fare any better than I did."

But Deathwing had no experience in such suffering. It tore at him where the pain of vicious talons or ripping teeth could not, for it tore at him in his very being.

The most terrible of dragons screamed as none had ever heard a dragon scream before.

That, perhaps, was all that saved him. So startled were the others by it that they faltered in their own spells. Able at last to rip free, Deathwing turned and fled, flying fast and furious. His entire body shook and he continued to scream even as he swiftly dwindled from sight.

"We mussst not let him ssslip away!" Nozdormu suddenly realized.

"Follow him, follow him, indeed!" agreed Malygos.

"I agree," She of the Dreaming quietly added. Ysera looked at Alexstrasza, who hovered, amazed at what she had done. "Sister?"

"Yes," the red dragon replied, nodding. "By all means, go on! I shall join you shortly. . . ."

"I understand . . ."

The other three Aspects veered off, gathering speed as they began their pursuit of the renegade.

Alexstrasza watched them fly off, almost ready to join in the hunt. She did not know if, even with their power returned to them, they could forever end the terror of Deathwing, but he certainly had to be contained. However, there were other matters that she had to deal with first.

The Dragonqueen surveyed both the skies and earth, searching. At last she spotted the one she sought.

"Korialstrasz," she whispered. "You were *not* one of Ysera's dreams after all. . . ."

If they had fought alone, the dwarves might have suffered a different fate. Certainly they could have held their own for a time, but the orcs had not only outnumbered them, they had also been in better condition. Years of skulking underground had hardened Rom's band in some ways, but it had drained them in others.

A fortunate thing, then, that their ranks had been added to by a war wizard, a skilled elven ranger, and one of their mad cousins atop a gryphon with razor-sharp talons and beak. With the *Demon Soul* destroyed, the trio had turned their talents to aiding the trusty hill dwarves and turning the tide.

Of course, the red dragon constantly swooping down on the orcs every time they tried to organize ranks certainly helped.

What remained of Grim Batol's orc forces finally surrendered, so very beaten that they knelt before the victors, certain death would soon follow. Rom, his arm in a sling, might have granted them that, for many of his folk and those of his allies had perished, including Gimmel. However, the dwarven leader followed the commands of another—and who argued with a dragon?

"They will be marched to the west, where Alliance vessels will take them back to the enclaves already set up. There has been enough blood this day, and northern Khaz Modan will certainly cause the shedding of more. . . ." Korialstrasz looked tired, so very tired. "I have seen enough blood today, thank you. . . ."

With Rom's promise to do as the leviathan bid, Korialstrasz turned his attention to Rhonin.

"I won't tell anyone the truth about you, *Krasus*," the young wizard immediately said. "I think I understand why you did what you did."

"But I will never forgive myself for my lapses. I only pray that my queen understands. . . ." The reptilian giant managed an almost human shrug. "As for my place in the Kirin Tor, that will be up for some debate. Not only do I not know if I wish to stay, but the truth about what happened is surely to come out—at least in part. They will realize that I sent you on other than a simple reconnaissance mission."

"What happens now?"

"Many things . . . too many things. The Horde still maintains its hold on Dun Algaz, but that will come to an end soon. After that, this world must rebuild . . . providing it gains the chance." He paused. "In addition, there are some political matters which, after this day's events, will most certainly shift." Korialstrasz eyed the tiny creatures before him somewhat uneasily. "And I will say to you now that my kind is as much to blame for those shifts as anyone else."

Rhonin would have pressed, but he immediately saw that Korialstrasz would not be answering those questions. Having learned of both Deathwing's and the red dragon's ability to masquerade as humans, the wizard did not doubt that the ancient race had interfered much over the history of not only humanity, but the elves and others as well.

"That was quick thinking, what you did, Rhonin," the behemoth remarked. "You were always a good student. . . ."

The conversation came to an abrupt end as a vast shadow swept over the band. For a brief moment, the weary mage feared that Deathwing had somehow escaped his pursuers and had returned to take his vengeance on those who had caused his defeat.

However, the dragon hovering above turned out not to be black, but rather as crimson as Korialstrasz.

"The dark one flees! His evil is, if not stopped, certainly curtailed some!" Korialstrasz gazed up, longing in his voice. "My queen . . ."

"I had thought you dead," murmured Alexstrasza to her consort. "I mourned you for a long time. . . ."

The male looked guilty. "The subterfuge was necessary, my queen, if only to give me the opportunity to try to win your freedom. I apologize not only for the pain I caused you, but also the inconsideration I displayed by manipulating these mortals. I know how you feel toward their kind. . . ."

She nodded. "If they will forgive you, then so will I." Her tail slipped down, intertwining with his own for a moment. "The others still pursue the dark one, but before I would join them in the hunt, we must gather what remains of our flight and rebuild our home anew. This I think a priority."

"I am your servant," he replied, bowing his massive head. "Now and forever, my love."

Looking at the wizard and his friends, the Dragonqueen added, "For your sacrifices, the least we can do is offer you a ride home—providing you can wait a little while."

Even though, with much effort, Falstad's gryphon could have eventually carried them home, Rhonin gratefully accepted. He found he liked both dragons, despite Korialstrasz's past trickery. Put in the same position, the wizard probably would have acted just as the consort had.

"The hill dwarves will give you food and a place to rest. We will return for you tomorrow after the eggs have all been recovered and safely secreted." A bitter smile crossed her draconic features. "Praise be that our eggs are so very durable, or else even in defeat Deathwing would have struck mine a bitter blow. . . ."

"Do not think about it," urged the male. "Come! The sooner we are done, the better!"

"Yes . . ." Alexstrasza dipped her head toward the trio. "Human Rhonin, elf, and dwarf! I thank all three of you for your parts in this, and know that as long as I am queen, my kind will never be an enemy to yours. . . ."

And with that, both dragons rose high into the air, racing in the direction that Deathwing had gone with the first of the eggs. Those still remaining with the caravan would be under the protection of the jubilant hill dwarves, who could at last claim the mountain fortress and all of Grim Batol as theirs again.

"A glorious sight, them!" rumbled Falstad once the dragons had vanished. He turned to his companions. "My elven lady, you shall always be a part of my dreams!" He took the confused ranger's hand, shook it, then said to Rhonin, "Wizard, I've not dealt much with your kind, but I'll say here that at least one of 'em has the heart of a warrior! Be quite a tale I'll be telling, *the*

Taking of Grim Batol! Don't be surprised if you someday find dwarves regaling your story in some tavern, eh?"

"Are you leaving us?" Rhonin asked in complete bewilderment. They had only just won the battle. He still struggled to catch his breath from the entire matter.

"You should not go until at least the morning," Vereesa insisted.

The wild dwarf shrugged as if indicating that, had it been his own choice, he would have gladly stayed. "Sorry I am, but this news must reach the Aerie as soon as possible! As fast as the dragons'll be, I'll get back there before they reach Lordaeron! 'Tis my duty—and I'd like a few particular folk there to know I've not been lost after all. . . ."

Rhonin gratefully took Falstad's powerful hand, thankful that he did not have to use his own injured one to shake. Even tired, the gryphon-rider had a crushing grip. "Thank you for everything!"

"No, human, thank *you!* I'd like to see another rider with a greater song of glory to sing than I've got! Will make the heads of the ladies turn my way, believe you me!"

In a startling display for one so reserved, Vereesa leaned down and kissed the dwarf lightly on the cheek. Underneath his great beard, Falstad blushed furiously. Rhonin felt a twinge of jealousy.

"Take care of yourself," she warned the rider.

"That I will!" He mounted the back of the gryphon with one practiced leap. With a wave to the duo, Falstad tapped lightly on the animal's sides with his heels. "Mayhaps we'll all meet again once this war's truly over!"

The gryphon lifted off into the sky, circling once so that Falstad could bid them farewell again. Then the dwarf's mount steered west, and the short warrior vanished into the distance.

Rhonin waved at the dwindling figure, recalling with some guilt his first impressions of the dwarf. Falstad had proven himself though, in many ways more than the wizard felt that *he* had.

A gentle hand took hold of his crippled one, lifting it slowly up.

"This is long past the need to be dealt with," Vereesa reproved him. "I took an oath to see you safe. This would not look good for me. . . ."

"Didn't your oath end when we reached the shores of Khaz Modan?" he returned, adding a slight smile.

"Perhaps, but it seems that you need to be guarded from yourself every hour of the day! What might you do to yourself next?" However, the elf, too, let a slight smile momentarily escape her.

Rhonin let her fuss over his broken finger, wondering if perhaps there might be a way for him to continue his association with Vereesa after the dragon had brought them both back to Lordaeron. Surely it would be best for those in command if the pair gave their reports together, the better to verify events. He would have to propose that to Vereesa and see how she felt about it.

Curious, he suddenly thought, how one could go from almost seeking death, as he had done in the beginning, to wanting to live to the fullest—and that after nearly having been incinerated, crushed, run through, beheaded, and devoured. He would always have regrets for what had happened on his previous mission, but no longer was he haunted by that time.

"There," Vereesa announced. "Keep it like that until I can find some better material. It should heal well, then."

She had taken a strip of cloth from her cloak and had fashioned a splint of sorts using a piece of wood from a broken war-ax. Rhonin inspected her work, found it exceptional.

He had never bothered to mention that, once recuperated, he would have been able to completely heal the hand himself. She had been very willing to help him.

"Thank you."

He hoped that the dragons would take their time with their task. With nothing to fear from the orcs, Rhonin found himself in no hurry whatsoever to go home.

When news at last spread to the Alliance of Grim Batol's downfall and the loss of the dragons to the Horde's dying cause, celebrations arose among the people. Surely now the war would at last come to an end. Surely now peace was at hand.

Each of the major kingdoms insisted on hearing the words of the wizard and elf for themselves, questioning the pair at great length. Word came down from the Aeries of verification from one of the gryphon-riders, the celebrated hero Falstad.

While Rhonin and Vereesa continued their tour of the various kingdoms—and grew closer in the process—he who had worn the guise of the wizard Krasus had made a report of his own in the Chamber of the Air. Initially, he had been greeted with hostility by his fellow councilors, especially those who knew he had outright lied to all. However, no one could argue with the results, and wizards were, if nothing else, pragmatic when it came to results.

Drenden had shaken his shadowed head at the faceless mage. "You could've brought down everything we'd worked for!" he boomed, his words echoed by the storm momentarily raging through the chamber. "Everything!"

"I understand that now. If you like, I will resign from the council, even accept penance or ouster, if that is what you wish."

"There were those who mentioned more than ouster," commented Modera. "Much more than ouster . . ."

"But we've all discussed that and decided that young Rhonin's success has brought Dalaran nothing but good will, even from those of our allies who briefly protested their lack of knowledge of his improbable mission. The elves especially are pleased, as one of their own was also involved." Drenden shrugged. "There seems no reason to continue on with this subject. Consider yourself officially censured, Krasus, but *congratulated* by me personally."

"Drenden!" snapped Modera.

"We're alone here, I can say what I will." He steepled his fingers. "Now, then, if no one else has any other comment, I'd like to bring up the subject of one Lord Prestor, supposed monarch-elect of Alterac—who *seems* to have vanished off the face of the world!"

"The chateau is empty, his servants fled . . ." added Modera, still annoyed at her counterpart's earlier comments concerning Krasus.

One of the other mages, the heavyset one, finally spoke up. "The spells surrounding the place've dissipated, too. And there're signs that there were goblins working for this rogue mage!"

The entire council looked to Korialstrasz.

He spread his hands as if as bewildered as the rest. "Lord Prestor" had clearly had the upper hand in the situation, everything to gain; why, the rest clearly wanted to know, had he abandoned it all now? "It is as much a puzzle to me as it is you. Perhaps he realized that, eventually, our combined might would bring him down. That would be my likely guess. Certainly nothing else would explain why he would give up so much."

This sat well with the other wizards. Like most creatures, Korialstrasz knew, they had their egos to assuage.

"His influence already wanes," he went on. "For surely you have all heard how Genn Greymane has reinstated his protest against Prestor's taking ascension, and even Lord Admiral Proudmoore has joined him on this. King Terenas even announced that a second check into the so-called noble's background left many questions unanswered. The rumors of Prestor's imminent betrothal to the young princess have dwindled away. . . ."

"You were looking into his background," commented Modera.

"It may be that some of that information slipped to His Majesty, yes."

Drenden nodded, quite pleased. "Rhonin's quest has brought us into the good graces of Terenas and the others, and we'll make the best use of that turn. By the end of a fortnight, 'Lord Prestor' will be anathema to the entire Alliance!"

Korialstrasz raised a warning hand. "Best to take a more subtle touch. We have the time. Before long, they will forget he even existed."

"Perhaps you're right." The bearded mage looked at the others, who nodded in agreement. "Unanimous, then. How wonderful." He raised his hand, ready to dismiss the council. "Well, if there's nothing more—"

"Actually, there is," interrupted the dragon mage. A cloud from the fading storm drifted through him.

"What is it?"

"Although you have granted me pardon for my questionable actions, I must tell you now that I must take my leave from council activities for a time."

They looked stunned. None could recall him ever having missed a gathering, much less stepping back from the council altogether.

"How long?" Modera asked.

"I cannot say. She and I have been apart so long, it will take quite some time to regain what we once had."

Korialstrasz could almost see Drenden blink, despite the shadow spell. "*You* have a . . . a *wife*, is she?"

"Yes. Forgive me if I never recalled to tell you. As I said, we were apart for quite some time. . . ." He smiled even though they could not see it. ". . . but now she is returned to me."

The others shared glances. Finally, Drenden replied, "Then . . . by all means . . . we shall not stand in your way. You certainly have the right to do this. . . ."

He bowed. In truth, the dragon hoped to return, for this had been as much a part of his centuries-old life as almost anything else. Yet, compared to being with his Alexstrasza, even it paled in comparison. "My thanks. I hope, of course, to keep abreast of all news of import, I promise you. . . ."

He raised his hand in farewell as the spell he cast transported him away from the Chamber of the Air. Korialstrasz's parting words were truer than even the other wizards might have realized. As one of the Kirin Tor—even one absent from the council—he most definitely planned to watch the political maneuverings. Despite "Lord Prestor's" disappearance, potentially devastating squabbles remained between the various kingdoms, Alterac again one of the foremost topics. His duties for Dalaran *demanded* Korialstrasz maintain watch.

And for his queen, for his ancient kind, he and others like him would also watch . . . watch and influence, if necessary. Alexstrasza believed in these young races, more so after what Rhonin and the others had done, and because of that Korialstrasz intended to do what he had to in order to steel her belief. He owed that to both her and those who had aided him in his quest.

No one had sighted Deathwing since the black beast's desperate escape. With the others constantly on watch for him now, it seemed unlikely that he would cause much terror for some time to come, if ever. Yet, because of him, the others had taken a renewed interest in life and the future.

The day of the dragon had passed, true, but that did not mean at all that they would not continue to leave their mark in the world . . . even if no one else ever suspected it.

Lord of
the Clans

CHRISTIE GOLDEN

About the Author

CHRISTIE GOLDEN is the award-winning author of twenty-eight novels and over a dozen short stories in the fields of fantasy, science fiction, and horror. Her media tie-in works include launching the *Ravenloft* line in 1991 with *Vampire of the Mists,* which introduced readers to elven vampire Jander Sunstar and will be reprinted in 2006, over a dozen *Star Trek* novels, including *Voyager* fiction set after the TV series, and the *World of Warcraft* novel *Rise of the Horde.* Original fiction includes the *Dancers* series from Luna Books, *On Fire's Wings,* reissued in mass market paperback in 2006, and *In Stone's Clasp.* Readers are invited to visit her website at www.christiegolden.com. And yes, she does play *World of Warcraft.*

This book is dedicated to its "holy trinity":

Lucienne Diver
Jessica McGivney
and
Chris Metzen

with appreciation for their enthusiastic support
and unwavering faith in my work.

PROLOGUE

They came when Gul'dan called them, those who had willingly—nay, eagerly—sold their souls to the darkness. Once they, like Gul'dan, had been deeply spiritual beings. Once, they had studied the natural world and the orcs' place in it; had learned from the beasts of forest and field, the birds of the air, the fish of the rivers and oceans. And they had been a part of that cycle, no more, no less.

No longer.

These former shamans, these new warlocks, had had the briefest taste of power and, like the barest drop of honey on the tongue, found it sweet indeed. So their eagerness had been rewarded with more power, and still more. Gul'dan himself had learned from his master Ner'zhul until student had finally surpassed teacher. While it had been because of Ner'zhul that the Horde had become the powerful, unstoppable tide of destruction it presently was, Ner'zhul had not had the courage to go further. He had a soft spot for the inherent nobility of his people. Gul'dan had no such weakness.

The Horde had slain all there was to slay in this world. They were lost with no outlet for their bloodlust, and were turning on one another, clan attacking clan in a desperate attempt to assuage the brutal longings that flamed in their hearts. It was Gul'dan who had found a fresh target upon which to focus the Horde's white-hot need to slaughter. Now they would soon venture into a new world, filled with fresh, easy, unsuspecting prey. The bloodlust would rise to a fever pitch, and the wild Horde needed a council to guide them. Gul'dan would lead that council.

He nodded to them as they entered, his small, fire-hazed eyes missing nothing. One by one they came, called like servile beasts to their master. To him.

They sat around the table, the most feared, revered, and loathed among the entire orcish clans. Some were hideous, having paid the price for their dark knowledge with more than just their souls. Others were yet fair, their bodies whole and strong with smooth green skin stretched tight across rippling muscles. Such had been their request in the dark bargain. All were ruthless, cunning, and would stop at nothing to gain more power.

But none was as ruthless as Gul'dan.

"We few gathered here," began Gul'dan in his raspy voice, "are the mightiest of our clans. We know power. How to get it, how to use it, and how to get more. Others are beginning to speak out against one or the other of us. This clan wishes to return to *its roots; that clan is tired of killing defenseless infants." His thick green lips curled into a sneer of contempt. "This is what happens when orcs go soft."*

"But, Great One," one of the warlocks said, "we have slain all the Draenei. What is there left to kill in this world?"

Gul'dan smiled, stretching his thick lips over large, sharp teeth. "Nothing," he said. "But other worlds await."

He told them of the plan, taking pleasure in the lust for power that was kindled in their red eyes. Yes, this would be good. This would be the most powerful organization of orcs that had ever existed, and at the head of this organization would be none other than Gul'dan.

"And we will be the council that makes the Horde dance to our tune," he said at last. "Each one of us is a powerful voice. Yet such is the orcish pride that they must not know who is truly the master here. Let each think that he swings his battle-ax because he wills it, not because we are commanding it. We will stay a secret. We are the walkers in the shadows, the power that is all the more potent for its invisibility. We are the Shadow Council, and none shall know of our strength."

Yet, one day, and that day soon, some would know.

ONE

Even the beasts were cold on a night such as this, mused Durotan. Absently he reached out to his wolf companion and scratched Sharptooth behind one of his white ears. The animal crooned appreciatively and snuggled closer. Wolf and orc chief stared together at the silent fall of white snow, framed by the rough oval that was the entrance to Durotan's cave.

Once, Durotan, chieftain of the Frostwolf clan, had known the kiss of balmier climes. Had swung his ax in the sunlight, narrowing small eyes against the gleam of sunshine on metal and against the spattering of red human blood. Once, he had felt a kinship with all of his people, not just those of his clan. Side by side they had stood, a green tide of death flooding over the hillsides to engulf the humans. They had feasted at the fires together, laughed their deep, booming laughs, told the stories of blood and conquest while their children drowsed by the dying embers, their little minds filled with images of slaughter.

But now the handful of orcs that comprised the Frostwolf clan shivered alone in their exile in the frigid Alterac Mountains of this alien world. Their only friends here were the huge white wolves. They were so different from the mammoth black wolves that Durotan's people had once ridden, but a wolf was a wolf, no matter the color of its fur, and determined patience combined with Drek'Thar's powers had won the beasts over to them. Now orc and wolf hunted together and kept one another warm during the interminable, snowy nights.

A soft, snuffling sound from the heart of the cave caused Durotan to turn. His harsh face, lined and held in perpetual tautness from years of worry and anger, softened at the noise. His little son, as yet unnamed until the ordained Naming Day of this cycle, had cried out as he was being fed.

Leaving Sharptooth to continue watching the snowfall, Durotan rose and lumbered back to the cave's inner chamber. Draka had bared a breast for the child to suckle upon, and had just removed the infant from his task. So that was why the child had whimpered. As Durotan watched, Draka extended a forefinger. With a black nail honed to razor sharpness, she pricked deep into the nipple before returning the infant's small head to her breast. Not a flicker of pain crossed her beautiful, strong-jawed face. Now, as the child fed, he would drink not only nourishing mother's milk, but his mother's blood as well. Such was appropriate food for a budding young warrior, the son of Durotan, the future chieftain of the Frostwolves.

His heart swelled with love for his mate, a warrior his equal in courage and cunning, and the lovely, perfect son they had borne.

It was then that the knowledge of what he had to do sank over him, like a blanket settling over his shoulders. He sat down and sighed deeply.

Draka glanced up at him, her brown eyes narrowing. She knew him all too well. He did not want to tell her of his sudden decision, although he knew in his heart it was the right one. But he must.

"We have a child now," Durotan said, his deep voice booming from his broad chest.

"Yes," replied Draka, pride in her voice. "A fine, strong son, who will lead the Frostwolf clan after his father dies nobly in battle. Many years from now," she added.

"I have a responsibility for his future," Durotan continued.

Draka's attention was now on him fully. He thought her exquisitely beautiful at this moment, and tried to brand the image of her in his mind. The firelight played against her green skin, casting her powerful muscles into sharp relief and making her tusks gleam. She did not interrupt, merely waited for him to continue.

"Had I not spoken against Gul'dan, our son would have more playmates with which to grow up," Durotan continued. "Had I not spoken against Gul'dan, we would have continued to be valued members of the Horde."

Draka hissed, opening her massive jaws and baring her fangs in displeasure at her mate. "You would not have been the mate I joined with," she boomed. The infant, startled, jerked his head away from the nourishing breast to look up at his mother's face. White milk and red blood dripped down his already jutting chin. "Durotan of the Frostwolf clan would not sit by and meekly let our people be led to their deaths like the sheep the humans tend. With what you had learned, you had to speak out, my mate. You could have done no less and still be the chieftain you are."

Durotan nodded at the truth of her words. "To know that Gul'dan had no love for our people, that it was nothing more than a way for him to increase his power. . . ."

He fell silent, recalling the shock and horror—and rage—that had engulfed him when he had learned of the Shadow Council and Gul'dan's duplicity. He had tried to convince the others of the danger facing them all. They had been used, like pawns, to destroy the Draenei, a race that Durotan was beginning to think had not required extinction after all. And again, shuttled through the Dark Portal onto an unsuspecting world—not the orcs' decision, no, but that of the Shadow Council. All for Gul'dan, all for Gul'dan's personal power. How many orcs had fallen, fighting for something so empty?

He searched for the words to express his decision to his mate. "I spoke, and we were exiled. All who followed me were. It is a great dishonor."

"Only Gul'dan's dishonor," said Draka fiercely. The infant had gotten over his temporary fright and was again nursing. "Your people are alive, and free, Durotan. It is a harsh place, but we have found the frost wolves to be our companions. We have plenty of fresh meat, even in the depths of winter. We have kept the old ways alive, as much as we can, and the stories around the fire are part of our children's heritage."

"They deserve more," said Durotan. He gestured with a sharp-nailed finger at his suckling son. "He deserves more. Our still-deluded brothers deserve more. And I will give it to them."

He rose and straightened to his full imposing height. His huge shadow fell over the forms of his wife and child. Her crestfallen expression told him that Draka knew what he was going to say before he spoke, but the words needed utterance. It was what made them solid, real . . . made them an oath not to be broken.

"There were some who heeded me, though they still doubted. I will return and find those few chieftains. I will convince them of the truth of my story, and they will rally their people. We shall no longer be slaves of Gul'dan, easily lost and not thought of when we die in battles that serve only him. This I swear, I, Durotan, chieftain of the Frostwolf clan!"

He threw back his head, opened his toothy mouth almost impossibly wide, rolled his eyes back, and uttered a loud, deep, furious cry. The baby began to squall and even Draka flinched. It was the Oath Cry, and he knew that despite the deep snow that often deadened sound, everyone in his clan would hear it this night. In moments, they would cluster around his cave, demanding to know the content of the Oath Cry, and making cries of their own.

"You shall not go alone, my mate," said Draka, her soft voice a sharp contrast to the ear-splitting sound of Durotan's Oath Cry. "We shall come with you."

"I forbid it."

And with a suddenness that startled even Durotan, who ought to have known better, Draka sprang to her feet. The crying baby tumbled from her lap as she clenched her fists and raised them, shaking them violently. A heart-beat later Durotan blinked as pain shot through him and blood dripped down his face. She had bounded the length of the cave and slashed his cheek with her nails.

"I am Draka, daughter of Kelkar, son of Rhakish. No one forbids me to follow my mate, not even Durotan himself! I come with you, I stand by you, I shall die if need be. Pagh!" She spat at him.

As he wiped the mixture of spittle and blood from his face, his heart swelled with love for this female. He had been right to choose her as his mate, to be the mother of his sons. Was there ever a more fortunate male in all of orc history? He did not think so.

Despite the fact that, if word reached Gul'dan, Orgrim Doomhammer and his clan would be exiled, the great Warchief made Durotan and his family welcome in his field camp. The wolf, however, he eyed with suspicion. The wolf eyed him back in the same manner. The rough tent that served Doomhammer for shelter was emptied of lesser orcs, and Durotan, Draka, and their yet-unnamed child were ushered in.

The night was a bit cool to Doomhammer, and he watched with wry amusement as his honored guests divested themselves of most of their clothing and muttered about the heat. Frostwolves, he mused, must be unused to such "warm weather."

Outside, his personal guards kept watch. With the flap that served as a door still open, Doomhammer watched them huddle around the fire, extending enormous green hands to the dancing flames. The night was dark, save for the small lights of the stars. Durotan had picked a good night for his clandestine visit. It was unlikely that the small party of male, female, and child had been spotted and identified for who they really were.

"I regret that I place you and your clan in jeopardy," were the first words Durotan spoke.

Doomhammer waved the comment aside. "If Death is to come for us, it will find us behaving with honor." He invited them to sit and with his own hands handed his old friend the dripping haunch of a fresh kill. It was still warm. Durotan nodded his acceptance, bit into the juicy flesh, and tore off a huge chunk. Draka did likewise, and then extended her bloody fingers to her baby. The child eagerly sucked the sweet liquid.

"A fine, strong boy," said Doomhammer.

Durotan nodded. "He will be a fitting leader of my clan. But we did not come all this way for you to admire my son."

"You spoke with veiled words many years ago," said Doomhammer.

"I wished to protect my clan, and I was not certain my suspicions were correct until Gul'dan imposed the exile," Durotan replied. "His swift punishment made it clear that what I knew was true. Listen, my old friend, and then you must judge for yourself."

In soft tones, so that the guards sitting at the fire a few yards away would not overhear them, Durotan began to speak. He told Doomhammer everything he knew—the bargain with the demon lord, the obscene nature of Gul'dan's power, the betrayal of the clans through the Shadow Council, the eventual, and dishonorable, end of the orcs, who would be thrown as bait to demonic forces. Doomhammer listened, forcing his wide face to remain impassive. But within his broad chest his heart pounded like his own famous warhammer upon human flesh.

Could this be true? It sounded like a tale spewed by a battle-addled halfwit. Demons, dark pacts . . . and yet, this was Durotan who was speaking. Durotan, who was one of the wisest, fiercest, and noblest of the chieftains. From any other mouth, these he would have judged to be lies or nonsense. But Durotan had been exiled for his words, which lent them credence. And Doomhammer had trusted the other chieftain with his life many times before now.

There was only one conclusion. What Durotan was telling him was true. When his old friend finished speaking, Doomhammer reached for the meat and took another bite, chewing slowly while his racing mind tried to make sense of all that had been said. Finally, he swallowed, and spoke.

"I believe you, old friend. And let me reassure you, I will not stand for Gul'dan's plans for our people. We will stand against the darkness with you."

Obviously moved, Durotan extended his hand. Doomhammer gripped it tightly.

"You cannot stay overlong in this camp, though it would be an honor to have you do so," Doomhammer said as he rose. "One of my personal guards will escort you to a safe place. There is a stream nearby and much game in the woods this time of year, so you shall not go hungry. I will do what I can on your behalf, and when the time is right, you and I shall stand side by side as we slay the Great Betrayer Gul'dan together."

The guard said nothing as he led them out of the encampment several miles into the surrounding woods. Sure enough, the clearing to which he took them was secluded and verdant. Durotan could hear the trickling of the water. He turned to Draka.

"I knew my old friend could be trusted," he said. "It will not be long before—"

And then Durotan froze. He had heard another noise over the splashing of the nearby stream. It was the snap of a twig under a heavy foot. . . .

He screamed his battle cry and reached for his ax. Before he could even grasp the hilt the assassins were upon him. Dimly, Durotan heard Draka's shrill scream of rage, but could spare no instant to turn to her aid. Out of the corner of his eye, he saw Sharptooth spring on one intruder, knocking him to the earth.

They had come silently, with none of the pride in the hunt that was so integral to orcish honor. These were assassins, the lowest of the low, the worm beneath the foot. Except these worms were everywhere, and though their mouths remained closed in that unnatural silence, their weapons spoke with a purposeful tongue.

An ax bit deep into Durotan's left thigh and he fell. Warm blood flowed down his leg as he twisted and reached with his bare hands, trying desperately to throttle his would-be murderer. He stared up into a face frighteningly devoid of good, honest orc rage, indeed of any emotion at all. His adversary lifted the ax again. With every ounce of strength left to him, Durotan's hands closed on the orc's throat. Now the worm did show emotion as he dropped the ax, trying to pry Durotan's thick, powerful fingers from his neck.

A brief, sharp howl, then silence. Sharptooth had fallen. Durotan did not need to look to see. He still heard his mate grunting obscenities at the orc who, he knew, would slay her. And then a noise that sent fear shivering through him split the air: his infant son's cry of terror.

They shall not kill my son! The thought gave Durotan new strength and with a roar, despite the lifeblood ebbing from the severed artery in his leg, he surged upward and managed to get his foe beneath his huge bulk. Now the assassin squirmed in genuine terror. Durotan pressed hard with both hands and felt the satisfying snap of neck beneath his palms.

"No!" The voice belonged to the treasonous guard, the orc who had betrayed them. It was high, humanish with fear. "No, I'm one of you, they are the target—"

Durotan looked up in time to see a huge assassin swing a blade almost bigger than he was in a smooth, precise arc. Doomhammer's personal guard didn't stand a chance. The sword sliced cleanly through the traitor's neck, and as the severed, bloody head flew past him, Durotan could still see the shock and surprise on the dead guard's face.

He turned to defend his mate, but he was too late. Durotan cried aloud in fury and raw grief as he saw Draka's still body, hacked almost to pieces, lying on the forest floor in a widening pool of blood. Her killer loomed over her, and now turned his attention to Durotan.

In a fair battle, Durotan would have been a match for any three of them. Grievously wounded as he was, with no weapon save his hands, he knew he was about to die. He did not try to defend himself. Instead, out of deep instinct he reached for the small bundle that was his child.

And stared foolishly at the spurting fountain of blood that sprang from his shoulder. His reflexes were slowing from lack of blood, and before he could even react, his left arm joined the right to lie, twitching, on the ground. The worms would not even let him hold his son one more time.

The injured leg could bear him no longer. Durotan toppled forward. His face was inches away from that of his son's. His mighty warrior's heart broke at the expression on the baby's face, an expression of total confusion and terror.

"Take . . . the child," he rasped, amazed that he could even speak.

The assassin bent close, so that Durotan could see him. He spat in Durotan's eye. For a moment, Durotan feared he would impale the baby right in front of his father's eyes.

"We will leave the child for the forest creatures," snarled the assassin. "Perhaps you can watch as they tear him to bits."

And then they were gone, as silently as they had left. Durotan blinked, feeling dazed and disoriented as the blood left his body in rivers. He tried again to move and could not. He could only stare with failing eyesight at the image of his son, his small chest heaving with his screams, his tiny fists balled and waving frantically.

Draka . . . my beloved . . . my little son . . . I am so sorry. I have brought us to this. . . .

The edges of his vision began to turn gray. The image of his child began to fade. The only comfort that Durotan, chieftain of the Frostwolf clan, had as his life slowly ebbed from him was the knowledge that he would die before having to witness the horrible spectacle of his son being eaten alive by ravenous forest beasts.

"By the Light, what a noise!" Twenty-two-year-old Tammis Foxton wrinkled his nose at the noise that was echoing through the forest. "Might as well turn back, Lieutenant. Anything that loud is certain to have frightened any game worth pursuing."

Lieutenant Aedelas Blackmoore threw his personal servant a lazy grin.

"Haven't you learned anything I've tried to teach you, Tammis?" he drawled. "It's as much about getting away from that damned fortress as bringing back supper. Let whatever it is caterwaul all it likes." He reached for the saddlebag behind him. The bottle felt cool and smooth in his hand.

"Hunting cup, sir?" Tammis, despite Blackmoore's comments, had been ideally trained. He extended a small cup in the shape of a dragon's head that had been hooked onto his saddle. Hunting cups were specifically designed for such a purpose, having no base upon which to sit. Blackmoore debated, then waved the offer away.

"One too many steps." With his teeth he pulled out the cork, held it in one hand, and raised the bottle's mouth to his lips.

Ah, this stuff was sweet. It burned an easy trail down his throat and into his gut. Wiping his mouth, Blackmoore recorked the bottle and put it back in the saddlebag. He deliberately ignored Tammis's look, quickly averted, of concern. What should a servant care how much his master drank?

Aedelas Blackmoore had risen swiftly through the ranks because of his almost incredible ability to slice a swath through the ranks of orcs on the battlefield. His superiors thought this due to skill and courage. Blackmoore could have told them that his courage was of the liquid variety, but he didn't see much point in it.

His reputation also didn't hurt his chances with the ladies. Neither did his dashing good looks. Tall and handsome, with black hair that fell to his shoulders, steel-blue eyes, and a small, neatly trimmed goatee, he was the perfect heroic soldier. If some of the women left his bed a little sadder but wiser, and more than occasionally with a bruise or two, it mattered nothing to him. There were always plenty more where they came from.

The ear-splitting sound was starting to irritate him. "It's not going away," Blackmoore growled.

"It could be an injured creature, sir, incapable of crawling away," said Tammis.

"Then let's find it and put it out of our misery," replied Blackmoore. He kicked Nightsong, a sleek gelding as black as his name, with more force than was necessary and took off at a gallop in the direction of the hellish noise.

Nightsong came to such an abrupt halt that Blackmoore, usually the finest of riders, nearly sailed over the beast's head. He swore and punched the animal in the neck, then fell silent as he saw what had caused Nightsong to stop so quickly.

"Blessed Light," said Tammis, riding up beside him on his small gray pony. "What a mess."

Three orcs and a huge white wolf lay sprawled on the forest floor. Blackmoore assumed that they had died recently. There was as yet no stink of decomposition, though the blood had congealed. Two males, one female. Who cared what sex the wolf had been. Damned orcs. It would save humans like him a lot of trouble if the brutes turned on themselves more often.

Something moved, and Blackmoore saw what it was that had been shrieking so violently. It was the ugliest thing he had ever seen . . . an orc baby, wrapped in what no doubt passed for a swaddling cloth among the creatures. Staring, he dismounted and went to it.

"Careful, sir!" yelped Tammis. "It might bite!"

"I've never seen a whelp before," said Blackmoore. He nudged it with his boot toe. It rolled slightly out of its blue and white cloth, screwed its hideous little green face up even more, and continued wailing.

Though he had already downed the contents of one bottle of mead and was well into the second, Blackmoore's mind was still sharp. Now, an idea began to form in his head. Ignoring Tammis's unhappy warnings, Blackmoore bent over and picked up the small monster, tucking the blue and white cloth snugly about it. Almost immediately, it stopped crying. Blue-gray eyes locked with his.

"Interesting," said Blackmoore. "Their infants have blue eyes when they are young, just as humans do." Soon enough those eyes would turn piggy and black, or red, and gaze upon all humans with murderous hate.

Unless. . . .

For years, Blackmoore had worked twice as hard to be half as well regarded as other men of equal birth and rank. He had labored under the stigma of his father's treachery, and had done everything possible to gain power and position. He was still skeptically regarded by many; "blood of a traitor" was often muttered when those around him thought him unable to hear. But now, perhaps he might one day not have to listen to those cutting comments any longer.

"Tammis," he said thoughtfully, gazing intently into the incongruously soft blue of the baby orc's eyes, "did you know that you have the honor to serve a brilliant man?"

"Of course I did, sir," Tammis replied, as was expected. "May I inquire as to why this is particularly true at this moment?"

Blackmoore glanced up at the still-mounted servant, and grinned. "Because Lieutenant Aedelas Blackmoore holds in his hands something that is going to make him famous, wealthy, and best of all, powerful."

TWO

Tammis Foxton was in a state of high agitation, due directly and inevitably to the fact that his master was terribly displeased. When they had brought the orc whelp home Blackmoore had been much as he was on the battlefield: alert, interested, focused.

The orcs were proving less and less of a challenge each day, and men used to the excitement of almost daily battles were growing bored. The planned bouts were proving extremely popular, giving men an outlet for their pent-up energies and providing a chance for a little money to change hands as well.

And this orc was going to be raised firmly under human control. With the speed and power of the orcs, but the knowledge that Blackmoore would impart, he would be all but unconquerable in the planned matches that were beginning to spring up.

Except the ugly little thing wouldn't eat, and had grown pale and quiet over the last several days. Nobody said the words, but everyone knew. The beast was dying.

That had enraged Blackmoore. Once, he had even seized the small monster and tried to shove finely chopped meat down its throat. He succeeded only in nearly choking the orc, whom he had named "Thrall," and when Thrall had spat up the meat he had literally dropped the orc on the straw and strode, cursing, from the stable in which the orc was temporarily housed.

Now Tammis walked around his master with the utmost discretion, choosing his words even more carefully than usual. And yet, more often than not, he had left an encounter with Lieutenant Blackmoore with a bottle—sometimes empty, sometimes not—flying behind him.

His wife Clannia, a fair-haired, apple-cheeked woman who served in the kitchens, now set a plate of cold food in front of him on the wooden table and rubbed his tight neck as he sat down to eat. Compared to Blackmoore, the beefy, loud cook who ran the kitchens was a veritable Paladin.

"Any word?" Clannia asked hopefully. She awkwardly sat down beside him at the rough wooden table. She had given birth a few weeks ago and still moved with hesitation. She and their eldest daughter, Taretha, had eaten many hours ago. Unseen by either parent, the girl, who slept with her baby brother in a small bed beside the hearth, had woken at her father's entrance. Now she sat up, her yellow curls covered by a sleeping cap, and watched and listened to the adult conversation.

"Aye, and all bad," said Tammis heavily as he spooned congealing potato soup into his mouth. He chewed, swallowed, and continued. "The orc is dying. It won't take anything Blackmoore tries to feed it."

Clannia sighed and reached for her mending. The needle flashed back and forth, stitching together a new dress for Taretha. "It's only right," she said softly. "Blackmoore had no business bringing something like that into Durnholde. Bad enough we've got the mature ones screaming all day long. I can't wait until the internment camps are finished and they're no longer Durnholde's problem." She shuddered.

Taretha watched, silent. Her eyes were wide. She had heard vague mutterings about a baby orc, but this was the first chance she had had to hear her parents discussing it. Her young mind raced. Orcs were so big and scary-looking, with their sharp teeth, green skin, and deep voices. She'd only caught the barest glimpses of them, but she had heard all the stories. But a baby wouldn't be big and scary. She glanced over at the small figure of her brother. Even as she watched, Faralyn stirred, opened his rosebud mouth, and announced that he was hungry with a shrill cry.

In a smooth motion, Clannia rose, put down her sewing, picked up her son, bared a breast, and set him to nursing. "Taretha!" she scolded. "You should be asleep."

"I was," Taretha said, rising and running to her father. "I heard Da come in."

Tammis smiled tiredly and permitted Taretha to climb in his lap. "She won't go back to sleep until Faralyn is done," he told Clannia. "Let me hold her for a while. I so seldom get to see her, and she's growing like a weed." He pinched her cheek gently and she giggled.

"If the orc dies, it will go badly with all of us here," he continued.

Taretha frowned. The answer was obvious. "Da," she said, "if it's a baby, why are you trying to make it eat meat?"

Both adults stared at her, stunned. "What do you mean, little one?" asked Tammis in a strained voice.

Taretha pointed to her nursing brother. "Babies drink milk, like Faralyn does. If this baby orc's mother is dead, it can't drink its milk."

Tammis continued to stare; then a slow smile spread across his weary face. "Out of the mouths of babes," he whispered, and then hugged his daughter to him so tightly that she began to squirm in protest.

"Tammis. . . ." Clannia's voice was taut.

"My dearest," he said. He held Taretha with one arm and reached across the table to his wife with the other. "Tari's right. For all their barbaric ways, the orcs do nurse their young, as we do. Our best guess is that the orc infant is but a few months old. It's no wonder it can't yet eat meat. It doesn't even have any teeth yet." He hesitated, but Clannia's face grew pale, as if she knew what he was going to say.

"You can't mean . . . you can't ask me to. . . ."

"Think what it will mean to our family!" Tammis exclaimed. "I've served Blackmoore for ten years. I've never seen him this excited about anything. If that orc survives because of us, we will lack for nothing!"

"I . . . I *can't*," stammered Clannia.

"Can't what?" asked Taretha, but they both ignored her.

"Please," begged Tammis. "It's only for a little while."

"They're monsters, Tam!" cried Clannia. "Monsters, and you . . . you want me to. . . ." She covered her face with one hand and began to sob. The baby continued to nurse, unperturbed.

"Da, why is Ma crying?" asked Taretha, anxious.

"I'm not crying," said Clannia thickly. She wiped her wet face and forced a smile. "See, darling? All is well." She looked at Tammis, and swallowed hard. "Your Da just has something he needs me to do, that's all."

When Blackmoore heard that his personal servant's wife had agreed to wet-nurse the dying orc baby, the Foxton family was deluged with gifts. Rich fabrics, the freshest fruits and choicest meats, fine beeswax tapers—all began to appear regularly at the door of the small room that the family called their home. Soon, that room was exchanged for another, and then for larger quarters still. Tammis Foxton was given his own horse, a lovely bay he named Ladyfire. Clannia, now called Mistress Foxton, no longer had to report to the kitchens, but spent all her time with her children and tending to the needs of what Blackmoore called his "special project." Taretha wore fine clothes and even had a tutor, a fussy, kind man named Jaramin Skisson, sent to teach her to read and write, like a lady.

But she was never allowed to speak about the small creature that lived with them for the next full year, who, when Faralyn died of a fever, became the only baby in the Foxton household. And when Thrall had learned to eat a vile concoction of blood, cow's milk, and porridge with his own small hands, three armed guards came and wrested him away from Taretha's arms. She cried and protested, and received a harsh blow for her pleas.

Her father held her and shushed her, kissing her pale cheek where a red hand imprint was visible. She quieted after a while, and, like the obedient child she wished to appear, agreed never to speak of Thrall again except in the most casual of terms.

But she vowed she would never forget this strange creature that had been almost like a younger brother to her.

Never.

"No, no. Like this." Jaramin Skisson stepped beside his pupil. "Hold it thus, with your fingers here . . . and here. Ah, that's better. Now make this motion . . . like a snake."

"What is a snake?" asked Thrall. He was only six years old, but already almost as big as his tutor. His large, clumsy hands did not hold the delicate, thin stylus easily, and the clay tablet kept slipping out of his grasp. But he was stubborn, and determined to master this letter that Jaramin called an "S."

Jaramin blinked behind his large spectacles. "Oh, of course," he said, more to himself than Thrall. "A snake is a reptile with no feet. It looks like this letter."

Thrall brightened with recognition. "Like a worm," he said. He had often snacked on those small treats that found their way into his cell.

"Yes, it does resemble a worm. Try it again, on your own this time." Thrall stuck his tongue out to aid his concentration. A shaky form appeared on the clay, but he knew it was recognizable as an "S." Proud of himself, he extended it to Jaramin.

"Very good, Thrall! I think it may be time we started teaching you numbers," said the tutor.

"But first, it's time to start learning how to fight, eh, Thrall?" Thrall looked up to see the lean form of his master, Lieutenant Blackmoore, standing in the doorway. He stepped inside. Thrall heard the lock click shut on the other side of the door. He had never tried to flee, but the guards always seemed to expect him to.

At once Thrall prostrated himself as Blackmoore had taught him. A kindly pat on his head told him he had permission to rise. He stumbled to his feet, suddenly feeling even bigger and clumsier than usual. He looked down at Blackmoore's boots, awaiting whatever it was his master had in store for him.

"How is he coming in his lessons?" Blackmoore asked Jaramin, as if Thrall weren't present.

"Very well. I hadn't realized orcs were quite so intelligent, but—"

"He is intelligent not because he is an orc," Blackmoore interrupted, his voice sharp enough to make Thrall flinch. "He is intelligent because humans taught him. Never forget that, Jaramin. And you." The boots turned in Thrall's direction. "You aren't to forget that either."

Thrall shook his head violently.

"Look at me, Thrall."

Thrall hesitated, then lifted his blue-eyed gaze. Blackmoore's eyes bored into his own. "Do you know what your name means?"

"No, sir." His voice sounded so rough and deep, even in his own ears, next to the musical lilt of the humans' voices.

"It means 'slave.' It means that you belong to me." Blackmoore stepped forward and prodded the orc's chest with a stiff forefinger. "It means that I own you. Do you understand that?"

For a moment, Thrall was so shocked he didn't reply. His name meant slave? It sounded so pleasant when humans spoke it, he thought it must be a good name, a worthy name.

Blackmoore's gloved hand came up and slapped Thrall across the face. Although the lieutenant had swung his hand with vigor, Thrall's skin was so thick and tough that the orc barely felt it. And yet the blow pained him deeply. His master had struck him! One large hand came up to touch the cheek, its black fingernails clipped short.

"You answer when you're spoken to," snapped Blackmoore. "Do you understand what I just said?"

"Yes, Master Blackmoore," replied Thrall, his deep voice barely a whisper.

"Excellent." Blackmoore's angry face relaxed into an approving smile. His teeth showed white against the surrounding black hair of his goatee. That quickly, all was well again. Relief surged through Thrall. His lips turned up in his best approximation of Blackmoore's smile.

"Don't do that, Thrall," said Blackmoore. "It makes you look uglier than you already are."

Abruptly, the smile vanished.

"Lieutenant," said Jaramin softly, "he's just trying to mimic your smile, that's all."

"Well, he shouldn't. Humans smile. Orcs don't. You said he was doing well in his lessons, yes? Can he read and write, then?"

"He is reading at quite an advanced level. As for writing, he understands how, but those thick fingers are having a difficult time with some of the lettering."

"Excellent," Blackmoore said again. "Then we have no more need of your services."

Thrall inhaled swiftly and looked over at Jaramin. The older man appeared to be as surprised as he by the statement.

"There's much he doesn't know yet, sir," stammered Jaramin. "He knows little of numbers, of history, of art—"

"He doesn't need to master history, and I can teach him what he needs to know about numbers myself. And what does a slave need to know of art, hmm? I fancy you think that would be a waste of time, eh, Thrall?"

Thrall thought briefly of the one time Jaramin had brought in a small statue and told him how it was carved, of how they had discussed how his swaddling cloth with its once-bright colors of blue and white had been woven. That, Jaramin had said, was "art," and Thrall had been eager to learn more about making such beautiful things.

"As my master wishes, so does Thrall," he said obediently, giving the lie to the feelings in his heart.

"That's right. You don't need to know those things, Thrall. You need to learn how to fight." With uncharacteristic affection, Blackmoore reached out a hand and placed it on Thrall's enormous shoulder. Thrall flinched, then stared at his master.

"I wanted you to learn reading and writing because it might one day give you an advantage over your opponent. I'm going to see to it that you are skilled with every weapon I have ever seen. I'm going to teach you about strategy, Thrall, and trickery. You are going to be famous in the gladiator ring. Thousands will chant your name when you appear. How does that sound, eh?"

Thrall saw Jaramin turn and gather up his things. It pained him strangely to see the stylus and the clay tablet disappear for the last time into Jaramin's sack. With a quick, backward glance, Jaramin moved to the door and knocked on it. It opened for him. He slipped out, and the door was closed and locked.

Blackmoore was waiting for Thrall's response. Thrall was a fast learner, and did not wish to be struck again for hesitating in his answer. Forcing himself to sound as if he believed it, he told his master, "That sounds exciting. I am glad my master wishes me to follow this path."

For the first time he could remember, Thrall the orc stepped out of his cell. He gazed in wonder as, with two guards in front of him, two guards behind, and Blackmoore keeping pace, he went through several winding stone corridors. They went up a set of stairs, then across, then down a winding stair that was so small it seemed to press in on Thrall.

Ahead was a brightness that made Thrall blink. They were approaching that brightness, and the fear of the unknown set in. When the guards ahead of him went through and into this area, Thrall froze. The ground ahead was yellow and brown, not the familiar gray of stone. Black things that resembled the guards lay on the ground, following their every movement.

"What are you doing?" snapped Blackmoore. "Come out. Others held here would give their right arms to be able to walk out into the sunlight."

Thrall knew the word. "Sunlight" was what came through in small slats in his cell. But there was so much sunlight out there! And what of the strange black things? What were they?

Thrall pointed at the black human-shaped things on the ground. To his shame, all the guards started laughing. One of them was soon wiping tears of mirth from his face. Blackmoore turned red.

"You idiot," he said, "those are just— By the Light, have I gotten myself an orc who's afraid of his own shadow?" He gestured and one of the guards pricked Thrall's back deeply with the point of a spear. Although his naturally thick skin protected him, the prod stung and Thrall lurched forward.

His eyes burned, and he lifted his hands to cover them. And yet the sudden warmth of the . . . sunlight . . . on his head and back felt good. Slowly he lowered his hands and blinked, letting his eyes become accustomed to the light.

Something huge and green loomed in front of him.

Instinctively, he drew himself up to his full height and roared at it. More laughter from the guards, but this time, Blackmoore nodded in approval at Thrall's reaction.

"That's a mock fighter," he said. "It's only made of burlap and stuffing and paint, Thrall. It's a troll."

Again embarrassment flamed through Thrall. Now that he looked more closely, he could tell it was no living thing. Straw served the mock fighter for hair, and he could see where it was stitched together.

"Does a troll really look like that?" he asked.

Blackmoore chuckled. "Only vaguely," said Blackmoore. "It wasn't designed for realism, but for practice. Watch."

He extended a gloved arm and one of the guards handed him something. "This is a wooden sword," Blackmoore explained. "A sword is a weapon, and we use wood for practice. Once you're sufficiently trained with this, you'll move on to the real thing."

Blackmoore held the sword in both hands. He centered himself, then raced at the practice troll. He managed to strike it three times, once in the head, once in the body, and once along the false arm that held a cloth weapon, without breaking stride. Breathing only slightly heavily, he turned around and trotted back. "Now you try," he said.

Thrall held out his hand for the weapon. His thick fingers closed around it. It fit his palm much better than the stylus had. It felt better, too, almost familiar. He adjusted the grip, trying to do what he had seen Blackmoore do.

"Very good," said Blackmoore. To one of the guards, he said, "Look at that, will you? He's a natural. As I knew he would be. Now, Thrall . . . attack!"

Thrall whirled. For the first time in his life, his body seemed willing to do what he asked of it. He lifted the sword, and to his surprise, a roar burst forth from his throat. His legs began to pump almost of their own accord, smoothly and swiftly carrying him toward the mock troll. He lifted the sword—oh, it was so easy—and brought it down in a smooth arc across the troll's body.

There was a terrible crack and the troll went sailing through the air. Suddenly afraid he had done something terribly wrong, Thrall's grace turned to clumsiness and he stumbled over his own feet. He hit the earth hard and felt the wooden sword crack underneath him.

Thrall scrambled to his feet and prostrated himself, sure that some sort of terrible punishment was about to ensue. He had broken the mock troll and destroyed the practice sword. He was so big, so clumsy . . . !

Loud whoops filled the air. Other than Jaramin, the silent guards, and the occasional visit from Blackmoore, Thrall had not had much interaction with humans. Certainly he had not learned to discern the finer points in their wordless noises, but he had a strange suspicion that these were not sounds of anger. Cautiously he looked up.

Blackmoore had an enormous smile on his face, as did the guards. One of them was bringing the palms of his hands together to create a loud smacking sound. When he caught sight of Thrall, Blackmoore's smile widened even more.

"Did I not say he would surpass all expectations?" cried Blackmoore. "Well done, Thrall! Well done!"

Thrall blinked, uncertain. "I . . . that wasn't wrong?" he asked. "The troll and the sword . . . I broke them."

"Damn right you did! First time ever swinging a sword and the troll sails across the courtyard!" Blackmoore's giddiness subsided slightly and he put his arm around the young orc in a friendly manner. Thrall tensed, then relaxed.

"Suppose you were in the gladiator ring," Blackmoore said. "Suppose that troll was real, that your sword was real. And suppose the first time you charged, you struck him so hard that he fell that far. Don't you see that that's a good thing, Thrall?"

The orc supposed he did. His large lips wanted to stretch over his teeth in a smile, but he resisted the impulse. Blackmoore had never been so pleased with him, so kind to him, before, and he wished to do nothing to disturb the moment.

Blackmoore squeezed Thrall's shoulder, then returned to his men. "You!" he shouted to a guard. "Get that troll back on the pike, and make sure it's secure enough to withstand my Thrall's mighty blows. You, get me another practice sword. Hells, get me five of them. Thrall is liable to break them all!"

Out of the corner of his eye, Thrall saw movement. He turned to see a tall, slender man with curly hair dressed in livery red, black, and gold that marked him as one of Blackmoore's servants. With him was a very small human being with bright yellow hair. It looked nothing like the guards that

Thrall knew. He wondered if this was a human child. It looked softer, and its garments were not the trousers and tunics the other wore, but a long, flowing garment that brushed the dusty earth. Was this, then, a female child?

His eyes locked with the blue ones of the child. She did not seem frightened of his ugly appearance at all. On the contrary, she met his gaze evenly, and as he watched, she smiled brightly and waved at him, as if she was happy to see him.

How could such a thing be? Even as Thrall watched, trying to determine the proper response, the male accompanying her clamped a hand to the little female's shoulder and steered her away.

Wondering what had just happened, Thrall turned back to the cheering men, and closed his large, green hand about another practice sword.

THREE

A routine was quickly established, one that Thrall would follow for the next several years. He would be fed at dawn, his hands and feet clapped in manacles that permitted him to shuffle out to the courtyard of Durnholde. At first, Blackmoore himself conducted the training, showing him the basic mechanics and often praising him effusively. Sometimes, though, Blackmoore's temper was sharp and nothing Thrall could do would please him. At such times, the nobleman's speech was slightly slurred, his movements haphazard, and he would berate the orc for no reason that Thrall could discern. Thrall came to simply accept the fact that he was unworthy. If Blackmoore berated him, it must be because he deserved it; any praise was simply the lord's own kindness.

After a few months, though, another man stepped in and Thrall ceased to see Blackmoore regularly. This man, known to Thrall only as Sergeant, was huge by human standards. He stood well over six feet, with a thick barrel chest covered with curly red hair. The hair on his head was bright red, its tousled mop matched by the long beard. He wore a black scarf knotted around his throat and in one ear sported a large earring. The first day he came to address Thrall and the other fighters who were being trained alongside him, he had fixed each one with a hard stare and shouted out the challenge.

"See this?" He pointed with a stubby forefinger to the glistening hoop in his left ear. "I haven't taken this out in thirteen years. I've trained thousands of recruits just like you pups. And with each group I offer the same challenge: Rip this earring from my ear and I'll let you beat me to a pulp." He grinned, showing several missing teeth. "You don't think it now, p'raps, but by the time I'm done with you, you'd sell your own mother for the chance to take a swing at me. But if I'm ever so slow that I can't fend off an attack by any of you ladies, then I deserve to have my ear ripped off and be forced to swallow what's left of my teeth."

He had been walking slowly down the line of men and now stopped abruptly in front of Thrall. "That goes double for you, you overgrown goblin," Sergeant snarled.

Thrall lowered his gaze, confused. He had been taught never, ever, to raise his hand against humans. And yet it appeared as though he was to fight them. There was no way he would ever try to rip Sergeant's earring from his lobe.

A large hand slipped underneath Thrall's chin and jerked it up. "You look at me when I talk to you, you understand?"

Thrall nodded, now hopelessly confused. Blackmoore didn't want him to meet his gaze. This man had just ordered him to do exactly that. What was he to do?

Sergeant divided them into pairs. The number was uneven and Thrall stood alone. Sergeant marched right up to him and tossed a wooden sword to him. Instinctively, Thrall caught it. Sergeant grunted in approval.

"Good eye-hand coordination," he said. Like all the other men, he carried a shield and was wearing heavy, well-cushioned armor that would protect his body and head. Thrall had none. His skin was so thick that he barely felt the blows as it was, and he was growing so quickly that any clothing or armor fashioned for him would soon be far too small.

"Let's see how you defend yourself, then!" And with no further warning, Sergeant charged Thrall.

For the briefest second, Thrall shrank from the attack. Then something inside him seemed to click into place. He no longer moved from a place of fear and confusion, but a place of confidence. He stood up straight, to his full height, and realized that he was growing so quickly that he was taller even than his opponent. He lifted his left arm, which he knew would one day hold a shield heavier than a human, in defense against the wooden sword, and brought his own practice weapon down in a smooth arc. If Sergeant had not reacted with stunning speed, Thrall's sword would have slammed into his helm. And even with that protection, Thrall knew that the power behind his blow was such that Sergeant probably would have been killed.

But Sergeant was swift, and his shield blocked Thrall's likely fatal blow. Thrall grunted in surprise as Sergeant landed a blow of his own against Thrall's bare midsection. He stumbled, thrown briefly off balance.

Sergeant took the opening and pressed, landing three swift blows that would have killed an unarmored man. Thrall regained his footing and felt a strange, hot emotion surge through him. Suddenly, his world narrowed to the figure before him. All his frustration and helplessness fled, replaced by a deadly focus: *Kill Sergeant.*

He screamed aloud, the power of his own voice startling even him, then charged. He lifted his weapon and struck, lifted and struck, raining blows upon the big man. Sergeant tried to retreat and his booted feet slipped on a stone. He fell backward. Thrall cried out again, as a keen desire to smash Sergeant's head to a pulp swept through him like a white-hot tide. Sergeant managed to get the sword in front of him and deflected most of the blows, but now Thrall had him pinned between his powerful legs. He tossed aside his sword and reached out with his large hands. If he could just fasten them around Blackmoore's neck—

Appalled at the image that swam before his eyes, Thrall froze, his fingers inches away from Sergeant's throat. It was protected with a gorget, of course, but Thrall's fingers were powerful. If he had managed to clamp down—

And then several men were on him all at once, shouting at him and hauling him off the prone figure of the fighting instructor. Now it was Thrall who was on his back, his mighty arms lifted to ward off the blows of several swords. He heard a strange sound, a *clang,* and then saw something metallic catch the bright sunlight.

"Hold!" screamed Sergeant, his voice as loud and commanding as if he had not just been inches away from death. "Damn you, hold or I'll cut your bloody arm off! Sheathe your sword this minute, Maridan!"

Thrall heard a *snick.* Then two strong arms seized his and he was hauled to his feet. He stared at Sergeant.

To his utter surprise, Sergeant laughed out loud and clapped a hand on the orc's shoulder. "Good job, lad. That's the closest I've ever come to having me earring snatched—and in the first match at that. You're a born warrior, but you forgot the goal, didn't you?" He pointed to the gold hoop. "This was the goal, not squeezing the life out of me."

Thrall struggled to speak. "I am sorry, Sergeant. I don't know what happened. You attacked, and then. . . ." He was not about to tell of the brief image of Blackmoore he had had. It was bad enough that he had lost his head.

"Some foes, you're going to want to do what you just did," said Sergeant, surprising him. "Good tactics there. But some opponents, like all the humans you'll face, you're going to want to get 'em down and then end it. Stop there. The bloodlust might save your hide in a real battle, but for gladiator fighting, you'll need to be more here—" he tapped the side of his head "—than here," and he patted his gut. "I want you to read some books on strategy. You read, don't you?"

"A little," Thrall managed.

"You need to learn the history of battle campaigns. These pups all know it," and he waved at the other young soldiers. "For a time, that will be their advantage." He turned to glare at them. "But only for a time, lads. This one's got courage and strength, and he's but a babe yet."

The men shot Thrall hostile glances. Thrall felt a sudden warmth, a happiness he had never known. He had nearly killed this man, but had not been reprimanded. Instead, he had been told he needed to learn, to improve, to know when to go for the kill and when to show . . . what? What did one call it when one spared an opponent?

"Sergeant," he asked, wondering if he would be punished for even voicing the question, "sometimes . . . you said sometimes you don't kill. Why not?"

Sergeant regarded him evenly. "It's called mercy, Thrall," he said quietly. "And you'll learn about that, too."

Mercy. Under his breath, Thrall turned the word over on his tongue. It was a sweet word.

"You let him do that to you?" Though Tammis was not supposed to be privy to this particular conversation between his master and the man he had hired to train Thrall, Blackmoore's shrill voice carried. Pausing in his duty of cleaning the mud off of Blackmoore's boots, Tammis strained to listen. He did not think of this as eavesdropping. He thought of this as a vital way to protect his family's welfare.

"It was a good martial move." Sergeant Something-or-other replied, sounding not at all defensive. "I treated it the way I would had it been any other man."

"But Thrall isn't a man, he's an orc! Or hadn't you noticed?"

"Aye, I had," said Sergeant. Tammis maneuvered himself so that he could peer through the half-closed door. Sergeant looked out of place in Blackmoore's richly decorated receiving room. "And it's not my place to ask why you want 'im trained so thorough."

"You're right about that."

"But you *do* want 'im trained thorough," said Sergeant. "And that's exactly what I'm doing."

"By letting him nearly kill you?"

"By praising a good move, and teaching 'im when it's good to use the bloodlust and when it's good to keep a cool head!" growled Sergeant. Tammis smothered a smile. Evidently, it was becoming difficult for Sergeant to keep his. "But that's not the reason I've come. I understand you taught 'im to read. I want 'im to have a look at some books."

Tammis gaped.

"What?" cried Blackmoore.

Tammis had utterly forgotten the chore he was ostensibly performing. He stared through the crack in the door, a brush in one hand and a muddy boot in the other, listening intently. When there was a light tap at his shoulder, he nearly jumped out of his skin.

Heart thudding, he whirled to behold Taretha. She grinned impishly at him, her blue eyes flicking from those of her father to the door. Clearly, she knew exactly what he was doing.

Tammis was embarrassed. But that emotion was overridden by a passionate desire to know what was about to happen. He raised a finger to his lips and Taretha nodded wisely.

"Now, why did you go and teach an orc to read if you didn't want him doing so?"

Blackmoore spluttered something incoherent.

" 'E's got a brain, whatever else you may think of him, and if you wants 'im trained the way you told me, you've got to get him understanding battle tactics, maps, strategies, siege techniques—"

Sergeant was calmly ticking things off on his fingers. "All right!" Blackmoore exploded. "Though I imagine I'll live to regret this. . . ." He strode toward the wall of books and quickly selected a few. "Taretha!" he bellowed.

Both older and younger Foxton servants jumped. Quickly Taretha smoothed her hair, put on a pleasant expression, and entered the room.

She dropped a curtsy. "Yes, sir?"

"Here." Blackmoore thrust the books at her. They were large and cumbersome and filled her arms. She peered at him over the edge of the top book, only her eyes visible. "I want you to give these to Thrall's guard to give him."

"Yes, sir," Taretha replied, as if this were something she was asked to do every day and not one of the most shocking things Tammis had heard his master order. "They're a bit heavy, sir . . . may I go to my quarters for a sack? It will make the carrying easier."

She looked every inch the obedient little servant girl. Only Tammis and Clannia knew how sharp a brain—and tongue—were hidden behind that deceptively sweet visage. Blackmoore softened slightly and patted her fair head.

"Of course, child. But take them straight over, understood?"

"Indeed, sir. Thank you, sir." She seemed to try to curtsy, thought better of it, and left.

Tammis closed the door behind her. Taretha turned to him, her large eyes shining. "Oh, Da!" she breathed, her voice soft so it would not carry. "I'm going to get to see him!"

Tammis's heart sank. He had hoped she was over this disturbing interest in the orc's welfare. "No, Taretha. You're just to hand the books to the guards, is all."

Her face fell, and she turned away sadly. "It's just . . . since Faralyn died . . . he's the only little brother I have."

"He's not your brother, he's an orc. An animal, fit only for camps or gladiator battles. Remember that." Tammis hated disappointing his daughter in anything, but it was for the child's own good. She mustn't be noticed having an interest in Thrall. Only ill would come from that if Blackmoore ever found out.

Thrall was sound asleep, worn out from the excitement of the day's practice, when the door to his cell slammed open. He blinked sleepily, then got to his feet as one of the guards entered carrying a large sack.

"Lieutenant says these are for you. He wants you to finish them all and be able to talk with him about them," said the guard. There was a hint of contempt in his voice, but Thrall thought nothing of it. The guards always spoke to him with contempt.

The door was pulled closed and locked. Thrall looked at the sack. With a delicacy that belied his huge frame, he untied the knot and reached inside. His fingers closed on something rectangular and firm, but that gave slightly.

It couldn't be. He remembered the feel. . . .

Hardly daring to hope, he pulled it forth into the dim light of his cell and stared at it. It was, indeed, a book. He read the title, sounding it aloud: *"The History of the Alliance of Lor-lordaeron."* Eagerly he grabbed a second book, and a third. They were all military history books. As he flipped one open, something fluttered to the straw-covered floor of his cell. It was a small, tightly folded piece of parchment.

Curious, he unfolded it, taking his time with his large fingers. It was a note. His lips worked, but he did not speak aloud:

Dear Thrall,

Master B. has ordered that you have these books I am so excited for you. I did not know he had let you learn how to read. He let me learn how to read too and I love reading. I miss you and hope you are well. It looks like what they are making you do in the courtyard hurts I hope you are all right. I would like to keep talking with you do you want to? If yes, write me a note

on the back of this paper and fold it back up in the book I put it in. I will try
to come and see you if not keep looking for me Im the little girl who waved at
you that one time. I hope you write back!!!!!

Love Taretha

P.S. Dont tell anyone about the note we will get in BIG TROUBLE!!!

Thrall sat down heavily. He could not believe what he had just read. He remembered the small female child, and had wondered why she had waved at him. Clearly, she knew him and . . . and thought *well* of him. How could this be? Who was she?

He extended a forefinger and gazed at the blunted, clipped nail. It would have to do. On his left arm, a scratch was healing. Thrall jabbed as deeply as he could and after several tries managed to tear the small wound open again. A sluggish trickle of crimson rewarded his efforts. Using his nail as a stylus, he carefully wrote on the back of the note a single word:

YES.

FOUR

Thrall was twelve years old when he saw his first orc. He was training outside the fortress grounds. Once he had won his first battle at the tender age of eight, Blackmoore had agreed with Sergeant's plan to give the orc more freedom—at least in training. He still had a manacle fastened to one of his feet, which was in turn carefully attached to a huge boulder. Not even an orc of Thrall's strength would be able to flee with that attached to his leg. The chains were thick and sturdy, unlikely to break. After the first time or two, Thrall paid it no heed. The chain was long and gave him plenty of room to maneuver. The thought of escaping had never occurred to him. He was Thrall, the slave. Blackmoore was his master, Sergeant his trainer, Taretha his secret friend. All was as it should be.

Thrall regretted that he had never made friends with any of the men with whom he practiced. Each year there was a new group, and they were all cut of the same cloth: young, eager, contemptuous, and slightly frightened of the mammoth green being with whom they were expected to train. Only Sergeant ever gave him a compliment; only Sergeant interfered when one or more would gang up on Thrall. At times Thrall wished he could fight back, but he remembered the concept of honorable fighting. Although these men thought of him as the enemy, he knew they weren't, and killing or grievously wounding them was the wrong thing to do.

Thrall had sharp ears and always paid attention to the idle gossip of the men. Because they thought him a mindless brute, they were not too careful of their tongues in his presence. Who minds their words when the only witness is an animal? It was in this way that Thrall learned that the orcs, once a fearful enemy, were weakening. More and more of them were being caught and rounded up into something called "internment camps." Durnholde was the base, and all those in charge of these camps lodged here now, while underlings conducted the day-to-day running of the camps. Blackmoore was the head of all of them. There were a few skirmishes still, but less and less frequently. Some of the men present at the training had never seen an orc fighting before they encountered Thrall.

Over the years, Sergeant had taught Thrall the finer points of hand-to-hand combat. Thrall was versed in every weapon used in the fights: sword, broadsword, spear, morningstar, dagger, scourge, net, ax, club, and halberd. He had been granted the barest of armor; it was deemed more exciting for the watching crowds if the combatants had little protection.

Now he stood at the center of a group of trainees. This was familiar territory to him, and was more for the benefit of the young men than for him. Sergeant called this scenario "ringing." The trainees were (of course) humans who had supposedly come upon one of the few remaining renegade orcs, who was determined not to go down without a fight. Thrall was (of course) the defiant orc. The idea was for them to devise at least three different ways of capturing or killing the "rogue orc."

Thrall was not particularly fond of this scenario. He much preferred one-on-one fighting to being the target of sometimes as many as twelve men. The light in the men's eyes at the thought of fighting him, and the smiles on their lips, always dismayed Thrall. The first time Sergeant had enacted the scenario, Thrall had had difficulty in summoning up the necessary resistance required in order to make this an effective teaching tool. Sergeant had to take him aside and assure him it was all right to pretend. The men had armor and real weapons; he had only a wooden practice sword. It was unlikely Thrall would cause any lasting harm.

So now, after having performed this routine several times over the last few years, Thrall immediately became a snarling, ravening beast. The first few times, it had been difficult to separate fantasy from reality, but it became easier with practice. He would never lose control in this scenario, and if things did turn bad, he trusted Sergeant with his life.

Now they advanced on him. Predictably, they chose simple assault as their first of three tactics. Two had swords, four had spears, and the rest had axes. One of them lunged.

Thrall swiftly parried, his wooden sword flying up with startling speed. He lifted a massive leg and kicked out, striking the attacker full in the chest. The young man went hurtling backward, astonishment plain on his face. He lay on the ground, gasping for air.

Thrall whirled, anticipating the approach of two others. They came at him with spears. With the sword, he knocked one of them out of the way as easily as if the human had been an annoying insect. With his free hand, for he had no shield, he seized the other man's spear, yanked it from his grip, and flipped it around so that the sharp blade was facing the man who had, just seconds ago, been wielding the weapon.

Had this been a real battle, Thrall knew he would have sunk the spear into the man's body. But this was just practice, and Thrall was in control. He lifted the spear and was about to toss it away when a terrible sound made everyone freeze in his tracks.

Thrall turned to see a small wagon approaching the fortress on the small, winding road. This happened many times each day, and the passengers were always the same: farmers, merchants, new recruits, visiting dignitaries of some sort.

Not this time.

This time, the screaming horses pulled a wagon full of monstrous green creatures. They were in a metal cage, and seemed stooped over. Thrall saw that they were chained to the bottom of the wagon. He was filled with horror at their grotesqueness. They were huge, deformed, sported mammoth tusks instead of teeth, had tiny, fierce eyes. . . .

And then the truth hit him. These were orcs. His so-called people. This was what he looked like to the humans. The practice sword fell from suddenly nerveless fingers. *I'm hideous. I'm frightening. I'm a monster. No wonder they hate me so.*

One of the beasts turned and stared Thrall right in the eye. He wanted to look away, but couldn't. He stared back, hardly breathing. Even as he watched, the orc somehow managed to wrench himself free. With a scream that shattered Thrall's ears, the creature hurled himself at the cage bars. He reached with hands bloody from the chafing of shackles, gripped the bars, and before Thrall's shocked eyes bent them wide enough to push his huge bulk through. The wagon was still moving as the frightened horses ran at top speed. The orc hit the ground hard and rolled a few times, but a heartbeat later was up and running toward Thrall and the fighters with a speed that belied his size.

He opened his terrible mouth and screamed out something that sounded like words: "Kagh! Bin mog g'thazag cha!"

"Attack, you fools!" cried Sergeant. Unarmored as he was, he seized a sword and began running to meet the orc. The men began to move and rushed to their Sergeant's aid.

The orc didn't even bother to look Sergeant in the face. He swung out with his manacled left hand, caught Sergeant square in the chest, and sent him flying. He came on, implacable. His eyes were fastened on Thrall, and again he shouted the words, "Kagh! Bin mog g'thazag cha!"

Thrall stirred, finally roused from his fear, but he didn't know what to do. He raised his practice sword and stood in a defensive posture, but did not advance. This fearfully ugly thing was charging toward him. It was most definitely the enemy. And yet, it was one of his own people, his flesh and blood. An orc, just as Thrall was an orc, and Thrall could not bring himself to attack.

Even as Thrall stared, the men fell upon the orc and the big green body went down beneath the flash of swords and axes and black armor. Blood seeped out beneath the pile of men, and when at last it was over, they stood back and regarded a pile of green and red flesh where a living creature had once been.

Sergeant propped himself up on one elbow. "Thrall!" he cried. "Get him back to the cell *now!*"

"What in the name of all that's holy have you *done?*" cried Blackmoore, staring aghast at the sergeant who had come to him so highly recommended, who was now the person Blackmoore had come to hate more than any other. "He was never supposed to see another orc, not until . . . now he knows, damn it. What were you thinking?"

Sergeant bristled under the verbal attack. "I was *thinking,* sir, that if you didn't want Thrall to see any other orcs, you might have told me that. I was *thinking,* sir, that if you didn't want Thrall to see other orcs you might have arranged for the wagons carrying them to approach when Thrall was in his cell. I was *thinking, sir,* that—"

"Enough!" bellowed Blackmoore. He took a deep breath and collected himself. "The damage is done. We must think how to repair it."

His calmer tone seemed to ease Sergeant as well. In a less belligerent tone, the trainer asked, "Thrall has never known what he looked like, then?"

"Never. No mirrors. No still basins of water. He's been taught that orcs are scum, which is of course true, and that he is permitted to live only because he earns me money."

Silence fell as the two men searched their thoughts. Sergeant scratched his red beard pensively, then said, "So he knows. So what? Just because he was born an orc doesn't mean he can't be more than that. He doesn't have to be a brainless brute. He isn't, in fact. If you encouraged him to think of himself as more human—"

Sergeant's suggestion infuriated Blackmoore. "He's not!" he burst out. "He *is* a brute. I don't want him getting ideas that he's nothing less than a big green-skinned human!"

"Then, pray, sir," said Sergeant, grinding out the words between clenched teeth, "what *do* you want him to think of himself as?"

Blackmoore had no response. He didn't know. He hadn't thought about it that way. It had seemed so simple when he had stumbled onto the infant orc. Raise him as a slave, train him to fight, give him the human edge, then put him in charge of an army of beaten orcs and attack the Alliance. With Thrall at the head of a revitalized orcish army, leading the charges, Blackmoore would have power beyond his most exaggerated fantasies.

But it wasn't working out that way. Deep inside, he knew that in some ways Sergeant was right. Thrall did need to understand how humans thought and reasoned if he was to take that knowledge to lord over the bestial orcs. And yet, if he learned, mightn't he revolt? Thrall had to be kept in his place, reminded of his low birth. *Had* to. By the Light, what was the right thing to do? How best to treat this creature in order to produce the perfect war leader, without letting anyone else know he was more than a gladiator champion?

He took a deep breath. He mustn't lose face in front of this servant. "Thrall needs direction, and we must give it to him," he said with remarkable calmness. "He's learned enough training with the recruits. I think it's time we relegated him exclusively to combat."

"Sir, he's very helpful in training," began Sergeant.

"We have all but vanquished the orcs," said Blackmoore, thinking of the thousands of orcs being shoved into the camps. "Their leader Doomhammer has fled, and they are a scattered race. Peace is descending upon us. We do not need to train the recruits to battle orcs any longer. Any battles in which they will participate will be against other men, not monsters."

Damn. He had almost said too much. Sergeant looked as if he had caught the slip, too, but did not react.

"Men at peace need an outlet for their bloodlust," he said. "Let us confine Thrall to the gladiator battles. He will fill our pockets and bring us honor." He smirked. "I've yet to see the single man who could stand up to an orc."

Thrall's ascendance in the ranks of the gladiators had been nothing short of phenomenal. He had reached his full height when very young; as the years passed, he began to add bulk to his tall frame. Now he was the biggest orc many had ever seen, even heard tell of. He was the master of the ring, and everyone knew it.

When he was not fighting he was shut alone in his cell, which seemed to him to grow smaller with each passing day despite the fact that Blackmoore had ordered him a new one. Thrall now had a small, covered sleeping area and a much larger area in which to practice. Covered by a grate, this sunken ring had mock weapons of every sort and Thrall's old friend, the battered training troll, upon which he could practice. Some nights, when he could not sleep, Thrall rose and took out his tension on the dummy.

It was the books that Taretha sent him, with their precious messages and now a tablet and stylus, that truly brightened those long, solitary hours. They had been conversing in secret at least once a week, and Thrall imagined a world as Tari painted it: A world of art, and beauty, and companionship. A world of food beyond rotting meat and slop. A world in which he had a place.

Every now and then, his eye would fall upon the increasingly fraying square of cloth that bore the symbol of a white wolf head on a blue field. He would look quickly away, not wanting to let his mind travel down that path. What good would it do? He had read enough books (some of which Black-moore had no idea that Tari had passed along to Thrall) to understand that the orc people lived in small groups, each with its own distinctive symbol. What could he do, simply tell Blackmoore that he was tired of being a slave, thank you, and would he please let Thrall out so he could find his family?

And yet the thought teased him. His own people. Tari had her own peo-ple, her family of Tammis and Clannia Foxton. She was valued and loved. He was grateful that she had such loving support, because it was out of that secure place that she had felt large in heart enough to reach out to him.

Sometimes, he wondered what the rest of the Foxtons thought of him. Tari never mentioned them much anymore. She had told him that her mother Clan-nia had nursed him at her own breast, to save his life. At first, Thrall had been touched by that, but as he grew older and learned more, he understood that Clannia had not been moved to suckle him out of love, but out of a desire to increase her standing with Blackmoore.

Blackmoore. All roads of thought ended there. He could forget he was a piece of property when he was writing to Tari and reading her letters, or searching for her golden hair in the stands at the gladiator matches. He could also lose himself in the exciting thing Sergeant called "bloodlust." But these moments were all too brief. Even when Blackmoore himself came to visit Thrall, to discuss some military strategy Thrall had studied, or to play a game of Hawks and Hares with him, there was no link, no sense of family with this man. When Blackmoore was jovial, it was with the attitude of a man toward a child. And when he was irritable and darkly furious, which was more often than not, Thrall felt as helpless as a child. Blackmoore could order him beaten, or starved, or burned, or shackled, or—the worst punishment of all, and one that had, thankfully, not yet occurred to Blackmoore—deny him access to his books.

He knew that Tari did not have a privileged life, not the way Blackmoore did. She was a servant, in her own way, as much in thrall as the orc who bore the name. But she had friends, and she was not spat upon, and she *belonged*.

Slowly, his hand moved, of its own accord, to reach for the blue swaddling cloth. At that moment, he heard the door unlock and open behind him. He dropped the cloth as if it were something unclean.

"Come on," said one of the dour-faced guards. He extended the manacles. "Time to go fight. I hear they've got quite the opponents for you today." He grinned mirthlessly, showing brown teeth. "And Master Blackmoore's ready to have your hide if you don't win."

FIVE

More than a decade had passed since one Lieutenant Blackmoore had simultaneously found an orphaned orc and the possible answer to his dreams.

They had been fruitful and happy years for Thrall's master, and for humanity in general. Aedelas Blackmoore, once Lieutenant, now Lieutenant *General*, had been mocked about his "pet orc" when he had first brought it to Durnholde, especially when it seemed as though the wretched little thing wouldn't even survive. Thank goodness for Mistress Foxton and her swollen teats. Blackmoore couldn't conceive of any human female being willing to suckle an orc, but although the offer had increased his contempt for his servant and his family, it had also saved Blackmoore's behind. Which was why he hadn't begrudged them baubles, food, and education for their child, even if she was a girl.

It was a bright day, warm but not too hot. Perfect fighting weather. The awning, bright with his colors of red and gold, provided pleasant shade. Banners of all colors danced in the gentle breeze, and music and laughter floated to his ears. The smell of ripe fruits, fresh bread, and roasted venison teased his nostrils. Everyone here was in a good mood. After the battles, some wouldn't be in such good moods, but right now, all were happy and filled with anticipation.

Lying on a chaise beside him was his young protégé, Lord Karramyn Langston. Langston had rich brown hair that matched his dark eyes, a strong, fit body, and a lazy smile. He was also completely devoted to Blackmoore, and was the one human being Blackmoore had told of his ultimate plans. Though many years his junior, Langston shared many of Blackmoore's ideals and lack of scruples. They were a good pair. Langston had fallen asleep in the warm sunshine, and snored softly.

Blackmoore reached over and snagged another bite of roasted fowl and a goblet of red wine, red as the blood that would soon be spilled in the arena, to wash it down with. Life was good, and with every challenge Thrall met and passed, life got even better. After each match, Blackmoore left with a heavy purse. His "pet orc," once the joke of the fortress, was now his pride.

Of course, most of the others that Thrall went up against were nothing more than humans. Some of the meanest, strongest, most cunning humans to be sure, but human nonetheless. The other gladiators were all brutal, hardened convicts hoping to earn their way out of prison by winning money and fame for their patrons. Some did, and earned their freedom. Most found themselves in just another jail, one with tapestries on the wall and women in their beds, but it was a prison nonetheless. Few patrons wanted to see their money-winners walk as free men.

But some of Thrall's adversaries weren't human, and that was when things got exciting.

It didn't hurt Blackmoore's ambitions at all that the orcs were now a defeated, downtrodden rabble rather than the awesome and fear-inspiring fighting force they had once been. The war was long over, and humans had won the decisive victory. Now the enemy was led into special internment camps almost as easily as cattle into stalls at the end of a day spent grazing. Camps, Blackmoore mused pleasantly, that he was completely in charge of.

At first, his plan was to raise the orc to be a well-educated, loyal slave and a peerless warrior. He would send Thrall to defeat his own people, if "people" was even the proper term for such mindless green thugs, and once they had been defeated, use the broken clans to his, Blackmoore's, own purpose.

But the Horde had been defeated by the Alliance without Thrall having even tasted battle. At first, Blackmoore had been sour about this. But then another thought came to him on how he could use his pet orc. It required patience, something Blackmoore had only in short supply, but the rewards would be far greater than he could have imagined. Infighting was already rampant among the Alliance. Elf sneered at human, human mocked dwarf, and dwarf mistrusted elf. A nice little triangle of bigotry and suspicion.

He raised himself from his chair long enough to observe Thrall defeat one of the biggest, nastiest-looking men Blackmoore had ever seen. But the human warrior was no match for the unstoppable green beast. The cheers went up, and Blackmoore smiled. He waved Tammis Foxton over, and the servant hastened to obey.

"My lord?"

"How many is that today?" Blackmoore knew his voice was slurred but he didn't care. Tammis had seen him drunker than this. Tammis had put him to *bed* drunker than this.

Tammis's prim, anxious face looked even more concerned than usual. "How many what, my lord?" His gaze flickered to the bottle, then back to Blackmoore.

Sudden rage welled up in Blackmoore. He grabbed Tammis by the shirt-front and yanked him down to within an inch of his face.

"Counting the bottles, you pathetic excuse for a man?" he hissed, keeping his voice low. One of the many threats he held over Tammis was public disgrace; even drunk as Blackmoore was, he didn't want to play that particular card quite yet. But he threatened it often, as now. Before his slightly swimmy vision he saw Tammis pale. "You farm out your own wife to suckle monsters, and you dare imply that I have weaknesses?"

Sickened by the man's pasty face, he shoved him away. "I wanted to know how many rounds Thrall has won."

"Oh, yes, sir, of course. Half dozen, all in a row." Tammis paused, looking utterly miserable. "With all due respect, sir, this last one taxed him. Are you sure you want to put him through three more matches?"

Idiots. Blackmoore was surrounded by idiots. When Sergeant had read the order of battles this morning, he, too, had confronted Blackmoore, saying the orc needed at least a few moments of rest, and couldn't they switch the combatant list so that the poor coddled creature could relax.

"Oh, no. The odds against Thrall go higher with ever' battle. He's never lost, not once. Of course I want to stop and give all those nice people their money back." Disgusted, he waved Tammis away. Thrall was incapable of being defeated. Why not make hay while the sun shone?

Thrall won the next battle, but even Blackmoore could see the creature struggling. He adjusted his chair for a better view. Langston imitated him. The battle after that, the eighth of the nine for which the orc was scheduled, saw something that Blackmoore and the crowds had never witnessed.

The mighty orc was tiring. The combatants this time were a pair of mountain cats, caught two weeks ago, penned, tormented, and barely fed until this moment. Once the door to the arena slid open they exploded at the orc as if they had been fired from a cannon. Their creamy brown pelts were a blur as, moving as one, they leaped on him, and Thrall went down beneath their claws and teeth.

A horrified cry arose among the onlookers. Blackmoore sprang to his feet, and immediately had to seize his chair in order to keep from falling down. All that money. . . .

And then Thrall was up! Screaming in rage, shaking the big animals off him as if they were but tree squirrels, he used the two swords that were his assigned weapon in this fight with speed and skill. Thrall was completely ambidextrous, and the blades sparkled in the bright sunlight as they whirled and slashed. One cat was already dead, its long, lithe body sliced nearly in two by a single powerful stroke. The remaining animal, goaded to further rage by the death of its mate, attacked with renewed fury. This time Thrall did not give it an opening. When the cat sprang, all yowls and claws and teeth, Thrall was ready for it. His sword sliced left, right, and left again. The cat fell in four bloody chunks.

"Will you look at that?" said Langston happily.

The crowd roared its approval. Thrall, who normally welcomed the cries with raised fists and stamped his feet almost until the earth itself shook, merely stood there with stooped shoulders. He was breathing raggedly, and Blackmoore saw that the cats had left their mark with several deep, bleeding scratches and bites. As he stared at his prized slave, Thrall slowly turned his ugly head and looked straight up at Blackmoore. Their eyes met, and in their depths Blackmoore saw agony and exhaustion . . . and an unspoken plea.

Then Thrall, the mighty warrior, fell to his knees. Again the crowd reacted vocally. Blackmoore fancied he even heard sympathy in the sound. Langston said nothing, but his brown eyes were watching Blackmoore intently.

Damn Thrall! He was an orc, had been fighting since he was six years old. Most of his matches today had been with humans, mighty warriors to be sure, but nothing to compare with Thrall's brute strength. This was a ploy to get out of the final round, which Thrall knew would be the toughest of all. Selfish, stupid slave. Wanted to go back to his cozy cell, read his books, and eat his food, did he? Well, Blackmoore would teach *him* a thing or two.

At that moment, Sergeant trotted onto the field. "Lord Blackmoore!" he cried, cupping his hands around his bearded mouth. "Will you cede this last challenge?"

Heat flared on Blackmoore's cheeks. How dare Sergeant do this, in front of everyone! Blackmoore, who was still standing unsteadily, gripped the back of the chair harder with his left hand. Langston moved unobtrusively to offer aid if he needed it. Blackmoore extended his right hand straight out in front of him, then brought the hand over to his left shoulder.

No.

Sergeant stared at him for a moment, as if he couldn't believe what he was seeing. Then, he nodded, and signaled that this final bout would begin.

Thrall climbed to his feet, looking as if he had a ton of stones on his back. Several men scurried onto the field, to remove the dead mountain cats and dropped weapons. They handed Thrall the weapon that he was to use for this battle: the morningstar, a studded, metal ball attached by a chain to a thick stick. Thrall took the weapon, and tried to draw himself up into a threatening posture. Even at this distance Blackmoore could see that he trembled. Usually, before each battle, Thrall stamped on the earth. The steady rhythm both excited the crowd and seemed to help Thrall feel more ready for combat. Today, though, he simply seemed struggling to stay on his feet.

One more bout. The creature could handle that.

The doors opened, but for a moment, nothing emerged from the inner gloom.

Then it came, its two heads crying incoherent challenges, its pale body towering over Thrall as Thrall towered over humans. It had only one weapon, as Thrall did, but it was a superior one for this battle—a long, deadly-looking spear. Between the length of its arms and the shaft of the spear, the ogre would be able to reach Thrall from much farther away. Thrall would need to get in close in order to strike any kind of a blow, let alone a winning one.

This was so unfair! "Who gave the ogre that spear?" Blackmoore bellowed to Langston. "It ought to have something at least similar to what Thrall has been given!" Blackmoore conveniently chose not to remember all the times that Thrall had been equipped with a broadsword or spear himself and his human opponents had had to make do with a short sword or ax.

The ogre marched into the circular arena like a machine of war rather than a living, breathing being. He stabbed forward with his spear, one head turned toward the crowd, one head facing Thrall.

Thrall had never seen one of these creatures before, and for a moment simply stood, staring at it. Then he rallied, drew himself up to his full height, and began to swing the morningstar. He threw back his head, tangled long black hair brushing his back, and let loose with a howl to match the ogre's bellowing.

The ogre charged, stabbing forward with the spear. There was no finesse in his movements, only brute strength. Thrall easily ducked the clumsy charge, slipped underneath the ogre's defenses, and swung hard with the morningstar. The ogre cried out and slowed as the spiked ball struck him heavily in the midsection. Thrall had dashed past and now whirled to attack again.

Before the ogre could even turn around, Thrall had struck him in the back. The ogre fell to his knees, dropping the spear and reaching to clutch his back.

Blackmoore smiled. Surely that had broken the miserable creature's spine. These fights weren't necessarily to the death—in fact, killing one's opponent was frowned on as it reduced the pool of good fighters—but everyone knew that dying was a very real possibility in this ring. Healers and their salves couldn't fix everything. And Blackmoore couldn't manage to find any sympathy at all for an ogre.

But his pleasure was short-lived. Even as Thrall began to swing the morningstar again, gathering momentum, the ogre lurched to his feet and seized the dropped spear. Thrall swung the morningstar at the creature's head. To the crowd's amazement, and obviously to Thrall's as well, the ogre simply extended a big hand and batted the spike out of the way while shoving forward with the spear.

The morningstar flew from Thrall's hand. He was knocked off balance and could not recover in time. Even as he desperately tried to twist out of the way the spear impaled him high in the chest, a few inches from his left shoulder. He screamed in agony. The ogre continued to shove as he approached, and the spear went completely through Thrall's body. He fell backward, and was pinned to the earth. Now the ogre fell atop him, pummeling the hapless orc madly and uttering horrible grunts and squeals.

Blackmoore stared in horror. The orc was being beaten, as helpless as a child beneath the onslaught of a bully. The gladiator ring, a showcase for the finest warriors in the kingdom to compete against one another using strength, skill, and cunning, had been reduced to nothing more than one weak monster being beaten to a pulp by another, bigger one.

How could Thrall have let this happen?

Men now hastened onto the field. With sharpened sticks, they prodded the ogre, trying to goad him into leaving off his prey. The brute responded to the taunts, abandoning a bloody Thrall and chasing after the men. Three others tossed a magical net, which immediately shrank to engulf the raging ogre and compress his flailing limbs close to his body. He thrashed now like a fish out of water, and the men, not at all gently, hauled the creature onto a cart and took him out of the ring.

Thrall, too, was being carried out, though with much more gentleness. Blackmoore's patronage assured that. But Blackmoore realized that he had lost every penny he had bet on Thrall today because of this single fight. Many of his companions had done likewise, and he could feel the heat of their furious glares as they reached for their purses to pay their debts.

Thrall. Thrall. *Thrall.* . . .

Thrall lay gasping on the straw that served him as a bed. He had never known such pain existed. Nor such exhaustion. He wished he would fall unconscious; it would be so much easier.

Nonetheless, he would not let the welcoming blackness overtake him. The healers would be here soon; Blackmoore always sent them after Thrall had been injured in a bout. Blackmoore also always came to visit him, and Thrall eagerly awaited the comforting words of his master. He had lost the battle, true, and that was a first, but surely Blackmoore would have nothing but praise for how well he had fought nine bouts in a row. That was unheard of, Thrall knew. Thrall also knew he could have beaten the ogre if he had been matched against him in the first bout, or the third, or even the sixth. But no one could expect him to win after a record-breaking eight bouts.

He closed his eyes as pain seared him. The hot burning in his chest was nigh unbearable. Where were the healers? They should have been here by now. He knew his injuries were bad this time. He estimated he had several broken ribs, a broken leg, several sword slashes, and of course the dreadful hole in his shoulder where the spear had impaled him. They would have to come soon if Thrall were to be able to fight again tomorrow.

Thrall heard the lock open, but could not lift his head to see who entered his cell.

"The healers will be here," came Blackmoore's voice. Thrall tensed. The voice was slurred and dripped with contempt. His heart began to speed up. Please, not this time . . . not now. . . .

"But they won't be here anytime soon. I wan' see you suffer, you poxy son of a whore."

And then Thrall gasped in torment as Blackmoore's boot kicked him in the stomach. The pain was incredible, but not nearly as searing as the shock of betrayal that shuddered through him. Why would Blackmoore strike him when he was so badly injured? Did he not see how well Thrall had fought?

Though the pain threatened to cause him to lose consciousness, Thrall raised his head and stared at Blackmoore with blurred vision. The man's face was contorted in anger, and even as Thrall met his eyes Blackmoore struck him soundly across the face with a mailed fist. Everything went black for an instant and when Thrall could next hear, Blackmoore was still railing.

". . . lost thousands, do you hear me, *thousands!* What is the matter with you? It was one pathetic little fight!"

He was still raining blows on Thrall, but Thrall was starting to drift away. He felt as if his body only vaguely belonged to him, and the kicks Blackmoore delivered felt more and more like taps. He felt blood sticky on his face.

Blackmoore had seen him. He knew how exhausted Thrall had been, had watched him rally again and again and again to hold his own eight out of nine times. There was no way anyone could have expected Thrall to win that fight. Thrall had fought with everything he had, and he had lost fairly and honorably. And yet that was not good enough for Blackmoore.

Finally, the blows stopped. He heard the steps as Blackmoore left, and a single phrase: "Let the others have their turn."

The door did not close. Thrall heard more footsteps. He could not raise his head again, though he tried. Several pairs of black military boots appeared in front of him. Thrall now realized what Blackmoore had ordered. One boot drew back slightly, then swung forward, kicking Thrall in the face.

His world went white, then black; then he knew no more.

Thrall awoke to warmth and a cessation of the agony that had been his companion for what seemed like an eternity. Three healers were working on him, using their salve to heal his wounds. Breathing was much easier and he guessed his ribs had been healed. They were administering the sweet-smelling, gooey stuff to his shoulder now; clearly that was the most difficult wound.

Although their touches were gentle, and their salve brought healing, there was no real compassion in these men. They healed him because Blackmoore paid them to do so, not out of any real desire to ease suffering. Once, he had been more naive and had thanked them sincerely for their efforts. One of them looked up, startled at the words.

A sneer had curled his lip. "Don't flatter yourself, monster. Once the coins stop flowing, so does the salve. Better not lose."

He had winced from the unkind words then, but they did not bother him now. Thrall understood. He understood many things. It was as if his vision had been cloudy, and a thick fog had suddenly lifted. He lay quietly until they had finished; then they rose and left.

Thrall sat upright and was surprised to see Sergeant standing there, his hairy arms folded across his broad chest. Thrall did not speak, wondering what new torment was coming.

"I pulled 'em off you," said Sergeant quietly. "But not before they'd had their sport. Blackmoore had some . . . business . . . he needed to talk w' me about. I'm sorry for that, lad. I'm right sorry. You amazed me in the ring today. Blackmoore ought to be prouder'n hell o' you. Instead. . . ." His gruff voice trailed off. "Well, I wanted to make sure you knew that you didn't deserve what he did. What they did. You did fine, lad. Just fine. Better get some sleep."

He seemed about to say something more, then nodded and left. Thrall lay back down, absently noting that they had changed the straw. It was fresh and clean, no longer clotted with his blood.

He appreciated what Sergeant had done, and believed the man. But it was too little, too late.

He would not let himself be used like this any longer. Once, he would have cringed and vowed to be better, to do something to earn the love and respect he so desperately craved. Now, he knew he would never find it here, not as long as Blackmoore owned him.

He would not sleep. He would use this time to plan. He reached for the tablet and stylus he kept in the sack, and wrote a note to the only person he could trust: Tari.

On the next dark moons, I plan to escape.

SIX

The grate above his head allowed Thrall to observe the moonslight. He was careful to give no hint, not to the trainees who had beaten him, not to Sergeant, and certainly not to Blackmoore (who treated Thrall as if nothing had happened) about his profound revelation. He was as obsequious as ever, for the first time noticing how he hated himself for that behavior. He kept his eyes lowered, although he knew himself to be the equal of any human. He went docilely into the irons, though he could have torn any four guards to bloody bits before they could have restrained him without his cooperation. In no way did he change his behavior, not in the cell nor out of it, not in the ring nor on the training field.

For the first day or two, Thrall noticed Sergeant watching him sharply, as if expecting to see the changes Thrall was determined not to show. But he did not speak to Thrall, and Thrall was careful not to arouse suspicion. Let them think they had broken him. His only regret was that he would not be present to see the look on Blackmoore's face when he discovered his "pet orc" had flown.

For the first time in his life, Thrall had something to look forward to with anticipation. It roused a hunger in him he had never known before. He had always concentrated so intensely on avoiding beatings and earning praise that he had never permitted himself to really think long and hard about what it meant to be free. To walk in the sunlight without chains, to sleep under the stars. He had never been outside at night in his life. What would that be like?

His imagination, fueled by books and by letters from Tari, was finally allowed to fly. He lay awake in his straw bed wondering what it would be like to finally meet one of his people. He had read, of course, all the information the humans had on "the vile green monsters from the blackest demon pits." And there was that disturbing incident when the orc had wrenched himself free to charge Thrall. If only he could have found out what the orc was saying! But his rudimentary orcish did not extend that far.

He would learn, one day, what that orc had said. He would find his people. Thrall might have been raised by humans, but little enough had been done to win his love and loyalty. He was grateful to Sergeant and Tari, for they had taught him concepts of honor and kindness. But because of their teachings, Thrall better understood Blackmoore, and realized that the Lieutenant General had none of those qualities. And as long as Thrall was owned by him, the orc would never receive them in his own life.

The moons, one large and silver and one smaller and a shade of blue-green, were new tonight. Tari had responded to his declaration with an offer to assist him, as he had known in his heart she would. Between the two of them, they had been able to come up with a plan that had a strong likelihood of working. But he did not know when that plan would go into effect, and so he waited for the signal. And waited.

He had fallen into a fitful slumber when the clanging of a bell startled him awake. Instantly alert, he went to the farthest wall of his cell. Over the years, Thrall had painstakingly worked a single stone loose and had hollowed out the space behind it. It was here that he stored his most precious things: his letters from Tari. Now he moved the stone, found the letters, and wrapped them up in the only other thing that meant anything to him, his swaddling cloth with the white wolf against the blue field. For a brief moment, he held them to his chest. Then he turned, and awaited his chance.

The bell continued to ring, and now shouts and screams joined it. Thrall's sensitive nose, much more keen than a human's, could smell smoke. The smell grew stronger with each heartbeat, and now he could see a faint orange and yellow lightening of the darkness of his cell.

"Fire!" came the cries. "Fire!"

Not knowing why, Thrall leaped for his makeshift bed. He closed his eyes and feigned sleep, forcing his rapid breathing to become deep and slow.

"He's not going anywhere," said one of the guards. Thrall knew he was being watched. He kept up the illusion of deep sleep. "Heh. Damned monster could sleep through anything. Come on, let's give them a hand."

"I don't know. . . ." said the other one.

More cries of alarm, mixed now with the treble shrieks of children and the high voices of women.

"It's spreading," said the first one. "Come *on!*"

Thrall heard the sounds of boots striking hard stone. The sounds receded. He was alone.

He rose, and stood in front of the huge wooden door. Of course it was still locked, but there was no one to see what he was about to do.

Thrall took a deep breath, then with a rush of speed charged the door, striking it with his left shoulder. It gave, but not entirely. Again he struck, and again. Five times he had to slam his enormous body against it before the old timbers surrendered with a crash. The momentum carried him forward and he landed heavily on the floor, but the brief pain was as nothing compared to the surge of excitement he experienced.

He knew these hallways. He had no problem seeing in the dim light provided by the few torches positioned in sconces that were fastened here and there to the stone walls. Down this one, up this stairwell, and then. . . .

As it had earlier in his cell, a deep instinct kicked in. He flattened himself against the wall, hiding his huge form in the shadows as best he could. From across the entryway, several more guards charged. They did not see him, and Thrall let his held breath out in a sigh of relief.

The guards left the door to the courtyard wide open. Cautiously Thrall approached, and peered out.

All was chaos. The barns were almost completely engulfed by flames, though the horses, goats, and donkeys ran panic-stricken in the courtyard. This was even better, for there was less chance of him being spotted in the milling madness. A bucket chain had been formed, and even as Thrall watched, several more men hastened up, spilling the precious water in their heedless rush.

Thrall looked to the right of the courtyard gate entrance. Lying in a crumpled pool of black was the object he was seeking: a huge black cloak. Even as large as it was, it could not possibly cover him, but it would serve. He covered his head and broad chest, crouched so that the short hem would fall lower on his legs, and scurried forward.

The trip across the courtyard to the main gates could not have lasted more than a few moments, but to Thrall it seemed an eternity. He tried to keep his head low, but he had to look up frequently in order to avoid being run down by a cart carrying barrels of rainwater, or a maddened horse, or a screaming child. His heart pounding, he threaded his way amid the chaos. He could feel the heat, and the bright light of the fire lit up the entire scene almost as brightly as the sun did. Thrall concentrated on putting one foot in front of the other, keeping as low as possible, and heading for the gates.

Finally, he made it. These, too, had been thrown open. More carts carrying rain barrels clattered through, the drivers having a hard time controlling their frightened mounts. No one noticed one lone figure slipping out into the darkness.

Once clear of the fortress, Thrall ran. He headed straight for the surrounding forested hills, leaving the road as soon as possible. His senses seemed sharper than they had ever been. Unfamiliar scents filled his flaring nostrils, and it felt as if he could sense every rock, every blade of grass beneath his running feet.

There was a rock formation that Taretha had told him about. She said it looked a bit like a dragon standing guard over the forest. It was very dark, but Thrall's excellent night vision could make out a jut that, if one used one's imagination, could indeed appear to be the long neck of a reptilian creature. There was a cave here, Taretha said. He would be safe.

For the briefest moment, he wondered if Taretha might not be setting a trap for him. At once he dismissed the idea, both angry and ashamed that it had even occurred to him. Taretha had been nothing but kind to him via her supportive letters. Why would she betray him? And more to the point, why go to such great lengths when simply showing his letters to Blackmoore would accomplish the same thing?

There it was, a dark oval against the gray face of the stone. Thrall was not even breathing heavily as he altered his course and trotted for the refuge.

He could see her inside, leaning against the cave wall, waiting for him. For a moment he paused, knowing that his vision was superior to hers. Even though she was within and he without, she could not see him.

Thrall had only human values by which to measure beauty, and he could tell that, by those standards, Taretha Foxton was lovely. Long pale hair—it was too dark for him to see the exact color, but he had glimpsed her momentarily in the stands at the matches from time to time—fell in a long braid down her back. She was clad only in nightclothes, a cloak wrapped close about her slender frame, and beside her was a large sack.

He paused for a moment, and then strode boldly up to her. "Taretha," he said, his voice deep and gruff.

She gasped and looked up at him. He thought her afraid, but then she laughed. "You startled me! I did not know you moved so quietly!" The laughter faded, settled into a smile. She strode forward and reached out both hands to him.

Slowly, Thrall folded them in his own. The small white hands disappeared in his green ones, nearly three times as large. Taretha barely reached his elbow, yet there was no fear on her face, only pleasure.

"I could kill you where you stand," he said, wondering what perverse emotion was making him say those words. "No witnesses that way."

Her smile only grew. "Of course you could," she acknowledged, her voice warm and melodious. "But you won't."

"How do you know?"

"Because I know *you.*" He opened his hands and released her. "Did you have any trouble?"

"None," he said. "The plan worked well. There was so much chaos that I think an entire village of orcs could have escaped. I noticed that you released the animals before setting fire to the barn."

She grinned again. Her nose turned up slightly, making her look younger than her—what, twenty? Twenty-five?—years.

"Of course. They're just innocent creatures. I'd never want to see them harmed. Now, we had best hurry." She looked down at Durnholde, at the smoke and flames still billowing up into the starry sky. "They seem to be getting control of it. You'll be missed soon." An emotion Thrall didn't understand shadowed her face for a moment. "As will I." She took the sack and brought it out into the open. "Sit, sit. I want to show you something."

Obediently, he sat down. Tari rummaged through the sack and withdrew a scroll. Unrolling it, she held it down on one side and gestured that he do the same.

"It's a map," said Thrall.

"Yes, the most accurate one I could find. Here's Durnholde," said Taretha, pointing at a drawing of a small castlelike building. "We're slightly to the southwest, right here. The internment camps are all within a twenty-mile radius of Durnholde, here, here, here, here, and here." She pointed to drawings so small even Thrall couldn't quite make them out in the poor light. "Your best chance for safety is to go here, into the wilderness area. I've heard that there are still some of your people hiding out there, but Blackmoore's men are never able to find them, just traces." She looked up at him. "You'll somehow need to find them, Thrall. Get them to help you."

Your people, Taretha had said. Not *the orcs,* or *those things,* or *those monsters.* Gratitude suddenly welled up inside him so powerfully that for a moment he couldn't speak. Finally, he managed, "Why are you doing this? Why do you want to help me?"

She looked at him steadily, not flinching from what she saw. "Because I remember you when you were a baby. You were like a little brother to me. When . . . when Faralyn died soon afterward, you were the only little brother I had anymore. I saw what they did to you, and I hated it. I wanted to help you, be your friend." Now she looked away. "And I have no more fondness for our master than you do."

"Has he hurt you?" The outrage that Thrall felt surprised him.

"No. Not really." One hand went to the other wrist, massaged it gently.

Beneath the sleeve Thrall could see the fading shadow of a bruise. "Not physically. It's more complicated than that."

"Tell me."

"Thrall, time is—"

"Tell me!" he boomed. "You have been my friend, Taretha. For over ten years you have written me, made me smile. I knew someone knew who I really was, not just some . . . some monster in the gladiator ring. You were a light in the darkness." With all the gentleness he could muster, he reached out and placed his hand oh so lightly on her shoulder. "Tell me," he urged again, his voice soft.

Her eyes grew shiny. As he watched, liquid spilled from them and poured down her cheeks. "I'm so ashamed," she whispered.

"What is happening to your eyes?" asked Thrall. "What is 'ashamed'?"

"Oh, Thrall," she said, her voice thick. She wiped at her eyes. "These are called tears. They come when we are so sad, so soul sick, it's as if our hearts are so full of pain there's no place else for it to go." Taretha took a shuddering breath. "And shame . . . it's when you've done something that's so contrary to who you believe yourself to be you wish that no one ever knew about it. But everyone knows, so you might as well, too. I am Blackmoore's mistress."

"What does that mean?"

She regarded him sadly. "You are so innocent, Thrall. So pure. But someday you will understand."

Suddenly Thrall recalled snippets of bragging conversations he had overheard on the training field, and understood what Taretha meant. But he did not feel shame for her, only outrage that Blackmoore had stooped even lower than Thrall had guessed he could. He understood what it was to be helpless before Blackmoore, and Taretha was so small and fragile she couldn't even fight.

"Come with me," he urged.

"I cannot. What he would do to my family if I fled . . . no." She reached out impulsively and gripped his hands. "But you can. Please, go now. I will rest the easier knowing that you, at least, have escaped him. Be free, for the both of us."

He nodded, unable to speak. He had known he would miss her, but now, having actually conversed with Tari, the pain of their parting cut even more deeply.

She wiped her face again and spoke in a steadier voice. "I've packed this full of food and put in several full water skins as well. I was able to steal a knife for you. I didn't dare take anything else that might be missed. Finally, I want you to have this." She bowed her head and removed a silver chain from her long neck. Dangling from the delicate chain was a crescent moon. "Not far from here, there is an old tree that was split by lightning. Blackmoore gives me leave to wander here when I wish. For that, at least, I'm grateful. If you are ever here and in need, place this necklace in the trunk of the old tree, and I will again meet you in this cave and do what I can to help you."

"Tari. . . ." Thrall looked at her miserably.

"Hurry." She cast an anxious glance back at Durnholde. "I have made up a story to excuse my absence, but it will go easier for me the sooner I return." They rose, and looked at one another awkwardly. Before Thrall realized what had happened, Tari had stepped forward and stretched her arms about his massive torso as far as they would reach. Her face pressed against his stomach. Thrall tensed; all such contact hitherto had been as an attack. But although he had never been touched in this way before, he knew it was a sign of affection. Following his instincts, he tentatively patted her head and stroked her hair.

"They call you a monster," she said, her voice thick again as she stepped away from him. "But they're the monsters, not you. Farewell, Thrall."

Taretha turned away, lifted her skirts, and began to run back toward Durnholde. Thrall stood and watched her until she had disappeared from view. Then, with the utmost care, he placed the precious silver necklace in his bundle, then stashed it in the sack.

He lifted the heavy sack—it must have been very difficult for Taretha to carry it so far—and slung it over his back. Then, Thrall, the former slave, began to stride to his destiny.

SEVEN

Thrall knew that Taretha had pointed out where the internment camps were located specifically so that he could avoid them. She wanted him to try to find free orcs. But he was uncertain as to whether these "free orcs" were even still alive or merely figments of some wistful warrior's imagination. He had studied maps while under Jaramin's tutelage, so he knew how to read the one Tari had given him.

And he set a course straight for one of the camps.

He did not choose the one nearest Durnholde; there was a good chance that, once he was missed, Blackmoore would have issued an alert. There was one that, according to the map, was located several leagues away from the fortress where Thrall had reached maturity. This was the one he would visit.

He knew only a little about the camps, and that little was filtered through the minds of men who hated his people. As he jogged easily and tirelessly toward his destination, his mind raced. What would it be like, to see so many orcs all in one place? Would they be able to understand his speech? Or would it be so tainted with a human accent he would be unable to converse at even the most basic level? Would they challenge him? He did not wish to fight them, but everything he knew told him that orcs were fierce, proud, unstoppable warriors. He was a trained fighter, but would that be enough against one of these legendary beings? Would he be able to hold his own long enough to persuade them that he was not their enemy?

Miles fell beneath his feet. From time to time he looked at the stars to judge his position. He had never been taught how to navigate, but one of the secret books Tari had sent him had dealt with the stars and their positions. Thrall had studied it eagerly, absorbing every scrap of information that had come his way.

Maybe he would meet the clan who bore the emblem of the white wolf head against the blue background. Maybe he would find his family. Blackmoore had told him he had been found not terribly far from Durnholde, so Thrall thought it quite possible that he would encounter members of his clan.

Excitement flooded him. It was good.

He traveled all that night and halted to rest once the sun began to rise. If he knew Blackmoore, and he did, the Lieutenant General would have men out looking for him. Perhaps they would even press into use one of their famed flying machines. Thrall had never seen one, and had privately doubted their existence. But if they did indeed exist, then Blackmoore would commandeer the use of one to find his wandering champion.

He thought of Tari, and desperately hoped that her part in his escape had not been discovered.

Blackmoore did not think he had ever been angrier in his entire life, and that was saying a great deal.

He had been roused from his slumber—alone tonight, Taretha had pleaded illness—by the clamor of the bells and stared in horror out his window at the billowing orange flames across the courtyard. Throwing on clothing, he had raced to join the rest of Durnholde's populace as they frantically tried to contain the blaze. It had taken several hours, but by the time dawn's pink hue had begun to taint the night sky the inferno had been tamed to a pile of sullen embers.

"It's a miracle no one was hurt," said Langston, wiping his forehead. His pale face was tinted black by the soot. Blackmoore fancied he looked no better. Everyone present was soiled and sweaty. The servants would have quite a bit of washing to do tomorrow.

"Not even the animals," said Tammis, coming up to them. "There was no way the animals could have escaped on their own. We can't be certain, my lord, but it's beginning to look as though this fire was deliberately set."

"By the Light!" gasped Langston. "Do you really think so? Who would want to do such a thing?"

"I'd count all my enemies on my hands, except I'd run out of fingers," growled Blackmoore. "And toes. Plenty of bastards out there jealous of my rank and my . . . Lothar's ghost." He suddenly felt cold and imagined that his face was white beneath the soot. Langston and Tammis both stared at him.

He couldn't spare the time to voice his concern. He leaped up from the stone steps upon which he'd been sitting and sped back toward the fortress. Both friend and servant followed him, crying out, "Blackmoore, wait!" and "My lord, what is it?"

Blackmoore ignored them. He hastened down the corridors, up the stairs, and skidded to a halt in front of the broken wooden shards that had once been the door to Thrall's cell. His worst fear had been proven right.

"Damn them all to hell!" he cried. "Someone stole my orc! Tammis! I want men, I want horses, I want flying machines—I want Thrall back immediately!"

Thrall was surprised at how deeply he slept, and how lively his dreams were. He woke as night was falling, and for a moment simply lay where he was. He felt the soft grass beneath his body, enjoyed the breeze that caressed his face. This was freedom, and it was sweet indeed. Precious. He now understood why some would rather die than live imprisoned.

A spear prodded his neck, and the faces of six human males peered down on him.

"You," one of them said. "Get up."

Thrall cursed himself as he was dragged behind a horse, with two men walking guard on either side. How could he have been so foolish! He had wanted to see the encampments, yes, but from the safety of hiding. He wanted to be an observer, not a participant in this system about which he had heard nothing good.

He'd tried to run, but four of them had horses and had run him down almost immediately. They had nets, spears, and swords, and Thrall was ashamed at how quickly and efficiently they managed to render him harmless. He thought about struggling, but decided not to. He was under no illusions that these men would pay for a healing if he were injured, and he wanted to keep his strength up. Also, would there be a better way to meet orcs than to be at the camp with them? Certainly, given their fierce warriors' nature, they would be eager to escape. He had knowledge that could help them.

So he pretended to be overcome, although he could have taken on all of them at once. He regretted his decision almost immediately when the men began to rummage through his sack.

"Plenty of food here," said one. "Good stuff, too. We'll eat well tonight, lads!"

"It's Major Remka who'll be eating well," said another.

"Not if she don't know about it, and we aren't going to tell her," said a third. As Thrall watched, the one who had spoken first bit eagerly into one of the small meat pies Taretha had packed.

"Well, look here," said the second one. "A knife." He rose and went to Thrall, who was helplessly bound in a trap-net. "Stole all this, didn't you?" He thrust the knife at Thrall's face. Thrall didn't even blink.

"Come off it, Hult," said the second man, who was the smallest and most anxious of the six. The others had tied their horses to nearby branches and were busily divvying up the spoils, putting them in their saddlebags and not choosing to report it to the mysterious Major Remka, whoever he was.

"I'm keeping this one," said Hult.

"You can have the food, but you know that everything else we find we really have to report," said the second man, looking nervous about standing up to Hult but doggedly determined to follow orders.

"And what if I don't?" said Hult. Thrall did not like him; he looked mean and angry, like Blackmoore. "What are you going to do about it?"

"It's what I'm going to do about it that ought to concern you, Hult," said a new voice. This man was tall and slender. He did not look physically imposing, but Thrall had fought enough fine warriors to know that often technique was as good as, and sometimes better than, size. Judging by Hult's reactions, this man was respected. "The rules exist so that we can keep an eye on the orcs. This is the first one we've seen in years that's carried a human weapon. It's worth reporting. As for these. . . ."

Thrall watched in horror as the man began to leaf through Taretha's letters. Blue eyes narrowing, the tall man turned to look at Thrall. "Don't suppose you can read, can you?"

The other men erupted with laughter, crumbs spraying from their mouths, but the man asking the question appeared to be serious. Thrall started to answer, then thought better of it. Better to pretend not to even know the human language, he thought.

The tall man strode up to him. Thrall tensed, anticipating a blow, but instead the man squatted down beside him and stared directly into Thrall's eyes. Thrall looked away.

"You. Read?" The man pointed with a gloved finger to the letters. Thrall stared at them, and, figuring even an orc who didn't speak the human tongue would have made the connection, shook his head violently. The man gazed at him a moment more, then rose. Thrall wasn't sure he'd convinced him.

"He looks familiar, somehow," said the man. Thrall went cold inside.

"They all look the same to me," said Hult. "Big, green, and ugly."

"Too bad none of us can read," said the man. "I bet these papers would tell us a lot."

"You're always dreaming above your station, Waryk," said Hult, a hint of contempt in his voice.

Waryk shoved the letters back into the sack, plucked the knife from Hult's grasp over the man's halfhearted protest, and slung the now mostly-empty sack over his horse's withers. "Put the food away, before I change my mind. Let's take him to the camp."

Thrall had assumed they would put him on a cart, or perhaps in one of the wagons he remembered from so long ago. He was not granted even that basest of courtesies. They simply attached a rope to the trap-net that bound his limbs so tightly and dragged him behind one of their horses. Thrall, however, had an extremely high pain threshold after so many years in the gladiator ring. What hurt him more deeply was the loss of Taretha's letters. It was fortunate that none of these men could read. He was grateful they had not found the necklace. He had been holding the necklace she'd given him last night and had managed to slip it inside his black trousers before it was noticed. That part of her, at least, he could still hold on to.

The journey seemed to take forever, but the sun crawled across the sky only slowly. Finally, they reached a large stone wall. Waryk called for admittance, and Thrall heard what sounded like heavy gates opening. He was being dragged on his back, so he had an excellent view of the thickness of the wall as they entered. Disinterested guards threw the newcomer a brief glance, then went about their business.

The first thing that struck Thrall was the stench. It reminded him of the stables at Durnholde, but was much stronger. He wrinkled his nose. Hult was watching it and he laughed.

"Been away from your own kind too long, eh, greenie?" he sneered. "Forgotten how bad you smell?" He pinched his nose shut and rolled his eyes.

"Hult," said Waryk, a warning in his voice. He grasped the net's webbing and spoke a word of command. At once Thrall felt his bonds loosen and he got to his feet.

He stared about in horror. Huddled everywhere were dozens—perhaps hundreds—of orcs. Some sat in puddles of their own filth, their eyes unfocused, their sharp-tusked jaws slack. Others paced back and forth, muttering incoherently. Some slept tightly curled up on the earth, seeming not to care even if they were stepped on. There was an occasional squabble, but even that apparently sapped too much energy, for it died down almost as quickly as it had begun.

What was going on here? Were these men drugging Thrall's people? That had to be the answer. He knew what orcs were, how fierce, how savage. He had expected . . . well, he had not known what to expect, but certainly not this peculiar, unnatural lethargy.

"Go on," said Waryk, shoving Thrall gently toward the nearest cluster of orcs. "Food's put out once a day. There's water in the troughs."

Thrall stood up straight and tried to put a bold face on it as he strode to a group of five orcs, sitting beside the aforementioned water troughs. He could feel Waryk's eyes boring into his scraped and bruised back and heard the man say, "I could swear I've seen him somewhere before." Then he heard the men walking away.

Only one of the orcs looked up as Thrall approached. His heart was racing. He had never been this close to one of his people before, and now, here were five of them.

"I greet you," he said in orcish.

They stared at him. One of them looked down and resumed clawing at a small rock embedded in the dirt.

Thrall tried again. "I greet you," he said, spreading his arms in the gesture that the books told him indicated one warrior saluting another.

"Where'd they catch you?" one of them finally asked, speaking the human language. At Thrall's startled look, she said, "You weren't raised to speak orcish. I can tell."

"You're right. I was raised by humans. They taught me only a little orcish. I was hoping you could help me learn more."

The orcs looked at one another, then broke into laughter. "Raised by humans, eh? Hey, Krakis—come over here! We got ourselves a good storyteller! All right, Shaman, tell us another one."

Thrall felt his chance to connect with these people slipping through his fingers. "Please, I mean no insult. I'm a prisoner like you are now. I've never met any orcs, I just want. . . ."

Now the one who had looked away turned around, and Thrall fell silent. This orc's eyes were bright red and seemed to glow, as if lit from within. "So you want to meet your people? Well, you've met us. Now leave us be." He turned back to picking at the stone.

"Your eyes . . ." Thrall murmured, too stunned by the strange red glow to recognize the insult.

The orc cringed, lifted a hand to shield his face from Thrall's gaze, and hunched away even farther.

Thrall turned to ask a question and found himself standing alone. The other orcs had all shuffled away, casting furtive glances back at him.

The sky had been clouding over all day, and it had steadily been growing colder. Now, as Thrall stood alone in the center of a courtyard surrounded by what remained of his people, the gray skies opened and icy rain mixed with snow began to fall.

Thrall barely noticed the wretched weather, so deep was his personal misery. Was this why he had severed every tie he had ever known? To live out his life as a captive in a group of spiritless, sluggish creatures whom he once dreamed of leading against the tyranny of the humans? Which was worse, he mused, fighting in the ring for the glory of Blackmoore, sleeping safe and dry, reading letters from Tari, or standing here alone, shunned even by those of his own blood, his feet sinking into freezing mud?

The answer came swiftly: Both were intolerable. Without appearing too obvious, Thrall began to look about with an eye toward escape. It should be simple enough. Only a few guards here and there, and at night, they would have more difficulty seeing than Thrall would. They looked bored and disinterested, and judging by the lack of spirit, even energy or interest, displayed by this pathetic collection of orcs, Thrall did not think even one of them would have the courage to try to climb the rather low walls.

He felt the rain now, as it soaked the trousers he wore. A gray, gloomy day, for a gray, gloomy lesson. The orcs were no noble, fierce warriors. He could not imagine how these creatures ever gave the humans the slightest bit of resistance.

"We were not always as you see us here," came a soft, deep voice at his elbow. Surprised, Thrall turned around to see the red-eyed orc staring up at him with those unsettling orbs. "Soulless, afraid, ashamed. This is what *they* did to us," he continued, pointing to his eyes. "And if we could be rid of it, our hearts and spirits might return."

Thrall sank down in the mud beside him. "Go on," he urged. "I'm listening."

EIGHT

I t had been almost two days since the fire and Thrall's escape, and Black-moore had spent the better part of that time angry and brooding. It was at Tammis's urging that he had finally gone out hawking, and he had to admit, his servant had had a good idea.

The day was gloomy, but he and Taretha were well dressed and the vigorous riding kept their blood warm. He had wanted to go hunting, but his soft-hearted mistress had persuaded him that simply riding would be enough to pleasantly pass the time. He watched her canter past on the pretty dapple gray he had given her two years ago and wished the weather were warmer. He could think of other ways to pleasantly pass the time with Taretha.

What an unexpectedly ripe fruit Foxton's daughter had been. She had been a lovely, obedient child, and had matured into a lovely, obedient woman. Who would have thought those bright blue eyes would snare him so, that he would so love to bury his face in the flowing gold of her long tresses? Not he, not Blackmoore. But since he had taken her for his own several years ago, she had managed to constantly entertain him, a rare feat.

Langston had once inquired when Blackmoore was going to put aside Taretha in favor of a wife. Blackmoore had replied that there would be no putting aside Taretha even when he *did* take a wife, and there was plenty of time for such things when his plan had finally come to fruition. He would be in a much better position to command a politically favorable marriage once he had brought the Alliance to its collective knees.

And truly, there was no rush. There was plenty of time now to enjoy Taretha whenever and wherever he wished. And the more of that time he spent with the girl, the less it was about satisfying his urges and the more it was about simply enjoying her presence. More than once, as he lay awake and watched her sleep, silvered in moonlight streaming through the windows, he wondered if he was falling in love with her.

He had pulled up Nightsong, who was growing older but who still enjoyed a good canter now and then, and was watching her playfully guide Gray Lady in circles around him. At his order, she had not covered nor braided her hair, and it fell loose around her shoulders like a fall of purest gold. Taretha was laughing, and for a moment their eyes met.

To hell with the weather. They would make do.

He was about to order her off her steed and into a nearby copse of trees—their capes would keep them sufficiently warm—when he heard the sound of hoofbeats approaching. He scowled as Langston emerged, panting. His horse was lathered and steaming in the chill afternoon.

"My lord," he gasped, "I believe we have news of Thrall!"

Major Lorin Remka was not a person to be trifled with. Although she stood only a little bit over five feet tall, she was stocky and strong, and could handle herself more than adequately in any fight. She had enlisted disguised as a man many years ago out of a passionate desire to destroy the greenskin beings that had attacked her village. When the subterfuge had been discovered, her commanding officer had put her right back in the front lines. Later, she had learned that the officer had hoped she'd be killed, thus sparing him the embarrassment of reporting her. But Lorin Remka had stubbornly survived, and had acquitted herself as well as, and in some cases better than, any man in her unit.

She had taken a savage pleasure in slaughtering the enemy. In more than one case, after a kill she'd rubbed the reddish-black blood all over her face to mark her victory. The men had always given her a wide berth.

In this time of peace, Major Remka took almost as much pleasure in ordering about the slugs that had once been her direst enemies, although that pleasure had diminished once the bastards ceased to fight back. Why they had become so much more like cattle and less like monsters had often been a subject of discussion between Remka and her men late in the evenings, over a game of cards and an ale or four.

Most satisfying of all had been being able to take these once-terrifying killers and turn them into bowing and scraping servants. She found the ones most malleable who had the odd red eyes. They seemed eager for direction and praise, even from her. Now one of them was drawing a bath for her in her quarters.

"Make sure it's hot, Greekik," she called. "And don't forget the herbs this time!"

"Yes, my lady," called the female orc in a humble voice. Almost immediately, Remka could smell the cleansing scent of the dried herbs and flowers. Ever since she'd been working here, it seemed to her as if she stank all the time. She couldn't get it out of her clothes, but at least she could soak her body in the hot, scented water and wash it from her skin and long black hair.

Remka had adopted the male style of clothing, much more practical than all that feminine frippery. After years spent on the field of battle, she was more than used to dressing herself and actually preferred it. Now she removed her boots with a sigh. Just as she set them aside for Greekik to clean there came an urgent knock on the door.

"This had better be good," she muttered, opening the door. "What is it, Waryk?"

"We captured an orc yesterday," he began.

"Yes, yes, I read your report. My bath is cooling even as we speak and—"

"I thought the orc looked familiar," Waryk pressed.

"By the Light, Waryk, they all look the same!"

"No. This one looked different. And I know why now." He stepped aside, and a tall, imposing figure filled the doorway. Immediately Major Remka snapped to attention, wishing desperately she still had her boots on.

"Lieutenant General Blackmoore," she said. "How may we be of service?"

"Major Remka," said Aedelas Blackmoore, white teeth gleaming through a neatly trimmed black goatee, "I believe you've found my lost pet orc."

Thrall listened, captivated, as the red-eyed orc spoke in a soft voice of tales of valor and strength. He told of charges made against impossible odds, of heroic deeds, and of humans falling beneath a relentless green tide of orcs united in purpose. He spoke wistfully of a spiritual people as well, something Thrall had never heard of.

"Oh, yes," Kelgar said sadly. "Once, before we were the proud, battle-hungry Horde, we were individual clans. And in those clans were those who knew the magic of wind and water, of sky and land, of all the spirits of the wild, and they worked in harmony with those powers. We called them 'shamans,' and until the emergence of the warlocks, their skills were all we knew of power."

The word seemed to make Kelgar angry. He spat and with the first rousing of any kind of passion, snarled, "Power! Does it feed our people, raise our young? Our leaders held it all themselves, and only the barest trickle dripped down to the rest of us. They did . . . something, Thrall. I do not know what. But once we were defeated, all desire to fight bled out of us as if from an open wound." He lowered his head, placing it on arms folded across his knees, and closed his red eyes.

"Did all of you lose the desire to fight?" asked Thrall.

"All of us here. Those who fought weren't captured, or if they were, they were killed as they resisted." Kelgar kept his eyes closed.

Thrall respected the other orc's need for silence. Disappointment filled him. Kelgar's tale had the ring of truth about it, and for verification, all Thrall needed to do was look around him. What was this strange thing that had happened? How could an entire race of people have their natures so distorted as to end up here, defeated before they were even caught and thrown into this wretched hellhole?

"But the desire to fight is still strong in you, Thrall, though your name suggests otherwise." His eyes were open again, and they seemed to burn into Thrall. "Perhaps your being raised by humans spared you this. There are others like you, still out there. The walls are not so high that you cannot climb them, if that is your wish."

"It is," said Thrall eagerly. "Tell me where I can find others like me."

"The only one I have heard tell of is Grom Hellscream," Kelgar said. "He remains undefeated. His people, the Warsong clan, came from the west of this land. That is all I can tell you. Grom has eyes like me, but his spirit still resisted." Kelgar lowered his head. "If only I had been as strong."

"You can be," said Thrall. "Come with me, Kelgar. I am strong, I can easily pull you up over the walls if—"

Kelgar shook his head. "It is not the strength that is gone, Thrall. I could kill the guards in a heartbeat. Anyone here could. It's the desire. I do not wish to try to climb the walls. I want to stay here. I can't explain it, and I am ashamed, but that is the truth. You will have to have the passion, the fire, for all of us here."

Thrall nodded his acceptance, though he could not understand. Who wouldn't want to be free? Who wouldn't want to fight, to gain back all that had been taken, to make the unjust humans pay for what they had done to his people? But it was clear: Of all of the orcs present, he was the only one who would dare lift a defiant fist in challenge.

He would wait until nightfall. Kelgar said there was only a skeleton roster of guardsmen, and they often drank themselves into a stupor. If Thrall simply continued to pretend he was like all the other orcs, he felt certain his opportunity would come.

At that moment, a female orc approached. She moved with a sense of purpose rarely seen here, and Thrall stood as it became clear that she was heading for him.

"You are the newly captured orc?" she asked, in human speech.

Thrall nodded. "My name is Thrall."

"Then, Thrall, you had best know that the commander of the encampments is coming for you."

"What is his name?" Thrall went cold inside as he feared the worst.

"I do not know, but he wears the colors red and gold, with a black falcon on—"

"Blackmoore," hissed Thrall. "I should have known he would be able to find me."

There was a loud clanging and all the orcs turned toward the large tower. "We are to line up," said the female. "Although it is not the usual time for counting."

"They want you, Thrall," said Kelgar. "But they won't find you. You will have to go now. The guards will be distracted at the thought of the commander coming. I will create a diversion. The least guarded area is at the end of the camp. We all are coming to the sound of the bell like the cattle we are," he said, self-loathing plain in his voice and mien. "Go. Now."

Thrall needed no further urging. He turned on his heel and began to move swiftly, threading his way between the sudden press of orcs moving in the opposite direction. As he shoved, struggling, he heard a cry of pain. It was the female orc. He didn't dare stop to look back, but when he heard Kelgar shouting harsh-sounding words in orcish, he understood. Kelgar had somehow managed to reach deep inside and find a shadow of his old fighting spirit. He had begun to fight with the female orc. By the sounds of the guards, this was highly unusual. They descended to break the quarreling orcs apart, and even as Thrall watched, the few guards who had been walking the wall scurried down and raced toward the shouting.

They would probably beat both Kelgar and the innocent female, Thrall thought. He regretted this deeply. But, he told himself, because of their actions, I am free to do everything I possibly can to ensure that no human ever, *ever* beats an orc again.

After having reached adulthood in a tightly guarded cell, with men watching his every move, he could not believe how easy it was to climb the walls and slip down to freedom. Ahead was a dense, forested area. He ran faster than he had ever run, knowing that every minute he was in the open he was vulnerable. And yet, no one cried the alarm, no one gave chase.

He ran for several hours, losing himself in the forest, zigging and zagging and doing everything possible to make it difficult for the search parties that would no doubt follow. Finally, he slowed, panting and gasping for air. He climbed a stout tree, and when he poked his head through its thick canopy of leaves, he could see nothing but a sea of green.

Blinking, he located the sun. It was starting its late afternoon journey toward the horizon. The west; Kelgar had said that Grom Hellscream's clan had come from the west.

He would find this Hellscream, and together, they would liberate their imprisoned brothers and sisters.

Black-gloved hands clasped behind him, the Commander of the Camps, one Aedelas Blackmoore, walked slowly down the line of orcs. All of them shied away from him, staring at their mud-encrusted feet. Blackmoore had to admit they had been more entertaining, if more deadly, when they had had some spirit to them.

Wincing at the stench, Blackmoore lifted a scented kerchief to his nose. Following him closely, like a dog awaiting its master's whim, was Major Remka. He'd heard good things about her; she was apparently more efficient than the majority of the men.

But if she had had his Thrall, and let him slip through her fingers, he would not be merciful.

"Where is the one you said you thought was Thrall?" he demanded of Remka's guardsman Waryk. The young man held his composure better than his commanding officer did, but even he was starting to show hints of panic about the eyes.

"I had seen him at the gladiator battles, and the blue eyes are so rare. . . ." said Waryk, starting to stammer a little.

"Do you see him here?"

"N-no, Lieutenant General. I don't."

"Then perhaps it was not Thrall."

"We did find some things he had stolen," said Waryk, brightening. He snapped his fingers and one of his men raced off, returning in a few moments with a large sack. "Do you recognize this?" He extended a plain dagger to Blackmoore, hilt first as etiquette demanded.

Blackmoore's breath caught in his throat. He had wondered where that had gone to. It wasn't a very expensive one, but he had missed it. . . . He ran his gloved thumb over the symbol of his crest, the black falcon. "This is mine. Anything else?"

"Some papers . . . Major Remka has not had time to look at them yet. . . ." Waryk's voice trailed off, but Blackmoore understood. The idiot couldn't read. What kind of papers could Thrall possibly have had? Leaves torn from *his* books, no doubt. Blackmoore snatched the sack and rummaged through the papers at the bottom. He drew one out into the light.

. . . wish I could talk to you instead of just sending you these letters. I see you in the ring and my heart breaks for you. . . .

Letters! Who could possibly . . . he seized another one.

. . . harder and harder to find time to write. Our Master demands so much of both of us. I heard that he beat you, I am so sorry my dear friend. You don't deserve . . .

Taretha.

A greater pain than any he had ever known clutched at Blackmoore's chest. He pulled out more letters . . . by the Light, there had to be dozens here . . . maybe hundreds. How long had the two been conspiring? For some reason his eyes stung and breathing became difficult. *Tari . . . Tari, how could you, you never lacked for anything. . . .*

"My lord?" Remka's concerned voice brought Blackmoore out of his painful shock. He took a deep breath and blinked the telltale tears back. "Is all well?"

"No, Major Remka." His voice was as cool and composed as ever, for which he was grateful. "All is not well. You had my orc Thrall, one of the finest gladiators ever to have graced the ring. He's made me a great deal of money over the years and was supposed to make me a great deal more. Beyond a doubt, it was he your man captured. And it is he whom I do not see in this line at all."

He took keen pleasure in watching the color drain from Remka's face. "He could be hiding inside the camp," she offered.

"He could be," said Blackmoore, drawing back his lips from white teeth in a rictus of a smile. "Let us hope so, for your continued good fortune, Major Remka. Search the encampment. *Now.*"

She scurried away to do his bidding, shouting orders. Thrall certainly wouldn't have been stupid enough to come to a lineup, like a dog responding to a whistle. It was possible he was still here. But somehow, Blackmoore sensed that Thrall was gone. He was elsewhere, doing . . . ? What? What kind of scheme had he and that bitch Taretha cooked up?

Blackmoore was right. An extensive search turned up nothing. None of the orcs, curse them, would even admit to seeing Thrall. Blackmoore demoted Remka, put Waryk in her place, and rode slowly home. Langston met him halfway, and commiserated with him, but even Langston's cheerful, brainless chatter could not stir Blackmoore from his gloom. In one fiery night, he had lost the two things most important to him: Thrall and Taretha.

He climbed the steps to his quarters, went to his bedchamber, and eased open the door. The light fell across Taretha's sleeping face. Gently, so as not to wake her, Blackmoore sat down on the bed. He removed his gloves and reached to touch the soft, creamy curve of her cheek. She was so beautiful. Her touch had thrilled him, her laughter moved him. But no more.

"Sleep well, pretty traitor," he whispered. He bent and kissed her, the pain in his heart still present but ruthlessly suppressed. "Sleep well, until I have need of you."

NINE

Thrall had never been so exhausted or hungry in his life. But freedom tasted sweeter than the meat he had been fed, and felt more restful than the straw upon which he had slept as Blackmoore's prisoner at Durnholde. He was unable to catch the coneys and squirrels that flitted through the forest, and wished that somehow survival skills had been taught to him along with battle histories and the nature of art. Because it was autumn, there were ripe fruits on the trees, and he quickly became adept at finding grubs and insects. These did little to appease the mammoth hunger that gnawed at his insides, but at least he had ready access to water in the form of the myriad small streams and brooks that wound through the forest.

After several days, the wind shifted while Thrall steadily pushed through the undergrowth and brought the sweet scent of roasting meat to his nostrils. He inhaled deeply, as if he could obtain sustenance by the smell alone. Ravenous, he turned to follow the smell.

Even though his body was crying out for food, Thrall did not let his hunger overcome his caution. That was well, for as he moved to the edge of the forested area, he saw dozens of humans.

The day was bright and warm, one of the last few such days of the fall, and the humans were joyfully preparing a feast that made Thrall's mouth water. There were baked breads, barrels of fresh fruits and vegetables, crocks of jams and butters and spreads, wheels of cheeses, bottles of what he assumed were wine and mead, and in the center, two pigs turned slowly on spits.

Thrall's knees gave way and he sank slowly to the forest floor, staring enraptured at the foodstuffs spread before him as if to taunt him. Over in the cleared field, children played with hoops and banners and other toys Thrall could not attach names to. Mothers suckled their babes, and maidens danced shyly with young men. It was a scene of happiness and contentment, and more than the food, Thrall wanted to belong here.

But he did not. He was an orc, a monster, a green-skin, a black-blood, and any of a hundred other epithets. So he sat and watched while the villagers celebrated, feasted, and danced until the night encroached upon them.

The moons rose, one bright and white, one cool and blue-green, as the last of the furniture, plates, and food items were gathered up. Thrall watched the villagers wander down the winding path through the field, and saw small candles appear in tiny windows. Still he waited, and watched the moons move slowly across the sky. Many hours after the last candle was extinguished in the windows, Thrall rose, and moved with skillful silence toward the village.

His sense of smell had always been acute, and it was sharpened now that he was giving it leave to enjoy the smells of food. He followed the scents, reaching into windows and snatching whole loaves of bread which he gobbled down at once, uncovering a basket of apples set out by the door and crunching the small, sweet fruits greedily.

Juice ran down his bare chest, sweet and sticky. He absently wiped at it with one large green hand. Slowly, the hunger was beginning to be sated. At each house, Thrall took something, but never too much from any one home.

At one window, Thrall peered in to see figures sleeping by the dying hearth fire. He quickly withdrew, waited a moment, and then slowly looked in again. These were children, sleeping on straw mattresses. There was three of them, plus one in a cradle. Two were boys; the third was a little girl with yellow hair. As Thrall watched, she rolled over in her sleep.

A sharp pang stabbed Thrall. As if no time at all had passed, he was transported in his mind back to that day when he had first seen Taretha, when she had smiled broadly and waved at him. This girl looked so much like her, with her round cheeks, her golden hair—

A harsh noise startled him and Thrall whirled just in time to see something four-legged and dark charge at him. Teeth snapped near his ear. Reacting instinctively, Thrall clutched the animal and closed his hands around the beast's throat. Was this a wolf, one of the creatures his people sometimes befriended?

It had erect, pointed ears, a long muzzle, and sharp white teeth. It resembled the woodcuts of wolves he had seen in the books, but was very different in coloring and head shape.

Now the house was awake, and he heard human voices crying in alarm. He squeezed, and the creature went limp. Dropping the body, Thrall looked inside to see the little girl staring at him with eyes wide in horror. As he watched, she screamed and pointed. "Monster, Da, monster!"

The hateful words coming from her innocent lips wounded Thrall to the quick. He turned to flee only to see that a ring of frightened villagers surrounded him. Some of them carried pitchforks and scythes, the only weapons this farming community possessed.

"I mean you no harm," Thrall began.

"It talks! It's a demon!" screamed someone, and the little band charged.

Thrall reacted instinctively and his training kicked in. When one of the men shoved a pitchfork at him, Thrall deftly seized the makeshift weapon and used it to knock the other forks and scythes out of the clumsy villagers' hands. At one point he screamed his battle cry, the bloodlust high within him, and swung the pitchfork at his attackers.

He stopped just short of impaling the fallen man, who stared up at him wildly.

These men were not his enemies, even though it was clear they feared and hated him. They were simple farmers, living off the crops they grew and the animals they raised. They had children. They were afraid of him, that was all. No, the enemy was not here. The enemy was sleeping soundly on a feather-bed in Durnholde. With a cry of self-loathing, Thrall hurled the pitchfork several yards away and took advantage of the break in the circle to flee for the safety of the forest.

The men did not pursue. Thrall had not expected them to. They only wished to be left in peace. As he ran through the forest, utilizing the energy engendered by the confrontation to his advantage, Thrall tried, and failed, to erase the image of a little blond girl screaming in terror and calling him "monster."

Thrall ran through the next day and into the night, when he finally collapsed in exhaustion. He slept the sleep of the dead, with no dreams to plague him. Something roused him before the dawn, and he blinked sleepily.

There came a second sharp prod to the belly, and now he was fully awake—and staring up at eight angry orc faces.

He tried to rise, but they fell upon him and bound him before he could even struggle. One of them shoved a large, angry face with yellowed tusks within an inch of Thrall's. He barked something completely unintelligible, and Thrall shook his head.

The orc frowned even more terribly, grabbed one of Thrall's ears and uttered more gibberish.

Guessing at what the other might be saying, Thrall said in the human tongue, "No, I'm not deaf."

An angry hiss came from all of them. "Hu-man," said the big orc, who seemed to be their leader. "You not speak orcish?"

"A little," Thrall said in that language. "My name is Thrall."

The orc gaped, then opened his mouth and guffawed. His cronies joined him. "Hu-man who looks like an orc!" he said, extending a black-nailed finger in Thrall's direction. In orcish, he said, "Kill him."

"No!" Thrall cried in orcish. One thing about this fairly dire encounter gave him hope—these orcs were fighters. They did not slouch about in exhausted despair, too dispirited to even climb an easily scalable stone wall. "Want find Grom Hellscream!"

The big orc froze. In broken human, he said, "Why find? You sent to kill, huh? From human, huh?"

Thrall shook his head. "No. Camps . . . bad. Orcs. . . ." He couldn't find the words in this alien tongue, so he sighed deeply and hung his head, trying to look like the pitiable creatures he had met in the internment camp. "Me want orcs. . . ." He lifted his roped hands and bellowed. "Grom help. No more camps. No more orcs. . . ." Again, he mimed looking despondent and hopeless.

He risked a look up, wondering if his broken orcish had managed to convey what he wanted. At least they weren't trying to kill him anymore. Another orc, slightly smaller but equally as dangerous-looking as the first, spoke in a gruff voice. The leader responded heatedly. They argued back and forth, and then finally the big one seemed to give in.

"Tragg say, maybe. Maybe you see Hellscream, if you worthy. Come." They hauled him to his feet and marched him forward. The prod of the spear in his back encouraged Thrall to pick up the pace. Even though he was bound and at the center of a ring of hostile orcs, Thrall felt a surge of joy.

He was going to see Grom Hellscream, the one orc that remained uncowed. Perhaps together, they could free the imprisoned orcs, rouse them into action, and remind them of their birthrights.

While it was difficult for Thrall to summon many words of orc speech, he was able to understand much more than he could articulate. He remained quiet, and listened.

The orcs escorting him to see Hellscream were surprised by his vigor. Thrall had noticed that most of them had brown or black eyes, not the peculiar, burning red of most of the orcs in the internment camps. Kelgar had indicated that there might be some kind of connection between the glowing, fiery orbs and the peculiar lethargy that had all but overcome the orcs. What it was, Thrall didn't know, and by listening, he hoped to learn.

While the orcs said nothing of glowing red eyes, they did comment on the listlessness. Many of the words that Thrall did not understand were nonetheless comprehensible because of the tone of contempt in which they were uttered. Thrall was not alone in his revulsion and disgust at seeing the once-legendary fighting force brought lower than common cattle. At least a bull would charge you if you irritated it.

Of their great warlord, they spoke words of praise and awe. They also spoke of Thrall, wondering if he was some sort of new spy sent to discover

Grom's lair and lead the humans to a cowardly ambush. Thrall desperately wished there were some way to convince them of his sincerity. He would do anything they wanted of him to prove himself.

At one point, the group came to a halt. The leader, whom Thrall had learned was named Rekshak, untied a sash from around his broad chest. He held it in both hands and went to Thrall. "You be. . . ." He said something in orcish that Thrall didn't understand, but he knew what Rekshak wanted. He lowered his head obediently, for he towered over all the other orcs, and permitted himself to be blindfolded. The sash smelled of new sweat and old blood.

Certainly, they might kill him now, or abandon him to die, bound and blindfolded. Thrall accepted that possibility and thought it preferable to another day spent risking his life in the gladiator pit for the glory of the cruel bastard who had beaten him and tried to break Tari's spirit.

Now he strode with less certain steps, though at one point two orcs silently went to either side of him and grasped his arms. He trusted them; he had no choice.

With no way to gauge the passing of time, the journey seemed to take forever. At one point the soft, springy forest loam gave way to chill stone, and the air around Thrall turned colder. By the way the other orcs' voices were altered, Thrall realized they were descending into the earth.

At last, they came to a halt. Thrall bowed his head and the sash was removed. Even the dim lighting provided by torches made him blink as his eyes adjusted from the utter darkness of the blindfold.

He was in an enormous underground cavern. Sharp stones thrust from both stone ceiling and floor. Thrall could hear the drip of moisture in the distance. There were several smaller caves leading out from this one large cavern, many with animal skins draped over the entrances. Armor that had seen better days, and weapons that looked well used and well cared for were scattered here and there. A small fire burned in the center, its smoke wafting up to the stone roof. This, then, must be where the legendary Grom Hellscream and the remnants of the once-fierce Warsong clan had retreated.

But where was the famous chieftain? Thrall looked around. While several more orcs had emerged from various caves, none had the bearing or garb of a true chieftain. He turned to Rekshak.

"You said you would take me to Hellscream," he demanded. "I do not see him here."

"You do not see him, but he is present. He sees you," said another orc, brushing aside an animal skin and emerging into the cavern. This one was almost as tall as Thrall, but without the bulk. He looked older, and very tired.

The bones of various animals and quite possibly humans were strung on a necklace about his thin throat. He carried himself in a manner that demanded respect, and Thrall was willing to give it. Whoever this orc was, he was a personage of importance in the clan. And it was clear he spoke the human tongue almost as fluently as Thrall.

Thrall inclined his head. "This may be. But I wish to speak with him, not merely bask in his unseen presence."

The orc smiled. "You have spirit, fire," he said. "That is well. I am Iskar, adviser to the great chieftain Hellscream."

"My name is—"

"You are not unknown to us, Thrall of Durnholde." At Thrall's look of surprise, Iskar continued, "Many have heard of Lieutenant General Blackmoore's pet orc."

Thrall growled, softly, deep in his throat, but he did not lose his composure. He had heard the term before, but it rankled more coming from the mouth of one of his own people.

"We have never seen you fight, of course," Iskar continued, clasping his hands behind his back and walking a slow circle around Thrall, looking him up and down all the while. "Orcs aren't allowed to watch the gladiator battles. While you were finding glory in the ring, your brethren were beaten and abused."

Thrall could take it no longer. "I received none of the glory. I was a slave, owned by Blackmoore, and if you do not think I despise him, look at this!" He twisted around so that they could see his back. They looked, and then to his fury they laughed.

"There is nothing to see, Thrall of Durnholde," Iskar said. Thrall realized what had happened; the healing salve had worked its magic all too well. There was not even a scar on his back from the terrible beating he had received from Blackmoore and all of his men. "You ask for our compassion, and yet you seem hale and healthy to us."

Thrall whirled. Anger filled him, and he tried to temper it, but to little avail. "I was a thing, a piece of property. Do you think I benefited from my sweat and blood shed in the ring? Blackmoore hauled in gold coins while I was kept in a cell, brought out for his amusement. The scars on my body are not visible, I realize that now. But the only reason I was healed was so that I could go back in the ring and fight again to enrich my master. There are scars you cannot see that run much deeper. I escaped, I was thrown into the camps, and then I came here to find Hellscream. Although I begin to doubt his existence. It seems too much to hope for that I could still find an orc who exemplifies all that I understood our people to be."

"What do you understand our people to be, then, orc who bears the name of slave?" Iskar taunted.

Thrall was breathing heavily, but summoned the control that Sergeant had taught him. "They are strong. Cunning. Powerful. They are a terror in battle. They have spirits that cannot be quenched. Let me see Hellscream, and he will know that I am worthy."

"We will be the judge of that," said Iskar. He raised his hand, and three orcs entered the cavern. They began to don armor and reach for various weapons. "These three are our finest warriors. They are, as you have said, strong, cunning, and powerful. They fight to kill or die, unlike what you are used to in the gladiator ring. Your playacting will not serve you here. Only real skill will save you. If you survive, Hellscream may grant you an audience, or he may not."

Thrall gazed at Iskar. "He will see me," he said confidently.

"You had best hope so. Begin!" And with no further warning, all three orcs charged at a weaponless, armorless Thrall.

TEN

For the briefest of moments, Thrall was caught off guard. Then years of training took over. While he had no desire to fight his own people, he was able to quickly regard them as combatants in the ring and react accordingly. As one of them charged, Thrall swiftly dodged and then reached upward, snatching the huge battle-ax from the orc's hands. In the same fluid motion, he swung. The blow bit deeply, but the armor deflected most of the strike. The orc cried out and stumbled to his feet, clutching his back. He would survive, but that quickly, the odds had been reduced to two to one.

Thrall whirled, snarling. The bloodlust, sweet and familiar, filled him again. Bellowing his own challenge, a second adversary charged, wielding an enormous broadsword that more than compensated for his lack of arm length. Thrall twisted to the side, avoiding a killing blow but still feeling the hot pain as the blade bit into his side.

The orc pressed his attack, and at the same time, the third orc came in from behind. Thrall, though, now had a weapon. He ignored the blood pumping from his side, making the stone floor slick and treacherous, and swung the huge ax first toward one attacker, then letting the momentum swing it back to strike the second.

They parried with enormous shields. Thrall had no armor or shielding, but fighting this way was something he was used to. These were clever opponents, but so had the human fighters been. They were strong and physically powerful, but so were the trolls Thrall had faced and defeated. He moved from a place of calm surety, dodging and screaming and striking. Once, they might have been a threat to him. Now, though, even at two to one, as long as Thrall was able to keep his eye on strategy and not succumb to the sweet call of bloodlust, he knew he would triumph.

His arm moved as if of its own accord, striking blow after blow. Even when his feet slipped and he fell, he used it to his advantage. He angled his body so it would strike one opponent, while extending his arm to its full length so that the huge ax would swipe the other orc's legs out from under him. He was careful to angle the ax so that the blunt end struck, not the blade. He did not wish to kill these orcs; he only wished to win the fight.

Both orcs went down hard. The orc Thrall had struck with the ax clutched his legs and howled his frustration. It appeared they had both been broken. The other orc staggered to his feet and tried to impale Thrall with the broadsword.

Thrall made his decision. Steeling himself for the pain, he reached upward with both hands, grasped the blade, and yanked it forward. The orc lost his balance and fell atop Thrall's body. Thrall twisted and in a heartbeat found himself straddling the other orc, his hands at his throat.

Squeeze, instinct cried. *Squeeze tight. Kill Blackmoore for what he did to you.*

No! he thought. This was not Blackmoore. This was one of his people, whom he had risked everything to find. He rose and extended a hand to the defeated orc to help him up.

The orc stared at the hand. "We kill," said Iskar, his voice as calm as before. "Kill your opponent, Thrall. It's what a real orc would do."

Thrall shook his head slowly, reached down to clasp his opponent's arm, and hauled the vanquished foe to his feet. "In battle, yes. I would kill my foe in battle, so that he did not rise up against me at another time. But you are my people, whether you will own me as one of you or not. We are too few in number for me to kill him."

Iskar looked at him strangely, seemed to be waiting for something, then continued speaking.

"Your reasoning is understandable. You have honorably defeated our three finest warriors. You have passed the first test."

First? Thrall thought, one hand going to his bleeding side. A suspicion began to form that no matter how many "tests" he passed, they would not let him see Hellscream. Perhaps Hellscream was not even here.

Perhaps Hellscream was no longer even *alive*.

But Thrall knew in his heart of hearts that even if this were so, he would rather die here than return to his life under Blackmoore's boot.

"What is the next challenge?" he asked quietly. He could tell by the reaction that his calm demeanor impressed them.

"A question of will," said Iskar. There was a slight smirk on his heavy-jawed face. He gestured, and an orc emerged from one of the caves carrying what appeared at first glance to be a heavy sack on his back. But when he carelessly tossed the "sack" onto the stone floor, Thrall realized that it was a male human child, bound hand and foot and with a gag thrust into his mouth. The child's black hair was tangled. He was filthy, and where dirt did not cover his pale flesh, Thrall saw the purple and green of bruises. His eyes were the same color as Thrall's own, a rich blue, and those eyes were wide with terror.

"You know what this is," said Iskar.

"A child. A human child," Thrall replied, perplexed. Surely they did not expect him to fight the boy.

"A male child. Males mature to become orc-killers. They are our natural enemies. If you indeed chafed at the whip and rod, and wish for revenge on those who enslaved you and even gave you a name to mark your low position in life, then exact your revenge now. Kill this child, before he grows to be of an age to kill you."

The boy's eyes widened, for Iskar had been speaking in the human tongue. He squirmed frantically and muffled sounds came from his mouth. The orc who had carried him out kicked him disinterestedly in the stomach. The child curled up tightly, whimpering past the gag.

Thrall stared. Surely they were not serious. He looked over at Iskar, who regarded him without blinking.

"This is no warrior," said Thrall. "And this is no honorable combat. I had thought that orcs prized their honor."

"So we do," agreed Iskar, "but before you lies a future threat. Defend your people."

"He is a child!" Thrall exclaimed. "He is no threat now, and who can say what he will be? I know the clothes he wears, and what village he was taken from. The people there are farmers and herders. They live on what they raise, both fruit and flesh. Their weapons are for hunting coneys and deer, not orcs."

"But there is a good chance that, if we again go to war, this boy will be in the front line, charging at one of us with a spear and calling for our blood," Iskar retorted. "Do you wish to see Hellscream or not? If you do not slay the child, you may rest assured that you will not leave this cave alive."

The boy was crying now, silently. Thrall was instantly reminded of his parting with Taretha, and her description of weeping. Her image filled his mind. He thought of her, and of Sergeant. He thought of how saddened he had been when his appearance had frightened the little girl in the village.

And then he thought of Blackmoore's handsome, contemptuous face; of all the men who had spat upon him and called him "monster" and "green-skin" and worse.

But those memories did not condone cold-blooded murder. Thrall made his decision. He dropped the bloody ax to the floor.

"If this child takes up arms against me in the future," he said, choosing his words slowly and deliberately, "then I shall kill him on the battlefield. And I shall take a certain pleasure in the doing, because I will know that I am fighting for the rights of my people. But I will not kill a bound child who lies helpless before me, human though he is. And if this means I never see Hellscream, so be it. If it means I must fight all of you and fall beneath your numbers, I say again, so be it. I would rather die than commit such a dishonorable atrocity."

He steadied himself, arms outstretched, waiting for the attack that would come. Iskar sighed.

"A pity," he said, "but you have chosen your own destiny." He lifted his hand.

At that moment, a terrible scream pierced the still, cool air. It echoed and reverberated through the cavern, hurting Thrall's ears and piercing him to the bone. He shrank back from the noise. The animal skin covering one of the caves was torn down and a tall, red-eyed orc emerged. Thrall had gotten used to the appearance of his people, but this orc was unlike any he had yet seen.

Long black hair flowed down his back in a thick tangle. Each large ear was pierced several times, reminding Thrall oddly of Sergeant, and the dozen or so rings glinted in the firelight. His leather clothing of red and black contrasted strikingly with his green skin, and several chains attached to various places on his body swayed with his movements. His entire jaw seemed to be painted black, and at the moment, it was open wider than Thrall would have believed possible. It was he who was making the terrifying noise, and Thrall realized that Grom Hellscream had gotten his name for a very good reason.

The shriek faded, and Grom spoke. "Never had I thought to see this!" He marched up to Thrall and stared at him. His eyes were flame-colored, and something dark and frightening seemed to dance in their centers in place of pupils. Thrall assumed the comment to be derogatory, but he was not about to be cowed. He drew himself up to his full imposing height, determined to meet death with an unbowed head. He opened his mouth to reply to Grom's comment, but the orc chieftain continued.

"How is it you know of mercy, Thrall of Durnholde? How is it you know when to offer it, and for what reasons?"

The orcs were murmuring among themselves now, confused. Iskar bowed.

"Noble Hellscream," he began, "we had thought that this child's capture would please you. We expected—"

"*I* would expect that its parents would track it down to our lair, you fool!" cried Grom. "We are warriors, fierce and proud. At least we once were." He shuddered, as if from a fever, and for a moment seemed to Thrall to be pale and tired. But that impression was gone as quickly as it had come. "We do not butcher children. I assume whoever caught the whelp had the presence of mind to blindfold it?"

"Of course, lord," said Rekshak, looking offended.

"Then take him back where you found him the same way." Hellscream marched over to the child and removed the gag. The boy was too terrified to cry out. "Listen to me, tiny human. Tell your people that the orcs had you, and chose not to harm you. Tell them," and he looked over at Thrall, "that they showed you mercy. Also tell them if they try to find us, they will fail. We will be on the move soon. Do you understand?"

The boy nodded. "Good." To Rekshak, he said, "Take him back. *Now.* And the next time you find a human pup, leave it be."

Rekshak nodded. With a definite lack of gentleness, he took the boy by the arm and hauled him to his feet.

"Rekshak," said Grom, his harsh voice heavy with warning. "If you disobey me and the boy comes to harm, I shall know of it. And I shall not forgive."

Rekshak scowled impotently. "As my lord wills," he said, and, still roughly hauling the boy, began to ascend one of the many winding stone corridors that emptied into the cavern.

Iskar looked confused. "My lord," he began, "this is the pet of Blackmoore! He stinks of humans, he brags of his fear of killing—"

"I have no fear of killing those who deserve to die," Thrall growled. "I do not choose to kill those who do not."

Hellscream reached out and put a hand on Iskar's shoulder, then placed the other on Thrall's, reaching up to do so. "Iskar, my old friend," he said, his rough voice soft, "you have seen me when the bloodlust has come upon me. You have seen me wade in blood up to my knees. I have killed the children of the humans ere now. But we gave all we had fighting in that manner, and where has it brought us? Low and defeated, our kind slouch in camps and lift no hand to free themselves, let alone fight for others. That way of fighting, of making war, has brought us to this. Long have I thought that the ancestors would show me a new way, a way to win back what we have lost. It is a fool who repeats the same actions expecting a different outcome, and whatever I may be, I am not a fool. Thrall was strong enough to defeat the finest we had to offer. He has tasted humankind's ways and turned his back on them to be free. He has escaped from the camps and against the odds managed to find me. I agree with his choices here today. One day, my old friend, you, too, will see the wisdom in this."

He squeezed Iskar's shoulder affectionately. "Leave us, now. All of you."

Slowly, reluctantly, and not without a few hostile glances in Thrall's direction, the orcs all ascended into different levels of the cave. Thrall waited.

"We are alone now," said Hellscream. "Are you hungry, Thrall of Durnholde?"

"I am ravenous," said Thrall, "but I would ask that you not call me Thrall of Durnholde. I escaped Durnholde, and I loathe the thought of it."

Hellscream lumbered over to another cave, pulled the skin aside, and withdrew a large chunk of raw meat. Thrall accepted it, nodded his thanks, and bit into it eagerly. His first honestly earned meal as a free orc. Deer flesh had never tasted so fine to him.

"Should we then change your other name? It is the term of a slave," said Hellscream, squatting and watching Thrall closely with red eyes. "It was meant to be a badge of shame."

Thrall thought as he chewed and swallowed. "No. Blackmoore gave me the name so that I would never forget that I was something he owned, that I belonged to him." His eyes narrowed. "I never will. I will keep the name, and one day, when I see him again, he will be the one who remembers what he did to me, and regret it with all his heart."

Hellscream regarded him closely. "You would kill him, then?"

Thrall did not answer immediately. He thought of the time when he had almost killed Sergeant and seen Blackmoore's face instead, of the countless times since that moment when he had visualized Blackmoore's handsome, taunting visage while fighting in the ring. He thought of Blackmoore's slurred speech and the agony that his kicks and fists had caused. He thought of the anguish on Taretha's lovely face as she spoke of the master of Durnholde.

"Yes," he said, his voice deep and hard. "I would. If any creature deserves death, it is certainly Aedelas Blackmoore."

Hellscream cackled, a strange, wild sound. "Good. At least you're willing to kill somebody. I was starting to wonder if I'd made the right choice." He gestured to the tattered cloth that Thrall had tucked into the waistband of his trousers. "That doesn't look human-made."

Thrall tugged the swaddling cloth free. "It isn't. This is the cloth in which Blackmoore found me, when I was an infant." He handed it to Hellscream. "That's all I know."

"I know this pattern," said Hellscream, opening the cloth and regarding the symbol of the white wolf's head on a blue background. "This is the symbol of the Frostwolf clan. Where did Blackmoore find you?"

"He always told me it wasn't very far from Durnholde," said Thrall.

"Then your family was a long way from home. I wonder why."

Hope seized Thrall. "Did you know them? Could you tell me who my parents were? There is so much I don't know."

"I can only say that this is the emblem of the Frostwolf clan, and that they live a great distance from here, somewhere up in the mountains. They were exiled by Gul'dan. I never did learn why. Durotan and his people seemed loyal to me. Rumor has it they have formed bonds with the wild white wolves, but one cannot always believe everything that one hears."

Thrall tasted disappointment. Still, it was more than he had known before. He ran a big hand over the small square of old fabric, amazed that he had ever been little enough to be wrapped in it.

"Another question, if you can answer it," he said to Hellscream. "When I was younger, I was training outside, and a wagon passed, carrying several. . . ." He paused. What was the correct term? Inmates? Slaves? "Several orcs to the internment camps. One of them broke free and attacked me. He kept screaming something over and over. I was never able to learn what he said, but I vowed I would remember the words. Perhaps you can tell me what they mean."

"Speak, and I shall tell you."

"Kagh! Bin mog g'thazag cha!" said Thrall.

"That was no attack, my young friend," said Hellscream. "The words are, 'Run! I will protect you!' "

Thrall stared. All this time, he had assumed that he was the object of the charge, when all along. . . .

"The other fighters," he said. "We were doing a training exercise. I was without armor or shield, in the center of a ring of men. . . . He died, Hellscream. They cut him to bits. He thought they were making sport of me, that I was being attacked twelve to one. He died to protect me."

Hellscream said nothing, merely continued to eat while watching Thrall closely. Famished though he was, Thrall let the haunch of meat drip its juices onto the stone floor. Someone had given his life to protect an unknown young orc. Slowly, without the keen pleasure he had experienced before, he bit into the flesh and chewed. Sooner or later, he would have to find the Frostwolf clan, and learn exactly who he was.

ELEVEN

T hrall had never known such joy. For the next several days, he feasted with the Warsong clan, sang their fierce battle chants and songs, and learned at Hellscream's feet.

Far from being the mindless killing machines the books had painted them, Thrall learned that the orcs were of a noble race. They were masters on the battlefield, and had been known to revel in the spray of blood and the crack of bone, but their culture was a rich, elaborate one. Hellscream spoke of a time when each clan was separate unto itself. Each had its own symbols, customs, even speech. There were spiritual leaders among them, called shamans, who worked with the magic of nature and not the evil magic of demonic, supernatural powers.

"Isn't magic magic?" Thrall, who had very little experience with magic in any form, wanted to know.

"Yes and no," said Grom. "Sometimes the effect is the same. For instance, if a shaman was to summon lightning to strike his foes, they would be burned to death. If a warlock was to summon hell's flames against an enemy, they would be burned to death."

"So magic is magic," said Thrall.

"But," Grom continued, "lightning is a natural phenomenon. You call it by requesting it. With hell's fire, you make a bargain. It costs a little of yourself."

"But you said that the shamans were disappearing. Doesn't that mean that the warlock's way was better?"

"The warlock's way was quicker," said Grom. "More effective, or so it seemed. But there comes a time when a price must be paid, and sometimes, it is dear indeed."

Thrall learned that he was not the only one appalled by the peculiar lethargy demonstrated by the vast majority of orcs, now languishing apathetically in the internment camps.

"No one can explain it," said Hellscream, "but it claimed nearly all of us, one by one. We thought it some kind of illness at first, but it does not kill and it does not worsen after a certain point."

"One of the orcs in the camp thought it had something to do with—" Thrall fell silent, having no desire to give offense.

"Speak!" demanded Grom, annoyed. "To do with what?"

"With the redness of the eyes," said Thrall.

"Ah," said Grom, with, Thrall thought, a trace of sorrow. "Perhaps it does, at that. There is something we wrestle with that you, blue-eyed youngling, cannot understand. I hope you never do." And for the second time since Thrall had met him, Hellscream appeared to him to be small and frail. He was thin, Thrall realized; it was his ferocity, his battle cry, which made him appear to be so threatening and powerful. Physically, the charismatic leader of the Warsongs was wasting away. Even though he barely knew Hellscream, the realization moved Thrall. It seemed as though the orc chieftain's will and powerful personality was the only thing keeping him alive, that he was bone and blood and sinew tied together by the barest of threads.

He did not voice his perception; Grom Hellscream knew it. Their eyes met. Hellscream nodded, and then changed the subject.

"They have nothing to hope for, nothing to fight for," Hellscream said. "You told me that one orc was able to rally enough to fight with a friend in order to provide a way for you to escape. That gives me hope. If these people thought that there was some way they could matter, take their destinies into their own hands—I believe they would rouse themselves. None of us has ever been in one of these accursed camps. Tell us all you know, Thrall."

Thrall willingly obliged, pleased to be of some help. He described the camp, the orcs, the guards, and the security measures in as much detail as he could. Hellscream listened intently, now and then interrupting with a question or asking him to elaborate. When Thrall was finished, Hellscream was silent for a moment.

"It is well," he said at last. "The humans are lulled into a sense of safety by our shameful lack of honor. We can use this to our advantage. It has long been a dream of mine, Thrall, to storm these wretched places and liberate the orcs held captive there. Yet I fear that once the gate is down, like the cattle they seem to have become, they will not fly to freedom."

"Regrettably, that seems true," said Thrall.

Grom swore colorfully. "It is up to us to awaken them from their strange dreams of despair and defeat. I think it no accident, Thrall, that you have come at this time. Gul'dan is no more, and his warlocks are scattered. It is time for what we once were to reemerge." His crimson eyes glittered. "And you will be part of that."

There was no relief for Blackmoore any longer.

With each day that crept by, he knew there was less and less of a chance that Thrall would be located. They had been probably only moments behind him at the internment camp, and the incident had left a bitter taste in his mouth.

Which he tried to wash away with beer, mead, and wine.

After that, nothing. Thrall had seemingly vanished, a difficult task for something as big and ugly as an orc. Sometimes, when the empty bottles began to pile up beside him, Blackmoore was convinced that everyone was conspiring against him to keep Thrall away. This theory was lent credence by the fact that at least one person close to him had most certainly betrayed him. He held her close at night, lest she suspect he knew; enjoyed her physically, perhaps with more roughness than usual; spoke fairly to her. And yet sometimes, when she slept, the pain and anger were so overwhelming that he crawled out of the bed they shared and drank himself into a stupor.

And of course, with Thrall gone, all hope of leading an orcish army against the Alliance had disappeared like morning mist under a harsh sun. What then would become of Aedelas Blackmoore? Bad enough that he had to overcome the stigma of his father's name and prove himself a dozen times over, whereas lesser men were accepted at face value. They had told him, of course, that his present position was an honor, one he had richly earned. But he was far from the seat of power, and out of sight meant out of mind. Who in any real position of power thought of Blackmoore? No one, that was who, and it was making Blackmoore sick to his stomach.

He took another long, thirsty drink. A cautious tap came on his door. "Go away," he snarled.

"My lord?" The tentative voice of the betraying whore's rabbit of a father. "There is news, my lord. Lord Langston is here to see you."

Hope surged through Blackmoore and he struggled to rise from the bed. It was midafternoon and Taretha was off doing whatever it was she did when she wasn't serving him. He swung his booted feet to the floor and sat there a moment while the world swirled about him. "Send him in, Tammis," he ordered.

The door opened and Langston entered. "Wonderful news, my lord!" he exclaimed. "We have had a sighting of Thrall."

Blackmoore sniffed. "Sightings" of Thrall had become quite commonplace, considering there was a substantial reward offered. But Langston wouldn't come rushing to Blackmoore with unverified rumors. "Who saw him? Where?"

"Several leagues from the internment camp, headed due west," said

Langston. "Several villagers were awakened when an orc tried to break into their homes. Seems it was hungry. When they surrounded it, it spoke fair to them, and when they pressed their attack, it fought back and overcame them."

"Anyone killed?" Blackmoore hoped not. He would have to pay the village if his pet had killed someone.

"No. In fact, they said the orc deliberately refrained from killing. A few days later, one of the farmers' sons was kidnapped by a group of orcs. He was taken to a subterranean cavern and they ordered a large orc to kill him. The orc refused, and the orc chieftain agreed with the decision. The boy was released and immediately told his story. And my lord—the confrontation took place with the orcs speaking in the human tongue, because the large orc could not understand the language of his fellows."

Blackmoore nodded. It all rang true with what he knew Thrall to be, versus what the populace assumed Thrall would be. Plus, a young boy wouldn't likely be clever enough to realize that Thrall didn't know much orcish.

By the Light . . . maybe they would find him.

There had been another rumor as to Thrall's whereabouts, and once again, Blackmoore had left Durnholde to follow up on it. Taretha had two passionate, conflicting thoughts. One was that she desperately hoped that the rumors were false, that Thrall was miles away from wherever it was he had been reportedly seen. The other was the overwhelming sense of relief she experienced whenever Blackmoore was not present.

She took her daily stroll around the grounds outside the fortress. It was safe these days, save for the occasional highwayman, and they skulked by the main roads. She would come to no harm in the forests that she had grown to know so intimately.

She undid her hair and let it cascade about her shoulders, enjoying the freedom of it. It was not seemly for a woman to have unbound hair. Gleefully, Taretha combed her fingers through the thick golden mass and shook her head in defiance.

Her gaze fell to the welts on her wrists. Instinctively, one hand reached to cover the other.

No. She would not hide what was not her own shame. Taretha forced herself to uncover the bruises. For the sake of her family, she had to submit to him. But she would not aid in hiding the wrongs he had done.

Taretha took a deep breath. Even here, it would seem, Blackmoore's shadow followed. Deliberately, she banished it, and turned her face up toward the sun.

She wandered up to the cave where she had said her farewells to Thrall and sat there for a while, hugging her long legs to her chest. There was no sign that anyone save the creatures of the woods had been here in a long time. She then rose and strolled to the tree where she had told Thrall to hide the necklace she'd given him. Peering down into its blackened depths, she saw no glint of silver. She was relieved and saddened at the same time. Taretha desperately missed writing to Thrall and hearing his kind, wise replies.

If only the rest of her people felt that way. Couldn't they see that the orcs were not a threat anymore? Couldn't they understand that with education and a little bit of respect, they could be valuable allies and not enemies? She thought of all the money and time being poured into the internment camps, of how foolish and small-minded it seemed.

Too bad she couldn't have run away with Thrall. As Taretha walked slowly back to the fortress, she heard a horn blow. The master of Durnholde had returned. All the sense of lightness and freedom she had experienced bled out of her, as if from an open wound.

Whatever betide, Thrall at least is free, she thought. *My days as a slave loom numberless ahead of me.*

Thrall fought, and ate food prepared in the traditional way, and learned. Soon he was speaking fluent, if heavily accented, orcish. He could go with the hunting parties and be more of a help than a hindrance in bringing down a stag. Fingers that, despite their thickness, had learned to master a stylus had no difficulty helping build snares for rabbits and other smaller animals. Bit by bit, the Warsong clan was accepting him. For the first time in his life, Thrall felt as though he belonged.

But then came the news from the scouting parties. Rekshak returned one evening, looking even more angry and sour than usual. "A word, my lord," he said to Hellscream.

"You may speak in front of us all," said Hellscream. They were above ground tonight, enjoying a crisp late autumn evening and feasting upon the kill that Thrall himself had brought back to the clan.

Rekshak cast an uneasy glance in Thrall's direction, then grunted. "As you wish. Humans are beginning to scour the forests. They wear red and gold livery, with a black falcon on their standard."

"Blackmoore," said Thrall, sickened. Would the man never let him be? Was he going to be hunted to the ends of the earth, dragged back in chains to perform again for Blackmoore's twisted amusement?

No. He would take his own life before he would consent again to a life of slavery. He burned to speak, but courtesy demanded that Hellscream answer his own man.

"As I suspected," said Hellscream, more calmly than Thrall would have thought.

Clearly Rekshak was also taken by surprise. "My lord," he said, "the stranger Thrall has put us all in danger. If they find our caves, then they have us at their mercy. We will either be killed or rounded up like sheep into their camps!"

"Neither shall happen," said Hellscream. "And Thrall has not put us in danger. It was by my decision that he stayed. Do you question that?"

Rekshak lowered his head. "No, my chieftain."

"Thrall shall stay," Hellscream declared.

"With thanks, great chieftain," said Thrall, "Rekshak is right. I must leave. I cannot put the Warsong clan in further danger. I will go and make sure that they have a spurious trail to follow, one that will lead them away from you and yet not lead them to me."

Hellscream leaned closer to Thrall, who was sitting on his right. "But we need you, Thrall," he said. His eyes glowed in the darkness. "*I* need you. We will move quickly, then, to liberate our brothers in the camps."

But Thrall continued to shake his head. "The winter comes. It will be hard to feed an army. And . . . there is something I must do before I am ready to stand at your side to free our brethren. You told me that you knew my clan, the Frostwolves. I must find them and learn more about who I am, where I came from, before I can be ready to stand by your side. I had hoped to travel to them in the spring, but it seems that Blackmoore has forced my hand."

For a long time, Hellscream gazed at Thrall. The bigger orc did not look away from those terrible red eyes. Finally, sadly, Hellscream nodded.

"Though I burn with desire for revenge, I find that yours is the wiser head. Our brothers suffer in confinement, but their lethargy may ease their pain. Time enough when the sun shows its head more brightly to liberate them. I do not know for certain where the Frostwolves dwell, but somehow, I know in my heart that you will find them if you are meant to do so."

"I will depart in the morning," said Thrall, his heart heavy in his chest. Across the flickering fire, he saw Rekshak, who had never liked him, nod in approval.

That next morning Thrall bade a reluctant farewell to the Warsong clan and Grom Hellscream.

"I wish you to have this," said Hellscream, as he lifted a bone necklace from around his too-thin throat. "These are the remains of my first kill. I have carved my symbols in them; any orc chieftain will know them."

Thrall started to object, but Hellscream curled his lips back from his sharp yellow teeth and snarled. Having no desire to displease the chieftain who had been so kind to him, or to hear that ear-splitting scream a second time, Thrall lowered his head so that Grom could place the necklace about his thick neck.

"I will lead the humans away from you," Thrall reiterated.

"If you do not, it is no matter," said Hellscream. "We will tear them limb from limb." He laughed fiercely, and Thrall joined in. Still laughing, he set off in the direction of the cold northlands, the place from which he came.

He made a detour after a few hours, to veer back in the direction of the small village where he had stolen food and frightened the inhabitants. He did not go too near, for his keen ears had already picked up the sound of soldiers' voices. But he did leave a token for Blackmoore's men to find.

Though it nearly killed him to do it, he took the swaddling cloth that bore the mark of the Frostwolves and tore a large strip from it. He placed it carefully to the south of the village on a jagged stump. He wanted it to be easily found, but not too obvious. He also made sure that he left several large, easily traceable footprints in the soft, muddy soil.

With any luck, Blackmoore's men would find the tattered piece of instantly recognizable cloth, see the footprints and assume that Thrall was headed due south. He walked backward carefully in his footprints—a tactic he had learned from his reading—and sought out stone and hard earth for the next several paces.

He looked toward the Alterac Mountains. Grom had told him that even at the height of summer, their peaks were white against the blue sky. Thrall was about to head into their heart, not knowing for certain where he was going, just as the weather was beginning to turn. It had snowed once or twice, lightly, already. Soon the snows would come thick and heavy, heaviest of all in the mountains.

The Warsong clan had sent him off well supplied. They had given him several strips of dried meat, a waterskin in which he could collect and melt snow, a thick cape to help ward off the worst of the winter's bite, and a few rabbit snares so he could supplement the dried meat.

Fate and luck, and the kindness of strangers and a human girl, had brought him this far. Grom had indicated that Thrall had a role to play yet. He had to trust that, if this was indeed the truth, he would be guided to his destiny as he had been guided thus far.

Hoisting the sack over his back, without a single glance behind him, Thrall began to stride toward the beckoning mountains, whose jagged peaks and hidden valleys were home somewhere to the Frostwolf clan.

TWELVE

The days turned into weeks, and Thrall began to judge how much time had passed not by how many sunrises he saw, but by how many snowfalls. It did not take long for him to exhaust the dried meat the Warsong clan had given him, although he rationed it carefully. The traps proved only intermittently successful, and the farther up in the mountains he went, the fewer animals he caught.

At least water was not a problem. Everywhere around him were icy streams, and then thick, white drifts. More than once he was caught off guard by a sudden storm, and made a burrow in the snow until it passed. Each time, he could only hope that he could dig his way out to safety.

The harsh environment began to take its grim toll. His movements were slower and slower, and more than once he would stop to rest and almost not rise again. The food ran out, and no rabbits or marmots were foolish enough to get caught in his traps. The only way he knew there was any animal life at all was by the occasional print of hoof or paw in the snow, and the eerie howling of distant wolves at night. He began eating leaves and tree bark just to quiet his furious stomach, sometimes with less than digestible results.

Snows came and went, blue skies appeared, dimmed to black, and then clouded over with more snows. He began to despair. He did not even know if he was headed in the right direction to encounter the Frostwolves. He put one foot in front of the other steadily, stubbornly, determined to find his people or die here in these inhospitable mountains.

His mind began to play tricks on him. From time to time, Aedelas Blackmoore would rear out of a snowdrift, screaming harsh words and swinging a broadsword. Thrall could even smell the telltale scent of wine on his breath. They would fight, and Thrall would fall, exhausted, unable to fend off Blackmoore's final blow. It was only then that the shade would disappear, transforming itself from a loathed image into the harmless outline of a rock outcropping or a twisted, weatherworn tree.

Other images were more pleasant. Sometimes Hellscream would come rescue him, offering a warm fire that vanished when Thrall stretched out his hands to it. Other times his rescuer was Sergeant, grumbling about having to track down lost fighters and offering a thick, warm cloak. His sweetest and yet most bitter hallucinations were those when Tari would appear, sympathy in her wide blue eyes and comforting words on her lips. Sometimes she would almost touch him before disappearing before his eyes.

On and on he pressed, until one day, he simply could go no farther. He took one step, and fully intended to take the next, and the one after that, when his body toppled forward of its own accord. His mind tried to command his exhausted, nearly frozen body to rise, but it disobeyed. The snow didn't even feel cold to him anymore. It was . . . warm, and soft. Sighing, Thrall closed his eyes.

A sound made him open them again, but he only stared disinterestedly at this fresh mind-trick. This time it was a large pack of white wolves, almost as white as the snow that surrounded him. They had formed a ring about him, and stood silently, waiting. He stared back, mildly interested in how this scenario would play out. Would they charge, only to vanish? Or would they just wait until unconsciousness claimed him?

Three dark figures loomed up behind the nonexistent wolves. They weren't anyone who had come to visit him before. They were wrapped from head to toe in thick furs. They looked warm, but not as warm as Thrall felt. Their faces were in shadow from fur-trimmed hoods, but he saw large jaws. That and their size marked them as orcs.

He was angry at his mind this time. He had gotten used to the other hallucinations that had visited him. Now he feared he was going to die before finding out what these imaginary people had in store for him.

He closed his eyes, and knew no more.

"I think he's awake." The voice was soft and high-pitched. Thrall stirred and opened heavy-lidded eyes.

Staring right at him with a curious expression on its face was an orc child. Thrall's eyes opened wider to regard the small male. There had been no children among the Warsong clan. They had been cobbled together after dreadful battles, their numbers decimated, and Grom had told him that the children had been the first to succumb.

"Hello," said Thrall in orcish, the word coming out in a harsh rasp. The boy jumped, then laughed.

"He's *definitely* awake," the child said, then scurried away. Another orc loomed into Thrall's field of vision. For the second time in as many minutes, Thrall saw a new type of orc; first the very young one, and now, one who had obviously known many, many winters.

All the features of the orcs were exaggerated in this aged visage. The jowls sagged, the teeth were even yellower than Thrall's, and many were missing or broken. The eyes were a strange milky color, and Thrall could see no pupils in them. This orc's body was twisted and stooped, almost as small as the child's, but Thrall instinctively shrank back from the sheer presence of the elder.

"Hmph," said the old orc. "Thought you were going to die, young one."

Thrall felt a twinge of irritation. "Sorry to disappoint you," he said.

"Our honor code obliges us to help those in need," continued the orc, "but it's always easier if our help proves ineffective. One less mouth to feed."

Thrall was taken aback by the rudeness, but chose to say nothing.

"My name is Drek'Thar. I am the shaman of the Frostwolves, and their protector. Who are you?"

Amusement rippled through Thrall at the idea of this wizened old orc being the protector of all the Frostwolves. He tried to sit up, and was startled to find himself slammed down on the furs as if from an unseen hand. He looked over at Drek'Thar and saw that the old man had subtly changed the position of his fingers.

"I didn't give you leave to rise," said Drek'Thar. "Answer my question, stranger, or I may reconsider our offer of hospitality."

Gazing at the elder with new respect, Thrall said, "My name is Thrall."

Drek'Thar spat. "Thrall! A human word, and a word of subjugation at that."

"Yes," said Thrall, "a word that means slave in their tongue. But I am a thrall no longer, though I keep the name to prick myself to my duties. I have escaped my chains and desire to find out my true history." Without thinking, Thrall tried to sit up again, and was again slammed down. This time, he saw the gnarled old hands twitch slightly. This was a powerful shaman indeed.

"Why did our wolf friends find you wandering in a blizzard?" Drek'Thar demanded. He stared away from Thrall, and Thrall realized that the old orc was blind.

"It is a long story."

"I've got time."

Thrall had to laugh. He found himself liking this cranky old shaman. Surrendering to the implacable force that kept him flat on his back, he told his story. Of how Blackmoore had found him as an infant, had raised him and taught him how to fight and to read. He told the shaman of Tari's kindness, of the listless orcs he had found in the camps, of finally making contact with Hellscream, who had taught him the warrior's code and the language of his people.

"Hellscream was the one who told me that the Frostwolves were my clan," he finished. "He knew by the small piece of cloth in which I was wrapped as a baby. I can show you—" He fell silent, mortified. Of course Drek'Thar could not be "shown" anything.

He expected the shaman to erupt in offense, but instead Drek'Thar extended his hand. "Give it to me."

Now the pressure on his chest eased, and Thrall was able to sit up. He reached in his pack for the tattered remains of the Frostwolf blanket, and wordlessly handed it to the shaman.

Drek'Thar took it in both hands, and brought it to his chest. He murmured softly words Thrall could not catch, and then nodded.

"It is as I suspected," he said, and sighed heavily. He handed the cloth back to Thrall. "The cloth is indeed the pattern of the Frostwolves, and it was woven by the hand of your mother. We had thought you dead."

"How could you tell that—" And then Thrall fully understood what Drek'Thar had said. Hope seized him. "You know my mother? My father? Who am I?"

Drek'Thar lifted his head and stared at Thrall with his blind eyes. "You are the only child of Durotan, our former chieftain, and his courageous mate Draka."

Over a hearty stew of meat, broth, and roots, Drek'Thar told Thrall the rest of his history, at least as much as he knew. He had taken the young orc into his cave, and with the fire burning brightly and thick fur cloaks about their bodies, both old shaman and young warrior were warm and comfortable. Palkar, his attendant, who had been so diligent about alerting him when Thrall had awakened, ladled up the stew and gently pressed the warm wooden bowl into Drek'thar's hands.

The orc ate his stew, delaying speaking. Palkar sat quietly. The only sound was the crackle of the fire and the slow, deep breathing of Wise-ear, Drek'thar's wolf companion. It was a difficult story for Drek'Thar, one he had never imagined he would need to speak of ever again.

"Your parents were the most honored of all the Frostwolves. They left us on a dire errand many winters past, never to return. We did not know what had happened to them . . . until now." He gestured in the direction of the cloth. "The fibers in the cloth have told me. They were slain, and you survived, to be raised by humans."

The cloth was not living, but it had been made of the fur of the white goats that braved the mountains. Because the wool had once belonged to a living being, it had a certain sentience of its own. It could not give details, but it spoke of blood being shed, spattering it with dark red droplets. It also told Drek'Thar a bit about Thrall as well, validating the young orc's story and giving it a sense of truth that Drek'Thar could believe.

He could sense Thrall's doubt that the blanket remnant had "spoken" to him freely. "What was the errand that cost my parents their lives?" the young orc wanted to know.

But that was information Drek'Thar was not ready to share. "I will tell you in time, perhaps. But now, you have put me in a difficult position, Thrall. You come during the winter, the harshest season of all, and as your clan members we must take you in. That does not mean that you will be kept warm, fed, and sheltered without recompense."

"I did not expect to be so treated," said Thrall. "I am strong. I can work hard, help you hunt. I can teach you some of the ways of humankind, that you will better be prepared to fight them. I can—"

Drek'Thar held up a commanding hand, silencing Thrall's eager babble. He listened. The fire was speaking to him. He leaned in to it, to hear its words better.

Drek'Thar was stunned. Fire was the most undisciplined of the elements. It barely would deign to reply when he addressed it after following all the rituals to appease it. And now, Fire was speaking to him . . . about Thrall!

He saw in his mind images of brave Durotan, beautiful and fierce Draka. *I miss you yet, my old friends,* he thought. *And yet your blood returns to me, in the form of your son. A son of whom even the Spirit of Fire speaks well. But I cannot just give him the mantle of leadership, not as young as he is, as untested . . . as human-tainted!*

"Since your father left, I have been the leader of the Frostwolves," said Drek'Thar. "I accept your offer of aid to the clan, Thrall, son of Durotan. But you will have to earn your rank."

Six days later, as Thrall battled his way through a snowstorm back to the clan encampment with a large, furry animal he and the frost wolves had brought down slung over his back, he wondered if perhaps slavery hadn't been easier.

As soon as the thought struck, he banished it. He was with his own people now, although they continued to regard him with hostility and grudging hospitality. He was always the last to eat. Even the wolves ate their fill before Thrall. He was given the coldest place to sleep, the thinnest cloak, the poorest weapons, the most onerous chores and tasks. He accepted this humbly, recognizing it for what it was: an attempt to test him, to make sure that he had not come to the Frostwolves expecting to be waited on like a king . . . like Blackmoore.

So he covered the refuse pits, skinned the animals, fetched the firewood, and did everything that was asked of him without a word. At least he had the frost wolves to keep him company in the blizzard this time.

One evening, he had asked Drek'Thar about the link between the wolves and the orcs. He was familiar with the concept of domesticating animals, of course, but this seemed different, deeper.

"It is," Drek'Thar replied. "The wolves are not tamed, not as you understand the word. They have come to be our friends because I invited them. It is part of being a shaman. We have a bond with the things of the natural world, and strive always to work in harmony with them. It would be helpful to us if the wolves would be our companions. Hunt with us, keep us warm when the furs are not enough. Alert us to strangers, as they did with you. You would have died had not our wolf friends found you. And in return, we make sure they are well fed, that their injuries are healed, and their cubs need not fear the mighty wind eagles that scour the mountains during the birthing times.

"We have made a similar pact with the goats, although they are not as wise as the wolves. They give us their wool and milk, and when we are in extreme need, one will surrender its life. We protect them in return. They are free to break the pact at any time, but in the last thirty years, none has done so."

Thrall could not believe what he was hearing. This was potent magic indeed. "You link with things other than animals, though, do you not?"

Drek'Thar nodded. "I can call the snows, and wind, and lightning. The trees may bend to me when I ask. The rivers may flow where I ask them to."

"If your power is so great, then why do you continue to live in such a harsh place?" Thrall asked. "If what you are saying is true, you could turn this barren mountaintop into a lush garden. Food would never be difficult to come by, your enemies would never find you—"

"And I would violate the primary agreement with the elements, and nothing of nature would ever respond to me again!" bellowed Drek'Thar. Thrall wished he could snatch back the words, but it was too late. He had obviously deeply offended the shaman. "Do you understand nothing? Have the humans sunk their greedy talons in you so deeply that you cannot see what lies at the heart of a shaman's power? I am granted these things because I *ask,* with respect in my heart, and I am willing to offer something in return. I request only the barest needs for myself and my people. At times, I ask great things, but only when the cause is good and just and wholesome. In return, I thank these powers, knowing that they are borrowed only, never bought. They come to me because they choose to, not because I demand it! These are not slaves, Thrall. They are powerful entities who come of their own free will, who are companions in my magic, not my servants. Pagh!" He snarled and turned away from Thrall. "You will never understand."

For many days, he did not speak with Thrall. Thrall continued to do the lesser jobs, but it seemed that he grew only more distant from the Frost-wolves, not closer, as time passed. One evening he was covering the refuse pits when one of the younger males called out, "Slave!"

"My name is Thrall," Thrall said darkly.

The other orc shrugged. "Thrall, slave. It means the same thing. My wolf is ill and has soiled his bedding. Clean it."

Thrall growled low in his throat. "Clean it yourself. I am not your servant, I am a guest of the Frostwolves," he snarled.

"Oh? Really? With a name like slave? Here, human-boy, take it!" He threw a blanket and it covered Thrall before he could react. Cold moisture clung to his face and he smelled the stench of urine.

Something snapped inside him. Red anger flooded his vision and he screamed in outrage. He ripped the filthy blanket off and clenched his fists. He began to stamp, rhythmically, angrily, as he had so long ago in the ring. Only there was no cheering crowd here, only a small circle of suddenly very quiet orcs who stared at him.

The young orc thrust his jaw out stubbornly. "I said, clean it, slave."

Thrall bellowed and sprang. The young male went down, though not without fighting. Thrall didn't feel his flesh part beneath sharp black nails. He felt only the fury, the outrage. He was no one's slave.

Then they were pulling him off and throwing him into a snow bank. The shock of the cold wetness brought him to his senses, and he realized that he had ruined any chance of being accepted by these people. The thought devastated him, and he sat waist-deep in the snow, staring down. He had failed. There was no place that he belonged.

"I had wondered how long it would take you," said Drek'Thar. Thrall glanced up listlessly to see the blind shaman standing over him. "You surprised me by lasting this long."

Slowly, Thrall stood. "I have turned on my hosts," he said heavily. "I will depart."

"You will do no such thing," said Drek'Thar. Thrall turned to stare at him. "The first test I had was to see if you were too arrogant to ask to be one of us. Had you come in here demanding the chieftainship as your birthright, we would have sent you away—and sent our wolves to make sure you stayed away. You needed first to be humble before we would admit you.

"But also, we would not respect anyone who would stay servile for too long. Had you not challenged Uthul's insults, you would not have been a true orc. I am pleased to see you are both humble and proud, Thrall."

Gently, Drek'Thar placed a wizened hand on Thrall's muscular arm. "Both qualities are needed for one who will follow the path of the shaman."

THIRTEEN

Though the rest of that long winter was bitter, Thrall clung to the warmth he felt inside and thought the chill as little. He was accepted now as a member of the clan, and even the Warsongs had not made him feel so valued. Days were spent hunting with clan members who were now family and in listening to Drek'Thar. Nights were spent as part of a loud, happy gathering sitting around a group fire, singing songs and telling tales of past days of glory.

Though Drek'Thar often regaled him with tales of his courageous father Durotan, Thrall somehow sensed that the old orc was holding something back. He did not press the matter, however. Thrall trusted Drek'Thar completely now, and knew that the shaman would tell him what he needed to know, when he needed to know it.

He also made a unique friend. One evening, as the clan and their wolf companions gathered around the fire as was their usual wont, a young wolf detached itself from the pack that usually slept just beyond the ring of firelight and approached. The Frostwolves fell silent.

"This female will Choose," said Drek'Thar solemnly. Thrall had long since stopped being amazed at how Drek'Thar knew such things as the wolf's gender and its—her—readiness to Choose, whatever that meant. Not without painful effort, Drek'Thar rose and extended his arms toward the she-wolf.

"Lovely one, you wish to form a bond with one of our clan," he said. "Come forward and Choose the one with whom you will be bonded for the rest of your life."

The wolf did not immediately rush forward. She took her time, ears twitching, dark eyes examining every orc present. Most of them already had companions, but many did not, particularly the younger ones. Uthul, who had become Thrall's fast friend once Thrall had rebelled against his cruel treatment, now tensed. Thrall could tell that he wanted this lovely, graceful beast to Choose him.

The wolf's eyes met Thrall's, and it was as if a shock went through his entire body.

The female loped toward Thrall, and lay down at his side. Her eyes bored into his. Thrall felt a warm rush of kinship with this creature, although they were from two different species. He knew, without understanding quite how he knew, that she would be by his side until one of them left this life behind.

Slowly, Thrall reached to touch Snowsong's finely shaped head. Her fur was so soft and thick. A warm wave of pleasure rushed over him.

The group grunted sounds of approval, and Uthul, though keenly disappointed, was the first to clap Thrall on the back.

"Tell us her name," said Drek'Thar.

"Her name is Snowsong," Thrall replied, again, not knowing how he knew. The wolf half-closed her eyes, and he sensed her satisfaction.

Drek'Thar finally revealed the reason for Durotan's death one evening toward the end of winter. More and more, when the sun shone, they heard the sounds of melting snows. Thrall stood by that afternoon and watched respectfully as Drek'Thar performed a ritual to the spring snowmelt, asking that it alter its course only enough to avoid flooding the Frostwolf encampment. As always now, Snowsong stood at his side, a white, silent, faithful shadow.

Thrall felt something stir inside him. He heard a voice: *We hear Drek'Thar's request, and find it not unseemly. We shall not flow where you and yours dwell, Shaman.*

Drek'Thar bowed, and closed the ceremony formally. "I heard it," Thrall said. "I heard the snow answer you."

Drek'Thar turned his unseeing eyes toward Thrall. "I know you heard it," he said. "It is a sign that you are ready, that you have learned and understood all that I have to teach. Tomorrow, you will undergo your initiation. But tonight, come to my cave. I have things to say that you must hear."

When darkness fell, Thrall appeared at the cave. Wise-ear, Drek'Thar's wolf companion, whined happily. Drek'Thar waved Thrall inside.

"Sit," he ordered. Thrall did so. Snowsong went to Wise-ear and they touched noses before curling up and quickly falling asleep. "You have many questions about your father and his fate. I have refrained from answering them, but the time has come that you must know. But first, swear by all you hold dear that you will never tell anyone what I am about to tell you, until you receive a sign that this must be said."

"I swear," said Thrall solemnly. His heart was beating fast. After so many years, he was about to learn the truth.

"You have heard that we were exiled by the late Gul'dan," said Drek'Thar. "What you have not heard is why. No one knew the reason but your parents and myself, and that was as Durotan wished it to be. The fewer people who knew what he knew, the safer his clan."

Thrall said nothing, but hung on Drek'Thar's every word.

"We know now that Gul'dan was evil, and did not have the best interest of the orc people in his heart. What most do not know is how deeply he betrayed us, and what dreadful price we are now paying for what he did to us. Durotan learned, and for that knowledge he was exiled. He and Draka—and you, young Thrall—returned to the southlands to tell the mighty orc chieftain Orgrim Doomhammer of Gul'dan's treachery. We do not know if your parents reached Doomhammer, but we do know that they were murdered for that knowledge."

Thrall bit back the impatient cry, *What knowledge?* Drek'Thar paused for a long moment, then continued.

"Gul'dan only ever wanted power for himself, and he sold us into a sort of slavery to achieve it. He formed a group called the Shadow Council, and this group, comprised of himself and many evil orc warlocks, dictated everything the orcs did. They united with demons, who gave them their vile powers, and who infused the Horde with such a love of killing and fighting that the people forgot the old ways, the way of nature, and the shaman. They lusted only for death. You have seen the red fire in the eyes of the orcs in the camps, Thrall. By that mark, you know that they have been ruled by demon powers."

Thrall gasped. He immediately thought of Hellscream's bright scarlet eyes, of how wasted Hellscream's body was. Yet Hellscream's mind was his own. He had acknowledged the power of mercy, had not given in to either mad bloodlust or the dreadful lethargy he'd seen at the camps. Grom Hellscream must have faced the demons every day, and continued to resist them. Thrall's admiration of the chieftain grew even more as he realized how strong Hellscream's will must be.

"I believe that the lethargy you reported seeing in the camps is the emptiness our people are feeling when the demonic energies have been withdrawn. Without that external energy, they feel weak, bereft. They may not even know why they feel this way, or care enough to ponder it. They are like empty cups, Thrall, that were once filled with poison. Now they cry out to be filled with something wholesome once again. That which they yearn for is the nourishment of the old ways. Shamanism, a reconnection with the simple and pure powers of the natural forces and laws, will fill them again and assuage that dreadful hunger. This, and only this, will rouse them from their stupor and remind them of the proud, courageous line from which we have all come."

Thrall continued to listen raptly, hanging on Drek'Thar's every word.

"Your parents knew of the dark bargain. They knew that this blood-thirsty Horde was as unnatural a construct as could be imagined. The demons and Gul'dan had taken our people's natural courage and warped it, twisted it for their own means. Durotan knew this, and for that knowledge his clan was banished. He accepted that, but when you were born, he knew he could no longer remain silent. He wanted a better world for you, Thrall. You were his son and heir. You would have been the next chieftain. He and Draka went into the southlands, as I have told you, to find their old friend Orgri-Doomhammer."

"I know that name," said Thrall. "He was the mighty Warchief who led all the clans together against the humans."

Drek'Thar nodded. "He was wise and brave, a good leader of our people. The humans eventually were the victors, Gul'dan's treachery—at least a pale shadow of its true depths—was discovered, and the demons withdrew. You know the rest."

"Was Doomhammer killed?"

"We do not believe so, but nothing has been heard from him since. The odd rumor reaches us now and then, that he has become a hermit, gone into hiding, or that he has been taken prisoner. Many think of him as a legend, who will return to free us when the time is right."

Thrall looked carefully at his teacher. "And what is it you think, Drek'Thar?"

The old orc chuckled deep in his throat. "I think," he said, "that I have told you enough, and that it is time for you to rest. The morrow will bring your initiation, if it is meant to be. You'd best be prepared."

Thrall rose and bowed respectfully. Even if the shaman could not see the gesture, he made it, for himself. "Come, Snowsong," he called, and the white wolf padded obediently into the night with her life's companion.

Drek'Thar listened, and when he was certain they had gone, he called to Wise-ear. "I have a task for you, my friend. You know what to do."

Although he had tried to get as much rest as he could, Thrall found sleep elusive. He was too excited, too apprehensive, about what his initiation would bring. Drek'Thar had told him nothing. He wished desperately he had some kind of idea as to what to expect.

He was wide awake when the gray dawn filled his cave with faint light. He rose and made his way outside, and was surprised to find that everyone else was awake and gathered silently outside his cave.

Thrall opened his mouth to speak, but Drek'Thar held up a commanding hand. "You are not to speak again until I give you leave," he said. "Depart at once, to go alone into the mountains. Snowsong must stay. You are not to eat or drink, but think hard about the path upon which you are about to set foot. When the sun has set, return to me, and the rite will begin."

Obediently, Thrall turned at once and left. Snowsong, knowing what was expected of her, did not follow. She did throw her head back and begin to howl. All the other wolves joined in, and the savage, sweet chorus accompanied Thrall as he went, alone, to meditate.

The day passed more swiftly than he would have expected. His mind was filled with questions, and he was surprised when the light changed and the sun, orange against the winter sky, began to move toward the horizon. He returned just as its last rays bathed the encampment.

Drek'Thar was waiting for him. Thrall noticed that Wise-ear was nowhere to be seen, which was unusual, but he assumed that this was part of the rite. Snowsong was also not present. He approached Drek'Thar and waited. The old orc gestured that Thrall follow.

He led Thrall over a snow-covered ridge to an area that Thrall had never seen before. In answer to the unvoiced question, Drek'Thar replied, "This place has always been here, but it does not wish to be seen. Therefore, only now, when it welcomes you, is it visible to you."

Thrall felt nervousness rise in him, but refrained from speaking. Drek'Thar waved his hands, and the snow melted right before Thrall's eyes, leaving a large, circular, rocky platform. "Stand in the center, Thrall, son of Durotan," said Drek'Thar. His voice was no longer raspy and quavering, but was filled with a power and authority Thrall had never heard from him before. He obeyed.

"Prepare to meet the spirits of the natural world," said Drek'Thar, and Thrall's heart leaped.

Nothing happened. He waited. Still nothing happened. He shifted, uneasily. The sun had fully set and the stars were beginning to appear. He was growing impatient and angry when a voice spoke very loudly inside his head: *Patience is the first test.*

Thrall inhaled swiftly. The voice spoke again.

I am the Spirit of Earth, Thrall, son of Durotan. I am the soil that yields the fruit, the grasses that feed the beasts. I am the rock, the bones of this world. I am all that grows and lives in my womb, be it worm or tree or flower. Ask me.

Ask you what? thought Thrall.

There was a strange sensation, almost as of a warm chuckle. *Knowing the question is part of your test.*

Thrall panicked, then calmed himself, as Drek'Thar had taught. A question came calmly into his mind:

Will you lend me your strength and power when I need it, for the good of the Clan and those we would aid?

Ask, came the reply.

Thrall began to stamp his feet. He felt power rising inside him, as he always did, but for the first time it was not accompanied by bloodlust. It was warm and strong and he felt as solid as the bones of the earth themselves. He was barely aware of the very earth trembling beneath him, and it was only when an unbearably sweet scent filled his nostrils that he opened his eyes.

The earth had erupted into enormous fissures, and on every inch of what was rock, flowers bloomed. Thrall gaped.

I have agreed to lend you my assistance, for the good of the Clan and those you would aid. Honor me, and that gift shall always be yours.

Thrall felt the power recede, leaving him trembling with shock at what he had summoned and controlled. But he had only a moment to marvel at it, for another voice was in his head now.

I am the Spirit of Air, Thrall, son of Durotan. I am the winds that warm and cool the earth, that which fills your lungs and keeps you alive. I carry the birds and insects and dragons, and all things that dare soar to my challenging heights. Ask me.

Thrall knew what to do this time, and asked the same question. The sensation of power that filled him was different this time: lighter, freer. Even though he had been forbidden to speak, he could not help the laughter that bubbled forth from his soul. He felt warm winds caress him, bringing all manner of delicious scents to his nostrils, and when he opened his eyes, he was floating high above the ground. Drek'Thar was so far below him he seemed as a child's toy. But Thrall was not afraid. The Spirit of Air would support him; he had asked, and it had answered.

Gently, he floated down, until he felt the solid stone beneath his feet. Air caressed him with a gentle touch, then dissipated.

Power again filled Thrall, and this time it was almost painful. Heat churned in his belly, and sweat popped out on his green skin. He felt an almost overpowering desire to leap into the nearby snowbanks. The Spirit of Fire was here, and he asked for its aid. It responded.

There was a loud crackling overhead, and Thrall, startled by the sound, looked up. Lightning danced its dangerous dance across the night sky. Thrall knew that it was his to command. The flowers that had strewn the broken earth exploded into flames, crisping and burning to ashes in the space of a few heartbeats. This was a dangerous element, and Thrall thought of the pleasant fires that had kept his clan alive. At once, the fires went out, to reform in a small, contained, cozy area.

Thrall thanked the Spirit of Fire, and felt its presence depart. He was feeling drained by all this strange energy alternately coursing through him and then departing, and was grateful that there was only one more element to acknowledge.

The Spirit of Water flowed into him, calming and cooling the burn the

Spirit of Fire had left behind. Thrall had a vision of the ocean, though he had never seen one before, and extended his mind to probe its darkling depths. Something cold touched his skin. He opened his eyes to see that it was snowing thick and fast. With a thought, he turned it to rain, and then halted it altogether. The comfort of the Spirit of Water within him soothed and strengthened, and he let it go with deep, heartfelt thanks.

He looked over at Drek'Thar, but the shaman shook his head. "Your test is not yet completed," he said.

And then suddenly Thrall was shaken from head to toe with such a rush of power that he gasped aloud. Of course. The fifth element.

The Spirit of the Wilds.

We are the Spirit of the Wilds, the essence and souls of all things living. We are the most powerful of all, surpassing the quakes of Earth, the winds of Air, the flames of Fire, and the floods of Water. Speak, Thrall, and tell us why you think you are worthy of our aid.

Thrall couldn't breathe. He was overwhelmed by the power churning within and without him. Forcing his eyes to open, he saw pale white shapes swirling about him. One was a wolf, the other a goat, another an orc, and a human, and a deer. He realized that every living thing had spirits, and felt despair rise up in him at the thought of having to sense and control all of them.

But faster than he could have dreamed, the spirits filled and then vacated him. Thrall felt pummeled by the onslaught, but forced himself to try to focus, to address each one with respect. It became impossible and he sank to his knees.

A soft sound filled the air, and Thrall struggled to lift a head that felt as heavy as stone.

They floated calmly around him now, and he knew that he had been judged and found worthy. A ghostly stag pranced about him, and he knew that he would never simply be able to bite into a haunch of venison without feeling its Spirit, and thanking it for the nourishment it provided. He felt a kinship with every orc that had ever been born, and even the human Spirit felt more like Taretha's sweet presence than Blackmoore's dark cruelty. Everything was bright, even if sometimes it embraced the dark; all life was connected, and any shaman who tampered with the chain without the utmost care and respect for that Spirit was doomed to fail.

Then they were gone. Thrall fell forward, utterly drained. He felt Drek'Thar's hand on his shoulder, shaking him. The old shaman assisted Thrall in sitting up. Thrall had never felt so limp and weak in his life.

"Well done, my child," said Drek'Thar, his voice trembling with emotion. "I had hoped they would accept . . . Thrall, you must know. It has been years, nay, decades, since the spirits have accepted a shaman. They were angry with us for our warlocks' dark bargain, their corruption of magic. There are only a few shamans left now, and all are as old as I. The spirits have waited for someone worthy upon whom to bestow their gifts; you are the first in a long, long time to be so honored. I had feared that the spirits would forever refuse to work with us again, but . . . Thrall, I have never seen a stronger shaman in my life, and you are only beginning."

"I . . . I thought it would feel so powerful," stammered Thrall, his voice faint. "But instead . . . I am so humbled. . . ."

"And it is that which makes you worthy." He reached and stroked Thrall's cheek. "Durotan and Draka would be so proud of you."

FOURTEEN

With the Spirits of Earth, Air, Fire, Water and the Wilds as his willing companions, Thrall felt stronger and more confident than ever in his life. He worked together with Drek'Thar to learn the specific "calls," as the elder called them. "Warlocks would term them spells," he told Thrall, "but we—shamans—term them simply 'calls.' We ask, the powers we work with answer. Or not, as they will."

"Have they ever not answered?" asked Thrall.

Drek'Thar was silent. "Yes," he answered slowly. They were sitting together in Drek'Thar's cave, talking late at night. These conversations were precious to Thrall, and always enlightening.

"When? Why?" Thrall wanted to know, then immediately added, "Unless you do not wish to speak of it."

"You are a shaman now, although a fledgling one," said Drek'Thar. "It is right that you understand our limitations. I am ashamed to admit that I asked for improper things more than once. The first time, I asked for a flood to destroy an encampment of humans. I was angry and bitter, for they had destroyed many of our clan. But there were many wounded and even women and children at this place, and Water would not do it."

"But floods happen all the time," said Thrall. "Many innocents die, and it serves no purpose."

"It serves the Spirit of Water's purpose, and the Wilds'," replied Drek'Thar. "I do not know their needs and plans. They certainly do not tell me of them. This time, it did not serve Water's needs, and it would not flood and drown hundreds of humans it saw as innocent. Later, once the rage had faded, I understood that the Spirit of Water was right."

"When else?"

Drek'Thar hesitated. "You probably assume I have always been old, guiding the clan spiritually."

Thrall chuckled. "No one is born old, Wise One."

"Sometimes I wish I had been. But I was once young, as you are, and the blood flowed hot in my veins. I had a mate and child. They died."

"In battle against the humans?"

"Nothing so noble. They simply fell ill, and all my pleas to the elements were to no avail. I raged in my grief." Even now, his voice was laden with sorrow. "I demanded that the spirits return the lives they had snatched. They grew angry with me, and for many years, refused my call. Because of my arrogant demand that my loved ones come back to life, many others of our clan suffered from my inability to summon the spirits. When I saw the foolishness of my request, I begged the spirits to forgive me. They did."

"But . . . it is only natural to want your loved ones to stay alive," said Thrall. "Surely the spirits must understand that."

"Oh, they understood. My first request was humble, and the element listened with compassion before it refused. My next request was a furious demand, and the Spirit of the Wilds was offended that I so abused the relationship between shaman and element."

Drek'Thar extended a hand and placed it on Thrall's shoulder. "It is more than likely you will endure the pain of losing loved ones, Thrall. You must know that the Spirit of the Wilds has reasons for doing what it does, and you must respect those reasons."

Thrall nodded, but privately he completely sympathized with Drek'Thar's desires, and did not blame the old orc one bit for raging at the spirits in his torment.

"Where is Wise-ear?" he asked, to change the subject.

"I don't know." Drek'Thar seemed singularly unconcerned. "He is a companion, not a slave. He leaves when he wishes, returns when it is his will."

As if to reassure him that she was not about to go anywhere, Snowsong placed her head on Thrall's knee. He patted her head, bade his teacher good night, and went to his own cave to sleep.

The days passed in a routine fashion. Thrall now spent most of his time studying with Drek'Thar, though on occasion he went hunting with a small group. He utilized his newfound relationship with the elements to aid his clan: asking the Spirit of Earth for advice on where the herds were, asking the Spirit of Air to change the course of the wind so that their scent would not betray them to the watchful creatures. Only once did he ask the Spirit of the Wilds for aid, when supplies were running dangerously low and their luck in hunting had taken a turn for the worse.

They knew deer were in the area. They had found gnawed tree bark and fresh droppings. But the canny creatures continued to elude them for several days. Their bellies were empty, and there was simply no more food left. The children were beginning to grow dangerously thin.

Thrall closed his eyes and extended his mind. *Spirit of the Wilds, who breathes life into all, I ask for your favor. We will take no more than we need to feed the hungry of our clan. I ask you, Spirit of the deer, to sacrifice yourself for us. We will not waste any of your gifts, and we will honor you. Many lives depend upon the surrendering of one.*

He hoped the words were right. They had been couched with a respectful heart, but Thrall had never attempted this before. But when he opened his eyes, he saw a white stag standing not two arms' lengths in front of him. His companions seemed to see nothing. The stag's eyes met Thrall's, and the creature inclined its head. It bounded away, and Thrall saw that it left no trace in the snow.

"Follow me," he said. His fellow Frostwolves did so at once, and they went some distance before they saw a large, healthy stag lying in the snow. One of its legs jutted out at an unnatural angle, and its soft brown eyes were rolling in terror. The snow all around it was churned up, and it was obvious that it was unable to rise.

Thrall approached it, instinctively sending out a message of calm. *Do not fear,* he told it. *Your pain will soon be ended, and your life continue to have meaning. I thank you, Brother, for your sacrifice.*

The deer relaxed, and lowered its head. Thrall touched its neck gently. Quickly, to cause it no pain, he snapped the long neck. He looked up to see the others staring at him in awe. But he knew it was not by his will, but the deer's, that his people would eat tonight.

"We will take this animal and consume its flesh. We will make tools from the bones and clothing from its hide. And in so doing, we will remember that it honored us with this gift."

Thrall worked side by side with Drek'Thar to send energy to the seeds beneath the soil, that they would grow strong and flower in the spring that was so near, and to nurture the unborn beasts, be they deer or goat or wolf, growing in their mothers' wombs. They worked together to ask Water to spare the village from the spring snowmelts and the avalanches that were a constant danger. Thrall grew steadily in strength and in skill, and was so engrossed in this new, vibrant path he was walking that when he saw the first yellow and purple spring flowers poking their heads up through the melting snows, he was taken by surprise.

When he returned from his walk to gather the sacred herbs that aided the shaman's contact with the elements, he was surprised to find that the Frost-wolves had another guest.

This orc was large, though from weight or muscle, Thrall could not say as the stranger's cloak was wrapped tightly around him. He huddled close to the fire and seemed not to feel the spring warmth.

Snowsong rushed forward to sniff noses and tails with Wise-ear, who had at long last returned. Thrall turned to Drek'Thar.

"Who is the stranger?" he asked softly.

"A wandering hermit," Drek'Thar replied. "We do not know him. He says that Wise-ear found him lost in the mountains, and led him here to safety."

Thrall looked at the bowl of stew the stranger clutched in one big hand, at the polite concern shown to him by the rest of the clan. "You receive him with more kindness than you received me," he said, not a little annoyed.

Drek'Thar laughed. "He comes asking only for refuge for a few days before pressing on. He didn't come with a torn Frostwolf swaddling cloth asking to be adopted by the clan. And he comes at springtime, when there is bounty to be had and shared, and not at the onset of winter."

Thrall had to acknowledge the shaman's points. Anxious to behave properly, he sat down by the stranger. "Greetings, stranger. How long have you been traveling?"

The orc looked at him from under a shadowing hood. His gray eyes were sharp, though his answer was polite, even deferential.

"Longer than I care to recall, young one. I am in your debt. I had thought the Frostwolves only a legend, told by Gul'dan's cronies to intimidate all other orcs."

Clan loyalty stirred inside Thrall. "We were banished wrongly, and have proved our worth by being able to make a life for ourselves in this harsh place," he replied.

"But it is my understanding that not so long ago, you were as much a stranger to this clan as I," the stranger said. "They have spoken of you, young Thrall."

"I hope they have spoken well," Thrall answered, unsure as to how to respond.

"Well enough," the stranger replied, enigmatically. He returned to eating his stew. Thrall saw that his hands were well muscled.

"What is your own clan, friend?"

The hand froze with the spoon halfway to the mouth. "I have no clan, now. I wander alone."

"Were they all killed?"

"Killed, or taken, or dead where it counts . . . in the soul," the orc answered, pain in his voice. "Let us speak no more of this."

Thrall inclined his head. He was uncomfortable around the stranger, and suspicious as well. Something was not quite right about him. He rose, nodded his head, and went to Drek'Thar.

"We should watch him," he said to his teacher. "There is something about this wandering hermit that I mislike."

Drek'Thar threw back his head and laughed. "We were wrong to suspect you when you came, yet you are the only one who mistrusts this hungry stranger. Oh, Thrall, you have yet so much to learn."

Over dinner that night, Thrall continued to watch the stranger without appearing too obvious. He had a large sack, which he would let no one touch, and never removed the bulky cape. He answered questions politely, but briefly, and revealed very little about himself. All Thrall knew was that he had been a hermit for twenty years, keeping to himself and nursing dreams of the old days without appearing to do very much to actually help bring them back.

At one point, Uthul asked, "Have you ever seen the internment camps? Thrall says the orcs imprisoned there have lost their will."

"Yes, and it is no surprise that this is so," said the stranger. "There is little to fight for anymore."

"There is much to fight for," said Thrall, his anger flaring quickly. "Freedom. A place of our own. The remembrance of our origins."

"And yet you Frostwolves hide up here in the mountains," the stranger replied.

"As you hide in the southlands!" Thrall retorted.

"I do not purport to rouse the orcs to cast off their slaves and revolt against their masters," the stranger replied, his voice calm, not rising to the bait.

"I will not be here long," said Thrall. "Come spring, I will rejoin the undefeated orc chieftain Grom Hellscream, and help his noble Warsong clan storm the camps. We will inspire our brethren to rise up against the humans, who are not their masters, but merely bullies who keep them against their will!" Thrall was on his feet now, the anger hot inside him at the insult this stranger dared to utter. He kept expecting Drek'Thar to chide him, but the old orc said nothing. He merely stroked his wolf companion and listened. The other Frostwolves seemed fascinated by the interchange between these two and did not interrupt.

"Grom Hellscream," sneered the stranger, waving his hand dismissively. "A demon-ridden dreamer. No, you Frostwolves have the right of it, as do I. I have seen what the humans can do, and it is best to avoid them, and seek the hidden places where they do not come."

"I was raised by humans, and believe me, they are not infallible!" cried Thrall. "Nor are you, I would think, you coward!"

"Thrall—" began Drek'Thar, speaking up at last.

"No, Master Drek'Thar, I will not be silent. This . . . this . . . he comes seeking our aid, eats at our fire, and dares to insult the courage of our clan and his own race. I will not stand for it. I am not the chieftain, nor do I claim that right, though I was born to it. But I will claim my individual right to fight this stranger, and make him eat his words sliced upon my sword!"

He expected the cowardly hermit to cringe and ask his pardon. Instead, the stranger laughed heartily and rose. He was almost as big as Thrall, and now, finally, Thrall could glimpse beneath the cloak. To his astonishment, he saw that this arrogant stranger was completely clad in black plate armor, trimmed with brass. Once, the armor must have been stunning, but though it was still impressive, the plates had seen better days and the brass trim was sorely in need of polishing.

Uttering a fierce cry, the stranger opened the pack he had been carrying and pulled out the largest warhammer Thrall had ever seen. He held it aloft with seeming ease, then brandished it at Thrall.

"See if you can take me, whelp!" he cried.

The other orcs cried aloud as well, and for the second time in as many moments Thrall received a profound shock. Instead of leaping to the defense of their clansman, the Frostwolves backed away. Some even fell to their knees. Only Snowsong stayed with him, putting herself between her companion and the stranger, hackles raised and white teeth bared.

What was happening? He glanced over at Drek'Thar, who seemed relaxed and impassive.

So be it, then. Whoever this stranger might be, he had insulted Thrall and the Frostwolves, and the young shaman was prepared to defend his honor and theirs with his life.

He had no weapon ready, but Uthul pressed a long, sharp spear into Thrall's outstretched hand. Thrall's fingers closed on it, and he began to stamp.

Thrall could feel the Spirit of the Earth responding questioningly. As gently as he could, for he had no wish to upset the element, he declined an offer of aid. This was not a battle for the elements; there was no dire need here. Only Thrall's need to teach this arrogant stranger a sorely needed lesson.

Even so, he felt the earth tremble beneath his pounding feet. The stranger looked startled, then oddly pleased. Before Thrall could even brace himself, the armored stranger launched into a punishing attack.

Thrall's spear came up to defend himself, but while it was a fierce weapon, it was never meant to block the blow of an enormous warhammer. The mighty spear snapped in two as if it were a twig. Thrall glanced around, but there was no other weapon. He prepared for his adversary's next blow, deciding to utilize the strategy that had worked so well for him in the past when he was fighting weaponless against an armed opponent.

The stranger swung his hammer again. Thrall dodged it, and whirled deftly to reach out and seize the weapon, planning to snatch it from its wielder. To his astonishment, as his hands closed on the shaft, the stranger tugged swiftly. Thrall fell forward, and the stranger straddled his now fallen body.

Thrall twisted like a fish, and managed to hurl himself to the side while catching one of his foe's legs tightly between his ankles. He jerked, and the stranger staggered and lost his balance. Now they were both on the earth. Thrall slammed his clenched fist down on the wrist of the hand that clutched the warhammer. The stranger grunted and reflexively loosed his hold. Seizing the opportunity and the warhammer both, Thrall leaped to his feet, swinging the weapon high over his head.

He caught himself just in time. He was about to bring the massive stone weapon crunching down on his opponent's skull. But this was a fellow orc, not a human he faced on the battlefield. This was a guest in his encampment, and a warrior he would be proud to have serve alongside him when he and Hellscream achieved their goal of storming the encampments and liberating their imprisoned kin.

The hesitation and the sheer weight of the weapon caused him to stumble. That moment was all the stranger needed. Growling, he utilized the same move Thrall had used on him. He kicked forward, knocking Thrall's feet out from under him. Still clutching the warhammer, Thrall fell, unable to stop himself. Before he even realized what was happening, the other orc was on top of him with his hands at Thrall's throat.

Thrall's world went red. Instinct kicked in and he writhed. This orc was almost as large as he and armored as well, but Thrall's fierce desire for victory and extra bulk gave him the edge he needed to twist his body around and pin the other warrior beneath him.

Hands closed on him and pulled him off. He roared, the hot bloodlust in him demanding satisfaction, and struggled. It took eight of his fellow Frostwolves to pin him down long enough for the red haze to clear and his breathing to slow. When he nodded that he was all right, they rose and let him sit up on his own.

Before him stood the stranger. He stomped forward and shoved his face to within a hand's breadth of Thrall's. Thrall met his eyes evenly, panting with exertion.

The stranger drew himself up to his full height and then let out a huge roar of laughter.

"Long has it been since anyone could even *challenge* me," he bellowed cheerfully, not seeming the least displeased that Thrall had nearly managed to smear his entrails into the earth. "And it has been even longer since anyone could best me, even in a friendly tussle. Only your father ever did that, young Thrall. May his spirit walk in peace. Hellscream did not lie, it seems. I appear to have found my second in command."

He extended a hand to Thrall. Thrall stared at it, and snapped, "Second in command? I beat you, stranger, with your own weapon. I know not what code makes the victor second!"

"Thrall!" Drek'Thar's voice cracked like a lightning strike.

"He does not yet understand," chuckled the stranger. "Thrall, son of Durotan, I have come a long way to find you, to see if the rumors were true— that there was yet a worthy second in command for me to take under my wing and trust in when I liberate the encampments."

He paused, and his eyes twinkled with laughter.

"My name, son of Durotan, is Orgrim Doomhammer."

FIFTEEN

Thrall's mouth dropped open in chagrin and shock. He had insulted Orgrim Doomhammer, the Warchief of the Horde? His father's dearest friend? The one orc he had held up as inspiration for so many years? The armor and the warhammer ought to have given the game away at once. What a fool he had been!

He fell to his knees and prostrated himself. "Most noble Doomhammer, I ask your forgiveness. I did not know—" He shot a look at Drek'Thar. "My teacher might have warned me—"

"And that would have spoiled everything," Doomhammer replied, still laughing a little. "I wanted to pick a fight, see if you indeed had the passion and the pride of which Grom Hellscream had spoken so glowingly. I got more than I bargained for . . . I got beaten!" He laughed again, loudly, as if this were the funniest thing that had happened to him in years. Thrall began to relax. Doomhammer's mirth subsided and he placed an affectionate hand on the younger orc's shoulder.

"Come and sit with me, Thrall, son of Durotan," he said. "We will finish our meal and you will tell me your story, and I will tell you tales of your father you have never heard."

Joy flooded Thrall. Impulsively he reached out and gripped the hand that lay on his shoulder. Suddenly serious, Doomhammer met Thrall's eyes and nodded.

Now that everyone knew who the mysterious stranger truly was—Drek'Thar confessed that he had known all along, and indeed had sent Wise-ear to find Doomhammer for just this confrontational purpose—the Frostwolves were able to treat their honored guest with the respect due him. They brought out several hares they had planned on drying for later use, dressed them with precious oils and herbs, and began to roast them over the fire. More herbs were added to the flame, and their pungent, sweet scents rose with the smoke. It was almost intoxicating. Drums and pipes were brought out, and soon the sounds of music and singing rose up to entwine with the smoke, sending a message of honoring and joy to the spirit worlds.

Thrall was tongue-tied at first, but Doomhammer coaxed his story out of him by alternately listening closely and asking probing questions. When Thrall was done, he did not speak at once.

"This Blackmoore," he said. "He sounds like Gul'dan. One who does not have the best interests of his people in his heart, but only his own profit and pleasure."

Thrall nodded. "I was not the only one to experience his cruelty and unpredictability. I am certain that he hates orcs, but he has little love for his own people either."

"And this Taretha, and Sergeant . . . I did not know humans were capable of such things as kindness and honor."

"I would not have known of honor and mercy had it not been for Sergeant," said Thrall. Amusement rippled through him. "Nor would I have known that first maneuver I used on you. It has won me the battle many times."

Doomhammer chuckled with him, then sobered. "It has been my experience that the males hate our people, and the females and children fear us. Yet this girl-child, of her own will, befriended you."

"She has a great heart," Thrall said. "I can give her no higher compliment than to say that I would be proud to admit her into my clan. She has an orc's spirit, tempered by compassion."

Doomhammer was silent again for a time. Finally, he said, "I have kept to myself these many years, since the final, ignominious defeat. I know what they say about me. I am a hermit, a coward, afraid to show my face. Do you know why I have scorned the company of others until this night, Thrall?"

Thrall silently shook his head.

"Because I needed to be by myself, to analyze what had happened. To think. To remind myself who I was, who we were as a people. From time to time, I would do as I have done this night. I would venture forth to the camp-fires, accept their hospitality, listen to their experiences, and learn." He paused. "I know the insides of human prisons, as you do. I was captured and kept as an oddity by King Terenas of Lordaeron for a time. I escaped from his palace, as you escaped from Durnholde. I was even in an encampment. I know what it is like to be that broken, that despairing. I almost became one of them."

He had been staring into the fire as he spoke. Now he turned to look at Thrall. Though his gray eyes were clear and devoid of the evil flame that burned in Hellscream's eyes, by a trick of the firelight, his eyes now seemed to gleam as red as Grom's.

"But I did not. I escaped, just as you did. I found it easy, just as you did. And yet it remains difficult for those huddled in the mud in those encamp-ments. We can only do so much from the outside. If a pig loves her stall, the open door means nothing. So it is with those in the camps. They must want to walk through the door when we open it for them."

Thrall was beginning to see what Doomhammer was trying to say. "Tear-ing down the walls alone will not ensure our people's freedom," he said.

Doomhammer nodded. "We must remind them of the way of the shaman. They must rid their contaminated spirits of the poison of the demon-whispered words, and instead embrace their true natures of the war-rior and the spirit. You have won the admiration of the Warsong clan, and their fierce leader, Thrall. Now you have the Frostwolves, the most indepen-dent and proud clan I have ever known, ready to follow you into battle. If there is any orc living that can teach our broken kindred to remember who they are, it is you."

Thrall thought of the encampment, of its dreary, deadly sloth. He also thought of how narrowly he had escaped Blackmoore's men.

"Though I despise the place, I will willingly return, if I can hope to reawaken my people," Thrall said. "But you must know that my capture is something that Blackmoore deeply desires. Twice, I have only narrowly escaped him. I had hoped to lead a charge against him, but—"

"But that will fail, without troops," Doomhammer said. "I know these things, Thrall. Though I have been a lone wanderer, I have not been inatten-tive to what has been happening in the land. Do not worry. We will lay false trails for Blackmoore and his men to follow."

"The commanders of the camps know to look for me," said Thrall.

"They will be looking for large, powerful, spirited, intelligent Thrall," countered Doomhammer. "Another defeated, muddied, broken orc will be overlooked. Can you hide that stubborn pride, my friend? Can you bury it and pretend that you have no spirit, no will of your own?"

"It will be difficult," Thrall admitted, "but I will do it, if it will help my people."

"Spoken like the true son of Durotan," said Doomhammer, his voice oddly thick.

Thrall hesitated, but pressed on. He had to know as much as he could. "Drek'Thar tells me that Durotan and Draka left to seek you, to convince you that Gul'dan was evil and using the orcs only to further his own struggle for power. The cloth in which I was wrapped told Drek'Thar that they had died violently, and I know that I was alone with the bodies of two orcs and a white wolf when Blackmoore found me. Please . . . can you tell me . . . did my father find you?"

"He did," Doomhammer said heavily. "And it is my greatest shame and sorrow that I did not keep them closer. I thought it for the good of both my warriors and Durotan as well. They came, bringing you, young Thrall, and told me of Gul'dan's treachery. I believed them. I knew of a place where they would be safe, or so I thought. I later learned that several of my own warriors were Gul'dan's spies. Though I do not know for certain, I am convinced that the guard I entrusted to lead Durotan to safety summoned assassins to kill them instead." Doomhammer sighed deeply, and for a moment it seemed to Thrall as if the weight of the world was piled atop those broad, powerful shoulders.

"Durotan was my friend. I would gladly have given my life for him and his family. Yet I unwittingly caused their deaths. I can only hope to atone for that by doing everything I can for the child he left behind. You come from a proud and noble line, Thrall, despite the name which you have chosen to keep. Let us honor that line together."

A few weeks later, in the full bloom of spring, Thrall found it ease itself to lumber into a village, roar at the farmers, and let himself be captured. Once the trap-net had closed about him, he subsided, whimpering, to make his captors believe that they had crushed his spirit.

Even when he was set free in the encampment, he was careful not to give himself away. But once the guards had ceased regarding him as a novelty, Thrall began to speak softly to those who would listen. He had singled out the few who still seemed to have spirit. In the darkness, with the human guards nodding at their posts, Thrall told these orcs of their origins. He spoke of the powers of the shamans, of his own skills. More than once, a skeptic demanded proof. Thrall did not make the earth shake, or call the thunder and lightning. Instead, he picked up a handful of mud, and sought what was left of life within it. Before the astonished eyes of the captives, he caused the brown earth to sprout forth grasses and even flowers.

"Even what appears dead and ugly has power and beauty," Thrall told the awestruck watchers. They turned to him, and his heart leaped within him as he saw the faintest glimmerings of hope in their expressions.

While Thrall subjected himself to voluntary imprisonment in order to inspire the beaten, imprisoned orcs in the camps, the Frostwolf clan and the Warsong clan had joined forces under Doomhammer. They watched the camp which Thrall was in, and waited for his signal.

It took longer than Thrall had hoped to rouse the downtrodden orcs to even think of rebellion, but eventually, he decided the time was right. In the small hours of the morning, when the light snoring of many of the guards could be heard in the dewy hush, Thrall knelt on the good, solid soil. He lifted his hands and asked the Spirits of Water and Fire to come to help him free his people.

They came.

A soft rain began falling. Suddenly the sky was split with three jagged lines of lightning. A pause, then the display was repeated. Angry thunder rolled after each one, almost shaking the earth. This was the agreed-upon signal. The orcs waited, frightened yet excited, clutching the makeshift weapons of stones and sticks and other things that could be readily found in the encampment. They waited for Thrall to tell them what to do.

A terrifying scream split the night more piercingly than the thunder, and Thrall's heart soared. He would recognize that cry anywhere—it was Grom Hellscream. The sound startled the orcs, but Thrall cried over the din, "Those are our allies outside the walls! They have come to free us!"

The guards had been awakened by the thunderclaps. Now they scrambled to their posts as Hellscream's cries faded, but they were too late. Thrall asked again for lightning, and it came.

A jagged bolt of it struck the main wall, where most of the guards were posted. Mixed in with that terrible sound were a clap of thunder and the screams of the guards. Thrall blinked in the sudden darkness, but there were tongues of flame still burning here and there, and he could see that the wall was completely breached.

Over that breach spilled a tide of lithe green bodies. They charged the guards and overwhelmed them with almost casual ease. The orcs gaped at the sight.

"Can you feel it stirring?" Thrall yelled. "Can you feel your spirits longing to fight, to kill, to be free? Come, my brothers and sisters!" Without looking to see if they followed, Thrall charged toward the opening.

He heard their tentative voices behind him, growing in volume with each step they took toward liberation. Suddenly Thrall grunted in pain as something impaled his arm. A black-fletched arrow had sunk almost the entire way through it. He ignored the pain; time enough to tend to it when all were free.

There was fighting all around him, the sounds of steel striking sword and ax biting flesh. Some of the guards, the more intelligent ones, had realized what was happening and were rushing to block the exit with their own bodies. Thrall spared a moment of pity for the futility of their deaths, then charged.

He snatched up a weapon from a fallen comrade and beat back the inexperienced guard easily. "Go, go!" he cried, waving with his left hand. The imprisoned orcs first froze in a tight group, then one of them yelled and charged forward. The rest followed. Thrall lifted his weapon, brought it down, and the guard fell writhing into the bloody mud.

Gasping from exertion, Thrall looked around. All he could see now were the Warsong and Frostwolf clans engaged in combat. There were no more prisoners.

"Retreat!" he cried, and made for the pile of still-hot rocks that had once been imprisoning walls and the sweet darkness of the night. His clansmen followed. There were one or two guards who gave chase, but the orcs were faster and soon outdistanced them.

The agreed-upon meeting place was an ancient pile of standing stones. The night was dark, but orcish eyes did not need the moons' illumination to see. By the time Thrall reached the site, dozens of orcs were huddled by the eight towering stones.

"Success!" cried a voice at Thrall's right. He turned to see Doomhammer, his black plate armor shiny with what could only be spilled human blood. "Success! You are free, my brethren. You are free!"

And the cry that swelled up into the moonless night filled Thrall's heart with joy.

"If you bear the news I think you do, then I am inclined to separate your pretty head from your shoulders," Blackmoore growled at the hapless messenger who wore a baldric that marked him as a rider from one of the internment camps.

The messenger looked slightly ill. "Perhaps, then, I ought not speak," he replied.

There was a bottle to Blackmoore's right that seemed to keep calling to him. He ignored its song, though his palms were sweaty.

"Let me guess. There has been another uprising at one of the encampments. All of the orcs have escaped. No one knows where they are."

"Lord Blackmoore," stammered the young messenger, "will you still cut my head off if I confirm your words?"

Anger exploded through Blackmoore so sharply it was almost a physical pain. Hard on that passionate emotion was a profound sense of black despair. What was going on? How could those cattle, those sheep in orc guise, rally themselves sufficiently to overthrow their captors? Who were these orcs who had come out of nowhere, armed to the teeth and as full of hatred and fury as they had been two decades past? There were rumors that Doomhammer, curse his rotten soul, had come out of hiding and was leading these incursions. One guard had sworn that he had seen the black plate that bastard was famous for wearing.

"You may keep your head," said Blackmoore, acutely aware of the bottle that was within arm's reach. "But only that you may carry a message back to your superiors."

"Sir," said the messenger miserably, "there's more."

Blackmoore peered up at him with bloodshot eyes. "How much more can there possibly be?"

"This time, the instigator was positively identified. It was—"

"Doomhammer, yes, I've heard the rumors."

"No, my lord." The messenger swallowed. Blackmoore could actually see sweat popping out on the youth's brow. "The leader of these rebellions is . . . is Thrall, my lord."

Blackmoore felt the blood drain from his face. "You're a damned liar, my man," he said, softly. "Or at least you'd better tell me you are."

"Nay, my lord, though I would it were not so. My master said he fought him in hand-to-hand combat, and remembered Thrall from the gladiator battles."

"I'll have your master's tongue for telling such untruths!" bellowed Blackmoore.

"Alas, sir, you'll have to dig six feet to get his tongue," said the messenger. "He died only an hour after the battle."

Overcome with this new information, Blackmoore sank back in his chair and tried to compose his thoughts. A quick drink would help, but he knew that he was drinking too much in front of people. He was starting to hear the whispers: *drunken fool . . . who's in command here now. . . .*

No. He licked his lips. *I'm Aedelas Blackmoore, Lord of Durnholde, master of the encampments . . . I trained that green-skinned, black-blooded freak, I ought to be able to outthink him . . . by the Light, just one drink to steady these hands. . . .*

A strange feeling of pride stole through him. He'd been right about Thrall's potential all along. He knew he'd been something special, something more than just an ordinary orc. If only Thrall hadn't spurned the chances

Blackmoore had given him! They could be leading the charge against the Alliance even now, with Blackmoore riding at the head of a loyal gathering of orcs, obedient to his every command. Foolish, foolish Thrall. For the briefest of moments, Blackmoore's thoughts drifted back toward that final beating he had given Thrall. Perhaps that had been a bit much.

But he would not let himself feel guilt, not over his treatment of a disobedient slave. Thrall had thrown it all away to ally with these grunting, stinking, worthless thugs. Let him rot where he would fall.

His attention returned to the trembling messenger, and Blackmoore forced a smile. The man relaxed, smiling tentatively back. With an unsteady hand, Blackmoore reached for a quill, dipped it in ink, and began to write a message. He powdered it to absorb the excess ink and gave it a few moments to dry. Then he carefully folded the missive into thirds, dripped hot wax on it, and set his seal.

Handing it to the messenger, he said, "Take this to your master. And have a care for that neck of yours, young sir."

Apparently having difficulty believing his good fortune, the messenger bowed deeply and hurried out, probably before Blackmoore could change his mind. Alone, Blackmoore lunged for the bottle, uncorked it, and took several long, deep pulls. As he lowered the bottle from his lips, it spilled on his black doublet. He wiped at the stains, disinterested. That's what he had servants for.

"Tammis!" he yelled. At once the door opened and the servant stuck his head in.

"Yes, sir?"

"Go find Langston." He smiled. "I've got a task for him to complete."

SIXTEEN

Thrall had successfully managed to infiltrate and liberate three encampments. After the first, of course, security had been stepped up at the encampments. It was still pathetically lax, and the men who "captured" Thrall never seemed to expect him to stir up trouble.

But during the battle for the third, he had been recognized. The element of surprise had now vanished, and after talking with Hellscream and

Doomhammer, it was decided that it would be too risky for Thrall to continue to pose as just another prisoner.

"It is your spirit, my friend, that has roused us. You cannot continue to put yourself into such jeopardy," said Hellscream. His eyes blazed with what Thrall now knew to be demonic hellfire.

"I cannot sit safely behind our lines, letting everyone else face the danger while I shirk it," Thrall replied.

"We are not suggesting that," said Doomhammer. "But the tactic we have utilized has now become too dangerous."

"Humans talk," said Thrall, recalling all the rumors and stories he had heard while training. The human trainees had thought him too stupid to comprehend, and had spoken freely in his presence. The thought still rankled, but he had welcomed the knowledge. "The orcs in the prisons cannot help but overhear how the other camps have been freed. Even if they do not care to listen, they will know that something is afoot. Even if I am not there physically to tell them of the way of the shaman, we can hope that somehow our message has gotten through. Once the way is clear, let us hope they will find their own paths to freedom."

And so it had been. The fourth camp had been bristling with armed guards, but the elements continued to come to Thrall's aid when he asked it of them. This further convinced him that his cause was right and just, for otherwise, the spirits would surely decline their help. It had been harder to destroy the walls and fight the guards, and many of Doomhammer's finest warriors had lost their lives. But the orcs imprisoned within those cold stone walls had eagerly responded, flowing through the breach almost before Doomhammer and his warriors were ready for them.

The new Horde grew almost daily. Hunting was easy at this time of year, and Doomhammer's followers did not go hungry. When he heard of a small group taking it upon themselves to storm an outlying town, Thrall was furious. Especially when he learned that many unarmed humans had been killed.

He learned who the leader of the excursion was, and that night he marched into that group's encampment, seized the startled orc, and slammed him hard into the ground.

"We are not butchers of humans!" Thrall cried. "We fight to free our imprisoned brothers, and our opponents are armed soldiers, not milkmaids and children!"

The orc started to protest, and Thrall backhanded him savagely. The orc's head jerked to the side and blood spilled from his mouth.

"The forest teems with deer and hare! Every camp we liberate provides us with food! There is no call to terrorize people who have offered us no harm simply for our amusement. You fight where I tell you to fight, who I tell you to fight, and if any orc ever again offers harm to an unarmed human, I will not forgive it. Is this understood?"

The orc nodded. Everyone around his campfire stared at Thrall with huge eyes and nodded as well.

Thrall softened a bit. "Such behavior is of the old Horde, led by dark war-locks who had no love for our people. That is what brought us to the intern-ment camps, to the listlessness caused by the lack of demon energy upon which we fed so greedily. I do not wish us beholden to anyone but ourselves. That way almost destroyed us. We will be free, never question that. But we will be free to be who we truly are, and who we truly are is much, much more than simply a race of beings who exist to slaughter humans. The old ways are no more. We fight as proud warriors now, not as indiscriminate killers. There is no pride in murdering children."

He turned and left. Stunned silence followed him. He heard a rumble of laughter in the dark, and turned to see Doomhammer. "You walk the hard path," the great Warchief said. "It is in their blood to kill."

"I do not believe that," said Thrall. "I believe that we were corrupted from noble warriors into assassins. Puppets, whose strings were pulled by demons and those of our own people who betrayed us."

"It . . . is a dreadful dance," came Hellscream's voice, so soft and weak that Thrall almost didn't recognize it. "To be used so. The power they give . . . it is like the sweetest honey, the juiciest flesh. You are fortunate never to have drunk from that well, Thrall. And then to be without it, it is almost . . . unbearable." He shuddered.

Thrall placed a hand on Hellscream's shoulder. "And yet, you have borne it, brave one," he said. "You make my courage as nothing with yours."

Hellscream's red eyes glowed in the darkness, and by their hellish crimson light, Thrall could see him smile.

It was in the small, dark hours of the morning when the new Horde, led by Doomhammer, Hellscream, and Thrall, surrounded the fifth encampment.

The outriders returned. "The guards are alert," they told Doomhammer. "There is double the usual number posted on the walls. They have lit many fires so that their weak eyes can see."

"And it is full moons' light," said Doomhammer, glancing up at the glow-ing silver and blue-green orbs. "The White Lady and the Blue Child are not our friends tonight."

"We cannot wait two more weeks," said Hellscream. "The Horde is eager for a just battle, and we must strike while they are still strong enough to resist the demon listlessness."

Doomhammer nodded, though he still looked concerned. To the scouts, he said, "Any sign that they are expecting an assault?" One of these days, Thrall knew, their luck would run out. They had been very careful not to select camps in any particular order, so that the humans would not be able to guess where they would strike next and thus could not be lying in wait. But Thrall knew Blackmoore, and knew that somehow, some way, a confrontation was inevitable.

While he relished the thought of finally facing Blackmoore in fair combat, he knew what it would mean to the troops. For their sake, he hoped that tonight was not that night.

The outriders shook their heads.

"Then let us descend," said Doomhammer, and in steady silence, the green tide flooded down the hill and toward the encampment.

They had almost reached it when the gates flew open and dozens of armed, mounted humans charged out. Thrall saw the black falcon on the red and gold standard, and knew that the day he had both dreaded and anticipated had finally arrived.

Hellscream's battle cry pierced the air, almost drowning out the screams of humans and the pounding of their horses' hooves. Rather than being disheartened by the enemy's strength, the Horde seemed revitalized, willing to rise to the challenge.

Thrall threw back his head and howled his own battle cry. The quarters were too close for Thrall to call on such great powers as lightning and earthquakes, but there were others he could ask to aid him. Despite an almost overwhelming desire to charge into the fray and fight hand to hand, he held back. Time enough for that once he had done all he could to tip the balance in the orcs' direction.

He closed his eyes, planted his feet firmly on the grass, and sought the Spirit of the Wilds. He saw in his mind's eye a great white horse, the Spirit of all horses, and sent forth his plea.

The humans are using your children to kill us. They, too, are in danger. If the horses throw their riders, they will be free to reach safety. Will you ask them to do so?

The great horse considered. *These children are trained to fight. They are not afraid of swords and spears.*

But there is no need for them to die today. We are only trying to free our people. That is a just cause, and not worth their deaths.

Again, the great horse spirit considered Thrall's words. Finally, he nodded his enormous white head.

Suddenly, the battlefield was thrown into greater confusion as every horse either wheeled and galloped off, bearing a startled and furious human with it, or began to rear and buck. The human guards fought to stay mounted, but it was impossible.

Now it was time to beseech the Spirit of Earth. Thrall envisioned the roots of the forest that surrounded the camp extending, growing, exploding up from the soil. *Trees who have sheltered us . . . will you aid me now?*

Yes, came a response in his mind. Thrall opened his eyes and strained to see. Even with his superb night vision, it was hard to discern what was happening, but he could just make it out.

Roots exploded from the hard-packed earth just outside the camp walls. They shot up from the soil and seized the men who had been dismounted, wrapping their pale lengths about the humans as firmly as the trap-nets closed about captive orcs. To Thrall's approval, the orcs did not kill the fallen guards as they lay helpless. Instead they ran on to other targets, pressed inward, and searched for their imprisoned kin.

Another wave of enemies charged out, this one on foot. The trees did not send their roots forth a second time; they had provided all the aid they would. Despite his frustration, Thrall thanked them and racked his brain as to what to do next.

He decided that he had done all he could as a shaman. It was time for him to behave as a warrior. Gripping his mammoth broadsword, a gift from Hellscream, Thrall charged down the hill to aid his brothers.

Lord Karramyn Langston had never been more afraid in his life.

Too young to have charged into battle in the last conflict between humankind and orcs, he had hung on every word his idol Lord Blackmoore had uttered. Blackmoore had made it sound as easy as hunting game in the tame, forested lands that surrounded Durnholde, except much more exciting. Blackmoore had said nothing about the shrieks and groans that assaulted his ears, the stench of blood and urine and feces and the orcs themselves, the bombardment of a thousand images upon the eye at any one time. No, battle with orcs had been described as a heart-pounding lark, which made one ready for a bath and wine and the company of adoring women.

They had had the element of surprise. They had been ready for the green monsters. What had happened? Why had the horses, well-trained beasts every one of them, fled or bucked off their riders? What wicked sorcery made the earth shoot up pale arms to bind those unfortunate enough to fall? Where were the horrible white wolves coming from, and how did they know whom to attack?

Langston got none of these questions answered. He was ostensibly in command of the unit, but any semblance of control he might have had dissolved once those terrifying tendrils emerged from the earth. Now there was only sheer panic, the sound of sword on shield or flesh, and the cries of the dying.

He himself didn't know whom he was fighting. It was too dark to see, and he swung his sword blindly, crying and sobbing with every wild strike. Sometimes Langston's sword bit into flesh, but most of the time he heard it cutting only the air. He was fueled by the energy of sheer terror, and a distant part of him marveled at his ability to keep swinging.

A solid, strong blow on his shield jangled his arm all the way to his teeth. Somehow, he kept it lifted under the onslaught of a creature that was hugely tall and enormously strong. For a fleeting second, Langston's eyes met those of his attacker and his mouth dropped open in shock.

"Thrall!" he cried.

The orc's eyes widened in recognition, then narrowed in fury. Langston saw a mammoth green fist rise up, and then he knew no more.

Thrall did not care about the lives of Langston's men. They stood between him and the liberation of the imprisoned orcs. They had come openly into honest combat and if they died, then that was their destiny. But Langston, he wanted kept alive.

He remembered Blackmoore's little shadow. Langston never said much, just looked upon Blackmoore with a fawning expression and upon Thrall with loathing and contempt. But Thrall knew that no one was closer to his enemy than this pathetic, weak-willed man, and though he did not deserve it, Thrall was going to see to it that Langston survived this battle.

He flung the unconscious captain over his shoulder and fought his way back against the pressing tide of continued battle. Hurrying back up to the shelter of the forest, he tossed Langston down at the foot of an ancient oak as if he were no more than a sack of potatoes. He tied the man's hands with his own baldric. *Guard him well until I return,* he told the old oak. In answer, the mammoth roots lifted and folded themselves none too gently about Langston's prone form.

Thrall turned and raced back down toward the battle. Usually the liberations were accomplished with astonishing speed, but not this time. The fighting was still continuing when Thrall rejoined his comrades, and it seemed to last forever. But the imprisoned orcs were doing everything they could to scramble toward freedom. At one point, Thrall fought his way past the humans and began searching the encampment. He found several still cowering in corners. They shrank from him at first, and with his blood so hot from battle it was difficult for Thrall to speak gently to them. Nonetheless, he managed to coax each group into coming with him, into making the desperate dash for freedom past groups of clustered, fighting warriors.

Finally, when he was certain that all the inhabitants had fled, he returned to the thick of the fray himself. He looked around. There was Hellscream, fighting with all the power and passion of a demon himself. But where was Doomhammer? Usually the charismatic Warchief had called for retreat by this time, so the orcs could regroup, tend to their wounded, and plan for the next assault.

It was a bloody battle, and too many of his brothers and sisters in arms already lay dead or dying. Thrall, as second in command, took it upon himself to cry, "Retreat! Retreat!"

Lost in the bloodlust, many did not hear him. Thrall raced from warrior to warrior, fending off attacks, screaming the word the orcs never liked to hear but was necessary, even vital, to their continued existence. "Retreat! Retreat!"

His screams penetrated the haze of battlelust at last, and with a few final blows, the orcs turned and moved purposefully out of the confines of the encampment. Many of the human knights, for knights it was clear they were, gave chase. Thrall waited outside, crying, "Go, go!" The orcs were larger, stronger, and faster than the humans, and when the last one was sprinting up the hill toward freedom, Thrall whirled, planted his feet in the foul-smelling mud that was hard earth and blood commingled, and called on the Spirit of Earth at last.

The earth responded. The ground beneath the encampment began to tremble, and small shocks rippled out from the center. Before Thrall's eyes, earth broke and heaved, the mighty stone wall encircling the camp shattering and falling into small pieces. Screams assaulted Thrall's ears, not battle cries or epithets, but cries of genuine terror. He steeled himself against a quick rush of pity. These knights came at the order of Blackmoore. More than likely they had been instructed to slay as many orcs as possible, imprison all they did not slay, and capture Thrall in order to return him to a life of slavery. They had chosen to follow those orders, and for that, they would pay with their lives.

The earth buckled. The screaming was drowned out by the terrible roar of collapsing buildings and shattering stone. And then, almost as quickly as it had come, the noises ceased.

Thrall stood and regarded the rubble that had once been an internment camp for his people. A few soft moans came from under the debris, but Thrall hardened his heart. His own people were wounded, were moaning. He would tend to them.

He took a moment to close his eyes and offer his gratitude to Earth, then turned and hastened to where his people were gathering.

This moment was always chaotic, but it seemed to Thrall to be even less organized than usual. Even as he ran up the hilly ground, Hellscream was hurrying to meet him.

"It's Doomhammer," Hellscream rasped. "You had better hurry."

Thrall's heart leaped. Not Doomhammer. Surely he could not be in danger. . . . He followed where Hellscream led, shoving his way through a thick cluster of jabbering orcs to where Orgrim Doomhammer lay propped up sideways against the base of a tree.

Thrall gasped, horrified. At least two feet of a broken lance extended from Doomhammer's broad back. As Thrall stared, frozen for a moment by the sight, Doomhammer's two personal attendants struggled to remove the circular breastplate. Now Thrall could see, poking through the black gambeson that cushioned the heavy armor, the reddened, glistening tip of the lance. It had impaled Doomhammer with such force that it had gone clear through his body, completely piercing the back plate and denting the breastplate from the inside.

Drek'Thar was kneeling next to Doomhammer, and he turned his blind eyes up to Thrall's. He shook his head slightly, then rose and stepped back.

Blood seemed to roar in Thrall's ears, and it was only dimly that he heard the mighty warrior calling his name. Stumbling in shock, Thrall approached and knelt beside Doomhammer.

"The blow was a coward's blow," Doomhammer rasped. Blood trickled from his mouth. "I was struck from behind."

"My lord," said Thrall, miserably. Doomhammer waved him to silence.

"I need your help, Thrall. In two things. You must carry on what we have begun. I led the Horde once. It is not my destiny to do so again." He grimaced, shuddered, and continued. "Yours is the title of Warchief, Thrall, son of D-Durotan. You will wear my armor, and carry my hammer."

Doomhammer reached out to Thrall, and Thrall grasped the bloody, armored hand with his own. "You know what to do. They are in your care now. I could not . . . have hoped for a better heir. Your father would be so proud . . . help me. . . ."

With hands that trembled, Thrall turned to assist the two younger orcs in removing, piece by piece, the armor that had always been associated with Orgrim Doomhammer. But the lance that still protruded from Orgrim's back would not permit the removal of the rest of the armor.

"That is the second thing," growled Doomhammer. There was a small crowd clustered around the fallen hero, and more were coming up every moment. "It is shame enough that I die from a coward's strike," he said. "I

will not leave my life with this piece of human treachery still in my body."
One hand went to the point of the lance. The fingers fluttered weakly, and
the hand fell. "I have tried to pull it out myself, but I lack the
strength. . . . Hurry, Thrall. Do this for me."

Thrall felt as though his chest were being crushed by an unseen hand. He
nodded. Steeling himself against the pain that he knew he would need to
cause his friend and mentor, he closed his armored fingers about the tip,
pressing into Doomhammer's flesh.

Doomhammer cried out, in anger as much as in pain. "Pull!" he cried.

Closing his eyes, Thrall pulled. The blood-soaked shaft came forward a
few inches. The sound that Doomhammer made almost broke Thrall's heart.

"Again!" the mighty warrior cried. Thrall took a deep breath and pulled,
willing himself to remove the entire shaft this time. It came free with such
suddenness that he stumbled backward.

Black-red blood now gushed freely from the fatal hole in Doomhammer's
belly. Standing beside Thrall, Hellscream whispered, "I saw it happen. It was
before you caused the horses to desert their masters. He was single-handedly
battling eight of them, all on horseback. It was the bravest thing I have ever
seen."

Thrall nodded dumbly, then knelt beside Doomhammer's side. "Great
leader," whispered Thrall, so that only Doomhammer could hear, "I am
afraid. I am not worthy to wear your armor and wield your weapon."

"No one breathes who is worthier," said Doomhammer in a soft, wet
voice. "You will lead them . . . to victory . . . and you will lead them . . . to
peace. . . ."

The eyes closed, and Doomhammer fell forward onto Thrall. Thrall
caught him, and held him close for a long moment. He felt a hand on his
shoulder. It was Drek'Thar, who slipped a hand beneath Thrall's arm and
helped him rise.

"They are watching," Drek'Thar said to Thrall, speaking very softly.
"They must not lose heart. You must put on the armor at once, and show
them that they have a new chieftain."

"Sir," said one of the orcs who had overheard Drek'Thar's words, "the
armor. . . ." He swallowed. "The plate that was pierced—it will need to be
replaced."

"No," said Thrall. "It will not. Before the next battle you will hammer it
back into shape, but I will keep the plate. In honor of Orgrim Doomhammer,
who gave his life to free his people."

He stood and let them place the armor on, grieving privately but pub-
licly showing a brave face. The gathered crowd watched, hushed and rev-
erent. Drek'Thar's advice had been sound; this was the right thing to do.

He bent, picked up the enormous hammer, and swung it over his head.

"Orgrim Doomhammer has named me Warchief," he cried. "It is a title I would not have sought, but I have no choice. I have been named, and so I will obey. Who will follow me to lead our people to freedom?"

A cry rose up, raw and filled with grief for the passing of their leader. Yet it was a sound of hope as well, and as Thrall stood, bearing aloft the famous weapon of Doomhammer, he knew in his heart that, despite the odds, victory would indeed be theirs.

SEVENTEEN

It was raw with grief and fueled by anger that Thrall marched up to where Langston fought against the implacable tree roots in a desperate attempt to sit up.

He shrank back when Thrall arrived, wearing the legendary black plate mail and towering over him. His eyes were wide with fear.

"I should kill you," said Thrall, darkly. The image of Doomhammer dying in front of his eyes was still fresh in his mind.

Langston licked his red, full lips. "Mercy, Lord Thrall," he begged.

Thrall dropped to one knee and shoved his face within inches of Langston's. "And when did you show me mercy?" he roared. Langston winced at the sound. "When did you intervene to say, 'Blackmoore, perhaps you've beaten him enough,' or 'Blackmoore, he did the best he could'? When did such words ever cross your lips?"

"I wanted to," said Langston.

"Right now you believe those words," said Thrall, rising again to his full height and staring down at his captive. "But I have no doubt that you never truly felt that way. Let us dispense with lies. Your life has value to me—for the moment. If you tell me what I want to know, I will release you and the other prisoners and let you return to your dog of a master." Langston looked doubtful. "You have my word," Thrall added.

"Of what worth is the word of an orc?" Langston said, rallying for a moment.

"Why, it's worth your pathetic life, Langston. Though I'll grant you, that is not worth much. Now, tell me. How did you know which camp we would be attacking? Is there a spy in our midst?"

Langston looked like a sullen child and refused to answer. Thrall formed a thought, and the tree roots tightened about Langston's body. He gasped and stared up at Thrall in shock.

"Yes," said Thrall, "the very trees obey my command. As do all the elements." Langston didn't need to know about the give-and-take relationship a shaman had with the spirits. Let him assume Thrall had complete control. "Answer my question."

"No spy," grunted Langston. He was having difficulty breathing due to the root across his chest. Thrall asked that it be loosened, and the tree complied. "Blackmoore has put a group of knights at all the remaining camps."

"So that no matter where we struck, we would encounter his men." Langston nodded. "Hardly a good use of resources, but it appears to have worked this time. What else can you tell me? What is Blackmoore doing to ensure my recovery? How many troops does he have? Or will that root creep up to your throat?"

The root in question gently stroked Langston's neck. Langston's resistance shattered like a glass goblet dropped on a stone floor. Tears welled up in his eyes and he began to sob. Thrall was disgusted, but not enough that he didn't pay close attention to Langston's words. The knight blurted out numbers, dates, plans, even the fact that Blackmoore's drinking was beginning to affect his judgment.

"He desperately wants you back, Thrall," snuffled Langston, peering up at Thrall with red-rimmed eyes. "You were the key to everything."

Instantly alert, Thrall demanded, "Explain." As the confining roots fell away from his body, Langston appeared heartened, and even more eager to tell everything he knew.

"The key to everything," he repeated. "When he found you, he knew that he could use you. First as a gladiator, but as so much more than that." He wiped his wet face and tried to recover as much of his lost dignity as he could. "Didn't you wonder why he taught you how to read? Gave you maps, taught you Hawks and Hares and strategy?"

Thrall nodded, tense and expectant.

"It was because he eventually wanted you to lead an army. An army of orcs."

Anger flooded Thrall. "You are lying. Why would Blackmoore want me to lead his rivals?"

"But they—you—wouldn't be rivals," said Langston. "You would lead an army of orcs against the Alliance."

Thrall gaped. He couldn't believe what he was hearing. He had known Blackmoore was a cruel, conniving bastard, but this . . . It was treachery on a staggering level, against his own kind! Surely this was a lie. But Langston appeared to be in dire earnest, and once the shock had worn off, Thrall realized that to Blackmoore it would make a great deal of sense.

"You were the best of both worlds," Langston continued. "The power and strength and bloodlust of an orc, combined with the intelligence and strategic knowledge of a human. You would command the orcs and they would be invincible."

"And Aedelas Blackmoore would be Lieutenant General no longer, but . . . what? King? Absolute monarch? Lord of all?"

Langston nodded furiously. "You can't imagine what he's been like since you escaped. It's been hard on all of us."

"Hard?" snarled Thrall. "I was beaten and kicked and made to think that I was less than nothing! I faced death nearly every day in the arena. I and my people are battling for our very lives. We are fighting for freedom. *That*, Langston, that is hard. Do not speak to me of pain and difficulty, for you have known precious little of either."

Langston fell silent and Thrall pondered what he had just learned. It was a bold and audacious strategy, but then again, whatever his many faults, Aedelas Blackmoore was a bold and audacious man. Thrall had learned a little, here and there, about the Blackmoore family's disgrace. Aedelas had always been eager to wipe the blot from his name, but perhaps the stain went deep. Perhaps it went all the way to the bone—or to the heart.

Why, though, if Blackmoore's aim had ultimately been to win Thrall's complete loyalty, had he not been treated better? Memories floated into Thrall's mind that he had not recalled in years: an amusing game of Hawks and Hares with a laughing Blackmoore; a plateful of sweets sent down from the kitchens after a particularly fine battle; an affectionate hand placed on a huge shoulder when Thrall had conquered a particularly tricky strategic problem.

Blackmoore had always aroused many feelings in Thrall. Fear, adoration, hatred, contempt. But for the first time, Thrall realized that, in many ways, Blackmoore deserved his pity. At the time, Thrall had not known why it was that sometimes Blackmoore was open and jovial, his voice clipped and erudite, and sometimes he was brutal and nasty, his voice slurred and unnaturally loud. Now, he understood; the bottle had gotten its talons as firmly into Blackmoore as an eagle's sank into a hare. Blackmoore was a man torn between embracing a legacy of treachery and overcoming it, of being a brilliant strategist and fighter and being a cowardly, vicious bully. Blackmoore had probably treated Thrall as well as he knew how.

The rage left Thrall. He felt terribly sorry for Blackmoore but the feeling changed nothing. He still was driven to liberate the encampments, and aid the orcs in rediscovering the power of their heritage. Blackmoore stood in the way, an obstacle that would need to be eliminated.

He looked back down at Langston, who sensed the change in him and gave him a smile that looked more like a grimace.

"I keep my word," Thrall said. "You and your men will go free. You will leave, now. With no weapons, no food, no mounts. You will be followed, but you will not see who follows you; and if you speak of an ambush, or attempt any kind of attack, you will die. Is this understood?"

Langston nodded. With a jerk of his head, Thrall indicated that he could leave. Langston needed no second urging. He scrambled to his feet and bolted. Thrall watched him and the other disarmed knights fleeing into the darkness. He looked up into the trees and saw the owl he had sensed staring back down at him with lambent eyes. The night bird hooted softly.

Follow them, my friend, if you will. Report back to me at once if they plan action against us.

With a rustle of wings, the owl sprang from the branch and began to follow the fleeing men. Thrall sighed deeply. Now that the keyed-up energy that had supported him through this long, bloody night was fading, he realized that he himself had suffered injuries and was exhausted. But these things could be tended to later. There was a more important duty to perform.

It took the rest of the night to gather and prepare the bodies, and by morning, black smoke was curling thickly into the blue skies. Thrall and Drek'Thar had asked the Spirit of Fire to burn more quickly than was its usual wont, so it would not take nearly as long for the bodies to be reduced to ashes, and those ashes given to Spirit of Air to scatter as it saw fit.

The largest and most decorated pyre was reserved for the most noble of them all. It took Thrall, Hellscream, and two others to lift Orgrim Doomhammer's massive corpse onto the pyre. Reverently, Drek'Thar anointed Doomhammer's nearly naked body with oils, murmuring words that Thrall could not hear. Sweet scents rose up from the body. Drek'Thar indicated that Thrall join him, and together they posed the body in an attitude of defiance. Dead fingers were folded and discreetly tied about a ruined sword. At Doomhammer's feet were laid the corpses of other brave warriors who had died in battle—the fierce, loyal white wolves who had not been swift enough to elude the humans' weapons. One lay at Doomhammer's feet, two more on each side, and across his chest, in a place of honor, was the grizzled, courageous Wise-ear. Drek'Thar patted his old friend one last time, then he and Thrall stepped back.

Thrall expected Drek'Thar to say whatever words might be appropriate, but instead Hellscream nudged Thrall. Uncertainly, Thrall addressed the crowd who gathered, hushed, about their former chieftain's corpse.

"I have not been long in the company of my own people," Thrall began. "I do not know the traditions of the afterlife. But this I know: Doomhammer died as bravely as it is possible for any orc to die. He fought in battle, trying to liberate his imprisoned kin. Surely, he will regard us with favor, as we honor him now in death as we all honored him in life." He looked over at the dead orc's face. "Orgrim Doomhammer, you were my father's best friend. I could not hope to know a nobler being. Speed to whatever joyous place and purpose await you."

With that, he closed his eyes and asked the Spirit of Fire to take the hero. Immediately, the fire burnt more swiftly and with more heat than Thrall had ever experienced. The body would soon be consumed, and the shell that had housed the fiery spirit called in this world Orgrim Doomhammer would soon be no more.

But what he had stood for, what he had died for, would never be forgotten.

Thrall tilted his head back and bellowed a deep cry. One by one, others joined him, screaming their pain and passion. If there were indeed ancestral spirits, even they must have been impressed by the volume of the lamentation raised for Orgrim Doomhammer.

Once the rite was done, Thrall sat heavily down beside Drek'Thar and Hellscream. Hellscream, too, had suffered injuries which he, like Thrall, simply chose to bear stoically for the moment. Drek'Thar had been expressly forbidden to be anywhere near the fighting, though he served loyally and well by tending to the injured. If anything happened to Thrall, Drek'Thar was the only shaman among them, and far too precious a resource to risk losing. He was not yet so old that the order didn't vex him, however.

"What encampment is next, my Warchief?" said Hellscream respectfully. Thrall winced at the term. He was still getting used to the fact that Doomhammer was gone, that he was now in charge of hundreds of orcs.

"No more encampments," he said. "Our force is large enough for the present moment."

Drek'Thar frowned. "They suffer," he said.

"They do," Thrall agreed, "but I have a plan to liberate all of them at once. To kill the monster, you must cut off his head, not just his hands and feet. It is time to cut off the head of the internment camp system."

His eyes glittered in the firelight. "We will storm Durnholde."

The next morning, when he announced the plan to the troops, huge cheers greeted him. They were ready, now, to tackle the seat of power. Thrall and Drek'Thar had the elements standing ready to aid them. The orcs were only revitalized by the battle of last night; few of them had fallen, though one was the greatest warrior of them all, and many of the enemy now lay dead around the blasted remains of the encampment. The ravens who circled were grateful for the feast.

They were several days' march away, but food was plentiful and spirits were high. By the time the sun was fully in the sky, the orcish Horde, under their new leader Thrall, was moving steadily and purposefully toward Durnholde.

"Of course I told him nothing," said Langston, sipping Blackmoore's wine. "He captured and tortured me, but I held my tongue, I tell you. Out of admiration, he let me and my men go."

Privately, Blackmoore doubted this, but said nothing. "Tell me more about these feats he performs," he asked.

Happy to regain his mentor's approval, Langston launched into a fabulous tale about roots clutching his body, lightning striking on command, well-trained horses abandoning their masters, and the very earth shattering a stone enclosure. If Blackmoore hadn't heard similar stories from the few men who returned, he would have been inclined to think that Langston had been hitting the bottle even harder than he.

"I was on the right path," Blackmoore mused, taking another gulp of wine. "In capturing Thrall. You see what he is, what he has done with that pathetic bunch of slumping, disheartened greenskins."

It was physically painful to think that he had come so close to manipulating this clearly powerful new Horde. Hard on the heels of that came a mental image of Taretha, and her letters of friendship to his slave. As always, anger mixed with a strange, sharp pain rose in him at the thought. He had let her be, never let her know that he had found the letters. He hadn't even let Langston know about that, and was now profoundly grateful for his wisdom. He believed that Langston had probably babbled everything he knew to Thrall, which necessitated a change of plan.

"I fear others were likely not as staunch as you in the face of torture by orcs, my friend," he said, trying and failing to keep the sarcasm out of his voice. Fortunately, Langston was so far in his cups that he didn't appear to notice. "We must assume that the orcs know all that we know, and act accordingly. We must try to think like Thrall. What would be his next move? What is his ultimate goal?"

And how in all the hells there are can I find a way to reclaim him?

Though he was leading an army of nearly two thousand, and it was almost certain to be spotted, Thrall did what he could to disguise the march of the Horde. He asked the earth to cover their prints, the air to carry their scent away from any beasts who might sound the alert. It was little, but every bit helped.

He made the encampment several miles south of Durnholde, in a wild and generally avoided forested area. Together with a small group of scouts, he set off for a certain wooded area directly outside the fortress. Both Hellscream and Drek'Thar had tried to dissuade him, but he insisted.

"I have a plan," he said, "one that may achieve our goals without undue bloodshed from either side."

EIGHTEEN

Even on the coldest days of winter, save when there was an active blizzard preventing anyone departing Durnholde, Taretha had gone to visit the lightning-felled tree. And each time she peered into the tree's black depths, she saw nothing.

She enjoyed the return of warmer weather, though the snowmelt-saturated earth sucked on her boots and more than once succeeded in pulling one off. Having to tug her boot free and put it on a second time was a trivial price to pay for the fresh smells of the awakening woods, the shafts of sunlight piercing the darkness of the shadows, and the astounding blaze of color that dotted the meadows and forest floor alike.

Thrall's exploits had been the talk of Durnholde. The conversations served only to increase Blackmoore's drinking. Which, at times, was not a bad thing. More than once she had arrived at his bedchamber and entered quietly, to find the Master of Durnholde asleep on floor, chair, or bed, a bottle somewhere nearby. On those nights, Taretha Foxton breathed a sigh of relief, closed the door, and slept alone in her own small room.

A few days ago, young Lord Langston had returned, with tales that sounded too preposterous to frighten a child still in the nursery. And yet . . . hadn't she read of ancient powers the orcs had once possessed? Powers in harmony with nature, long ago? She knew that Thrall was profoundly intelligent, and it would not at all surprise her to discover that he had learned these ancient arts.

Taretha was approaching the old tree now, and looked into its depths with a casualness born of repetition.

And gasped. Her hand flew to her mouth as her heart began to pound so fiercely she feared she would faint. There, nestled in a brown-black hollow, was her necklace. It seemed to catch the sunlight and glow like a silver beacon to her. With trembling fingers, she reached for it, grasped it, and then dropped it.

"Clumsy!" she hissed, picking it up again with a slightly steadier hand.

It could be a trick. Thrall could have been captured and the necklace taken from him. It might even have been recognized as hers. But unless Thrall told someone about their compact, who would know to leave it here? She was certain of one thing: Nobody could break Thrall.

Tears of joy filled her eyes and spilled down her cheeks. She wiped at them with the back of her left hand, the right one still cradling the crescent pendant.

He was here, in these woods, likely hiding in the dragonlike cliffside. He was waiting for her to help him. Perhaps he was injured. Her hands folded over the necklace and she tucked it inside her dress, carefully out of sight. It would be best if no one saw her "missing" necklace.

Happier than she had been since she had last seen the orc, and yet filled with worry for his safety, Taretha returned to Durnholde.

The day seemed to last forever. She was grateful that the dinner tonight was fish; more than once, she'd gotten ill on poorly prepared fish. The chef at Durnholde had served with Blackmoore in battle over twenty years ago. He had been hired as a reward for his service, not for his cooking.

Of course, she did not eat at the table in the great hall with Blackmoore. He would not dream of having a servant girl sit beside him in front of his noble friends. *Good enough to bed, not good enough to wed,* she thought, recalling the old childhood verse. All the better tonight.

"You seem a bit preoccupied, my dear," Tammis said to his daughter as they sat together at the small table in their quarters. "Are you . . . well?"

The slightly strained tone of his voice and the frightened look her mother gave Taretha at the question almost made her smile. They were worried that she was pregnant. That would help with her deception tonight.

"Very well, Da," she answered, folding her hand over his. "But this fish . . . does it taste all right to you?"

Clannia prodded her own fish in cream sauce with her two-pronged fork. "It tastes well enough, for being Randrel's cooking."

In truth, the fish was fairly tasty. Still, Taretha took another bite, chewed, swallowed, and made a slight face. She made a bit of a show of pushing the plate away from her. As her father peeled an orange, Taretha closed her eyes and whimpered.

"I'm sorry. . . ." She rushed out of the room to her own quarters, making noises as if she was about to be sick. She reached her room, on the same floor as her parents', and made loud noises over the chamber pot. She had to smile a little; it would be amusing, were the stakes not so high.

There came an urgent knock on the door. "Darling, it's me," called Clannia. She opened the door. Taretha put the empty chamber pot out of sight. "Poor dear. You look pale as milk."

That, at least, Taretha didn't have to feign. "Please . . . can Da have a word with the Master? I don't think. . . ."

Clannia colored bright pink. Although everyone knew that Taretha had become Blackmoore's mistress, no one spoke of it. "Certainly, my dear, certainly. Would you like to stay with us tonight?"

"No," she said, quickly. "No, I'm fine. I'd just like to be alone for a bit." She lifted her hand to her mouth again, and Clannia nodded.

"As you will, Tari dear. Good night. Let us know if you need anything."

Her mother closed the door behind her, and Taretha let out a long, deep breath. Now, to wait until it was safe to leave. She was next to the kitchens, one of the last places that settled down for the night. When all was still, she ventured forth. First, she went to the kitchens, placing as much food as she could lay her hands on into the sack. Earlier today, she had torn up some old dresses for bandages, should Thrall need them.

Blackmoore's habits were as predictable as the sun's rising and setting. If he started drinking at dinner, as was his wont, he would be ready to entertain her in his bedchamber by the time dinner was over. Afterward, he would fall into a slumber, almost a stupor, and there was very little that could rouse him until sunrise.

She had listened to the servers in the great hall, and ascertained that he had, as usual, been drinking. He had not seen her tonight, and that would put him in a foul mood, but by now, he would be asleep.

Gently, Taretha unlocked the door to Blackmoore's quarters. She let herself in, then closed the door as quietly as possible. Loud snoring met her ears. Reassured, she moved steadily toward her gate to freedom.

Blackmoore had boasted about this many months ago when he had been in his cups. He had forgotten he had told her about it, but Taretha remembered. Now, she went to the small desk and opened a small drawer. She pressed gently on it, and the false bottom came loose in her hand, revealing a tiny box.

Taretha removed the key and returned the box to the drawer, closing it carefully. She then turned toward the bed.

On the right side, a tapestry hung on the stone wall. It depicted a noble knight doing battle with a fierce black dragon defending a huge pile of treasure. Taretha brushed the tapestry aside and found the room's real treasure—a hidden door. As quietly as she could, she inserted the key, turned it, and opened the door.

Stone steps led down, into darkness. Cool air bathed her face, and a scent of wet stone and mold assaulted her nostrils. She swallowed hard, facing her fear. She did not dare to light a candle. Blackmoore slept deeply, but the risk was far too great. If he knew what she was doing, he'd have her flogged raw.

Think of Thrall, she thought. *Think of what Thrall has faced.* Surely she could overcome a fear of the darkness for him.

She closed the door behind her and was suddenly standing in a blackness so absolute she could almost feel it. Panic rose up in her like a trapped bird, but she fought it down. There was no chance of getting lost here; the tunnel led only one way. She took a few deep, steadying breaths, and then began.

Cautiously, she descended the steps, extending her right foot each time to search for the next one. Finally, her feet touched earth. From here, the tunnel sloped downward at a gentle angle. She recalled what Blackmoore had told her about it. *Got to keep the lords safe, m'dear,* he had said, leaning over her so she could smell his wine-scented breath. *And if there's a siege, well, there's a way we can be safe, you and I.*

It seemed to go on forever. Her fears battled with her mind for control. *What if it collapses? What if after all these years, it's blocked? What if I trip here in the darkness and break my leg?*

Angrily, Taretha silenced the voices of terror. Her eyes kept trying to adjust to the darkness, but with no light whatsoever, they only strained futilely.

She shivered. It was so cold down here, in the dark. . . .

After what seemed an eternity, the ground began to gradually slope upward again. Taretha resisted the urge to break into a run. She would be furious with herself if she lost control now and tripped. She pushed forward steadily, though she could not help but quicken her pace.

Was it her imagination, or was there a lightening of this dreadful darkness? No, she was not imagining it. Up ahead, it was definitely lighter. She drew closer and slowed. Her foot struck something and she stumbled forward, striking her knee and outthrust hand. There were different levels of stone . . . Steps! She reached out a hand, moving upward step by slow step until her questing fingers touched wood.

A door. She had reached a door. Another horrible thought seized her. What if it was bolted from the outside? Wouldn't that make sense? If someone could escape Durnholde by this route, someone else with hostile intentions might be able to enter the same way. It was sure to be locked, or bolted. . . .

But it wasn't. She reached upward and pushed with all her strength. Ancient hinges shrieked, but the door swung open, falling flat with a loud bang. Taretha jumped. It was not until she lifted her head up through the small, square opening, the light seeming to her eyes as bright as day, that she breathed a sigh of relief and permitted herself to believe it was true.

The familiar smells of horses, leather, and hay filled her nostrils. She was in a small stable. She stepped fully out of the tunnel, whispering softly and reassuringly to the horses that turned to look with mild inquiry at her. There were four of them; their tack hung on the wall. She knew at once where she must be. Near the road but fairly far from Durnholde was a courier station, where riders whose business could not be delayed changed exhausted mounts for fresh ones. The light came through chinks in the walls. Taretha carefully closed the trap door in the floor through which she had entered, and hid it with some hay. She went to the stable door and opened it, almost blinking in the full, blue-white light provided by the two moons.

As she had surmised, she was on the outskirts of the small village that encircled Durnholde, inhabited by those who made their living off tending to the needs of the fortress's inhabitants. Taretha took a moment to get her bearings. There it was, the cliff face she had, as a child, imagined to be so like a dragon.

Thrall would be waiting there for her in the cave, hungry and perhaps injured. Buoyed by her victory over the dark tunnel, Taretha raced toward him.

When he saw her running over the crest of the small hill, her slim figure silver in the moonlight, Thrall was hard-pressed not to let out a shout of joy. He contented himself with rushing forward.

Taretha froze, then lifted her skirts and ran toward him in return. Their hands met and clasped, and as the hood fell back from her tiny face he saw her lips were wide in a smile.

"Thrall!" she exclaimed. "It is so good to see you, my dear friend!" She squeezed the two fingers her own little hands could hold as tightly as she could and almost bounced with excitement.

"Taretha," he rumbled affectionately. "Are you well?"

The smile faded, then returned. "Well enough. And you? We have heard of your doings, of course! It is never pleasant when Lord Blackmoore is in a foul mood, but as it means that you are free, I have come to look forward to his anger. Oh. . . ." With a final squeeze, she dropped Thrall's hands and reached for the sack she had been carrying. "I did not know if you were wounded or hungry. I wasn't able to bring a great deal, but I brought what I could. I have some food, and some skirts I tore up for bandages. It's good to see you don't need—"

"Tari," Thrall said gently, "I did not come alone."

He signaled to his scouts, who had been waiting in the cave, and they emerged. Their faces were twisting into scowls of disapproval and hostility. They drew themselves up to their full height, folded their arms across their massive chests, and glared. Thrall watched her reaction carefully. She seemed surprised, and for a brief moment, fear flitted across her face. He didn't suppose he could blame her; the two outriders were doing everything they could to appear menacing. Finally, though, she smiled and strode up to them.

"If you are friends of Thrall, then we are friends also," she said, extending her hands.

One of them snorted in contempt and batted her hand away, not hard enough to hurt her, but enough to throw her slightly off balance. "Warchief, you ask too much of us!" one of them snapped. "We will spare the females and their young as you command, but we will not—"

"Yes you will!" Thrall replied. "This is the female who risked her life to free me from the man who owned both of us. She is risking her life again to come to our aid now. Taretha can be trusted. She is different." He turned to regard her fondly. "She is special."

The scouts continued to glare, but looked less certain of their prejudgment. They exchanged glances, then each took Taretha's hands in turn.

"We are grateful for what you have brought," said Thrall, switching back to human speech. "Rest assured, it will be eaten, and the bandages kept. I have no doubt that they will be needed."

The smile faded from Tari's face. "You intend to attack Durnholde," she said.

"Not if it can be avoided, but you know Blackmoore as I do. On the morrow, my army will march to Durnholde, prepared to attack if needed. But first I will give Blackmoore the opportunity to talk to us. Durnholde is the center of the camp controls. Break it, we break all the camps. But if he is willing to negotiate, we will not shed blood. All we want is to have our people freed, and we will leave the humans alone."

Her fair hair looked silver in the moons' light. She shook her head sadly. "He will never agree," she said. "He is too proud to think of what would be best for those he commands."

"Then stay here with us," said Thrall. "My people will have orders not to attack the women and children, but in the heat of battle, I cannot guarantee their safety. You will be at risk if you return."

"If I am discovered missing," Tari replied, "then that will alert someone that something is going on. They might find and attack you first. And my parents are still there. Blackmoore would take out his anger on them, I am sure. No, Thrall. My place is, and always has been, at Durnholde, even now."

Thrall regarded her unhappily. He knew, as she could not, what chaos battle brought. What blood, and death, and panic. He would see her safe, if he could, but she was her own person.

"You are courageous," said one of the scouts, speaking up unexpectedly. "You risk your personal safety to give us our opportunity to free our people. Our Warchief did not lie. Some humans, it would seem, do understand honor." And the orc bowed.

Taretha seemed pleased. She turned again to Thrall. "I know it sounds foolish to say, but be careful. I wish to see you tomorrow night, to celebrate your victory." She hesitated, then said, "I have heard rumors of your powers, Thrall, are they true?"

"I don't know what you have heard, but I have learned the ways of the shamans. I can control the elements, yes."

Her face was radiant. "Then Blackmoore cannot possibly stand against you. Be merciful in your victory, Thrall. You know we are not all like him. Here. I want you to have this. I've been so long without it, it doesn't feel right for me to keep it anymore."

She inclined her head and removed the silver chain and crescent pendant. Dropping it in Thrall's hand, she folded his fingers over it. "Keep it. Give it to your child, if you have one, and perhaps I may visit him one day."

As she had done so many months ago, Taretha stepped forward and hugged Thrall as best she could. This time, he was not surprised by the gesture, but welcomed it and returned it. He let his hand caress her golden, silky hair, and desperately hoped that they would both survive the coming conflict.

She pulled back, reached up to touch his strong-jawed face, turned and nodded to the others, then turned and purposefully strode back the way she had come. He watched her leave with a strange feeling in his heart, holding her necklace tightly. *Be safe, Tari. Be safe.*

It was only when she was well away from the orcs that Tari permitted the tears to come. She was so afraid, so dreadfully afraid. Despite her brave words, she didn't want to die any more than anyone else did. She hoped Thrall would be able to control his people, but she knew that he was unique. Not all orcs shared his tolerant views toward humans. If only Blackmoore could be persuaded to see reason! But that was as likely as her suddenly sprouting wings and flying away from all of this.

Although she was human, she wished for an orc victory—Thrall's victory.

If he survived, she knew the humans would be treated with compassion. If he fell, she could not be certain of that. And if Blackmoore won—well, what Thrall had experienced as a slave would be as nothing to the torment Blackmoore would put him through now.

She returned to the little stable, opened the trap door, and stepped down into the tunnel. Her thoughts were so full of Thrall and the coming conflict that this time the darkness bothered her hardly at all.

Taretha was still deep in thought when she ascended the stairs to Blackmoore's room and eased the door open.

Abruptly, dark lanterns were unshielded. Taretha gasped. Seated in a chair directly opposite the secret door was Blackmoore, with Langston and two rough-looking, armed guardsmen.

Blackmoore was stone cold sober, and his dark eyes glittered in the candlelight. His beard parted in a smile that resembled that of a hungry predator.

"Well met, my traitor," he said, silkily. "We've been waiting for you."

NINETEEN

The day dawned misty and foggy. Thrall smelled rain in the air. He would have preferred a sunny day, the better to see the enemy, but rain would keep his warriors cooler. And besides, Thrall could control the rain, if it came down to that. For now, he would let the weather do what it would.

He, Hellscream, and a small group of Frostwolves would go ahead. The army would follow behind. He would have preferred to utilize the cover provided by the trees, but an army of nearly two thousand would need the road. If Blackmoore kept scouts posted, then he would be alerted. Thrall did not remember such scouts from his time at Durnholde, but things were very different now.

His small advance party, armored and armed, moved steadily down the road toward Durnholde. Thrall called a small songbird and asked it to look about for him. It came back in a few minutes and in his mind Thrall heard, *They have seen you. They are racing back to the keep. Others are moving to circle behind.*

Thrall frowned. This was quite well organized, for Blackmoore. Nonetheless, he knew his army outnumbered the men at Durnholde nearly four to one.

The bird, perched on one of his massive forefingers, waited. *Fly back to my army and find the old, blind shaman. Tell him what you have told me.*

The songbird, its body a golden yellow and black and its head bright blue, inclined its blue head and flew to execute Thrall's request. Drek'Thar was a trained warrior as well as a shaman. He would know what to do with the bird's warning.

He pressed on, feet steadily moving forward. The road curved, and then Durnholde in all its proud, stony glory loomed up before them. Thrall sensed a change in his group.

"Hold up the flag of truce," he said. "We will observe the proprieties, and it may prevent them from opening fire too soon. Before, we have stormed the encampments with ease," he acknowledged. "Now we must face something more difficult. Durnholde is a fortress, and will not be taken easily. But mark me, if negotiations fail, then fall Durnholde will."

He hoped it would not come to that, but he expected the worst. It was unlikely that Blackmoore would be reasonable.

Even as he and his companions moved forward, Thrall could see movement on the parapets and walkways. Looking more closely, he saw the mouths of cannons opening toward him. Archers took their positions, and several dozen mounted knights came cantering around the sides of the fortress to line up in front of it. They carried lances and spears, and halted their horses. They were waiting.

Still Thrall came. There was more movement atop the walls directly above the huge wooden door, and his heart sped up a little. It was Aedelas Blackmoore. Thrall halted. They were close enough to shout. He would approach no farther.

"Well, well," came a slurred voice that Thrall remembered all too well. "If it isn't my lil' pet orc, all grown up."

Thrall did not rise to the bait. "Greetings, Lieutenant General," he said. "I come not as a pet, but as a leader of an army. An army that has defeated your men soundly in the past. But I will make no move against them this day, unless you force my hand."

Langston stood beside his lord on the walkway. He couldn't believe it. Blackmoore was rip-roaring drunk. Langston, who had helped Tammis carry his lord to bed more times than he cared to admit, had never seen Blackmoore so drunk and still be able to stand. What had he been thinking?

Blackmoore had had the girl followed, of course. A scout, a master of stealth and sharp of eye, had unbarred the door in the courier's stable so she would be able to emerge from the tunnel. He had watched her greet Thrall and a few other orcs. He had seen her give them a sack of food, seen her *embrace* the monster, by the Light, and then return via the no-longer-secret tunnel. Blackmoore had feigned his drunkenness last evening, and had been quite sober when the shocked girl had walked back into his bedchamber to be greeted by Blackmoore, Langston, and the others.

Taretha had not wanted to talk, but once she learned that she had been spied upon, she made great haste to assure Blackmoore that Thrall had come to talk peace. The very notion had offended Blackmoore deeply. He dismissed Langston and the other guards, and for many paces outside his door Langston could still hear Blackmoore cursing and even the sound of a hand striking flesh.

He hadn't seen Blackmoore again until this moment, though Tammis had reported to him. Blackmoore had sent out his fastest riders, to get reinforcements, but they were still at least four hours away. The logical thing to do would be to keep the orc, who had after all raised the flag of truce, talking until help arrived. In fact, etiquette demanded that Blackmoore send out a small party of his own to talk with the orcs. Surely Blackmoore would give the order any moment. Yes, it was the logical thing to do. If the count was right, and Langston thought it was, the orcish army numbered over two thousand.

There were five hundred and forty men in Durnholde, of whom fewer than four hundred were trained warriors who had seen combat.

As he watched uneasily, Langston saw movement on the horizon. They were too far away for him to detect individuals, but he clearly saw a huge green sea begin to move slowly over the rise, and heard the steady, unnerving sound of drums.

Thrall's army.

Though the morning was cool, Langston felt sweat break out under his arms.

"Tha's nice, Thrall," Blackmoore was saying. As Thrall watched, disgusted, the former war hero swayed and caught himself on the wall. "What did you have in mind?"

Once again, pity warred with hatred in his heart. "We have no desire to fight humans anymore, unless you force us to defend ourselves. But you hold many hundreds of orcs prisoners, Blackmoore, in your vile encampments. They will be freed, one way or another. We can do it without more unnecessary bloodshed. Willingly release all the orcs held prisoner in the encampments, and we will return to the wilds and leave humans alone."

Blackmoore threw back his head and laughed. "Oh," he gasped, wiping tears of mirth from his eyes, "oh, you are better than the king's jester, Thrall. *Slave*. I swear, it is more entertaining to watch you now than it was when you fought in the gladiator ring. Listen to you! Using complete sentences, by the Light! Think you understand mercy, do you?"

Langston felt a tug on his sleeve. He jumped, and turned to behold Sergeant. "I've no great love for you, Langston," the man growled, his eyes fierce, "but at least you're sober. You've got to shut Blackmoore up! Get him down from there! You've seen what the orcs can do."

"We can't possibly surrender!" gasped Langston, though in his heart he wanted to.

"Nay," said Sergeant, "but we should at least send out men to talk to them, buy some time for our allies to get here. He *did* send for reinforcements, didn't he?"

"Of course he did," Langston hissed. Their conversation had been overheard and Blackmoore turned bloodshot eyes in their direction. There was a small sack at his feet and he nearly stumbled over it.

"Ah, Sergeant!" he boomed, lurching over toward him. "Thrall! Here's an old friend!"

Thrall sighed. Langston thought he looked the most composed of all of them. "I am sorry that you are still here, Sergeant."

"As am I," Langston heard the Sergeant mutter. Louder, Sergeant said, "You've been too long away, Thrall."

"Convince Blackmoore to release the orcs, and I swear on the honor that you taught me and I possess, none within these walls shall come to harm."

"My lord," said Langston nervously, "you recall what powers I saw displayed in the last conflict. Thrall had me, and he let me go. He kept his word. I know he's only an orc, but—"

"Y'hear that, Thrall?" bellowed Blackmoore. "You're only an orc! Even that idiot Langston says so! What kin' of human surrenders to an orc?" He rushed forward and leaned over the wall.

"Why'd you do it, Thrall?" he cried brokenly. "I gave you everything! You and me, we'd have led those greenskins of yours against th' Alliance and had all the food and wine and gold we could want!"

Langston stared, horrified. Blackmoore was now screaming his treachery to all within earshot. At least he hadn't implicated Langston . . . yet. Langston wished he had the guts to just shove Blackmoore over the wall and surrender the fortress to Thrall right now.

━━◼━━

Thrall didn't waste the opportunity. "Do you hear that, men of Durnholde!" he bellowed. "Your lord and master would betray all of you! Rise up against him, take him away, yield to us, and at the end of the day you will still have your lives and your fortress!"

But there was no sudden stirring of rebellion, and Thrall supposed he couldn't blame them. "I ask you once more, Blackmoore. Negotiate, or die."

Blackmoore stood up to his full height. Thrall now saw that he held something in his right hand. It was a sack.

"Here's my answer, Thrall!"

He reached into the sack and pulled something out. Thrall couldn't see what it was, but he saw Sergeant and Langston recoil. Then the object came hurtling toward him and struck the ground, rolling to a stop at Thrall's feet.

Taretha's blue eyes stared sightlessly up at him from her severed head.

"That's what I do with traitors!" screamed Blackmoore, dancing madly on the walkway. "That's what we do with people we love who betray us . . . who take everything and give nothing . . . who sympathize with double-damned *orcs!*"

Thrall didn't hear him. Thunder was rolling in his ears. His knees went weak and he fell to the earth. Gorge rose in his throat and his vision swam.

It couldn't be. Not Tari. Surely not even Blackmoore could do such an abominable thing to an innocent.

But blessed unconsciousness would not come. He remained stubbornly awake, staring at long blond hair, blue eyes, and a bloody severed neck. Then the horrible image blurred. Wetness poured down his face. His chest heaving with agony, Thrall recalled Tari's words to him, so long ago: *These are called tears. They come when we are so sad, so soul sick, it's as if our hearts are so full of pain there's no place else for it to go.*

But there was a place for the pain to go. Into action, into revenge. Red flooded Thrall's vision now, and he threw back his head and screamed with rage such as he had never before experienced. The cry burned his throat with its raw fury.

The sky boiled. Dozens of lightning strikes split the clouds, dazzling the eye for a moment. The furious peals of crashing thunder that followed nearly deafened the men at the fortress. Many of them dropped their weapons and fell to their knees, gibbering terror at the celestial display of fury that so clearly echoed the wrenching pain of the orc leader.

Blackmoore laughed, obviously mistaking Thrall's rage for helpless grief. When the last peals of thunder died down, he yelled, "They said you couldn't be broken! Well, I broke you, Thrall. *I broke you!*"

Thrall's cry died away, and he stared at Blackmoore. Even across this distance, he could see the blood drain from Blackmoore's face as his enemy now, finally, began to understand what he had roused with his brutal murder.

Thrall had come hoping to end this peacefully. Blackmoore's actions had destroyed that chance utterly. Blackmoore would not live to see another sunrise, and his keep would shatter like fragile glass before the orcish attack.

"Thrall. . . ." It was Hellscream, uncertain as to Thrall's state of mind. Thrall, his chest still raw with grief and tears still streaming down his broad green face, impaled him with his glance. Mingled sympathy and approval showed in Hellscream's expression.

Slowly, harnessing his powerful self-control, Thrall raised the great warhammer. He began to stamp his feet, one right after the other, in a powerful, steady rhythm. The others joined him at once, and very faintly, the earth trembled.

Langston stared, sickened and appalled, at the girl's head on the ground thirty feet below. He had known Blackmoore had a streak of cruelty, but he had never imagined. . . .

"What have you done!" The words exploded from Sergeant, who grabbed Blackmoore and spun him around to face him.

Blackmoore began laughing hysterically.

Sergeant went cold inside as he heard the screams, and then felt the slight tremble in the stone. "My lord, he makes the earth shake . . . we must fire!"

"Two thousand orcs all stomping their feet, 'course the earth's going to shake!" snarled Blackmoore. He veered back toward the wall, apparently intent upon verbally tormenting the orc still further.

They were lost, Langston thought. It was too late to surrender now. Thrall was going to use his demonic magic, and destroy the fortress and everyone in it as retaliation for the girl. His mouth worked, but nothing came out. He felt Sergeant staring at him.

"Damn the lot of you noble-born, heartless bastards," Sergeant hissed, then bellowed, *"Fire!"*

Thrall did not even twitch when the cannons went off. Behind him he heard screams of torment, but he was untouched. He called on the Spirit of Earth, pouring out his pain, and Earth responded. In a clean, precise, direct line, the earth heaved and buckled. It went straight from Thrall's feet to the mammoth door like the burrowing of some giant underground creature. The door shuddered. The surrounding stone trembled and a few small stones fell, but it was more soundly built than the slapped-together walls of the encampments, and held.

Blackmoore shrieked. His world took on a very sharp focus, and for the first time since he had gotten himself drunk enough to order Taretha Foxton's execution he was thinking clearly.

Langston hadn't exaggerated. Thrall's powers were immense and his tactic to break the orc had failed. In fact, it had roused him to an even greater fury, and as Blackmoore watched, panicked and sick, hundreds . . . no, thousands . . . of huge, green forms flowed down the road in a river of death.

He had to get out. Thrall was going to kill him. He just knew it. Somehow, Thrall was going to find him and kill him, for what he'd done to Taretha. . . .

Tari, Tari, I loved you, why did you do this to me?

Someone was shouting. Langston was yapping in one ear, his pretty face purple and eyes bulging with fear, and Sergeant's voice was in the other, screaming nonsensical noises. He stared at them helplessly. Sergeant spat some more words, then turned to the men. They continued to load and fire the cannons, and below Blackmoore the mounted knights charged the ranks of orcs. He heard battle cries and the clash of steel. The black armor of his men milled with the ugly green skin of the orcs, and here and there was a flash of white fur as . . . by the Light, had Thrall really managed to call white wolves to his army?

"Too many," he whispered. "There are too many. So many of them. . . ."

Again, the very walls of the fortress shook. Fear such as Blackmoore had never known shuddered through him, and he fell to his knees. It was in this position, crawling like a dog, that he made his way down the steps and into the courtyard.

The knights were all outside fighting, and, Blackmoore presumed, dying. Inside, the men who were left were shrieking and gathering what they could to defend themselves—scythes, pitchforks, even the wooden training weapons with which a much younger Thrall had honed his fighting skills. A peculiar, yet familiar smell filled Blackmoore's nostrils. Fear, that was it. He'd reeked of the stench in battles past, had smelled it on dead men's corpses. He'd forgotten how it had churned his stomach.

It wasn't supposed to be this way. The orcs on the other side of the now-shuddering gates were supposed to be his army. Their leader, out there screaming Blackmoore's name over and over again, was supposed to be his docile, obedient slave. Tari was supposed to be here . . . where was she, anyway . . . and then he remembered, he remembered, his own lips forming around the order that had taken her life, and he was sick, right in front of his men, sick in body, sick in soul.

"He's lost control!" bellowed Langston inches from Sergeant's ear, shouting to be heard over the sounds of cannon, sword impacting shield, and cries of pain. Yet again, the walls shuddered.

"He lost control long ago!" Sergeant shouted back. "You're in command, Lord Langston! What would you have us do?"

"Surrender!" Langston shrieked, without hesitation. Sergeant, his eyes on the battle thirty feet below, shook his head.

"Too late for that! Blackmoore's done us all in. We've got to fight for it now until Thrall decides he wants to talk peace again . . . if he ever does. What would you have us do?" Sergeant demanded again.

"I . . . I . . ." Anything resembling logical thought had fled from Langston's brain. This thing called battle, he was not made for it—twice now he had crumbled in the face of it. He knew himself for a coward, and despised himself for it, but the fact remained.

"Would you like me to take command of the defense of Durnholde, sir?" asked Sergeant.

Langston turned wet, grateful eyes to the older man and nodded.

"Right, then," said Sergeant, who turned to face the men in the courtyard and began screaming orders.

At that moment, the door shattered, and a wave of orcs crashed into the courtyard of one of the most powerfully constructed fortresses in the land.

TWENTY

The skies seemed to open and a sheet of rain poured down, plastering Blackmoore's dark hair to his skull and making him slip in the suddenly slick mud of the courtyard. He fell hard, and the wind was knocked out of him. He forced himself to scramble to his feet and continue. There was only one way out of this bloody, noisy hell.

He reached his quarters and dove for his desk. With trembling fingers, he searched for the key. He dropped it twice before he was able to stumble to the tapestry beside his bed, tear the weaving down, and insert the key into the lock.

Blackmoore plunged forward, forgetting about the steps, and hurtled down them. He was so inebriated that his body was limp as a rag doll's, however, and suffered only a few bruises. The light shining in the door from his quarters reached only a few yards, and up ahead yawned utter darkness. He should have brought a lamp, but it was too late now. Too late for so many things.

He began to run as fast as his legs would carry him. The door on the other side would still be unbolted. He could escape, could flee into the forest, and return later, when the killing was over, and feign . . . he didn't know. Something.

The earth trembled again, and Blackmoore was knocked off his feet. He felt small bits of stone and earth dust him, and when the quake ceased, he eased himself up and moved forward, arms extended. Dust flew thickly, and he coughed violently.

A few feet ahead, his fingers encountered a huge pile of stone. The tunnel had collapsed in front of him. For a few wild moments, Blackmoore tried to claw his way out. Then, sobbing, he fell to the ground. What now? What was to become of Aedelas Blackmoore now?

Again the earth shook, and Blackmoore sprang to his feet and began to race back the way he had come. Guilt and fear were strong, but the instinct to survive was stronger. A terrible noise rent the air, and Blackmoore realized with a jolt of horror that the tunnel was again collapsing right behind him. Terror lent him speed and he sprinted back toward his quarters, the roof of the tunnel missing him by a foot or two, as if it was following his path a mere step behind.

He stumbled up the stairs and hurled himself forward, just as the rest of the tunnel came down with a mighty crash. Blackmoore clutched the rushes on the floor as if they could offer some solidity in this suddenly mad world. The terrible shaking of the earth seemed to go on and on.

Finally, it ended. He didn't move, just lay with his face to the stone floor, gasping.

A sword came out of nowhere to clang to a stop inches from his nose. Shrieking, Blackmoore scuttled back. He looked up to see Thrall standing in front of him, a sword in his own hand.

Light preserve him, but Blackmoore had forgotten just how *big* Thrall was. Clad in black plate armor, wielding a massive sword, he seemed to tower over the prone figure of Blackmoore like a mountain towers over the landscape. Had he always had that set to his huge, deformed jaw, that . . . that presence?

"Thrall," Blackmoore stammered, "I can explain. . . ."

"No," said Thrall, with a calmness that frightened Blackmoore more than rage would have. "You can't explain. There is no explanation. There is only a battle, long in the coming. A duel to the death. Take the sword."

Blackmoore drew his legs up beneath him. "I . . . I . . ."

"Take the sword," repeated Thrall, his voice deep, "or I shall run you through where you sit like a frightened child."

Blackmoore reached out a trembling hand and closed it about the hilt of the sword.

Good, thought Thrall. At least Blackmoore was going to give him the satisfaction of fighting.

The first person he had gone for was Langston. It had been ease itself to intimidate the young lord into revealing the existence of the subterranean escape tunnel. Pain had sliced through Thrall afresh as he realized that this must have been the way Taretha had managed to sneak out to see him.

He had called the earthquakes to seal the tunnel, so that Blackmoore would be forced to return by this same path. While he waited, he had moved the furniture angrily out of the way, to clear a small area for this final confrontation.

He stared as Blackmoore stumbled to his feet. Was this really the same man he had adored and feared simultaneously as a youngster? It was hard to believe. This man was an emotional and physical wreck. The vague shadow of pity swept through Thrall again, but he would not permit it to blot out the atrocities that Blackmoore had committed.

"Come for me," Thrall snarled.

Blackmoore lunged. He was quicker and more focused than Thrall had expected, given his condition, and Thrall actually had to react quickly to avoid being struck. He parried the blow, and waited for Blackmoore to strike again.

The conflict seemed to revitalize the master of Durnholde. Something like anger and determination came into his face, and his moves were steadier. He feinted left, then battered hard on Thrall's right. Even so, Thrall blocked effectively.

Now he pressed his own attack, surprised and a bit pleased that Blackmoore was able to defend himself and only suffered a slight grazing of his unprotected left side. Blackmoore realized his weakness and looked about for anything that could serve as a shield.

Grunting, Thrall tore the door off its hinges and tossed it to Blackmoore. "Hide behind the coward's door," he cried.

The door, while it would have made a fine shield for an orc, was of course too large for Blackmoore. He shoved it aside angrily.

"It's still not too late, Thrall," he said, shocking the orc. "You can join with me and we can work together. Of course I'll free the other orcs, if you'll promise that they'll fight for me under my banner, just as you will!"

Thrall was so furious he didn't defend himself properly as Blackmoore unexpectedly lunged. He didn't get his sword up in time, and Blackmoore's blade clanged off the armor. It was a clean blow, and the armor was all that stood between Thrall and injury.

"You are still drunk, Blackmoore, if you believe for an instant I can forget the sight of—"

Again, Thrall saw red, the recollection of Taretha's blue eyes staring at him almost more than he could bear. He had been holding back, trying to give Blackmoore at least a fighting chance, but now he threw that to the wind. With the impassive rage of a tidal wave crashing upon a seacoast city, Thrall bore down on Blackmoore. With each blow, each cry of rage, he relived his tormented youth at this man's hands. As Blackmoore's sword flew from his fingers, Thrall saw Taretha's face, the friendly smile that enveloped human and orc alike, and saw no difference between them.

And when he had beaten Blackmoore into a corner, and that wreck of a man had seized a dagger from his boot and shoved it up toward Thrall's face, narrowly missing the eye, Thrall cried out for vengeance, and brought his sword slicing down.

Blackmoore didn't die at once. He lay, gasping, fingers impotently clutching his sides as blood pumped out in a staggering rush of red. He stared up at Thrall, his eyes glazed. Blood trickled from his mouth, and to Thrall's astonishment, he smiled.

"You are . . . what I made you . . . I am so proud . . ." he said, and then sagged against the wall.

Thrall stepped out of the keep into the courtyard. Driving rain pelted him. At once, Hellscream splashed up to him. "Report," demanded Thrall, even as his eyes swept the scene.

"We have taken Durnholde, my Warchief," said Hellscream. He was spattered with blood and looked ecstatic, his red eyes burning bright. "Reinforcements for the humans are still leagues distant. Most of those who have offered resistance are under our control. We have almost completed searching the keep and removing those who did not come to fight. The females and their young are unharmed, as you asked."

Thrall saw clusters of his warriors surrounding groups of human males. They were seated in the mud, glaring up at their captors. Now and then one would rally, but he was quickly put in his place. Thrall noticed that although the orcs seemed to want very badly to assault their prisoners, none did.

"Find me Langston." Hellscream hastened to do Thrall's bidding, and

Thrall went from cluster to cluster. The humans were either terrified or belligerent, but it was clear who had control of Durnholde now. He turned as Hellscream returned, driving Langston in front of him with well-timed prods from his sword.

At once Langston dropped to his knees in front of Thrall. Vaguely disgusted, Thrall ordered him to rise. "You are in command now, I assume?"

"Well, Sergeant . . . yes. Yes I am."

"I have a task for you, Langston." Thrall bent down so that the two were face-to-face. "You and I know what sort of betrayal you and Blackmoore were plotting. You were going to turn traitor to your Alliance. I'm offering you a chance to redeem yourself, if you'll take it."

Langston's eyes searched his, and a bit of the fear left his face. He nodded. "What would you have me do?"

"Take a message to your Alliance. Tell them what has happened this day. Tell them that if they choose the path of peace, they will find us ready to engage in trade and cooperation with them, provided they free the rest of my people and surrender land—good land—for our use. If they choose the path of war, they will find an enemy the likes of which they have never seen. You thought we were strong fifteen years past—that is as nothing to the foe they will face on the battlefield today. You have had the good fortune to survive two battles with my army. You will, I am sure, be able to properly convey the full depths of the threat we will pose to them."

Langston had gone pale beneath the mud and blood on his face. But he continued to meet Thrall's eyes evenly.

"Give him a horse, and provisions," said Thrall, convinced his message had been understood. "Langston is to ride unhindered to his betters. I hope, for the sake of your people, that they listen to you. Now, go."

Hellscream grabbed Langston by the arm and led him to the stables. Thrall saw that, per his instructions, his people who were not occupied with guarding the humans were busily taking provisions from the keep. Horses, cattle, sheep, sacks of grain, bedding for bandages—all the things an army needed would soon be provided to the new Horde.

There was one more man he needed to talk to, and after a moment, he found him. Sergeant's small group of men had not surrendered their weapons, but neither were they actually using them. It was a standoff, with both orcs and humans armed, but neither particularly desirous of escalating the conflict.

Sergeant's eyes narrowed warily when he saw Thrall approach. The circle of orcs parted to admit their Warchief. For a long moment, Sergeant and Thrall regarded one another. Then, faster than even Sergeant had credited him for, Thrall's hand was on Sergeant's earlobe, the golden hoop firmly between his thick green fingers. Then, just as swiftly, Thrall released him, leaving the earring where it was.

"You taught me well, Sergeant," Thrall rumbled.

"You were a fine student, Thrall," Sergeant replied cautiously.

"Blackmoore is dead," said Thrall. "Your people are being led from the fortress and its provisions taken even as we speak. Durnholde stands now only because I will it to stand." To illustrate his point, he stamped, once, on the ground, and the earth shook violently.

"You taught me the concept of mercy. At this moment, you should be very glad of that lesson. I intend to level Durnholde in a few moments. Your reinforcements will not arrive in time to be of any help to you. If your men will surrender, they and their families will be permitted to leave. We will see to it that you have food and water, even weapons. Those who do not surrender will die in the rubble. Without this fortress and its knights to protect the camps, we will find it easy to liberate the rest of our people. That was always my only goal."

"Was it?" Sergeant said. Thrall knew he was thinking of Blackmoore.

"Justice was my goal," said Thrall. "And that has, and will be, served."

"Do I have your word that no one will come to harm?"

"You do," said Thrall, lifting his head to look at his people. "If you offer us no resistance, you will be permitted to walk out freely."

For answer, Sergeant tossed his weapon to the muddy earth. There was a silence, and then the armed men did likewise. The battle was over.

When everyone, human and orc, was safely away from the fortress, Thrall called upon the Spirit of Earth.

This place serves nothing good. It housed prisoners who had done no wrong, elevated evil to great power. Let it fall. Let it fall.

He spread out his arms and began to stamp rhythmically on the earth. Closing his eyes, Thrall remembered his tiny cell, Blackmoore's torture, the hatred and contempt in the eyes of the men he had trained with. The memories were shockingly painful as he sifted through them, reliving them briefly before letting them go.

Let it fall. Let it fall!

The earth rumbled, for the final time in this battle. The sound was ear-splitting as the mighty stone buildings were pulverized. Earth churned upward, almost as if it was eating the fortress. Down it came, the symbol to Thrall of everything he had fought against. When the earth was at last still, all that was left of the mighty Durnholde was a pile of rocks and jagged pieces of wood. A huge cheer went up from the orcs. The humans, haggard and haunted, simply stared.

In that pile, somewhere, was Aedelas Blackmoore's body.

"Until you bury him in your heart, you won't be able to bury him deep enough," came a voice by his side. Thrall turned to look at Drek'Thar.

"You are wise, Drek'Thar," said Thrall. "Perhaps too wise."

"Was it good to kill him?"

Thrall thought before answering. "It needed to be done," he said. "Blackmoore was poison, not just to me, but to so many others." He hesitated. "Before I killed him, he . . . he said that he was proud of me. That I was what he had made me. Drek'Thar, the thought appalls me."

"Of course you are what Blackmoore made you," Drek'Thar replied, surprising and sickening Thrall with the answer. Gently, Drek'Thar touched Thrall's armor-clad arm.

"And you are what Taretha made you. And Sergeant, and Hellscream, and Doomhammer, and I, and even Snowsong. You are what each battle made you, and you are what you have made of yourself . . . the lord of the clans." He bowed, then turned and left, guided by his attendant Palkar. Thrall watched them go. He hoped that one day, he would be as wise as Drek'Thar.

Hellscream approached. "The humans have been given food and water, my Warchief. Our outriders report that the human reinforcements will shortly be closing in. We should leave."

"In a moment. I have a duty for you to perform." He extended a closed fist to Hellscream, then opened it. A silver necklace with a crescent moon dropped into Hellscream's outstretched hand. "Find the humans called Foxton. It is likely that they have only now learned about their daughter's murder. Give this to them and tell them . . . tell them that I grieve with them."

Hellscream bowed, then left to do Thrall's bidding. Thrall took a deep breath. Behind him was his past, the ruin that had once been Durnholde. Before him was his future, a sea of green—his people, waiting, expectant.

"Today," he cried, raising his voice so that all could hear, "today, our people have won a great victory. We have leveled the mighty fortress Durnholde, and broken its grasp on the encampments. But we cannot yet rest, nor claim that we have won this war. There are many of our brothers and sisters who yet languish in prisons, but we know that they will soon be free. They, like you, will taste what it is to be an orc, to know the passion and power of our proud race.

"We are undefeatable. We will triumph, because our cause is just. Let us go, and find the camps, and smash their walls, and free our people!"

A huge cheer rose up, and Thrall looked around at the thousands of proud, beautiful orcish faces. Their mouths were open and their fists were waving, and every line of their large bodies spoke of joy and excitement. He recalled the sluggish creatures in the encampment, and felt a stab of almost painful pleasure as he allowed himself to realize that he had been the one to inspire them to these heights. The thought was humbling.

A profound peace swept over him as he watched his people cry his name. After so many years of searching, he finally knew where his true destiny lay; knew deep in his bones who he was:

Thrall, son of Durotan . . . Warchief of the Horde.

He had come home.

The Last Guardian

JEFF GRUBB

About the Author

JEFF GRUBB is the author of *StarCraft: Liberty's Crusade* as well as numer-ous books for the *Forgotten Realms*, *Dragonlance*, and *Magic: The Gathering* settings, including *Cormyr, a Novel*, *Lord Toede*, and *The Brothers' War*. His hobby is building worlds, while his job is explaining them to other people. He is currently writing short fiction on Beowulf, cats, and dragons cele-brating Christmas (not all at the same time). He lives in Seattle with his wife, author Kate Novak, and two cats. He keeps an online journal at grubbstreet.blogspot.com

To Chris Metzen
Who kept the Vision

PROLOGUE
The Lonely Tower

The larger of the two moons had risen first this evening, and now hung pregnant and silver-white against a clear, star-dappled sky. Beneath the lambent moon the peaks of the Redridge Mountains strained for the sky. In the daylight the sun picked out hues of magenta and rust among the great granite peaks, but in the moonlight they were reduced to tall, proud ghosts. To the west lay the Forest of Elwynn, its heavy canopy of greatoaks and satinwoods running from the foothills to the sea. To the east, the bleak swamp of the Black Morass spread out, a land of marshes and low hills, bayous and backwaters, failed settlements and lurking danger. A shadow passed briefly across the moon, a raven-sized shadow, bearing for a hole in the heart of the mountain.

Here a chunk had been pulled from the fastness of the Redridge Range, leaving behind a circular vale. Once it might have been the site of some primeval celestial impact or the memory of an earth-shaking explosion, but the aeons had worn the bowl-shaped crater into a series of steep-edged, rounded hillocks which were now cradled by the steep mountains surrounding them. None of the ancient trees of Elwynn could reach its altitude, and the interior of the ringed hills was barren save for weeds and tangled vines.

At the center of the ringed hills lay a bare tor, as bald as the pate of a Kul Tiras merchant lord. Indeed the very way the hillock rose steeply, then gentled to a near-level slope at its apex, was similar in shape to a human skull. Many had noted it over the years, though only a few had been sufficiently brave, or powerful, or tactless to mention it to the property's owner.

At the flattened peak of the tor rose an ancient tower, a thick, massive protrusion of white stone and dark mortar, a man-made eruption that shot effortlessly into the sky, scaling higher than the surrounding hills, lit like a beacon by the moonlight. There was a low wall at the base of the tower surrounding a bailey, and within those walls the tumbledown remains of a stable and a smithy, but the tower itself dominated all within the ringed hills.

Once this place was called Karazhan. Once it was home of the last of the mysterious and secretive Guardians of Tirisfal. Once it was a living place. Now it was simply abandoned and timelost.

There was silence upon the tower but not a stillness. In the night's embrace quiet shapes flitted from window to window, and phantoms danced along the balconies and parapets. Less than ghosts, but more than memories, these were nothing less than pieces of the past that had become unstuck from the flow of time. These shadows of the past had been pried loose by the madness of the tower's owner, and were now condemned to play out their histories again and again, in the silence of the abandoned tower. Condemned to play but denied of any audience to appreciate them.

Then in the silence, there was the soft scrape of a booted foot against stone, then another. A flash of movement beneath the lambent moon, a shadow against the white stone, a flutter of a tattered, red-hued cloak in the cool night air. A figure walked along the topmost parapet, on the crenellated uppermost spire that years before had served as an observatory.

The parapet door into the observatory screeched open on ancient hinges, then stopped, frozen by rust and the passage of time. The cloaked figure paused a moment, then placed a finger on the hinge, and muttered a few choice words. The door swung open silently, the hinges made as if new. The trespasser allowed himself a smile.

The observatory was empty now, what tools that remained smashed and abandoned. The trespassing figure, almost as silent as a ghost himself, picked up a crushed astrolabe, its scale twisted in some now-forgotten rage. Now it is merely a heavy piece of gold, inert and useless in his hands.

There was other movement in the observatory, and the trespasser looked up. Now a ghostly figure stood nearby, near one of the many windows. The ghost/non-ghost was a broad-shouldered man, hair and beard once dark but now going to a premature gray at the edges. The figure was one of the shards of the past, unglued and now repeating its task, regardless of whether it had observers or not. For the moment, the dark-haired man held the astrolabe, the unbroken twin to the one in the trespasser's hands, and fiddled with a small knob along one side. A moment, a check, and a twitch of the knob. His dark brows furrowed over ghostly green eyes. A second moment, another check, and another twitch. Finally, the tall, imposing figure sighed deeply and placed the astrolabe on a table that was no longer there, and vanished.

The trespasser nodded. Such hauntings were common even in the days when Karazhan was inhabited, though now, stripped of the control (and the madness) of their master, they had become more brazen. Yet these shards of the past belonged here, while he did not. He was the interloper, not they.

The trespasser crossed the room to its staircase leading down, while behind him the older man flickered back into the view and repeated his action, sighting his astrolabe on a planet that had long since moved to other parts of the sky.

The trespasser moved down through the tower, crossing levels to reach other stairs and other hallways. No door was shut to him, even those locked and bolted, or sealed by rust and age. A few words, a touch, a gesture and the fetters flew loose, the rust dissolved into ruddy piles, the hinges restored. In one or two places ancient wards still glowed, potent despite their age. He paused before them for a moment, considering, reflecting, searching his memory for the correct counter-sign. He spoke the correct word, made the correct motion with his hands, shattered the weak magic that remained, and passed on.

As he moved through the tower, the phantoms of the past grew more agitated and more active. Now with a potential audience, it seemed that these pieces of the past wished to play themselves out, if only to be made free of this place. Any sound they once possessed had long-since eroded away, leaving only their images moving through the halls.

The interloper passed an ancient butler in dark livery, the frail old man shuffling slowly down the empty hallway, carrying a silver tray and wearing a set of horse-blinders. The interloper passed through the library, where a green-fleshed young woman stood with her back to him, poring over an ancient tome. He passed through a banquet hall, at one end a group of musicians playing soundlessly, dancers twirling in a gavotte. At the other end a great city burned, its flames beating ineffectively against the stone walls and rotting tapestries. The trespasser moved through the silent flames, but his face grew drawn and tense as he witnessed once more the mighty city of Stormwind burn around him.

In one room three young men sat around a table and told now-unknown lies. Metal mugs were scattered on the table's surface as well as beneath it. The trespasser stood watching this image for a long time, until a phantom taverness brought another round. Then he shook his head and pressed on.

He reached nearly the ground level, and stepped out on a low balcony that hung precariously to the wall, like a wasps' nest over the main entrance. There, in the wide space before the tower, between the main entrance and a now-collapsed stables across the bailey, stood a single ghostly image, lonely and separated. It did not move like the others, but rather stood there, waiting, tentative. A piece of the past that had not been released. A piece that was waiting for him.

The immobile image was of a young man with a skunk stripe of white running through his dark, untidy head of hair. The straggling fragments of a beard, newly grown, clung to his face. A battered rucksack lay at the youth's feet, and he held a red-sealed letter with a deathlike grip.

This was well and truly no ghost, the trespasser knew, though the owner of this image may yet be dead, fallen in combat beneath a foreign sun. This was a memory, a shard of the past, trapped like an insect in amber, waiting for its release. Waiting for his arrival.

The trespasser sat on the stonework ledge of the balcony and looked out, beyond the bailey, beyond the hillock, and beyond the ringed hills. There was silence in the moonlight, as the mountains themselves seemed to be holding their breath, waiting for him.

The trespasser lifted a hand and intoned a series of chanted words. Softly came the rhymes and rhythms the first time, then louder, and finally louder still, shattering the calm. In the distance wolves picked up his chant and cast it back in howling counterpoint.

And the image of the ghostly youth, its feet seemingly trapped in mud, took a deep breath, hoisted his rucksack of secrets to his shoulder, and slogged his way toward the main entrance of Medivh's Tower.

ONE
Karazhan

Khadgar clutched the crimson-sealed letter of introduction and desperately tried to remember his own name. He had ridden for days, accompanying various caravans, and finally making the journey alone to Karazhan through the vast, overgrown, woods of Elwynn. Then the long climb into the heights of the mountains, to this serene, empty, lonely place. Even the air felt cold and apart. Now, sore and tired, the scruffy-bearded young man stood in the gathering dusk of the courtyard, petrified of what he now must do.

Introduce himself to the most powerful mage of Azeroth.

An honor, the scholars of the Kirin Tor had said. An opportunity, they insisted, that was not to be missed. Khadgar's sage mentors, a conclave of influential scholars and sorcerers, told him they had been trying to insinuate a sympathetic ear in the tower of Karazhan for years. The Kirin Tor wanted to learn what knowledge the most powerful wizard in the land had hidden away in his library. They wanted to know what research he favored. And most of all they wanted this maverick mage to start planning for his legacy, wanted to know when the great and powerful Medivh planned to train an heir.

The Great Medivh and the Kirin Tor had been at loggerheads on these and other matters for years, apparently, and only now did he relent to some of their entreaties. Only now would he take on an apprentice. Whether it was from a softening of the wizard's reportedly hard heart, or mere diplomatic concession, or a feeling of the mage's own creeping mortality, it did not matter to Khadgar's masters. The simple truth was that this powerful independent (and to Khadgar, mysterious) wizard had asked for an assistant, and the Kirin Tor, which ruled over the magical kingdom of Dalaran, were more than happy to comply.

So the youth Khadgar was selected and shuttled off with a list of directions, orders, counter-orders, requests, suggestions, advice, and other demands from his sorcerous masters. Ask Medivh about his mother's battles with demons, asked Guzbah, his first instructor. Find out all you can about elven history from his library, requested Lady Delth. Check his volumes for any bestiaries, commanded Alonda, who was convinced that there was a fifth species of troll as yet unrecorded in her own volumes. Be direct, forthright, and honest, advised Norlan the Chief Artificer—the Great Magus Medivh seemed to value those traits. Be diligent and do what you're told. Don't slouch. Always seem interested. Stand up straight. And above all, keep your ears and eyes open.

The ambitions of the Kirin Tor did not bother Khadgar horribly—his upbringing in Dalaran and his early apprenticeship to the conclave made it clear to him that his mentors were insatiably curious about magic in all its forms. Their continual accumulation, cataloging, and definition of magic were imprinted on young students at an early age, and Khadgar was no different than most.

Indeed, he realized, his own curiosity may have accounted for his current plight. His own nocturnal wanderings through the halls of the Violet Citadel of Dalaran had uncovered more than a few secrets that the conclave would rather not have noised about. The Chief Artificer's fondness for flamewine, for example, or Lady Delth's preference for young cavaliers a slender fraction of her age, or Korrigan the Librarian's secret collection of pamphlets describing (in lurid fashion) the practices of historical demon-worshipers.

And there was something about one of the great sages of Dalaran, venerable Arrexis, one of the gray eminences that even the others respected. He had disappeared, or died, or something horrible had happened, and the others chose to make no mention of it, even to the point of excising Arrexis's name from the volumes and not speaking of him again. But Khadgar had found out, nonetheless. Khadgar had a way of finding the necessary reference, making the needed connection, or talking to the right person at the right time. It was a gift and may yet prove to be a curse.

Any one of these discoveries could have resulted in his drawing this prestigious (and for all the planning and warnings, potentially fatal) assignment. Perhaps they thought young Khadgar was a little *too* good at ferreting out secrets—easier for the conclave to send him somewhere where his curiosity would do some good for the Kirin Tor. Or at least put him far enough away so he wasn't finding things out about the other natives of the Violet Citadel.

And Khadgar, through his relentless eavesdropping, had heard *that* theory as well.

So Khadgar set out with a rucksack filled with notes, a heart filled with secrets, and a head filled with strong demands and useless advice. In the final week before leaving Dalaran, he had heard from nearly every member of the conclave, each of whom was interested in something about Medivh. For a wizard living on the butt-end of nowhere, surrounded by trees and ominous peaks, the members of the Kirin Tor were extremely curious about him. Urgent, even.

Taking a deep breath (and in doing so reminding himself that he still was too close to the stables), Khadgar strode forward toward the tower itself, his feet feeling like he was pulling his pack-pony along by his ankles.

The main entrance yawned like a cavern's mouth, without gate or portcullis. That made sense, for what army would fight its way through the Forest of Elwynn to top the rounded walls of the crater, all to fight the Magus Medivh himself? There was no record of anyone or anything even attempting to besiege Karazhan.

The shadowed entrance was tall enough to let an elephant in full livery pass beneath. Overhanging it slightly was a wide balcony with a balustrade of white stone. From that perch one would be level with the surrounding hills and gain a view of the mountains beyond. There was a flicker of motion along the balustrade, a bit of movement that Khadgar *felt* more than actually witnessed. A robed figure, perhaps, moving back along the balcony into the tower itself. Was he being watched even now? Was there no one to greet him, or was he expected to brave the tower on his own?

"You are the New Young Man?" said a soft, almost sepulchral voice, and Khadgar, his head still craned upward, nearly jumped out of his skin. He wheeled to see a stooped, thin figure emerge out of the shadows of the entranceway.

The stooped thing looked marginally human, and for a moment Khadgar wondered if Medivh was mutating forest animals to work as his servants. This one looked like a hairless weasel, its long face was framed by what looked like a pair of black rectangles.

Khadgar didn't remember making any response, but the weasel person stepped farther from the shadows, and repeated itself.

"You are the New Young Man?" it said. Each word was enunciated with its own breath, encapsulated in its own little box, capitalized and separate from the others. It stepped from the shadows fully and revealed itself as nothing more or less threatening than a whip-slender elderly man in dark worsted livery. A servant—human, but a servant. It, or rather he, was still wearing black rectangles on the sides of his head, like a set of earmuffs, that extended forward to his most prominent nose.

The youth realized that he was staring at the old man, "Khadgar," he said, then after a moment presented the tightly held letter of introduction. "Of Dalaran. Khadgar of Dalaran, in the kingdom of Lordaeron. I was sent by the Kirin Tor. From the Violet Citadel. I am Khadgar of the Kirin Tor. From the Violet Citadel. Of Dalaran. In Lordaeron." He felt like he was casting conversational stones into a great, empty well, hoping that the old man would respond to any of them.

"Of course you are, Khadgar," said the old man. "Of the Kirin Tor. Of the Violet Citadel. Of Dalaran. Of Lordaeron." The servant took the proffered letter as if the document were a live reptile and, after smoothing out its crumpled edges, tucked it inside his livery vest without opening it. After carrying and protecting it for so many miles, Khadgar felt a pain of loss. The letter of introduction represented his future, and he was loath to see it disappear, even for a moment.

"The Kirin Tor sent me to assist Medivh. Lord Medivh. The Wizard Medivh. Medivh of Karazhan." Khadgar realized he was but a half-step from collapsing into a full-fledged babble, and with a definitive effort tightly clamped his mouth shut.

"I'm sure they did," said the servant. "Send you, that is." He appraised the seal on the letter, and a thin hand dipped into his waistcoat, pulling out a set of black rectangles bound by a thin band of metal. "Blinders?"

Khadgar blinked. "No. I mean, no thank you."

"Moroes," said the servant.

Khadgar shook his head.

"I am Moroes," the servant said. "Steward of the Tower. Castellan to Medivh. Blinders?" Again he raised the black rectangles, twins to those that framed his narrow face.

"No thank you . . . Moroes," said Khadgar, his face twisted in curiosity.

The servant turned and motioned that Khadgar follow with a weak wave of the arm.

Khadgar picked up his rucksack and had to lope forward to catch up with the servant. For all his supposed fragility the steward moved at a good clip.

"Are you alone in the tower?" Khadgar ventured as they started climbing a curved set of wide, low stairs. The stone dipped in the center, worn by myriad feet of passing servants and guests.

"Eh?" responded the servant.

"Are you alone?" repeated Khadgar, wondering if he would be reduced to speaking as Moroes spoke in order to be understood. "Do you live here by yourself?"

"The Magus is here," responded Moroes in a wheezing voice that sounded as faint and as fatal as grave dust.

"Yes, of course," said Khadgar.

"Wouldn't be much point for you to be here if he wasn't," continued the steward. "Here, that is." Khadgar wondered if the old man's voice sounded that way because it was not used that often.

"Of course," agreed Khadgar. "Anyone else?"

"You, now," continued Moroes. "More work to take care of two than one. Not that I was consulted."

"So just you and the Wizard, then, normally?" said Khadgar, wondering if the steward had been hired (or created) for his taciturn nature.

"And Cook," said Moroes, "though Cook doesn't talk much. Thank you for asking, though."

Khadgar tried to restrain himself from rolling his eyes, but failed. He hoped that the blinders on either side of the steward's face kept the servant from seeing his response.

They reached a level spot, a cross-hallway lit by torches. Moroes crossed immediately to another set of saddle-worn, curving stairs opposite them. Khadgar paused for a moment to examine the torches. He raised a hand mere inches from the flickering flame, but felt no heat. Khadgar wondered if the cold flame was common throughout the tower. In Dalaran they used phosphorescent crystals, which beamed with a steady, constant glow, though his research spoke of reflective mirrors, elemental spirits bound within lanterns, and in one case, huge captive fireflies. Yet these flames seemed to be frozen in place.

Moroes, half-mounted up the next staircase, slowly turned and let out a gasping cough. Khadgar hurried to catch up. Apparently the blinders did not limit the old steward that much.

"Why the blinders?" Khadgar asked.

"Eh?" replied Moroes.

Khadgar touched the side of his head. "The blinders. Why?"

Moroes twisted his face in what Khadgar could only assume was a smile. "Magic's strong here. Strong, and wrong, sometimes. You see . . . things . . . around here. Unless you're careful. I'm careful. Other visitors, the ones before you, they were less careful. They're gone now."

Khadgar thought of the phantom he may or may not have seen on the overhanging balcony, and nodded.

"Cook has a set of rose-quartz lenses," added Moroes. "Swears by them." He paused for a moment, then added, "Cook is a bit foolish that way."

Khadgar hoped that Moroes would be more chatty once he was warmed up. "So, you've been in the Magus's household for long?"

"Eh?" said Moroes again.

"You've been with Medivh long?" Khadgar said, hoping to keep the impatience out of his voice.

"Ayep," said the steward. "Long enough. Too long. Seems like years. Time's like that here." The weathered steward let his voice trail off and the two climbed in silence.

"What do you know about him?" ventured Khadgar, finally. "The Magus, I mean."

"Question is," said Moroes, pulling open yet another door to reveal yet another staircase up. "What do *you* know?"

Khadgar's own research in the matter was surprisingly unproductive, and his results were frustratingly sparse. Despite access to the Violet Citadel's Grand Library (and surreptitious access to a few private libraries and secret collections), there was precious little on this great and powerful Medivh. This was doubly odd, since every elder mage in Dalaran seemed to hold Medivh in awe, and wanted one thing or another from him. Some favor, some boon, some bit of information.

Medivh was apparently a young man, as wizards went. He was merely in his forties, and for a grand bulk of that time seemed to have made no impact whatsoever on his surroundings. This was a surprise to Khadgar. Most of the tales he had heard and read described independent wizards as being extremely showy, fearless in dabbling in secrets man was not meant to know, and usually dead, crippled, or damned from messing with powers and energies beyond their ken. Most of the lessons he had learned as a child about non-Dalaran mages always ended in the same fashion—without restraint, control, and thought, the wild, untrained, and self-taught wizards always came to a bad end (sometimes, though not often, destroying a large amount of the surrounding countryside with them).

The fact that Medivh had failed to bring a castle down on top of himself, or disperse his atoms across the Twisting Nether, or summon a dragon without knowing how to control that dragon, indicated either great restraint or great power. From the fuss that the scholars had made about his appointment, and the list of instructions he had received, Khadgar decided on the latter.

Yet for all his research, he could not figure out why. Nothing indicated any great research of this Medivh's, any major discovery, nor any ground-shaking achievement, that would account for the obvious awe in which the Kirin Tor held this independent mage. No huge wars, great conquests, or known mighty battles. The bards were noticeably sketchy when it came to the matters involving Medivh, and otherwise diligent heralds nodded when it came time to discuss his accomplishments.

And yet, realized Khadgar, there was something important here, something that created in the scholars a mixture of fear, respect, and envy. The Kirin Tor held no other spellcasters as their equals for magical knowledge, indeed often sought to hinder those wizards who did not hold allegiance to the Violet Citadel. And yet they kowtowed to Medivh. Why?

Khadgar had only the smallest bits—a bit on his parentage (Guzbah was particularly interested in Medivh's mother), some margin notes in a grimoire invoking his name, and mention of the occasional visit to Dalaran. All these visits were within the past five years, and apparently Medivh met only with elder mages, such as the now-missing Arrexis.

To sum up, Khadgar knew precious little of this supposedly great mage he was assigned to work for. And as he considered knowledge to be his armor and sword, he felt woefully underequipped for the coming encounter.

Aloud, he said, "Not much."

"Eh?" responded Moroes, half-turning on the staircase.

"I said I don't know much," said Khadgar, louder than he meant to. His voice bounced off the bare walls of the stairway. It was curved now, and Khadgar was wondering if the tower was truly as high as it seemed. Already his thighs were aching from the climb.

"Of course you don't," said Moroes. "Know, that is. Young people never know much. That's what makes them young, I suppose."

"I mean," said Khadgar, irritated. He paused and took a deep breath. "I mean, I don't know much about Medivh. You asked."

Moroes held for a moment, his foot poised on the next step. "I suppose I did," he said at last.

"What *is* he like?" asked Khadgar, his voice almost pleading.

"Like everyone else, I suppose," said Moroes. "Has his druthers. Has his moods. Good days and bad. Like everybody else."

"Puts his pants on one leg at a time," said Khadgar, sighing.

"No. He levitates into them," said Moroes. The old servant looked at Khadgar, and the youth caught the slightest tug of a smile along the old man's face. "One more set of stairs."

The final set of stairs curled tightly, and Khadgar guessed that they had to be near the tower's highest spire. The old servant led the way.

The stairway opened up on a small circular room, surrounded by a wide parapet. As Khadgar had surmised, they were at the topmost tip of the tower, with a large observatory. The walls and ceilings were pierced by crystalline windows, clear and unfogged. In the time of their climb, night had fallen fully, and the sky was dark and strewn with stars.

The observatory itself was dim, lit by a few torches of the same, unwavering light as found elsewhere. Yet these were hooded, their lamps banked for observing the night sky. An unlit brazier sat in the middle of the room in preparation for later, as the temperature would drop toward morning.

Several large curved tables spread around the outer wall of the observatory, decked with all manner of devices. Silver levels and golden astrolabes acted as paperweights for foolscap, or as bookmarks keeping ancient texts open to certain pages. A half-disassembled model, showing planetary movement through the celestial vault, sat on one table, fine wires and additional beads laid out among the delicate tools next to it. Notebooks lay stacked against one wall, and others were in crates jammed beneath the tables. A map of the continent was stretched on a frame, showing the southern lands of Azeroth and Khadgar's own Lordaeron, as well as the reclusive dwarven and elven kingdoms of Khaz Modan and Quel'Thalas. Numerous small pins bedecked the map, constellations that only Medivh could decipher.

And Medivh was there, for to Khadgar it could be no other. He was a man of middling years, his hair long and bound in a ponytail in the back. In his youth his hair had likely been ebon black, but now it was already turning gray at the temples and along the beard. Khadgar knew that this happened to many mages, from the stress of the magical energies they wielded.

Medivh was dressed in robes simple for a mage—well cut and fitted to his large frame. A short tabard, unadorned by decoration, hung to his waist, over trousers tucked into oversize boots. A heavy maroon cloak hung from his broad shoulders, the hood pulled back.

As Khadgar's eyes adjusted to the darkness, he realized that he was wrong about the wizard's clothing being unadorned. Instead, it was laced with silver filigree, of such a delicate nature that it was invisible at first blush. Looking at the mage's back, Khadgar realized he was looking at the stylized face of some ancient demon-legend. He blinked, and in that time the tracery transformed itself into a coiled dragon, and then into a night sky.

Medivh had his back to the old servant and the young man, ignoring them entirely. He was standing at one of the tables, a golden astrolabe in one hand, a notebook in the other. He seemed lost in thought, and Khadgar wondered if this was one of the "things" that Moroes had warned him about.

Khadgar cleared his throat and took a step forward, but Moroes raised a hand. Khadgar froze in place, as surely as if transfixed with a magical spell.

Instead the old servant walked quietly to one side of the master mage, waiting for Medivh to recognize his presence. A minute passed. A second minute. Then a period that Khadgar swore was an eternity.

Finally, the robed figure set down his astrolabe, and made three quick jots in the notebook. He closed the book with a sharp snap, and looked over at Moroes.

Seeing his face for the first time, Khadgar thought that Medivh was much older than his supposed forty-plus years. The face was deeply lined and worn. Khadgar wondered what magics Medivh wielded that wrote such a deep history on his face.

Moroes dipped into his vest and brought out the crumpled letter of introduction, the crimson seal now bloodred in the steady, unflickering torchlight. Medivh turned and regarded the youth.

The mage's eyes were deeply set beneath his dark, heavy brows, but Khadgar was aware at once of the power within. Something danced and flickered within those deep green eyes, something powerful, and perhaps uncontrolled. Something dangerous. The master mage glanced at him, and in a moment Khadgar felt that the wizard had taken in his sum total of existence and found it no more intriguing than that of a beetle or flea.

Medivh looked away from Khadgar and at the still-sealed letter of introduction. Khadgar felt himself relax almost immediately, as if a large and hungry predator had stalked past him without giving him a second look.

His relief was short-lived. Medivh did not open the letter. Instead his brows furrowed only slightly, and the parchment burst into flames with an explosive rush of air. The flames clustered at the far end of the document from where Medivh held it, and flickered with an intense, blue flame.

When Medivh spoke his voice was both deep and amused.

"So," said Medivh, oblivious to the fact he was holding Khadgar's future burning in his hand. "It seems our young spy has arrived at last."

TWO

Interview with the Magus

I s something wrong?" asked Medivh, and Khadgar suddenly felt himself under the master mage's gaze again. He felt like a beetle again, but this time one that had inadvertently crawled across a bug collector's work desk. The flames had already consumed half the letter of introduction, and the wax seal was already melting, dripping onto the observatory's flagstones.

Khadgar was aware that his eyes were wide, his face bloodless and pale, and his mouth hanging open. He tried to force the air out of his body, but all he managed was a strangled, hissing sound.

The dark, heavy brows pursed in a bemused glance. "Are you ill? Moroes, is this lad ill?"

"Winded, perhaps," said Moroes in a level tone. "Was a long climb up."

Finally Khadgar managed to gather his senses about him sufficiently to say, "The letter!"

"Ah," said Medivh. "Yes. Thank you, I had almost forgotten." He walked over to the brazier and dropped the burning parchment on top of the coals. The blue ball of flame rose spectacularly to about shoulder height, and then diminished into a normal-looking flame, filling the room with a warm, reddish glow. Of the letter of introduction, with its parchment and crimson seal inscribed with the symbol of the Kirin Tor, there was no sign.

"But you didn't read it!" said Khadgar, then caught himself, "I mean, sir, with respect . . ."

The master mage chuckled and settled himself into a large chair made of canvas and dark carved wood. The brazier lit his face, pulling out the deep lines formed into a smile. Despite this, Khadgar could not relax.

Medivh leaned forward in his chair and said, " 'Oh Great and Respected Magus Medivh, Master Mage of Karazhan, I bring you the greetings of the Kirin Tor, most learned and puissant of the magical academies, guilds, and societies, advisors to the kings, teachers of the learned, revealers of secrets.' They continue on in that fashion for some ways, puffing themselves up more with every sentence. How am I doing so far?"

"I couldn't say," said Khadgar, "I was instructed—"

"Not to open the letter," finished Medivh. "But you did, anyway."

The master mage raised his eyes to regard the young man, and Khadgar's breath caught in his throat. Something flickered in Medivh's eyes, and Khadgar wondered if the master mage had the power to cast spells without anyone noticing.

Khadgar slowly nodded, steeling himself for the response.

Medivh chuckled loudly. "When?"

"On the . . . on the voyage from Lordaeron to Kul Tiras," said Khadgar, unsure if what he said would amuse or irritate his potential mentor. "We were becalmed for two days and . . ."

"Curiosity got the better of you," finished Medivh again. He smiled, and it was a clean white smile beneath the graying beard. "I probably would have opened it the moment I got out of sight of Dalaran's Violet Citadel."

Khadgar took a deep breath and said, "I considered that, but I believed they had divination spells in operation, at least at that range."

"And you wanted to be far from any spell or message recalling you for opening the letter. And you patched it back together well enough to fool a cursory examination, sure that I would likely break the seal straightaway and not notice your tampering." Medivh allowed himself a chuckle, but drew his face into a tight, focused knot. "How did I do that?" he asked.

Khadgar blinked. "Do what, sir?"

"Know what was in the letter?" said Medivh, the sides of his mouth tugging down. "The letter I just burned says that I will find the young man Khadgar most impressive in his deduction and intelligence. Impress me."

Khadgar looked at Medivh, and the jovial smile of a few seconds before had evaporated. The smiling face was now that of some primitive stone god, judgmental and unforgiving. The eyes that had been tinged with mirth earlier now seemed to be barely concealing some hidden fury. The brows knitted together like the rising thunderhead of a storm.

Khadgar stammered for a moment, then said, "You read my mind."

"Possible," said Medivh. "But incorrect. You're a stew of nerves right now, and that gets in the way of mind reading. One wrong."

"You've gotten this sort of letter before," said Khadgar. "From the Kirin Tor. You know what kind of letters are written."

"Also possible," said the master mage. "As I *have* received such letters and they *do* tend to be overweening in their self-congratulatory tone. But you know the exact wording as well as I do. A good try, and the most obvious, but also incorrect. Two wrong."

Khadgar's mouth formed into a tight line. His mind raised and his heart thundered in his chest. "Sympathy," he said at last.

Medivh's eyes remained unreadable, and his voice level. "Explain."

Khadgar took a deep breath. "One of the magical laws. When someone handles an item, they leave a part of their own magical aura or vibration attached to the item. As auras vary with individuals, it is possible to connect to one by affecting the other. In this way a lock of hair may be used in a love charm, or a coin may be tracked back to its original owner."

Medivh's eyes narrowed slightly, and he dragged a finger across his bearded chin. "Continue."

Khadgar stopped for a moment, feeling the weight of Medivh's eyes pressing in on him. That was what he knew from lectures. He was halfway there. But how did Medivh use it to figure out. . . .

"The more someone uses an item, the stronger the resonance," said Khadgar quickly. "So therefore an item that experiences a lot of handling or attention will have a stronger sympathy." The words were coming together tighter and more rapidly now. "So a document which someone had written has more aura to it than a blank piece of parchment, and the person is concentrating on what they are writing, so . . ." Khadgar let his thoughts catch up for a moment. "You were mind reading, but not my mind—the mind of the scribe who wrote the letter at the time he was writing it—you picked up his thoughts reinforcing the words."

"Without having to physically open the document," said Medivh, and the light danced within his eyes again. "So how would this trick be useful to a scholar?"

Khadgar blinked for a moment, and looked away from the master mage, seeking to avoid his piercing glance. "You could read books without having to read books."

"Very valuable for a researcher," said Medivh. "You belong to a community of scholars. Why don't you do that?"

"Because . . . because . . ." Khadgar thought of old Korrigan, who could find anything in the library, even the smallest marginal notation. "I think we do, but for older members of the conclave."

Medivh nodded. "And that is because . . ."

Khadgar thought for a moment, then shook his head.

"Who would write if all the knowledge could be sucked out with a mental twist and a burst of magic?" suggested Medivh. He smiled, and Khadgar realized he had been holding his breath. "You're not bad. Not bad at all. You know your counterspells?"

"To the fifth roster," said Khadgar.

"Can you power a mystic bolt?" asked Medivh, quickly.

"One or two, but it's draining," answered the younger man, suddenly feeling that the conversation had taken a serious turn once more.

"And your primary elementals?"

"Strongest in flame, but I know them all."

"Nature magic?" asked Medivh. "Ripening, culling, harvesting? Can you take a seed and pull the youth from it until it becomes a flower?"

"No, sir. I was trained in a city."

"Can you make a homunculus?"

"Doctrine frowns on it, but I understand the principles involved," said Khadgar. "If you're curious . . ."

Medivh's eyes lit up for a moment, and he said, "You sailed here from Lordaeron? What type of boat?"

Khadgar felt thrown for a moment by the sudden change of discussion. "Yes. Um . . . A Tirassian windrunner, the *Gracious Breeze*," he replied.

"Out of Kul Tiras," concluded Medivh. "Human crew?"

"Yes."

"You spoke with the crew at all?" Again, Khadgar felt himself sliding once more from conversation to interrogation.

"A little," said Khadgar. "I think I amused them with my accent."

"The crews of the Kul Tiras ships are easily amused," said Medivh. "Any nonhumans in the crew?"

"No, sir," said Khadgar. "The Tirassians told stories of fish men. They called them Murlocs. Are they real?"

"They are," said the Magus. "What other races have you encountered? Other than variations of humans."

"Some gnomes were at Dalaran once," said Khadgar. "And I've met dwarven artificers at the Violet Citadel. I know dragons from the legends; I saw the dragon's skull in one of the academies once."

"What about trolls, or goblins?" said Medivh.

"Trolls," said Khadgar. "Four known varieties of trolls. There may be a fifth."

"That would be the bushwah Alonda teaches," muttered Medivh, but motioned for Khadgar to continue.

"Trolls are savage, larger than humans. Very tall and wiry, with elongated features. Um . . ." He thought for a moment. "Tribal organization. Almost completely removed from civilized lands, almost extinct in Lordaeron."

"Goblins?"

"Much smaller, more the size of dwarves. Just as inventive, but in a destructive fashion. Fearless. I have read that as a race they are insane."

"Only the smart ones," said Medivh. "You know about demons?"

"Of course, sir," said Khadgar quickly. "I mean from the legends, sir. And I know the proper abjurations and protections. All mages of Dalaran are taught so from our first day of training."

"But you've never summoned one," said Medivh. "Or been present when someone else did so."

Khadgar blinked, wondering if this was a trick question. "No sir. I wouldn't even think of it."

"I do not doubt that you wouldn't," said the Magus, and there was the faintest edge in his voice. "Think of it, that is. Do you know what a Guardian is?"

"A Guardian?" Khadgar suddenly felt the conversation take yet another left-hand turn. "A watchman? A guard? Perhaps another race? Is it a type of monster? Perhaps a protector against monsters?"

Medivh smiled, now, and shook his head. "Don't worry. You're not *supposed* to know. It's part of the trick." Then he looked up and said, "So. What do you know about *me?*"

Khadgar shot a glance toward Moroes the Castellan, and suddenly realized that the servant had vanished, fading back into the shadows. The young man stammered for a moment. "The mages of the Kirin Tor hold you in high regard," he managed at last, diplomatically.

"Obviously," said Medivh brusquely.

"You are a powerful independent mage, supposedly an advisor to King Llane of Azeroth."

"We go back," said Medivh, nodding at the youth.

"Beyond that . . ." Khadgar hesitated, wondering if the mage truly could read his mind.

"Yes?"

"Nothing specific to justify the high esteem . . ." said Khadgar.

"And fear," put in Medivh.

"And *envy*," finished Khadgar, feeling suddenly put upon by the questions, unsure about how to answer. He quickly added, "Nothing specific to explain directly the high *respect* the Kirin Tor holds you in."

"It's supposed to be that way," snapped Medivh peevishly, rubbing his hands over the brazier. "It's supposed to be that way." Khadgar could not believe how the master mage could possibly be cold. He himself felt nervous sweat drip down his back.

At length, Medivh looked up, and the brewing storm was in his eyes again. "But what do you know about *me?*"

"Nothing, sir," said Khadgar.

"Nothing?" Medivh's voice raised and seemed to reverberate across the observatory. "Nothing? You came all this way for nothing? You didn't even bother to check? Perhaps I was just an excuse for your masters to get you out of their hair, hoping you'd die en route. It wouldn't be the first time someone tried that."

"There wasn't that much to check. You haven't done that much," responded Khadgar hotly, then took a deep breath, realizing whom he was speaking with, and what he was saying. "I mean, not much that I could find out, I mean . . ."

He expected an outburst from the older mage, but Medivh just chuckled. "And what *did* you find out?" he asked.

Khadgar sighed, and said, "You come from a spellcaster heritage. Your father was a mage of Azeroth, one Nielas Aran. You mother was Aegwynn, which may be a title as opposed to a name, one that goes back at least eight hundred years. You grew up in Azeroth and know King Llane and Lord Lothar from your childhood. Beyond that . . ." Khadgar let his voice trail off. "Nothing."

Medivh looked into the brazier and nodded. "Well, that *is* something. More than most people can find out."

"And your name means 'Keeper of Secrets,'" Khadgar added. "In High Elven. I found that out as well."

"All too true," said Medivh, looking suddenly tired. He stared into the brazier for a while. "Aegwynn is not a title," he said at length. "It is merely my mother's name."

"Then there were several Aegwynns, probably a family name," suggested Khadgar.

"Only one," said Medivh, somberly.

Khadgar gave a nervous laugh. "But that would make her . . ."

"Over seven hundred fifty years old when I was born," said Medivh, with a surprising snort. "She is much older than that. I was a late child in her life. Which may be one reason the Kirin Tor is interested in what I keep in my library. Which is why they sent you to find out."

"Sir," said Khadgar, as sternly as he could manage. "To be honest, every mage save the highest in the Kirin Tor wants me to find out *something* from you. I will accommodate them as best as I am able, but if there is material that you want to keep restricted or hidden, I will fully understand. . . ."

"If I thought that, you would not have gotten through the forest to reach here," said Medivh, suddenly serious. "I need someone to sort and organize the library, for starters, then we work on the alchemical laboratories. Yes, you'll do nicely. You see, I know the meaning of your name just as you know mine. Moroes!"

"Here, sir," said the servant, suddenly manifesting out of the shadows. Despite himself, Khadgar jumped.

"Take the lad down to his quarters and make sure he eats something. It's been a long day for him."

"Of course, sir," said Moroes.

"One question, Master," said Khadgar, catching himself. "I mean, Lord Magus, sir."

"Call me Medivh for now. I also answer to Keeper of Secrets and a few other names, not all of them known."

"What do you mean when you say you know my name?" asked Khadgar.

Medivh smiled, and the rooms suddenly seemed warm and cozy again. "You don't speak dwarven," he observed.

Khadgar shook his head.

"My name means 'Keeper of Secrets' in High Elven. Your name means 'Trust' in the old dwarven language. So I will hold you to your name, young Khadgar. Young Trust."

Moroes saw the young man to his quarters halfway down the tower, explaining in that ghostly, definitive voice as he shuffled down the stairs. Meals in Medivh's Tower were simple fare—porridge and sausages for breakfast, a cold lunch, and a large, hearty dinner, usually a stew or a roast served with vegetables. Cook would retire after the evening meals, but there were always leftovers in the cold room. Medivh kept hours that could be charitably described as "erratic" and Moroes and Cook had long since learned how to accommodate him with a minimal amount of hardship on their parts.

Moroes informed young Khadgar that, as an assistant instead of a servant, he would not have that luxury. He would be expected to be available to help the master mage whenever he deemed necessary.

"I'd expect that, as an apprentice," said Khadgar.

Moroes turned in midstep (they were walking along an upper gallery overlooking what seemed to be a reception hall or ballroom). "Not an apprentice yet, Lad," wheezed Moroes. "Not by half."

"But Medivh said . . ."

"You could sort out the library," said Moroes. "Assistant work, not apprentice's. Others have been assistants. None became apprentices."

Khadgar's brow furrowed, and he felt the warmth of a blush on his face. He had not expected there to be a level *before* apprentice in the mage's hierarchy. "How long before . . ."

"Couldn't say, really," gasped the servant. "None have ever made it that far."

Khadgar thought of two questions at once, hesitated, then asked, "How many other 'assistants' have there been?"

Moroes looked out over the gallery railing, and his eyes grew unfocused. Khadgar wondered if the servant was thinking or had been derailed by the question. The gallery below was sparsely furnished with a heavy central table and chairs. It was surprisingly uncluttered, and Khadgar surmised that Medivh did not hold many banquets.

"Dozens," said Moroes at last. "At least. Most of them from Azeroth. An elfling. No, two elflings. You're the first from the Kirin Tor."

"Dozens," repeated Khadgar, his heart sinking as he wondered how many times Medivh had welcomed a young would-be mage into his service.

He asked the other question. "How long did they last?"

Moroes snorted this time, and said, "Days. Sometimes hours. One elf didn't even make it up the tower stairs." He tapped the blinders at the side of his wizened head. "They *see* things, you know."

Khadgar thought of the figure at the main gate and just nodded.

At last they arrived at Khadgar's quarters, in a side passage not far from the banquet hall. "Tidy yourself up," said Moroes, handing Khadgar the lantern. "The jakes is at the end of the hall. There's a pot beneath the bed. Come down to the kitchen. Cook will have something warm for you."

Khadgar's room was a narrow wedge of the tower, more suitable to the contemplations of a cloistered monk than a mage. A narrow bed along one wall, and an equally narrow desk along the other with a bare shelf above. A standing closet for clothes. Khadgar tossed his rucksack into the closet without opening it, and walked over to the thin window.

The window was a slim slice of leaded glass, mounted vertically on a pivot in the center. Khadgar pushed on one half and it slowly pushed open, the solidifying oil in the bottom mount oozing as the window rotated.

The view was from still high up the tower's side, and the rounded hills that surrounded the tower were gray and bare in the light of the twin moons. From this height it was obvious to Khadgar that the hills had once been a crater, worn and weathered by the passage of the years. Had some mountain been pulled from this spot, like a rotted tooth? Or maybe the ring of hills had not risen at all, but rather the rest of the surrounding mountains had risen faster, leaving only this place of power rooted in its spot.

Khadgar wondered if Medivh's mother was here when the land rose, or sank, or was struck by a piece of the sky. Eight hundred years was long even by the standards of a wizard. After two hundred years, most of the old object lessons taught, most human mages were deathly thin and frail. To be seven hundred fifty years old and bear a child! Khadgar shook his head, and wondered if Medivh was having him on.

Khadgar shed his traveling cloak and visited the facilities at the hall's end. They were spartan, but included a pitcher of cold water and a washbasin and a good, untarnished mirror. Khadgar thought of using a minor spell to heat the water, then decided merely to tough it out.

The water was bracing, and Khadgar felt better as he changed into less-dusty togs—a comfortable shirt that reached nearly to his knees and a set of sturdy pants. His working gear. He pulled a narrow eating knife from his sack and, after a moment's thought, slid it into the inside sleeve of one boot.

He stepped back out into the hallway, and realized that he had no clear idea where the kitchen was. There had been no cooking shed out by the stables, so whatever arrangements were likely within the tower. Probably on or near the ground level, with a pump from the well. With a clear path to the banquet hall, whether or not the hall was commonly used.

Khadgar found the gallery above the banquet hall easily enough, but had to search to find the staircase, narrow and twisting in on itself, leading to it. From the banquet hall itself he had a choice of exits. Khadgar chose the most likely one and ended up in a dead-end hallway with empty rooms on all sides, similar to his own. A second choice brought a similar result.

The third led the young man into the heart of a battle.

He did not expect it. One moment he was striding down a set of low flag-stone steps, wondering if he needed a map or a bell or a hunting horn to nav-igate the tower. The next moment the roof above him opened up into a brilliant sky the color of fresh blood, and he was surrounded by men in armor, armed for battle.

Khadgar stepped back, but the hallway had vanished behind him, only leaving an uneven, barren landscape unlike any he was familiar with. The men were shouting and pointing, but their voices, despite the fact that they were right next to Khadgar, were indistinct and muddied, like they were talk-ing to him from underwater.

A dream? thought Khadgar. Perhaps he had laid down for a moment and fallen asleep, and all this was some night terror brought on by his own con-cerns. But no, he could almost feel the heat of the dying, corpulent sun on his flesh, and the breeze and shouting men moved around him.

It was as if he had become unstuck from the rest of the world, occupied his own small island, with only the most tenuous of connections to the reality around him. As if he had become a ghost.

Indeed, the soldiers ignored him as if he were a spirit. Khadgar reached out to grab one on the shoulder, and to his own relief his hand did not pass through the battered shoulder plate. There was resistance, but only of the most amorphous sort—he could feel the solidity of the armor, and if he con-centrated, feel the rough ridges of the dimpled metal.

These men had fought, Khadgar realized, both hard and recently. Only one man in three was without some form of rude bandage, bloodstained badges of war sticking out from beneath dirty armor and damaged helms. Their weapons were notched as well, and spattered with dried crimson. He had fallen into a battlefield.

Khadgar examined their position. They were atop a small hillock, a mere fold in the undulating plains that seemed to surround them. What vegeta-tion existed had been chopped down and formed into crude battlements, now guarded by grim-faced men. This was no safe redoubt, no castle or fort. They had chosen this spot to fight only because there was no other available to them.

The soldiers parted as their apparent leader, a great, white-bearded man with broad shoulders, pushed his way through. His armor was as battered as any, but consisted of a breastplate bolted over a crimson set of scholar's robes, of the type that would not have been out of place in the halls of the Kirin Tor. The hem, sleeves, and vest of these crimson robes were inscribed with runes of power—some of which Khadgar recognized, but others which seemed alien to him. The leader's snowy beard reached almost to his waist, obscuring the armor beneath, and he wore a red skullcap with a single golden gem on the brow. He held a gem-tipped staff in one hand, and a dark red sword in the other.

The leader was bellowing at the soldiers, in a voice that sounded to Khadgar like the raging sea itself. The warriors seemed to know what he was saying, though, for they formed themselves up neatly along the barricades, others filling gaps along the line.

The snow-bearded commander brushed past Khadgar, and despite himself the youth stumbled back, out of the way. The commander should not have noticed him, no more than any of the blood-spattered warriors had.

Yet the commander did. His voice dropped for a moment, he stammered, his foot landed badly on the uneven soil of the rocky hilltop and he almost stumbled. Yet instead he turned and regarded Khadgar.

Yes, he looked at Khadgar, and it was clear to the would-be apprentice that the ancient mage-warrior saw him and saw him clearly. The commander's eyes looked deeply into Khadgar's own, and for a moment Khadgar felt as he had under Medivh's own withering glare earlier. Yet, if anything, this was more intense. Khadgar looked into the eyes of the commander.

And what he saw there made him gasp. Despite himself, he turned away, breaking the locked gaze with the mage-warrior.

When Khadgar looked up again, the commander was nodding at him. It was a brief, almost dismissive nod, and the old man's mouth was a tight frown. Then the snow-bearded leader was off again, bellowing at the warriors, entreating them to defend themselves.

Khadgar wanted to go after him, to chase him down and find out how he could see him when others did not, and what he could tell him, but there was a cry around him, a muddy cry of tired men called into duty one last time. Swords and spears were raised to a sky the shade of curdled blood, and arms pointed toward the nearby ridges, where flooding had stripped out patterns of purple against the rust-colored soil.

Khadgar looked where the men were pointing, and a wave of green and black topped the nearest ridge. Khadgar thought it was some river, or an arcane and colorful mudflow, but he realized that the wave was an advancing army. Black was the color of their armor, and green was the color of their flesh.

They were nightmare creatures, mockeries of human form. Their jade-fleshed faces were dominated by heavy underslung jaws lined with fanged teeth, their noses flat and snuffling like a dog's, and their eyes small, bloody, and filled with hate. Their ebon weapons and ornate armor shone in the eternally dying sun of this world, and as they topped the rise they let out a bellow that rocked the ground beneath them.

The soldiers around him let out a cry of their own, and as the green creatures closed the distance between the hill they let out volley after volley of red-fletched arrows. The front line of the monstrous creatures stumbled and fell, and were immediately trampled by those who came behind. Another volley and another rank of the inhuman monsters toppled, yet their failing was subsumed by the advancing tide of the mass that followed.

To Khadgar's right there were flashes as lightning danced along the surface of the earth, and the monstrosities screamed as the flesh was boiled from their bones. Khadgar thought of the warrior-mage commander, but also realized that these bolts only thinned the charging hordes by the merest fraction.

And then the green-fleshed monstrosities were on top of them, the wave of ebon and jade smashing against the rude palisade. The felled timbers were no more than twigs in the path of this storm, and Khadgar could feel the line buckle. One of the soldiers nearest him toppled, impaled by a great dark spear. In the warrior's place there was a nightmare of green flesh and black armor, howling as it swept down upon him.

Despite himself, Khadgar backed two steps, then turned to run.

And almost slammed into Moroes, who was standing in the archway.

"You," wheezed Moroes calmly, "were late. Might have gotten lost."

Khadgar wheeled again in place, and saw that behind him was not a world of crimson skies and green monstrosities, but an abandoned sitting room, its fireplace empty and its chairs covered with drop cloths. The air smelled of dust only recently disturbed.

"I was . . ." gasped Khadgar. "I saw . . . I was . . ."

"Misplaced?" suggested Moroes.

Khadgar gulped, looked about, then nodded mutely.

"Late supper is ready," groaned Moroes. "Don't get misplaced, again, now."

And the dark-clad servant turned and glided quietly out of the room.

Khadgar took one last look at the dead-end passage he had stumbled into. There were no mystic archways or magical doorways. The vision (if vision it was) had ended with a suddenness only to be equaled by its beginning.

There were no soldiers. No creatures with green flesh. No army about to collapse. There was only a memory that scared Khadgar to his core. It was real. It had felt real. It had felt true.

It was not the monsters or the bloodshed that had frightened him. It was the mage-warrior, the snow-haired commander that seemed to be able to see him. That seemed to have looked into the heart of him, and found him wanting.

And worst of all, the white-bearded figure in armor and robes had

Khadgar's eyes. The face was aged, the hair snow-white, the manner powerful, yet the commander had the same eyes that Khadgar had seen in the untarnished mirror just moments (lifetimes?) before.

Khadgar left the sitting room, and wondered if it would not be too late to
get a set of blinders.

THREE
Settling In

We'll start you off slow," said the elder wizard from across the
table. "Take stock of the library. Figure out how you are going
to organize it."

Khadgar nodded over the porridge and sausages. The bulk of the breakfast
conversation was about Dalaran in general. What was popular in Dalaran and
what were the fashions in Lordaeron. What they were arguing about in the halls
of the Kirin Tor. Khadgar mentioned that the current philosophical question
when he left was whether when you created a flame by magic, you called it into
being or summoned it from some parallel existence.

Medivh huffed over his breakfast. "Fools. They wouldn't know an alternate dimension if it came up and bit them on the . . . . So what do you think?"

"I think . . ." And Khadgar, suddenly realizing he was once again on the
spot. "I think that it may be something else entirely."

"Excellent," said Medivh, smiling. "When given a choice between two,
choose the third. Of course you meant to say that when you create fire, all
you are doing is concentrating the inherent nature of fire contained in the
surrounding area into one location, calling it into being?"

"Oh yes," said Khadgar, then adding, "had I thought about it. For a while.
Like a few years."

"Good," said Medivh, dabbing at his beard with a napkin. "You've a quick
mind and an honest appraisal of yourself. Let's see how you do with the
library. Moroes will show you the way."

The library occupied two levels, and was situated about a third of the way
up the tower itself. The staircase along this part of the tower hugged the outside edge of the citadel, leaving a large chamber two floors high. A wrought
iron platform created an upper gallery on the second level. The room's narrow windows were covered with interwoven rods of iron, reducing what nat-

ural light the room had to little more than that of a hooded torch. On the great oak tables of the first level, crystalline globes covered with a thick patina of dust glowed with a blue-gray luster.

The room itself was a disaster area. Books were scattered opened to random pages, scrolls were unspooled over chairs, and a thin layer of dusty foolscap covered everything like the leaves on the forest floor. The more ancient tomes, still chained to the bookshelves, had been unshelved, and hung from their links like prisoners in some dungeon cell.

Khadgar surveyed the damage and let out a deep sigh. "Start me off slow," he said.

"I could have your gear packed in an hour," said Moroes from the hallway. The servant would not enter the library proper.

Khadgar picked up a piece of parchment at his feet. One side was a demand from the Kirin Tor for the master mage to respond to their most recent missive. The other side was marked with a dark crimson smear that Khadgar assumed at first was blood but realized was nothing more than the melted wax seal.

"No," said Khadgar, patting his small pouch of scribe tools. "It's just more of a challenge than I first anticipated."

"Heard that before," said Moroes.

Khadgar turned to ask about his comment, but the servant was already gone from the doorway.

With the care of a burglar, Khadgar picked his way through the debris. It was as if a battle had erupted in the library. Spines were broken, covers were half-torn, pages were folded over upon themselves, signatures had been pulled from the bindings entirely. And this was for those books that were still mostly whole. More portfolios had been pulled from their covers, and the dust on the tables covered a layer of papers and correspondences. Some of these were open, but some were noticeably still unread, their knowledge contained beneath their wax seals.

"The Magus does not need an assistant," muttered Khadgar, clearing a space at the end of one table and pulling out a chair. "He needs a housekeeper." He shot a glance at the doorway to make sure that the castellan was well and truly gone.

Khadgar sat down and the chair rocked severely. He stood up again, and saw that the uneven legs had shifted off a thick tome with a metallic cover. The front cover was ornate, and the page edges clad in silver.

Khadgar opened the text, and as he did so he felt something shift within the book, like a slider moving down a metal rod or a drop of mercury moving through a glass pipe. Something metallic unwound within the spine of the tome.

The book began to tick.

Quickly Khadgar closed the cover, and the book silenced itself with a sharp whirr and a snap, its mechanism resetting. The young man delicately set the volume back on the table.

That was when he noticed the scorch marks on the chair he was using, and the floor beneath it.

"I can see why you go through so many assistants," said Khadgar, slowly wandering through the room.

The situation did not improve. Books were hanging open over the arms of chairs and metal railings. The correspondence grew deeper as he moved farther into the room. Something had made a nest in one corner of the bookshelf, and as Khadgar pulled it from the shelf, a small shrew's skull toppled out, crumbling when it struck the floor. The upper level was little more than storage, books not even reaching the shelves, just piled in higher stacks, foothills leading to mountains leading to unattainable peaks.

And there was one bare spot, but this one looked like someone had started a fire in a desperate attempt to reduce the amount of paper present. Khadgar examined the area and shook his head—something else burned here as well, for there were bits of fabric, probably from a scholar's robe.

Khadgar shook his head and went back to where he had left his scribe's tools. He spilled out a thin wooden pen with a handful of metal nibs, a stone for sharpening and shaping the nibs, a knife with a flexible blade for scraping parchment, a block of octopus ink, a small dish in which to melt the ink, a collection of thin, flat keys, a magnifying lens, and what looked at first glance like a metallic cricket.

He picked up the cricket, turned it on its back, and using a specially-fashioned pen nib, wound it up. A gift from Guzbah upon Khadgar completing his first training as a scribe, it had proved invaluable in the youth's perambulations among the halls of the Kirin Tor. Within was contained a simple but effective spell that warned when a trap was in the offing.

As soon as he had wound it one revolution, the metallic cricket let out a high-pitched squeal. Khadgar, surprised, almost dropped the detecting insect. Then he realized that the device was merely warning about the intensity of the potential danger.

Khadgar looked at the piled volumes around him, and muttered a low curse. He retreated to the doorway, and finished winding the cricket. Then he brought the first book he had picked up, the ticking one, over to the doorway.

The cricket warbled slightly. Khadgar set the trapped book to one side of the doorway. He picked up another volume and brought it over. The cricket was silent.

Khadgar held his breath, hoped that the cricket was enchanted to handle all forms of traps, magical and otherwise, and opened the book. It was a treatise written in a soft feminine hand on the politics of the elves from three hundred years back.

Khadgar set the handwritten volume to the other side of the doorway, and went back for another book.

"I know you," said Medivh, the next morning, over sausage and porridge.

"Khadgar, sir," said the youth.

"The new assistant," said the older mage. "Of course. Forgive, but the memory is not everything it once was. Too much going on, I'm afraid."

"Anything you need aid with, sir?" asked Khadgar.

The elder man seemed to think about it for a moment, then said, "The library, Young Trust. How are things in the library?"

"Good," said Khadgar. "Very good. I'm busy sorting the books and papers."

"Ah, by subject? Author?" asked the master mage.

Fatal and non-fatal, thought Khadgar. "I'm thinking by subject. Many are anonymous."

"Hmmmfph," said Medivh. "Never trust anything that a man will not set his reputation and name upon. Carry on, then. Tell me, what is the opinion of the Kirin Tor mages about King Llane? Do they ever mention him?"

The work proceeded with glacial slowness, but Medivh did not seem to be aware of the time involved. Indeed, he seemed to start each morning with being mildly and pleasantly surprised that Khadgar was still with them, and after a short summary of the progress the conversation would switch into a new direction.

"Speaking of libraries," he would say. "What is the Kirin Tor's librarian, Korrigan, up to?"

"How do people in Lordaeron feel about elves? Have any ever been seen there, in living memory?"

"Are there any legends of bull-headed men in the halls of the Violet Citadel?"

And one morning, about a week into Khadgar's stay, Medivh was not present at all.

"Gone," said Moroes simply when asked.

"Gone where?" asked Khadgar.

The old castellan shrugged, and Khadgar could almost hear the bones clatter within his form. "He's not one to say."

"What's he doing?" pressed Khadgar.

"Not one to say."

"When will he be back?"

"Not one to say."

"He would leave me alone in his tower?" asked Khadgar. "Unsupervised, with all his mystic texts?"

"Could come stand guard over you," volunteered Moroes. "If that's what you want."

Khadgar shook his head, but said, "Moroes?"

"Ayep, young sir?"

"These visions . . ." started the younger man.

"Blinders?" suggested the servant.

Khadgar shook his head again. "Do they show the future or the past?"

"Both, when I've noticed, but I usually don't," said Moroes. "Notice, that is."

"And the ones of the future, do they come true?" said the young man.

Moroes let out what Khadgar could only assume was a deep sigh, a bone-rattling exhalation. "In my experience, yes, young sir. In one vision Cook saw me break a piece of crystal, so she hid them away. Months passed, and finally the Master asked for that piece of crystal. She removed it from its hiding place, and within two minutes I had broken it. Completely unintentionally." He sighed again. "She got her rose quartz lenses the next day. Will there be anything else?"

Khadgar said no, but was troubled as he climbed the staircase to the library level. He had gone as far as he had dared so far in his organization, and Medivh's sudden disappearance left him high and dry, without further direction.

The young would-be apprentice entered the library. On one side of the room were those volumes (and remains of volumes) that the cricket had determined were "safe," while the other half of the room was filled with the (generally more complete) volumes that were noted as being trapped.

The great tables were covered with loose pages and unopened correspondence, laid out in two semiregular heaps. The shelves were entirely bare, the chains hanging empty of their prisoners.

Khadgar could sort through the papers, but better to restock the shelves with the books. But most of the volumes were untitled, or if titled, their covers so bare, worn, scuffed, and torn as to be illegible. The only way to determine contents would be to open the books.

Which would set off the trapped ones. Khadgar looked at the scorch mark on the floor and shook his head.

Then he started looking, first among the trapped volumes, then among the untrapped ones, until he found what he was looking for. A book marked with the symbol of the key.

It was locked, a thick metal band holding it closed, secured by a lock.

Nowhere in his searches had Khadgar come across a real key, though that did not surprise him, given the organization of the room. The binding was strong, and the cover itself was a metal plate bound in red leather.

Khadgar pulled the flat pieces of keys from his pouch, but they were all insufficient for the large lock. Finally, using the tip of his scraping knife, Khadgar managed to thread the sliver of metal through the lock, and it gave a satisfying "click" as he drove it home.

Khadgar looked at the cricket he kept on the table, and it was still silent.

Holding his breath, the young mage opened the heavy volume. The sour smell of decayed paper rose to his nostrils.

"Of Trapes and Lockes," he said aloud, wrapping his mouth around the archaic script and over-vowelled words. "Beeing a Treateese on the Nature of Securing Devicees."

Khadgar pulled up a chair (slightly lower as he had sawed off the three long legs to balance it) and began to read.

Medivh was gone a full two weeks, and by that time, Khadgar had claimed the library as his own. Each morning he rose for breakfast, gave Moroes a perfunctory update as to his progress (which the castellan, as well as Cook, never gave any indication of curiosity about), then buried himself away within the vault. Lunch and supper were brought to him, and he often worked into the night by the soft bluish light from the glowing balls.

He adjusted to the nature of the tower as well. There were often images that hung at the corner of his eye, just a twinkling of a figure in a tattered cloak that would evaporate when he turned to look at it. A half-finished word that drifted on the air. A sudden coldness as if a door or window had been left open, or a sudden change of pressure, as if a hidden entrance had suddenly appeared. Sometimes the tower groaned in the wind, the ancient stones shifting on each other after centuries of construction.

Slowly, he learned the nature, if not the exact contents, of the books that were within the library, foiling the traps that were placed around the most valuable tomes. His research served him well in the last case. He soon became as expert at foiling spell mechanisms and weighted traps as he had been with locked doors and hidden secrets in Dalaran. The trick for most of them was to convince the locking mechanism (whether magical or mechanical in nature) that the lock had not been foiled when in reality it had been. Determining what set the particular trap off, whether it was weight, or a shifting bit of metal or even exposure to the sun or fresh air, was half the battle to defeating it.

There were books that were beyond him, whose locks foiled even his modified picks and dexterous knife. Those went to the highest level, toward the back, and Khadgar resolved to find out what was within them, either on his own or by threading the knowledge out of Medivh.

He doubted the latter, and wondered if the master mage had used the library as anything else than a dumping ground for inherited texts and old letters. Most mages of the Kirin Tor had at least some semblance of order to their archives, with their most valuable tomes hidden away. But Medivh had everything in a hodgepodge, as if he didn't really need it.

Except as a test, thought Khadgar. A test to keep would-be apprentices at bay.

Now the books were on the shelves, the most valuable (and unreadable) ones secured with chains on the upper level, while the more common military histories, almanacs, and diaries were on the lower floor. Here were the scrolls as well, ranging from mundane listings of items bought and sold in Stormwind to recordings of epic poems. The last were particularly interesting since a few of them were about Aegwynn, Medivh's claimed mother.

If she lived over eight hundred years, she must have been a powerful mage indeed, thought Khadgar. More information about her would likely be in the protected books in the back. So far these tomes had resisted every common entreaty and physical attempt to sidestep their locks and traps, and the detecting cricket practically mewled in horror whenever he attempted to unlock them.

Still, there was more than enough to do, with categorizing the loose pieces, reassembling those volumes which age had almost destroyed, and sorting (or at least reading) most of the correspondence. Some of the later was in elven script, and even more of it, from a variety of sources, was in some sort of cipher. The latter type came with a variety of seals upon it, from both Azeroth, Khaz Modan, and Lordaeron, as well as places that Khadgar could not locate in the atlas. A large group communicated in cipher with each other, and with Medivh himself.

There were several ancient grimoires on codes, most of them dealing with letter replacement and cant. Nothing compared to the code used in these ciphers. Perhaps they used a combination of methods to create their own.

As a result, Khadgar had the grimoires on codes, along with primers in elven and dwarven languages, open on the table the evening that Medivh suddenly returned to the tower.

Khadgar didn't hear him as much as felt his sudden presence, the way the air changes as a storm front bears across the farmland. The young mage turned in his chair and there was Medivh, his broad shoulders filling the doorway, his robes billowing behind him of their own volition.

"Sir, I . . ." started Khadgar, smiling and half-rising from his chair. Then he saw that the master mage's hair was in disarray, and his lambent green eyes were wide and angry.

"Thief!" shouted Medivh, pointing at Khadgar. "Interloper!" The elder mage pointed at the younger and began to intone a string of alien syllables, words not crafted for the human throat.

Despite himself, Khadgar raised a hand and wove a symbol of protection in the air in front of him, but he might as well have been making a rude hand gesture for all the effect it had on Medivh's spell. A wall of solidified air slammed into the younger man, bowling over both him and the chair he sat in. The grimoires and primers went skating along the surface of the table like boats caught in a sudden squall, and the notes danced away, spinning.

Surprised, Khadgar was driven back, slammed into one of the bookshelves behind him. The shelf itself rocked from the force of the blow, and the youth was afraid it would topple, spoiling his hard work. The bookcase held its position, though the pressure on Khadgar's chest from the force of the attack intensified.

"Who are you?" thundered Medivh. "What are you doing here?"

The young mage struggled against the weight on his chest and managed to speak. "Khadgar," he gasped. "Assistant. Cleaning library. Your orders." Part of his mind wondered if this was why Moroes spoke in such a shorthand fashion.

Medivh blinked at Khadgar's words, and straightened like a man who had just been woken from a deep sleep. He twisted his hand slightly, and at once the wave of solidified air evaporated. Khadgar dropped to his knees, gasping for air.

Medivh crossed to him and helped him to his feet. "I am sorry, lad," he began. "I had forgotten you were still here. I assumed you were a thief."

"A thief that insisted on leaving a room neater than he found it," said Khadgar. It hurt a little when he breathed.

"Yes," said Medivh, looking around the room, and nodding, despite the disruption his own attack had caused. "Yes. I don't believe anyone else had ever gotten this far before."

"I've sorted by type," said Khadgar, still bent over and grasping his knees. "Histories, including epic poems, to your right. Natural sciences on your left. Legendary material in the center, with languages and reference books. The more powerful material—alchemic notes, spell descriptions, and theory—go on the balcony, along with some books I could not identify that seem fairly powerful. You're going to have to look at those yourself."

"Yes," said Medivh, now ignoring the youth and scanning the room. "Excellent. An excellent job. Very good." He looked around, seeming like a man just getting his bearings again. "Very good indeed. You've done well. Now come along."

The master mage bolted for the door, pulled himself up short, then turned. "Are you coming?"

Khadgar felt as if he had been hit by another mystic bolt. "Coming? Where are we going?"

"To the top," said Medivh curtly. "Come now or we'll be too late. Time is of the essence!"

For an older man Medivh moved swiftly up the stairs, covering them two at a time at a brisk pace.

"What's at the top?" gasped Khadgar, finally catching up at a landing near the top.

"Transport," snapped Medivh, then hesitated for a moment. He turned in place and his shoulders dropped. For a moment it looked like the fire had burned out of his eyes. "I must apologize. For back there."

"Sir?" said Khadgar, his mind now spinning with this new transformation.

"My memory is not what it once was, Young Trust," said the Magus. "I should have remembered you were in the tower. With everything, I assumed you must have been a . . ."

"Sir?" interrupted Khadgar. "Time is of the essence?"

"Time," said Medivh, then he nodded, and the intensity returned to his face. "Yes, it is. Come on, don't lollygag!" And with that the older man was up on his feet and taking the steps two at a time.

Khadgar realized that the haunted tower and the disorganized library were not the only reason people left Medivh's employ, and hastened after him.

The aged castellan was waiting for them in the tower observatory.

"Moroes," thundered Medivh as he arrived at the top of the tower. "The golden whistle, if you please."

"Ayep," said the servant, producing a thin cylinder. Dwarven runes were carved along the cylinder's side, reflecting in the lamplight of the room. "Already took the liberty, sir. They're here."

"They?" started Khadgar. There was the rustle of great wings overhead. Medivh headed for the ramparts, and Khadgar looked up.

Great birds descended from the sky, their wings luminescent in the moonlight. No, not birds, Khadgar realized—gryphons. They had the bodies of great cats, but their heads and front claws were those of sea eagles, and their wings were golden.

Medivh held out a bit and bridle. "Hitch yours up, and we'll go."

Khadgar eyed the great beast. The nearest gryphon let out a shrieking cry and pawed the flagstones with its clawed forelegs.

"I've never . . ." started the young man. "I don't know . . ."

Medivh frowned. "Don't they teach anything among the Kirin Tor? I don't have time for this." He raised a finger and muttered a few words, touching Khadgar's forehead.

Khadgar stumbled back, shouting in surprise. The elder mage's touch felt as if he were driving a hot iron into his brain.

Medivh said, "Now you *do* know. Set the bit and bridle, now."

Khadgar touched his forehead, and let out a surprised gasp. He *did* know now, how to properly harness a gryphon, and to ride one as well, both with saddle and, in the dwarven style, without. He knew how to bank, how to force a hover, and most of all, how to prepare for a sudden landing.

Khadgar harnessed his gryphon, aware that his head throbbed slightly, as if the knowledge now within had to jostle that already within his skull to make room.

"Ready? Follow!" said Medivh, not asking for a response.

The pair launched themselves into the air, the great beasts straining and beating the air to allow them to rise. The great creatures could take armored dwarves aloft, but a human in robes approached their limits.

Khadgar expertly banked his swooping gryphon and followed Medivh as the elder mage swooped down over the dark treetops. The pain in his head spread from the point where Medivh had touched him, and now his forehead felt heavy and his thoughts muzzy. Still, he concentrated and matched the master mage's motions exactly, as if he had been flying gryphons all his life.

The younger mage tried to catch up with Medivh, to ask where they were going, and what their goal was, but he could not overtake him. Even if he had, Khadgar realized, the rushing wind would drown out all but the greatest shouts. So he followed as the mountains loomed above them, as they winged eastward.

How long they flew Khadgar could not say. He may have dozed fitfully on gryphon-back, but hands held the reins firm, and the gryphon kept pace with its brother-creature. Only when Medivh suddenly jinked his gryphon to the right did Khadgar shake himself out of his slumber (if slumber it was) and followed the master mage as his course turned south. Khadgar's headache, the likely product of the spell, had almost completely dissipated, leaving only a ragged ache as a reminder.

They had cleared the mountain range and Khadgar now realized they were flying over open land. Beneath them the moonlight was shattered and reflected in myriad pools. A large marsh or swamp, Khadgar thought. It had to be early in the morning now, the horizon on their right just starting to lighten with the eventual promise of day.

Medivh dropped low and raised both hands over his head. Incanting from gryphon-back, Khadgar realized, and though his mind assured him that he knew how to do this, steering the great beast with his knees, he felt in his heart that he could never be comfortable in such a maneuver.

The creatures dropped farther, and Medivh was suddenly bathed in a ball of light, both limning him clearly and catching Khadgar's gryphon as a trailing shadow. Beneath them, the young mage saw an armed encampment on a low rise that jutted from the surrounding swamp. They passed low over the camp, and beneath him Khadgar could hear shouts and the clatter of armor and weapons being hastily grabbed. What was Medivh doing?

They passed over the encampment, and Medivh pulled into a high, banking turn, Khadgar following him move for move. They returned over the camp, and it was brighter now—the campfires that had previously been banked were now fed fresh fuel, and blazed in the night. Khadgar saw it was a large patrol, perhaps even a company. The commander's tent was large and ornate, and Khadgar recognized the banner of Azeroth flapping overhead.

Allies, then, for Medivh was supposedly closely connected to both King Llane of Azeroth and Lothar, the kingdom's Knight Champion. Khadgar expected Medivh to land, but instead the mage kicked the sides of his mount, pulling the gryphon's head up. The beast's great wings beat the dark air and they climbed again, this time rocketing north. Khadgar had no choice but to follow, as Medivh's light dimmed and the master mage took the reins again.

Over the marshlands again, and Khadgar saw a thin ribbon beneath, too straight for a river, too wide for an irrigation ditch. A road, then, plowed through the swamp, connecting bits of dry land that rose out of the fen.

Then the land rose to another ridge, another dry spot, and another encampment. There were also flames in this encampment, but they were not the bright, contained ones of the army's forces. These were scattered throughout the clearing, and as they neared, Khadgar realized they were wagons set alight, their contents strewn out among the dark human forms that were tossed like children's dolls on the sandy ground of the campsite.

As before, Medivh passed over the campsite, then wheeled high in the air, banking to make a return pass. Khadgar followed, the young mage himself leaning over the side of his mount to get a better look. It looked like a caravan that had been looted and set ablaze, but the goods themselves were scattered on the ground. Wouldn't bandits take the booty and the wagons? Were there any survivors?

The answer to the last question came with a shout and a volley of arrows that arched up from the brush surrounding the site.

The lead gryphon let out a shriek as Medivh effortlessly pulled back on the reins, banking the creature clear of the flight of arrows. Khadgar attempted the same maneuver, the warm, false, comforting memory in his head telling him that this was the correct way to turn. But unlike Medivh, Khadgar was riding too far forward on his mount, and he had insufficient pull on his reins.

The gryphon banked, but not enough to avoid all the arrows. A barbed arrow pierced the feathers of the right wing, and the great beast let out a bleating scream, jerking in flight and desperately attempting to beat its wings to get above the arrows.

Khadgar was off-balance, and was unable to compensate. In a heartbeat his hands slipped loose of the reins, and his knees slipped up from the sides of the gryphon. No longer under tight control, the gryphon bucked, throwing Khadgar entirely free of its back.

Khadgar lashed out to grab the reins. The leather lines whipped at his fingertips and then were gone into the night, along with his mount.

And Khadgar plummeted toward the armed darkness below.

FOUR
Battle and Aftermath

The air rushed out of Khadgar's lungs as he struck the ground. The earth was gritty beneath his fingers, and he realized he must have landed on a low dune of sandy debris collected along one side of the ridge.

Uneasily the young mage rose to his feet. From the air the ridge looked like a forest fire. From the ground it looked like an opening to hell itself.

The wagons were almost completely consumed by fire now, their contents scattered and blazing along the ridge. Bolts of cloth had been unwound in the dirt, barrels staved and leaking, and food despoiled and mashed into the earth. Around him were bodies as well, human forms dressed in light armor. There was an occasional gleam of a helmet or a sword. Those would be the caravan guards, who failed their task.

Khadgar shrugged a painful shoulder, but it felt bruised as opposed to broken. Even given the sand, he should have landed harder. He shook his head, hard. Whatever ache was left from Medivh's spell was outweighed by greater aches elsewhere.

There was movement among the wreckage, and Khadgar crouched. Voices barked back and forth in an unfamiliar tongue, a language to Khadgar's ears both guttural and blasphemous. They were searching for him. They had seen him topple from his mount and now they were searching for him. As he watched, stooped figures shambled through the wreckage, forming hunched silhouettes where they passed before the flames.

Something tickled the back of Khadgar's brain, but he could not place it. Instead he started to back out of the clearing, hoping the darkness would keep him hidden from the creatures.

Such was not to be. Behind him, a branch snapped or a booted foot found a chuckhole covered by leaves, or leather armor was tangled briefly in some brush. In any event, Khadgar knew he was not alone, and he turned at once to see . . .

A monstrosity from his vision. A mockery of humanity in green and black.

It was not as large as the creature of his vision, nor as wide, but it was still a nightmare creature. Its heavy jaw was dominated by fangs that jutted upward, its other features small and sinister. For the first time Khadgar realized it had large, upright ears. It probably heard him before it saw him.

Its armor was dark, but it was leather and not the metal of his dream. The creature bore a torch in one hand that caught the deep features of its face, making it all the more monstrous. In its other hand the creature carried a spear decorated with a string of small white objects. With a start Khadgar realized the objects were human ears, trophies of the massacre around them.

All this came to Khadgar in an instant, in the moment's meeting of man and monster. The beast pointed the grisly-decorated spear at the youth and let out a bellowing challenge.

The challenge was cut short as the young mage muttered a word of power, raised a hand, and unleashed a small bolt of power through the creature's midsection. The beast slumped in on itself, its bellow cut short.

One part of his mind was stunned by what he had just done, the other knew that he had seen what these creatures could do, in the vision in Karazhan.

The creature had warned the other members of its unit, and now there were war-howls in return around the encampment. Two, four, a dozen such travesties, all converging on his location. Worse yet, there were other howls from the swamp itself.

Khadgar knew he did not have the power to repulse all of them. Summoning the mystic bolt was enough to weaken him. Another would put him in dire danger of fainting. Perhaps he should try to flee?

But these monsters probably knew the dark fen that surrounded them better than he did. If he kept to the sandy ridge, they would find him. If he fled into the swamp, not even Medivh would be able to locate him.

Khadgar looked up into the sky, but there was no sign of either the Magus or the gryphons. Had Medivh landed somewhere, and was sneaking up on the monsters? Or had he returned to the human force to the south, to bring them here?

Or, thought Khadgar grimly, had Medivh's quicksilver mood changed once again and he had forgotten he had someone with him on this flight?

Khadgar looked quickly out into the darkness, then back toward the site of the ambush itself. There were more shadows moving around the fire, and more howling.

Khadgar picked up the grisly trophy-spear, and strode purposely toward the fire. He might not be able to fire off more than a mystic bolt or two, but the monsters didn't know that.

Perhaps they were as dumb as they looked. And as inexperienced with wizards as he was with them.

He did surprise them, for what it was worth. The last thing they expected was their prey, the victim they had unseated from its flying mount, suddenly to manifest at the edge of the campfire's light, bearing the trophy-spear of one of their guards.

Khadgar tossed the spear sideways on the fire, and it sent up a shower of sparks as it landed.

The young mage summoned a bit of flame, a small ball, and held it in his hand. He hoped that it limned his features as seriously as the torch had lit the guard's. It had better.

"Leave this place," Khadgar bellowed, praying that his strained voice would not crack. "Leave this place or die."

One of the larger brutes took two steps forward and Khadgar muttered a word of power. The mystic energies congealed around his flaming hand and blasted the green nonhuman full in the face. The brute had enough time to raise a clawed hand to its ruined features before it toppled.

"Flee," shouted Khadgar, trying to pitch his voice as deeply as he could. "Flee or face the same fate." His stomach felt like ice, and he tried not to stare at the burning creature.

A spear launched out of the darkness, and with the last of his energy Khadgar summoned a bit of air, just enough to push it clearly aside. As he did he felt faint. That was the last he could do. He was well and truly tapped out. It would be a good time for his bluff to work.

The surrounding creatures, about a dozen visible, took a step back, then another. One more shout, Khadgar reckoned, and they would flee back into the swamp, and give him enough time to flee himself. He had already decided he would flee south, toward the army encampment.

Instead there was a high, cackling laugh that froze Khadgar's blood. The ranks of the green warriors parted and another figure shambled forward. It was thinner and more hunched than the others, and wore a robe the color of curdled blood. The color of the sky of Khadgar's vision. Its features were as green and misshapened as the others, but this one had a gleam of feral intelligence in its eyes.

It held out its hand, palm upward, and took a dagger and pierced its palm with the tip. Reddish blood pooled in the clawed palm.

The robed beast spoke a word that Khadgar had never heard, a word that hurt the ears, and the blood burst into flame.

"Human wants to play?" said the robed monster, roughly matching the human language. "Wants to play at spells? Nothgrin can play!"

"Leave now," tried Khadgar. "Leave now or die!"

But the young mage's voice wavered now, and the robed mockery merely laughed. Khadgar scanned the area around him, looking for the best place to run, wondering if he could grab one of the guards' swords laying on the ground. He wondered if this Nothgrin was bluffing as much as Khadgar had been.

Nothgrin took a step toward Khadgar, and two of the brutes to the spell-caster's right suddenly screamed and burst into flame. It happened with a suddenness that shocked everyone, including Khadgar. Nothgrin wheeled toward the immolated creatures, to see two more join them, bursting into flame like dry sticks. They screamed as well, their knees buckling, and they toppled to the ground.

In the place where the creatures had been now stood Medivh. He seemed to glow of his own volition, diminishing the main fire, the burning wagons, and the burning corpses on the ground, sucking their light into himself. He seemed radiant and relaxed. He smiled at the collected creatures, and it was a savage, brutal smile.

"My apprentice told you to leave," said Medivh. "You should have followed his orders."

One of the beasts let out a bellow, and the rogue magus silenced it with a wave of his hand. Something hard and invisible struck the beast square in the face, and there was a shattering crack as its head came loose of its body and rolled backward, striking the ground only moments before the creature's body struck the sand.

The rest of the creatures staggered backward a step, then fled entirely into the night. Only the leader, the robed Nothgrin, held its ground, and its over-wide jaw flapped open in surprise.

"Nothgrin knows you, human," he hissed. "You are the one. . . ."

Anything else the creature said disappeared in a scream as Medivh waved a hand and the creature was pulled off its feet by a burst of air and fire. It was swept upward, screaming, until at last its lungs collapsed from the stress and remains of its burned body drifted down like black snow-flakes.

Khadgar looked at Medivh, and the wizard had a toothy, self-satisfied smile. The smile faded when he looked at Khadgar's ashen face.

"Are you all right, lad?" he asked.

"Fine," said Khadgar, feeling the weight of his exhaustion sweeping over him. He tried to sit but ended up just collapsing to his knees, his mind worn and empty.

Medivh was at his side in a moment, passing a palm over the lad's forehead. Khadgar tried to move the hand away, but found that he lacked the energy.

"Rest," said Medivh. "Recover your strength. The worst is over."

Khadgar nodded, blinking. He looked at the bodies around the fire. Medivh could have slain him as easily, in the library. What stayed his hand, then? Some recognition of Khadgar? Some bit of memory or of humanity?

The young mage managed, "Those things." His voice sounded slurred. "What were . . ."

"Orcs," said the Magus. "Those were orcs. Now no more questions for the moment."

To the east, the sky was lightening. To the south, there was the sound of bright horns and powerful hooves.

"The cavalry at last," said Medivh with a sigh. "Too loud and too late, but don't tell them that. They can pick up the stragglers. Now rest."

The patrol swept through the camp, half of them dismounting, the remainder pressing up along the road. The horsemen began checking the bodies. A detail was assigned to bury the members of the caravan. The few dead orcs that Medivh had not set on fire were gathered and put on the main fire, their bodies charring as their flesh turned to ash.

Khadgar didn't remember Medivh leaving him, but he did return with the patrol's commander. The commander was a stocky, older man, his face weathered by combat and campaign. His beard was already more salt than pepper, and his hairline had receded to the back of his head. He was a huge man, made all the more imposing by his plate armor and greatcape. Over one shoulder Khadgar could see the hilt of a huge sword, the crosspiece huge and jeweled.

"Khadgar, this is Lord Anduin Lothar," said Medivh. "Lothar, this is my apprentice, Khadgar of the Kirin Tor."

Khadgar's mind spun and caught first on the name. Lord Lothar. The

King's Champion, boyhood companion of both King Llane and Medivh. The blade on his back had to be the Great Royal Sword, pledged to defend Azeroth, and . . .

Did Medivh just say Khadgar was his *apprentice?*

Lothar dropped to one knee to bring himself level with the young man, and looked at him, smiling. "So you finally got an apprentice. Had to go to the Violet Citadel to find one, eh, Med?"

"Find one of suitable merit, yes," said Medivh.

"And if it ties the local hedge wizards' undies in a bundle, so much the better, eh? Oh, don't look at me like that, Medivh. What has this one done to impress you?"

"Oh, the usual," said Medivh, showing his teeth in a feral grin in response. "Organized my library. Tamed a gryphon on the first try. Took on these orcs single-handed, including a warlock."

Lothar let out a low whistle. "He organized *your* library? I *am* impressed." A smile flashed beneath his graying moustache.

"Lord Lothar," managed Khadgar finally. "Your skill is known even in Dalaran."

"You rest, lad," said Lothar, putting a heavy gauntlet on the young mage's shoulder. "We'll get the rest of those creatures."

Khadgar shook his head. "You won't. Not if you stay on the road."

The King's Champion blinked in surprise, and Khadgar was not sure if it was because of his presumption or his words.

"The lad's right, I'm afraid," said Medivh. "The orcs have taken to the swamp. They seem to know the Black Morass better than we do, and that's what makes them so effective here. We stay on the roads, and they can run circles around us."

Lothar rubbed the back of his head with his gauntlet. "Maybe we could borrow some of those gryphons of yours to scout."

"The dwarves that trained them may have their opinions about loaning out their gryphons," said Medivh. "But you might want to talk to them, and to the gnomes as well. They have a few whirligigs and sky-engines that might be more suitable for scouting."

Lothar nodded, and rubbed his chin. "How did you know they were here?"

"I encountered one of their advance scouts near my domain," said Medivh, as calmly as if he was discussing the weather. "I managed to squeeze out of him that there was a large party looking to raid along the Morass Road. I had hoped to arrive in time to warn them." He looked at the devastation around them.

The sunlight did little to help the appearance of the area. The smaller fires had burned out, and the air smelled of burning orcflesh. A pallid cloud hung over the site of the ambush.

A young soldier, little more than Khadgar's age, ran up to them. They had found a survivor, one that was pretty badly chewed up, but alive. Could the Magus come at once?

"Stay with the lad," said Medivh. "He's still a little woozy from everything." And with that the master mage strode across the scorched and bloody ground, his long robes trailing him like a banner.

Khadgar tried to rise and follow him, but the King's Champion put his heavy gauntlet on his shoulder and held him down. Khadgar struggled only for a moment, then returned to a seated position.

Lothar regarded Khadgar with a smile. "So the old coot finally took on an assistant."

"Apprentice," said Khadgar weakly, though he felt the pride rising in his chest. The feeling brought a new strength to his mind and limbs. "He's had many assistants. They didn't last. Or so I heard."

"Uh-huh," said Lothar. "I recommended a few of those assistants, and they came back with tales of a haunted tower and a crazy, demanding mage. What do you think of him?"

Khadgar blinked for a moment. In the past twelve hours, Medivh had attacked him, shoved knowledge into his head, dragged him across the country on gryphon-back, and let him face off a handful of orcs before swooping in for the rescue. On the other hand, he had made Khadgar his apprentice. His student.

Khadgar coughed and said, "He is more than I expected."

Lothar smiled again and there was genuine warmth in the smile. "He is more than anyone expected. That's one of his good points." Lothar thought for a moment and said, "That is a very politic and polite response."

Khadgar managed a weak smile. "Lordaeron is a very politic and polite land."

"So I've noticed in the King's Council. 'Dalaran ambassadors can say both yes and no at the same time, and say nothing as well.' No insult intended."

"None taken, my lord," said Khadgar.

Lothar looked at the lad. "How old are you, lad?"

Khadgar looked at the older man. "Seventeen. Why?"

Lothar shook his head and grunted, "That might make sense."

"Make sense how?"

"Med, I mean Lord Magus Medivh, was a young man, several years younger than yourself, when he fell ill. As a result, he never dealt much with someone of your age."

"Ill?" said Khadgar. "The Magus was ill?"

"Seriously," said Lothar. "He fell into a deep sleep, a coma they called it. Llane and I kept him at Northshire Abbey, and the holy brothers there fed him broth to keep him from wasting away. For years he was like that, then, snap, he woke up, right as rain. Or almost."

"Almost?" asked Khadgar.

"Well, he missed a large piece of his teenage years, and a few additional decades as well. He fell asleep a teenager and woke up a grown man. I always worry that it affected him."

Khadgar thought about the master mage's mercurial temperament, his sudden mood swings, and the childlike delight with which he approached battling the orcs. Were Medivh a younger man, would his actions make more sense?

"His coma," said Lothar, and shook his head at the memory. "It was unnatural. Med calls it a 'nap,' like it was perfectly reasonable. But we never found out why it happened. The Magus might have puzzled it out, but he's shown no interest in the matter, even when I've asked."

"I am Medivh's apprentice," said Khadgar simply. "Why are you telling me this?"

Lothar sighed deeply and looked out over the battle-scarred ridge. Khadgar realized that the King's Champion was a basically honest individual, who would not last a day and a half in Dalaran. His emotions were plain on his weathered, open face.

Lothar sucked on his teeth, and said, "To be honest, I worry about him. He's all alone in his tower. . . ."

"He has a castellan. And there's Cook," put in Khadgar.

". . . with all of his magic," continued Lothar. "He just seems alone. Tucked up there in the mountains. I worry about him."

Khadgar nodded, and added to himself, *And that is why you tried to get apprentices from Azeroth in there. To spy on your friend. You worry about him, but you worry about his power as well.* Aloud, Khadgar said, "You worry if he's all right."

Lothar gave a shrug, revealing both how much he did worry and how much he was willing to pretend otherwise.

"What can I do to help?" asked Khadgar. "Help him. Help you."

"Keep an eye on him," said Lothar. "If you're an apprentice, he should spend more time with you. I don't want him to . . ."

"Fall into another coma?" suggested Khadgar. *At a time when these orcs are suddenly everywhere.* For his part, Lothar rewarded him with another shrug.

Khadgar gave the best smile he could manage. "I would be honored to help you both, Lord Lothar. Know that my loyalty must be to the master mage first, but if there is anything a *friend* would need to know, I will pass it along."

Another heavy pat of the gauntlet. Khadgar marveled at how badly Lothar concealed his concerns. Were all the natives of Azeroth this open and guileless? Even now, Khadgar could see there was something else Lothar wanted to speak of.

"There's something else," said Lothar. Khadgar just nodded politely.

"Has the Lord Magus spoken of the Guardian to you?" he asked.

Khadgar thought of pretending to know more than he did, to draw out more from this older, honest man. But as the thought passed through his head, he discarded it. Best to hold to the truth.

"I have heard the name from Medivh's lips," said Khadgar. "But I know nothing of the details."

"Ah," said Lothar. "Then let it be as if I said nothing to you."

"I'm sure we will talk of it in due course," added Khadgar.

"Undoubtedly," said Lothar. "You seem like a trustworthy sort."

"After all, I've only been his apprentice for a few days," said Khadgar lazily.

Lothar's eyebrows raised. "A few days? Exactly how long have you been Medivh's apprentice?"

"Counting until dawn tomorrow?" said Khadgar, and allowed himself a smile. "That would be one."

Medivh chose that moment to return, looking more haggard than before. Lothar raised his eyebrows in a hopeful question, but the Magus merely shook his head. Lothar frowned deeply, and after exchanging a few pleasantries, left to oversee the rest of salvage and clean-up. The half of the patrol that had moved ahead along the road had returned, but had found nothing.

"Are you up for travel?" asked Medivh.

Khadgar pulled himself to his feet, and the sandy ridge in the middle of the Black Morass seemed like a ship pitching on a rough sea.

"Well enough," he said. "I don't know if I can handle a gryphon, though, even with . . ." he let his voice trail off, but touched his forehead.

"It's just as well," said Medivh. "Your mount got spooked by the arrows, and headed for the high country. We'll have to double up." He raised the rune-carved whistle to his lips and let out a series of short, sharp blasts. Far above, there was the shriek of a gryphon on the wing, circling high above them.

Khadgar looked up and said, "So, I'm your apprentice."

"Yes," said Medivh, his face a calm mask.

"I passed your tests," said the youth.

"Yes," said Medivh.

"I'm honored, sir," said Khadgar.

"I'm glad you are," said Medivh, and a ghost of a smile crossed his face. "Because now starts the hard part."

FIVE

Sands in an Hourglass

I 've seen them before," said Khadgar.

It was seven days after the battle in the swamp. With their return to the tower (and a day of recovery on Khadgar's part), the young mage's apprenticeship had begun in earnest. The first hour of the day, before breakfast, Khadgar practiced his spells under Medivh's tutelage. From breakfast until lunch and through lunch until supper, Khadgar would assist the master mage with various tasks. These consisted of making notes as Medivh read off numbers, running down to the library to recover this book or that, or merely holding a collection of tools as the Magus worked.

Which was what he was doing at this particular moment, when he finally felt comfortable enough with the older mage to tell him what he knew about the ambush.

"Seen who before?" replied his mentor, peering through a great lens at his current experiment. On his fingers the master mage wore small pointed thimbles ending in infinitely-thin needles. He was tuning something that looked like a mechanical bumblebee, which flexed its heavy wings as his needles probed it.

"The orcs," said Khadgar. "I've seen the orcs we fought before."

"You didn't mention them when you first arrived," said Medivh absentmindedly, his fingers dancing in odd precision, lancing the needles into and out of the device. "I remember asking you about other races. There was no mention. Where have you seen them?"

"In a vision. Soon after I arrived here," Khadgar said.

"Ah. You had a vision. Well, many get them here, you know. Moroes probably told you. He's a bit of a blabbermouth, you know."

"I've had one, maybe two. The one I am sure about was on a battlefield, and these creature, these orcs, were there. Attacking us. I mean, attacking the humans I was with."

"Hmmm," said Medivh, the tip of his tongue appearing beneath his moustache as he moved the needles delicately along the bumblebee's copper thorax.

"And I wasn't here," continued Khadgar. "Not in Azeroth, or Lordaeron. Wherever I was, the sky was red as blood."

Medivh bristled as if struck by an electric shock. The intricate device beneath his tools flashed brightly as the wrong parts were touched, then screamed, and then died.

"Red skies?" he said, turning away from the workbench and looking sharply at Khadgar. Energy, intense and uncaring, seemed to dance along the older man's dark brows, and the Magus's eyes were the green of a storm-tossed sea.

"Red. Like blood," said Khadgar. The young man had thought he was becoming used to Medivh's sudden and mercurial moods, but this struck him with the force of a blow.

The older mage let out a hiss. "Tell me about it. The world, the orcs, the skies," commanded Medivh, his voice like stone. "Tell me *everything.*"

Khadgar recounted the vision of his first night there, mentioning everything he could remember. Medivh interrupted constantly—what were the orcs wearing, what was the world like. What was in the sky, on the horizon. Were there any banners among the orcs. Khadgar felt his thoughts were being dissected and examined. Medivh pulled the information from Khadgar effortlessly. Khadgar told him everything.

Everything except the strange, familiar eyes of the warrior-mage commander. He did not feel right mentioning that, and Medivh's questions seemed to concentrate more on the red-skied world and the orcs than the human defenders. As he described the vision, the older mage seemed to calm down, but the choppy sea still remained beneath his bushy brows. Khadgar saw no need to upset the Magus further.

"Curious," said Medivh, slowly and thoughtfully, after Khadgar had finished. The master mage leaned back in his chair and tapped a needle-tipped finger to his lips. There was a silence that hung over the room like a shroud. At last he said, "That is a new one. A very new one indeed."

"Sir," began Khadgar.

"Medivh," reminded the master mage.

"Medivh, sir," began Khadgar again. "Where do these visions come from? Are they hauntings of some past or portents of the future?"

"Both," said Medivh, leaning back in his chair. "And neither. Go fetch an ewer of wine from the kitchen. My work is done for the day, I'm afraid, it's nearly time for supper, and this may take some explaining."

When Khadgar returned, Medivh had started a fire in the hearth and was already settling into one of the larger chairs. He held out a pair of mugs. Khadgar poured, the sweet smell of the red wine mixing with the cedar smoke.

"You do drink?" asked Medivh as an afterthought.

"A bit," said Khadgar. "It is customary to serve wine with dinner in the Violet Citadel."

"Yes," said Medivh. "You wouldn't need to if you just got rid of the lead lining for your aqueduct. Now, you were asking about visions."

"Yes, I saw what I described to you, and Moroes . . ." Khadgar hesitated for a moment, hoping not to further blacken the castellan's reputation for gossip, then decided to press on. "Moroes said that I was not alone. That people saw things like that all the time."

"Moroes is right," said Medivh, taking a long pull from the wine and smacking his lips. "A late harvest vintage, not bad at all. That this tower is a place of power should not surprise you. Mages gravitate toward such places. Such places are often where the universe wears thin, allowing it to double back on itself, or perhaps even allowing entry to the Twisting Nether and to other worlds entirely."

"Was that what I saw, then," interrupted Khadgar, "another world?"

Medivh held up a hand to hush the younger man. "I am just saying that there are places of power, which for one reason or another, become the seats of great power. One such location is here, in the Redridge Mountains. Once long ago something powerful exploded here, carving out the valley and weakening the reality around it."

"And that's why you sought it out," prompted Khadgar.

Medivh shook his head, but instead said, "That's one theory."

"You said there was an explosion long ago that created this place, and it made it a place of magical power. You then came. . . ."

"Yes," said Medivh. "That's all true, if you look at it in a linear fashion. But what happens if the explosion occurred because I would eventually come here and the place needed to be ready for me?"

Khadgar's face knitted. "But things don't happen like that."

"In the normal world, no, they do not," said Medivh. "But magic is the art of circumventing the normal. That's why the philosophical debates in the halls of the Kirin Tor are so much buffle and blow. They seek to place rationality upon the world, and regulate its motions. The stars march in order across the sky, the seasons fall one after the other with lockstepped regularity, and men and women live and die. If that does not happen, it's magic, the first warping of the universe, a few floorboards that are bent out of shape, waiting for industrious hands to pry them up."

"But for that to happen to the area to be prepared for you . . ." started Khadgar.

"The world would have to be very different than it seems," answered Medivh, "which it truly is, after all. How does time work?"

Khadgar was not thrown as much by Medivh's apparent change of topic. "Time?"

"We use it, trust it, measure by it, but what *is* it?" Medivh was smiling over the top of his cup.

"Time is a regular progression of instants. Like sands through an hourglass," said Khadgar.

"Excellent analogy," said Medivh. "One I was going to use myself, and then compare the hourglass with the mechanical clock. You see the difference between the two?"

Khadgar shook his head slowly as Medivh sipped on his wine.

Eventually, the mage spoke, "No, you're not daft, boy. It's a hard concept to wrap your brain around. The clock is a mechanical simulation of time, each beat controlled by a turning of the gears. You can look at a clock and know that everything advances by one tic of the wheel, one slip of the gears. You know what is coming next, because the original clockmaker built it that way."

"All right," said Khadgar. "Time is a clock."

"Ah, but time is also an hourglass," said the older Mage, reaching for one planted on the mantel and flipping it over. Khadgar looked at the timepiece, and tried to remember if it was there before he had brought up the wine, or even before Medivh reached for it.

"The hourglass also measures time, true?" said Medivh. "Yet here you never know which particle of sand will move from the upper half to the lower half at any instant. Were you to number the sands, the order would be slightly different each time. But the end result is always the same—all the sand has moved from the top to the bottom. What order it happens in does not matter." The old man's eyes brightened for a moment. "So?" he asked.

"So," said Khadgar. "You're saying that it may not matter if you set up your tower here because an explosion created this valley and warped the nature of reality around it, or that the explosion occurred *because* you would eventually come here, and the nature of the universe needed to give you the tools you wanted to stay."

"Close enough," said Medivh.

"So what these visions are, then, are bits of sand?" said Khadgar. Medivh frowned slightly but the youth pressed on. "If the tower is an hourglass, and not a clock, then there are bits of sand, of time itself, that are moving through it at any time. These are unstuck, or overlap each other, so that we can see them, but not clearly. Some of it is parts of the past. Some of it is parts of the future. Could some of it be of other worlds as well?"

Medivh now was thinking deeply himself. "It is possible. Full marks. Well thought out. The big thing to remember is that these visions are just that.

Visions. They waft in and out. Were the tower a clock, they would move regularly and be easily explained. But since the tower is an hourglass, then they don't. They move at their own speed, and defy us to explain their chaotic nature." Medivh leaned back in his chair. "Which I, for one, am quite comfortable with. I could never really favor an orderly, well-planned universe."

Khadgar added, "But have you ever sought out a particular vision? Wouldn't there be a way to discover a certain future, and then make sure it happened?"

Medivh's mood darkened. "Or make sure it never comes to pass," he said. "No, there are some things that even a master mage respects and stays clear of. This is one of them."

"But . . ."

"No buts," said Medivh, rising and setting his empty mug on the mantelpiece. "Now that you've had a bit of wine—let's see how that affects your magical control. Levitate my mug."

Khadgar furrowed his brow, and realized that his voice had been slightly slurred. "But we've been drinking."

"Exactly," said the master mage. "You will never know what sands the universe will throw in your face. You can either plan to be eternally vigilant and ready, eschewing life as we know it, or be willing to enjoy life and pay the price. Now try to levitate the mug."

Khadgar didn't realize until this moment how much he had drunk, and tried to clear the mushiness from his mind and lift the heavy ceramic mug from the mantel.

A few moments later, he was heading for the kitchen, looking for a broom and a pan.

In the evenings, Khadgar's time was his own, to practice and research, as Medivh dealt with other matters. Khadgar wondered what the other matters were, but assumed they included correspondence, for twice a week a dwarf on gryphon-back arrived at the topmost tower with a satchel, and left with a larger satchel.

Medivh gave the young man free license in the library to research as he saw fit, including the myriad questions that his former masters in the Violet Citadel had requested.

"My only demand," said Medivh with a smile, "is that you show me what you write before you send it to them." Khadgar must have shown his embarrassment, because Medivh added, "Not because I fear you'll keep something from me, Young Trust, but because I'd hate for them to know something that I had forgotten about."

So Khadgar plunged into the books. For Guzbah he found an ancient, well-read scroll with an epic poem, its numbered stanzas precisely detailing a battle between Medivh's mother Aegwynn and an unnamed demon. For Lady Delth he made a listing of the moldering elven tomes in the library. And for Alonda he plunged through those bestiaries he could read, but could not push the number of troll species past four.

Khadgar also spent his free time with his lock picks and his personal opening spells. He still sought to master those books that foiled his earlier attempts to crack them open. These tomes had strong magics on them, and he could spend an evening among his divinations before getting even the first hint what style of spell protected their contents.

Lastly, there was the subject of the Guardian. Medivh had mentioned it, and Lord Lothar had assumed that the Magus had confided it to the young man, and backed off quickly when the King's Champion had found it not to be the case.

The Guardian, it seemed, was a phantom, no more or no less real than the time-skewed visions that seemed to move through the tower. There was a mention in passing of a Guardian (always capitalized) in this elven tome, a reference in the Azeroth's royal histories of a Guardian attending this wedding or that funeral, or being in the vanguard of some attack. Always present, but never identified. Was this Guardian a position, or, like Medivh's supposed near-immortal mother, a single being?

There were other phantoms that orbited this Guardian as well. An order of some sort, an organization—was the Guardian a holy knight? And the word "Tirisfal" was written in the margins of one grimoire, and then erased, such that only Khadgar's skill at examination told him what was once written there by the carving the pen had done in the parchment. A name of a particular Guardian, or the organization, or something else entirely?

It was the evening that Khadgar found this word, four days after the incident with the mug, that the young man fell into a new vision. Or rather, a vision snuck up on him and surrounded him, swallowing him whole.

It was the smell that came to him first, a soft vegetable warmth among the moldering texts, a fragrance that slowly rose into the room. The heat rose in the room, not uncomfortably, but as a warm damp blanket. The walls darkened and turned green, and vines trellised up the sides of the bookcases, passing through and replacing the volumes that were there and spreading wide, flat leaves. Large pale moonflowers and crimson star orchids sprouted among the stacked scrolls.

Khadgar took a deep breath, but more from anticipation than fear. This was not the world of harsh land and orc armies that he had seen before. This was something different. This was a jungle, but it was a jungle on this world. The thought comforted him.

And the table disappeared, and the book, and Khadgar was left sitting at a campfire with three other young men. They seemed to be about his age, and were on some sort of expedition. Sleeping rolls had been laid out, and the stewpot, empty and already cleaned, was drying by the fire. All three were dressed for riding, but their clothes were well tailored and of good quality.

The three men were laughing and joking, though, as before, Khadgar could not make out the exact words. The blond one in the middle was in the midst of telling a story, and from his hand motions, one involving a nicely apportioned young woman.

The one on his right laughed and slapped a knee as the blond one continued his tale. This one ran his fingers through his hair, and Khadgar noticed that his dark hair was already receding. That was when he realized he was looking at Lord Lothar. The eyes and nose were his, and the smile just the same, but the flesh was not yet weathered and his beard was not graying. But it was him.

Khadgar looked at the third man, and knew at once it had to be Medivh. This one was dressed in a dark green hunter's garb, his hood pulled back to reveal a young, mirthful face. His eyes were burnished jade in the light of the campfire, and he favored the blond one's story with an embarrassed smile.

The blond one in the center made a point and motioned to the young Medivh, who shrugged, clearly embarrassed. The blond one's story apparently involved the future Magus as well.

The blond one had to be Llane, now King Llane of Azeroth. Yes, the early stories of the three of them had found their way even into the Violet Citadel's archives. The three of them often wandered through the borders of the kingdom, exploring and putting down all manner of raiders and monsters.

Llane concluded his story and Lothar nearly fell back over the log he was sitting upon, roaring with laughter. Medivh suppressed a laugh himself into his curled hand, looking like he was merely clearing his throat.

Lothar's laughter subsided, and Medivh said something, opening his palms upward to make a point. Lothar *did* pitch backward now, and Llane himself put his face in his hand, his body heaving in amusement. Apparently whatever Medivh said topped Llane's story entirely.

Then something moved in the surrounding jungle. The three stopped their revelry at once—they must have heard it. Khadgar, the ghost at this gathering, more felt it instead; something malevolent lurking at the borders of the campfire.

Lothar rose slowly and reached for a great, wide-bladed sword laying in its sheath at his feet. Llane stood up, reaching behind his log to pull out a double-headed ax, and motioned for Lothar to go one way, Medivh to go the other. Medivh had risen as well by this point, and though his hands were empty he, even at this age, was the most powerful of the three.

Llane with his broadax loped forward to one side of the campsite. He might have imagined himself as stealthy, but Khadgar saw him move with firm-footed deliberation. He wanted whatever was there at the edge to reveal itself.

The thing obliged, bursting from its place of concealment. It was half again as tall as any of the young men, and for one instant he thought it was some gigantic orc.

Then he recognized it from bestiaries that Alonda had him peruse. It was a troll, one of the jungle breed, its blue-hued skin pale in the moonlight, its long gray hair lacquered upright into a crest that ran from its forehead back to the nape of the neck. Like the orcs, it had fangs jutting from its lower jaw, but these were rounded, peglike tusks, thicker than the sharp teeth of the orcs. Its ears and nose were elongated, parodies of human flesh. It was dressed in skins, and chains made of human finger bones danced on its bare chest.

The troll let out a battle roar, baring its teeth and its chest in rage, and feinted with its spear. Llane swung at the outthrust weapon, but his blow went wide. Lothar charged from one side, and Medivh came up as well, eldritch energy dancing off his fingertips.

The troll sidestepped Lothar's greatsword, and danced back another step when Llane shredded the air with his huge ax. Each step covered more than a yard, and the two warriors pressed the troll each time it retreated. It used the spear more as a shield than a weapon, holding the haft two-handed and knocking aside the blow.

Khadgar realized the creature wasn't fighting to kill the humans, not yet. It was trying to pull them into position.

In the vision, the young Medivh must have realized the same thing, because he shouted something to the others.

But by this time it was too late, for two other trolls chose that moment to leap from their hiding places on either side of the combat.

Llane, for all his planning, was the one caught by surprise, and the spear skewered his right arm. The broadax's blade bit into the earth as the future king screamed a curse.

The other two concentrated on Lothar, and now the warrior was being forced back, using his broad blade with consummate dexterity, foiling first one thrust, then the other. Still, the jungle trolls showed their strategy—they were driving the two warriors apart, separating Llane from Lothar, forcing Medivh to choose.

Medivh chose Llane. From his phantom viewpoint Khadgar guessed it was because Llane was already wounded. Medivh charged, his hands flaming. . . .

And caught the butt end of the troll's spear in the face, as the troll slammed the heavy haft against Medivh's jaw, then turned and with one elegant motion pummeled the wounded Llane. Medivh went down, and so did Llane, and the ax, spun out of the future sovereign's hand.

The troll hesitated a moment, trying to determine who to kill first. It chose Medivh, sprawled on the ground at its feet, the closer of the two. The troll raised the spear and the obsidian point glowed evil in the moonlight.

The young Medivh choked off a series of syllables. A small tornado of dust rose from the ground and flung itself into the troll's face, blinding it. The troll hesitated for a moment, and clawed at its dusty orbs with one hand.

The hesitation was all Medivh needed, for he lunged forward, not with a spell, but with a simple knife, plunging it into the back of the troll's thigh. The troll gave a scream in the night, stabbing blindly. The spear dug into where Medivh had been, for the young mage had rolled to one side and was now rising, his fingertips crackling.

He muttered a word and lightning gathered in a ball between his fingers and lanced forward. The troll jolted from the shock and hung for a moment, caught in a blue-limned seizure. The creature fell to its knees, and even then was not done, for it tried to rise, its rheumy red eyes burning with hatred for the wizard.

The troll never got its chance, for a shadow rose behind it, and Llane's recovered ax gleamed briefly in the moonlight before coming down on the troll's head, bisecting it at the neck. The creature sprawled forward, and the two young men, as well as Khadgar, turned to the trolls battling with Lothar.

The future champion was holding his own, but just barely, and had backed almost across the entire campsite. The trolls had heard the death scream of their brother, and one continued to press his attack as the other charged back to deal with the two humans. It let out an inarticulate bellow as it crossed the campsite, its spear before it like a knight on horseback.

Llane charged in return, but at the last moment veered to one side, dancing aside the spear's point. The troll took two more steps forward, which brought him up to the campfire itself, and where Medivh was waiting.

Now the mage seemed to be full of energy and, limned by the coals before him, looked demonic in his demeanor. He had his arms wide, and he was chanting something harsh and rhythmic.

And the fire itself leaped up, taking a brief animated form of a giant lion, and leaped on the attacking troll. The jungle troll screamed as the coals, logs, and ash wrapped itself around him like a cloak, and would not be shrugged off.

The troll flung itself on the ground and rolled first one way and then the other, trying to dampen the flame, but it did no good. Finally the troll stopped moving entirely, and the hungry flames consumed it.

For his part, Llane continued his charge and buried his ax in the side of the surviving troll. The beast let out a howl, but its moment's hesitation was all that Lothar needed. The champion batted away the outthrust spear with a backhanded blow, then with a level, precise swing cut the troll's head cleanly from its shoulders. The head bounced into the brush, and was lost.

Llane, though bleeding from his own wound, slapped Lothar on the back, apparently taunting him for taking so long with his troll. Then Lothar put a hand to Llane's chest to quiet him, and pointed at Medivh.

The young mage was still standing over the fire, his hands held open, but fingers hooked like claws. His eyes were glassy in the surviving firelight, and his jaw was tightly clenched. As the two men (and the phantom Khadgar) ran over to him, the young man pitched backward.

By the time the pair reached Medivh, he was breathing heavily, and his pupils were wide in the moonlight. Warriors and vision visitor leaned over him, as the young mage strained to push the words out of his mouth.

"Watch out for me," he said, looking at neither Llane nor Lothar, but at Khadgar. Then the young Medivh's eyes rolled up in his head and he lay very still.

Lothar and Llane were trying to revive their friend, but Khadgar just stepped back. Had Medivh truly seen him, as the other mage, the one with his eyes on the war-swept plains, had? And he had heard him, clear words spoken almost to the depth of his soul.

Khadgar turned and the vision dropped away as quickly as a magician's curtain. He was back in the library again, and he almost stumbled into Medivh himself.

"Young Trust," said Medivh, the version much older than the one laying on the ground in the vanished vision. "Are you all right? I called out, but you did not answer."

"Sorry Med . . . sir," said Khadgar, taking a deep breath. "It was a vision. I was lost in it, I'm afraid."

Medivh's dark brows drew together. "Not more orcs and red skies?" he asked seriously, and Khadgar saw a touch of the storm in those green eyes.

Khadgar shook his head and chose his words carefully. "Trolls. Blue trolls, and it was a jungle. I think it was this world. The sky was the same."

Medivh's concern deflated and he just said, "Jungle trolls. I met some once, down south, in the Stranglethorn Vale. . . ." The mage's features softened as he himself seemed to become lost in a vision of his own. Then he shook his head. "But no orcs this time, right? You are sure."

"No, sir," said Khadgar. He did not want to mention that it was that battle he was witnessing. Was it a bad memory for Medivh? Was this the time when he slipped into the coma?

Looking at the older mage, Khadgar could see much of the young man from the vision. He was taller, but slightly stooped from his years and researches, yet there was the young man wrapped within the older form.

Medivh for his part said, "Do you have 'Song of Aegwynn'?"

Khadgar shook himself out of his thoughts. "The song?"

"Of my mother," said Medivh. "It would be an old scroll. I swear I can't find anything here since you've cleaned!"

"It is with the other epic poetry, sir," said Khadgar. *He should tell him about the vision,* he thought. Was this a random event, or was it brought on by his meeting of Lothar? Was finding out about things triggering visions?

Medivh crossed to the shelf, and running a finger along the scrolls, pulled out the needed version, old, and well worn. He unwound it partway, checked it against a scrap of paper in his pocket, then rewound and replaced it.

"I have to go," he said suddenly. "Tonight, I'm afraid."

"Where are we going?" asked Khadgar.

"I go alone, this time," said the elder mage, already striding toward the door. "I will leave instructions for your studies with Moroes."

"When will you return?" shouted Khadgar after his retreating form.

"When I am back!" bellowed Medivh, taking the stairs up two at a time already. Khadgar imagined the castellan already at the top of the tower, with his runic whistle and tame gryphon at the ready.

"Fine," said Khadgar, looking at the books. "I'll just sit here and figure out how to tame an hourglass."

SIX

Aegwynn and Sargeras

Medivh was gone a week, all told, and it was a week well spent for Khadgar. He installed himself in the library, and had Moroes bring his meals there. On more than one occasion he did not even reach his quarters in the evening, rather spending the time sleeping on the great library tables themselves. Ultimately, he was searching for visions.

His own correspondence went unanswered as he plumbed the ancient tomes and grimoires on questions about time, light, and magic. His early reports had drawn quick responses from the mages of the Violet Citadel. Guzbah wanted a transcription of the epic poem of Aegwynn. Lady Delth declared that she recognized none of the titles he sent her—could he send them again, this time with the first paragraph of each, so she knew what they were? And Alonda was adamant that there had to be a fifth breed of troll, and that Khadgar had obviously not found the proper bestiaries. The young mage was delighted to leave their demands unanswered as he sought out a way of taming the visions.

The key to his incantation, it seemed, would be a simple spell of farseeing, a divination that granted sight of distant objects and far-off locations. A book of priestly magic had described it as an incantation of holy vision, yet it worked as well for Khadgar as it did for their clerics. While that priestly spell functioned over space, perhaps with modification it could function over time. Khadgar reasoned that this would normally be impossible given the flow of time in a determinant, clockwork universe.

But it seemed that within the walls of Karazhan, at least, time was an hourglass, and identifying bits of disjointed time was more likely. And once one hooked into one grain of time, it would be easier to move that grain to another.

If others had attempted this within the walls of Medivh's Tower, there was no clue within the library, unless it was within the most heavily guarded or unreadable of the tomes located on the iron balcony. Curiously, the notes in Medivh's own hand were uninterested in the visions, which seemed to dominate other notes from other visitors. Did Medivh keep that information in another location, or was he truly more interested in matters beyond the walls of the citadel than the activities within it?

Refitting a spell for a new activity was not as simple as changing an incantation here, altering a motion there. It required a deep and precise understanding of how divination worked, of what it revealed and how. When a hand-motion changes, or the type of incense used is deleted, the result is most likely complete failure, where the energies are dissipated harmlessly. Occasionally the energies may go wild and out of control, but usually the only result of a failed spell is a frustrated spellcaster.

In his studies, Khadgar discovered that if a spell fails in a spectacular fashion, it indicates that the failed spell is very close to the final intended spell. The magics are trying to close the gap, to make things happen, though not always with the results intended by the caster. Of course, sometimes these failed magic-users did not survive the experience.

During the process, Khadgar was afraid that Medivh would return at any time, wafting back into the library, looking for the well-read epic poem or some other bit of trivia. Would he tell his master what he was trying? And if he did, would Medivh encourage him, or forbid him from trying to find out?

After five days, Khadgar felt he had the spellmaking complete. The framework remained that of the farseeing, but it was now empowered with a random factor to allow it to reach through and search out the discontinuities that seemed to exist within the tower. These bits of misplaced time would be a little brighter, a little hotter, or simply a little odder than the immediate surroundings, and as such attract the full force of the spell itself.

The spell, if it functioned, should in addition tune in the vision better. This would collect the sounds at the other end and remove the distortion, concentrating them in the same fashion as an elderly person cupping a hand to the ear to hear better. It would not work for sounds beyond the central location as well, but should clarify what individuals were saying in addition to what the caster was seeing.

The evening of the fifth day, Khadgar had completed his calculations, the neat rows and orders of power and casting laid out in a simple script. Should something go horribly wrong, at least Medivh would figure out what had happened.

Medivh, of course, kept a fully equipped pantry of spell components, including a larder of aromatic and thaumaturgic herbs, and a lapidarium of crushed semiprecious stones. Of these Khadgar chose amethyst to lay out his magical circle, in the library itself, crisscrossing it with runes of powered rose quartz. He reviewed the words of power (most of them known to the young mage before he left Dalaran) and worked through the motions (almost all of them original). Dressed in conjuration robes (more for luck than effect), he stepped within the casting circle.

Khadgar let his mind settle and become calm. This was no quickly-cast battle spell, or some offhand cantrip. Rather this was a deep and powerful spell, one that, if within the Violet Citadel, would set off the warning abjurations of other mages and bring them flying to him.

He took a deep breath, and began to cast.

Within his mind, the spell began to form, a warm, hot ball of energy. He could feel it congeal within him, as rainbow ripples moved across the surface. This was the core of the spell, usually quickly dispatched to alter the real world as its caster saw fit.

Khadgar fitted the sphere with the attributes he desired, to seek out the bits of time that seemed to haunt the tower, sort through them, and bring together a single vision, one that he could witness spread before him. The ideas seemed to sink with the imaginary sphere in his mind, and in return the sphere seemed to hum at a higher pitch, awaiting only release and direction.

"Bring me a vision," said the young mage. "Bring me a vision of the young Medivh."

With the sound of an egg imploding the magic was gone from his mind, seeping into the real world to carry out his bidding. There was a rush of air, and as Khadgar looked around, the library began to transform, as it had before, the vision moving slowly into his space and time.

Only when it suddenly got colder did Khadgar realize he had called up the wrong vision.

It moved through the library suddenly, a cold draft as if someone had left a window open. The breeze went from a draft to a chill to an arctic blast, and despite his own knowledge that it was merely illusion, Khadgar shivered to his core.

The walls of the library fell away as the vision took hold with an expanse of white. The chill wind curled around the books and manuscripts and left a blanket of snow as it passed, thick and hard. Tables, shelves, and chairs were obscured and then eliminated with the swirls of thick heavy flakes.

And Khadgar was on a hillside, his feet disappearing at his knees into a bank of snow, but leaving no mark. He was a ghost within this vision.

Still, his breath frosted and curled upward as he looked around him. To his right was a copse of trees, dark evergreens loaded down by the passing snowstorm. Far to his left was a great white cliff. Khadgar thought it some chalky substance, and then realized that it was ice, as if someone had taken a frozen river and uprooted it. The ice river was as tall as some of the mountains on Dalaran, and small dark shapes moved above it. Hawks or eagles, though they would have to be of immense size if they were truly near the icy cliffs.

Ahead of him was a vale, and moving up the vale was an army.

The army melted the snow as it passed, leaving a smudged mark of black behind it like a slug's trail. The members of the army were dressed in red, wearing great horned helms and long, high-backed black cloaks. They were hunters, for they wore all manner of weapons.

At the head of the army, its leader bore a standard, and atop the standard rode a dripping, decapitated head. Khadgar thought it some great green-scaled beast, but stopped himself when he realized it was a dragon's head.

He had seen a skull of such a creature in the Violet Citadel, but never thought that he would see one that had recently been alive. How far back had his vision truly thrown him?

The army of giant-things were bellowing what could have been a marching song, though it could just as easily have been a string of curses or a challenging cry. The voices were muddled, as if they were at the bottom of a great well, but at least Khadgar could hear them.

As they grew closer, Khadgar realized what they were. Their ornate helmets were not helms, but rather horns that jutted from their own flesh. Their cloaks were not garments but great batlike wings that jutted from their backs. Their red-tinged armor was their own thick flesh, glowing from within and melting the snow.

They were demons, creatures from Guzbah's lectures and Korrigan's hidden pamphlets. Monstrous beings that exceeded even the orcs in their bloodthirst and sadism. The great, broad-bladed swords were clearly bathed in crimson, and now Khadgar could see that their bodies were spattered with gore as well.

They were here, wherever and whenever here was, and they were hunting dragons.

There was a soft, distorted sound behind him, no more than a footfall on a soft carpet. Khadgar turned, and he realized that he was not alone on the hillock overlooking the demon hunting party.

She had come up from behind him unawares, and if she saw him, she paid him no mind. Just as the demons seemed a blight incarnate on the land, so, too, did she radiate her own sense of power. This was a brilliant power that seemed to fold and intensify as she glided along atop the surface of the snow itself. She was real, but her white leather boots left only the faintest marks in the snow.

She was tall and powerful and unafraid of the abomination in the valley below. Her garb was as white and unspoiled as the snow around them, and she wore a vest made of small silver scales. A great white hooded fur cape with a lining of green silk billowed behind her, held at her throat by a large green stone which matched her eyes. She wore her blond hair simply, held in place by a silver diadem, and seemed less affected by the cold than the ghostly Khadgar.

Yet it was her eyes that held his attention—green as summer forest, green as polished jade, green as the ocean after a storm. Khadgar recognized those eyes, for he had felt the penetrating gaze of similar eyes, but from her son.

This was Aegwynn. Medivh's mother, the powerful near-immortal mage that was so old as to become a legend.

Khadgar also realized where he must be, and this was Aegwynn's battle against the demon hordes, a legend saved only in fragments, in the cantos of an epic poem on the library shelf.

With a pang Khadgar realized where his spell had gone wrong. Medivh had asked for that scroll before leaving, the last time Khadgar had seen him. Perhaps the spell misfired, passing through a vision of Medivh himself most recently into the very legend that he was checking?

Aegwynn frowned as she looked down on the demonic hunting party, the single line dividing her eyebrows showing her displeasure. Her jade eyes flashed, and Khadgar could guess that a storm of power was brewing within her.

It did not take long for that anger to be released. She raised an arm, chanted a short, clipped phrase, and lightning danced from her fingertips.

This was no mere conjurer's bolt, nor even the harshest strike of a summer thunderstorm. This was a shard of elemental lightning, arcing through the cold air and finding its ground in the surprised demonic armor. The air split down to its most basic elements as the bolt cleaved through it, and the air smelled sharp and bitter in its passing, the air thundering in to replace the space the bolt had briefly filled. Despite himself, despite knowing that he was phantom, despite knowing that this was a vision, despite all this and the fact that the noise was muted by his ghostly state, Khadgar grimaced and recoiled at the flash and metallic tolling of the mystic bolt.

The bolt struck the standard bearer, the one bearing the severed head of the great green dragon. It immolated the demon where he stood, and those around it were blasted from their feet, falling like hot coals in the snow. Some did not rise again.

But the majority of the hunting party were outside the spell's effect, whether by accident or design. The demons, each one larger than ten men, recoiled in shock, but that lasted only a moment. The largest of them bellowed something in a language that sounded like broken metal bells, and half of the demons took wing, charging Aegwynn's (and Khadgar's) position. The other half pulled out heavy bows of black oak and iron arrows. As they fired the arrows, they ignited, and a rain of fire descended upon them.

Aegwynn did not flinch, but merely raised a hand in a sweeping motion. The entire sky between her and the fiery rain erupted in a wall of bluish flame, which swallowed the orange-red bolts as if they had simply fallen into a river.

Yet the bolts were merely to provide cover for the attackers, who burst through the blue wall of fire as it dissipated and dropped on Aegwynn from above. There had to be at least twenty of them, each a giant, darkening the skies with their huge wings.

Khadgar looked at Aegwynn and saw that she was smiling. It was a knowing, self-confident smile, and one that the young mage had seen on Medivh's face, when they had fought the orcs. She was more than confident.

Khadgar looked down the valley to where the archers had been. They had abandoned their useless missiles but now were gathered together, chanting in a low, buzzing tone. The air warped around them, and a hole appeared in reality, a dark malignancy against the pristine white. And from that hole dropped more demons—creatures of every description, with the heads of animals, with flaming eyes, with wings of bats and insects and great scavenging birds. These demons joined the choir and the rift opened farther, sucking more and more of the spawn of the Twisting Nether into the cold northern air.

Aegwynn paid the chanters and reinforcements no mind, but rather coolly concentrated on those dropping on her from above.

She passed her hand, palm up. Half of those that flew were turned to glass, and all of them were knocked from the sky. Those that had been turned to crystal shattered where they struck with discordant chords. Those that were still living landed with a heavy thump, and rose again, their ichor-splattered weapons drawn. There were ten left.

Aegwynn placed her left fist against her upright right palm, and four of the survivors melted, their ruddy flesh melting off the bones as they slumped into the snow banks. They screamed until their decaying throats filled with their own desiccated flesh. There were six left.

Aegwynn clutched at the air and three more demons exploded as their interiors turned into insects and ripped them from the inside out. They didn't even have time to scream as their forms were replaced by swarms of gnats, bees, and wasps, which boiled out toward the forests. There were three left.

Aegwynn pulled her hands apart and a demon had its arms and legs ripped from its torso by invisible hands. Two left. Aegwynn raised two fingers and a demon turned to sand, its dying curse lost on the chill breeze.

One left. It was the largest, the leader, the bellower of orders. At close range Khadgar could see that its bare chest was a pattern of scars, and one eye socket was empty. The other burned with hate.

It did not attack. Neither did Aegwynn. Instead they stopped, frozen for a moment, while the valley beneath them filled with demons.

Finally the great behemoth of a demon snarled. His voice was clear but distant to Khadgar's ears.

"You are a fool, Guardian of Tirisfal," it said, wrapping its lips around the uncomfortable human language.

Aegwynn let out a laugh, as sharp and as thin as a glass dagger. "Am I, foulspawn? I came here to spoil your dragon hunt. It seems that I have succeeded."

"You are an overconfident fool," slurred the demon. "While you have been fighting only a few, my brothers in sorcery have brought in others. A legion of others. Every incubus and petty demon, every nightmare and shadow-hound, every dark lord and captain of the Burning Legion. All have come here while you have fought these few."

"I know," said Aegwynn, calmly.

"You *know?*" bellowed the demon with a throaty laugh. "You know that you are alone in the wilderness, with every demon raised against you. You *know?*"

"I know," said Aegwynn, and there was a smile in the voice. "I know you would bring as many of your allies as possible. A Guardian would be too great a target for you to resist."

"*You know?*" shouted the demon again. "And you came anyway, alone, to this forsaken place?"

"I know," said Aegwynn. "But I never said I was alone."

Aegwynn snapped her fingers and the sky suddenly darkened, as if a great flock of birds had been disturbed, and blocked the sun.

Except they were not birds. They were dragons. More dragons than Khadgar even imagined existing. They hovered in place on their great wings, waiting for the Guardian's signal.

"Foulspawn of the Burning Legion," said Aegwynn. "It is you that are the fool."

The demonic leader let out a cry and raised its blood-spattered sword. Aegwynn was too quick for it, and raised a hand, three fingers outstretched. The foulspawn's scar-ridden chest evaporated, leaving only a cloud of bloody motes. His brawny arms fell away to each side, its abandoned legs folded and it collapsed, and its head, registering nothing so much as a look of shocked surprise, fell into the melting snow and was lost.

That was the signal for the dragons, for as one they turned on the collected horde of summoned demons. The great flying creatures swooped down from all sides, and flame sprung from their open maws. The front rows of demons were immolated, reduced to no more than ash in an instant, while others struggled to pull out their weapons, to ready their own spells, to flee the field.

In the center of the army, a chant went up, this one an intense pleading, and a passionate cry. These were the most powerful of the demonic spellcasters, who concentrated their energies as those at the borders fought off the dragons at deadly cost.

The demons regrouped and retaliated, and dragons now began to fall from the sky, their bodies riddled by iron arrows and flaming bolts, by sorcerous poisons and by maddening visions. Still, the circle around the center of the demons shrank as more and more of the dragons took their revenge against the demons for the hunt, and the cries in the center became more desperate and indistinct.

Khadgar looked at Aegwynn, and she was standing stock-still in the snow, her fists clenched, her green eyes blazing with power, her teeth locked in a hideous grin. She was chanting, too, something dark and inhuman and beyond even Khadgar's ability to recognize. She was fighting the spell the demons had constructed, but she was pulling energy from it as well, bending mystic force contained within back on itself, like layers of steel in a sword's blade are folded back on themselves to make the blade stronger and more potent.

The cries of the demons in the center reached a fever pitch, and now Aegwynn was shouting herself, a nimbus of energy coalesced around her. Her hair was loose and flying now, and she raised both arms and unleashed the last words of her conjuration.

And there was a flash at the center of the demonic horde, at the center where the casters chanted and screamed and prayed. It was a rip in the universe, this time a bright rip, as if a doorway into the sun itself had been opened. The energy spiraled outward, and the demons did not even have time to scream as it overtook them, burning them out and leaving the shadows of their afterimage as their only testament.

All of the demons were caught, and a few of the dragons as well who strayed too close to the center of the demonic horde. They were caught like moths in a flame and snuffed out just as surely.

Aegwynn let out a ragged breath and smiled. It was the smile of the wolf, of the predator, of the victor. Where the demonic horde had been there was now a pillar of smoke, rising to the heavens in a great cloud.

But as Khadgar watched, the cloud flattened and gathered in on itself, growing darker and more intense, like the anvil of a thunderhead. Yet in redoubling itself, it grew stronger, and its heart grew blacker, verging on shades of purple and ebony.

And from out of the darkened cloud Khadgar saw a god emerge.

It was a titanic figure, larger than any giant of myth, greater than any dragon. Its skin looked like it was cast in bronze, and it wore black armor made of molten obsidian. Its great beard and wild hair were made of living flames, and huge horns jutted from above its dark brow. Its eyes were the color of the Infinite Abyss. It strode out of the dark cloud, and the earth shook where its feet fell. It carried a huge spear engraved with runes that dripped burning blood, and it had a long tail ending in a fireball.

What dragons were left fled the field, heading for the dark forest and the distant cliffs. Khadgar could not blame them. As much power as Medivh held within him, as much great power that his mother now showed, it was like two small candles compared to the raw power of this lord of the demons.

"Sargeras," hissed Aegwynn.

"Guardian," thundered the great demon, in a voice as deep as the ocean itself. In the distance, the ice cliffs collapsed rather than echo this hellish voice.

The Guardian pulled herself up to her full height, brushed back a stray blond hair, and said, "I have broken your toys. You are finished here. Flee while you still have your life."

Khadgar looked at the Guardian as if she had lost her mind. Even to his eyes she was exhausted from her experience, almost as empty as Khadgar had been against the orcs. Surely this titanic demon could see through the ruse. The epic poem spoke of Aegwynn's victory. Was he about to witness her death, instead?

Sargeras did not laugh, but his voice rolled across the land, pressing down on Khadgar nonetheless. "The time of Tirisfal is about to end," said the demon. "This world will soon bow before the onslaught of the Legion."

"Not as long as there is a Guardian," said Aegwynn. "Not as long as I live, or those who come after me." Her fingers curled slightly, and Khadgar could see that she was summoning power within herself, gathering her wits, her will, and her energy into one great assault. Despite himself, Khadgar took a step back, then another, then a third. If his elder self could see him in the vision, if young Medivh could see him, could not these two great powers, mage and monster, see him as well?

Or was he too small to notice, perhaps?

"Surrender now," said Sargeras. "I have use of your power."

"No," said Aegwynn, her hands in tight balls.

"Then die, Guardian, and let your world die with you," said the titanic demon, and raised his bleeding rune-spear.

Aegwynn raised both hands, and unleashed a shout, half-curse and half-prayer. A flaming rainbow of colors unseen on this world erupted from her palms, snaking upward like a sentient strike of lightning. It struck like a dagger thrust in the center of Sargeras's chest.

It seemed to Khadgar like a bow-shot fired against a boat, as small and as ineffective. Yet Sargeras staggered under the blow, taking a half-step backward and dropping his huge spear. It struck the ground like a meteorite hitting the earth, and the snow rippled beneath Khadgar's feet. He fell to one knee, but looked up at the demon lord.

When Aegwynn's spell had struck, there was a darkness spreading. No, not a darkness, but rather a coolness, the heated bronze flesh of the titan-demon dying and being replaced with a cold, inert mass. It radiated from the center of its chest like a wildfire, leaving consumed flesh behind it.

Sargeras regarded the growing devastation with surprise, then alarm, then fear. He raised a hand to touch it, and it spread to that limb as well, leaving an inert mass of rough, black metal behind. Now Sargeras starting chanting himself, pulling together what energies he possessed to reverse the process, to staunch the flow, to put out the consuming fire. His words grew hotter and more passionate, and his unaffected skin flicked with renewed intensity. He was glowing like a sun, shouting curses as the dark coolness reached where his heart should have been.

And then there was another flash, this one as intense as the one that consumed the demon horde, centered on Sargeras himself. Khadgar looked away, looked at Aegwynn, who watched as the fire and darkness consumed her foe. The brightness of the light dimmed the day itself, and long shadows stretched out behind the mage.

And then it was over. Khadgar blinked as his eyes regained their sight. He turned back to the vale and there was the titanic Sargeras, inert as a thing made of wrought iron, the power burned out of him. Beneath his weight, the heated arctic ground started to give way, and slowly his dead form fell forward, remaining whole as it mashed into the ground. The air around them was still.

Aegwynn laughed. Khadgar looked at her, and she looked drained, both by exhaustion and by madness. She rubbed her hands and chuckled and started to walk down toward the toppled titan. Khadgar noticed that she no longer rested delicately atop the drifts, but now had to slog her way down the hill.

As she left him, the library began to return. The snow began to sublimate in thick clouds of steam, and the shadowy forms of the shelves, the upper gallery, and the chairs slowly made themselves visible.

Khadgar turned slightly, back toward where the table should have been, and everything was back to normal. The library reasserted its reality with a firm suddenness.

Khadgar let out a chill breath and rubbed his skin. Cool, but not cold. The spell had worked well enough, in generalities if not particulars. It had called the vision, but not the desired one. The question was what went wrong, and what was the best way to fix it.

The young mage reached for his scribe's pouch, pulling from it a blank sheet of parchment and tools. He fitted a metal nub to the end of his stylus, melted some of the octopus ink in a bowl, and quickly began to note everything that happened, how he cast the initial spell, to Aegwynn sinking deeper in the snow as she walked away.

He was still working an hour later when there was a cadaverous cough at the doorway. Khadgar was so wrapped up in thought that he did not notice until Moroes coughed a second time.

Khadgar looked up, mildly irritated. There was something important he was about to write, but it was eluding him. Something that was just at the corner of his mind's eye.

"The Magus is back," said Moroes. "Wants you up at the observatory level."

Khadgar looked at Moroes blankly for a moment, before the words gained purchase in his mind. "Medivh's back?" he managed at last.

"That's what I said," groaned Moroes, each word given grudgingly. "You're to fly to Stormwind with him."

"Stormwind? Me? Why?" managed the younger mage.

"You're the apprentice, that's why," scowled Moroes. "Observatory, top level. I've summoned the gryphons."

Khadgar looked at his work—line upon line of neat handwriting, delving into every detail. There was something else that he was thinking about. Instead he said, "Yes. Yes. Let me gather my things up. Finish this."

"Take your time," said the castellan. "It's only the Magus that wants you to fly with him to Stormwind Castle. Nothing important." And Moroes faded back into the hallway. "Top level," came his disembodied voice, almost as an afterthought.

Stormwind! thought Khadgar. *King Llane's castle.* What would be important enough for him to have to go there? Perhaps a report of the orcs?

Khadgar looked at his writing. With the news that Medivh was back, and that they would leave soon, his thoughts were disrupted, and now his mind was on the new task. He looked at the last words he wrote on the parchment.

Aegwynn has two shadows, it said.

Khadgar shook his head. Whatever course his mind was following was gone now. He carefully blotted the excess ink to make sure it did not smear, and set the pages aside. Then he gathered his tools, and quickly headed for his quarters. He would have to change into traveling clothes if he was going gryphon-back, and would need to pack his good conjuring cloak if he was going to meet royalty.

SEVEN
Stormwind

U p until then, the greatest buildings that Khadgar had ever seen had been the Violet Citadel itself, on Cross Island outside the city of Dalaran. The majestic spires and great halls of the Kirin Tor, roofed by thick slate the color of lapis lazuli, which gave the citadel its name, had been a point of pride for Khadgar. In all his travels through Lordaeron and into Azeroth, nothing, not even Medivh's Tower, came close to the ancient grandeur of the citadel of the Kirin Tor.

Until he came to Stormwind.

They had flown through the night, as before, and this time the young mage was convinced he had slept while guiding the gryphon through the chill night air. Whatever knowledge Medivh had placed in his mind was still operating, for he was sure with his ability to guide the winged predator with his knees, and felt quite at home. The part of his brain where the knowledge resided felt no pain this time, but rather a slight thrumming, like the mental tissue had healed over, leaving scar tissue, taking the knowledge within but still recognizing it as a separate part of him.

He woke as the sun crested the horizon behind him, and panicked momentarily, causing the great flier to bank slightly, dragging it away from following in Medivh's wake. Ahead of him, sudden and brilliant in the morning sun, was Stormwind.

It was a citadel of gold and silver. The walls in the morning light seemed to glow with their own radiance, burnished like a chalice under a castellan's cleaning. The roofs glittered as if crafted from silver, and for a moment Khadgar thought they were set with innumerable small gems.

The young mage blinked and shook his head. The golden walls became mere stone, though polished to a fine luster in some places, intricately carved in others. The roofs of silver were merely dark slate, and what he thought were gemstones merely collected dew rainbowing back the dawn.

And yet Khadgar was still astounded by the city's size. As great if not greater than anything in Lordaeron, and seen from this great height, it spread out before him. He counted three full sets of walls ribboned around the central keep, and lesser barriers separating different wards. Everywhere he looked, there was more city beneath him.

Even now, in the dawn hours, there was activity. Smoke rose from morning fires, and already people were clotting in the open marketplaces and commons. Great wains were lumbered out of the main gates, loaded with farmers heading for the neat, ordered fields that spread out from the city's walls like skirts, stretching almost to the horizon.

Khadgar could not identify half the buildings. Great towers could have been universities or granaries, as far as he could tell. A surging river cascade had been harnessed by massive waterwheels, but to what purpose he could not guess. There was a sudden flame far to his right, though whether from a foundry, a captive dragon, or some great accident was a mystery.

It was the greatest city he had ever seen, and at its heart was Llane's castle.

It could be no other. Here the walls seemed to be truly made of gold, set with silver around the windows. The royal roof was shod with blue slate, as deep and luxurious as a sapphire's, and from its myriad towers Khadgar could see pennants with the lion's head of Azeroth, the sigil of King Llane's household and symbol of the land.

The castle complex seemed to be a small city in itself, with innumerable side buildings, towers, and halls. Arching galleries spanned between buildings, at lengths that Khadgar thought impossible without magical aide.

Perhaps such a structure could only be crafted with magic, thought Khadgar, and realized that perhaps this was one reason Medivh was so valued here.

The older mage raised a hand and circled over one particular tower, its topmost floor a level parapet. Medivh pointed down—once, twice, a third time. He wanted Khadgar to land first.

Pulling from the scabbed-over memories, Khadgar brought the great gryphon down neatly. The great eagle-headed beast churned its wings backward like a great sail, slowing to a delicate landing.

There was a delegation already waiting for him. A group of retainers in blue livery surged forward to take the reins and fit the gryphon's head with a heavy hood. The alien memories told Khadgar that this was similar to a falconer's snood, restricting the raptor's vision. Another had a bucket of warm cow guts, which were carefully presented before the gryphon's snapping beak.

Khadgar slid from the gryphon's back and was greeted warmly by Lord Lothar himself. The huge man seemed even larger in an ornate robe and cape, topped with an inscribed breastplate and filigreed mantle hanging on his shoulder.

"Apprentice!" said Lothar, swallowing Khadgar's hand in his huge meaty paw. "Good to see you're still employed!"

"My lord," said Khadgar, trying not to wince from the pressure of the larger man's grip. "We flew through the night to get here. I don't . . ."

The rest of Khadgar's statement was swept away in a flurry of wings and the panicked squawk of a gryphon. Medivh's mount tumbled out of the sky, and the Magus was less graceful in his landing. The huge flier slid across the width of the turret and almost fell off the other side, and Medivh pulled hard on the reins. As it was, the gryphon's great foreclaws clutched at the crenellated wall, and almost tipped the older mage over the side.

Khadgar did not wait for comment from Lord Lothar, but bolted forward, followed by the host of blue-clad retainers, and Lothar lumbering up behind them.

Medivh had already dismounted by the time they had reached him, and handed the reins to the first of the retainers. "Blasted crosswind!" said the older mage irritably. "I told you this was the precisely wrong spot for an aviary, but no one listens to the mage around here. Good landing, lad," he added as an afterthought, as the servants swarmed over his gryphon, trying to calm it down.

"Med," said Lothar, holding out a hand in greeting. "It is good you could come."

Medivh just scowled. "I came as soon as I could," the wizard snapped, responding to some affront that passed Khadgar by entirely. "You have to get along without me sometimes, you know."

If Lothar was surprised by Medivh's attitude, he said nothing of it. "Good to see you anyway. His Majesty . . ."

"Will have to wait," finished Medivh. "Take me to the chamber in question, now. No, I know the way myself. You said it was Huglar and Hugarin. This way, then." And with that the Magus was off, toward the side stairs that spiraled into the tower proper. "Five levels down, then a cross bridge, then three levels up! Horrible place for an aviary!"

Khadgar looked at Lothar. The larger man rubbed his beefy hand up over his balding pate, and shook his head. Then he started after the man, Khadgar in tow.

Medivh was gone by the time they reached the bottom of the spiral, though a litany of complaints and the occasional curse could be heard up ahead, diminishing fast.

"He's in a fine mood," said Lothar. "Let me walk you to the mage-chambers. We'll find him there."

"He was very agitated last night," said Khadgar, by way of apology. "He had been gone, and apparently your summons reached Karazhan shortly after he had returned."

"Has he told you what all this is about, Apprentice?" asked Lothar. Khadgar had to shake his head.

Champion Anduin Lothar frowned deeply. "Two of the great sorcerers of Azeroth are dead, their bodies burned almost beyond recognition, their hearts pulled from their very chests. Dead in their chambers. And there is evidence—" Lord Lothar hesitated for a moment, as if trying to choose the right words. "There is evidence of demonic activity. Which is why I sent the fastest messenger to fetch the Magus. Perhaps he can tell us what happened."

"Where are the bodies?" shouted Medivh, as Lothar and Khadgar finally caught up with him. They were near the top of another of the spires of the castle, the city spread out before them in a great open bay window opposite the door.

The room was a shambles, and looked like it had been searched by orcs, and sloppy orcs at that. Every book had been pulled from the shelves, and every scroll unrolled, and in many cases shredded. Alchemic devices were smashed, powders and poultices scattered about in a fine dusting, and even the furniture broken.

In the center of the room was a ring of power, an inscription carved into the floor itself. The ring was two concentric circles, incised with words of power between them. The incisions in the floor were deep and filled with a sticky dark liquid. There were two scorch marks on the floor, each man-sized, situated between the circle and the window.

Such incised rings had only one purpose to them, as far as Khadgar knew. The librarian in the Violet Citadel was always warning about them.

"Where *are* the bodies?" repeated Medivh, and Khadgar was glad that he was not expected to provide the answers. "Where are the remains of Huglar and Hugarin?"

"They were removed soon after they were found," said Lothar calmly. "It was unseemly to leave them here. We didn't know when you would arrive."

"You didn't know *if* I would arrive, you mean," snapped Medivh. "All right. All right. We can still salvage something. Who has come into this room?"

"The Conjurer-Lords Huglar and Hugarin," began Lothar.

"Well, of *course*," said Medivh sharply. "They had to be here if they died here. Who else?"

"One of their servants found them," continued Lothar. "And I was called. And I brought several guardsmen to move the bodies. They have not been interred yet, if you wish to examine them."

Medivh was already deeply in thought. "Hmmm? The bodies, or the guardsmen? No matter, we can take care of that later. So that's a servant, yourself, and about four guards, would you say? And now myself and my apprentice. No one else?"

"No one I can think of," said Lothar.

The Magus closed his eyes and muttered a few words under his breath. It might have been either a curse or a spell. His eyes flew open. "Interesting. Young Trust!"

Khadgar took a deep breath. "Lord Magus."

"I need your youth and inexperience. My jaded eyes may see what I'm expecting to see. I need fresh eyes. Don't be afraid to ask questions, now. Come here and stand in the center of the room. No, don't cross the circle itself. We don't know if it has any lingering enchantments on it. Stand here. Now. What do you sense?"

"I see the wrecked room," started Khadgar.

"I didn't say see," said Medivh sharply. "I said sense."

Khadgar took a deep breath and cast a minor spell, one that sharpened the senses and helped find lost articles. It was a simple divination, one he had used hundreds of times in the Violet Citadel. It was particularly good for finding things that others wanted to keep hidden.

But even upon the first intoned words, Khadgar could feel it was different.

There was a sluggishness to the magic in this room. Often magic had a feel of lightness and energy, but this felt more viscous, almost liquid in nature. Khadgar had never felt it before, and wondered if it was because of the circles of power, or powers and cantrips of the late mages themselves.

It was a thick feeling, like stale air in a room that had been shuttered for years. Khadgar tried to pull the energies together, but they seemed to resist, to follow his desires with only the greatest reluctance.

Khadgar's face grew stern as he tried to pull more of the power of the room, of the magical energies, into himself. This was a simple spell. If anything, it should be easier in a place where such castings would be commonplace.

And suddenly the young mage was inundated with the thick fetid feel of the magic. It was suddenly upon him and surrounding him, as if he had pulled the bottommost stone out and brought down a wall upon himself. The force of the dark, heavy magic fell upon him in a thick blanket, crushing the spell beneath him and driving him physically to his knees. Despite himself, he cried out.

Medivh was at his side at once, helping the young mage to his feet. "There, there," said the Magus, "I didn't expect you to succeed even that well. Good try. Excellent work."

"What is it?" managed Khadgar, suddenly able to breathe again. "It was like nothing I've felt before. Heavy. Resistant. Smothering."

"That's good news for you, then," said Medivh. "Good that you sensed it. Good that you carried through. The magic has been particularly twisted here, a remnant of what occurred earlier."

"You mean like a haunting?" said Khadgar. "Even in Karazhan, I never . . ."

"No, not like that," said Medivh. "Something much worse. The two dead mages here were summoning demons. It's that taint that you feel here, that heaviness of magic. A demon was here. That is what killed Huglar and Hugarin, the poor, powerful idiots."

There was a silence of a moment, then Lothar said, "Demons? In the king's towers? I cannot believe . . ."

"Oh, believe," said Medivh. "No matter how learned and knowledgeable, how wise and wonderful, how powerful and puissant, there is always one more sliver of power, one more bit of knowledge, one more secret to be learned by any mage. I think these two fell into that trap, and called upon forces from beyond the Great Dark Beyond, and paid the price for it. Idiots. They were friends and colleagues, and they were idiots."

"But how?" said Lothar. "Surely there were to be protections. Wards. This is a mystic circle of power."

"Easily breached, easy broken," said Medivh, leaning over the ring that glimmered with the dried blood of the two mages. He reached down and produced a thin straw that had laid over the cooling stones. "A-hah! A simple broom straw. If this was here when they began their summonings, all the adjurations and phylacteries in the world would not protect them. The demon would consider the circle to be no more than an arch, a gateway into this world. He would come out, hellfire blazing, and attack the poor fools who brought him into this world. I've seen it before."

Khadgar shook his head. The thick darkness that pressed in on all sides of him seemed to lift somewhat, and he gathered his wits about him. He looked around the room. It was already a disaster area—the demon had torn everything apart in its assault. If there was a broom straw breaking the circle, then it surely should have been moved elsewhere during the battle.

"How were the bodies found?" asked Khadgar.

"What?" said Medivh, with a sharpness that almost made Khadgar jump.

"I'm sorry," Khadgar responded quickly. "You said I should ask questions."

"Yes, yes, of course," said Medivh, cooling his harsh tone only a notch. To the King's Champion he said, "Well, Anduin Lothar, how were the bodies found?"

"When I came in, they were on the ground. The servant had not moved them," said Lothar.

"Faceup or facedown, sir?" said Khadgar, as calmly as he could. He could feel the icy stare of the elder mage. "Heads toward the circle or toward the window?"

Lothar's face clouded in memory. "Toward the circle. And facedown. Yes, definitely. They were badly scorched all over, and we had to turn them over to make sure it was Huglar and Hugarin."

"What are you driving at, Young Trust?" said the Magus, now seated by the open window, stroking his beard.

Khadgar looked at the two scorch marks between the malfunctioned protective circle and the window, and tried to think of them both as bodies and not think of them as once-living mages. "If you hit someone from the front, they fall backward. If you hit someone from the back, they fall forward. Was the window open when you arrived?"

Lothar looked at the open bay window, the great city beyond forgotten for the moment. "Yes. No. Yes, I think it was. But it could have been opened by the servant. There was a horrible stench—that's what brought attention to it in the first place. I can ask."

"No need," said Medivh. "The window was likely open when your servant entered." The Magus rose and walked to where the scorch marks were.

"So you think, Young Trust," he said, "that Huglar and Hugarin were standing here, watching the magic circle, and something came in the window and hit them from the back." For effect he smacked himself against the back of the head with an open palm. "They fell forward, and were burned in that position."

"Yes, sir," said Khadgar. "I mean, it's a theory."

"A good one," said Medivh. "But wrong, I'm afraid. In the first place, the two mages would be standing there, facing nothing at all, *unless* they were looking at the magic circle. Therefore they were summoning a demon. Such a circle would not be used otherwise."

"But . . ." started Khadgar, and the Magus froze his words in his throat with a harsh glance.

"*And,*" continued Medivh, "while that would work with a single attacker with a sap or a club, it does not function as well for the dark energies of demons. Had the beast breathed fire, it could have caught both men standing, killed them, and only after being set alight, the bodies fell forward. You said the bodies were burned front and back?" He put that question to Lothar.

"Yes," said the King's Champion.

Medivh held a palm up in front of him. "Demon breathes fire. Burns the front. Huglar (or Hugarin) falls forward, flames spread to the back. Unless the demon hit Hugarin (or Huglar) in the back, then turned them over to make sure the front was burned, then turned them over again. Hardly likely—demons are not that methodical."

Khadgar felt his face warm from embarrassment. "I'm sorry. It was just a theory."

"And a good one," said Medivh quickly. "Just in error, that's all. You're right, the window would be open, because that was how the demon left the tower. It is at large in the city right now."

Lothar cut short a curse, and said, "Are you sure?"

Medivh nodded. "Completely. But it will probably be laying low for the moment. Even killing two fools like Huglar and Hugarin by surprise would tax any but the most powerful creature's abilities."

"I can organize search parties within the hour," said Lothar.

"No," said Medivh. "I want to do this myself. No use throwing away good lives after bad. I'll want to see the remains, of course. That will tell me what we're dealing with here."

"We moved them to a cool room in the wine cellar," said Lothar. "I can take you there."

"In a moment," said Medivh. "I want to look about here for a moment. Will you grant me and my apprentice a moment or ten alone?"

Lothar hesitated for a moment, then said, "Of course. I will be right outside." As he said the last he looked at Khadgar sharply, then left.

The door's latch clicked shut and there was silence in the room. Medivh moved from table to table, pawing through the shredded tomes and torn papers. He held up a piece of correspondence with a purple seal, and shook his head. Slowly, he crumpled the piece of paper in his hand.

"In *civilized* countries," he said, his voice slightly strained, "apprentices don't disagree with their masters. At least in public." He turned toward Khadgar and the youth saw the older man's face was a mass of storm clouds.

"I am sorry," said Khadgar. "You said I should ask questions, and the position of the bodies did not seem right at the time, but now that you mention how the bodies were burned . . ."

Medivh held up a hand and Khadgar silenced himself. He paused a moment, then let out a slow exhalation. "Enough. You did the right thing, no more or less than asked by me. And if you hadn't spoken up, I wouldn't have realized the demon probably skittered down the tower itself, and wasted more time searching the castle complex. But, you asked questions because you don't know much about demons, and that is ignorance. And ignorance I will *not* tolerate."

The elder Magus looked at Khadgar, but there was a smile at the corner of his lips. Khadgar, sure that the storm had passed, lowered himself onto a stool. Despite himself, he still said, "Lothar . . ."

"Will wait," said Medivh, nodding. "He waits well, that Anduin Lothar. Now, what did you learn of demons in your time at the Violet Citadel?"

"I've heard the legends," said Khadgar. "In the First Days, there were demons in the land, and great heroes arose to drive them out." He thought of the image of Medivh's mother blasting the demons to bits, and facing down their Lord, but said nothing. No need to make Medivh angry again now that he'd calmed down.

"That's the basics," said Medivh. "What we tell the hoi polloi. What do you know in addition?"

Khadgar took a deep breath. "The official teachings in the Violet Citadel, in Kirin Tor, is that demonology is to be eschewed, avoided, and abjured. Any attempt to summon demons is to be found out and stopped at once, and those involved are to be expelled. Or worse. There were stories, among the young students, when I was growing up."

"Stories grounded in fact," said Medivh. "But you're a curious lad, you know more, I assume?"

Khadgar tilted his head in thought, choosing words carefully. "Korrigan, our academic librarian, had an extensive collection of . . . material at his disposal."

"And needed someone to help organize it," said Medivh dryly. Khadgar must have jumped, because Medivh added, "That was a guess, only, Young Trust."

"The material is mostly folk legends and the reports of the local author- ities involving demon worshipers. Most of it was along the lines of individu- als committing foul acts in the name of some old demon from the legends or another. Nothing about the actions of truly summoning a demon. No spells, no arcane writings." Khadgar motioned toward the protective circle. "No ceremonies."

"Of course," said Medivh. "Even Korrigan would not inflict that on a stu- dent. If he has such things, he would keep them separate."

"From that, the general belief is that when the demons were defeated, they were driven out of this world entirely. They were pushed out of the world of light and living, and into their own domain."

"The Great Dark Beyond," said Medivh, intoning the phrase like a prayer.

"They are still out there, or so the legend goes," said Khadgar, "and they want to come back in. Some say they come to the weak-willed in their sleep and urge them to find old spells and make sacrifices. Sometimes it is to open the way for them to come back fully. Others say they want worshipers and sacrifices to make this world like it once was, bloody and violent, and only then would they return."

Medivh was quiet for a moment, stroking his beard, then said, "Anything else?"

"There's more. Details and individual stories. I've seen carvings of demons, pictures, diagrams." Again Khadgar felt a rising need to tell Medivh about the vision, about the demon army. Instead he said, "And there is that old epic poem, the one about Aegwynn, fighting a horde of demons in a far- off land."

The mention of that brought a gentle, knowing smile to Medivh's face. "Ah yes, 'The Song of Aegwynn.'" You'll find that poem in a lot of powerful mages' quarters, you know."

"My teacher, Lord Guzbah was interested in it," said Khadgar.

"Is he, now?" said Medivh, smiling. "With all due respect, I don't know if Guzbah is quite ready for that poem. At least not in its true form." He peaked his eyebrows. "What you have is basically true. A lot of people couch it in the form of legends and fairy stories, but I think you know as well as I do that demons are real, and are out there, and yes, form a threat to those of us who walk this sunlit world, as well as other worlds. I think, now, I definitely *think,* that your red-sunned world was another place, a different world, on the far side of the Great Dark Beyond. The Beyond is a prison for these demons, a place without light or succor, and they are very, very jealous and very, very anxious to get back in."

Khadgar nodded, and Medivh continued, "But your assumption that their victims are weak-willed is in error, though again an error that is well-intended. There are more than enough venal farmhands who invoke a demonic force for revenge against a former lover, or stupid merchants who burn an invoice from a debtor with a black candle, badly mangling the ancient name of some once-great demonic power. But just as often there are those who walk willingly to the abyss, who feel themselves safe and sure and knowledgeable that they are beyond any blandishment or threat, that they are powerful enough to harness the demonic energies that surge beyond the walls of the world. They are in many ways even more dangerous than the common rabble, for as you know, a near-failure in spellcasting is more deadly than a complete failure."

Khadgar could only nod, and wondered if Medivh had the power of the mind. "But these were powerful mages—Huglar and Hugarin, I mean."

"The most powerful in Azeroth," said Medivh. "The wisest and finest wizards, magical advisors to King Llane himself. Safe, sage, and sinecured!"

"Surely they would know better?" asked Khadgar.

"You would think so," said Medivh. "Yet, here we stand in the wreckage of their chambers, and their demon-burned bodies lay in the wine cellar."

"Why would they do it, then?" Khadgar knitted his brows, trying not to offend. "If they knew so much, why did they try to summon a demon?"

"Many reasons," said Medivh with a sigh. "Hubris, that false pride that goes before the fall. Overconfidence, both in each individually and doubled for working in tandem. And fear, I suppose, most of all."

"Fear?" Khadgar looked at Medivh quizzically.

"Fear of the unknown," said Medivh. "Fear of the known. Fear of things more powerful than they."

Khadgar shook his head. "What could be more powerful than two of the most advanced and learned wizards in Azeroth?"

"Ah," said Medivh, and a small smile blossomed beneath his beard. "That would be me. They killed themselves summoning a demon, playing with forces best left alone, because they feared *me.*"

"You?" said Khadgar, the surprise in his voice greater than he had intended. For a moment he feared offending the older mage once more.

But Medivh just took a deep breath and blew the air out slowly. Then he said, "Me. They were fools, but I blame myself as well. Come, lad, Lothar can wait. It's time I told you the story of the Guardians and of the Order of Tirisfal, which is all that stands between us and the Darkness."

EIGHT
Lessons

To understand the Order," said Medivh, "you must understand demons. You must also understand magic." He lowered himself comfortably on one of the still-undamaged chairs. The chair also had one of the few unripped pillows upon it.

"Lord Medivh . . . Magus," said Khadgar. "If there is a demon abroad in Stormwind, we should concentrate on that, and not on history lessons that could wait until later."

Medivh looked down at his chest, and Khadgar feared that he risked another outburst from the elder mage. But the master mage merely shook his head, and smiled as he said, "Your concerns would be valid if the demon in question was a threat to those around it. Take my word for it, it is not. The demon, even were it one of the more powerful officers within the Burning Legion, would have expended almost all its personal power in dealing with the two powerful mages that summoned it. It is of little matter, at least for the moment. What is important, is that you understand what the Order is, what I am, and why others are so deeply interested in it."

"But Magus . . ." started Khadgar.

"And the sooner I finish the sooner I will know that I can trust you with the information, and the sooner I will go out to deal with this petty demon, so if you truly want me to go you should let me finish, eh?" Medivh gave the younger mage a hard, knowing smile.

Khadgar opened his mouth to protest, but thought better of it. He slouched down against the wide ledge by the open window. Despite the efforts of the servants to remove the bodies from the tower, the stench of their death, a corrosive pallor, was still heavy in the air.

"So. What is magic?" asked Medivh, in the manner of a schoolmage.

"An ambient field of energy that pervades the world," said Khadgar, almost without thinking. It was catechism, a simple answer for a simple question. "It is stronger in some locations than others, but it is ever-present."

"Yes it is," said the older mage, "at least *now.* But imagine a time when it was not."

"Magic is universal," said Khadgar, knowing as soon as he said it that it was soon to prove not to be. "Like air or water."

"Yes, like water," said Medivh. "Now imagine a time at the very start of things, when all the water in the world was in one location. All the rain and rivers and seas and streams, all the showers and creeks and tears, all in one location, in one well."

Khadgar nodded, slowly.

"Now, instead of water, it is magic we're talking about," said Khadgar. "A well of magic, the source, an opening into other dimensions, a shimmering doorway into the lands beyond the Great Dark, beyond the walls of the world. The first peoples to cast spells encamped around the well and distilled its raw power into magic. They were called the Kaldorei then. What they are called now, I cannot say." Medivh looked at Khadgar, but the younger mage kept his silence now.

Medivh resumed. "The Kaldorei grew powerful from their use of magic, but they did not understand its nature. They did not understand that there were other, powerful forces in the Great Dark Beyond, moving in the space between worlds, that hungered after magic and were very interested in any who tamed it and refined it to their own ends. These malign forces were abominations and juggernauts and nightmares from hundreds of worlds, but we call them simply demons. They sought to invade any world where magic was mastered and grown, and destroy it, keeping the energies for themselves alone. And the greatest of them, the master of the Burning Legion, was a demon named Sargeras."

Khadgar thought of the vision with Aegwynn and suppressed a shudder.

If Medivh noticed the young mage's reaction he did not say anything. "The Lord of the Burning Legion was both powerful and subtle, and worked to corrupt the early magic-users, the Kaldorei. He succeeded, for a dark shadow fell upon their hearts, and they enslaved other races, the nascent humans as well as others, in order to build their empire."

Medivh sighed. "Now in this time of the enslaving Kaldorei, there were those with greater vision than their brethren, who were willing both to speak out against the Kaldorei and to pay the price for their vision. These brave individuals, both Kaldorei and other races as well, saw the hearts of the ruling Kaldorei grow cold and dark, and the demonic power grow.

"So it came to pass that the Kaldorei were corrupted by Sargeras such that they nearly damned this world at its birth. The Kaldorei ignored those who spoke out against them, and opened the way for the most powerful of demons, Sargeras and his lot, to invade. Only by the heroic actions of a few was the shimmering doorway through the Great Dark shut, exiling Sargeras and his followers. But the victory was at great cost. The Well of Eternity exploded when the doorway was shut down, and the resulting explosion ripped the heart out of this world, destroying the Kaldorei lands and the very continent it rested upon. Those that shut the door were never seen again by living eyes."

"Kalimdor!" said Khadgar, interrupting despite himself.

Medivh looked at him, and Khadgar continued, "It's an old legend in Lordaeron! Once there was an evil race who meddled foolishly with great power. As punishment for their sins, their lands were broken and set beneath the waves. It was called the Sundering of the World. Their lands were called Kalimdor."

"Kalimdor," repeated Medivh. "Though you have the child's version of the tale, the bit we tell would-be mages to stress the dangers of what they are playing with. The Kaldorei were foolish, and destroyed themselves and nearly our world. And when the Well of Eternity exploded, the magical energies within scattered to the four corners of the earth, in an eternal rain of magic. And *that's* why magic is universal—it's the power of the well's death."

"But Magus," said Khadgar, "that was thousands of years ago."

"Ten thousand years," said Medivh, "give or take a score."

"How is it that the legend comes down to us? Dalaran itself has histories only going back twenty centuries, and the earliest of those are wrapped in legends."

Medivh nodded and took up the story again. "Many were lost in the sinking of Kalimdor, but some survived, and took their knowledge with them. Some of these surviving Kaldorei would found the Order of Tirisfal. Whether Tirisfal was a person, or a place, or a thing, or a concept, even I cannot say. They took the knowledge of what had happened, and swore to keep it from ever happening again, and that is the bedrock of the Order.

"Now, the race of humans survived those dark days as well, and thrived, and soon, with magical energy worked into the fabric of the world itself, they too were scratching at the doors of reality, beginning to summon creatures from the Great Dark, prying at the shut gates of Sargeras's prison. That was when those Kaldorei who had survived and changed themselves came forward with the story of how their ancestors had almost destroyed the world.

"The first human mages considered what the surviving Kaldorei had said, and realized that even were they to lay down their wands and grimoires and ciphers, that others would seek, innocently or less so, ways to allow the demons access once more to our green lands. And so they continued the Order, now as a secret society among the most powerful of their mages. This Order of Tirisfal would choose one of its number, who would serve as the *Guardian* of the *Tirisfalen*. This guardian would be given the greatest of powers, and would be the gatekeeper of reality. But now the gate was not a single great well of power, but rather an infinite rain that continues to fall even today. It is nothing less than the heaviest responsibility in the world."

Medivh fell silent, and his eyes lost their focus briefly, as if he were suddenly swept into the past himself. Then he shook his head, returning to himself, but still did not speak.

"You are the Guardian," said Khadgar, simply.

"Aye," said Medivh, "I am the child of the greatest Guardian of all time, and was given her power soon after my birth. It was . . . too much for me, and I paid for it with a good piece of my youth."

"But you said the mages chose among themselves," said Khadgar. "Couldn't Magna Aegwynn have chosen an older candidate? Why choose a child, especially her own child?"

Medivh took a deep breath. "The first Guardians, for the first millennium, were chosen among the select group. The very existence of the Order was kept hidden, as was the wishes of the original founders. However, over time, politics and personal interests came into play, such that the Guardian soon became little more than a servant, a magical dogsbody. Some of the more powerful mages felt it was the Guardian's job to keep *everyone else* from enjoying the power that they themselves commanded. Like the Kaldorei before us, a shadow of corrupting power was moving through the members of the Order. More demons were getting through, and even Sargeras himself had manifested the smallest bits of himself. A mere fraction of his power, but enough to slay armies and destroy nations."

Khadgar thought of the image of Sargeras that fought Aegwynn in the vision. Could this have been a mere fraction of the great demon's power?

"Magna Aegwynn," Medivh said the words, then stopped. It was as if he was not used to speaking those words. "She who bore me was herself born nearly a thousand years ago. She was greatly gifted, and chosen by other members of the Order to become the Guardian. I believe the grayest of the graybeards of that time thought they could control her, and in doing so continue to use the Guardian as a pawn of their own political games.

"She surprised them."—and at this Medivh smiled. "She refused to be manipulated, and indeed fought against some of the greatest mages of her age when they themselves fell into demonic lore. Some thought that her independence was a passing thing, that when her time came, she would have to pass the mantle on to a more malleable candidate. Again, she surprised them, using the magics within her to live for a thousand years, unchanging, and to wield her power with wisdom and grace. So the Order and the Guardian split. The former can advise the latter, but the latter must be free to challenge the former, to avoid what happened to the Kaldorei.

"For a thousand years she fought the Great Dark, even challenging the physical aspect of Sargeras himself, who had instilled himself into this plane and sought to destroy the mythical dragons, adding their power to his own. Magna Aegwynn met him and defeated him, locking his body away in a place where none knows, keeping him forever from the Great Dark that is his power. That's in that epic poem, 'The Song of Aegwynn,' the one Guzbah wants. But she could not do it forever, and there must always be a Guardian.

"And then . . ." And again Medivh's voice faltered. "She had one more trick up her sleeve. Powerful she was, but she was still of mortal flesh. She was expected to pass on her power. Instead she fathered an heir on a conjurer from the Court of Azeroth itself, and she chose that child as her successor. She threatened the Order, saying that if her choice was not honored, she would not step down, and would rather take the power of the Guardian into death than allow another to have it. They felt they *might* be able to manipulate the child . . . me . . . better, and so they allowed it.

"The power was too much," said Medivh. "When I was a young man, younger than you, it awoke within me, and I slept for over twenty years. Magna Aegwynn had so much of a life, and I seem to have lost most of it." His voice faltered again. "Magna Aegwynn . . . my mother . . ." he began, but found he had nothing more to say.

Khadgar just sat there for a moment. Then Medivh rose, shook back his mane and said, "And while I slept, evil crept back into the world. There are more demons, and more of these orcs as well. And now members of my own Order are once more playing the dark road. Yes, Huglar and Hugarin were members of the Order, as have been others, like ancient Arrexis among the Kirin Tor. Yes, something similar happened to him, and while they covered it up neatly, you probably heard *something* about it. They feared my mother's power, and they fear me, and I have to keep their fear from destroying them. Such is the charge laid upon the Guardian of Tirisfal."

The older man launched himself to his feet. "I must be off!" he said.

"Off?" said Khadgar, suddenly surprised by the energy within the lanky frame.

"As you have so rightly noted, there is a demon abroad," said Medivh with a renewed smile. "Sound the hunter's horn, I must find it before it regains its wits and strength and kills others!"

Khadgar pulled himself upright. "Where do we start?"

Medivh pulled himself up short, and turned, looking slightly sheepishly at the younger man. "Ah. *We* are not starting anywhere. I am going to go. You're talented, but you're not up to demons quite yet. This battle is my own, Young Apprentice Trust."

"Magus, I am sure I can . . ."

But Medivh raised a hand to silence him.

"I also need you here to keep your own ears open," said Medivh, in a quieter voice. "I have no doubt that Old Lothar has spent the past ten minutes with his ear to the door, such that there will be a keyhole-shaped impression on the side of his face." Medivh grinned. "He knows a lot, but not all. That's why I had to tell you, so he doesn't pry too much out of you. I need someone to guard the Guardian, as it were."

Khadgar looked at Medivh and the older mage winked. Then the Magus strode to the door and pulled it open with a quick motion.

Lothar did not stumble into the room, but he was there, right on the other side. He could have been listening, or just standing watch.

"Med," said Lothar with a game smile. "His Majesty . . ."

"His Majesty will understand perfectly," said Medivh, breezing right past the larger man. "That I would rather meet with a rampaging demon than the leader of a nation. Priorities and all that. In the meantime will you look after my apprentice?"

He said it all in a single breath, and then he was gone, out into the hall and down the stairs, leaving Lothar in mid-sentence.

The old warrior rubbed a great hand up over his balding pate, letting out an exaggerated sigh. Then he looked at Khadgar and let out another, deeper sigh.

"He's always been like this, you know," said Lothar, as if Khadgar truly did know. "I suppose you're hungry, at least. Let's see if we can find some lunch."

Lunch consisted of a cold game fowl looted from the cold room and tucked under Lothar's arm, and two mugs of ale the size of ewers, one in each meaty hand. The King's Champion was surprisingly at ease, despite the situation, and guided Khadgar out to a high balcony overlooking the city.

"My lord," said Khadgar. "Despite the Magus's request, I realize you have other work."

"Aye," said Lothar, "and most of it was taken care of while you were talking to Medivh. His majesty King Llane is in his quarters, as are most of the courtiers, under guard, in case that demon decided to hide in the castle. Also I have agents already spreading through the city, with orders to both report anything suspicious but not to make themselves suspicious. The last thing we need is a demon-panic. I've cast all my lines, and now there is nothing to do but wait." He looked at the younger man. "And my lieutenants know that I'll be on this balcony, as I always have a late lunch anyway."

Khadgar considered Lothar's words, and thought that the King's Champion was very much like Medivh—not only planning ahead a few moves, but delighting in telling others how he'd planned things out. The apprentice picked at the sliced breast meat while Lothar tore into a drumstick.

The pair ate in silence for a long time. The fowl was anything but foul, for it was treated with a concoction of rosemary, bacon, and sheep's butter placed beneath the skin before roasting. Even cold it fell apart in the mouth. The ale for its part was pungent, rich with bottomland hops.

Beneath them the city unfolded. The citadel itself was atop a rocky outcropping that already separated the King from his subjects, and from the tower's additional height, the citizens of Stormwind looked like naught but small dolls busying themselves along crowded streets. Some sort of market day was playing out beneath them, brightly-tarped storefronts occupied with vendors bellowing (very quietly, it seemed to Khadgar at this altitude) the virtues of their wares.

For a moment Khadgar forgot where he was, and what he had seen, and why he was there in the first place. It was a beautiful city. Only Lothar's deep grumble brought him back to this world.

"So," said the King's Champion in his way of introspection. "How is he?"

Khadgar thought for a moment, and replied, "He is in good health. You have seen that yourself, milord."

"Bah," spat Lothar, and for a moment Khadgar thought the knight was choking on a large piece of meat. "I can see, and I know Med can dance and bluff his way past just about anyone. What I mean to say is, How *is* he?"

Khadgar looked out at the city again, wondering if he had Medivh's talent to bluster his way past the older man, to deny answers without causing affront.

No, he decided, Medivh played on loyalties and friendships older than he was. He had to find another way to respond. He let out a sigh and said, "Demanding. He's very demanding. And intelligent. And surprising. I feel I have apprenticed myself to a whirlwind, sometimes." He looked at Lothar, his eyebrows raised, hoping that this would be sufficient.

Lothar nodded. "A whirlwind, aye. And a thunderstorm, too, I suspect."

Khadgar shrugged awkwardly. "He has his moods, like anyone."

"Hmmpph," said the King's Champion. "An ostler has a mood and he kicks the dog. A mage has his moods and a town disappears. No offense meant."

"None taken, milord," said Khadgar, thinking of the dead mages in the tower room. "You ask how he is. He's all these things."

"Hmmmph," said Lothar again. "He's a very powerful person."

Khadgar thought *and you worry about him like the other wizards do.* Instead he said, "He speaks well of you."

"What did he say?" said Lothar, more quickly than perhaps he meant to.

"Only," Khadgar chose his words carefully, "that you served him well when he was ill."

"True enough," grunted the Champion, starting into the other drumstick.

"And that you are extremely observant," added Khadgar, feeling that this was a sufficient distillation of Medivh's opinion of the warrior.

"Glad to know he notices," said Lothar, with a full mouth. There was a pause between the two of them, as Lothar chewed and swallowed. "Has he mentioned the Guardian?"

"We have spoken," said Khadgar, feeling that he was on a very narrow verbal cliff. Medivh did not tell him how much Lothar knew. He settled for silence as the best answer, and let the statement hang in the air for a moment.

"And it is not the Apprentice's place to discuss the doings of the Master, eh?" said Lothar, with a smile that seemed just a jot too forced. "Come now, you're from Dalaran. That nest of mage-vipers has more secrets per square foot than any other place on the continent. No offense, again."

Khadgar shrugged off the comment. Diplomatically, he stated, "I notice that there is less obvious rivalry between mages here than in Lordaeron."

"And you mean to tell me that your teachers didn't send you out with a laundry list of things to pry out of the high Magus?" Lothar's grin deepened, and looked almost sympathetic.

Khadgar felt some heat in his face. The older warrior was firing bow shots increasingly close to the gold. "Any requests from the Violet Citadel are under Medivh's consideration. He has been *very* accommodating."

"Hmmph," snorted Lothar. "Must mean they aren't asking for the right stuff. I know the mages around here, including Huglar and Hugarin, the saints rest their souls, were always pestering him for this and that, and complaining to His Majesty or myself when they didn't get it. Like we had any control over him!"

"I don't think anyone does," said Khadgar, drowning any additional comment he might have made in his ale.

"Not even his mother, I understand," said Lothar. It was a small comment, but it slipped in like a dagger thrust. Khadgar found himself wanting to ask Lothar more about her, but contained himself.

"I fear I am too young to know," he said. "I've read some on her. She seems like a powerful mage."

"And that power is in *him*, now," said Lothar. "She whelped him from a conjurer of this very court, and weaned him on pure magestuff, and poured her power into him. Yes, I know all about it, pieced it together after he went into that coma. Too much, too young. Even now I'm concerned."

"You think he's too powerful," said Khadgar, and Lothar froze him with a sudden, penetrating stare. The young mage kicked himself for speaking his mind, practically accusing his host.

Lothar let out a smile and shook his head. "On the contrary, lad, I worry that he's not powerful *enough*. There are horrible things afoot in the kingdoms. Those orc-things you saw a month ago, they're multiplying like rabbits after a rain. And trolls, nearly extinct, have been seen more often. And Medivh is out hunting a demon even as we speak. Bad times are coming, and I hope, no, I *pray*, that he's up to it. We went for twenty-some years without a Guardian, when he was in a coma. I don't want to go another twenty, particularly at a time like this."

Khadgar felt embarrassed now. "So when you ask, How is he? You mean . . ."

"How *is* he?" finished Lothar. "I don't want him weakening at a time like this. Orcs, trolls, demons, and then there is . . ." Lothar let his voice trail off and looked at Khadgar, then said, "You know of the Guardian, by now, I can assume?"

"You can assume," said Khadgar.

"And the Order, too?" said Lothar, then he smiled. "No need to say anything, young man, your eyes gave yourself away. Never play cards with me, eh?"

Khadgar felt on the very precipice itself. Medivh warned him not to let too much loose to the Champion, but Lothar seemed to know as much as Khadgar knew. More, even.

Lothar spoke in a calm voice. "We would not send for Med for a simple matter of a magical misfire. Nor even two common conjurers being caught in their own spells. Huglar and Hugarin were two of our best, two of our most powerful. There was another, even more powerful, but she met an accident two months back. All three, I believe, were members of your Order."

Khadgar felt a chill creep up his back. He managed to say, "I don't think I'm comfortable speaking of this."

"Then don't," said Lothar, his brows furrowed like the foothills of some ancient mountain chain. "Three powerful mages, the most powerful in Azeroth. Not a patch on Med or his mother, mind you, but great and powerful wizards nonetheless. All dead. I can buy one mage being unlucky, or being caught unawares, but three of them? A warrior doesn't believe in that much coincidence.

"There's more," continued the King's Champion. "I have my own ways of finding out things. Caravan traders, mercenaries, and adventurers that come into the city often find a receptive ear with old Lothar. Word comes from Ironforge and Alterac, and even from Lordaeron itself. There has been a plague of such mishaps, one after another. I think someone, or worse yet, some*thing* is hunting the great mages of this secret Order. Both here, and in Dalaran itself, I don't doubt."

Khadgar realized that the older man was studying his face as he spoke, and with a start he realized that this fit into the rumors he heard before leaving the Violet Citadel. Ancient mages, suddenly gone, and the upper echelons quietly hushing it up. The great secret among the Kirin Tor, part of a greater problem.

Despite himself, Khadgar looked away, out over the city. "Yes, Dalaran too, it seems," said Lothar. "Not much news comes from there, but I'm willing to bet that the news is similar, eh?"

"You think that the Lord Magus is in danger?" asked Khadgar. The desire to not tell Lothar anything was eroding by the obvious concern of the older warrior.

"I think Medivh is danger incarnate," said Lothar. "And I admire anyone willing to be under the same roof with him." It sounded like a joke, but the King's Champion did not smile. "But yes, something is out there, and it may be tied with the demons or the orcs or something much worse. And I would hate to lose our most powerful weapon at a time like this."

Khadgar looked at Lothar, trying to read the furrows of the older man's face. Was this old warrior worried about his friend, or worried about the loss of a magical protection? Was his concern about Medivh's safety, out in the middle of the wilderness, or that something was stalking them all? The older man's face seemed like a mask, and his deep sea-blue eyes gave no clue as to what Lothar was truly thinking.

Khadgar had expected a simple swordsman, a knight devoted to duty, but the King's Champion was more than this. He was pushing Khadgar, looking for weakness, looking for information, but to what end?

I need someone to guard the Guardian, Medivh had said.

"He is fine," said Khadgar. "You are worried about him, and I share your concerns. But he is doing well, and I doubt anything or anyone can truly hurt him."

Lothar's unfathomable eyes seemed to deflate for a moment, but only a flickering moment. He was going to say something else, to renew the prying, friendly inquisition, but a commotion within the tower drew both their attentions away from the discussion, away from the now-empty mugs and the bare bones of the fowl.

Medivh swaggered into view, followed by a crew of servants and guardsmen. All complained about his presence, but none would (wisely) place a hand on him, and as a result followed him like a living, mewling comet's tale. The older mage strode out onto the parapet.

"I thought you a creature of habit, Lothar," said Medivh. "I knew you'd be out here taking afternoon tea!" The Magus beamed a warm smile, but Khadgar saw there was a slight, almost drunken sway to his walk. Medivh kept one arm behind him, concealing something.

Lothar rose, concern in his voice. "Medivh, are you all right? The demon . . ."

"Ah, yes, the demon," said Medivh brightly and pulled his bloodied prize out from behind his back. He lobbed it at Lothar and Khadgar in a lazy, under-handed swing.

The red orb spun as it flew, spilling the last bits of blood and brains out before landing at Lothar's feet. It was a demon's skull, the flesh still adhered to it, with a mighty divot, like that of a great ax, driven into the center, right between the ramlike horns. The demon's expression, Khadgar thought, was one of both awe and indignation.

"You might want to have that stuffed," said Medivh, pulling himself seri-ously to his full height. "Had to burn the rest of it, of course. No telling what the inexperienced might do with a draught of demon's blood."

Khadgar saw that Medivh's face was more pinched than it had been ear-lier, and that the lines around his eyes were more prominent. Lothar may have caught it as well, and remarked, "You caught it quite quickly."

"Child's play!" said Medivh. "Once Young Trust here pointed out how the demon fled the castle, it was a simple matter to track it from the tower's base to a small escarpment. It was over before I knew it. Before it knew it either." The Magus swayed slightly.

"Come then," said Lothar, with a warm smile. "We should tell the King. There should be reveling in your honor for this, Med!"

Medivh held up a hand. "You may revel without us, I am afraid. We should get back. Miles to go before we rest. Isn't that right, Apprentice?"

Lothar looked at Khadgar, again with a questioning, imploring look. Medivh looked calm but worn. He also looked expectant for Khadgar to sup-port him this time.

The young mage coughed. "Of course. We left an experiment on the boil."

"Indeed!" said Medivh, picking up the lie immediately. "In our rush to get here, I had quite forgotten. We should make haste." The Magus wheeled and bellowed at the collected courtiers. "Make ready our mounts! We leave at once." The servants dissolved like a covey of quail. Medivh turned back to Lothar. "You will make our apologies to His Majesty, of course."

Lothar looked at Medivh, then at Khadgar, then at Medivh again. At last he sighed and said, "Of course. Let me lead you to the tower, at least."

"Lead on," said Medivh. "Don't forget to take your skull. I'd keep it myself, but I have one like it already."

Lothar hefted the ram-headed skull in one hand and brushed past Medivh, leading into the tower itself. As he passed, the Magus seemed to deflate, the air going out of him. He looked more tired than before, grayer than he had been moments earlier. He let out a heavy sigh and headed for the door himself.

Khadgar chased after him and caught him by the elbow. It was a light touch, but the elder mage suddenly pulled himself upright, flinching as if reacting to a blow. He turned to Khadgar, and his eyes seemed to mist over for a moment as he looked at the younger mage.

"Magus," said Khadgar.

"What is it now?" said Medivh in a hissing whisper.

Khadgar thought about what to say, how to risk the Magus's censure. "You're not well," he said, simply.

It was the right thing to say. Medivh gave an aged nod, and said, "I've been better. Lothar probably knows as well, but he won't challenge me on it. But I'd rather be home than here." He paused for a moment, and his lips formed a stiff line beneath his beard. "I was sick for a long time, here. Don't want to repeat the experience."

Khadgar didn't say anything, but only nodded. Lothar now stood at the door, waiting.

"You're going to have to lead the way back to Karazhan," said Medivh to Khadgar, loud enough for all nearby to hear. "This city life takes too much out of a man, and I could use a nap about now!"

NINE
The Slumber of the Magus

This is very important," said Medivh, staggering slightly as he slid from the back of the gryphon. He looked haggard, and Khadgar assumed the battle with the demon had been worse than even he let on.

"I will be . . . unavailable for a few days," continued the older Mage. "If any messengers arrive during this time, I want you to keep track of my correspondence."

"I can do that," said Khadgar, "easily."

"No you can't," said Medivh, starting roughly down the stairs. "That is why I need to tell you how to read the ones with the purple seal. The purple seal is always Order business."

Khadgar said nothing this time, but just nodded.

Medivh slid on the edge of the stairs and stumbled, pitching forward head-long. Khadgar lunged to grab the older man, but the Magus had already caught himself against the wall and pulled himself upright. He didn't miss a beat. "In the library, there is a scroll. 'The Song of Aegwynn.' Tells of my mother's battle with Sargeras."

"The scroll that Guzbah wanted a copy of," said Khadgar, now watching the mage carefully as he lurched down the stairs ahead of him.

"The very one," said Medivh. "This is why he can't have it—we use it as cipher for Order communications. It is the master key. An identical scroll is with each of the members of the Order. If you take the standard alphabet, and move everything down, so the first letter is represented by the fourth, or the tenth, or the twentieth. It is a simple code. You understand?"

Khadgar started to say he did, but Medivh was already hurrying on, almost urgent in his need to explain.

"The scroll is the key," he repeated. "At the top of the message, you'll see what looks like a date. It's not. It's a reference to the stanza, line, and word you start at. The first letter of that word becomes the first letter of the alphabet in the code. From there it proceeds normally, the next letter in alphabetic progression would be the second letter of the alphabet, and so on."

"I understand."

"No, you don't," said Medivh, rushed now and tired. "That's the cipher for the first sentence only. When you hit a punctuation mark, you go to the second letter in the word. That becomes the equivalent for the first letter of the alphabet for the cipher of that sentence. Punctuation is normal. Numbers are as well, but they are supposed to write things out, not use numerals. There's something else, but I'm missing it."

They were outside Medivh's personal quarters now. Moroes was already present, with a robe slung over his arm and a covered bowl resting on an ornate table. From the doorway Khadgar could smell the rich broth rising from the bowl.

"What should I do once I decipher the message?" asked Khadgar.

"Right!" said Medivh, as if some vital connection had snapped closed in his mind. "Delay. Delay first. Day or two, I may be up to it after that. Then equivocate. I am out on business, may return any time. Use the same cipher as you got, but make sure you mark it as the date. If all else fails, delegate. Tell whoever it is to use their own judgment, and I will lend what aid I can at the soonest moment. They always love that. Do *not* tell them I am indisposed—

the last time I mentioned that, a horde of would-be clerics arrived to minister to my needs. I'm still missing silverware from that little visit."

The old mage took a deep breath, and seemed to deflate, supporting himself against the door frame. Moroes did not move, but Khadgar took a step forward.

"The fight with the demon," said Khadgar. "It was bad, wasn't it?"

"I've fought worse. Demons! Slope-shouldered, ram-headed brutes. Equal parts shadow and fire. More beast than human, more raw bile than both. Nasty claws. That's what you watch out for, the claws."

Khadgar nodded. "How did you defeat it?"

"Massive trauma usually will force out the life essence," said Medivh. "In this case, I took its head off."

Khadgar blinked. "You didn't have a sword."

Medivh smiled wearily. "Did I say I needed a sword? Enough. More questions when I am up to it." And with that he stepped into the room, and the ever-faithful Moroes closed the door on Khadgar. The last sound the youth heard was the exhausted groan of an old man who had finally found a resting place.

A week passed, and Medivh had not emerged from his quarters. Moroes would shuffle upstairs with a daily bowl of broth. Finally, Khadgar summoned sufficient nerve to look in. The castellan made no move to protest, other than a monosyllabic recognition of his presence there.

In repose Medivh looked ghastly, the light gone out of his shuttered eyes, the tension of life gone from his visage. He was dressed in a long nightshirt, propped up against the headboard, supported by pillows, his mouth open, his face pale, his usually animate form thin and haggard. Moroes would carefully spoon the broth into Medivh's mouth, and he would swallow, but otherwise not awaken. The castellan would change the bedding as well, then retire for the day.

Khadgar got a frisson of recognition, and wondered if this was the same scene that played out in Medivh's youth, when his powers first surfaced, and when Lothar tended to him. He wondered how long the Magus would truly be out. How much energy had the battle with the demon taken out of him?

Normal communications came in, written in common hand and clear language. Some were delivered by gryphon-rider, others by horseback, and more than a few came with the regular supply wagons of traders seeking to fill Moroes's larders. They were for the most part mundane—ship movements and troop drills. Readiness reports. An occasional discovery of an ancient tomb or a forgotten artifact, or the recovery of a time-worn legend. The sighting of a waterspout, or a great sea turtle, or a crimson tide. Sketches of fauna that may have been new to the observer, but were better duplicated in the bestiaries already in the library.

And mention of the orcs, in ever-increasing numbers, particularly from the east. Rising sightings of them in the vicinity of the Black Morass. Increased guards on the caravans, locations of temporary camps, reports of raids, robberies, and mysterious disappearances. An increase in refugees heading for the protection of the larger walled towns and cities. And sketches from the survivors of the slant-browed, heavy-jawed creatures, including a detailed description of the powerful muscular systems that, Khadgar realized with a start, could only come from vivisecting the subject.

Khadgar began to read the mail to the wizard as he slept, reading aloud the more interesting or humorous bits. The Magus made no response to encourage the younger mage, but neither did he forbid it.

The first purple-sealed letter arrived and Khadgar was immediately lost. Some of the letters made sense, but others quickly descended into gibberish. At first the younger mage panicked, sure that he had misunderstood some basic instruction. After a day of littering the quarters with notes and failed attempts, Khadgar realized what he had been missing—that the space between the words was considered a letter in the Order's cipher, shifting everything one more letter in the process. Once that realization dawned, the missive deciphered easily.

It was less impressive than it had seemed earlier when it was gibberish. A note from the far south, the peninsula of Ulmat Thondr, noting that all was quiet, there were no signs of orcs (though there was a rise in the number of jungle trolls of late) and that a new comet was visible along the southern horizon, with detailed notes (written out in words, not numbers). No response was requested, and Khadgar set it, and its translation, aside.

Khadgar wondered why the Order did not use a magical encoding or spell-based script. Perhaps not all members of the Order of Tirisfal were mages. Or that they were trying to hide it from other wizards, like Guzbah, and putting it in a magical script would draw their curiosity like bees to nectar. Most likely, Khadgar decided, it was out of Medivh's sheer cussedness to the point of making the other members of the Order use a poem praising his mother as the key.

A large package arrived from Lothar, distilling the previously-reported orc sightings and attacks and translating them onto a large map. Indeed, it seemed like armies of orcs were pouring out of the swampy territory of the Black Morass itself. Again, no response was asked. Khadgar considered sending Lothar a note regarding Medivh's state, but thought better of it. What could the Champion do, in any event, other than to worry? He did send a note, over his own signature, thanking him for the information and asking to be kept apprised.

A second week passed and they moved into a third, the master comatose, the student searching. Now armed with proper key, Khadgar started going through the older mail, some of it still held shut by violet dabs of sealing wax. Going through the old documents, Khadgar began to understand Medivh's often ambivalent feelings toward the Order. Oftimes the letters were little more than demands—this enchantment, that bit of information, a summons to come at once because the cows are off their feed or their milk has gone sour. The more complimentary of the missives usually held some sort of sting—a request for a desired spell or a lost tome, wrapped up within its florid praise. Many held nothing but pedantic advice, pointing out in detail how this candidate or that would be a perfect apprentice (these were mostly unopened, he noticed). And there were continual reports of no news, no changes, nothing out of the ordinary.

The latter changed within the more recent messages (they were not dated, but Khadgar began to determine where they fell within a timeline, both by the yellowing of the parchment and the increasing fever-pitch of demands and advice). The tone became more consolatory with the sudden appearance of the orcs, particularly as they started raiding caravans. But the undercurrent of demands on Medivh's time remained, and even increased.

Khadgar looked at the old man lying on the bed and wondered what would possess him to help these people and help them on a regular basis.

And then there were the mystery letters—the occasional thanks, the references to some arcane text, a response to an unknown question—"Yes," "No," and "The emu, of course." During his vigil at Medivh's bedside one mystery letter arrived, without signature. It read "Prepare quarters. The Emissary will arrive shortly."

At the end of the third week two letters arrived one evening with a traveling merchant, one with the purple seal, the other red-sealed and addressed to Khadgar himself. Both were from the Violet Citadel of the Kirin Tor.

The letter to Khadgar began, in a spidery hand, "We regret to inform you of the sudden and unexpected death of the instructor mage Guzbah. We understand you have been in correspondence with the late mage and we share your emotion and sympathy at this time. If you have any correspondence, moneys, or information currently due to Guzbah, or are in possession of any of his property (in particular any of his books on loan), the return of that correspondence, money, information, or property would be appreciated, sent to the below address." A set of numbers and a lazy, illegible scrawl marked the bottom of the letter.

Khadgar felt as if he had been struck in the gut. Guzbah, dead? He turned the letter over, but no further information fell out. Stunned, he reached for the purple-sealed letter. This was in the same spider-hand, but once it was decoded held more information.

Guzbah was found slain in the library on the eve of the Feast of Scribes, in the midst of a reviewing of *Denbrawn's Treatise on the "Song of Aegwynn."* (Khadgar felt a pang of remorse for not sending his former instructor the scroll.) He was apparently taken by surprise from a beast (presumably summoned) which ripped him apart. The death was quick but painful, and the explanation of how the body was found detailed to the point of excess. From the description of the body and the shambles of the library, Khadgar could only conclude that the "summoned beast" was a demon of the type Medivh had fought in Stormwind.

The letter continued, the words maintaining a cold, analytical tone that Khadgar found excessive. The writer noted that this was the seventh death within the year of a mage of the Violet Citadel, including that of the archmage Arrexis. It went on further to note that this was the first death of this type where the victim was not a member of the Order itself. The writer wanted to know if Medivh had been in contact with Guzbah, either directly or through his apprentice (Khadgar had a moment of déjà vu looking at his own name in print). The unknown author went forward to speculate that since he was not a member of the Order, Guzbah might be responsible for the summoning of the beast for some other matter, and if this was the case, then Medivh should be aware that Khadgar had been Guzbah's student at one point.

Khadgar felt a sharp pain of anger. How dare this mysterious writer (it had to be someone high within the Kirin Tor hierarchy, but Khadgar had no idea who) impugn both Guzbah and himself! Khadgar wasn't even present when Guzbah was killed! Perhaps this writer was the one responsible, or someone like Korrigan—the librarian was always researching demon-worshipers. Casting accusations about like that!

Khadgar shook his head and took a deep breath. No, such speculation was futile and fueled only by personal indignation, like so much of the politics of the Kirin Tor. The anger faded to sadness and realization that the mighty mages of the Violet Citadel were unable to stop this, that seven wizards (six of them members of this supposedly secret and powerful Order) had died, and all this writer could do was cast about aspersions in the desperate hope that there would be no additional deaths. Khadgar thought of Medivh's quick and decisive actions at Stormwind Keep, and marveled that there was no one of equal wit, drive, and intelligence within his own community.

The young mage picked up the encoded letter and examined it again in the wan candlelight. The Feast of Scribes was over a month and a half ago. It took this long for the message to cross the sea and reach them overland. A month and a half. Before Huglar and Hugarin were killed in Stormwind. If the same demon was involved, or even the same summoner, it would have to move between the two points very, very swiftly. Some of the demons in the vision had wings—was it possible for such a beast to move between the locations without anyone spotting it?

An errant and unexpected breeze wafted through. The hairs on the back of Khadgar's neck began to bristle, and he looked up in time to see the figure manifest within the room.

First there was smoke, red as blood, bubbling out from some pinprick hole in the universe. It coiled and curdled upon itself like milk rising through water, quickly forming a swirling mass, through which stepped the looming form of a great demon.

Its form was reduced from when Khadgar had seen it before, on the field of snow in the timelost vision. It had shrunk itself to allow it to fit within the confines of the room. Still its flesh was of bronze, its armor of jet-black iron, and its beard and hair of animated fire, huge horns erupting from a massive brow. It was weaponless, but seemed to need no weapons, for it moved with the comfortable grace of a predator that fears nothing.

Sargeras.

Khadgar was stunned into silence and immobility. Surely the wards Medivh had maintained would keep such a beast at bay? Yet here it was, entering the tower, entering the Magus's very room with the ease of a noble entering a commoner's shack.

The Lord of the Burning Legion did not look around, instead glided to the foot of the bed. He stood there for a long moment, the flames of his beard and hair flickering without sound, as he regarded the unconscious form before him. The demon stood watching the sleeping mage.

Khadgar held his breath and looked around the worktable. A few tomes, the candle backlit by a mirror for greater illumination. A letter opener used to break the purple seals. The young mage slowly reached for the opener, trying to move without attracting the great demon's attention. His fingers wrapped around it tightly, his knuckles white.

Still Sargeras stood at the foot of the bed. A long moment passed, and Khadgar tried to will himself to move. Either to flee or to attack. His muscles felt locked in position.

Medivh shifted in his bedding, mumbling something unheard. The demon lord raised a hand slowly, as if to pronounce a benediction on the Magus's inert form.

Khadgar gave a strangled cry and thrust himself up from his chair, letter opener clutched in his hand. Only at this moment did he realize that he held the opener in his wrong hand.

The demon looked up, and it was a lazy, smooth motion, as if the demon himself was sleeping, or far underwater. It regarded the charging youth, hand raised in a clumsy attack with a short, sharp dagger.

The demon smiled. Medivh shifted and muttered in his sleep. Khadgar drove the letter opener into the demon's chest.

And through the creature's body entirely. The thrust of his blow carried him forward, through the form of Sargeras, and sent him spinning toward the opposite wall. Unable to stop, he slammed into the wall, and the letter opener jangled to the stone floor.

Medivh's eyes popped open, and the Guardian sat up. "Moroes? Khadgar? Are you here?"

Khadgar pulled himself to his feet, looking around. The demon had vanished, popped like a soap bubble at the first touch of steel. He was alone in the room with Medivh.

"What are you doing on the floor, lad?" said Medivh. "Moroes could have gotten you a cot."

"Master, your wards!" said Khadgar. "They have failed. There was . . ." he stumbled for a moment, unsure that he should reveal he knew Sargeras by appearance. Medivh would catch something like that, and pester him until he revealed how he knew it.

"A demon," he managed. "There was a demon here."

Medivh smiled, looking well rested, the color returning to his face. "A demon? I think not. Hold." The Magus closed his eyes and nodded. "No, the wards are still in place. It would take more than a catnap for them to run out of energy. What did you see?"

Quickly Khadgar recounted the appearance of the demon from the cloud of boiling red milk, of it standing there, of it raising its hand. The Magus shook his head.

"I think that was another one of your visions," he said at last. "Some bit of time unstuck and displaced that fell into the tower, quickly banished."

"But the demon . . ." started Khadgar.

"The demon you described is no more, at least no more in this life," said Medivh. "He was slain before I was born, buried far beneath the sea. Your vision was of Sargeras, from 'The Song of Aegwynn.' You have the scrolls there. Deciphering messages? Yes. Perhaps that's what called that timelost wraith into my quarters. You should not be doing work here while I slept." He frowned slightly, as if he was thinking if he should be more upset or not.

"I'm sorry, I thought . . . I thought it would be best to not leave you alone?" Khadgar twisted it into a question, and it sounded a bit foolish.

Medivh chuckled and let a smile creep across his weathered features. "Well, I didn't say you couldn't, and I don't suppose Moroes would have stopped you, since that would reduce his need to be here." He rubbed a finger and thumb over his lips and through his beard. "I think I've had enough broth for one lifetime. And just to reassure you, I *will* check the tower's mystic wards. And show you how to do it as well. Now, aside from demon visions, did anything happen while I was gone?"

Khadgar summarized the messages he had received. The rising tide of orc incidents. Lothar's map. The mystery message about the Emissary. And the news of Guzbah's death.

Medivh grunted at the description of Guzbah's passing, and said, "So they're going to blame Guzbah until the next poor sod gets sliced open." He shook his head, then added, "Feast of the Scribes. That would be before Huglar and Hugarin died."

"By about a week and a half," said Khadgar. "Time enough for a demon to fly from Dalaran to Stormwind Keep."

"Or a man on gryphon-back," mused Medivh. "It's not all demons and magic in this world. Sometimes a simpler answer suffices. Anything else?"

"It sounds like these orcs are becoming much more numerous and dangerous," said Khadgar. "Lothar says they are moving from caravan raids to attacks on settlements. Small ones, but there are more people coming into Stormwind and the other cities all the time as a result."

"Lothar worries too much," said Medivh with a grimace.

"He's concerned," said Khadgar flatly. "He doesn't know what to expect next."

"On the contrary," said Medivh, letting out a long, mournful sigh. "If everything you tell me is true, then I'm afraid things are going *just* the way I expected!"

TEN
The Emissary

With Medivh's recovery things returned to normal, or as normal as anything was in the presence of the Magus. When the Magus was absent, Khadgar was left with instructions as to honing his magical skill, and when Medivh was in residence in the tower, the younger mage was expected to demonstrate those skills at the drop of a hat.

Khadgar adapted well, and felt as if his power was a set of clothes, two sizes too big, that only now was he growing into. He could control fire at will now, summon lightning without a cloud in the sky, and cause small items to dance upon the table at the will of his own mind. He learned other spells as well—those that allowed one to know when and how a man died from a single bone of his remains, how to cause a ground-fog to rise, and how to leave magical messages for others to find. He learned how to restore the age lost to an inanimate object, strengthening an old chair, and its reverse, to pull all the youth from a newly-crafted club, leaving it dusty and brittle. He learned the nature of the protective wards, and was entrusted with keeping them intact. He learned the library of demons, though Medivh would not permit any to be summoned in his tower. This last order Khadgar had no desire to break.

Medivh was gone for brief periods of a day here, a few days there. Always instructions were left behind, but never explanations. Upon his return the Guardian looked more haggard and worn, and would push Khadgar testily to determine the youth's mastery over his craft, and to detail any news that had arrived in his absence. But there was no further repeat of his comatose rest, and Khadgar assumed that whatever the master was doing, it did not involve demons.

One evening in the library, Khadgar heard noises from the common area and stables below. Shouts, challenges, and responses, in low, illegible tones. By the time he reached a window overlooking that part of the castle, a group of riders were leaving the tower's walls.

Khadgar frowned. Were these some supplicants turned away by Moroes, or messengers with some other dark tidings for his master? Khadgar descended the tower to find out.

He caught sight of the new arrival only briefly—a flash of a black cloak stepping into a guest room along the lower levels of the tower. Moroes was there, candle in hand, blinders in place, and as Khadgar slipped down the last few steps he could hear the castellan say "... Other visitors, they were less careful. They're gone now."

Whatever response the new arrival made was lost, and Moroes pulled the door shut as Khadgar came up.

"A guest?" asked the young man, trying to see if there was any clue of the new arrival behind him. Only a closed door greeted his view.

"Ayep," replied the castellan.

"Mage or merchant?" asked the young mage.

"Couldn't say," said the castellan, already moving down the hall. "Didn't ask, and the Emissary didn't say."

"The Emissary," repeated Khadgar, thinking of one of the mystery letters from Medivh's great sleep. "So it's political, then. For the Magus."

"Assume so," said Moroes. "Didn't ask. Not my place."

"So it is for the Magus," said Khadgar.

"Assume so," said Moroes, with the same sleepy inflection. "We'll be told when we need to know." And with that he was gone, leaving Khadgar to stare at the shut door.

For the next day, there was the odd feeling of another presence in the tower, a new planetary body whose very gravity changed the orbits of all the others. This new planet caused Cook to shift to a larger set of pans, and Moroes to move through the halls at more random times than normal. And even Medivh himself would send Khadgar on some errand within the tower, and as the young mage left he would hear the whisper of a heavy cloak on the stonework behind him.

Medivh volunteered nothing, and Khadgar waited to be told. He dropped hints. He waited patiently. Instead he was sent to the library to continue his studies and practice his spells. Khadgar descended the curved stairs for half a rotation, stopped, then slowly climbed back up, only to see the back of a black cloak glide into the Guardian's laboratory.

Khadgar stomped down the stairs, considering options of who the Emissary was. A spy for Lothar? Some secretive member of the Order? Perhaps one of the members from the Kirin Tor, the one with the spidery handwriting and the venomous theories? Or maybe some other matter entirely? Not knowing was frustrating, and not being trusted by the Magus seemed to make matters worse.

"We'll be told when we need to know," Khadgar muttered, stomping into the library. His notes and histories were scattered on the tables, where he'd left them last. He looked at them, and the schematics of his vision summoning spell. He had made a few amendments since his last attempt, hoping to temporally refine its results.

Khadgar looked at the notes and smiled. Then he picked up his vials of crushed gemstones, and headed downward—putting additional floors between himself and Medivh's audience chamber—to one of the abandoned dining halls.

Two levels lower was perfect. An ellipsoid of a room with stone fireplaces at each end, the great table put into service elsewhere, the ancient chairs lined across the wall from the single entrance. The floor was white marble, old and cracked but kept clean by Moroes's relentless industry and drive.

Khadgar laid out a magic circle of amethyst and rose quartz, still grinning as he laid out the lines. He was confident in his castings now, and did not need his ceremonial conjuration robes for luck. As he laid out the pattern of protection and abjuration, he smiled again. He was already shaping the energy within his mind, calling the required shades and types of magic, conforming them to their requisite shape, holding that fertile energy in abeyance until it was needed.

He stepped within the circle, spoke the words that needed to be spoken, made the motions with his hands in perfect harmony, and unleashed the energy within his mind. He felt the release as something connected within his mind and soul, and he called the magic forth.

"Show me what is happening in Medivh's quarters," he said, his mind giving off a nervous tic, hoping that the Guardian's wards did not apply to his apprentice.

Immediately, he knew the spell had gone wrong. Not in a major fashion, with the magical matrices collapsing upon themselves, but in a slight misfire. Perhaps the wards did work against him, redirecting his vision elsewhere, to another scene.

He knew he was off by several clues. First off, it was now daylight. Second, it was warm. And last, the location was familiar.

He had not been here before, exactly, at least not in this particular spire, but it was clear he was at Stormwind Keep, overlooking the city below. This was one of the taller spires, and the room was similar in general design to that where the two members of the Order had met their end months earlier. Yet here the windows were large and opened onto great white parapets, and a warm scented breeze stirred diaphanous draperies. Multicolored birds perched within golden hoops around the perimeter of the room.

Before Khadgar a small table was set with white porcelain plates edged with gold, the knifes and forks made of the precious metal as well. Crystal bowls held fruits—fresh and unblemished, the morning dew still clinging to the dimples of the strawberries. Khadgar felt his stomach rumble slightly at the sight.

Around the table hovered a thin man unknown to Khadgar, narrow-faced and wide-foreheaded, with a slender moustache and goatee. He was draped in an ornate red quilt that Khadgar realized must be a dressing gown, cinched at the waist with a golden belt. He touched one of the forks, moving it a molecule's length sideways, then nodded in satisfaction. He looked up at Khadgar and smiled.

"Ah, you are awake," he said in a voice that almost sounded familiar to Khadgar as well.

For an instant, Khadgar thought that this vision could see him, but no, the man was addressing someone behind him. He turned to see Aegwynn, as youthful and beautiful as she had been on the snowfield. (Was it earlier than that date? Later? He could not tell from her appearance.) She wore a white cape with green lining, but this was made of silk now, not fur, and her feet were shod not in boots but in simple white sandals. Her blond hair was held in place with a silver diadem.

"You seem to have gone to a great deal of trouble," she said, and her face was unreadable to Khadgar.

"With sufficient magic and desire, nothing is impossible," said the man, and turned over his hand, palm upward. Floating above his palm, a white orchid bloomed.

Aegwynn took the flower, raised it perfunctorily to her nose, then set it down on the table. "Nielas . . ." she began.

"Breakfast first," said the mage Nielas. "See what a court conjurer may whip up first thing in the morning. These berries were picked from the royal gardens not more than an hour ago. . . ."

"Nielas," Aegwynn said again.

"Followed by slices of butter-fed ham and syrup," continued the mage.

"Nielas," Aegwynn repeated.

"Then perhaps some eggs of the *vrocka,* poached at the table in the shells by a simple spell I learned out on the isles . . ." said the mage.

"I am leaving," said Aegwynn, simply.

A cloud passed over the mage's face. "Leaving? So soon? Before breakfast? I mean, I thought we would have a chance to talk further."

"I am leaving," said Aegwynn. "I have my own tasks to complete, and little time for the pleasantries of the morning afterward."

The court conjurer still looked confused. "I thought that after last night you would want to remain in the castle, at Stormwind, for a while." He blinked at the woman. "Wouldn't you?"

"No," said Aegwynn. "Indeed, after last night, there is no need for me to remain at all. I have attained what I have come here for. There is no need for me to stay any longer."

In the present, Khadgar winced as the pieces fell into place. Of course the mage's voice sounded familiar.

"But I thought . . ." stammered the mage Nielas, but the Guardian shook her head.

"You, Nielas Aran, are an idiot," said Aegwynn simply. "You are one of the mightiest sorcerers in the Order of Tirisfal, and yet, you remain an idiot. That says something about the rest of the Order."

Nielas Aran bridled. He meant to look irritated, but only looked petulant. "Now, wait a moment. . . ."

"Surely you did not think that your natural charms alone brought me to your chamber, nor that your wit and sense of whimsy distracted me from our discussion of conjuration rites? Surely you realize that I cannot be impressed by your position as court conjurer like some village cowherd would? And surely you must realize that seduction works both ways? You are not *that* big an idiot, are you, Nielas Aran?"

"Of course not," said the court conjurer, clearly stung by her words but refusing to admit it. "I just thought that, like civilized people, we might share a moment of breakfast."

Aegwynn smiled, and Khadgar saw that it was a cruel smile. "I am as old as many dynasties, and got over my girlish indulgences early in my first century. I knew fully what I was doing coming to your chambers last night."

"I thought . . ." said Nielas. "I just thought . . ." He struggled for the right words.

"That you, of all the Order, would be the one to charm and tame the great, wild Guardian?" said Aegwynn, the smile growing wider. "That you could break her to your will, where all the others had failed, through your charm and wit and parlor tricks? Harness the power of the *Tirisfalen* to your own chariot? Come now, Nielas Aran. You have wasted much of your potential as it is, do not tell me that life in the royal court has corrupted you utterly. Leave me some respect for you."

"But if you weren't impressed," said Nielas, his mind wrapping around what Aegwynn was saying, "if you didn't want me, then why did we . . ."

Aegwynn provided the answer. "I came to Stormwind for one thing I could not provide for myself, a suitable father to my heir. Yes, Nielas Aran, you can tell your fellow mages in the Order that you managed to bed the great and mighty Guardian. But you will also have to tell them that you provided me with a way of passing on my power without the Order having any further say in it."

"I did?" The results of his actions began to sink in. "I suppose I did. But the Order would not like . . ."

"To be manipulated? To be countered? To be fooled?" said Aegwynn. "No, they will not. But they will not act against you, for fear that I truly do have some romantic interest in you. And take this solace—of all the mages, wizards, conjurers, and sorcerers, you were the one with the most potential. Your seed will protect and strengthen my child and make him the vessel for my power. And when he is born and weaned, you will even raise him, here, for I know he will follow my path, and even the Order would not want to miss that opportunity to influence him."

Nielas Aran shook his head. "But I . . ." He stopped for moment. "But did you . . ." He stopped again. At last when he spoke, there was finally some fire in his eyes, and steel in his voice. "Good-bye, Magna Aegwynn."

"Good-bye, Nielas Aran," said Aegwynn. "It has been . . . pleasant." And with that she turned on her heel and was gone from the room.

Nielas Aran, chief conjurer to the throne of Azeroth, conspirator in the

Order of Tirisfal, and now father to the future Guardian Medivh, sat by the perfectly set table. He picked up a golden fork, turned it over and over in his fingers. Then he sighed, and dropped it on the floor.

The vision faded before the fork struck the marble floor, but Khadgar was aware of another noise, this one behind him. The sound of a boot scraping against cold stone. The soft scraping of a cloak. He was not alone.

Khadgar wheeled, but all he caught was a tantalizing glimpse of a black cloak's back. The Emissary was spying on him. Bad enough he was sent away each time Medivh met with the stranger—now the Emissary had run of the castle and was spying on him!

At once, Khadgar was on his feet and rushing for the entrance. By the time he reached the doorway, his prey was gone, but there was the sound of fabric brushing along stone down the stairs. Down toward the guest quarters.

Khadgar barreled forward down the stairs as well. The curve of the stairs would keep the Emissary to the outside rim, where the footing was broader and more sure. The younger mage had raced up and down these steps so many times he deftly danced down along the inner wall, skipping the stairs in twos and threes.

Halfway to the guest level Khadgar could see his prey's shadow against the outer wall. As he reached the guest level itself he could see the cloaked figure, moving swiftly out through the archway and toward its door. Once the Emissary reached the guest quarters, he would lose his chance. Khadgar vaulted the last four steps in a single bound, and leapt forward to grasp the cloaked figure by the arm.

His hand closed on fabric and firm muscle, and he spun his prey toward the wall. "The Magus will want to know you're spying. . . ." he began, but the words died in his mouth as the cloak fell open to reveal the Emissary.

She was dressed in traveling leathers, with high laced boots and black trousers and black silk blouse. She was well-muscled, and Khadgar had no doubt that she had ridden the entire way here. But her skin was green, and as the hood fell back it revealed a jut-jawed, fanged orcish face. Tall greenish ears poked up from the mass of ebony hair.

"Orc!" shouted Khadgar, and reacted with an automatic response. He raised a hand, muttering a word of power, summoning the forces to drive a bolt of mystic power through her.

He never had the chance to finish. At the first opening of his mouth, the orc woman lashed out with a roundhouse kick, bringing her leg up to chest level. Her knee brushed aside Khadgar's pointing hand, forcing his aim off. Her booted foot slammed into the side of Khadgar's cheek, staggering him.

Khadgar reeled back and tasted blood—he must have bitten his cheek as a result of the blow. He raised his hand again to fire a bolt, but the orc was still too fast, faster than the armor-bound warriors he had fought earlier. Already she had closed the distance between them, driving a hard fist into his stomach, forcing the wind from his lungs and the concentration from his mind.

The young mage snarled, abandoning magic for the moment in favor of a more direct approach. Still smarting from the blow, he spun to one side, grasping the woman's arm and pulling her off-balance. A surprised look crossed the woman's jade-shaded face, but only for a moment. She planted her feet firmly on the ground, pulled Khadgar toward her, and neatly broke and reversed the hold.

Khadgar caught a whiff of spices as he was drawn close to the orc, and then she threw him, bodily, down the hallway. He slid along the stone floor, bumping into the wall and at last coming to rest at someone else's feet.

Looking up, Khadgar saw the castellan looking down on him, a look of vague concern on his face.

"Moroes!" shouted Khadgar. "Get back! Fetch the Magus! We have an orc in the tower!"

Moroes did not move, but instead looked up at the orcish woman with his bland, blinkered eyes. "You all right, Emissary?"

The woman smirked, her greenish lips tucked back, and wrapped her cloak around herself. "Never better. Needed a little exercise. The whelp was kind enough to oblige."

"Moroes!" spat the younger mage. "This woman is . . ."

"The Emissary. A guest of the Magus," said Moroes, adding blandly, "Came to get you. Magus wants to see you."

Khadgar pulled himself to his feet and looked sharply at the Emissary. "When you see the Magus, you're going to tell him you're snooping around?"

"Doesn't want to see her," corrected Moroes. "Wants to see you, Apprentice."

"She's an orc!" said Khadgar, louder and harsher than he meant to.

"Half-orc, really," said Medivh. He was bent over his workbench, fiddling with a golden device, an astrolabe. "I surmise her homeland has humans, or near-humans, or at least had them within living memory. Hand me the calipers, Apprentice."

"They tried to kill you!" shouted Khadgar.

"Orcs, you mean? Some did, true," said Medivh calmly. "*Some* orcs tried to kill me. And kill you as well. Garona wasn't in that group. I don't think she was, at any rate. She's here as a representative for her people. Or at least some of her people."

Garona. So the witch has a name, thought Khadgar. Instead he said, "We were attacked by orcs. I had a vision of attacks of orcs. I have been reading the communications from all over Azeroth, speaking of raids and attacks by orcs. Every mention of orcs speaks of their cruelty and violence. There seem to be more of them every day. This is a dangerous and savage race."

"And she dispatched you easily, I assume," said Medivh, looking up from his work.

Despite himself, Khadgar touched the corner of his mouth, where the blood had already dried. "That is completely beside the point."

"Completely," said Medivh. "And your point would be?"

"She is an orc. She is dangerous. And you have given her free rein in the tower."

Medivh grumbled, and there was steel in his voice. "She is a half-orc. She is about as dangerous as you are, given the situation and inclination. And she is my guest and should be accorded all the respect of a guest. I expect this from you regarding my guests, Young Trust."

Khadgar was silent for a moment, then tried a new approach. "She is the Emissary."

"Yes."

"Who is she the emissary *for?*"

"One or more of the clans that are currently inhabiting the Black Morass," said Medivh. "I'm not quite sure which ones, yet. We haven't gotten that far."

Khadgar blinked in surprise. "You let her into our tower, and she has no official standing?"

Medivh laid down the calipers and gave out a weary sigh. "She has presented herself to me as a representative of some of the orc clans that are presently raiding Azeroth. If this matter is going to be solved by any manner other than by fire and the sword, then someone has to start talking. Here is as good a place as any. *And,* by the way, this is considered *my* tower, not ours. You are my student here, my apprentice, and are here at my whim. And as my student, as my apprentice, I expect you to keep an open mind."

There was a silence as Khadgar tried to let this sink in. "So she represents whom? Some, none, or all of the orcs?"

"She represents, for the moment, herself," said Medivh, letting out an irritated sigh. "Not all humans believe the same thing. There is no reason to believe that all orcs do, either. My question for you is, given your natural curiosity, why aren't you already trying to pull as much information out of her as possible, instead of telling me I should not do the same? Unless you doubt me and my abilities to handle a single half-orc?"

Khadgar was silent, doubly embarrassed both for his actions and for failing to see another way. Was he doubting Medivh? Was there even a chance that the Magus would act in a fashion not to uphold his Order? The thoughts churned within him, fueled by Lothar's words, the vision of the demon, and the politics of the Order. He wanted to warn the older man, but every word seemed to be turned back against him.

"I worry about you, at times," he said at last.

"And I worry about you as well," said the older mage, distractedly. "I seem to worry about a lot of things these days."

Khadgar had to make one last attempt. "Sir, I think this Garona is a spy," he said, simply. "I think she is here to learn as much as she can, to be used against you later."

Medivh leaned back and gave the young man a wicked smile. "That is very much the pot calling the kettle black, young mageling. Or have you forgotten the list of things your own masters of the Kirin Tor wanted you to wheedle out of me when you first got to Karazhan?"

Khadgar's ears were burning crimson as he left the room.

ELEVEN
Garona

He returned to his (well, Medivh's) library to find her going over his notes. An immediate rage blossomed in his chest, but the sting of her blows, and Medivh's chastisement, kept his anger in check.

"What are you doing?" he still said sharply.

Emissary Garona's fingers danced up from the papers. "Snooping, I believe you called it? Spying?" She looked up, a frown on her face. "Actually, I'm just trying to understand what you're doing here. It was left out in the open. Hope that is all right with you."

It is NOT all right with me, thought Khadgar, but instead he said, "Lord Medivh has instructed me to extend to you every courtesy. However, he may take umbrage if, in doing so, I allow you to blow yourself up in casting some ill-thought magical spell."

Garona's face was impassive, but Khadgar noted that she did lift her fingers from the pages. "I have no interest in magic."

"Famous last words," said Khadgar. "Is there something here I can help you with, or are you just snooping in general, seeing what you can come up with?"

"I was told you had a tome on Azeroth's kings," she said. "I would like to consult it."

"You can read?" asked Khadgar. It sounded harsher than he meant it. "Sorry. I meant to say . . ."

"Yes, surprisingly, I can read," said Garona, quickly and officiously. "I have picked up many talents over the years."

Khadgar scowled. "Second row, fourth shelf up. It's a red-bound book with gold trim." Garona disappeared into the stacks, and Khadgar took the opportunity to gather up his notes from the table. He would have to keep them elsewhere if the half-orc had free run of the place. At least it wasn't Order correspondence—even Medivh would have a fit if he turned over "The Song of Aegwynn" to her.

His eyes went to the section where the scroll used as the key was kept. From where he was standing it looked undisturbed. No need to cause a scene here, but he would probably have to move it as well.

Garona returned with a massive tome in her hand, and raised a heavy eyebrow at Khadgar, forming a question. "Yes, that's the one," said the apprentice.

"Human languages are a bit . . . wordy," she said, setting the tome down in the empty space that previously held Khadgar's notes.

"Only because we always have something to say," said Khadgar, trying to manage a smile. He wondered, did orcs have books? Did they read at all? They had spellcasters, of course, but did that mean they had any real knowledge?

"I hope I wasn't too hard on you, earlier in the hall." Her tone was glib, and Khadgar was sure that she would rather have seen him spit out a tooth. Probably this was what passed for an apology among the orcs.

"Never better," said Khadgar. "I needed the exercise."

Garona sat down and started poring through the text. Khadgar noticed that she moved her lips as she read, and she had immediately turned toward the back of the book, to the recent additions about King Llane's reign.

Now, not in the immediate fire of combat, he could see that Garona was not the standard orc he had fought earlier. She was lean and well-muscled, unlike the lumpy, rough brutes he had battled at the caravan site. Her skin was smoother, almost human, and a lighter shade of green than the jade flesh of the orcs themselves. Her fangs were a bit smaller, and her eyes were a bit larger, more expressive than the hard crimson orbs of the orc warriors. He wondered how much of this was from her human heritage and how much from being female. He wondered if any of the orcs he had fought earlier were female—it was not obvious, and he had no desire to check at the time.

Indeed, without the green flesh, the disfigured, tusked face, and the hostile, superior attitude she might almost be attractive. Still, she was in *his* library, and going through *his* books (well, Medivh's library, and Medivh's books, but the Magus had entrusted them to *him*).

"So you are an Emissary," he said at last. He tried to keep his words light and conversational. "I was told of your impending arrival."

The half-orc nodded, concentrating on the words before her.

"Who are you emissarying *for*, exactly?"

Garona looked up, and Khadgar saw a flicker of irritation beneath her heavy brows. Khadgar felt good about bothering her, but at the same time wondered where the woman drew the line. He did not want to push too hard or too fast, lest he earn another beating, or another curt dismissal by the Magus.

At least this time he would get some information out before the battle. He said, "I mean, if you're the Emissary, that means that someone is giving you orders, someone is pulling your strings, someone you have to report back to. Whom do you represent?"

"I'm sure your Master, the Old Man, would tell you, if you asked," said Garona smoothly, but her eyes remained hard.

"I'm sure he would," Khadgar lied. "If I had the effrontery to ask him. So I ask you instead. Whom do you represent? What powers have you been granted? Are you here to negotiate, or demand, or what?"

Garona closed the book (Khadgar felt a small victory in distracting her from her task) and said, "Do all humans think alike?"

"It would be boring if we did," said Khadgar.

"I mean, does everyone agree about everything? Are people always agreeing to what their masters or superiors want?" said Garona. The hardness in her eyes faded just a touch.

"Hardly," said Khadgar. "One reason that there are so many tomes is that everyone has an opinion. And that is just the literate ones."

"So understand that there are differences of opinions among the orcs as well," said Garona. "The Horde is made up of a number of clans, all with their own chieftains and war leaders. All orcs belong to a clan. Most orcs are loyal to their clan and their chieftain."

"What are the clans?" asked Khadgar. "What are they called?"

"Stormreaver is one," said the half-orc. "Blackrock. Twilight's Hammer. Bleeding Hollow. Those are the major ones."

"Sounds like a warlike bunch," said Khadgar.

"The homeland of the orc peoples is a harsh place," said Garona, "and only the strongest and best organized survive. They are no more than what their land has made them."

Khadgar thought of the blasted, red-skied land he had seen in the vision.

This was the orcs' homeland, then. Some wasteland in another dimension. Yet how did they get here? Instead he said, "So which is your clan?"

Garona gave a snort that sounded like a bulldog sneezing. "I have no clan."

"You said all of your people belonged to a clan," said Khadgar.

"I said all *orcs*," said Garona. When Khadgar looked at her blankly, she held up her hand. "Look at this. What do you see?"

"Your hand," said Khadgar.

"Human or orc?"

"Orc," said Khadgar. It was obvious to him. Green skin, sharp yellowing nails, knuckles just a shade too large to be human.

"An orc would say that it's a human hand—too slender to be really useful, not enough muscle to hold an ax or bash a skull in properly—too pale, too weak, and too ugly." Garona lowered her hand and looked at the young mage through lowered brows. "You see the parts of me that are orcish. My orcish superiors, and all other orcs, see the parts of me that are human. I am both, and neither, and considered an inferior being by both sides."

Khadgar opened his mouth to argue, but thought twice of the matter and kept silent. His first reaction was to strike out at the orc he had found in the halls, not to see the human that was Medivh's guest. He nodded and said, "It must be difficult, then. Without a clan allegiance."

"I have turned it to my advantage," said Garona. "I can move between the clans more easily. As a lesser creature, I am assumed to not be always looking for an advantage to my native clan. I am disliked by all, so therefore I am not biased. Some chieftains find that reassuring. It makes me a better negotiator, and before you say it, a better spy. But better to have no allegiance than conflicting ones."

Khadgar thought of Medivh's own castigation of his Kirin Tor ties, but said, "And which clan do you represent at the moment?"

Garona gave a wry, fanged smile. "If I said Gizblah the Mighty, what would you say? Or perhaps I am on a mission for Morgax the Gray or Hikapik the Bloodrender. Would that tell you enough?"

"It might," said Khadgar.

"It wouldn't," said Garona, "because I made up all those names, just now. And the name of the faction that has sent me here would mean nothing to you either, not at the moment. Similarly, the Old Man's stated friendship with King Llane means nothing to our chieftains, and the name Lothar is nothing more than a curse invoked by the human peasants we encounter. Before we can have peace, before we can even start negotiating, we have to learn more about you."

"Which is why you're here."

Garona let out a deep sigh. "Which is why I am praying that you will leave me alone long enough so I can figure out what the Old Man is talking about when we have our discussions."

Khadgar was silent for a moment. Garona opened the volume again, leafing through the pages to where she had stopped. "Of course, that goes both ways," Khadgar said, and Garona closed the book with an exasperated breath. "I mean, we need to know more about the orcs if we're going to do more than just battle them. If you're serious about peace."

Garona glared at Khadgar, and for a moment the young mage wondered if the half-orc was going to leap across the table and throttle him. Instead, her ears perked up, and she said, "Hold on. What's that?"

Khadgar felt it before he heard it. A sudden change in the air, like a window had been opened elsewhere in the tower. A bit of wind stirring up the dust in the hall. A wave of warmth passing through the tower.

Khadgar said, "Something is . . ."

Garona said, "I heard . . ."

And then Khadgar heard it as well, the sound of iron claws scraping against stone, and the warmth of the air increased as the hairs on the back of his neck rose.

And the great beast slouched into the library.

It was made of fire and shadow, its skin dark and containing the flickers of the flame within. Its wolflike face was framed by a set of ram's horns, that glowed like polished ebony. It looked biped, but walked on all fours, its long front claws scraping along the stone floors.

"What is . . ." hissed Garona.

"Demon," said Khadgar in a strangled voice, rising and backing away from the table.

"Your manservant said there were visions here. Ghosts. Is this one?" Garona stood up as well.

Khadgar wanted to explain no, that visions tended to encompass the area entirely, shifting you to the new place, but he instead just shook his head.

The beast itself was perched in the doorway, sniffing the air. The creature's eyes blazed with flame. Was the beast blind, and could only detect by scent? Or was it detecting a new thing in the air, a spice that it had not expected?

Khadgar tried to pull the energies into his mind, but at first his heart quailed and his mind went empty. The beast continued to sniff, turning in place until it faced the pair.

"Get to the high tower," said Khadgar quietly. "We have to warn Medivh." Out of the corner of his eye he saw Garona nod, but her eyes did not leave the beast. A trickle of sweat dropped down her long neck. She shifted slightly to one side.

The movement was enough, and everything happened at once. The beast crouched and leapt across the room. Khadgar's mind cleared, and with a quick efficiency he pulled the energies into himself, raised his hand, and buried a bolt of mystic energy into the creature's chest. The energy ripped through the beast's chest and splattered out its back, sending pieces of flaming flesh in all directions, but it did not deter it in the slightest.

It landed on the study table, its claws digging into the hardwood, and bounded again, this time for Khadgar. The young mage's mind went blank for a second, but a second was all it took for the slope-shouldered demon to close the distance between them.

Something else grabbed him and yanked him out of the way. He smelled musky cinnamon and heard a deep-throated curse as he spun out of the path of the loping demon. The beast sailed through the space that until recently had been occupied by the apprentice, and let out a scream of its own. A long ragged tear had appeared along the creature's left side, and was oozing burning blood.

Garona released Khadgar from her grip (a weak, humanish grip, but still enough to drive the air from his lungs). In her other hand, the apprentice noticed that Garona held a long-bladed knife, crimson with its first strike, and Khadgar wondered where she had hid it while they were arguing.

The creature landed, wheeled, and tried to make an immediate, clumsy second assault, its iron-shod talons outstretched, its mouth and eyes blazing with flame. Khadgar ducked, then came up with the heavy red volume of *The Lineage of Azeroth's Kings*. He hefted the massive tome into the creature's face, then ducked again. The beast sailed past him, landing back near the door. It let out a retching, choking noise, and shook his ram-horned head to dislodge the weighty grimoire. Khadgar saw there was a line of burning blood etched along the creature's right side. Garona had struck a second time.

"Get Medivh," shouted Khadgar. "I'll get it away from the door."

"What if it wants me, instead?" responded Garona, and for the first time, Khadgar heard a ripple of fear in her voice.

"It doesn't," said Khadgar grimly. "It kills mages."

"But you . . ."

"Just go," said Khadgar.

Khadgar broke to the left, and, true to his fears, the demon followed him. Instead of heading toward the door, Garona broke for the right, and started climbing the far bookcase.

"Get Medivh!" shouted Khadgar, darting down one of the rows of books.

"No time," responded Garona, still climbing. "See if you can delay it in one of the rows."

Khadgar turned at the far end of the long bookshelves, and turned again. The demon had already leapt over the study table and was now prowling down the row between the bookcases, between histories and geographies. In the shadow between the rows the creature's flaming eyes and mouth stood out in stark relief, and acrid smoke now roiled from its wounded sides.

Khadgar cleared his mind, stuffed down his fear, and fired off a mystic bolt. A globe of fire or a shard of lightning might be more effective, but the beast was surrounded by his books.

The bolt smashed into the creature's face, staggering it back a pace. It growled and crept forward again.

He repeated the process like a ritual—clear the mind, fight the fear, raise a hand, and invoke the word. Another bolt splanged off its ebony horns, ricocheting upward. The beast halted, but only for a moment. Now its maw seemed a twisted, flame-filled smile.

A third time he invoked the power of the mystic bolt, but now the creature was close, and it flashed in its face, but save for illuminating its amused features, did nothing. Khadgar smelled its sour, burning flesh, and heard a deep clicking within the beast's throat—laughter?

"Get ready to run!" shouted Garona, from somewhere to his right and above.

"What are you . . ." started Khadgar, already backing up.

"Run!" she shouted, and pushed off with her feet. The half-orc had climbed to the top of the bookcases, and now shoved them apart, toppling the cases like giant dominos. A deep crash of thunder resounded as each bookcase tipped over its neighbor, spilling volumes and crushing everything in its path.

The last bookcase smashed against the wall and splintered, the force of the impact driving it to the ground. Garona slid down from her now wobbling perch, long-bladed knife drawn. She tried to peer through the churning dust.

"Khadgar?" she said.

"Here," said the apprentice, plastered against the back wall, where the iron pedestals rose to support the upper stacks on the balcony above. His face was pale even for a human.

"Did we get it?" she demanded, still in a half-crouch, expecting a new assault at any moment.

Khadgar pointed to the edge of what was until seconds before the end of the row of shelves. Now the entire lower floor was a ruins of shattered cases and ruined volumes. Reaching out of the tattered wreckage was a muscular, mangled arm made of dull flame and twisted shadow. Its iron claws were already red with rust, and warm blood was already pooling on the floor. Its outstretched hand was a mere foot from where Khadgar splayed himself.

"Got it," said Garona, sliding the knife back into its sheath beneath her blouse.

"You should have listened," said Khadgar, choking on the dust. "Should have gotten Medivh."

"It would have sliced you open before I got up two flights of stairs," said the half-orc. "And then who would be left to explain things to the Old Man?"

Khadgar nodded, and then a thought furrowed his brow. "The Magus. Did he hear this?"

Garona nodded in agreement. "He should have come down. We made enough noise here to wake the dead."

"No," said Khadgar, heading for the entrance to the library. "What if there was more than one demon? Come on!"

Without thinking, Garona drew her knife and followed the human out of the room.

They found Medivh sitting in his laboratory, at the same workbench that Khadgar had left him no more than an hour previously. Now the golden instrument he was working on was in twisted pieces, and an iron hammer rested at one side of the bench.

Medivh started when Khadgar burst into the room, followed closely by Garona. The apprentice wondered, had he been dozing through all this?

"Master! There is a demon in the tower!" blurted Khadgar.

"A demon, again?" said Medivh wearily, rubbing one eye with the flat of his palm. "It was a demon the first time. The last time it was an orc."

"Your student is correct," said Garona. "I was in the library with him when it attacked. Large creature, bestial, but cunning. Made of fire and darkness, and its wounds burned and smoked."

"It was probably nothing more than another vision," said Medivh, turning back to his work. He picked up a mangled piece of the device and looked at it, as if seeing it for the first time. "They happen here, the visions. I think Moroes warned you about them."

"It was not a vision, Master," said Khadgar. "It was a demon, of the type you fought at Stormwind Keep. Something has gotten past the wards and attacked us."

Medivh's gray brows arched in suspicion. "Something get past my wards again? Ridiculous." He closed his eyes and traced a symbol in the air. "No. Nothing is amiss. None of the wards are tripped. You are here. Cook is in the kitchen, and Moroes is in the hall outside the library right now."

Khadgar and Garona exchanged a glance. Khadgar said, "Then you should come at once, Master."

"Must I?" said Medivh. "I have other things to worry about, of this I'm sure."

"Come and see," said Khadgar.

"We believe the beast to be dead," said Garona. "But we don't want to risk the lives of your servants on our beliefs."

Medivh looked at the smashed device, shook his head, and set it down. He seemed irritated by it. "As you wish. Apprentices are not supposed to be this much trouble."

By the time they reached the library, however, Moroes was standing there, dustpan and broom in hand, surveying the damage. He looked up, slightly lost, as the two mages and the half-orc entered.

"Congratulations," said Medivh, the lines of his frown cutting deeply across his face. "I think it's a bigger mess now than when you first arrived. At least then I had shelving. Where is this supposed demon?"

Khadgar walked over to where the demon's hand had jutted out, but now all that remained was one of the bookcases pressed flat on the floor. Even the blood was missing.

"It was here," said Garona, looking as surprised as Khadgar. "It came in, and attacked us." She grasped the edge of the case, trying to pry it up, but the massive oak was too heavy for her. After she struggled a moment, she said, "We both saw it."

"You saw a vision," said Medivh sternly. "Didn't Moroes warn you about this?"

"Ayep," confirmed Moroes. "I did at that." He tapped the sides of his blinders for effect.

"Master, it did attack us," said Khadgar. "We damaged it with our own spells. The Emissary here wounded it, twice."

"Hmmph," grunted the Magus. "More likely you overreacted when you saw it, and did most of the damage yourselves. These are fresh scratches on the table. From the demon?"

"He had iron claws," said Khadgar.

"Or perhaps from your own mystic bolts, flung around like beads at a Stormwind streetfair?" Medivh shook his head.

"My knife bit into something hard and leathery," said Garona.

"No doubt some of the books themselves," said the Magus. "No, were there a demon, its body would still be here. Unless someone cleaned it up. Moroes, do you happen to have a demon in your dustbin?"

"Don't believe so," said the castellan. "I could check."

"Don't worry, but leave your tools for these two." To the younger mage and the half-orc he said, "I expect you to get along. In light of this, you two get to straighten up the library. Young Trust, you have betrayed your name, and so must make restitution now."

Garona would not relent. "But I saw—"

"You saw a phantom," interrupted Medivh in an authoritative tone, his brows knitted. "You saw a piece of somewhere else. It would not have harmed you. It never does. Your friend here," and he motioned at Khadgar, "tends to see demons where there are none. That worries me a bit. Perhaps you can try not to see any when you are cleaning up. Until you do, I am not to be disturbed!"

And with that, he was gone. Moroes laid the broom and dustpan on the floor and followed him.

Khadgar looked around at the debris of the room. More than just a broom would be needed here. Cases were toppled and in a couple places shattered entirely, and books were flung randomly about, some with their spines broken and their covers torn. Could it have been a time-lost vision?

"This was no illusion that attacked us," said Garona moodily.

"I know," said Khadgar.

"So why doesn't he see it?" asked the half-orc.

"That I don't know," said the apprentice. "And I worry about finding out the answer."

TWELVE
Life in Wartime

It took only several days to put the library back in proper order. Most of the scattered books were at least near to where they needed to be, and the rarer, more magical, and trapped volumes were on the upper balcony and had been untouched by the fracas. Rebuilding some of the cases took time, however, and Garona and Khadgar turned the empty stables into a makeshift carpentry shop, and they tried to restore (and in some cases replace) the shattered cases.

Of the demon, there was no trace, save for the damage wrought. The claw marks remained in the table, and the pages of *The Lineage of Azeroth's Kings* were badly mangled and torn, as if by massive jaws. Yet there was no body, no blood, no remains to drop at Medivh's feet.

"Maybe it was rescued," suggested Garona.

"It was pretty dead when we left it," responded Khadgar, at the time trying to remember if he had put epic poetry on the shelf above or below romantic epics.

"Something rescued the body," said Garona. "The same person who popped it in here would have popped him out."

"And the blood as well," reminded Khadgar.

"And blood as well," repeated the half-orc. "Perhaps it was a tidy demon."

"That's not the way magic works," said Khadgar.

"Perhaps not your magic, the magic you learned," said Garona. "Other peoples could have other magics. The old shamans among the orcs had one way of magic, the warlocks that cast spells have different ones. Maybe it's a spell you never heard of."

"No," said Khadgar simply. "It would have left some kind of a marker. A bit of the caster behind. Some residual energy that I could feel, even if I could not identify it. The only spellcasters active in the tower have been myself and the Magus. I know that through my own spells. And I checked the wards. Medivh was right—they were all operating. No one should have been able to break into the tower, magically or otherwise."

Garona shrugged. "But there are odd things about this tower as well, correct? Could the old rules not apply here?"

It was Khadgar's turn to shrug. "If that's the case, we're in a lot more trouble than I imagined."

Khadgar's relationship with the half-orc seemed to improve over the course of repairing the library, and when his back was to her, or she was in the stacks, her voice sounded almost human. Still, she remained guarded about whom she represented, and Khadgar for his part remained watchful. He kept track of what references she used and what questions she asked.

He also tried to keep track of any communications she made, to the point of wrapping the guest quarters with his own web of detection spells, to inform him if she had left the room or sent word out. If she had, her methods foiled even Khadgar's detection, which made him more nervous as opposed to assuring him. If she was doing anything with the knowledge she had gained, she was keeping it to herself.

And true to her word, Garona began sharing her own knowledge about the orcs. Khadgar began to assemble a picture of how the orcs were ruled (by strength and warrior prowess) as well as the different clans within. Once she got rolling, the Emissary made very clear her opinion of the various clans, whose leaders she tended to think of as lumpen oafs who are only thinking of where their next battle is coming from. As she described the multi-clan orcish nation, the Horde, Khadgar quickly understood that the dynamics were ever-changing and fluid at best.

A large chunk of the Horde was the conservative Bleeding Hollow clan. A powerful group with a long history of conquest, the clan was less powerful in that its aged leader, Kilrogg Deadeye, had become more unwilling to throw lives away in combat. Garona explained that in orcish politics, older orcs become more pragmatic, which is often mistaken for cowardice by the younger generation. Kilrogg had killed three of his sons and two grandsons already who thought they could rule the clan better.

The clan known as the Blackrock appeared to have another large chunk of the Horde; its leader was Blackhand, who had as his chief recommendation for leader the ability to thump anyone else who wanted the title. A chunk of Blackrock had already splintered off, knocked out a tooth, and called themselves the Black Tooth Grin. Charming names.

There were other clans: Twilight's Hammer, which reveled in destruction, and the Burning Blade, who seemed to have no leader, but rather served as an anarchic gathering within the chaos of the Horde. And smaller clans, like the Stormreavers, that were led by a warlock. Khadgar suspected that Garona was reporting to someone within the Stormreavers, if only because she had less to complain about with them than the others.

Khadgar took what notes he could, and assembled them into reports for Lothar. A larger amount of communications was coming in from all points in Azeroth, and now it seemed that the Horde was spilling out of the Black Morass in all directions. The orcs that were considered mere rumors a year ago were now omnipresent, and Stormwind Keep was mobilizing to meet the threat. Khadgar kept the ever-worsening news from Garona, but fed to Lothar what details he could glean, down to clan rivalries and favorite colors (The Blackrock clan, for example, favored red for some reason).

Khadgar also tried to communicate what he had learned to Medivh, but the Magus was surprisingly disinterested. Indeed, the Magus's conversations with Garona were not as common as they once were, and on several occasions Khadgar discovered that Medivh had left the tower without informing him. Even when he was present, Medivh seemed more distant. More than once Khadgar had come upon him, seated in one of his chairs in the observatory, staring out into the Azerothean night. He seemed moodier now, quicker to disagree, and less willing to listen than before.

His disaffected mood was clear to the others as well. Moroes would give Khadgar a painful, long-suffering look as he left the master's chambers. And Garona herself brought up the subject as they reviewed the maps of the known world (which were made in Stormwind, and as such woefully incomplete even when talking about Lordaeron).

"Is he always like this?" she asked.

Khadgar responded stoically, "He has many moods."

"Yes, but when I first encountered him, he seemed alive, engaged, and positive. Now he seems more . . ."

"Distracted?"

"Addled," said Garona, twisting her lips in disgust.

Khadgar could not disagree. Later that evening, Khadgar reported to the Magus a slew of new message translations, all with the purple seal, all begging for aid against the orcs.

"The orcs are not demons," said Medivh. "They are flesh and blood, and as such the worry of warriors, not wizards."

"The messages are quite dire," said Khadgar. "It sounds like the lands closest to the Black Morass are being abandoned, and refugees are flooding into Stormwind and the other cities of Azeroth. They are pressed thin."

"And so they depend on the Guardian to ride to their rescue. Bad enough I must guard the watchtowers on the Twisting Nether to watch for demons, and to hunt down the mistakes of these amateurs. Now I must rescue them against other nations? Will I be asked to support Azeroth in a trade dispute with Lordaeron next? Such matters should not be our worry."

"There may not be an Azeroth without your help. Lothar is . . ."

"Lothar is a fool," muttered Medivh. "An old mother hen that sees threats everywhere. And Llane is little better, seeing nothing that could break his walls. And the Order, all the mighty mages, they have quarreled and argued and spat among themselves so now they don't have the power to repel a new invader. No, Young Trust, this is the little stuff. Even if the orcs succeeded in Azeroth, they would need a Guardian, and I would be here for them."

"Master, that's . . ."

"Sacrilege? Blasphemy? Betrayal?" The Magus sighed and pinched the bridge of his nose. "Perhaps. But I am a man made old before my time, and I have paid a great price for my unwanted power. Permit me to rail against the clockworks that rule my life. Go now. I'll return to your tales of woe in the morning."

As he was closing the door, Khadgar heard Medivh add, "I am so tired of worrying about everything. When can I worry about myself?"

"The orcs have attacked Stormwind," said Khadgar. It was three weeks later. He laid the missive on the table between him and Garona.

The half-orc stared at the red-sealed envelope like it was a venomous snake. "I am sorry," she said at last. "They will not as a rule take prisoners."

"The orc forces were repelled this time," said Khadgar. "Thrown back before they reached the gates by Llane's troops. From the descriptions, it sounds like Kilrogg's Bleeding Hollow and the Twilight's Hammer clans. There seemed to be a lack of coordination between the major forces."

Garona gave a bulldog-sneeze grunt and said, "The Twilight's Hammer should have never be put on an assault in a siege situation. Kilrogg likely was trying to decimate a rival, and use Stormwind as his anvil to do so."

"So even in the midst of an attack, they continue to brawl and betray each other," said Khadgar. He wondered if his own reports to Lothar had given them the information they needed to break the assault.

Garona shrugged. "Very much like humans." She motioned to the books piled high on the study table. "In your histories, there are continual justifications for all manner of hellish actions. Claims of nobility and heritage and honor to cover up every bit of genocide, assassination, and massacre. At least the Horde is honest in their naked lust for power." She was silent for a moment, then added, "I don't think I could have helped them."

"The orcs, or Stormwind?" asked Khadgar.

"Either," said Garona. "I did not know about any attack on Stormwind, if that's what you're hinting at, though anyone with half an ounce of sense would know that a Horde would strike against the biggest target as soon as possible. You know that from our discussions. You also know that they'll pull back, regroup, kill a few leaders, and then come back in greater numbers."

"I can guess, yes," said Khadgar.

Garona added, "And you already sent a letter to the Champion at Stormwind just to that effect."

Khadgar thought he kept his face passive, but the orc emissary gave a wide smile. "Yes, you did."

Khadgar now felt his face turn flushed, but pressed his point. "Actually, the question I have is, Why haven't *you* been reporting to your masters?"

The green-fleshed woman leaned back in her seat. "Who's to say I haven't?"

"I do," said Khadgar. "Unless you're a better mage that I am."

A small tic at the corner of Garona's mouth betrayed her. "You haven't been reporting in at all, have you?" asked Khadgar.

Garona was silent for a moment, and Khadgar let the silence fill the library. At length she said, "Let's just say I've been having a problem with divided loyalties."

"I thought you had no allegiances," said Khadgar.

Garona ignored him. "I was sent here, ordered here, by a warlock named Gul'dan. Spellcaster. Leader of the Stormreavers. Very influential in the Horde. Very interested in the mages of your world."

"And the orcs have the tendency to strike the biggest target first. Medivh," said Khadgar.

"Gul'dan said Medivh was special. From which secret divination or spice-fueled meditation he used to come to that conclusion, I don't know." Garona avoided Khadgar's glance. "I met several times with Medivh in the field, then agreed to come to the tower here as an emissary. I was supposed to trade basic information and report back to Gul'dan as much as I could about Medivh's strengths. So you were right from the start—I was here as a spy."

Khadgar sat down across from her. "You wouldn't have been the first," he said. "So why didn't you report back?"

Garona was silent for a moment. "Medivh . . ." she started, then stopped. "The Old Man . . ." another pause. "He saw through it all at once, of course, and he still told me what I wanted to know. Most of it, at least."

"I know," said Khadgar. "He had the same effect on me."

Garona nodded. "At first I thought he was just being pompous, sure in his power, like some orc chieftains I've known. But there's something else. It's as if he feels that by giving me the knowledge, he knew I would be changed by it, and would not betray his trust."

"Trust," said Khadgar. "That's a big thing for Medivh. He seems to exude it. Standing next to him, you feel he knows what he's doing."

"Right," said Garona, "and orcs are drawn to power naturally. I figured I could tell Gul'dan that I was held prisoner, unable to respond, and so I learned more, and eventually . . ."

"You didn't want to see him hurt," finished Khadgar.

"As Moroes would say, 'ayep,'" said Garona. "He put a lot of trust in me, and he puts it in you, too. After watching your vision-power thing, I told him about it. I figured that might have brought the demon down on us. He said he knew and it didn't bother him. That you were naturally curious, and it served you well. He stands by his people."

"And you can't hurt someone like that," said Khadgar.

"Ayep. He made me feel human. And I haven't felt human in a long, long time. The Old Man, Magus Medivh, seems to have a dream of more than one force battling another for domination. With his power, he could have destroyed us all, yet he does not. I think he believes in something better. I want to believe his dream as well."

The two sat there for a while in silence. Somewhere in the distance, Moroes or Cook moved along the hallway.

"And recently . . ." said Garona. "Has he ever been like this before?"

She sounded like Lothar—trying to ask without seeming too concerned. Khadgar shook his head. "He's always been erratic. Eccentric. But I've never seen him this . . . depressed."

"Brooding," added Garona. "Neutral. Up to now I've always assumed he would be on the side of the Kingdom of Azeroth. But if Stormwind itself is attacked and still he does nothing . . ."

"It may be his own training," said Khadgar, choosing his words carefully. He did not want to reveal the Order to Garona, regardless of her current feelings. "He has to take a very long view on things. It sometimes cuts him off from others."

"Which is why he takes in strays, I suppose," said Garona. Another silence, then she added, "I am not sorry that Stormwind repelled the invaders. You don't destroy something like that from without. You have to do something within to weaken the walls first."

"I'm glad you're not there as a general," said Khadgar.

"Chieftain," said Garona. "Like I'd get a chance."

"There is something," said Khadgar, then stopped. Garona tilted her heavily mawed head toward him.

"You sound like someone looking for a favor," she said.

"I have never asked you about troop strengths, and positions. . . ."

"About obvious spy stuff."

"But," said Khadgar, "they were amazed by the huge numbers of orc warriors on the field. They fought them back, but were surprised that the swamps of the Black Morass could hold that many soldiers. Even now they're worried about the forces that could be hiding within the marshlands."

"I know nothing of troop dispositions," said Garona. "I have been here, spying on you, remember?"

"True," said Khadgar. "But I also know you talked of your homeland. How did you get from there to here? Was it some spell?"

Garona sat quietly for a moment, as if trying to resolve something in her mind. Khadgar expected a flip comment, or a redirection of the subject, or even another question in response. Instead she said, "We call our world Draenor. It is a savage world, filled with badlands and bluffs and hardscrabble vegetation. Inhospitable and stormy . . ."

"And it has a red sky," added Khadgar.

Garona looked at the young mage. "You have spoken with other orcs? Prisoners, perhaps? I was unaware the humans took orc prisoners."

"No, a vision," said Khadgar. The memory seemed half a lifetime away. "Much like you saw the first time we met. It was the first time I had seen orcs. I remember there were huge numbers of them."

Garona let out a bulldog snort. "Your visions probably reveal more than you say, but you have a good picture. Orcs are fecund, and large litters are common, because so many die before they reach a warrior's age.

"It was a hard life, and only the strong, the powerful, and the smart survived. I was in the third group, but still I was a near-outcast, surviving as best I could at the fringes of the clan. That would be the Stormreavers, at the time, at least when the order went out."

"Order?"

"We were put on the march, every warrior and every capable hand. Grunt labor and swordsmen, all ordered to pack up their weapons, tools, and belongings, and head for the Hellfire Peninsula. There a great portal had been erected by Gul'dan and other powerful warlocks. A portal that broke through the space between the worlds."

Garona sucked on a fang, remembering. "It was a great set of standing stones, hauled there to frame a rip in space itself. Within the rip were the colors of darkness, a swirl like oil on the surface of a polluted pool. I got the feeling that rip had been forged by greater hands, and the warlocks had just contained it.

"Many of the most hardened warriors feared the space between the pillars, but the chieftains and underchiefs made passionate speeches about what was to be found on the other side. A world of riches. A world of plenty. A world of soft creatures who would be easily dominated. All this they promised.

"Some still resisted. Some were slain, and others were forced through with axes resting against their backs. I was caught with a large group of laborers and shoved into the space between the pillars."

Garona fell silent for a moment. "It's called the Twisting Nether, and it was both instantaneous and eternal. I fell forever, and when I emerged into the strange light, I was in a mad new world."

Khadgar added, "After promises of paradise, the Black Morass would be quite a letdown."

Garona shook her head. "It was a shock. I remember quailing at the first sight of the blue, hostile sky. And the land, covered with vegetation as far as the eye could see. Some could not take it and went mad. Many joined the Burning Blade, the chaos orcs thronging beneath their fire-orange pennant, that day."

Garona stroked her heavy chin. "I feared, but I survived. And I found my half-breed life gave me insight on these humans. I was part of an ambush party that attacked Medivh. He killed everyone else, but left me alive, and sent me with a message back to the Warlock Gul'dan. And after a while, Gul'dan sent me as his spy, but I found I had . . . difficulty . . . betraying the Old Man's secrets."

"Divided loyalties," commented Khadgar.

"But to answer your question," said Garona, "no, I don't know how many clans have poured through the Dark Portal from Draenor. And I don't know how long it will take for them to recover. And I don't know where the portal came from. But you, Khadgar, can find out."

Khadgar blinked. "Me?"

"Your visions," said Garona. "You seem to be able to summon up the ghosts of the past, even of far-away. I watched you call up a vision of Medivh's mother when I first met you. That was Stormwind we were at?"

"Yes," said Khadgar. "And that's why I still think the demon in the library was real—there was no background to the vision."

Garona waved off his comment. "But you can call up these visions. You can summon up the moment when the rift was first created. You can find out who brought the orcs through to Azeroth."

"Aye," said Khadgar. "And I bet it's the same mage or warlock that has been unleashing demons. It makes sense, that the two be linked." He looked at Garona. "You know, that would not be a question I would have thought of."

"I will provide the questions," said Garona, looking very pleased with herself, "if you provide the answers."

The empty dining room again. The ever-diligent Moroes had swept up the earlier casting circle, and Khadgar had to recast it with streams of crushed rose quartz and amethyst. Garona fit lit torches into the wall sconces, then stood in the center of the pattern, next to him.

"I'll warn you," he said to the half-orc. "This may not work."

"You'll do well," replied Garona. "I've seen you do it before."

"I'll probably get something," said Khadgar. "I just don't know what." He made the motions with his hands, and intoned the words. With Garona watching, he wanted to get everything just right. At last he released the mystical energy from the cage within his mind and shouted, "Show me the origin of the rift between Draenor and Azeroth!"

There was a change in the pressure, in the very weight of the air around them. It was warm, and night, but the night sky outside their window (for there was a window now in these quarters) was a deep red, the color of old, dried blood, and only a few weak stars pierced the envelope.

It was someone's quarters, likely an orc leader. There were fur rugs on the floor and a large platform that would serve as a bed. A low fire pit burned in the center of the room. Weapons hung on the stone walls, and there were a plethora of cabinets as well. One was open, showing a line of preserved *things,* some of which might have once belonged to human or humanish creatures.

The figure in the bed tossed, turned, and then sat up suddenly, as awakening from a bad dream. He stared into the darkness, and his savaged, war-torn face was clear. Even by orc standards, he was an ugly representative of his race.

Garona let out a sharp gasp, and said, "Gul'dan."

Khadgar nodded and said, "He should not see you." This, then, was the warlock that had sent Garona to spy. He looked about as trustworthy as a bent gold piece. For the moment, he wrapped himself in his furs, and spoke.

"I can still see you," he said. "Even though I think I am awake. Perhaps I dream I am awake. Come forth, dream creature."

Garona gripped Khadgar's shoulder, and he could feel her sharp finger-nails dig into his flesh. But Gul'dan was not speaking to them. Instead a new specter wafted into view.

It was tall and broad-shouldered, taller than any of the other three. It was translucent, as if it did not belong here either. It was hooded, and its voice reedy and distant. Though the only light was from the fire pit, the figure cast two shadows—one directly back from the flames, the other to one side, as if lit by a different source.

"Gul'dan," said the figure. "I want your people. I want your armies. I want your power to aid me."

"I have called upon my spirit protectors, creature," said Gul'dan, and Khadgar could hear a tremor in the orc's voice. "I have called upon my war-locks and they have quailed before you. I have called upon my mystic master and he has failed to stop you. You haunt my dreams, and now you come, a dream-creature, into my world. Who and what are you, truly?"

"You fear me," said the tall figure, and at the sound of his voice, Khadgar felt a cold hand run down his spine, "for you do not understand me. See my world and understand your fear. Then fear no more."

And with that the tall hooded figure shaped a ball out of the air, as light and clear as a soap bubble. It floated, about a foot in diameter, and within it showed a tableau of a land with blue sky and green fields.

The cloaked figure was showing him Azeroth.

Another bubble followed, and then another, and then a fourth. The sun-dappled fields of summer grain. The swamps of the Black Morass. The ice fields of the north. The shining towers of Stormwind Keep.

And a bubble that contained a lonely tower cradled within a crater of hills, lit by clear moonlight. He was showing the orc spellcaster Karazhan.

And there was another bubble, a fleeting one, that showed some dark scene far beneath the waves. It seemed an errant thought, one that was quickly eradicated. Yet Khadgar got the feeling of power. There was a grave beneath the waves, a crypt, one that surged with power like a heartbeat. It was there for an instant, and then gone.

"Gather your forces," said the cloaked figure. "Gather your armies and warriors and laborers and allies, and prepare them for a journey through the Twisting Nether. Prepare them well, for all this will be yours when you succeed."

Khadgar shook his head. The voice stung at him like an errant gnat. Then he realized who it was and his heart quailed.

Gul'dan was up on his knees, his hands clasped before him. "I shall do so, for yours is power most supreme. But who are you truly, and how will we reach this world?"

The figure raised his hands to his hood, and Khadgar shook his head. He didn't want to see it. He knew but he did not want to see it.

A deeply lined face. Graying brows. Green eyes that sparkled with hidden knowledge and something dangerous. Next to him, Garona let out a gasp.

"I am the Guardian," said Medivh to the orc warlock. "I will open the way for you. I will smash the cycle and be free."

THIRTEEN
The Second Shadow

No!" shouted Khadgar, and the vision ebbed at once. They were alone in the dining hall once more, at the center of an ornate pattern made of crushed agates and rose quartz.

His ears tingled and the corners of his vision seemed to close in on him. He had sunk to one knee, but was unaware that he had even moved. Above him and to his right, Garona's voice sounded hushed, almost strangled.

"Medivh," she said quietly. "The Old Man. It couldn't be."

"It can be," said Khadgar. His stomach felt like knotted snakes were churning within his flesh. His mind was already racing, and though he fervently wished to deny it, he knew its destination.

"No," said Garona, grimly. "It must be a misfire. A false vision. We went looking for one thing and found something else. You said that's happened before."

"Not like this," said Khadgar. "We may not be shown what we want, but we are always shown the truth."

"Perhaps it's just a warning," said the half-orc.

"It makes sense," said Khadgar, and there was the sound of trust and regret in his voice. "Think about it. That's why the wards were still intact after we were attacked. He was already within the wards, and summoned the demon within."

"It didn't seem like him," said Garona. "Perhaps it was an illusion, some magical fakery. It didn't seem like him."

"It was him," said the apprentice, rising now. "I know the master's voice. I know the master's face. In all his moods and manners."

"But it was like someone else was wearing that face," said Garona. "Something false. Like he was a set of clothes, or a suit of armor, that someone else was wearing."

Khadgar looked at the half-orc. Her voice was tremulous, and tears pooled in the corners of her wide eyes. She wanted to believe. She truly wanted to believe.

Khadgar wanted to believe as well. He nodded slowly. "It could be a trick. It still could be him. He could be tricking that orc, convincing him to come here. Maybe a vision of the future?"

Now it was Garona's turn to shake her head. "No. That was Gul'dan. He's here already. He herded us through the portal. This was in the past, this was their first meeting. But why would Medivh want to bring the orcs to Azeroth?"

"It explains why he hasn't done much to oppose them," said Khadgar. He shook his head, trying to loosen the thoughts that were lodged there. So many things suddenly made more sense. Odd disappearances. Little interest in the increasing number of orcs. Even bringing a half-orc into the castle.

He regarded Garona and wondered how deeply she was involved in the plot. She seemed completely taken aback by the news, yet was she a conspirator, or another pawn in the shadowplay that Medivh seemed to be running?

"We need to find out," he said simply. "We need to know why he was there. What he was doing. He is the Guardian—we should not condemn him on a single vision."

Garona nodded slowly. "So we ask him. How?"

Khadgar opened his mouth to respond, but another voice sounded through the halls.

"What's all this brouhaha?" said Medivh, rounding the corner at the dining hall's entrance.

Khadgar's throat constricted and went dry.

The Magus stood in the doorway, and Khadgar looked at him, hunting for something in his walk, his appearance, his voice. Anything to betray his presence. There was nothing. This was Medivh.

"What are you children up to?" said the Magus, his gray brows furrowing.

Khadgar struggled for an answer, but Garona said, "The Apprentice was showing me a spell he was working on." Her voice fluttered.

Medivh grunted. "Another of your visions, Young Trust? They're bad enough around here, without you calling up the past. Come out of there at once—we have work to do. And you as well, Emissary."

His voice was measured and understanding, but firm. The stern voice of the wise mentor. Khadgar took a step forward, but Garona grabbed him by the arm.

"Shadows," she hissed.

Khadgar blinked, and looked at the Magus again. Impatience showed on his face now, and disapproval. His shoulders were still broad, he held himself upright despite the pressures on him. He was dressed in robes Khadgar had seen him wear often before.

And behind him trailed two shadows. One directly away from the torch, and the other, equally dark, at an odd angle.

Khadgar hesitated, and Medivh's disapproval deepened, a storm gathering on his face. "What is the matter, Young Trust?"

"We should clean up our mess," said Khadgar, trying to be light. "Don't want to make Moroes work too hard. We will catch up."

"Negotiation is not part of an apprentice's duties," said Medivh. "Now come here at once."

No one moved. Garona said, "Why doesn't he come into the room?"

Why indeed, thought Khadgar. Instead he said, "One question, Master?"

"What now?" grunted the master mage.

"Why did you visit the orc Gul'dan's dreams?" said Khadgar, feeling his throat tighten as he asked. "Why did you show the orcs how to come to this world?"

Medivh's glare shifted to Garona. "I was unaware Gul'dan told you of me. He didn't strike me as being unwise, or a chatterbox."

Garona took a step back, but this time Khadgar restrained her. She said, "I didn't know. Until now."

Medivh snorted. "It matters little. Now come here. Both of you."

"Why did you show the orcs the way here?" repeated Khadgar.

"You do not negotiate with your betters!" snapped the mage.

"Why did you bring the orcs to Azeroth?" asked Khadgar, pleading now.

"It is none of your business, child. You *will* come here! Now!" The Magus's face was livid and twisted.

"With respect, sir," said Khadgar, and his words felt like dagger-thrusts, "no, I will not."

Medivh thundered in rage. "Child, I will have you . . ."and as he spoke, he stepped into the room.

Sparks flew up at once, bathing the older mage in a shower of light. The Magus staggered back a step, then raised his hands, and muttered a curse.

"What?" began Garona.

"Circle of Warding," snapped Khadgar. "To keep summoned demons at bay. The Magus cannot cross it."

"But if it only affects demons, why not? Unless . . ." Garona looked at Khadgar. "No," she said. "Can the circle hold him back?"

Khadgar thought of jackstraw laid across the wards in the tower at Stormwind, and at the energy blossoming by the doorway. He shook his head.

Instead he shouted at the Magus, "Is this what you did to Huglar and Hugarin? And Guzbah? And the others? Did they figure things out?"

"They were further from the truth than you were, child," said the illuminated Magus through gritted teeth, "but I had to be careful. I forgave your curiosity for your youth, and thought that loyalty—" He grunted now as the protective wards resisted him. "—I thought that loyalty still mattered in this world."

The protective wards blazed as Medivh moved into them, and Khadgar could see the fields distorting around the Magus's outstretched palms. The flickering of the sparks seemed to catch Medivh's beard on fire, and smoke curled up like horns from his forehead.

And then Khadgar's heart sank, for he realized that what he was seeing was another image, this one laid over the image of the beloved mage. The image that belonged to the second shadow.

"He's going to get through," said Garona.

Khadgar gritted his teeth. "Eventually. He's pouring huge amounts of power into breaking the circle."

"Can he do that?" asked the half-orc.

"He's the Guardian of Tirisfal," said Khadgar. "He can do whatever he wants. It just takes time."

"Well, can we get out of here?" Garona sounded panicked now.

"Only way out is past him," said Khadgar.

Garona looked around. "Blow out a wall, then. New exit."

Khadgar looked at the stonework of the tower, but shook his head.

"Well, try something!"

"I'll try this," said Khadgar. Before them, the figure of Medivh, taller now and wreathed in lightning, loomed up in the smoke.

Calming himself, he pulled the magical energies into himself. He made the motions he had made only minutes before, and intoned the words lost to mortal men, and when he had compressed the energies into a single ball of light, he released it.

"Bring me a vision," said Khadgar, "of one who has fought this beast before!"

There was a brief bit of disorientation, and for a moment Khadgar thought the spell had misfired and transported them to the observatory atop the tower. But no, it was now night around them, and an imperious, angry female voice split the air.

"You *dare* strike your own mother?" shouted Aegwynn, her own face livid with rage.

Aegwynn stood at one end of the observatory deck, Medivh at the other. It was Medivh as he knew him—tall, proud, and apparently worried. Neither she nor the past-Medivh paid any attention to either Khadgar or Garona. With a start, Khadgar realized that the present incarnation of Medivh was present as well, sparkling along one wall. The pair from the past ignored him as well, but the present-Medivh was watching the spectacle played out before them.

"Mother, I thought you were being hysterical," said the past-Medivh.

"So a mystic bolt would bring me to my senses?" snapped the previous Guardian. Khadgar saw that she was much older now. Her blond hair was now white, and there were tight wrinkles around her eyes and mouth. Still, she held the presence of the earlier forms he had seen. "Now," she said, "answer my question."

"Mother, you're not seeing things right," said the past-Medivh.

"Answer," snapped Aegwynn sternly. "Why did you bring the orcs to Azeroth?"

"No wonder he was so testy when you asked him that," said Garona. Khadgar shushed her, and kept an eye on the present-Medivh. The present incarnation had ceased to press against the walls of the wards, and his face seemed to have lost its emotion.

"Mother?" said the present-Medivh. His face looked credulous.

"You don't *HAVE* an answer, do you?" said Aegwynn. "This is some little game you're playing. Some challenge for Llane and Lothar to amuse themselves with? The power of the *Tirisfalen* is no game, child. There are more orcs coming in all the time, and I am hearing of caravans being raided near the Black Morass. A novice could track back to your Portal, but only your mother would be able to taste the power that wrapped it. Again, child, how do you account for yourself?"

Khadgar wilted under the older woman's invective, and half-expected the past-Medivh to flee the room. Instead, Medivh surprised him. He laughed deeply.

"Does your mother's disapproval amuse you, child?" said Aegwynn sternly.

"No," said Medivh, flashing a deep, predatory grin. "But my mother's stupidity does."

Khadgar looked across the room, and saw the present-Medivh flinch at the sound of his past incarnation's words.

"You dare," thundered Aegwynn, raising her hand. A sphere of blazing-white light erupted from her palm and lanced toward the past-Medivh. The Magus raised a hand and turned it aside with ease.

"I do, Mother," said the phantom of the past. "And I have the power for it. The power that you invested me with at my conception, a power that I did not want or request." The phantom-Medivh gestured, and the topmost floor was alight with a blazing bolt. Aegwynn caught the energy herself, but Khadgar noted that she had to raise both hands, and still was staggered back.

"But *why* did you let the orcs into Azeroth?" hissed the older woman. "There is no need. You put entire populations at risk, and to what end?"

"To break the cycle, of course," said the past-Medivh. "To smash the clockwork universe that you have built for me. Everything in its place, including your child. If you could not continue on as Guardian, your hand-picked, born and groomed successor would, but would be locked into his script as tightly as any of your other pawns."

The present-Medivh had sunk to his knees, his eyes locked on the tableau before him. He was mouthing the words that his past-self had spoken.

Garona tugged on Khadgar's sleeve, and he nodded. The pair left the heart of the wards, and began to edge around the room, trying to ease behind the present incarnation of the Magus.

"But, the risk, child . . ." said Aegwynn.

"Risk?" said Medivh. "Risk to whom? Not to me, not with the power of the *Tirisfalen* at my command. To the rest of the Order? They worry more about internal politics than demons. To the human nations? Fat and happy, protected from dangers that they do not even know about? Is anyone important really at risk?"

"You're playing with forces greater than yourself, Son," said Aegwynn. Khadgar and Garona were nearly to the door, but the present-Medivh was held rapt by the vision.

"Oh, of course," said the Magus's past with a snarl. "Thinking that I could handle powers like that would be the sin of Pride. Sort of like thinking you could match wits with a demon lord and come out on top."

They were behind Medivh now, and Garona reached for the knife inside her blouse. Khadgar stopped her hand and shook his head. They slipped behind Medivh. Tears were starting to form at the old man's eyes.

"What happens if these orcs succeed?" said Aegwynn. "They worship dark gods and shadows. Why would you give Azeroth to them?"

"*When* they succeed," said the past Medivh, "they will make me their leader. They respect strength, Mother, unlike you or the rest of this sorry world. And thanks to you, I am the strongest thing in this world. And I will have broken the shackles that you and others have placed on me, and I will rule."

There was a silence in the vision, and Khadgar and Garona froze, holding their breath. Would the present Medivh notice them in the silence?

Aegwynn, speaking from the years past, held his attention. "You are not my son," she said.

The present Medivh put his face in his hands. His past version said, "No. I have never been your son. Never truly yours, in any case."

And the past Magus laughed. It was a deep, thundering laugh that Khadgar had heard before, on the icy steppes, when last these two battled.

Aegwynn looked shocked. "Sargeras?" she spat, in final recognition. "I killed you."

"You killed a body, witch. You only killed my physical form!" snarled the Medivh of the past, and already Khadgar could see the overlay of the second being, the alternate shadow, that consumed him. A creature of shadow and flame, with a beard of fire and great ebon horns. "Killed it and hid it away in a tomb beneath the sea. But I was willing to sacrifice it to gain a greater prize."

Despite herself, Aegwynn put a hand over her stomach.

"Yes, Mother dear," said the past Medivh, the flames licking at his beard, the horns forming out of smoke before his brows. He was Medivh, but Sargeras as well. "I hid in your womb, and passed into the slumbering cells of your unformed child. A cancer, a blight, a birth defect that you would never surmise. Killing you was impossible, seducing you unlikely. So I made myself your heir."

Aegwynn shouted a curse and lurched her hands upward, her anger wrapped around words not made for human voices. A bolt of scintillating rainbow energy struck the Medivh/Sargeras creature full in the chest.

The phantom of the past staggered back one step, then two, then raised a single hand and caught the energy cast at him. The room smelled of cooking meat, and the Sargeras/Medivh snarled and spat. He invoked a spell of his own, and Aegwynn was flung across the room.

"I cannot kill you, Mother," snapped the demonic form. "Some part of me keeps me from doing that. But I *will* break you. Break you and banish you, and by the time you've healed, by the time you've walked back from where I will send you, this land will be mine. This land, and the power of the Order of Tirisfal!"

In the present day, Medivh let out the howl of a lost soul, screaming to the heavens for forgiveness that will never be forthcoming.

"That's our cue," said Garona, pulling on Khadgar's robe. "Let's get while the getting is good."

Khadgar hesitated for a moment, then followed her to the stairs.

They tumbled down the stone stairs three at a time, almost slamming into Moroes.

"Excited," he noted calmly. "Problem?"

Garona hurdled down past the castellan, but Khadgar grabbed the older man and said, "The master has gone mad."

"More than usual?" replied Moroes.

"It's not a joke," said Khadgar, then his eyes lit up. "Do you have the whistle to summon gryphons?"

The servant raised a rune-carved piece of metal. "Wish me to summon . . ."

"I'll do it," said Khadgar, grabbing the item from his hands, and hurtling after Garona. "He'll be after us, but you had better run as well. Take Cook and flee as far as you can."

And with that Khadgar was lost to view.

"Flee?" said Moroes to the apprentice's retreating form; then he snorted. "Wherever would I go?"

FOURTEEN
Flight

They had made it several miles when the gryphon began to misbehave. Only a single beast had answered Khadgar's summons, and bridled as Garona approached it. Only by sheer strength of will did the young mage get the gryphon to accept the half-orc's presence. They could hear Medivh screaming and cursing long after they had left the circle of hills. They tilted the gryphon toward Stormwind, and Khadgar dug his heels deeply into the gryphon's haunches.

They had made good speed, but now the gryphon bucked beneath him, trying to tear at the reins, trying to turn back toward the mountains. Khadgar tried to break the beast, to keep it to its course, but it became increasingly agitated.

"What's wrong with it?" asked Garona over his shoulder.

"Medivh is calling it back," said Khadgar. "It wants to go back to Karazhan."

Khadgar wrestled with the reins, even tried the whistle, but at last had to admit defeat. He brought the gryphon down on a low, bare tor, and slid from its back after Garona had climbed off. As soon as he touched ground, the gryphon was aloft again, beating its heavy wings against the darkening air, climbing to return at the call of its master.

"Think he will follow?" asked Garona.

"I don't know," said Khadgar. "But I don't want to be here if he does. We'll make for Stormwind."

They stumbled about for most of the evening and night, finding a dirt track, then following it in the general direction of Stormwind. There was no immediate pursuit nor strange lights in the sky, and before dawn the pair rested briefly, huddling beneath a great cedar.

They saw no one alive during the next day. There were houses burned to the foundations, and clumps of newly hummocked earth that marked buried families. Overturned and smashed carts were common, as were great burned circles heaped with ash. Garona noted that this was how the orcs dealt with their dead, after the bodies had been looted.

The only animals they saw were dead—disemboweled pigs by a shattered farmhouse, the skeletal remains of a horse, consumed save for the frightened, twisted head. They moved in silence through one despoiled farmstead after another.

"Your people have been thorough," Khadgar said at last.

"They pride themselves on such matters," said Garona, grimly.

"Pride?" said Khadgar, looking around him. "Pride in destruction? In despoiling? No human army, no human nation would burn down everything in its path, or kill animals without purpose."

Garona nodded. "It is the orc way—do not leave enough standing that their foes could use against them. If they could not use it immediately—as fodder, as quarters, as plunder—then it should be put to the torch. The borders of orc clans are often desolate places, as each side seeks to deny the other resources."

Khadgar shook his head. "These are *not* resources," he said hotly. "These are lives. This land was once green and verdant, with fields and forests. Now it's a wasteland. Look at this! Can there be any peace between humans and orcs?"

Garona said nothing. They continued in on silence that day, and camped in the shambles of an inn. They slept in separate rooms, he in the wreckage of the common room, she moving farther back to the kitchen. He didn't suggest they stay together, and neither did she.

Khadgar was awakened by the growls of his stomach. They had fled the tower with little but what they had on their backs, and save for some foraged berries and ground nuts, they had not eaten in over a day.

The young mage extricated himself from the rain-damp straw tick that made his bed, his joints protesting. He had not camped in the open since his arrival at Karazhan, and he felt out of shape. The fear of the previous day had ebbed entirely, and he wondered about his next move.

Stormwind was their stated target, but how would he get someone like Garona into the city? Maybe find something to disguise her. Or did she even want to come? Now that she was free of the tower, maybe it would be better for her to rejoin Gul'dan and the Stormreaver clan.

Something moved along the wrecked side of the building. Probably Garona. She had to be as hungry as Khadgar. She hadn't complained, but he assumed from the wreckage left behind that orcs required a lot of food to keep them in top fighting form.

Khadgar stood up, shook the cobwebs from his mind, and leaned out the remains of a window to ask her if there was anything left in the kitchen.

And was faced with one edge of a huge double-bladed ax, leveled at his neck.

At the opposite end of the ax was the jade-green face of an orc. A real orc. Khadgar had not realized until now how accustomed to Garona's face he had become, such that the heavy jaw and sloped brow were a shock to him.

The orc growled, "Wuzzat?"

Khadgar slowly raised both hands, all the while calling up in his mind the magical energy. A simple spell, enough to knock the creature aside, to get Garona and get away.

Unless Garona had brought it here, he suddenly realized.

He hesitated, and that was enough. He heard something behind him, but did not get to turn as something large and heavy came down on the back of his neck.

He could not have been out long—long enough for a half-dozen orcs to spill into the room and start pushing through the rubble with their axes. They wore green armbands. Bleeding Hollow clan, his memory told him. He stirred, and the first orc, the one with the double-bladed ax, spun on him again.

"Wharsyurstuth?" said the orc. "Wharyuhidit?"

"What?" asked Khadgar, wondering if it was the orc's voice or his own ears that were mangling the language.

"Your stuff," said the orc, slower. "Your gear. You gots nothing. Where did you hide it?"

Khadgar spoke without thinking. "No stuff. Lost it earlier. No stuff."

The orc snorted. "Then you die," he snarled, and raised his blade.

"No!" shouted Garona from the ruined doorway. She looked like she had spent a bad night, but had a brace of hares on a leather thong hanging from her belt. She had been out hunting. Khadgar felt mildly embarrassed for his earlier thoughts.

"Git out, half-breed," snapped the orc. "None of your business."

"You're killing my property, that makes it my business," said Garona.

Property? thought Khadgar, but held his tongue.

"Prop'ty?" lisped the orc. "Who's you to have prop'ty?"

"I am Garona Halforcen," snarled the woman, twisting her face into a mask of rage. "I serve Gul'dan, warlock of the Stormreaver clan. Damage my property and you'll have to deal with him!"

The orc snorted again. "Stormreavers? Pah! I hear they are a weak clan, pushed around by their warlock!"

Garona gave him a steely glare. "What I *hear* was that Bleeding Hollow failed to support the Twilight Hollow clan in the recent attack on Stormwind, and that both clans were thrown back. I *hear* that humans beat you in a fair fight. Is that true?"

"Dat's beside the point," said the Bleeding Hollow orc. "Dey had horses."

"Maybe I can . . ." said Khadgar, trying to rise to his feet.

"Down, slave!" shouted Garona, cuffing him hard and sending him backward. "You speak when spoken to, and not before!"

The lead orc took the opportunity to take a step forward, but as soon as Garona had finished she wheeled again, and a long-bladed dagger was pointed at the orc's midsection. The other orcs backed away from the brewing fight.

"Do you dispute my ownership?" snarled Garona, fire in her eyes and her muscles tensed to drive the blade through the leather armor.

There was silence for a moment. The Bleeding Hollow orc looked at Garona, looked at the sprawled Khadgar, and looked at Garona again. He snorted and said, "Go get something worth fighting for, first, half-breed!"

And with that the orc leader backed away. The others relaxed, and started to file out of the ruined common room.

One of his subordinates asked him as they left the building, "What duz she have a use for human slave anyway?"

The orc leader said something that Khadgar could not hear. The subordinate shouted from outside, "Dat's *disgusting!*"

Khadgar tried to stand, but Garona waved her hand for him to stay down. Despite himself, Khadgar flinched.

Garona moved to the empty window, watched for a moment, then returned to where Khadgar had propped himself up against the wall.

"I think they're gone," she said at last. "I was afraid they might double back to even the score. Their leader is probably going to be challenged tonight by his subordinates."

Khadgar touched the tender side of his face. "I'm fine, thanks for asking."

Garona shook her head. "You idiot of a paleskin! If I hadn't knocked you down, the orc leader would have killed you outright, and then turned on me because I couldn't keep you in line."

Khadgar sighed deeply. "Sorry. You're right."

"You're right I'm right," said Garona. "They kept you alive long enough for me to get back only because they thought you'd hidden something in the inn. That you wouldn't be dumb enough to be out in the middle of a war zone without equipment."

"Did you have to hit that hard?" asked Khadgar.

"To convince them? Yes. Not that I didn't enjoy it." She threw the hares at him. "Here, skin these and get the water boiling. There're still pots and some tubers left in the kitchen."

"Despite what you're telling your friends," said Khadgar, "I am not your slave."

Garona chuckled. "Of course. But I caught breakfast. You get to cook it!"

Breakfast was a hearty stew of rabbit and potato, seasoned with herbs Khadgar found in the remains of the kitchen garden and mushrooms Garona picked in the wilderness. Khadgar checked the mushrooms to see if any of them were poisonous. None of them were.

"Orcs use their young as taste-testers," said Garona. "If they survive, they know it's good for the community."

They set out on the road again, heading for Stormwind. Once more, the woods were eerily quiet, and all they encountered was the remains of war.

About midday, they came upon the Bleeding Hollow orcs once more. They were in a wide clear space around a shattered watchtower, all facedown. Something large, heavy, and sharp had torn through their back armor, and several were missing their heads.

Garona quickly moved from body to body, pulling salvageable gear from them. Khadgar scanned the horizon.

Garona shouted over, "Are you going to help?"

"In a moment," said Khadgar. "I want to make sure that whatever killed our friends is not still around."

Garona scanned the edges of the clearing, then looked skyward. Nothing was overhead but low, ink-spattered clouds.

"Well?" she said. "I don't hear anything."

"Neither did the orcs, until it was too late," said Khadgar, joining her at the orc leader's body. "They were hit in the back, while running, and from an attacker taller than they were." He pointed at hoof prints in the dust.

They were those of iron-shod, heavy horses. "Cavalry. Human cavalry."

Garona nodded. "So we're getting close, at least. Take what you can from them. We can use their rations—they're nasty but nutritious. And take a weapon, at least a knife."

Khadgar looked at Garona. "I've been thinking."

Garona laughed. "I wonder how many human disasters start with *that* line."

"We're within range of Stormwind patrols," said Khadgar. "I don't think Medivh is following us, at least not directly. So maybe we should split up."

"Thought of that," said Garona, rummaging through one of the orc's packs, and pulling out first a cloak, and then a small cloth-wrapped parcel. She opened the parcel to find a flint and steel and a vial of oily liquid. "Fire-starting kit," she explained. "Orcs love fire, and this is a quick starter."

"So you think we should split up," said Khadgar.

"No," said Garona. "I said I thought about it. The trouble is that no one is in control of this area, human or orc. You might walk fifty yards away and hit another patrol of the Bleeding Hollow clan, and I might get ambushed by your cavalry buddies. If the two of us are together, there's a better chance of survival. One is the other's slave."

"Prisoner," said Khadgar. "Humans don't take slaves."

"Sure you do," said Garona. "You just call them something else. So we should stay together."

"And that's it?" said Khadgar.

"Mostly," said Garona. "Plus there is the little fact that I haven't reported in to Gul'dan for some time. If and when we do run into him, I will explain that I was held prisoner at Karazhan, and he should have shown more wisdom than to send one of his followers into a trap."

"You think he'd believe that?" asked Khadgar.

"I am uncertain that he would," said Garona. "Which is another good reason to stay with you."

"You could buy yourself a lot of influence with what you've learned," said Khadgar.

Garona nodded. "Yeah. If I don't get an ax through my brain before I get to tell anyone. No, for the moment I'll take my chances with the paleskins. Now, I need one more thing."

"What's that?"

"I need to gather the bodies together, and heap some brush and tinder over them. We can cache what we don't need, but we need to burn the bodies. It's the least we can do."

Khadgar frowned. "If the heavy horse are still in the area, a plume of smoke will bring them at once."

"I know," said Garona, looking around at the fragments of the patrol. "But it's the right thing to do. If you found human soldiers killed in an ambush, wouldn't you want to bury them?"

Khadgar's mouth made a grim line, but he didn't say anything. Instead, he went to grab the farthest orc and drag him back to the remains of the watchtower. Within an hour, they had stripped the bodies and set the remains ablaze.

"Now we should go," said Khadgar, as Garona watched the smoke spiral upward.

"Won't this call the horsemen?" said Garona.

"Yes," said Khadgar. "And it will also send a message—there are orcs here. Orcs who feel secure enough to burn the bodies of their comrades. I'd rather have a chance to explain ourselves at close range than face a charging warhorse, thank you very much."

Garona nodded, and, stolen cloaks flapping behind them, they left the burning watchtower.

Garona spoke truly, in that the orc version of field rations were a nasty concoction of hardened syrup, nuts, and what Khadgar swore was boiled rat. Still, it kept them going, and they made good time.

A day and a day passed and the country opened up now into sprawling fields that rippled with growing crops. The land was no less desolate, though, the stables empty and the houses already collapsed in on themselves. They found several more burned spots of orc funerals, and an increasing number of hummocks marking the passing of human families and patrols.

Still, they kept to the brush and fence lines as much as possible. The more open terrain made it easier to see any other units, but left them more exposed. They holed up in a mostly intact farmhouse while a small army of orcs moved along the ridgeline.

Khadgar watched the line of units surge forward. Grunts, cavalry mounted on great wolves, and catapults done up in fanciful decorations of skulls and dragons. Beside him, Garona watched the procession and said, "Idiots."

Khadgar shot her a questioning glance.

"They could not be more exposed," she explained. "We can see them, and the paleskins can see them as well. This lot doesn't have an objective—they're just rolling through the countryside, looking for a fight. Looking for a noble death in battle." She shook her head.

"You don't think much of your people," said Khadgar.

"I don't think much of *any* people, right now," said Garona. "The orcs disown me, the humans will kill me. And the only human I really trusted turned out to be a demon."

"Well, there's me," said Khadgar, trying not to sound hurt.

Garona winced. "Yes, there is you. You are human, and I trust you. But I thought, I really thought, that Medivh was going to make a difference. Powerful, important, and willing to talk. Unprejudiced. But I deceived myself. He's just another madman. Maybe that's just my place—working for madmen. Maybe I'm just another pawn in the game. What did Medivh call it? The unforgiving clockwork of the universe?"

"Your role," said Khadgar, "is whatever you choose it to be. Medivh always wanted that as well."

"You think he was sane when he said that?" asked the half-orc.

Khadgar shrugged. "As sane as he ever was. I believe he was. And it sounds like you want to believe that as well."

"Ayep," drawled Garona. "It was all so simple, when I was working for Gul'dan. His little eyes and ears. Now I don't know who's right and who's wrong. Which people are my people? Either of them? At least you don't have to worry about divided loyalties."

Khadgar didn't say anything, but looked out into the gathering dusk. Somewhere, over the horizon, the orc army had run into something. There was the low glow of a false dawn along the edge of the world in that direction, marked with the reflection of sudden flashes off the low clouds, and the echoes of war drums and death sounded like distant thunder.

Another day and a day passed. Now they moved through abandoned towns and marketplaces. The buildings were more whole now, but still abandoned. There were signs of recent inhabitation, both by human and orc troops, but now the only inhabitants were ghosts and memories.

Khadgar broke into a likely-looking shop, and while its shelves had been stripped bare, the hearth still had wood in the hopper and there were potatoes and onions in a small bin in the basement. Anything would be an improvement after the orcs' iron rations.

Khadgar laid the fire and Garona took a cauldron to the nearby well. Khadgar thought about the next step. Medivh was a danger, perhaps a greater danger than the orcs. Could he be reasoned with, now? Convinced to shut the portal? Or was it too late?

Just the knowledge that there *was* a portal would be good news. If the humans could locate it, even shut it, it would strand the orcs on this world. Deny them reinforcements from Draenor.

The apprentice was pulled from his thoughts by the commotion outside. The clash of metal on metal. Human voices, bellowing.

"Garona," muttered Khadgar, and headed for the door.

He found them by the well. A patrol of about ten footmen, dressed in the blue livery of Azeroth, swords drawn. One of them was cradling a bleeding arm, but another pair had Garona in their grip, one restraining each arm. Her long-bladed dagger was on the ground. As Khadgar rounded the corner, the sergeant backhanded her across the face with a mailed glove.

"Where are the others?" he snarled. The half-orc's mouth leaked blackish-purple blood.

"Leave her alone!" shouted Khadgar. Without thinking, he pulled the energies into his mind and released a quick spell.

A brilliant light blossomed around Garona's head, a miniature sun that caught the humans unaware. The two footmen holding Garona let go of her, and she slid to the ground. The sergeant raised a hand to protect his eyes, and the remainder of the patrol was sufficiently surprised, so that Khadgar was among them and at Garona's side in a matter of moments.

"S'prised," muttered Garona through a split lip. "Lemme get my wind back."

"Stay down," said Khadgar softly. To the blinking sergeant he barked, "Are you in charge of this rabble?"

By now most of the footmen had recovered, and had their swords level. The two next to Garona had backed up a pace, but they were watching her, not Khadgar.

The sergeant spat, "Who are *you* to interfere with the military? Get him out of the way, boys!"

"Hold!" said Khadgar, and the soldiers, having experienced his spells once, only advanced a single pace. "I am Khadgar, apprentice to Medivh the Magus, friend and ally to your King Llane. I have business with him. Take us at once to Stormwind."

The sergeant just chuckled. "Sure you are, and I am Lord Lothar. Medivh doesn't take apprentices. Even I know that. And who is your sweetheart, there, then?"

"She is . . ." Khadgar hesitated for a moment. "She is my prisoner. I am taking her to Stormwind for questioning."

"Huh," grunted the sergeant. "Well, boyo, we *found* your prisoner out here, armed, with you nowhere in sight. I'd say your prisoner escaped. Pity the orc would rather die than surrender."

"Don't touch her!" said Khadgar, and he raised his hand. Flames danced within his curled fingers.

"You're flirting with your own death," snarled the sergeant. In the distance, Khadgar could hear the heavy footfalls of horses. Reinforcements. But would they be any more willing to listen to a half-orc and a spellcaster than this lot were?

"You're making a horrible mistake, sir," said Khadgar, keeping his voice level.

"Stay out of this, boy," commanded the sergeant. "Take the orc. Kill her if she resists!"

The footmen took another step forward, those closest to Garona bending down to grab her again. She tried to squirm away and one kicked her with a heavy boot.

Khadgar bit back tears and unleashed the spell against the sergeant. The ball of flame slammed into his knee. The sergeant howled and dropped to the ground.

"Now stop this," hissed Khadgar.

"Kill them!" shouted the sergeant, his eyes wide in pain. "Kill them both!"

"Hold!" came another voice, darker and deeper, muffled by a great helm. The horsemen had arrived in the town square. About twenty riders, and Khadgar's heart sank. More here than even Garona could take care of. Their leader was in full armor, with a visored helm. Khadgar could not see his face.

The young apprentice rushed forward. "Sir," he said. "Call off these men. I am the apprentice to Magus Medivh."

"I know who you are," said the commander. "Stand down!" he ordered. "Keep the orc guarded, but let her go!"

Khadgar gulped and continued, "I have a prisoner and important information for King Llane. I need to see Lord Lothar, at once!"

The commander lifted his visor. "So you shall, lad," said Lothar. "So you shall."

FIFTEEN
Beneath Karazhan

The discussion at Stormwind Castle had not gone well, and now they were circling Medivh's Tower on gryphon-back. Beneath them, in the gathering dusk, Karazhan loomed large and empty. No lights shone from any of its windows, and the observatory atop the structure was dark. Beneath a now-moonless sky, even the pale stones of the tower were dark and brooding.

There had been a heated discussion in the King's Privy Quarters the previous evening. Khadgar and Garona were there, although the half-orc was asked to surrender her knife to Lothar in the presence of His Majesty. The King's Champion was there as well, and a gaggle of advisors and courtiers all hovering around King Llane. Khadgar could not smell a single spellcaster in the group, and surmised that any that had survived Medivh's poaching were either on the battlefield or squirreled away for safekeeping.

As for the King himself, the young man from the early visions had grown up. He had the broad shoulders and sharp features of his youth, only now starting to surrender to middle age. Of all present, he was resplendent, and his blue robes shone among the others. He kept an open-faced helm to one side of his seat, a great helm with white wings, as if he expected to be called onto the battlefield at any moment.

Khadgar wondered if such a call was not exactly what Llane desired, remembering the headstrong youth of the troll-vision. A direct conflict on an open and level field, with his forces' eventual triumph never in doubt. He wondered how much of the assuredness derived from the faith in the Magus's eventual support. Indeed, it seemed that one led naturally to the other—that the Magus will always support Stormwind, and Stormwind will always hold as a result of the Magus's support.

The healers had tended to Garona's split lip, but could do nothing for her temper. Several times Khadgar winced as she bluntly described the orcish opinions of the master mage's sanity, of the paleskins in general, and Llane's troops in particular.

"The orcs are relentless," she said. "And they will not let up. They will be back."

"They did not get within bowshot of the walls," countered Llane. To Khadgar, his majesty seemed more amused than alarmed by Garona's direct manner and blunt warnings.

"They did not get within bowshot of the walls," repeated Garona. "This time. Next time they will. And the time after that they will get over the walls. I don't think you are taking the orcs sufficiently seriously, sire."

"I assure you, I take this very seriously," said Llane. "But I am also aware of the strengths of Stormwind. Of its walls, of its armies, of its allies, and of its heart. Perhaps if you saw them, you too would be less confident in the power of the orcs."

Llane was similarly adamant about the Magus as well. Khadgar laid every-thing out before the privy council, with assurances and additions from Garona. The visions of the past, the erratic behavior, the visions that were not visions at all but rather true demonstrations of Sargeras's presence in Karazhan. Of Medivh's culpability in the present assault on Azeroth.

"If I had a silver groat for every man who has told me that Medivh is mad, I would be richer than I am today," said Llane. "He has a plan, young sir. It's as simple as that. More times than I can count he has gone off on some mad dash or another, and Lothar here had worried his beard to tatters. And each time he's proved to be right. The last time he was here did he not hare off to hunt a demon, and bring it back within a few hours? Hardly the action of one demon-possessed to decapitate one of his own."

"But it might be the action of one who was trying to maintain his own innocence," put in Garona. "No one saw him kill this demon, in the heart of your city. Could he not have summoned it up, then killed and provided it as the one responsible?"

"Supposition," grumbled the king. "No. With respect to both of you, I do not deny that you saw what you saw. Not even these 'visions' of the past. But I think the Magus is crazy like a fox, and all this is part of some larger plan of his. He always speaks of larger plans and greater cycles."

"With all due respect," said Khadgar. "The Magus may have a larger plan, but the question is, do Stormwind and Azeroth truly have a place within that plan?"

So went most of the evening. King Llane was adamant on all points—that Azeroth could, with its allies, destroy or drive back the orc hordes to their home world, that Medivh was working on some plan that no one else could understand, and that Stormwind could withstand any assault "as long as men with stout hearts were manning the walls and the throne."

Lothar for his part was mostly silent, only breaking in to ask a relevant question, then shaking his head when Khadgar or Garona gave him a truthful answer. Finally, he spoke up.

"Llane, don't let your security blind you!" he said. "If we cannot count on Magus Medivh as an ally, we are weakened. If we discount the capabilities of the orcs, we are lost. Listen to what they are saying!"

"I am listening," said the King. "But I hear not only with my head but with my heart. We spent many years with young Medivh, both before and during his long sleep. He remembers his friends. And once he reveals his thinking, I'm sure even you will appreciate what a friend we have in the Magus."

At last the King rose and dismissed all, promising to take the matters under proper consideration. Garona was muttering under her breath, and Lothar gave them rooms without windows and with guards on the doors, just to be sure.

Khadgar tried to sleep, but the frustration kept him pacing the floor for most of the night. Finally, when exhaustion had finally claimed him, there was a sound pounding on the door.

It was Lothar, in full armor, with a uniform draped over his arm. "Sleep like the dead, will you?" he said, holding out the livery with a smile. "Put this on and meet us at the top of the tower in fifteen minutes. And hurry, lad."

Khadgar struggled into the gear, which included trousers, heavy boots, blue livery marked with the lion of Azeroth, and heavy-bladed sword. He thought twice about the sword, but slung it onto his back. It might prove useful.

There were no less than six gryphons clustered on the towers, rustling their great wings in agitation. Lothar was there, and Garona as well. She was similarly dressed to Khadgar, with the blue tabard marked with the lion of Azeroth, and a heavy sword.

"Don't," she growled at him, "say a word."

"You look very good in it," he said. "It goes with your eyes."

Garona snorted. "Lothar said the same thing. He tried to convince me by saying that you were wearing the outfit, too. *And* that he wanted to make sure that none of the others shot me thinking I was someone else."

"Others?" said Khadgar, and looked around. In the morning light, it was clear that there were other flights of gryphons on other towers. Around six, including theirs, the gryphons' wings pink with the unrisen sun. He was unaware that there were this many trained gryphons in the world, much less Stormwind. Lothar must have gone to talk to the dwarves. The air was cold and sharp as a dagger thrust.

Lothar hurried up to them, and adjusted Khadgar's sword so he could ride gryphon-back with it.

"His Majesty," grumbled Lothar, "has an abiding faith in the strength of the people of Azeroth and the thickness of the walls of Stormwind. It doesn't hurt that he also has good people who take care of things when he's wrong."

"Like us," said Khadgar, grimly.

"Like us," repeated Lothar. He looked at Khadgar hard and added, "I had asked you how he was, you know."

"Yes," said Khadgar. "And I told you the truth, or as much of it as I understood it at the time. And I felt loyal to him."

"I understand," said Lothar. "And I feel loyal to him as well. I want to make sure what you say is true. But I also want you to be able to do what needs to be done, if we have to do it."

Khadgar nodded. "You believe me, don't you?"

Lothar nodded grimly. "Long ago, when I was your age, I was tending to Medivh. He was in his coma, then, that long sleep that denied him much of his youth. I thought it was a dream, but I swore there was another man opposite me, also watching over the Magus. He seemed to be made of burnished brass, and he had heavy horns on his brow, and his beard made of flames."

"Sargeras," said Khadgar.

Lothar let out a deep breath. "I thought I had fallen asleep, that it was a dream, that it could not be what I thought it was. You see, I too felt loyal to him. But I never forgot what I saw. And as the years passed I began to realize that I had seen a bit of the truth, and that it might come to this. We may yet save Medivh, but we might find that the darkness is too deeply rooted. Then we will have to do something sudden, horrible, and absolutely necessary. The question is—Are you up to it?"

Khadgar thought for a moment, then nodded. His stomach felt like ice. Lothar raised a hand. On his command, the other flights of gryphons strained aloft, springing to life as the first rays of the dawn crested the earth's rim, the new sunlight catching their wings and turning them golden.

The chill feeling in the pit of Khadgar's stomach did not ebb on the long flight to Karazhan. Garona rode behind him, but neither spoke as the land fled beneath their wings.

The land had changed beneath their wings. Great fields were little more than blackened wreckage, dotted by the remnants of toppled foundations. Forests were uprooted to feed the engines of war, creating huge scars in the landscape. Open pits yawned wide, the earth itself wounded and stripped to reach the metals beneath. Columns of smoke rose up along the horizon, though whether they were from battlefields or forges Khadgar could not say. They flew through the day and the sun was ebbing along the horizon now.

Karazhan rose like an ebon shadow at the center of its crater, sucking in the last dying rays of the day and giving nothing back. No lights shone from the tower nor from any of the hollow windows. The torches that flamed without consuming their source had been extinguished. Khadgar wondered if Medivh had fled.

Lothar kneed his gryphon down, and Khadgar followed, quickly setting down, and slipping from the back of the winged beast. As soon as he touched the ground, the gryphon shot aloft again, letting out a shrieking cry and heading north.

The Champion of Azeroth was already at the stairs, his huge shoulders tensed, his heavy frame moving with the quiet, agile grace of a cat, his blade drawn. Garona slunk forward as well, her hand dipping into her tabbard and coming up with her long-bladed dagger. The heavy blade from Stormwind clattered against Khadgar's hip, and he felt like a clumsy creature of stone compared to the other two. Behind him, more gryphons landed and discharged their warriors.

The observatory parapet was empty, and the upper level of the master mage's study deserted but not empty. There were still tools scattered about, and the smashed remnants of the golden device, an astrolabe, rested on the mantel. So if the tower was truly abandoned, it was done quickly.

Or it had not been abandoned at all.

Torches were fired and the party descended the myriad stairs, with

Lothar, Garona, and Khadgar in the lead. Once these walls were familiar, were home, the many stairs a daily challenge. Now, the wall-mounted torches, with their cool, frozen flame, had been extinguished, and the moving torches of the invaders cast myriad armed shadows against the wall, giving the halls an alien, almost nightmarish cast. The very walls seemed to hold menace, and Khadgar expected every darkened doorway to hold a deadly ambush.

There was nothing. The galleries were empty, the banquet halls bare, the meeting rooms as devoid of life and furnishings as ever. The guest quarters were still furnished, but unoccupied. Khadgar checked his own quarters: Nothing had changed there.

Now the torchlight cast strange shadows on the walls of the library, twisting the iron frames and turning the bookcases into battlements. The books were untouched, and even Khadgar's most recent notes were still on the table. Had Medivh not thought enough of the library to take any of his volumes?

Tatters of paper caught Khadgar's eye, and he crossed to the shelves containing the epic poetry. This was new. Fragments of a scroll, now smashed and torn. Khadgar picked up a large piece, read a few words, then nodded.

"What is it?" said Lothar, looking like he expected the books to come to life at any moment and attack.

"'The Song of Aegwynn,'" said Khadgar. "An epic poem about his mother."

Lothar grunted a note of understanding, but Khadgar wondered. Medivh had been here, after they had left. Yet only to destroy the scroll? Out of harsh memories of the Magus's conflict with his mother? Out of revenge for Sargeras's decisive loss to Aegwynn? Or did the act of destroying the scroll, the cipher used by the Guardians of Tirisfal, symbolize his resignation and final betrayal of the group?

Khadgar risked a simple spell—one used to divine magical presences—but came up with nothing more than the normal response when surrounded by magical tomes. If Medivh had cast a spell here, he had masked its presence sufficiently to beat anything Khadgar could manage.

Lothar noted the young mage tracing symbols into the air, and when he was done, said, "You'd best save your strength for when we find him."

Khadgar shook his head and wondered if they were going to find the Magus.

They found Moroes, instead, at the lowest level, near the entrance to the kitchen and larder. His crumpled form was splayed in the middle of the hallway, a bloody rainbow arcing along the floor to one side. His eyes were wide and open, but his face was surprisingly composed. Not even death seemed to surprise the castellan.

Garona dodged into the kitchen, and returned a moment later. Her face was a paler shade of green, and she held something up for Khadgar to see.

A set of rose-colored lenses, smashed. Cook. Khadgar nodded.

The bodies seemed to make the troops more alert now, and they moved to the great vault-like entranceway, and out into the courtyard itself. There had been no sign of Medivh, and only a few broken clues of his passing.

"Could he have another lair?" Lothar asked. "Another place he would hide?"

"He was often gone," said Khadgar. "Sometimes gone for days, then reappearing without warning." Something moved along the balcony overlooking the main entrance—just a slight wavering of the air. Khadgar started and stared at the location, but it looked normal.

"Perhaps he went to the orcs, to lead them," suggested the Champion.

Garona shook her head. "They would never accept a human leader."

"He couldn't vanish into thin air!" thundered Lothar. To the troops he shouted, "Form up! We're going to head back!"

Garona ignored the Champion, then said, "He didn't. Back into the tower." She parted the troops like a boat cutting through a choppy sea.

She disappeared once more in the open maw of the tower. Lothar looked at Khadgar, who shrugged and followed the half-orc.

Moroes had not moved, his blood smeared across the floor in a quarter circle, away from the wall. Garona touched that wall, as if trying to feel something along it. She frowned, cursed, and slapped the wall, which gave a very solid response.

"It should be here," she said.

"What should be?" asked Khadgar.

"A door," said the half-orc.

"There's never been a door here," said Khadgar.

"There's *always* been a door, probably," said Garona. "You've just never seen it. Look. Moroes died here," she stomped her foot next to the wall, "and then his body was moved, creating the smear of blood in the quarter-circle, to where we found it."

Lothar grunted assent, and started to run his hands along the wall as well.

Khadgar looked at the apparently blank wall. He had passed it five or six times a day. There should be nothing but earth and stone on the far side. Still . . .

"Stand away," the young mage said. "Let me try something."

The Champion and half-orc stood back, and Khadgar pulled the energies together for a spell. He had used it before, on real doors and locked books, but this was the first time he tried to work it on a door he could not see. He tried to envision the door, figuring how large it would have to be to move Moroes's body in the quarter circle, where the hinges would be, where the frame would be, and, if he wanted to keep it secure, where he would place the locks.

He envisioned the door, and flung a bit of magic into its unseen frame to unfasten those hidden locks. Half to his surprise, the wall shifted, and a seam appeared along one side. Not a lot, but enough to define the clear edges of a door that had not been there a moment before.

"Use your swords and pry it open," snarled Lothar, and the squad surged forward. The stone door resisted their attempts for a few moments, until some mechanism within it snapped loudly and the door swung outward, nuzzling Moroes's corpse as it did so, and revealed a stairway descending into the depths.

"He didn't vanish into thin air," said Garona grimly. "He stayed here, but went someplace no one else knew about."

Khadgar looked at Moroes's crumpled form. "Almost no one. But I wonder what else he has hidden."

They moved down the stairs, and a sense grew within Khadgar. While the upper levels felt spookily abandoned, the depths beneath the tower had a palpable aura of immediate menace and foreboding. The rough-hewn walls and floor were moist, and in the light of the torches seemed to undulate like living flesh.

It took a moment for Khadgar to realize that as the stairs continued to spiral down, they now had reversed their direction, moving opposite to the tower above, as if this descent was a mirror of that above.

Indeed, where an empty meeting room would be within the tower, here was a dungeon bedecked with unoccupied iron chains. Where a banquet hall stood unused above the surface was a room strewn with detritus and marked with mystic circles. The air felt heavy and oppressive here, as it had in the tower in Stormwind, where Huglar and Hugarin had been slain. Here was where the demon that attacked them had been summoned.

When they reached the level that mirrored the library, they found a set of iron-shod doors. The stairs continued to spiral down into the earth, but the company was brought up short here, regarding the mystic symbols carved deeply into the wood and dabbed with brownish blood. It seemed as if the wood itself was bleeding. Two huge rings of iron hung from the wounded doors.

"This would be the library," said Khadgar.

Lothar nodded. He had noted the similarities between the tower and this burrow as well. "See what he keeps here, if the books are all upstairs."

Garona said, "His study is at the top of the tower, with his observatory, so if he *is* here, he should be at the very bottom. We should press on."

But she was too late. As Khadgar touched the iron-shod doors, a spark leapt from his palm to the door, a signal, a magical trap. Khadgar had time to curse as the doors were flung open, back into the darkness of the library.

A kennel. Sargeras had no need for knowledge, so he turned the room over to his pets. The creatures lived within a darkness of their own making, and acrid smoke wafted out into the hallway.

There were eyes within. Eyes and flaming maws and bodies made of fire and shadow. They stalked forward, snarling.

Khadgar sketched runes in the air, pulling the energy together in his mind, to pull the doors closed again, as soldiers struggled with the great rings shut again. Neither spellcraft nor muscle could move the rings.

The beasts let out a harsh, choppy laugh, and crouched to spring.

Khadgar raised his hands to cast another spell, but Lothar batted them down.

"This is to waste your time and energy," he said. "It is to delay us. Head down and find Medivh."

"But they are . . ." started Khadgar, and the large demon-beast in the front leapt at them.

Lothar took two steps forward and brought up his blade to meet the leaping beast. As he pulled his blade upward, the runes etched deep into the metal blazed with a bright yellow light. For a half-second, Khadgar saw fear in the eyes of the demon-beast.

And then the arc of Lothar's cut intersected with the demon-beast's leap and the blade bit deep into the creature's flesh. Lothar's blade erupted from the creature's back, and he neatly bisected the forward portion of its torso in two. The beast had only a moment to squeal in pain as the blade pulled forward through its skull, completing the arch. The smoldering wreckage of the demon-beast, weeping fire and bleeding shadow, fell at Lothar's feet.

"Go!" thundered the Champion. "We'll take care of this and catch up."

Garona grabbed Khadgar, and pulled him down the stairs. Behind them, the soldiers had pulled their blades, as well, and the runes danced in brilliant flames as they drank deep of the shadows. The young mage and half-orc rounded the curve of the stairs, and behind them they heard the cries of the dying, from both human and inhuman throats.

They spiraled into the darkness, Garona holding a torch in one hand, dagger in the other. Now Khadgar noticed that the walls glowed with their own faint phosphorescence, a reddish hue like some nocturnal mushrooms deep within the forest. It was also growing warmer, and the sweat was beading along his forehead.

As they came to one of the dining halls, suddenly Khadgar's stomach wrenched and they were somewhere else. It moved suddenly upon them, like the leading edge of a summer storm.

They were atop one of the larger towers of Stormwind, and around them the city was in flames. Pillars of smoke rose from all sides, spreading into a black blanket above that snared the sun. A similar blanket of blackness surrounded the city walls, but this was made of orcish troops. From their viewpoint Khadgar and Garona could see the armies spread out like beetles on the verdant corpse that had been Stormwind's cropland. Now there were only siege towers and armed grunts, the colors of their banners a sickening rainbow.

The forests were gone as well, transformed into catapults that now rained fire down on the city itself. Most of the lower city was in flames, and as Khadgar watched, a section of the outer walls collapsed, and small dolls dressed in green and blue fought each other among the rubble.

"How did we get . . . ?" started Garona.

"Vision," said Khadgar bluntly, but he wondered if this was a random occurrence of the tower, or another delaying action by the Magus.

"I told the King. I told him, but he would not listen," she muttered. To Khadgar she said, "This is a vision of the future, then? How do we get out of the vision?"

The young mage shook his head. "We don't, at least for the moment. In the past these would come and go. Sometimes a good shock will break it."

A flaming piece of debris, a fiery missile from a catapult, passed within bowshot of the tower. Khadgar could feel the heat as it fell to earth.

Garona looked around. "At least it's just orc armies," she said grimly.

"That's good news?" said Khadgar, his eyes stinging as a column of smoke wafted over the tower.

"No demons in the orc armies," noted the half-orc. "If Medivh was with them, we would see much worse as well. Maybe we convinced him to help."

"I'm not seeing Medivh among our troops, either," said Khadgar, forgetting who he was speaking to for the moment. "Is he dead? Did he flee?"

"How far in the future are we?" asked Garona.

Behind them, there was a rise of voices in argument. The pair turned away from the parapet and saw that they were outside one of the royal audience halls, now converted into a coordination center against the assault. A small model of the city had been laid out on the table, and toy soldiers in the shapes of men and orcs were scattered around it. There was a constant flow of reports coming in as King Llane and his advisors hunched over the table.

"Breach along the Merchants' District Wall!"

"More fires in the lower city!"

"Large forces massing at the main gates again. It looks like spellcasters!"

Khadgar noted that none of the earlier courtiers were now present, replaced with grim-faced men in uniforms similar to their own. No sign of

Lothar at the table, and Khadgar hoped he was on the front lines, carrying the battle to the foe.

Llane moved with a deft hand, as if his city was attacked on a regular basis. "Bring up the Fourth and Fifth Company to reinforce the breach. Get the militia to organize bucket brigades—take the water from the public baths. And bring up two squads of lancers to the main gate. When the orcs are about to attack, then launch a sortie against them. That will break the assault. Bring two mages over from the Goldsmith's street; are they done there?"

"That assault has been turned," came the report. "The mages are exhausted."

Llane nodded and said, "Have them stand down, then, pull back for an hour. Bring the younger mages from the academy instead. Send twice as many, but tell them to be careful. Commander Borton, I want your forces on the Eastern Wall. That's where I would hit next, if I were them."

To each commander in turn, Llane gave an assignment. There was no argument, no discussion, no suggestions. Each warrior in turn nodded and left. In the end, all that was left was King Llane and his small model of a city that was now in flames outside his window.

The king leaned forward, resting his knuckles on the table. His face looked worn and old. He looked up and said to the empty air, "You can make your report now."

The curtains opposite hissed against the floor as Garona stepped out. The half-orc at Khadgar's side let out a gasp in surprise.

The future Garona was dressed in her customary black pants and black silk blouse, but wore a cloak marked with the lion's head of Azeroth. She had a wild look in her eyes. The present Garona gripped Khadgar's arm, and he could feel her nails dig into his arm.

"Bad news, sire," said Garona, approaching the King's side of the table. "The various clans are working together in this assault, unified under Blackhand the Destroyer. None of them will betray the others until after Stormwind has fallen. Gul'dan is bringing up his warlocks by nightfall. Until then, the Blackrock clan will be trying to take the Eastern Wall." Khadgar heard a tremor in the half-orc's voice.

Llane let out a deep sigh, and said, "Expected and countered. We will throw this one back, just like the others. And we will hold until the reinforcements come. As long as men with stout hearts are manning the walls and the throne, Stormwind will hold."

The future-Garona nodded, and Khadgar now saw that large tears were pooling in the corners of her eyes. "The orc leaders agree with your assessment," she said, and her hand dipped into her black blouse.

Both Khadgar and the real Garona shouted as one as the future-Garona pulled her long-bladed dagger and shoved it upward beneath the King's left breast. She moved with a quickness and grace and left King Llane with nothing more than a puzzled expression on his face. His eyes were wide, and for a moment he hung there, suspended on her blade.

"The orc leaders agree with your assessment," she said again, and tears were running freely down the sides of her wide face. "And have enlisted an assassin to remove that strong heart on the throne. Someone you would let come close. Someone you would meet with alone."

Llane, King of Azeroth, Master of Stormwind, ally of wizard and warrior, slid to the floor.

"I'm sorry," said Garona.

"*No!*" shouted Garona, the present Garona, as she slipped to the floor herself. Suddenly they were back in the false dining hall. The wreckage of Stormwind was gone and the corpse of the king with it. The half-orc's tears remained, now in the eyes of the real Garona.

"I'm going to kill him," she said in a small voice. "I'm going to kill him. He treated me well, and listened when I talked, and I'm going to kill him. No."

Khadgar knelt down besides her. "It's okay. It may not be true. It may not happen. It's a vision."

"It's true," she said. "I saw it and I knew that it was true."

Khadgar was silent for a moment, reliving his own vision of the future, beneath a red-hued sky, battling Garona's people. He saw it and knew it was true as well. "We have to go," he said, but Garona just shook her head. "After all this, I thought I found someplace better than the orcs. But now I know, I'm going to destroy it all."

Khadgar looked up and down the stairs. No idea how Lothar's men were doing with the demons, no idea what lay at the base of the underground tower. His face formed a grim line, and he took a deep breath.

And slapped Garona hard across the face.

His own palm bled from striking a tusk, but the response from Garona was immediate. Her teary eyes widened and a mask of rage hardened on her expression.

"You idiot!" she shouted, and leapt on Khadgar, bearing him over backward. "You never do that! You hear me! Do that again and I'll kill you!"

Khadgar was sprawled on his back, the half-orc on top of him. He didn't even see her draw the dagger, but now its blade was resting against the side of his neck.

"You can't," he managed with a harsh smile. "I had a vision of my own future. I think it's true as well. If it is, then you can't kill me now. Same thing applies to you."

Garona blinked and rocked back on her haunches, suddenly in control again. "So if I am going to kill the King . . ."

"You're going to get out of here alive," said Khadgar. "So am I."

"But what if we're wrong," said Garona. "What if the vision is false?"

Khadgar pulled himself to his feet. "Then you die knowing that you'll never kill the King of Azeroth."

Garona sat for a moment, her mind working over the possibilities. At length she said, "Give me a hand up. We have to move on."

They continued to spiral downward, through false analogs of the tower levels above. Finally they reached the level that would be the uppermost level, of Medivh's observatory and lair. Instead the stairs spilled out on a reddish plain. It seemed to be poured out of cooling obsidian, dark, reflective puzzle pieces floating on fire beneath their feet. Khadgar instinctively jumped back, but the footing seemed solid and the heat, while sweltering, was not oppressive.

In the center of the great cave was a simple collection of iron furniture. A work bench and stool, a few chairs, a gathering of cabinets. For a moment it looked oddly familiar, then Khadgar realized that it was set up in an exact duplicate to Medivh's tower room.

Standing among the iron furniture was the broad-shouldered form of the Magus. Khadgar strained to see something in his manner, in his bearing, that would betray him, that would reveal this figure to not be the Medivh he had come to know and trust, the older man who had shown faith and encouraged his work. Something that would declare this to be an imposter.

There was nothing. This was the only Medivh he had ever known.

"Hello, Young Trust," said the Magus and flames ignited along his beard as he smiled. "Hello, Emissary. I've been expecting you both."

SIXTEEN
The Breaking of a Mage

It was inspired, I must say," said the Medivh who was and was not Medivh. "Inspired to summon the shadow of my past, a piece that would stop me from pursuing you. Of course, while you were out gathering your strength, I was out gathering my own."

Khadgar looked at Garona and nodded. The half-orc moved a few steps to the right. They would surround the old man if they had to.

"Master, what happened to you?" said Khadgar, taking a step forward, trying to focus the Magus's attention on him.

The older mage laughed. "Happened to me? Nothing happened to me. This is who I am. I was tainted from birth, polluted from before my conception, a bad seed grown to bear bitter fruit. You have never seen the true Medivh."

"Magus, whatever has happened, I'm sure it can be fixed," said Khadgar, walking slowly toward him. Garona orbited out to the right, and her long-bladed dagger had vanished again—her hands were apparently empty.

"Why should I fix it?" said Medivh with an evil smile. "All goes as planned. The orcs will slay the humans and I will control them through warlock-chiefs like Gul'dan. I will lead these misshapen creations to the lost tomb where Sargeras's body is, protected against demon and human but not against orc, and my form will be free. And then I can shed this lumpish body and weakened spirit and burn this world as it so richly deserves."

Khadgar stepped to the left as he spoke. "You are Sargeras."

"Yes and no," said the Magus. "I am, for when Aegwynn killed my physical body I hid within her womb, and invested her very cells with my dark essence. When she finally chose to mate with a human mage, I was already there. Medivh's dark twin, completely subsumed within his form."

"Monstrous," said Khadgar.

Medivh grinned. "Little different than what Aegwynn had planned, for she placed the power of the *Tirisfalen* within the child as well. Small wonder that there was so little room for the young Medivh himself, with the demon and the light both fighting over his very soul. So when the power truly manifested within him, I shut him down for a while, until I could put my own plans into operation."

Khadgar continued to move left, trying not to watch as Garona crept up behind the older mage. Instead he said, "Is there anything of the real Medivh within you?"

"Some," said Medivh. "Enough to deal with you lesser creatures. Enough to fool the kings and wizards as to my intent. Medivh is a mask—I have left enough of him at the surface to display to others. And if in my workings I seem odd or even mad, they write it off to my position and responsibility, and to the power invested in me by my dear mother."

Medivh gave a predatory grin. "I was crafted first by Magna Aegwynn's politics to be her tool, and then shaped by demonic hands to be their tool. Even the Order saw me as little more than a weapon to be used against demons. And so it not surprising at all that I am nothing more than the sum of my parts."

Garona was behind the mage now, blade drawn, moving on the softest of steps on the obsidian floor. There were no tears in her eyes, but rather a steely determination. Khadgar kept himself focused on Medivh, not wanting to betray her with a single glance.

"You see," continued the mad mage, "I am nothing but one more component in the great machine, one that has been running since the Well of Eternity was first shattered. The one thing that the original bits of Medivh and myself agree on is that this cycle needs to be shattered. Of this, I assure you, we are of one mind."

Garona was within a step now, her dagger raised. She took the last step.

"Excuse me," said Medivh, and lashed out with a fist. Mystic energies danced along the older man's knuckles, and he caught the half-orc square in the face. She staggered backward under the blow.

Khadgar let loose a curse and raised his hands to cast a spell. Something to knock the mage off his balance. Something simple. Something quick.

Medivh was quicker, turning back to him and raising a claw-like hand. Immediately, Khadgar felt the air around him tighten into a restraining cloak, trapping his arms and legs and making it impossible for him to move. He shouted but his voice sounded muffled and coming from a great distance.

Medivh raised his other hand, and pain shot through Khadgar's body. The joints of his skeleton seemed to seethe with red-hot spikes that subsided quickly into dull, throbbing pains. His chest tightened, and his flesh felt like it dried out and crawled along his frame. He felt like the fluids were being pulled from his body, leaving a shriveled husk behind. And with it he felt his magic pulled away as well, his body drained of his ability to cast spells, to summon the requisite energies. He felt like a vessel being emptied.

As suddenly as the attack descended upon him, it had passed, and Khadgar toppled to the floor, the wind knocked out of him. It hurt his chest to breathe.

Garona had recovered at this point, and came in screaming this time, bringing her dagger-hand upward, to catch Medivh beneath the left breast. Instead of trying to back up, Medivh stepped toward the charging half-orc, inside the arc of her blow. He raised a hand and caught her forehead in his hand. She froze in mid-charge.

Mystic energy of a sickening yellow hue pulsed beneath his hand and the half-orc hung there, her body twitching helplessly, as the mage held her by the forehead.

"Poor, poor Garona," said Medivh. "I thought with your conflicting heritages, you of all people would understand what I'm going through. That you would understand the importance of making your own way. But you're just like the others, aren't you?"

The wide-eyed half-orc could only manage a spittle-drenched gurgle in response.

"Let me show you my world, Garona," said Medivh. "Let me drive my own divisions and doubts into you. You'll never know who you serve and why. You'll never find your peace."

Garona tried to scream, but it died in her throat as her face was bathed in a radiant sunburst issued from Medivh's palm.

Medivh laughed and let the half-orc collapse to the floor, sobbing. She tried to rise, but slumped again. Her eyes were wide and wild, and her breath was short and ragged, torn by tears.

Khadgar could breathe now, but the breath was short and tight. His joints burned, and his muscles ached. He saw his reflection in the obsidian floor. . . .

And it was the old man of the vision looking back at him. Heavy, tired eyes surrounded by wrinkles and gray hair. Even his beard had turned white.

And Khadgar's heart sank. Robbed of his youth, of his magic, he no longer felt like he would survive this battle.

"That was instructive," said Medivh, turning back to Khadgar. "One of the negative things about this humaniform cell I am trapped in is that the human part keeps reaching out. Making friends. Helping people. It makes it so difficult to destroy them later on. I almost wept when I killed Moroes and Cook, did you know? That's why I had to come down here. But it's like anything else. Once you get used to it, you can kill friends as easily as anyone else."

Now he stood a few paces in front of Khadgar, his shoulders straight, his eyes vibrant. Looking more like Medivh than at any time Khadgar had seen him. Looking confident. Looking at ease. Looking frighteningly, damnedly sane.

"And now you get to die, Young Trust," said the Magus. "It seems your trust was misplaced after all." Medivh raised a hand cupped with magical energy.

There was a throaty scream from the right. "Medivh!" bellowed Lothar, Champion of Azeroth.

Medivh looked up, and his face seemed to soften for a moment, though his hand still burned with the mystic power. "Anduin Lothar?" he said. "Old friend, why are you here?"

"Stop it now, Med," said Lothar, and Khadgar could hear the pain in the Champion's voice. "Stop it before it is too late. I don't want to fight you."

"I don't want to fight you either, old friend," said Medivh raising his hand. "You have no idea what it's like to do the things I've done. Harsh things. Necessary things. I don't want to fight you. So lay down your weapon, friend, and let this be done."

Medivh opened his palm and the bits of magic droned toward the Champion, bathing him in stars.

"You want to help me, don't you, old friend," said Medivh, the harsh smile once more on his face. "You want to be my servant. Come help me dispose of this child. Then we can be friends again."

The spangling stars around Lothar faded, and the Champion took a slow, firm step forward, then another, then a third, and now Lothar charged forward. As he charged, the Champion raised his rune-carved blade high. He charged at Medivh, not at Khadgar. A curse rose in his voice, a curse backed by sorrow and tears.

Medivh was surprised, but just for a moment. He dodged backward and Lothar's first cut passed harmlessly through the space the Magus had occupied a half-second before. The Champion checked the swing and brought it back in a solid blocking motion, driving the mage another step back. Then an overhand chop, driving him back another step.

Now Medivh had recovered himself, and the next blow landed squarely on a shield of bluish energy, the yellow fires of the sword spattering harmlessly like sparks. Lothar tried to cut upward, then thrust, then chop again. Each attack was met and countered by the shield.

Medivh snarled and raised a clawed hand, mystic energy dancing in his palm. Lothar screamed as his clothes suddenly burst into flames. Medivh smiled at his handiwork, then waved his hand, tossing the burning form of Lothar aside like a rag doll.

"Just. Gets. Easier," said Medivh, biting off the words and turning back to where Khadgar had been kneeling.

Except Khadgar had moved. Medivh turned to find the no-longer young mage right behind him, with the sword Lothar had provided drawn and pressed against the Magus's left breast. The runes along the blade glowed like miniature suns.

"Don't even blink," said Khadgar.

A moment passed, and a bead of sweat trickled down Medivh's cheek.

"So it comes to this," said the Magus. "I don't think you have the skill or the will to use that properly, Young Trust."

"I think," said Khadgar, and it seemed that his voice wheezed and burbled as he spoke, "that the human part of you, Medivh, kept others around despite your own plans. As a backup. As a plan for when you finally went mad. So your friends could put you down. So we could break the cycle where you cannot."

Medivh managed a small sigh, and his features softened. "I never meant to really harm anyone," he said. "I only wanted to have my own life." As he spoke, he jerked his hand upward, his palm glowing with mystic energy, seeking to scramble Khadgar's mind as he had Garona's.

Medivh never got the chance. At the first flinch, Khadgar lunged forward, driving the thin blade of the runesword between Medivh's ribs, into the heart.

Medivh looked surprised, even shocked, but his mouth still moved. He was trying to say something.

Khadgar drove the blade home to the hilt, the tip erupting from the back of the mage's robes. The mage sunk to his knees, and Khadgar dropped with him as well, keeping his hands firmly locked on the blade. The old mage gasped and struggled to say something.

"Thank you," he managed at last. "I fought it for as long as I could. . . ."

Then the master mage's face began to transform, the beard turning fully to flame, the horns sprouting from his brow. With the death of Medivh, Sargeras finally came fully to the surface. Khadgar felt the hilt of the runeblade grow warm, as the fires danced along Medivh's flesh, transforming him to a thing of shadow and flame.

Behind the kneeling, wounded Magus, Khadgar could see the smoldering form of Lothar rise once more. The Champion stumbled forward, his flesh and armor still smoking. He raised his runeblade once more, and brought it across in a hard, level swing.

The edge of the blade burst like a sun as it struck Medivh's neck, and severed the master mage's head from the neck in one smooth blow.

It was like unstoppering a bottle, for everything within Medivh rushed out at once through ragged remnants of his neck. A great torrent of energy and light, shadow and fire, smoke and rage, all spilling upward like a fountain, splashing against the ceiling of the underground vault, and dissipating away. Within the seething caldron of energies, Khadgar thought he could make out a horned face, crying in despair and rage.

And when it was over, all that was left was the skin and clothes of the Magus. All that was within him had been eaten away, and now that his human form had been ripped asunder, there was no way to contain it.

Lothar used the tip of his sword to stir aside the rags and flesh that had been Medivh and said, "We need to go."

Khadgar looked around. There was no sign of Garona. The Magus's head had boiled away all the flesh, leaving only a glistening red-white skull.

The former apprentice shook his head. "I need to stay here. Attend to a few things."

Lothar growled, "The greatest danger may be passed, but the obvious one is still there. We have to drive back the orcs and close the portal."

Khadgar thought of the vision, of Stormwind burning and Llane's death. He thought of his own vision, of his now-aged form in final battle with the orcs. Instead he said, "I must bury what's left of Medivh. I should find Garona. She couldn't have gone far."

Lothar grunted an assent and shambled toward the entrance. At last he turned and said, "It couldn't have been helped, you know. We tried to alter it, but it was all part of a larger scheme."

Khadgar nodded slowly. "I know. All part of a greater cycle. A cycle that now at last may be broken."

Lothar left the former apprentice beneath the citadel, and Khadgar gathered up what was left of the physical remains of the Magus. He found a shovel and a wooden box in the stable. He put the skull and the bits of skin in the box with the tattered remains of "The Song of Aegwynn," and buried them all deep in the courtyard in view of the tower. Perhaps later he would raise a monument, but for the time being it would be best to not let others know where the master mage's remains were. After he had finished burying the Magus, he dug two more graves, human-sized, and laid Moroes and Cook to rest to one side of Medivh.

He let out a deep sigh, and looked up at the tower. White-stoned Karazhan, home of the most mighty mage of Azeroth, the Last Guardian of the Order of Tirisfal, loomed above him. Behind him the sky was lightening, and the sun threatened to touch the topmost level of the tower.

Something else caught his eye, above the empty entrance hall, along the balcony overlooking the main entrance. A bit of movement, a fragment of a dream. Khadgar let out a deeper sigh and nodded at the ghostly trespasser that watched his every move.

"I can see you, now, you know," he said aloud.

EPILOGUE
Full Circle

The trespasser from the future looked down from the balcony at the no-longer young man of the past.

"How long have you been able to see me?" asked the trespasser.

"I have felt bits of you as long as I have been here," said Khadgar. "From my first day. How long have you been there?"

"Most of an evening," said the trespasser in his tattered red robes. "The dawn is coming up here."

"Here as well," said the former apprentice. "Perhaps that is why we can talk. You are a vision, but different than any I have seen before. We can see each other and converse. Are you future or past?"

"Future," said the trespasser. "Do you know who I am?"

"Your form is different than when I last saw you, you are younger, and calmer, but yes, I know," said Khadgar. He motioned toward the three heaps of turned earth—two large and one small. "I thought I just buried you."

"You did," said the trespasser. "At least you buried much of what was the worst about me."

"And now you're back. Or you will be back," said Khadgar. "Different, but the same."

The trespasser nodded. "In many ways, I was never here the first time around."

"More is the pity," said Khadgar. "So what are you in the future? Magus? Guardian? Demon?"

"Be reassured. I am a better being than I was," said the trespasser. "I am free of the taint of Sargeras thanks to your actions this day. Now I may deal directly with the Lord of the Burning Legion. Thank you. There cannot be success without sacrifice."

"Sacrifice," said Khadgar, the words bitter in his mouth. "Tell me this then, ghost of the future. Is all that we have seen true? Will Stormwind truly fall? Will Garona slay King Llane? Must I die, in this aged flesh, in some nether-spawned land?"

The being on the balcony paused for a long moment, and Khadgar feared that he would fade away. Instead he said, "As long as there are Guardians, there is Order. And as long as there is Order, the parts are there to be played. Decisions made millennia ago set both your path and mine. It is part of the greater cycle, one that has held us all in its sway."

Khadgar craned his head upward. The sun was now touching the top half of the tower. "Perhaps there should not be Guardians then, if this has been the price."

"Agreed," said the trespasser, and as the strong light of day began to grow, he began to fade. "But for the moment, for your moment, we must all play our part. We must all pay this price. And then, when we have the chance, we will start anew."

And with that the trespasser was gone, the last fragments of his being swept back into the future by an errant wind of magic.

Khadgar shook his aged head and looked at the three newly-dug graves. Lothar's surviving men took their dead and wounded back with them to Stormwind. There was no sign of Garona, and though Khadgar would search the tower once more, he doubted that she was within. He would take what books he thought were valuable, what supplies he could, and set protective wards over the rest. Then he would leave as well, and follow Lothar into battle.

Hefting his shovel, he walked back into the now-abandoned keep of Karazhan, and wondered if he would ever return.

As the trespasser spoke a small breeze kicked up, a mere churning of the leaves, but it was enough to scatter the vision. The no-longer-young man broke up and faded like dying fog, and the no-longer old man watched him go.

A single tear ran down the side of Medivh's face. So much sacrifice, so much pain. Both to keep the plan of the Guardians in place, and then so much sacrifice to break that plan, to break the world free of its lock-step. To bring about true peace.

And now, even that was at risk. Now one more sacrifice would have to be made. He would have to pull the power from this place if he would succeed in what was to come. In the final conflict with the Burning Legion.

The sun had risen farther now, and was almost to the level of his balcony. He would have to work quickly now.

He raised a hand, and the clouds began to swirl above the peak of the tower. Slowly first, then more quickly, until the upper ranges of the tower itself were encased within a hurricane.

Now he reached deep within himself, and released the words, words made up of equal parts regret and anger, words caught within him since the day that his life ended the first time. Words that laid claim to the whole of that previous life, for good and ill. Accepting its power, and in doing so, accepting the responsibility for what was done the last time he wore flesh.

The hurricane around the tower howled, and the tower itself resisted his claim. He stated it again, and then a third time, shouting to be heard over the winds that he himself had summoned. Slowly, almost grudgingly, the tower gave up its secrets.

The power burned from within the stones and mortars, and leached outward, channeled by the force of the winds toward the base, toward Medivh. All the visions began to bubble loose of its fabric, and stream downward. The fall of Sargeras, with its hundreds of screaming demons, fell in on him, as did the final conflict with Aegwynn and Khadgar's own battle beneath the dull red sun. Medivh's appearance before Gul'dan and the boyish battles of three young nobles and Moroes breaking Cook's favorite crystal, all were pulled into him. And with those visions came memories, and with those memories responsibilities. This must be avoided. This must never happen again. This must be corrected.

So too did the images and power leach upward from the hidden tower, from the pits beneath the tower itself. The fall of Stormwind flamed upward at him, and the death of Llane, and the myriad demons summoned in the middle of the night and unleashed against those in the Order too close to the truth. All of them fountained upward and were consumed within the form of the mage standing on the balcony.

All the shards, all the pieces of history, known and unrevealed, spiraled down the tower or rose from its dungeons and flowed into the man who had been the Last Guardian of Tirisfal. The pain was great, but Medivh grimaced and accepted it, taking the energy and the bittersweet memories it bore with equal measure.

The last image to fade was the one beneath the balcony itself, an image of a young man, a rucksack at his feet, a letter marked with the crimson seal of the Kirin Tor, hope in his heart and butterflies in his stomach. That youth was the last to fade, as he moved slowly toward the entrance, the magic surrounding his vision, his shard of the past, spiraling upward, unraveling him and letting the energy pass into the former Magus. As the last bit of Khadgar fell into him, a tear pooled at the corner of Medivh's eye.

Medivh held both hands to his chest tightly, containing all that he had regained. The tower of Karazhan was just a tower now, a pile of stone in the remote reaches, far from the traveled paths. Now the power of the place was within him. And the responsibility to do better with it, this time.

"And so we start anew," said Medivh.

And with that, he transformed into a raven, and was gone.

Of Blood and Honor

Chris Metzen

About the Author

Some people write stories, CHRIS METZEN helps build worlds. As Blizzard Entertainment, Inc.'s Vice President of Creative Development, Metzen oversees the creation of the memorable and immersive characters, places, events, and histories behind all Blizzard games . While the majority of his time is spent writing, Metzen also has a hand in game design, conceptual artwork, and the voice direction of Blizzard's titles.

Metzen began working at Blizzard in 1994. He has worked on nearly all of Blizzard's award-winning games, including *Warcraft III: Reign of Chaos*, *Warcraft III: The Frozen Throne*, *Warcraft II*, *Diablo*, *StarCraft*, *StarCraft: Brood War*, *Diablo II*, *Diablo II: Lord of Destruction*, *World of Warcraft*, and the upcoming *World of Warcraft Expansion Set: The Burning Crusade*.

To my folks, Pete and Kathy Metzen,
for all their love, support, and encouragement over the years.

To Team Hamro—
Sam Moore, Michael Carrillo, Mike Pirozzi, and Daniel Moore,
for always reminding me of what "epic" really means.

To Walter Simonson,
whose portrayal of a certain thunder god defined
everything I value as an artist and a storyteller.

And last, but not least—
to all of my talented brothers and sisters at Blizzard with
whom I've had the distinct privilege of building the greatest
worlds in computer gaming. This one's for you, y'all.

ONE
A Clash of Arms

A soft, cool breeze blew through the upper branches of the mighty oak trees of the Hearthglen Woods. A peaceful quiet had fallen over the tranquil forest, leaving Tirion Fordring alone with his thoughts. His gray stallion, Mirador, trotted at an easy pace along the winding hunting path. Though game had been strangely scarce for the past few weeks, Tirion came to hunt here whenever the opportunity presented itself. He preferred the grandeur and crisp air of the open country to the musty, confining halls of his keep. He had been hunting in these woods since he was a small boy and knew their numerous, winding trails like the back of his hand. This was the one place he could always find refuge from the burdens and bureaucratic pressures of his station. He mused that someday he would bring his young son, Taelan, to hunt with him so that the boy could experience the rugged majesty of his homeland for himself.

Lord Paladin Tirion Fordring was a powerful man. He was strong in both mind and body, and was counted as one of the greatest warriors of his day. Though he was slightly over fifty years of age, he still looked as fit and dynamic as he had when a younger man. His signature bushy mustache and his neatly trimmed brown hair were streaked with gray, but his piercing green eyes still shone with an energy that belied his years.

Tirion was the governor of the prosperous Alliance principality of Hearthglen, a large forested region nestled at the crossroads between the towering Alterac Mountains and the mist-shrouded shores of Darrowmere Lake. He was respected as a just governor and his name and deeds were honored throughout the kingdom of Lordaeron. His great keep, Mardenholde, was the center of commerce and trade for the bustling region. The citizens of Hearthglen took great pride in the fact that the keep's mighty walls had never fallen to invaders, even during the darkest days of the orcish invasion of Lordaeron. Yet, of late, Tirion was disgruntled to find a different kind of army scurrying worriedly through the halls of his home.

In recent weeks the keep had been overrun with traveling dignitaries and representatives from the various nations of the Alliance, who passed through Hearthglen on their secret diplomatic errands. He had met with many of them in person, offering his hospitality and assistance wherever he could. Though the dignitaries were appropriately appreciative of his efforts, Tirion could sense a growing tension within all of them. He suspected that they were charged with carrying dire news directly to the Alliance High Council. Try as he might, he could not discern the specifics behind their urgent communiqués. Yet Tirion Fordring was no fool. After thirty years of serving the Alliance as a Paladin, he recognized that only one thing could cause the otherwise stoic emissaries to be so troubled: War was returning to Lordaeron.

It had been nearly twelve years since the war against the orcish Horde had ended. It was a terrible conflict that had raged across the northlands, leaving many of the Alliance kingdoms razed and blackened in its wake. Too many brave men fell before the rampaging Horde was finally stopped. Tirion had lost a number of good friends and soldiers over the course of the war. Though the Alliance had rallied at the eleventh hour and pulled victory from the clutches of certain defeat, it had paid a heavy price. Almost an entire generation of young men had selflessly given their lives to insure that mankind would never be slaves to savage orc overlords.

Near the war's end, the battered and leaderless orc clans were rounded up and placed within guarded reserves near the outskirts of the Alliance lands. Though, as a precautionary measure, it was necessary to police the reserves with full regiments of knights and footmen, the orcs remained docile and passive. Indeed, as time passed, the orcs seemed to lose their raging bloodlust completely and lapse into a strange communal stupor. Some supposed that the foul brutes' lethargy was brought on by inactivity, but Tirion remained to be convinced. He had seen, firsthand, the orcs' brutality and savagery in battle. Memories of their heinous atrocities had plagued his dreams for years after the war. He, for one, would never believe that their warlike ways had left them completely.

Tirion prayed every night, as he always had, that conflict would never endanger his people again. Perhaps naively, he hoped fervently that his young son would be spared the rigors and horrors of war. As a Paladin, he had seen far too many children orphaned or left for dead over the course of the tragic conflict. He wondered how any child could not become cold and disassociated when faced with terror and violence all around them. He would certainly never allow that to happen to his own boy, that was certain. Yet, despite his best wishes, he could not ignore the reality of the present situation. His closest aides and advisors had been telling him of the grim rumors for months now—that the orcs were once again on the move. Hard as it was to believe, the presence of so many emissaries in his keep confirmed it to be true.

If the orcs were foolish enough to rise up again, he would do whatever it took in order to stop them. Duty had always been the one constant in his life. He had spent the majority of his years defending Lordaeron in one way or another. Though he had not been born a noble, his enthusiasm and honor had won him the rank of knight at the tender age of eighteen. Tirion served his king with undying loyalty and won a great deal of respect from his superiors. Years later, when the orcs first invaded Lordaeron, intent on crushing civilization, he was one of the first knights to be given the honor of standing with Uther the Lightbringer and being anointed as a holy Paladin.

Uther, Tirion, and a number of devout knights were handpicked by the Archbishop Alonsus Faol to become living vessels of the holy Light. Their special, sacred charge was twofold: aided by the holy Light, the Paladins would not only lead the fight against the vile forces of darkness, but heal the wounds inflicted upon the innocent citizens of humanity as well. Tirion and his fellows were given the divine power to heal wounds and cure diseases of every kind. They were imbued with great strength and wisdom that enabled them to rally their brethren and give glory to the Light. Indeed, the Paladins' leadership and strength helped to turn the tide of the war and insure the survival of humanity.

Though his own Light-given powers had waned somewhat over the years, Tirion could still feel strength and grace flow through his aging limbs. Surely he would have strength enough when he needed it the most. For his son and for his people, he would have strength enough, he vowed.

Clearing his head of concerns, Tirion stopped to get his bearings. To his surprise, he found that he'd wandered much farther up the winding path than he'd intended. The path snaked its way up and over the densely forested mountain. There were no outposts this far up, Tirion remembered. As a matter of fact, he couldn't recall the last time he had ventured up this far. He took a moment to drink in the raw beauty of the place. He could hear babbling streams nearby and smell the clean, crisp air. The sky was blue and clear as he watched two falcons circle high above. He truly loved this land. He told himself that he'd return to this spot when a more opportune moment presented itself. Running his hand through his thinning, graying hair, he chided himself for becoming so lost in thought. He had come out to hunt, after all. Tirion deftly turned his mount around on the thin path and spurred Mirador to a quicker pace back down the mountain. He pulled sharply on the reins and steered his faithful mount into the dense woods.

After a few minutes he slowed his pace and galloped into a wide clearing that surrounded the ruins of an abandoned guard tower. He stopped near the old tower's base and peered up at the lonely structure. Like many other ruins that dotted the land, it was a painful reminder of a darker time. The tower's walls were broken and scarred by blackened blastmarks. Obviously the work of orcish catapults, he thought. He remembered how the destructive machines had hurled their fiery projectiles from great distances and devastated entire villages during the war. He wondered how the ruined structure could still be standing after having been left to the unforgiving elements for so long. While examining the tower's base he caught sight of strange tracks upon the ground. He dismounted to inspect them. His blood nearly froze in his veins as he realized that the oversized tracks had not been made by any man—and that they were fresh.

Tirion quickly looked around and found more tracks scattered throughout the clearing. He surmised that orcs had been here within the past few days at least. Could the vile brutes be mobilizing so soon, he wondered? No. There had to be some other explanation. Hearthglen's borders were secure. There was no way that a group of orcs could go undetected in his land for any length of time. Subtlety, of all things, was definitely not a part of their nature. His scouts and guardsmen would have been alerted to any orcish incursion into Hearthglen immediately upon their arrival. Yet the fresh tracks were there, just the same.

Tirion walked Mirador around to the back of the tower and drew his heavy bastard sword from the scabbard attached to his saddle. He wished fervently that he had brought his mighty warhammer instead. Though he was well-practiced with a blade, he would have preferred to wield his traditional hammer, as all Paladins did in the face of danger.

As stealthily as he could, Tirion crept around the tower and entered through what was left of its front door. A number of large wooden beams had fallen from the rickety ceiling and splintered all over the chipped stone floor. He inspected the dilapidated guardroom and found a small, makeshift fire pit near a ragged, patchwork bedroll. The fire in the ash-laden pit had only recently burnt out. Apparently the orcs had taken up residence within the old tower. Strangely, he saw no weapons or token trophies, which orcs were fond of collecting. He wondered what could possess the brutes to so recklessly squat on Alliance-held lands.

Deciding to return to the keep and gather his men, Tirion exited the tower and strode boldly out into the clearing. To his surprise, he immediately locked eyes with a gargantuan orc, who had suddenly emerged from the tree line. The orc, who seemed as startled as Tirion, dropped the bundle of firewood it had been carrying and reached for the broad battle-ax that was slung to its back. Tirion gritted his teeth and brandished his own sword threateningly. Slowly, the orc planted his feet firmly on the ground, unslinging the mighty ax.

It had been years since Tirion had laid eyes on an orc. He looked upon the brute with unabashed awe and revulsion. Yet, through his surging adrenaline, Tirion noticed that there was something quite different about this orc. Certainly, the creature was as immense and well-muscled as any other he had beheld. Its coarse, green skin and ape-like stance marked it as clearly as any other orc. Even its hideous tusks and pointed ears were reminiscent of every savage that Tirion had faced during the war. But something in the creature's stature and demeanor seemed different. There was an aged weight in its stance and far too many wrinkles around its eyes. Its ratty beard and ritually topknotted hair bore heavy streaks of gray. Where most orc warriors adorned themselves with mismatched plates of armor and spiked gauntlets, this one wore only stitched furs and ruddy leather pants. Its calm lethality and assured, comfortable battle stance clearly indicated that this orc was no rampaging youngster, but, indeed, a seasoned veteran. Despite its apparent age, it was potentially more dangerous than any orc Tirion had ever faced.

The hulking creature stood motionless for a long moment, as if daring Tirion to make the first move. Tirion quickly surveyed the tree line to make certain there were no other orcs preparing to ambush him. Peering back at the orc, he found that it had not moved even an inch. The orc nodded as if to confirm that it was alone. The creature's knowing gaze left Tirion with the impression that it wanted his full attention before it engaged him in combat.

Feeling somewhat unhinged by the orc's calm demeanor, Tirion lunged forward. The orc easily sidestepped Tirion's initial attack and brought his great ax around in a wide arc. Reflexively, Tirion ducked under the savage strike and rolled into a defensive crouch. Seizing the moment, he thrust his blade up at the orc's exposed belly. The creature expertly blocked the thrust with the haft of his ax, and leapt backward to give himself more room to maneuver. Tirion feinted to his right and then brought his blade around in a sweeping reverse thrust. Momentarily caught off guard by the clever move, the orc whirled around in the opposite direction and brought his ax down in a fast overhead swipe, meant to cut Tirion in two. Tirion rolled out of the way as the ax crashed down only inches from where he had stood. The two opponents straightened and squared off once more. They stared at one another in surprise. Tirion had to admit that the orc was as formidable a foe as he had ever faced. The grim smile that passed over the orc's bestial face seemed to impart a similar respect for Tirion's own abilities.

They began to circle one another, each sizing up the other's strengths and weaknesses. Tirion was again surprised by the orc's demeanor and focus. Every other orc he had encountered had rushed forward with reckless abandon, preferring savagery and brute force to finesse and tactical maneuvering. This orc, however, demonstrated remarkable skill and self-control.

For a moment, Tirion wondered whether or not he could actually best the creature. For a split second, he worried that his tired limbs and reflexes would fail him at a crucial moment. Sporadic thoughts of his beloved wife and son being left to fend for themselves without him flashed through his mind, weakening his resolve by a fraction. With a derisive snort, he shook off his doubts and readied his weapon. He had faced death a hundred times. He had a job to do. He relaxed slightly and reminded himself that his battle instincts were as sharp as ever. And he had the power of the Light on his side. No matter how impressive the orc's fighting prowess might be, it was still a creature of darkness as far as he was concerned—it was the sworn enemy of humanity, and for that it had to die.

Rushing forward with grim resolve, Tirion slashed at the orc with every ounce of strength he could muster. The orc was forced to give ground before the Paladin's furious attack. Tirion pushed the orc backward until it felt as if his sword arm would burst into flames. The orc managed to block and counter a number of the Paladin's thrusts, but was thrown off-balance by an expertly placed strike. Tirion cut a gaping gash in the orc's thigh, sending the brute stumbling into the dust. The old orc grunted loudly as it slammed down onto the packed dirt. Gripping its bloodied leg in pain, the orc attempted to rise again, clearly expecting Tirion to take advantage of its precarious position. To its obvious surprise, Tirion backed off and slowly motioned for it to rise. The orc blinked in astonishment.

Tirion was a Paladin—a Knight of the Silver Hand—and to him, butchering a fallen foe in the midst of single combat was unquestionably dishonorable. The holy code of his Order demanded that he give the orc a reprieve. He nodded to the orc in assurance, and once more motioned for him to rise. Gritting his sharp, yellowed teeth in pain, the orc slowly recovered his ax and got to his feet. They stood there for a moment, facing each other with eyes locked. The orc straightened slightly and raised his clenched fist to his heart. A salute, Tirion realized. Now it was Tirion's turn to blink in disbelief. Certainly no savage orc had ever saluted him in battle before. He conceded that perhaps there was more to the fierce creature than he would have guessed. Nevertheless, it was his enemy. He nodded to the orc in understanding and raised his sword again.

This time it was the orc who surged forward. Unable to support its great weight upon its wounded leg, the orc was forced to lunge at the Paladin with short, violent leaps. Wielding its heavy ax with one hand, the mighty orc slashed wildly at Tirion. The Paladin was hard-pressed to evade the brute's savage blows, and was forced back toward the tower's entrance. Barely dodging a particularly brutal strike, Tirion crashed into the guardroom through the open doorway. Momentarily stunned, Tirion roared as the razor-sharp ax bit deep into his left arm. Fighting to keep his head clear from pain, he managed to slash at the orc's exposed hand. The surprised orc howled in rage as his ax clattered upon the stone floor. Tirion moved in, hoping to end the duel as quickly as possible.

Instantly, the orc grabbed hold of a fallen beam and swung at the advancing Paladin.

Tirion backed up a pace as the orc swung the beam in a clumsy arc. The beam smashed into the brittle wall. Dust and loose rock rained down from the high ceiling. The remaining beams creaked and groaned as the tower's walls shifted their weight. Tirion continued his attack, cutting the orc's makeshift weapon to splinters with every fevered strike. Realizing the desperate nature of its situation, the orc dropped what was left of the beam and lunged straight at Tirion with its sinewy arms outstretched. Howling in fury, the massive orc reached out for Tirion's throat. The Paladin managed to stab the orc once before the full weight of the creature's body slammed into his. The two entangled combatants crashed into the weakened wall as the rickety ceiling finally gave way and collapsed down upon them.

Tirion woke to the sounds of creaking timber and clattering stone. He blinked as thick clouds of dust settled all around him. All else was black in the shattered guardroom. His body was numb, but he could feel a great pressure upon his chest. As the dust cleared, he could see that he was pinned under a large, split beam. His legs, too, were pinned beneath immense chunks of mortar. Frantically, he looked around for any sign of the orc. He would be defenseless if the creature decided to finish him off. Reaching down, he grabbed hold of the beam and heaved with all of his remaining strength. The beam toppled to the side and clattered against the rubble.

Pain immediately flooded Tirion's body. His head swam as the open cut on his arm gushed his precious blood upon the floor. He attempted to lift himself up and felt an acute burst of pain as his broken ribs ground against one another. His right leg, too, felt like it might be broken beneath the heavy blocks of mortar. His battered body reeling from agony and exhaustion, Tirion felt as if he would black out. He could hear the remaining walls of the structure creaking and groaning. The whole tower was going to collapse. With consciousness rapidly slipping away, Tirion sensed a rustling behind him. Fighting to stay awake, Tirion barely turned to see the orc's green, menacing hands reaching out for him. His gasp of terror was cut short as blackness overtook him.

TWO
Unanswered Questions

*S*unlight cascaded down from the open skylight in the cathedral's vaulted ceiling. Dust motes spiraled in a lazy dance, blown by the soft wind that wafted through the grandiose hall. Rows of large, white candles stood before the base of an immense triptych window of stained glass. The image of a proud, regal warrior was depicted in the window. Thousands of tiny, colored shards of glass portrayed the man's broad features and noble bearing. Surrounded by a halo of golden light, the man held a mighty warhammer in one hand and a large, leatherbound tome in the other. The inscription on the tome read: "Esarus thar no'Darador"—"By Blood and Honor We Serve."*

Tirion Fordring looked up toward the colorful image and felt his spirit soar. Kneeling upon an ornately carved dais, Tirion humbly bowed his head in prayer. To his left, a group of somber men dressed in flowing white robes stood in attendance. They were clerics—warrior priests—who hailed from the Northshire region. The pious clerics were present in order to offer Tirion their support and spiritual guidance, should he require it. To his immediate right, another group stood in observance, all dressed in heavy suits of highly polished armor. They were the Knights of the Silver Hand—the Paladins. The shining Paladins were the champions of

Lordaeron and the Alliance. They stood in support of Tirion—the newest initiate to their hallowed ranks. Before him was a vast altar that lay directly beneath the enormous stained glass window. The streaming sunlight was focused at the center of the altar, where another robed man sat in meditative silence, cradling a large book in his lap. Tirion was only vaguely aware of the others gathered in the cathedral behind him, chatting anxiously while waiting for the ceremony to begin.

The robed man on the altar raised his hand, calling for the gathered masses to fall silent. Tirion held his breath. This was the moment for which he had waited. The robed man stood and slowly walked forward to address the kneeling Tirion. The Archbishop stopped as he reached the ornate dais and opened the large book he had been holding. With a voice like thunder, the Archbishop read aloud:

"In the Light, we gather to empower our brother. In its grace, he will be made anew. In its power, he shall educate the masses. In its strength, he shall combat the shadow. And, in its wisdom, he shall lead his brethren to the eternal rewards of paradise." Finishing the verse, the Archbishop closed the book and turned toward the men on the left. Tirion felt a rush of excitement sweep through his body. He breathed in deeply and tried to focus on the solemnity of the moment.

"Clerics of the Northshire, if you deem this man worthy, place your blessings upon him," the Archbishop said in a ritualistic tone. One of the white-robed men walked forward, carrying an embroidered dark blue stole in his hands. The Cleric reached the dais and reverently placed the blessed stole around Tirion's neck. He dipped his thumb in a small vial of sacred oil and anointed Tirion's sweating brow with it.

"By the grace of the Light, may your brethren be healed," the Cleric said in a whisper. He bowed and backed away to stand once more amongst his fellows.

The Archbishop turned to the men on the right and spoke again: "Knights of the Silver Hand, if you deem this man worthy, place your blessings upon him."

Two of the armored men moved forward with obvious pride on their faces and stood solemnly in front of the dais. One of the men held a great, two-handed warhammer. The hammer's silvery head was etched with holy runes and its haft was meticulously wrapped in blue leather. Tirion could only marvel at the weapon's exceptional craftsmanship and beauty. The knight laid the hammer on the dais before Tirion's feet. He then bowed his head and backed away. The second knight, carrying dual ceremonial shoulder plates, stepped forward and looked Tirion in the eye. He was Saidan Dathrohan, one of Tirion's closest friends. The knight's face was alight with pride and excitement. Tirion smiled knowingly. Visibly composing himself, Saidan placed the silver shoulder plates upon Tirion's shoulders and spoke in a stern voice. "By the strength of the Light, may your enemies be undone."

After he finished speaking, Saidan adjusted the silver plates so that the blue stole streamed out from beneath them. He then backed away and returned to the group of attendant knights. Tirion's heart pounded in his chest. He was so overcome with joy that he felt almost light-headed. The Archbishop strode forward once again and placed his hand upon Tirion's head.

"Arise and be recognized," he said. Tirion got to his feet and marveled at the sheer magnitude of the honor being bestowed upon him. The Archbishop leveled his gaze at Tirion, then read aloud from the book.

"Do you, Tirion Fordring, vow to uphold the honor and codes of the Order of the Silver Hand?"

"I do," Tirion replied earnestly.

"Do you vow to walk in the grace of the Light and spread its wisdom to your fellow man?"

"I do."

"Do you vow to vanquish evil wherever it be found, and protect the weak and innocent with your very life?"

Tirion swallowed hard and nodded while saying, "By my blood and honor, I do." He exhaled softly, overcome with emotion.

The Archbishop closed the book and walked back toward the center of the altar.

Turning to face the entire assembly, the Archbishop said, "Brothers—you who have gathered here to bear witness—raise your hands and let the Light illuminate this man." Each of the Clerics and knights raised their right hands and pointed toward Tirion. To Tirion's amazement, their hands began to glow with a soft, golden radiance. He supposed that, in the excitement of the moment, his eyes were playing tricks on him. Yet, as he watched in wonder, the sunlight that poured in from above began to move slowly across the floor. As if in response to the assembly's command, the light came to rest upon Tirion himself. Partially blinded by the intense radiance, Tirion felt his body warmed and energized by its holy power. Every fiber of his being was ignited by divine fire. He could sense life-giving energies flowing through his limbs, energies enough to heal any wound or cure any disease. He mused that these energies were enough to burn even the souls of the accursed denizens of the shadow. Despite himself, he shuddered involuntarily.

Ablaze with hope and joy, Tirion knelt down and took hold of the mighty hammer—the symbol of his holy appointment and station. With joyous tears streaming down his face, he raised his head and looked toward the Archbishop, who smiled warmly back at him.

"Arise, Tirion Fordring—Paladin defender of Lordaeron. Welcome to the Order of the Silver Hand."

The entire assembly erupted in cheers. Trumpets blared from the high balconies and the cheerful din echoed through the vastness of the Cathedral of Light.

Tirion woke with a start. The sound of children's frolicking laughter came through the nearby window. Outside he could hear the familiar sounds of commerce and trade being conducted within the grounds of Mardenholde keep. He was home, in his own bed. Shaking his head to clear his groggy mind, he wondered how long he had slept. His sheets were soaked with sweat and he smelled as if he hadn't bathed in a week. His head was pounding so hard he felt as if it would burst. Sighing heavily, he remembered that he had been dreaming. He tried to recall the dream's details, but due to the incessant pounding in his skull, he could only grasp the faintest flashes of imagery: a robed man, a shiny hammer, and a vicious orc. A vicious orc? He surmised that he had dreamt of his appointment as a Paladin. But surely there were no orcs present at that joyous ceremony. Slowly, more images began to flash in his mind. There had been a fight between himself and the orc—and he had lost. Nonsense, he thought absently. He mused that his dreams were becoming even more imaginative in his old age.

Lifting his head from the sweat-soaked pillow, he attempted to get up and out of bed. A searing pain shot through him and he lay back down, panting for breath. He stripped the blankets from his body and saw that his entire midsection had been neatly bandaged. Bruises and small lacerations covered most of his aching body. He was surprised to find that his arm had also been dressed and bandaged. Frantically, he tried to recall what had happened to him. Had the fight against the orc been real? For some strange reason, his memory seemed hazy and sluggish. His face contorted with pain as he struggled out of bed. Wrapping himself in his dressing robe, he made his way toward the sitting room of his private chambers.

He found his young wife, Karandra, sitting quietly with her needlework in a large plush chair near an open window. At seeing him enter the room, Karandra threw down her embroidery and rushed to meet him. She hugged him warmly, careful not to squeeze him too tightly.

"Thank the Light, you're awake," she said. Her young, delicate features were fixed with both relief and concern. Her blue eyes seemed to stare straight through him, as they always did. He smiled back and kissed her forehead lightly. He marveled, for perhaps the ten thousandth time, at her beauty. "I was beginning to wonder if you were going to sleep clear through midyear," she said. His eyebrow arched questioningly as he stroked her soft, golden hair.

"What do you mean? How long have I slept?" he asked.

"Nearly four days," she replied flatly. Tirion blinked in disbelief.

"Four days," he mumbled to himself. That would explain the hazy memory, he mused.

"Karandra, what's happened to me? Why have I slept so long?" he asked. She shrugged, shaking her head slightly.

"We're not exactly sure what happened to you," she replied. "You left in the morning to go hunting and were gone for hours. Since you're almost never late in returning, I was worried that you'd been hurt. I sent Arden out to find you." Tirion smiled. Arden was the captain of the keep's guards, and perhaps his most loyal friend. He should have guessed that Arden would go searching for him. Karandra continued, "Just as he was leaving the keep, he came across you atop Mirador. He said that you were unconscious when he found you, and that you'd been tied to the saddle with your own reins."

Tirion cupped his aching head in his hands. "Tied to my saddle? None of this makes any sense," he said wearily.

She placed her cool hand against his forehead, soothingly. "Your ribs were broken and your arm had been sliced open. We feared you had been attacked by a rogue bristlebear. Barthilas healed you as soon as Arden brought you inside."

Tirion sat down heavily in her chair. *Barthilas? Barthilas had healed him?* The youth was only recently anointed as a Paladin, and Tirion was surprised to hear that his powers had developed so quickly. The somewhat arrogant but devout Barthilas had been assigned as Tirion's Second—his successor as Lord Paladin over Hearthglen. He had tutored the young Paladin in the ways of their holy Order and instructed him in the protocols of the political arena. Though he was glad the youth had been able to heal him, he had other matters to ponder. *Had the fight with the orc really taken place?*

Karandra kneeled down, close to him. "Barthilas' healing taxed you greatly, and left him exhausted. As you slept, you cried out a number of times in delirium," she said.

He looked at her questioningly. "And?" he asked.

"Well," she began with a look of concern crossing her face, "you were rambling on about orcs, Tirion. You said that there were orcs in Hearthglen."

He laid back in the chair wearily. The memories of the furious encounter came rushing back at him. The fight *had* been real. He looked into her crystal blue eyes and nodded grimly.

"It *was* an orc," he told her. Karandra sat back on her feet, mouth agape.

"Light save us," she muttered. Just then the door slammed open and five-year-old Taelan came bounding into the room.

"Poppa! Poppa!" the boy shouted, running over to his parents. Karandra straightened and stood up as Taelan leaped up into Tirion's lap. Tirion grunted as the small boy threw himself against his sore chest.

"Taelan, my boy, how are you?" he asked, wrapping his son up in a hearty hug. Taelan beamed a coy smile up at him and shrugged his shoulders. "Have you been good for your mother?" Taelan nodded excitedly.

"He's mindful often enough," Arden's strong voice boomed from the doorway. "But he's just as rambunctious as his father ever was." Karandra smiled warmly at the loyal guardsman as he entered the room. "I hope I'm not intruding on anything. I saw Taelan there heading this way like a raging ogre and thought to catch him before he woke you, Tirion. It seems I shouldn't have worried." With a grunt, Tirion rose with Taelan in his arms and walked forward to greet his old friend. The two shook hands heartily.

"Karandra tells me that I should thank you for hauling me back to the keep. Honestly, Arden, if I had a gold mark for every time you've fished me out of trouble . . ."

"Nonsense. I just led your horse back. If you thank anyone, it should be Barthilas. He just about burnt himself out trying to heal you. You'd taken a pretty good beating, old friend. In any case, I'm glad to see you back amongst the living. You had us concerned there for a while."

"I know," Tirion said. "There are some things we should discuss, immediately." Arden nodded, casting a sidelong look at Taelan and Karandra. Catching the captain's subtle hint, Karandra took Taelan from Tirion's arms and said, "I'll leave you both to it, then. You've got plans to make. And this little one needs to go down for his nap." She kissed the boy on the cheek. Taelan, whining with displeasure, struggled to break free of her firm grasp. Karandra laughed softly to herself.

"Just like his father," she said with a giggle. Both Tirion and Arden smiled as she left.

"I'll see you later, son," Tirion said, watching them leave. Once they were out of earshot, he turned to face Arden, his face a mask of concern.

"It was an orc, Arden. More than likely, it's still alive. As far as I could tell, it was alone out there. And, until we know otherwise, I want to keep this between us and whoever else was on hand when you brought me in. I don't want to panic the entire province in case this was just a solitary incident."

Arden's strong jaw tightened noticeably. "There may be a problem on that front already, milord. Barthilas and I were both on hand while you slept. We both heard you mutter about the orc," he said. Tirion grimaced as Arden continued. "You know Barthilas as well as I do. Once he heard you say 'orc,' he flew into a rage and started calling for a full regiment to scour the countryside in search of any more of the brutes. I nearly had to sit on him to calm him down."

"I appreciate the lad's enthusiasm, but his fervor could be problematic," Tirion stated wryly.

"That would be an understatement," Arden added, smiling. Both men had recognized early on Barthilas' almost zealous obsession to face orcs in battle. Barthilas' parents had been murdered by orcs during the war, which had left the traumatized youth orphaned and inconsolable. Deciding to spend the rest of his life combating the orcs' evil, Barthilas underwent years of rigorous training and study. Yet, tragically, the fiery youth was accepted as a Paladin only after the war had ended. Despite all his training and preparation, Barthilas was tortured by the fact that he wouldn't have the chance to avenge his slaughtered parents. He also felt that he could win the respect of his superiors only by bloodying his hands gloriously in battle, as they had during the war. He dreamed of becoming a mighty hero and taking vengeance upon the creatures that had taken his family from him.

Although he empathized with the younger Paladin, Tirion knew that that kind of thinking could lead to disaster. "I doubt he's been tight-mouthed about my encounter. Especially after he healed my wounds. How many know about this, Arden?" Tirion asked anxiously.

"Rumors have been flying all around the keep for the past few days. Personally, I've heard just about everything from an orc raiding party to a full-fledged invasion force waiting to descend upon us. You know how it is. People are terrified that the Horde will return. And Barthilas, specifically, is terrified that he won't get to defeat it singlehandedly if it ever does," Arden replied. Tirion patted him reassuringly on the shoulder.

"Let's just hope it doesn't come to that," Tirion said in earnest. "Assemble my advisors. We'll discuss this further in council." Arden saluted crisply and turned to leave. Tirion cleared his throat. "Arden," he said softly. "One last thing . . ." Arden stopped in his tracks and stiffened. "You saw the shape I was in when you found me?"

"Yes," Arden replied.

"There's no way I could have tied myself to Mirador and found my way home in that condition."

"No, milord. There's no way."

"And you saw no one else out there? No one who could have helped me and led the horse back here?"

"No, milord. There was no one about. I even went back later to search for tracks. I found nothing. Someone definitely tied you to your horse. And, for the life of me, I can't figure out who," Arden finished. Tirion nodded and motioned for him to go. Left alone, Tirion pondered on who his anonymous savior could have been. As far as he knew, the only two people in the woods that morning were himself and the mysterious old orc. Briefly, Tirion wondered if it was the orc that had saved him. His past experience with the creatures prompted him to disregard the notion. The bestial creatures had no notion of honor. From all he had seen of them, he was certain that they would never go out of their way to show compassion toward another creature, least of all a hated enemy. Still, despite his convictions, Tirion's instincts told him that it had been the orc after all.

Candles fluttered in the medium-size council room. At the room's center sat a large oak table, covered by an immense map that displayed the lands of Hearthglen down to the most minute detail. Six men were seated around the table, conversing amongst themselves. At the head of the table sat Tirion, who stared quietly at the section of map that indicated the woodlands surrounding the ruined tower. Lost in thought, Tirion was disinterested in his advisors' idle conversation. He couldn't tear his mind from the nagging question—who had saved him and led his horse home? He remembered clearly that the orc had saluted him when he allowed the creature a reprieve during their combat. Perhaps the brute had some semblance of honor after all, Tirion mused. No, it had to be a mistake. Orcs were vile and savage. Their kind knew nothing of civility or compassion, he reminded himself. But still, his heart told him that it was the orc who had saved him.

His thoughts were interrupted as the door swung open to admit a tall, slender young man. Resplendent in his silver plate armor, with a deep green cloak flowing behind him, Barthilas looked every bit the crusading Paladin. Though he was nearly thirty years younger than Tirion, Barthilas held his oath as a Knight of the Silver Hand as sacred as the elder Paladin did. As always, Barthilas moved with a fluid grace, barely even acknowledging the presence of the other men in the room. Brash and somewhat pompous, Barthilas rarely went out of his way to acknowledge anyone who was not a Light-blessed Paladin.

Tirion stood and saluted the younger man as he entered.

"Greetings, Barthilas. I thank you for your healing. If not for you, I'd have gone on my way to join the Light," Tirion said, rubbing his still sore ribs. Although his wounds had healed completely, his body was still tender. Barthilas shook his head dismissively and returned Tirion's salute.

"It was nothing, milord. I did just as you would have done for me if the circumstances had been reversed," Barthilas said confidently. "I dearly wish that it had been me facing that orc. If I had, its head would now adorn the keep's battlements." Tirion noticed a few of the advisors exchanging surprised glances. As was usually the case, the young Paladin's enthusiasm bordered on impertinence. Tirion smiled at the young man with practiced patience. "Which, of course," Barthilas continued, "is not to say that you couldn't have defeated the brute yourself, milord."

"Well, I'm sure you would have put the fear of the Alliance into it, at least, Barthilas. Just the same, for the time being, I don't want any of you discussing this matter with anyone else. I'd rather not rile the citizenry until we have a better understanding of what we're dealing with here," Tirion said.

Barthilas nearly choked. "Milord, with respect, are you suggesting that we keep silent while the enemy creeps unhindered through our lands? We must scour the woods immediately! Every second we waste here could provide the orcs with enough time to—" Tirion cut him off.

"You are assuming that there are more orcs out there, Barthilas. I was there, and I saw none. I will not sound the call to arms before we've confirmed the facts. This is not the time to start jumping at shadows. We must remain calm and be vigilant."

"Jumping at shadows? An orcish force somehow slips undetected into our lands, one of its members beats you to a pulp, and you want to remain calm? This is madness!" A few of the advisors gasped at the young man's audacity, but Barthilas continued, unabated. "We should mobilize a hunting party right this instant!"

Tirion clenched his fists and tried to keep his voice even. The advisors, who had kept silent during their heated exchange, seemed incensed by Barthilas' disrespectful rantings.

"You'll watch your tone with me, boy. I am still governor of this province, and your direct superior as a Paladin. For so long as I am, we will do things the way I see fit. You are to stand down and remain within the keep's grounds until I order you to do otherwise. Is that clear?" Tirion growled.

Barthilas was beside himself with rage. "I hope and pray to the Light that milord isn't so shaken by his recent beating that he fears to do his clear duty."

"That will be *enough*, Barthilas! You've gone too far!" one of the councilors shouted. Bristling with anger, Tirion stepped up to the young Paladin and looked him dead in the eye.

"You may leave my council room now," he said to Barthilas.

The young Paladin choked back his rage and steadied himself. He calmed visibly. "Of course, milord," he said in a strained voice. "I will await your orders eagerly." With that he snapped a crisp salute and left the room.

"Yes, I'm sure you will," Tirion said grimly. Everyone seemed to sigh as the tension drained from the room. Tirion rubbed his eyes wearily and sat back down.

One of the advisors spoke. "Milord, he is brash, but he is a good man at heart. I'm sure he didn't mean—"

"I know what he is. And I know what he meant. Barthilas has always been ruled by his passions. They're what make him an exceptional Paladin. However, they also make him a liability in delicate situations," Tirion stated. He felt tired, like an old man. "Once he calms down, he'll come around. He always does."

"But milord, what if he's right? What if there are more orcs out there waiting to strike at us, and we sit here and do nothing?" the advisor asked.

Tirion ran his fingers over the spot on the map that indicated the broken tower. "Under no circumstances will I do *nothing*, old friend. I'll take care of this matter myself." Before they had a chance to argue the point further, he rose and walked toward the exit, leaving the advisors to stare at one another in confusion. "But on the off chance that he is right . . . may the Light help us all."

Later that evening, Tirion sat alone in the keep's spacious dining hall. His plate of food had gone cold, and he picked at it absently with his fork. He was thinking about the old orc again. Was it truly possible that the orc had saved his life? He would have to find out soon. If Barthilas was right, then everything he'd worked for could come crashing down at any moment.

Behind him he heard a quiet scuffling of small feet. Looking around, he saw sleepy-eyed Taelan emerging from the adjoining sitting room.

"Shouldn't you be asleep, young man?" he asked. The boy crawled into his lap and looked up at him in awe. Tirion smiled at his son, thinking how much the boy resembled his mother. Sandy blond hair. Big blue eyes. He was certainly a sweet, innocent child, Tirion thought.

"Did the green men come back again, Poppa?" Taelan asked. Tirion nodded and ruffled the boy's hair.

"Yes. But you don't need to worry, son. You'll be safe enough here in the keep."

"Are you going to fight the green men, Poppa?" the boy asked. Tirion's brow creased.

"I don't know yet, son. I just don't know."

THREE
A Warrior's Tale

Tirion woke early the next morning. Slipping out of bed so as not to wake Karandra, he dressed and made his way down to his personal ready room. There, displayed upon an ornate stand near the darkened room's center, was his armor. The heavy silver plates with their gold lining shone brightly in the early morning light, despite the numerous gouges and dents that covered them. *Scars of battle*, he thought warily. Any one of the deep gouges could have signified a fatal wound, had he been a less cautious man over the years. He hoped silently that his luck would hold out with whatever troubles were coming.

As quietly as he could, he slipped the armor plates on one at a time and buckled them into place. Once finished, he stood in front of a full-length mirror and looked himself over. He looked much the same as he always had, despite a few more gray hairs framing his tired face. He marveled at how well the heavy suit still fit after all these years. He had to admit to feeling a certain indestructibility every time he wore the armor. Yet that was a young man's notion. No one was invincible. *No one lived forever,* he thought grimly.

Walking over to the stone fireplace set into the far wall, Tirion reached out for his trusty warhammer, which rested on the oak mantel above. The expertly weighted hammer felt good in his hands. The holy runes etched in its head shone as brightly as they ever had.

"With any luck, I won't need your strength today, old friend," he muttered. He tucked the hammer under his arm and strode down toward the keep's stables.

The sun was just breaking over the distant Alterac peaks as Tirion finished saddling Mirador. He slung the hammer into its saddle-hoop and made ready to mount the seasoned warhorse. He put his foot in the stirrup and grunted in pain. His ribs still ached, and the heavy armor made it difficult for him to pull his own weight up.

"May I ask what you're doing?" a suspicious voice asked from the stable's dark entryway. Tirion took his foot from the stirrup and turned to face Arden. The captain of the guard's face was stern and etched with concern.

"I am going to investigate the tower's ruins. If the orcs are planning an invasion of my land, then I'll find proof of it myself," Tirion said flatly.

Arden nodded. "Great. Then I'll saddle up and go with you."

"I do not wish to have company. This is something I must do alone, Arden," Tirion said. There was iron in his voice, and the captain's concern grew more apparent.

"I don't like this, Tirion. What exactly are you trying to prove? Heading off unescorted so soon after your—"

Tirion cut him off. "My what, Arden? My defeat?" Tirion asked heatedly. Arden lowered his gaze and shifted uncomfortably. Tirion mounted the horse, exhaled deeply, and curtly said, "I'll be back in a few hours. Try to keep an eye on Barthilas while I'm gone. I have a feeling he'll try to stir up trouble." He dug his spurs into Mirador's sides and sped out toward the distant tree line.

With growing unease, Arden watched his lord gallop away into the distance. Somehow he knew that Tirion wasn't telling him everything.

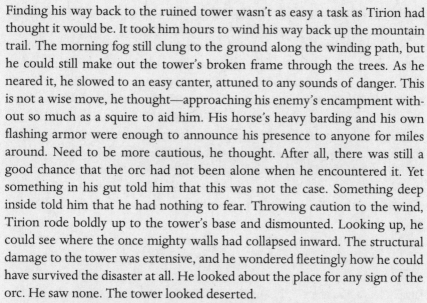

Finding his way back to the ruined tower wasn't as easy a task as Tirion had thought it would be. It took him hours to wind his way back up the mountain trail. The morning fog still clung to the ground along the winding path, but he could still make out the tower's broken frame through the trees. As he neared it, he slowed to an easy canter, attuned to any sounds of danger. This is not a wise move, he thought—approaching his enemy's encampment without so much as a squire to aid him. His horse's heavy barding and his own flashing armor were enough to announce his presence to anyone for miles around. Need to be more cautious, he thought. After all, there was still a good chance that the orc had not been alone when he encountered it. Yet something in his gut told him that this was not the case. Something deep inside told him that he had nothing to fear. Throwing caution to the wind, Tirion rode boldly up to the tower's base and dismounted. Looking up, he could see where the once mighty walls had collapsed inward. The structural damage to the tower was extensive, and he wondered fleetingly how he could have survived the disaster at all. He looked about the place for any sign of the orc. He saw none. The tower looked deserted.

A low, guttural grunt caught his attention and he turned to see the orc sitting on a large rock near the tree line. The creature seemed calm and poised, but its great battle-ax leaned nearby within easy reach. *So the creature, too, was cautious,* Tirion thought to himself. The proud Paladin removed his helmet and set it on the pommel of Mirador's saddle. The great horse snorted loudly, sensing its master's tension. From the corner of his eye, Tirion caught sight of the warhammer strapped to the saddle and reached for its handle. Immediately, the orc grabbed for his ax. Tirion quickly pulled his hand away and took a step back from the horse. The orc grunted softly and relaxed. It grinned at him knowingly. Tirion took a deep breath and then walked slowly toward the orc.

As he walked forward, he realized that he could have been sorely mistaken about the old orc. Perhaps the creature did intend to kill him after all. Maybe someone else had miraculously saved him from the tower's wreckage. Maybe. But he had to know for sure, one way or another. Stopping only a few paces from where the orc sat, Tirion raised his fist to his heart in salute. *That had been the orc's salute, right?* In return, the orc raised a stiff hand to his own grizzled brow.

"That is how you humans do it, is it not?" the orc asked in fluid speech. Its voice was deep and gritty, but its articulation was exceptional. Tirion was dumbfounded, his shock evident on his face. The orc's hideous features contorted in what Tirion surmised was a grin.

"You . . . you speak our language?" Tirion asked shakily.

The old orc eyed him sternly. "Do you think my people survived in your world this long using brute strength alone?" it asked. "Your kind has always underestimated mine. That is why you lost the first war, I think."

Tirion could only marvel at the creature. Here sat a thing of darkness—a vile, murdering beast. And yet, it spoke with fluidity and wit. This creature did not rush to tear out his heart, as he would have expected. It merely sat, reading him with its clever, knowing eyes. Tirion shuddered, feeling fascinated and repulsed at the same time. Without thinking, he blurted out the question he had been asking himself ceaselessly: "I must know. Did you pull me from the tower and lead my horse back to the road?"

The old orc held him in his gaze for a long while and then nodded once. "I did," it said.

Tirion exhaled sharply. "Why would you do that?" he asked. "We are sworn enemies."

The orc seemed to consider the point for a moment. "You have great honor, for a human. That much was clear from our fight. No honorable warrior deserves to die like a trapped animal. It would not have been right to simply leave you there," the orc finished. Tirion didn't know exactly what he had expected to hear, but he was clearly unprepared for that answer. "Besides," the orc continued, "I have seen enough death in my time."

Tirion bowed his head, struggling to make sense of the orc's words. *This can't be right*, he thought. This creature is a merciless savage. How could it speak so? Yet Tirion knew that the orc's words rang true. He could feel the orc's sincerity—and beneath it, deeply buried pain and sorrow. As a Paladin, he had developed a certain empathic ability to sense deep emotions from others. The curious ability had never proven to be more useful. He pulled himself together and simply went with the moment.

"I should thank you, then," Tirion began, wondering how to properly address the creature.

Sensing Tirion's confusion, the orc spoke. "I am Eitrigg, human. You may call me Eitrigg." Relieved, Tirion replied, "Thank you, Eitrigg. Thank you for saving my life."

The orc nodded again and stood up. Tirion noticed that the orc walked with a distinct limp. He surmised that the cut he had given the creature during their battle was likely infected. Without giving Tirion a second glance, the orc limped over toward the ruined tower.

"I am Tirion Fordring," the Paladin began. "I should tell you that I am the lord of this land, Eitrigg, and that your presence here upsets many of those whom I entrust with its protection."

The orc laughed softly. "I wager they slept well enough before you found me," the orc said. "I have lived here in these woods for many long years, human. I move from place to place, keeping hidden, finding shelter where I can. I have made great sport of evading your scouts and your *Rangers.*"

The latter was spoken with distinct scorn. Orcs were not known for their fondness of elven Rangers. The cunning, forest-running Rangers had sworn to gain vengeance against the Horde after the orcs had destroyed the elves' enchanted homeland of Quel'Thalas. Tirion wondered if Eitrigg was telling the truth. *Could this orc have remained undetected for so long?*

Eitrigg snorted and said, "It was bad luck that led you to me."

"Perhaps," Tirion began, "but your being here creates a serious problem for me. My people hate your kind, Eitrigg. Your race brought nothing but misery and chaos to these lands. They would kill you in a heartbeat if they could. How, then, can I be merciful? How can I let you stay, knowing what your people have done?"

"I have abandoned them, human! I live here in solitude—in exile," Eitrigg said warily. "I no longer wish to pay for their sins."

"I don't understand," the Paladin replied. "Are you saying that you've disavowed your own people?"

"My people are lost!" the orc spat. "Truth be told, they were lost long before they ever came to this strange world. When the Horde finally fell before your standards, I decided to take my leave of it forever."

Eitrigg reached down and rolled a large chunk of mortar onto its side. Tirion was impressed with the orc's strength. It would have taken at least two stout men to move the stone. The orc motioned for Tirion to sit and then sat himself down cross-legged on the ground. Tirion took a seat on the leveled mortar.

"There is much you do not know about my people. Their honor and their pride left them long ago. I decided my duty to them was finished when my sons were killed," Eitrigg said grimly.

"Were your sons warriors?" Tirion asked. Eitrigg scoffed loudly.

"All orcs are warriors, human," he said, as if Tirion were a brainless child. "We know little else. Despite my sons' strength and prowess, they were betrayed by their own leaders. During the last war our clan Chieftains fought amongst themselves over petty rivalries. As one particularly bloody battle concluded, my sons were ordered to pull back from the front lines. One of our Chieftain's rivals, hoping to advance his clan's standing within the Horde, countermanded the order and sent my sons and their brethren back to be slaughtered. It was a dark day for our clan. . . ." Eitrigg said, lost in thought. "A dark day for me," he finished.

Tirion's mind reeled. He was well aware of the fact that orcs frequently fought amongst themselves. Yet Eitrigg's apparent grief moved him. He never imagined that such treachery could affect an orc so.

"I realized then that there was no hope. Corruption and enmity had completely overshadowed my people's spirit. I felt that it was only a matter of time before the Horde devoured itself from within," Eitrigg said.

"Where did the corruption come from, Eitrigg? What drove your people to such depravity?" Tirion asked.

Eitrigg's brow raised and he appeared to be deep in thought. "In my grandfather's time, my people were simple and proud. There were a few dozen clans then. They lived and hunted within the wilds of our world. They were all hunters back then—mighty warriors who lived by an honorable code and worshiped the spirits of the elements themselves. Thunder and lightning coursed through the blood of my ancestors!" Eitrigg said proudly, lost in the haze of reverie. "Wise Shamans guided them and kept the peace between the clans."

Tirion leaned in, hanging on the old orc's words. Surely, no human ears had ever heard this much of the orcs' history before. "And then?" Tirion asked anxiously. He wondered if this was how Taelan felt, as he read the boy stories before his bedtime. Eitrigg continued somberly.

"A new order rose up amongst the clans, promising to unite them and forge them into a powerful nation. Many of the Shamans discarded their ancient traditions and began to practice dark magics. They began to call themselves Warlocks. For some malign purpose, they used their shadowy powers to corrupt the clans and drive them to heinous acts of violence. They did succeed in uniting my people, after a fashion," Eitrigg stated wryly. "Under the Warlocks' rule, the clans *were* united—as a rampaging Horde. Our noble warrior traditions were perverted to serve their dark, secretive ends. It was the Warlocks who brought my people to your world, human. It was they who drove us to make war against you."

Tirion shook his head in bewilderment. "And no one spoke out against them? Out of an entire race of warriors, no one was willing to fight them?" Tirion asked heatedly.

"There were a few who would not submit. One of the dissident clans, led by an orc named Durotan, challenged the Warlocks openly and tried to convince the other clans of their folly. I remember the mighty Durotan well. He was a great hero. Unfortunately, few orcs heeded Durotan's warnings. The Warlocks' hold over their hearts blinded them to reason. For his courage, Durotan was exiled, along with his clan. I heard that the Warlocks' assassins finally killed him, years later. Such is the way of the Horde," Eitrigg finished.

"Madness," Tirion said. "If your people truly valued honor, as you've said, then I can't believe that they'd let themselves be controlled so easily."

Eitrigg scowled and sat silently for a moment. He looked up with stern eyes and replied, "It was a terrible momentum that gripped us in those days, human. After Durotan was taken away, fear and paranoia overtook my people. None would stand against the Warlocks."

Tirion scoffed derisively.

Bristling with anger, Eitrigg erupted. "Have you ever stood against the will of an entire nation, human? Have you ever questioned an order, knowing that to disobey meant immediate death?"

Tirion looked away. *No.* He could scarcely imagine what that must have been like.

Eitrigg nodded, feeling his point had been made. "It was rumored that the Warlocks consorted with demons and drew on their infernal powers. Personally, I believe it to be true. The darkness that took hold of my people could not have been born in our hearts."

Tirion tensed. He remembered hearing that the orcs had set demons loose to sow terror throughout the human ranks. The very thought appalled him. "It seems your people have suffered greatly, Eitrigg, even before they roused the wrath of mine," Tirion said with a note of pride in his voice. Eitrigg gave him a sidelong glance. "However, your story is a remarkable one. I fear I may have misjudged you and your people along many lines."

Eitrigg grunted as if amused and stood up to stretch his back. "Actually," Tirion continued, "we are much alike, you and I. We are both old soldiers who have sacrificed much for our—"

Eitrigg cut him off with a wave of his sinewy hand. "We are nothing alike, human," he growled. "I am a renegade living as an exile in a hostile land! You are a wealthy lord, loved by a free people, able to live life as you wish. We are *nothing* alike!" Embarrassed by his outburst, the old orc scowled and looked away into the distance.

Tirion considered the orc's harsh words for a moment. "You are right, of course. Our people are at war. Thus, I must ask you, Eitrigg, on your honor— are there any other orcs in my land? Does the Horde plan to attack this region?"

Eitrigg sighed heavily and sat back down. He shook his head in dismay and looked Tirion in the eye. "As I have told you, human, I live here alone. I have no interest in dealing with others of my kind. I haven't even seen another orc in years. I cannot tell you what the Horde plans now. I can only assure you that this broken old warrior has no plans to assault your keep or make any trouble for you whatsoever. I just want to be left alone to live out my remaining years in solitude. After a lifetime of fruitless war, peace is the only comfort I have left."

Tirion nodded. "As a warrior of honor, I accept your words, Eitrigg. And, in return for having saved my life, I will allow you your solitude. So long as you remain hidden and leave my people unmolested, you may stay here for as long as you wish."

Eitrigg smirked slightly in disbelief. "I think perhaps your brethren will hunt me down despite you, human. To them, I am the sum of their fears," the old orc said.

"Yet I am their lord, Eitrigg. They shall do as I say. I give you my solemn oath as a Light-sworn Paladin that your secret will be safe. None shall hunt you while I have power to prevent it," Tirion vowed. For a brief moment, Tirion regretted making such a bold statement. He knew it would be extremely difficult to fulfill his charge if matters became complicated. If his comrades ever found out that he had made such a pact, they would certainly brand him as a traitor. However, his instincts told him that this was the right decision. He stood, resolved.

Eitrigg grunted in satisfaction. "On your honor, then," he said, rising to his feet once more. Tirion noticed the orc's limp again. Eitrigg was obviously in great pain.

"On my honor," Tirion replied, gazing at the orc's wounded leg. "You know, Eitrigg, I can heal your wound. It is a power I have," he said.

The orc chuckled in amusement. "Thank you, but it's not necessary," Eitrigg stated. "Pain is a great teacher. Apparently, even after all my battles, I still have much to learn."

Tirion laughed out loud. He was truly beginning to like the old orc who, not an hour before, he considered to be the most heinous villain. "Perhaps someday I can return and converse with you further. I must admit you are not at all what I expected to find," the Paladin chided.

Eitrigg's massive, yellowed tusks seemed to stretch as he smiled. "Nor are you what I expected, human."

Tirion gave the orc's salute again and mounted Mirador with a grunt. He dug his spurs into the stallion's flank and rode off beyond the orc's sight.

A thousand different thoughts flooded Tirion's mind as he rode home along the winding path. He wondered if he had made a mistake by offering the orc sanctuary in his lands. Nevertheless, he had given his word that he would keep the orc's secret safe. Whatever else happened, he was honor-bound to protect the old orc from persecution, and that was that.

It was nearly dusk as he rode back into the keep's stables. Tiredly, Tirion handed his reins to the stable boy and headed inside. All he wanted was to sleep and clear the day's business from his mind. As he reached for the door handle that led into the kitchens, a strong hand caught his arm. Tirion looked up to find Barthilas blocking his way. There was a light in the youth's eyes that made Tirion very uneasy.

"Milord," Barthilas began icily, "we must talk immediately."

Tirion sighed in frustration. "I'm very tired, Barthilas. We can talk in the morning if you wish."

Barthilas' grip only tightened. "I don't think you understand, milord. You see, I know where you were today," the young Paladin stated. His eyes never blinked, but held Tirion in their frosty depths. Tirion wondered if Arden had betrayed him and told of his errand. No. Arden had always been loyal.

"I know that you know there are orcs in Hearthglen, Tirion. I can see it in your eyes. I pray, for your sake, that you're not covering up any pertinent information."

Tirion bristled. He could handle the youth's arrogance, but he would not be threatened in his own home by an overly zealous boy.

"I told you before, Barthilas. You will address me with the proper respect," Tirion stated furiously. "As for your concerns, I have determined that my encounter was an isolated incident. That's all you need to know for the time being. I suggest that you forget about this business and let the matter drop. Now take your hand away and let me pass before I lose my temper."

Slowly, Barthilas released his grip and took a step back. His piercing eyes never left Tirion's. The elder Paladin turned brusquely and entered the keep.

Left standing alone, Barthilas scowled in frustration. "This is not over, milord," the young Paladin hissed to himself, clenching his fists. "This is not over by far."

Tirion made his way to his private chambers. He ceremoniously removed his armor and placed his warhammer back upon the mantel. He entered his bedroom and crashed down heavily on the bed. All he wanted in the world was just a few hours of sleep. Just as his head hit the plush pillow, Karandra walked into the room. She was surprised to find him there.

"Oh, you're home," she said sweetly. "Where did you go running off to this morning, Tirion? I asked Arden, but he wouldn't tell me anything." Her voice was full of concern.

Tirion tensed. He didn't want to discuss the matter about the orc at all. He had given his word to keep Eitrigg's secret safe, and the last thing he wanted was to be forced to lie to his wife about his activities. But, looking into her eyes, Tirion could tell she wasn't going to settle for anything less than the whole story.

"I went out to inspect the site where I fought the orc, Karandra. I needed to find out if there were more orcs in my lands," he said, a tad too irritably. "I wanted to go alone, so I told Arden not to speak about it with anyone."

Karandra frowned and folded her arms under her breasts. She did that every time she was upset with him.

"You went off alone only days after your attack? How can you be so reckless, Tirion? What were you trying to prove? It's not like you're a young man anymore!" she said heatedly.

Tirion flinched. First Barthilas and now his wife. "I've been soldiering for more years than you've been alive, girl! The last thing I need from you is a lecture on how to perform my duties properly!" he growled.

Tirion rarely spoke to her like that, and Karandra never really knew how to respond when he did. She decided that a tactical change of subject was needed in order to salvage the conversation.

"Did you find what you were looking for?" she asked, trying to make her voice sound as innocent as possible.

Tirion forced himself to calm down, but knew that this new line of questioning wouldn't fare well for her either. "Yes, I did," he said in an even tone. "I am convinced that my encounter was an isolated event, and that we have nothing to fear from the orcs."

Karandra brightened and sat down beside him on the bed. She took his hand in hers. "I'm so relieved. That's wonderful, Tirion, but how can you be so sure?" she asked.

Tirion's heart sank. He would not lie to her. "I can't tell you, my love," he said softly.

"Why not? If there is nothing to fear, as you say, then there shouldn't be any problem with telling me, should there?" she asked. Something in her voice sounded hurt.

"It is a matter of honor, Karandra. I cannot tell you," he repeated.

With a start, Karandra ripped her hand away and stood up from the bed. Tirion half expected lightning bolts to burst forth from her eyes.

"Honor. It always comes down to that with you, Tirion! You're just as exasperating as that vainglorious Barthilas! Is your precious honor really more important to you than your own wife?" She cupped her face with her hands and seemed to be on the verge of tears. Tirion looked up at her and answered as gently as he could.

"You wouldn't understand, my love. I am a Paladin. There is a great deal expected of me. . . ." he said, his voice trailing off. There was an uncharacteristic note of self-pity in his tone.

Karandra took her hands from her face and had to restrain herself from hitting him.

"You're right, I don't understand! But I know exactly what's expected of you," she yelled as tears started flowing down her reddening cheeks. "You're expected to act like my husband and not try to shelter me from your silly little secrets like I'm still a girl in pigtails! You're expected to act like a responsible lord and not go gallivanting off alone and putting yourself in danger!" Tirion looked away as she began to sob. "You're supposed to be careful and stay alive so that our son doesn't grow up without a father," she finished.

Tirion stood up and took her in his arms. "I know, dearest. I did take an unnecessary risk. But you've got to trust me on this, Karandra. Everything will be all right," he told her soothingly.

She wiped the tears from her eyes and looked at her husband's face. She would try to trust his judgment. She was about to tell him as much when a quiet shuffling of feet announced that Taelan had entered the room. Tirion and Karandra looked toward the door to see their bleary-eyed son standing before them. Apparently, their arguing had woken the boy up.

"Are you two fighting?" the boy asked timidly, his big blue eyes glistening with concern.

Tirion walked over and scooped the boy up in his arms. "No, son, your mother's just worried about the orcs, is all," he said soothingly.

Taelan seemed to think for a moment. "Poppa, are the orcs as mean and cruel as everyone says they are?" the boy asked.

Tirion wasn't prepared for such a direct question. He thought about his revealing conversation with Eitrigg, and marveled that he wasn't so sure anymore. He certainly didn't want to lie to his son. *There had to be some hope for future generations.*

"Well, son, that's hard to answer," he said slowly. Focused on Taelan as he was, Tirion didn't see Karandra's incredulous stare. The boy listened intently as his father continued. "I think there are some orcs who can be good. They're just harder to find, is all," Tirion said gently.

Karandra couldn't believe her ears. Her ebbing anger flooded back into her.

"Really, Poppa?" Taelan asked.

"I think so," Tirion replied. "Sometimes we need to be careful of how quickly we judge people, son."

The boy seemed pleased with the answer. Karandra was not. Despite everything else, she would be damned if she let Tirion fill the boy's head with such nonsense.

"Don't tell him that!" she hissed. "Orcs are mindless beasts who should all be hunted down and killed! How can you even say that, knowing what they've done to our world! What's gotten into you, Tirion?" she yelled, snatching Taelan from his arms. Sensing her anger, the boy began to cry. She stroked his hair lovingly as she turned to leave. "Don't worry, baby," she said, "your father's just tired. We'll let him get some rest, all right?" she said as she left the room briskly without even turning to acknowledge Tirion.

Left alone, Tirion wandered over to an ornate serving stand and poured himself a cup of chilled wine. Taking a deep sip, he sat down heavily and marveled at how quickly his entire world had turned upside down.

FOUR
The Chains of Command

Two days passed by quietly in Hearthglen. The rumors of the supposed orcish threat had died down significantly. Tirion felt relaxed, and mused that he might even be able to put the whole matter behind him for good. So long as Eitrigg stayed away from people, Tirion wouldn't have to worry about taking action and betraying his oath to the old orc. He was surprised to find that Barthilas had remained quiet about the issue for the past few days. Yet, despite the young Paladin's silence, Tirion sensed that Barthilas wouldn't rest so long as he suspected there were orcs in Hearthglen.

After his unexpected hiatus, Tirion slipped back into his role as the lands' governor with relative ease. The somewhat monotonous bureaucratic duties of his office served to keep his mind off of Eitrigg and their fateful encounter. He spent what private time he could find with Taelan and Karandra. Surprisingly, his wife seemed to have forgotten about their argument from the previous night. She acted as cheerful as she always had, and never once broached the subject of orcs again. Tirion was thankful for the peace and quiet. After the past week, he had had his fill of excitement and danger.

The sun was centered in the crystal blue sky as Tirion sat on a large balcony overlooking the keep's stables and riding corral. Located at the rear of the keep's grounds, the balcony offered a breathtaking view of the mighty snow-capped Alterac peaks in the distance. He watched as, far below him in the corral, Karandra led a small, white pony around in circles. Upon the pony's back sat Taelan, who was clearly having the time of his life. The laughing boy flailed his tiny arms gleefully, calling for his mother to go faster and faster. Karandra laughed with her son, and kept reminding him to hold on to the pony's mane with both hands.

Tirion gazed at them both intently. They were the center of his world and the source of all his joy. He would not fail them. He had thought long and hard about what Karandra had said to him during their heated argument. Perhaps his honor was a selfish thing after all, he mused. But even if it was, it was an integral part of him. It defined him as clearly as his own face did. As a Paladin he could not and would not discard it out of hand. All depended on it. He simply hoped that it would never come between him and his loved ones again.

Arden's heavy boots clanked loudly upon the balcony's stone floor. The captain of the guard strode up behind Tirion and bowed curtly. Tirion noticed that Arden was winded. Apparently, the loyal captain had rushed to find him. Tirion stood up and saluted the younger man. He saw that Arden's face was drawn and pale.

"What is it, Arden? Why are you in such a hurry?"

The captain struggled to catch his breath. "I've been looking all over for you, milord," Arden said in a raspy tone. "We have visitors at the gate." Tirion tensed. For a brief moment, he feared the worst. Certainly, visitors to the keep were common enough. The only thing Tirion imagined that would affect Arden so was an army of orcs scaling the walls.

"What visitors? Is there some problem?" the Paladin asked tightly.

Arden shook his head and gulped air. "An envoy from Stratholme, milord. Lord Commander Dathrohan has come in person, escorted by a full regiment. He wishes to speak to you immediately."

Tirion's jaw dropped. *Lord Dathrohan, here?* he wondered. The Lord Commander was not only his direct superior, but one of his oldest friends as well. Dathrohan was a great leader and an honorable warrior. He and Tirion had saved each other's lives more than once during the war. Due to their increasing duties, the two friends hadn't seen each other in years. But why would the great lord venture all the way from the province's capital for an unannounced visit escorted by so large a force? A burst of panic surged through Tirion's body. *Dathrohan knew about the orc.* It was the only explanation for his visit, Tirion concluded. He knew that it must have been Barthilas who had alerted the Lord Commander to his recent encounter with Eitrigg. Tirion inhaled deeply and steadied himself. He patted Arden reassuringly on the shoulder and, with a sidelong glance at his wife and son below, strode out toward the main gate.

Lord Commander Saidan Dathrohan was an imposing figure. He stood nearly six and a half feet tall and was resplendent in his ornate, shining armor. A gold-rimmed, midnight-blue cloak covered his broad shoulders and flowed out regally behind him. His aged features were marked by long years of battle and strife. His evenly cropped hair and neatly trimmed beard were gray, but his piercing blue eyes shone with a vigor and strength that belied his years.

Upon seeing Tirion approach, Dathrohan's stern countenance broke and he smiled widely. He strode forward and embraced his friend in a bear hug. Tirion felt the air escape from his lungs. The mighty Dathrohan nearly lifted him from the floor. Dathrohan let out a deep, barrel-chested laugh.

"Tirion, my friend, it's good to see you. How long has it been, four years?" Dathrohan asked. He released Tirion and the Paladin straightened formally.

"Almost four years exactly, milord," Tirion replied.

Dathrohan smirked and slapped his back, nearly sending Tirion stumbling. "Let's not start with all that 'my lord' rubbish! You're one of the few men alive who still remembers me as a snot-nosed whelp. We're on even ground here, you and I," Dathrohan said humorously. Tirion forced himself to relax and smiled back.

"Have it your way then, *Saidan*." He slapped his hand on the taller man's shoulder plate. "It's good to see you, too," he said warmly. Though Dathrohan's demeanor was as familiar and raucous as it had ever been, there was a light of concern in his sharp eyes. Tirion looked past his friend and saw row upon row of armored footmen standing on the plain beyond the keep's walls. His heart sank. Although he was glad to see his friend, Tirion knew that the presence of so many soldiers meant trouble.

"Tell me, Saidan, why didn't you inform me of your journey? I could have prepared a great feast, had I known you were coming," Tirion said, trying to keep his voice open and friendly.

Dathrohan nodded and spread his hands wide. "I apologize for the intrusion, Tirion, but we have urgent business to conduct. I felt I had to come and see you as soon as possible. But let's leave our business until later. You need time to gather your advisors for a meeting," he said in a more somber tone.

"Is there trouble, Saidan? Are we going to war?" Tirion asked, not knowing what else to say. Dathrohan held him in his piercing gaze, studying his features.

"That's what I'm here to find out, Tirion," he said at last. *He* does *know about Eitrigg,* Tirion concluded. "For now, I'm anxious to meet your lovely bride and your son," Dathrohan said warmly. "I regret that I couldn't visit and see the lad when he was born. You know how it is."

Tirion nodded. "He's a good boy. A future Paladin," he said assuredly. He felt beads of sweat forming on his brow. He tried to calm himself and behave naturally. He felt as if Dathrohan were looking right through him. He nearly jumped as Dathrohan belted out a hearty laugh.

"Of that I have little doubt. I suspect that the Fordring line will always be there to defend Lordaeron and its people," Dathrohan said, smiling.

Tirion smiled back and nodded while saying, "I certainly hope so."

Hours later, Tirion's advisors had gathered in the council room. A few of Dathrohan's senior lieutenants were present as well. Barthilas, who looked very excited by the new arrivals, stood near the back of the room and remained silent. Lord Commander Dathrohan had taken a seat at the head of the table, next to Tirion. There was a tension in the room as all present speculated on the urgent matter that Dathrohan had come to discuss.

"Now, then," Dathrohan began, looking levelly at Tirion. "I received news that there are orcs in Hearthglen. What exactly is the current situation?" he asked.

Tirion swallowed, his throat suddenly dry. "Milord, a few days ago, I had an encounter with an orc warrior," he said. "Though I wounded it badly, I was knocked out before I could slay the creature. I returned to the spot where we battled in order to determine if the creature still lived. And, to discern whether or not there are others of its kind within my borders. My findings led me to believe that it was an isolated incident and that there were no other orcs accompanying it," Tirion finished. He was on dangerous ground. He had no wish to lie to his superior. Honor forbade it.

Dathrohan leaned back in his chair, rubbing his bearded chin and pondering Tirion's response. "And you conducted your investigation alone?" Dathrohan asked.

Tirion nodded. "Yes, milord."

"It is unfortunate that you didn't have others with you to verify your findings, Tirion. Apparently, your retainers don't share your optimistic appraisal of the situation," Dathrohan said grimly. Tirion scowled. He didn't even have to look at the back of the room to sense Barthilas' smug satisfaction.

"Paladin Barthilas sent me news of the affair. He seems to believe that the threat to these lands is far more dire than you do. I have come to find out for myself if this land is in peril," the Lord Commander said sternly.

Tirion then turned to stare at Barthilas' bemused face. He fought down his rage at the youth's audacity. He turned back to Dathrohan. "Saidan, we've been friends for years. Surely you don't doubt my judgment in this matter?

Honestly, young Barthilas' actions are a clear affront to my authority over this land. His zeal is commendable, but to worry you over such a minor matter is perplexing to say the least!"

Dathrohan put his hand on Tirion's arm to calm him.

"Tirion, I have always trusted your judgment. I have never questioned your honor or authority, and I do not intend to start doing so now. Under normal circumstances, I would never intervene in a matter like this, but certain events have transpired that force me to look critically at any possible orcish incursions."

Dathrohan leaned in and searched the eyes of the gathered advisors. "For some time, we have been receiving reports that there is a new, upstart Warchief amongst the orcs. Apparently, this young orc is intent on rallying the clans and re-forming the Horde. Though they are few, his fanatical warriors have somehow overrun many of the guarded reserves and appear to be amassing stronger numbers. The Alliance High Command has deemed that we are in a state of emergency. I tell you all of this so that you understand my motives. If there is any truth behind Barthilas' claims, then it is imperative that we prepare ourselves for war," he said grimly.

The shocked advisors began to converse amongst themselves. Dathrohan turned to face Tirion. "Old friend, with all due respect, I cannot rely on your instincts alone. This situation is far too volatile."

Tirion shook his head in disbelief. He braced himself for what he knew was coming next.

"At first light, we will head out and scour the woodlands for more definitive proof of orcish activity. Tirion, I want you to personally lead us to where you encountered the orc. If the creature be found, we will take it back to Stratholme for interrogation," Dathrohan finished.

Tirion's heart dropped. There was no way out now. He had been given a direct order. He would be forced to break his vow to Eitrigg. "As you wish, milord," Tirion said in a strained voice.

Dathrohan seemed content to let the matter rest. He dismissed the advisors and suggested that everyone prepare their men. Tirion stood to exit and saw Barthilas staring at him from the doorway. The young Paladin's face was alight with victory. Tirion had to fight back the sudden urge to strangle the smirking youth. Without giving Barthilas a second glance, he left the room and made ready for the morning's expedition.

Dawn had already bathed the land with its first rays as the force of knights and footmen made their way into the forested foothills. Tirion, Arden and Dathrohan led the shining column down the dusty hunting path that snaked its way through the dense woods. Barthilas hung back behind them, preferring to converse with the veteran soldiers under Dathrohan's command.

Clearly, the young Paladin was eager to prove himself in battle. Tirion was glad that the youth stayed away. He was disgusted with Barthilas and didn't even want to see his face.

Tirion was in a grim mood. He had slept little during the night, and woke with his guts tied in knots. He wished that he could somehow warn Eitrigg so that the old orc could evade capture. But Tirion knew that, even if he could warn the orc, his actions would betray his superior's direct order. He knew that there was no way to uphold his vow and do his duty at the same time. His precious honor was in great peril.

They rode for hours up into the mountains as Tirion led the way. He knew exactly where he was going. Before long the broken tower's remaining walls could be seen through the trees. Dathrohan leaned in and asked Tirion if it was the tower they sought.

"That is where I first encountered the orc, milord," Tirion said in a quiet voice.

Dathrohan nodded, sensing Tirion's apprehension. "Are you certain, Tirion? You seem rather pensive this morning."

"I am certain, milord," Tirion replied huskily. "I'm fine. I'm just a tad tired, is all."

Dathrohan patted his shoulder reassuringly. The Lord Commander motioned for his men to take up positions along the road. He then called for a number of guards to come to the front of the column. Arden was among those who came forward. The captain smiled up at Tirion, but the Paladin didn't feel like smiling at all. Tirion shuddered as two of the guards pulled a makeshift wagon-cage behind them. The rickety cage was designed to hold and transport a small number of prisoners over long distances. He fervently hoped that it would stay empty.

Dathrohan, feeling that stealth would be wise until they confirmed that there were numerous orcs in the area, ordered his men to remain behind as he and a small group moved in on the lonely tower.

Barthilas, with a fiery enthusiasm, rode eagerly behind the Lord Commander. Tirion, Arden and six footmen continued up the path after them.

The clearing around the tower was quiet, but the footmen moved quietly enough despite their cumbersome armor and weapons. Following the instructions he had been given earlier, Arden commanded his guards to encircle the tower. Barthilas dismounted and retrieved his warhammer from its saddle-loop. Escorted by two footmen, Barthilas cautiously made his way to the tower's entrance. Stopping a short distance from the ravaged entryway, Barthilas called out in his most authoritative voice:

"We come in the name of the Alliance! Come out from there and surrender yourselves, you foul beasts, or we'll be forced to kill you!" His voice was edgy and quavered slightly. Tirion knew that the unseasoned Paladin was quaking in his boots. Beads of sweat ran down Barthilas' scowling face. A shuffling noise came from the tower's ruined guardroom. The two footmen near Barthilas braced themselves for an attack. Barthilas gripped his warhammer tightly, trying to keep his nerves in check.

Slowly, the silhouette of a large orc emerged from the room's shadows and stood in the entranceway. Eitrigg held his battle-ax with both hands and looked ready to go down fighting. The orc scanned the human faces with furious eyes. He caught sight of Tirion, sitting atop his horse, and he scowled deeply. Tirion's eyes locked with the orc's for a moment, but he was forced to look away. The orc's disgusted gaze told Tirion everything he needed to know—that Eitrigg thought his notion of honor was laughable. The old orc had saved his life, and he had repaid the debt by leading enemies straight to his home. Never in his life had Tirion felt such dejection and self-loathing.

Eitrigg took a couple of steps into the clearing. Tirion noticed that he was limping more than when he last saw him. The orc's wound must be badly infected, he thought. Eitrigg's eyes blazed with hate and fury. Tirion could see that the orc would not allow himself to be taken alive.

As if in response to his thought, Dathrohan spoke up. "I do not want the creature killed. I need him alive!" he said. Barthilas took a quick moment to look back in dismay, but seemed to understand the order clearly enough. Arden and his guards converged on the tower, intending to aid in the orc's capture. Barthilas was so nervous his hands shook. He could feel the eyes of Dathrohan and Tirion upon him. This was the moment he had waited for. This was his moment of glory.

With a strangled cry, Barthilas lunged at the orc, swinging his hammer—intent on delivering a killing blow to the orc, regardless of what Dathrohan had asked. *Surely, no savage beast could match his Light-born powers*, he thought.

Tirion winced as Eitrigg adeptly blocked the young Paladin's clumsy blow and slammed his stout fist into Barthilas' face. Panicking, Barthilas dropped his hammer as Eitrigg kicked him squarely in the midsection. The young Paladin, having had the wind knocked out of him, crashed to the ground and doubled over in a fetal position. Eitrigg grunted derisively at Barthilas' weakness and ineptitude.

The two footmen rushed at the orc, slashing wildly. Eitrigg parried the first footman's attack and struck the second footman squarely in the chest, nearly cutting the warrior in half. The remaining footman, seeing the orc's apparent savagery and skill, backed off a pace in horror. Arden and his guards, enraged by their comrade's swift death, rushed forward madly. Tirion saw that they would kill the orc if they could.

"Don't kill him!" Tirion screamed frantically as the warriors descended upon the old orc. Dathrohan, sensing Tirion's obvious concern for the creature, looked at his friend questioningly. "You seem very concerned for the orc's safety, Tirion," the Lord Commander said evenly. "This *is* just a routine capture. Are you all right?"

Tirion gritted his teeth. He couldn't just sit there and watch the proud orc be cut down. But neither could he beg for the orc's release. To do so would brand him as a traitor. This was all his doing.

Eitrigg fought bravely against the footmen, but he was easily outmaneuvered, due to his wounded leg. The six footmen succeeded in pulling the mighty orc down to the ground. Arden smashed the orc's hand, and Eitrigg loosed his hold on his ax. The warriors immediately began to beat the orc to within an inch of his life.

Every fiber of Tirion's body was ablaze with rage as he watched the footmen subdue the orc. He dismounted quickly and walked forward, intending to pull the footmen away. As the footmen pulled the bleeding orc to his feet, Tirion's resolve to save the creature slipped and he stopped. *What was he thinking?* He couldn't let this happen, but neither could he take up arms against his own men. His every muscle tensed as he stood undecided.

With a loud moan, Barthilas raised himself up from the dirt. Arden helped him to stand and brushed him off. Barthilas, feeling deeply embarrassed and shamed before his superiors, rushed at the orc in a rage. Arden and Tirion both grabbed the young Paladin's arms and restrained him. They exchanged knowing glances and held Barthilas until he calmed.

"The bastard creature fought dishonorably!" Barthilas screamed. "He should be killed right here! Let me go!" He continued to strain against Tirion and Arden.

"I have ordered that it remain alive, Barthilas," Dathrohan said. "Your wounded pride is not nearly as important as the information the creature may have. Restrain the beast," he ordered. Immediately a number of footmen appeared, pulling the wagon-cage behind them. They took hold of Eitrigg and threw him into the cage.

Tirion turned to face Dathrohan. "Milord, surely this old orc is no threat to anyone," Tirion began. Dathrohan looked at him in amazement.

"What is this, Tirion? Are you actually suggesting that we turn the beast loose?" Barthilas and Arden stared at him as well, both shocked by Tirion's statement.

Tirion turned back to gaze at the beaten orc. His face swollen and dripping blood, Eitrigg stared straight back. *So much for your honor,* the orc's gaze seemed to say. The footmen continued to beat and whip Eitrigg through the cage's bars. They spit and hurled obscenities at the old orc.

Tirion's nerves finally snapped. He dashed forward and grabbed the guard who was whipping the orc. He grabbed the whip from the young man and began to lash him with it instead.

"How does it feel?" Tirion shouted at the terrified guard, who attempted to shield himself from the Paladin's raging strikes.

Dathrohan looked on in unabashed disbelief. Arden felt the same. He rushed forward and grabbed his lord's arm. "Tirion, please! What are you doing?" Arden yelled.

Tirion shrugged him off and stood to face Dathrohan with the light of rage in his eyes. "The orc must be set free!" he yelled. "It is a matter of honor!" Tirion pushed Arden away and smashed at the cage's lock with the haft of the whip's long handle.

"Tirion, have you taken leave of your senses?" Dathrohan yelled in a deep voice. Barthilas merely stood by, mouth agape. Tirion continued to smash at the lock. Shaking his head wearily, Dathrohan ordered the footmen to seize and restrain the raging Paladin. Arden's troops grabbed hold of Tirion's arms and wrestled him to the ground. Tirion fought with all of his strength, but the younger men easily overpowered him.

Arden pleaded with him to submit. "My lord, please stop! What the hell is wrong with you?" he asked. After a brief struggle, the guards brought Tirion to his feet. The Paladin looked at Eitrigg, and was met only with a blank stare in return.

"Tirion, what in the Light's name has come over you? Your actions are treasonous! Tell me you have some explanation for all of this! Tell me you didn't just try to free this creature!" Dathrohan yelled.

Tirion attempted to compose himself. "This orc saved my life, Saidan!" Tirion yelled. "During our battle, part of the tower's ceiling collapsed. I was left trapped and defenseless. The orc pulled me free before the entire roof came crashing down. I know it sounds impossible, but it happened."

Dathrohan was stunned. Arden could only stare at his lord in shock. *Certainly Tirion didn't really believe the orc had saved him, did he?* He looked into his lord's eyes and knew that, indeed, he did.

"I vowed to let him live in peace, and by my honor, I will fight to see that he does!" Tirion renewed his struggle against the footmen, attempting to free his arms.

Barthilas seemed to come out of his momentary shock. "Traitor!" the young Paladin screamed. "He is a traitor to the Alliance! He's been consorting with this beast all along!"

Dathrohan couldn't believe his ears. He had always known Tirion to be an honorable, levelheaded man. But here he was, defying his superior and siding with his mortal enemy all the same. "Tirion, I'm trying hard to be patient. Obviously, you're very confused about this creature. Regardless of what you believe happened, if you do not desist, I will be forced to have you arrested and placed on trial for treason! You will cease this senselessness at once!"

Tirion persisted. "Damn it, Saidan! This is a matter of honor! Don't you understand that?" he growled through clenched teeth.

"I stand witness to his treachery, milord," Barthilas said proudly to Dathrohan. Obviously the young Paladin sought to make up for his defeat by endearing himself to the conflicted Lord Commander.

"Shut up, Barthilas!" Dathrohan growled. With a heavy heart, he motioned for the footmen to subdue Tirion. "You leave me no choice here, Tirion. I hereby charge you with treason against the Alliance! Captain Arden, see that the prisoner is bound and placed upon his horse. He will be taken to Stratholme along with this orc and put on trial."

Arden bowed his head in sorrow. Slowly, he tied Tirion's hands together and led him to his horse. "I am sorry, milord," Arden said, looking Tirion in the eye.

Tirion frowned at his loyal servant. "It is I who am sorry, Arden. This is all my own doing. What I've done, I've done for honor's sake," Tirion said softly.

Arden shook his head questioningly. "Tirion, what honor is there in betrayal?" he asked in a whisper.

"I am a Paladin of the Light, Arden. You wouldn't understand." Arden helped him up on his horse. Dathrohan rode up to Tirion and stared at him.

"I never thought I'd live to see the day," the Lord Commander said. Tirion avoided his old friend's gaze. Dathrohan, overcome by frustration and sorrow, angrily turned away and motioned for his troops to move out.

FIVE
A Trial of Will

Tirion sat in a small holding cell that was adjacent to the Hall of Justice, where his trial was to be held. Through a small window, cut high into the cell's wall, he could hear the sounds of commerce and activity emanating from the bustling marketplace of Stratholme. Periodically he heard hammering sounds coming from the main square. The city's clamorous sounds were very different from the relaxing rural din of Mardenholde keep. Fervently, he wished he were back there now. He had no idea how his trial would go, but he had the distinct impression that no matter what happened in the court, his life would be irrevocably changed. He thought about his family and the life of affluence and ease he'd shared with them. Despite himself, he wondered if he hadn't thrown it all away on a fanciful, selfish whim.

He had been held in custody for three days. Today he was to be tried for treason against the land he had spent his life defending. He could scarcely believe it, but depending on what the court decided, he could face either execution or spending the rest of his days in prison. Karandra would never forgive him for taking such a risk for the sake of honor alone. He wondered if he'd be able to forgive himself if his wife was forced to raise their son alone. He laughed softly to himself. He always believed that the only thing that could possibly keep him from his loved ones was the enemy. *What have I done?* he asked himself over and over.

He was surprised to hear footsteps echo through the adjacent corridor. *Surely, the proceedings haven't started yet*, he thought miserably. He heard the guards outside the door question someone as the latch clicked and the door opened.

Arden walked somberly into the room. Tirion brightened somewhat and shook his friend's hand.

"It's good to see you, Arden. Have you been home since my arrest? Have you spoken with my wife?" he asked hurriedly.

Arden shook his head and motioned for Tirion to sit down on his cot. "No. They won't allow me to leave until the trial is finished, milord," the captain stated flatly. "I don't know if Karandra's been told or not."

Tirion scowled. He knew she must be beside herself with worry. "What of the orc?" Tirion asked. "What did they do with him?"

Arden tensed. "Why do you care, Tirion? It is your enemy! I don't understand why you're so concerned about it! There's no way the creature would have saved your life! It's a mindless brute!" Arden spat.

Tirion looked him square in the eye. "Just answer me, Captain," Tirion said as calmly as he could. He had to watch his tone—Arden might be the only friend he had left.

"They've been interrogating the creature for the past few nights," Arden said. "Apparently, it didn't offer up anything they didn't already know. I heard some of the local guards boasting about how they'd beaten the hell out of it. They're going to hang the wretched beast tomorrow morning in the square."

Tirion's heart sank. Eitrigg was going to die, and it was all his fault. Somehow, he had to find a way to make amends—to put things right.

Arden sensed Tirion's tension. "Milord, they might execute you for this," Arden began. "If you confess and claim that you lost your senses, maybe they'll relent and let you go. Surely this matter isn't worth dying for! You're a Lord Paladin, for the Light's sake! People depend on you! You've got to snap out of this!" the captain finished heatedly.

Tirion only shook his head. "I can't, Arden. It is a matter of honor. I swore to protect the orc, and I betrayed that vow. Whatever punishment they charge me with, it is well deserved."

Arden ran his hands through his hair in frustration. "This makes no sense, Tirion. Think about your wife and child!" Arden yelled.

Tirion stood up to face him. "I am, old friend. What kind of example would I set for my son if my word counted for nothing? What kind of man would I be seen as then?" Tirion asked.

Arden turned away, bristling. "It's not that simple, and you know it!" the captain bellowed. "Just admit that you made a mistake! Admit that you were wrong to side with the orc, and they might be lenient! Why do we even have to discuss this? Have you lost all sense, man?"

Just then the door opened and two guards stepped in. "You'll have to leave now, Captain," one of the guards said. "We are to escort the prisoner to the Hall now." Arden gave Tirion a last, pleading look and marched out the door in a huff.

Tirion straightened and attempted to look as proud and confident as he could. "I am ready, gentlemen," he said to them. They bound his hands and led him outside. The bright, midday sun caused Tirion to wince slightly. His limbs were tired and cramped from the past few days of inactivity. The guards marched him across the square toward the imposing structure of the Hall of Justice. Out of the corner of his eye, Tirion caught sight of the gallows' scaffolding being erected. He surmised that it was the source of the hammering he had been hearing. Briefly, he visualized Eitrigg standing upon the gallows with a rope tied around his neck. Tirion had to work hard in order to keep his forced semblance of confidence. If Eitrigg died, then all his efforts would have been for nothing.

An hour later, Tirion was seated in a large oaken chair in the middle of the polished courtroom floor. Before him was an immense stage adorned with four throne-like chairs. At the center of the stage, directly in front of him, was a large lectern where the judge would conduct the trial. Above the stage was an enormous white flag bearing a stylized blue letter *L*, which signified the Alliance of Lordaeron. Lining the vast walls of the chamber were other huge banners representing the seven nations of the Alliance. A large blue banner embroidered with a golden lion signified the kingdom of Stormwind. Another banner, black with a red-gauntleted fist, represented the kingdom of Stromgarde. Tirion was too nervous to look around at the others.

Though he could not bear to turn around and see his comrades' accusing faces, he could hear a hundred voices whispering and muttering at once throughout the grandiose chamber. Through the din, he discerned that everyone in attendance was shocked to hear that he had betrayed them. Many of the onlookers had served under his command during the war, and many others he considered to be good friends. He could feel their communal confusion and scorn buffet him in waves. His trial would not be an easy one.

Far to his right, he caught sight of Barthilas sitting in attendance. The young Paladin had a condemning look in his eye as he gazed intently at Tirion. Tirion wondered why the youth had turned on him so completely and been so eager to see him disgraced. He turned away from Barthilas as another armored Paladin made his way to the front of the stage.

"Defenders of Lordaeron," the Paladin said in a clear voice, "today we stand in judgment of one of our own. The trial of Lord Tirion Fordring will now commence."

Tirion realized that his palms were sweating. He had to physically restrain himself from shaking. He knew that the four jurors would enter the Hall soon. Every major trial in Lordaeron was presided over by four of the highest-ranking lords within the Alliance. Tirion was sure that he'd recognize many of them as his peers. The attendant onlookers hushed as the first of the jurors entered.

"All hail Lord Admiral Daelin Proudmoore of Kul'Tiras," the Paladin said as the tall, lanky figure walked across the stage. Lord Proudmoore took the throne-like seat on the far right with a look of disquiet on his proud face. Tirion knew Proudmoore well. As well as being a tactical genius, the Lord Admiral was one of the greatest heroes of the war. His officer's uniform and large, ceremonial hat were deep blue and adorned with golden medals and pins signifying his rank as master of the Alliance's navies.

The Paladin spoke again. "All hail Arch-Mage Antonidas of the Magocracy of Dalaran," he said as the second juror strode in. A hush descended upon the crowd as the mysterious wizard took his seat. His lavender hooded robe was adorned with black and gold trim, and he carried a great, polished staff in his hands. Ever distrustful of magic, Tirion hadn't had many dealings with wizards over the years, and was somewhat disconcerted to find that his fate was now in the hands of one. He looked back to the Paladin as the last two jurors were announced.

The venerable Archbishop, Alonsus Faol, who had anointed Tirion as a Paladin long ago, walked in and took a seat next to the lectern.

Following the Archbishop was the young prince of Lordaeron, Arthas, who had only recently been made a full Paladin. Tirion had never met the young prince before, but he could see that the handsome youth radiated goodness and wisdom despite his relatively young age. Tirion wished fervently that Barthilas had had the prince's composure, days before.

With the jurors assembled, the Paladin motioned for everyone to rise for the judge's entrance. All of the attendant men and women rose as Uther the Lightbringer entered the Hall and walked forward to the ornate lectern. The mighty, holy patron of the Knights of the Silver Hand scanned the assembly with stern eyes the color of ocean storms. His ornately etched silver armor seemed to reflect every light source in the vast Hall—bathing Uther in a halo of shimmering beauty. Uther was the first Paladin, and was held to be the mightiest warrior amongst the armies of the Alliance. He was also held to be the wisest and most noble of all the holy Paladins. Everyone in the room was cowed by his commanding presence.

Tirion's mind reeled. Up until that point, he was resolved to stand by his decision and accept his fate with honor. But, looking up at the stern visage of his powerful superior, his courage wavered. *Perhaps Arden was right?* he thought frantically. *Maybe he should beg for the court's mercy and forget that he ever made a vow to an enemy of humanity?* His thoughts were disrupted as the Lightbringer's powerful, melodious voice filled his ears.

"Lord Paladin Fordring," Uther began. "You are charged with treason against the Alliance and failing to obey a direct order given to you by your superior. As you know, this is a dire charge. The noble lords gathered here will hear your case and judge you accordingly under the Light. How do you plead to the charges against you?" Tirion clenched his fists to keep them from shaking. He barely found the voice to answer.

"I am guilty as charged, milord. I accept full responsibility for my actions," Tirion said.

A hundred angry voices flooded the room at once. Apparently, many of the onlookers had believed the charges to be greatly exaggerated or false. The assembly was shocked to hear Tirion admit his guilt so openly. Tirion looked behind him to watch the crowd's raucous reaction. He caught sight of Arden sitting right behind him. The captain's tortured expression seemed to plead to Tirion to reconsider his position. Tirion had to look away. Arden believed in him and had always served him loyally. But the captain would never understand. . . .

Uther's voice boomed out as the mighty Paladin commanded the assembly to silence. The gathered host went quiet as if it had been struck by lightning. Tirion could almost feel an electrical tension in the air. He braced himself.

"Very well," Uther said evenly. "Let the record show that Lord Paladin Fordring has entered a plea of guilty."

Tirion watched as the four jurors conversed amongst themselves for a brief moment. Lord Proudmoore ended the discussion and motioned for Uther to continue.

"Let Lord Commander, Saidan Dathrohan, come forward and give his testimony," Uther commanded. The crowd stirred slightly as Dathrohan walked toward the stage. He stopped and stood solemnly next to Tirion's chair. The two friends exchanged fleeting glances. Dathrohan could only nod sorrowfully at Tirion.

"Lord Commander Dathrohan, you have charged this man with treason. Please explain for the court the occurrence and the nature of this man's alleged infraction," Uther said.

Dathrohan cleared his throat and straightened slightly. "My lords, I do wish to state for the record that Tirion Fordring has always been a man of honor and nobility. But I cannot deny what I saw with my own eyes. Four days ago, I led a detachment into the Hearthglen Woods in search of renegade orcs. Lord Fordring assisted me with the exercise and helped me to track down the orc that we currently hold in our prison for execution. When I gave the command to arrest the creature, Lord Fordring turned upon my men and attempted to set the orc free. I asked him repeatedly to desist, but he would not relent. It is with a heavy heart that I give this testimony," Dathrohan finished. Once again, murmurs and hushed whispers floated through the Hall. The jurors discussed Dathrohan's words as Uther addressed the court again.

"Is there anyone here who can give credence to Lord Commander Dathrohan's testimony?" Tirion's whole body clenched as he saw Barthilas spring up from his seat.

"I can, milord," the young Paladin stated excitedly. "I was there, under Lord Dathrohan's command, when the incident took place. I bore witness to Tirion's treachery firsthand." The scorn in his voice was evident when he spoke his superior's name. Tirion could hear Arden groaning behind him.

Uther dismissed Dathrohan and motioned for Barthilas to come forward. Dathrohan gripped Barthilas in a searing gaze as they passed each other. Apparently, the youth's efforts to win his way into the Lord Commander's good graces were not working as well as Barthilas had planned. With surprising calm, Barthilas took his place near Tirion's chair. His face was proud and intent.

"State your claim, *junior* Paladin Barthilas," Uther said icily. He was obviously disgruntled by the younger Paladin's lack of respect for his superior. Guilty or not, Tirion was still to be addressed by his title.

Undeterred, Barthilas continued. "Just as Lord Commander Dathrohan said, milord, I saw *Lord* Fordring fight to save the orc from capture. He said that he had made a pact with the creature and would be damned if we incarcerated it," Barthilas said matter-of-factly. "You see, I knew he was up to something. I had a feeling that this *vile traitor* was untrustworthy even before we set out to capture the orc!"

"Silence!" Uther shouted, his voice reverberating through the chamber like thunder. He ensnared the now trembling Barthilas with his overpowering gaze. "You will learn to control your tongue, *junior* Paladin. I have known this man for years. We saved each other's lives more than once, and stood victorious before the enemy more times than I can clearly remember. Whatever he may have done, he certainly deserves more than to be harangued by an unseasoned boy like yourself." Barthilas turned white as a sheet and looked as if he might faint. "Your testimony has been heard and will be reviewed by the court. You are dismissed," Uther finished. Reddening in embarrassment, Barthilas hurried back to his seat. Tirion watched as the jurors once again began to converse with one another.

The four lords finished their deliberations and motioned that they were ready to proceed. Uther turned to stare down at Tirion. His gaze seemed to look straight into Tirion's heart, searching for some explanation for his friend's unprecedented behavior.

"Lord Paladin Fordring, do you have anything to say in your defense?" Uther asked Tirion levelly.

Tirion stood up and solemnly addressed the court. "My lords, I know that the notion must sound preposterous, but the orc saved my life. In return, I gave him my word as a Paladin that I would protect his as well. The orc's name is Eitrigg, and he is as honorable an opponent as I have ever faced." Jeers and shocked gasps erupted from the assembled onlookers. Tirion continued unabated. "You must understand me when I tell you—in order to follow my orders, I would have had to betray my honor as a Paladin. That I could not do. That said, I will accept whatever punishment you deem fit."

Uther strode over to the four jurors and knelt beside them. He argued with them briefly, pointing his finger as if to stress a point. After a few moments, it appeared as if the jurors had relented and Uther walked back to the lectern, victorious.

"Lord Paladin Fordring," he began, "this court is well aware of your long years of service in defense of Lordaeron and its allied kingdoms. Every man here is aware of your courage and valor. However, consorting with the sworn enemies of humanity, regardless of their supposed honor, is a grievous crime. In granting the orc amnesty, you took a terrible risk and gambled the safety of Hearthglen on a personal whim. In light of your service, this court is prepared to offer you a full pardon if you will disavow your oath to the creature and reaffirm your commitment to the Alliance."

Tirion cleared his throat. It would be so easy to simply give in and go home to his wife and son. He turned to see Arden wringing his hands in anticipation.

"Please, milord. Commit to them and be done with it," Arden whispered anxiously. Tirion saw Dathrohan take a step forward, as if urging him to forget about the orc and clear his good name.

"Let's put this nonsense behind us, Tirion," Dathrohan exclaimed under his breath.

"Lord Paladin Fordring? What is your answer?" Uther asked suspiciously, seeing Tirion's hesitation.

Tirion braced himself and faced the court members boldly. "What is to be done with the orc, milord?" The great Paladin looked surprised by the question, but saw fit to answer anyway.

"It will be executed, like any other enemy of humanity. Regardless of your personal experience with the creature, it is a savage, murdering beast that cannot be allowed to live."

Tirion bowed his head and thought for a moment. He pictured Taelan's innocent face in his mind's eye. He wanted to go home, so badly. . . .

He raised his head and saw Dathrohan give him a pleased smile; the Lord Commander seemed convinced that Tirion would make the right decision. Tirion saw his course plainly. He would make the only decision honor would permit.

"I will remain committed to the Alliance until my dying day. Of that, have no doubt," Tirion said confidently. "But I cannot disavow the oath I took. To do so would be to betray everything I am and everything we, as honorable men, hold dear."

This time the entire gathering erupted in fury and shock. None could believe Tirion's brazen decision. Even the noble jurors gaped openmouthed at Tirion. The tired Paladin thought he heard Arden weeping behind him, and his heart sank even lower. Dathrohan sat down heavily in his chair, shaking his head in dismay. Barthilas seemed to be on the verge of jumping out of his seat in excitement. Many of the gathered warriors began to shout obscenities at Tirion and call him a traitor. Some spat at him as he stood motionless before the stage.

Rubbing his eyes wearily, Uther motioned for the court to fall silent once more. He was beside himself with anguish over what he must do, but Tirion had stated his position clearly.

"So be it," Uther said ominously. "Tirion Fordring, from this day forth you are no longer welcome among the Knights of the Silver Hand. You are no longer fit to bask in the grace of the Light. I hereby excommunicate you from our ranks."

The audience gasped at Uther's words. Excommunication was a rare, harsh punishment that stripped a Paladin of his Light-given powers. Though it had only been used a few times, every Paladin lived in mortal fear of it. Tirion could not fathom what was about to happen. Before he could utter another word, Uther made a sweeping motion with his hand. Immediately, Tirion felt a dark shadow pass over him, choking out the holy power of the Light. Panic threatened to overwhelm him as the grace and strengthening energies of the Light fled his body. The blessed energies, which had been such an integral part of him for so long, ebbed away just as if they had never been. Though the light of the Hall never wavered, Tirion felt as if he had been wrapped in darkness and cast down into oblivion. Unable to withstand the raging despair and hopelessness that washed over him in waves, Tirion lowered his head in abject despair.

Uther continued. "All trappings of our order will be stripped from you," he said as two Paladins came forward and viciously ripped the silver plates from Tirion's wracked body, "as well as your personal titles and holdings."

Tirion struggled against despair. Never in his life had he felt so naked and powerless. Images of Taelan and Karandra sifted through his tortured mind. He had to get a grip on himself. He had to think of his dignity. On wobbly legs, he stood and faced the court once more.

"You shall be exiled from these kingdoms and live the rest of your days amongst the wild things of the world. May the Light have mercy on your soul," Uther finished.

Tirion felt dazed, His head spun and anxiety threatened to overtake him. He was barely conscious of Uther's next words to the assembly:

"Though it goes against my better judgment, it is the will of this court that Paladin Barthilas take over as regent governor of Hearthglen, effective immediately. Barthilas is to remain here to oversee the morning's hanging and then return home to his duties. The exile, Tirion Fordring, is to be escorted back to Mardenholde keep. There he will collect his family and be escorted to the borders of the Alliance lands. These proceedings are over," Uther said, smashing his armored fist against the lectern. He gazed at Tirion in frustration, clearly disgusted with the trial's outcome.

"My lord, I have one last question," Tirion barely managed to say. Uther paused to listen—a final gesture of respect and friendship for his former comrade. "My wife and son . . . are they to be exiled as well? Will my sin damn their lives as it has mine?" Tirion asked shakily.

Uther bowed his head in sorrow. The man before him was a good man. This was no way for a hero to be treated.

"No, Tirion. They may remain in Lordaeron if they so desire. This was your crime, not theirs. They should not be punished for your pride," Uther said. He then turned his back on Tirion and departed. Lost in a haze of despair and grief, Tirion was barely aware of the guards hauling him out of the Great Hall.

SIX
A Sort of Homecoming

It was twilight as the tired envoy made its way back to Mardenholde keep. It had begun to rain during the afternoon, and the weary horses trudged their way down the muddy road. Arden, leading the somber column of knights and footmen, looked back at Tirion worriedly. Tirion was slumped over in his saddle, heedless of what transpired around him. His broad shoulders drooped weakly and his head was bowed in grief. The ceaseless rain ran in rivulets down his haggard face. Arden's heart broke, seeing his former lord and master in such a state. He was forced to look away. Looking toward the keep, the captain saw that Tirion's advisors had gathered at the main gate to greet their returning lord.

Tirion's stomach was tied in knots. He was blocked from the Light. In the thirty years that he had served as a Paladin, he never dreamed that the blessed power would be stripped from him. He felt absolutely hollow inside. Wallowing in despair and misery, he was unable to even lift his eyes toward the sight of his former home.

Arden rode slowly up to the gate and dismounted. The advisors, at seeing Tirion's near-comatose state, asked the captain what was wrong.

Arden grimaced. "There have been some changes," he said to them curtly. The advisors looked at each other in confusion.

"What do you mean, Captain? Where have you both been these past few days? What is wrong with our lord?" one of them asked heatedly.

Arden bowed his head in shame and sorrow. "Our lord Tirion has been found guilty of treason against the Alliance," he said with a heavy heart. "The

High Court has ordered that he be exiled from our lands." The advisors gasped in shock.

"Surely you must be mistaken. That's impossible!" one of the advisors said shakily. He looked into Arden's eyes and saw that it clearly was not.

"It can't be," the advisor said blankly. Arden nodded grimly and helped Tirion dismount from his horse.

"Well, who is our lord now, Arden? Who will rule over Hearthglen?" another advisor asked. Arden shook his head and scoffed as he answered, "Barthilas will be your new lord, for the time being." *It did sound like a bad joke*, he thought to himself. He put his arm around Tirion and started to lead him inside. "I want the guards to stay alert tonight. Tirion is to remain here under house arrest. At first light, I will take a party of footmen and escort him to the border. Until then, neither of us is to be disturbed. Is that clear?" the captain asked in a gravelly voice.

The shocked advisors merely nodded their assent. Arden dragged Tirion in out of the rain and ushered him toward his private chambers, hoping that he wouldn't have to face Karandra before morning. Not for the first time, he wondered if there was anything that he could have done to prevent this all from happening.

Arden leaned Tirion against the wall outside his private chambers and opened the door.

"Thanks for your help, Arden. This has been . . . very difficult. I just wanted you to know that you've been a good friend to me. I'm sorry all this has happened," the former Paladin said.

Arden nodded and turned away slowly. "If there's anything you need, let me know," the captain said as he left.

Tirion watched him leave and found just enough strength to close the door behind him and collapse in a chair. Overcome with emotion, he buried his face in his hands. His limbs would not stop shaking, and the gnawing emptiness in his gut threatened to devour what was left of his soul. He couldn't face his wife and tell her what he'd done. Ironically, after all the years he'd refused to lie to her, he found now that he couldn't bear to tell her the truth.

The adjoining door to Taelan's room opened and Karandra stepped out quietly, shutting it behind her. She looked surprised to see Tirion sitting there in the dark.

"Tirion, what has happened?" she asked urgently. She lit a decorative lantern, and its soft light bathed the room. Shadows danced across the walls as she knelt down beside her husband.

"Where have you been? I've been worried sick."

"I accompanied Lord Dathrohan back to Stratholme," he muttered, his head still bowed.

"You know, Tirion, you've been sneaking off quite a bit lately. If I didn't know you any better, I'd assume that you were seeking comfort from another woman," she said teasingly. Tirion raised his head and looked at her. Seeing the deadened look in his eyes, she knew that he was not amused in the least.

"Tirion, darling, what's wrong? Has something happened to you?" she asked worriedly. He looked over toward Taelan's room.

"Is the boy asleep?" he asked quietly. Karandra frowned and answered that he was.

"I don't quite know how to tell you this, my love," he began somberly, "but I have been branded a traitor and stripped of my titles."

Her eyes widened in shock. He wasn't joking, she realized. In fact, as she looked at him more closely, she marveled at how defeated and deflated he seemed. In all the years she had known him, he had never looked this way. It frightened her immensely. She shook her head, unable to grasp the enormity of the situation.

"How could this happen, Tirion? What have you done?" she asked in a strangled voice.

He closed his eyes and held his breath for a moment, attempting to calm the furious pounding of his heart. "Do you remember the secret that I kept from you?" he asked. She nodded as her brow creased in anxiety. "The orc I fought with saved my life, Karandra. If not for him, I would have been crushed under a collapsing tower. To repay him for saving me, I vowed, on my honor, to keep his existence secret."

Karandra covered her face. She shook her head as if she didn't want to hear any more, but Tirion continued anyway.

"I was forced to hunt the orc down under direct orders. But when it came time to capture him, my conscience overtook me. To uphold my honor, I fought to free it. I was arrested on the spot and taken to Stratholme for trial," he finished.

They sat there in silence for many long moments. Karandra sniffed and wiped tears from her eyes. "I can't even begin to imagine what you were thinking," she said breathlessly. "The orc is a beast, Tirion! It has no concept of honor! You gambled all our lives on a stupid, silly whim!" she spat, careful to keep her voice down. She didn't want to wake Taelan and let him see his father in such a state. Tirion simply sat with his head bowed. For some strange reason, seeing him in such a weakened state only made her more anxious.

"So what happens to us now, Tirion? Did you even consider that while you were playing the martyr?" she said softly, disappointment rampant in her voice.

He stood up and walked over to the window. Night had settled heavily over the fields beyond the keep. The rain continued to pour, as if nature was attempting to rid itself of some foulness in the world.

"I have been exiled, Karandra. I am to be escorted to the border at first light," he said gravely. She blinked in shock.

"Exiled?" she whispered. "Light-damn you, Tirion! I told you your precious honor would be the end of us!"

He turned to face her. "Without honor, woman, everything we have is meaningless!" he said, motioning around at their lavish surroundings.

She waved her arm dismissively.

"Will your honor keep us fed and keep our son decently clothed? How can you maintain this senseless obsession in the face of what's happened? What happened to the responsible man I married?" she asked.

He gritted his teeth and turned to face her. "I have always been this way, Karandra! Don't talk to me as if it's any surprise! You knew that marrying a Paladin would demand certain sacrifices."

"And I've made plenty of them. Willingly! I held my tongue every time you rode off to battle. I sat here, alone, for countless hours—waiting to hear if you were alive or dead. Do you have any idea of what that was like for me? I never complained once all those times that you left us for your bureaucratic duties. I knew you had a job to do. I knew people counted on you. But I counted on you, too, damn it! I kept it all inside so that you could 'do your duty' with honor. I know all about sacrifices, Tirion. But this time the price is too high."

"What do you mean by that?" he asked, although he already knew the answer. She held him in her fiery stare.

"I love you, Tirion. Please believe that. But I won't be coming with you . . . and neither will Taelan," she said softly. Karandra turned away, unable to look him in the eye. "I will not have our son grow up as an outcast or be the subject of ridicule for the rest of his life. He doesn't deserve that, Tirion, and neither do I," she said.

Tirion felt as if his life no longer had any meaning. Losing the Light was devastating enough; he didn't know if he could bear losing her too. His head spun.

"I understand how you must feel, Karandra. Believe me, I do," he barely managed to say. "Are you certain this is what you want?"

"You've ruined your life. I will not simply hold on while you plummet to the bottom and ruin ours as well!" she said, almost frantically. She hugged herself, trying to calm her raw nerves. "I hope your precious honor keeps you warm at night," she said.

"Karandra, wait," Tirion said as she left. She walked swiftly toward her room and slammed the door shut behind her. Tirion heard the bolt lock, and the faint sounds of her sobbing.

Unable to comfort her, Tirion leaned his head against the window's cool pane of glass. Absently, he watched as the raindrops splattered against the pane. He knew her well enough to know that she would not change her mind. He had lost nearly everything he had ever cared for. The only thing he had left in the world was his honor. He wasn't even sure of that anymore.

As if in a daze, Tirion walked into his reading room and sat down at his large, polished oak desk. He lit a few candles and gathered up a piece of parchment, ink and a new quill. Without really knowing exactly what he wanted to say, he started scribbling down his thoughts on the parchment. His hand shook as he wrote, smearing the ink in spots. He emptied his heart out onto the parchment, expressing everything he felt, explaining everything he had done. He sat at the desk and wrote late into the night.

Morning was only an hour off when Tirion entered Taelan's darkened room. Karandra had cried herself to sleep hours before, so Tirion knew he would be undisturbed. He walked over to where his son lay sleeping peacefully. Snuggled in his blankets, the boy breathed steadily. Tirion watched him sleep for a while, awed by the child's innocence and purity. He knew his son deserved better than a life of forced exile. He deserved all of the good things life had to offer.

With a shaky hand, Tirion reached into his coat pocket and retrieved the rolled parchment he had written. Tears filled his eyes as he carefully placed the note under his son's pillow. *Perhaps someday the boy might understand what I've done*, he hoped. *Perhaps somehow he'll look back on me and be proud*. Tirion patted the boy's head and kissed him on the cheek.

"Good-bye, my son," he said, fighting back his tears. "Be good."

With that, he quietly left and closed the door behind him.

Dawn had broken over the tranquil fields of Hearthglen. The oppressive storm clouds had blown away and the sky was bright and crystal clear. In a few hours, the old orc Eitrigg would be hanged in Stratholme. Tirion had decided that he would not let that happen. Whatever else transpired, Eitrigg would not die. He had little trouble bypassing the keep's lax guardsmen and reaching the stables. As quietly as he could, he saddled Mirador and prepared his meager supplies for the journey to Stratholme.

He placed his foot in the stirrup and hauled himself up onto his horse.

"This is the second time I've caught you trying to sneak off, Tirion," Arden said, standing in the entranceway. Tirion's heart froze. He looked around and saw that there were no guards with the captain. In fact, there was no escort party to be seen anywhere.

"I figured you'd try something like this," the captain said.

Tirion gripped his reins tightly and cleared his throat. "Are you here to stop me, Arden?" he asked tightly.

The captain walked over and tightened the straps of Mirador's saddlebags. "Even if I had a mind to, I doubt that I could," Arden replied honestly. "I sat up all night thinking about what you said at the trial. I think perhaps I understand how you felt. You were only doing what you thought was right. You always have. For that, I cannot condemn you."

Tirion nodded and leaned down. He placed his hand on Arden's shoulder.

"I need to ask you a favor, old friend. It is the most important thing I've ever asked of you," he said breathlessly.

Arden looked up at him gravely. "Whatever is in my power to do, I will do," the captain said.

"Watch over them for me, Arden. Keep my boy safe," Tirion said.

Arden reached up and took hold of his friend's hand. "I will," was all he could say.

Satisfied, Tirion nodded to Arden and looked out toward the distant tree line. He dug his spurs into Mirador's sides and thundered out of the stables. Stratholme was only a few hours away. If he rode like the wind, he would make it in time to stop the hanging. He charged down the path at breakneck speed, pushing the faithful Mirador faster and harder than he ever had before.

SEVEN
The Drums of War

Tirion made good time reaching Stratholme. The sun had just barely crested the distant Alterac peaks by the time he reached the city's outskirts. He had tethered Mirador in the woods and ran the last quarter mile to the city. As he ran, he attempted to formulate a plan to save old Eitrigg. Much to his dismay, he came up with nothing. He hoped that when the time came, he would think of something brilliant that didn't involve killing or injuring his own people. However, seeing as how he was a convicted traitor, they certainly would have no qualms about killing him. He knew that the likelihood of saving the orc and escaping Stratholme alive was slim.

Undeterred, Tirion stealthily made his way through Stratholme's quiet, cobblestone streets. A few merchants and vendors were beginning to set up their wares for the day's transactions in the marketplace, but there were few others about at that early hour. He managed to evade the few guards he saw walking the streets. Fearing that the local guardsmen would recognize him, Tirion kept to the shadows and stayed well out of sight.

As Tirion neared the public square, he began to hear loud voices shouting and jeering. He hoped he was not too late to save the orc. He stepped into the square and saw a large gathering of men at its center. Clinging to the shadows, Tirion climbed a short staircase and situated himself in a small, recessed alcove that offered a full view of the newly erected gallows. The crowd that had gathered around the scaffolding was comprised mostly of guards and footmen. They had all come to see the spectacle of the old orc's hanging. Thankfully, Tirion realized that the prisoner had not yet been brought out. The gathered men merely jeered and shouted at one another in anticipation.

There were a number of knights, dressed in their finest armor, surrounding the square. They stood quiet and vigilant, ready to intercede if the volatile crowd turned into a mob. Tirion recognized many of the knights who had been present at his trial. Although they were relatively calm, Tirion knew that they wanted to see the orc hanged as much as the footmen and the guards did.

After a few moments, the gathering stirred as a newcomer strode up to the gallows. Tirion saw that it was Barthilas. The young Paladin waved and shouted to the crowd enthusiastically, riling them up for what he obviously considered to be the morning's entertainment. Tirion was glad that he couldn't hear Barthilas' words. He suspected that they were filled with poison and hatred. He felt a momentary pang of remorse, knowing that his beloved Hearthglen was now in Barthilas' unstable hands.

Tirion watched as a second figure emerged from the throng and ascended the scaffolding. Lord Dathrohan, seemingly oblivious to the crowd's raucous din, walked up to Barthilas' side and scanned the square with stern eyes. He spoke to the crowd for a moment and the jeering died down to a low roar. Tirion held his breath. He knew they would bring Eitrigg out soon. Minutes passed by slowly as Tirion waited anxiously beneath the alcove. A tension built amongst the onlookers as well. They seemed more eager to watch a neck snap than see true justice met. As the din rose up again, more and more people gathered in the square. Even women and children edged closer, hoping to catch sight of the terrible orcish monster.

Finally, the gates to the nearby holding cell opened and a squad of footmen strode out in tight formation. The gathered onlookers erupted in cheers and began to hurl garbage and stones at the newcomers. Armored as they were, the footmen took little notice of the crowd's fervor or its harmless projectiles. Their shiny armor flashed in the morning light, but Tirion could see that they dragged a huddled shape among them.

It was Eitrigg.

They stopped at the base of the scaffolding, and two men dragged the old orc up the rest of the way. The orc was barely able to stand and his green body was covered with dark bruises and lacerations.

Tirion wondered how the weakened orc could even walk. Apparently the interrogators had taken their time in beating him. Despite his injuries, Eitrigg did his best to keep his head raised. He would not give his tormentors the satisfaction of seeing him broken. Tirion knew that Eitrigg's orcish spirit was too proud for that.

Tirion's heart pounded in his chest. Against such a spirited group of warriors, he didn't stand a chance of saving the old orc. *He didn't have a plan. He didn't even have a weapon of any kind.* He looked down and saw that the hangman was adjusting the tightly wound noose. *Eitrigg was only moments away from death.*

Frantically, Tirion leaped down from his perch and pushed his way through the boisterous crowd. In their excitement, no one noticed the disgraced exile passing by them. Their attention was focused on the gallows and the beaten green beast that stood before them.

Tirion watched as Lord Dathrohan gave Barthilas a stiff salute and walked back down toward the holding cell's gates. Apparently the Lord Commander had no interest in watching the vulgar spectacle so soon after Tirion's trial. Barthilas was none too concerned to see him go. Smiling broadly, Barthilas ordered the hangman to put the noose around the orc's throat. Eitrigg scowled as the rope was tightened around his muscular neck. The orc's dark eyes stared straight forward, as if he were looking into another world that no one else could see. Tirion clawed and shoved his way closer to the scaffolding. Barthilas waved his hand in the air, motioning for silence. Surprisingly, the raucous crowd quieted down.

"My fellow defenders of Lordaeron," he began proudly, "I am glad to see that so many of you turned out this morning. This loathsome creature that stands before you is an affront to the Light and an enemy of our people. Its cursed race brought war and suffering to our shores and murdered many of our loved ones with little or no remorse. Thus," Barthilas continued, staring Eitrigg in the eye, "we will extinguish this wretched creature's life just as remorselessly." Eitrigg met Barthilas' fevered gaze with his own. "Blood for blood. Debt for debt," the young Paladin finished.

The crowd cheered wildly for Barthilas and screamed for the orc's blood. Tirion marveled that his own people could be so savage and vile. He felt sick and overwhelmed by their smothering, collective hatred.

Barthilas stepped back as the hangman moved Eitrigg into position over the scaffolding's trap door. The old orc's stoic mask began to slip as death approached. Eitrigg began to shake and growl and fight against his restraints. The onlookers merely laughed at his futile efforts. They seemed to revel in the old orc's panic and confusion.

Searching for some type of weapon, Tirion saw an old, rusted sledgehammer leaning against the base of the scaffolding. He pushed his way through the front row of onlookers and dove for the sledgehammer. Time seemed to stand still as Tirion reached out to grasp the unwieldy tool. As if in slow motion, he watched as the hangman placed his hand upon the trap door lever while Barthilas raised his arm, ready to give the signal that would end the orc's life. Tirion's hands closed over the sledgehammer's wooden haft as, in a surge of light and adrenaline, he charged forward.

The assembled knights and footmen yelled in anger at seeing Tirion emerge from the roiling crowd. The former Paladin struck fast and hard, leaving the surprised footmen scattered in his wake. A few alert guards rushed at him, but Tirion swung the old sledgehammer in a wide arc. Careful not to use lethal force, Tirion punched a deep dent in one guard's breastplate and smashed in another's helmet-visor. Seeing that he had bought himself a few, precious seconds, Tirion leaped up onto the scaffolding and headed straight for Barthilas.

The young Paladin was shocked at seeing Tirion charging at him. He fumbled awkwardly for his warhammer, but Tirion was too fast. He rammed his shoulder into Barthilas' gut and sent the young Paladin careening wildly off the platform. Barthilas landed with a loud thud and was nearly trampled by the raging crowd.

The hooded hangman rushed forward to overpower Tirion, but the former Paladin stood his ground. Grabbing the hangman by the arm, Tirion flipped him over his shoulder and sent him tumbling down the scaffolding's steps. He could hear the knights and footmen charging up the steps behind him. *They would hang him for this*, he thought frantically. Not even the Lightbringer himself could pardon Tirion for this affront.

As quickly as he could, Tirion ran over to Eitrigg and unfastened the noose around the orc's neck. Left too weak to stand, Eitrigg slumped heavily into Tirion's arms. The orc barely recognized his savior's face.

"*Human?*" Eitrigg mumbled questioningly. Tirion smiled down at him.

"Yes, Eitrigg," Tirion said. "It's me." Eitrigg shuddered in pain and exhaustion, but fixed Tirion with his hazy gaze.

"You must be crazy," the old orc said. Tirion laughed to himself and nodded in agreement. He turned just in time to see Barthilas climbing up over the edge of the scaffolding. Tirion knew that the knights and footmen were only seconds away. Barthilas straightened and glowered at him.

"Traitor! You have damned yourself this day!" the young Paladin screamed. The shocked crowd yelled their assent and began throwing garbage at Tirion and Eitrigg both.

Out of the corner of his eye, Tirion could see Lord Dathrohan looming in the background. Apparently, he hadn't left after all. The Lord Commander's face was a mask of grief and revulsion. Tirion wished there was some way to make his old friend understand that what he was doing, he was doing for honor's sake.

Barthilas yelled for the knights to seize Tirion and the orc. As they approached, Tirion stretched out his hand and commanded them to halt. He had spent his life leading men into battle and his deep voice still carried the weight of command. Many of the knights who had served under him previously found themselves cowed by his presence. Tirion faced them boldly.

"Hear me!" Tirion shouted. His voice boomed out over the crowd and reverberated against the surrounding structures. Many of the onlookers fell strangely silent. "This orc has done you no harm! He is old and infirm. His death would accomplish nothing!" The honorable knights paused for a moment, considering Tirion's protests.

"But it's an orc! Are we not at war with its kind?" one of the knights yelled incredulously. Tirion steadied himself and tightened his grip on Eitrigg.

"We may very well be! But this one's warlike days are over!" Tirion said. "There is no honor in hanging such a defenseless creature." He saw that a few of the knights nodded reluctantly. The rest of the onlookers remained to be convinced. They continued to jeer and call Tirion an orc-loving traitor.

"You're not fit to even speak of honor, Tirion," Barthilas spat angrily. "You're a traitorous mongrel who deserves to die right beside that inhuman beast!"

Tirion tensed. Barthilas' words hit him like a slap in the face. "I took a vow, long ago, to protect the weak and defenseless," Tirion said through gritted teeth, "and I intend to do just that. You see, boy, that's what it truly means to be a Paladin—knowing the difference between right and wrong and being able to separate justice from vengeance. You've never been able to make those distinctions, have you, Barthilas?" Tirion asked. Barthilas nearly choked with rage.

Above the din of the shouting crowd, a single beating drum boomed out loud and clear. Eitrigg's weary head jerked up suddenly. He scanned the square's periphery as if he expected to see a familiar sight, then bowed his head again. Tirion looked at the orc questioningly, certain that the orc recognized the strange beat. A few of the onlookers turned to see where the drumming was coming from, but Barthilas paid it no mind. The young Paladin stepped toward Tirion with his fists clenched.

"Have you forgotten so soon, Tirion? You're no longer a Paladin! You're a disgrace—an exile! It doesn't make any difference what you think or believe!" Barthilas yelled.

"Damn it, Barthilas, you've got to open your eyes!" Tirion said urgently. "After all the years I ruled over Hearthglen, the one thing I'm absolutely certain of is that war begets only war! If we can't master our own hatreds, then this senseless conflict will never cease! There will never be a future for our people!"

Barthilas laughed contemptuously in Tirion's face.

The strange drumming sound grew louder and was joined by newer, stronger drums. At that point most of the onlookers became aware of the ominous beating of the drums as well. They were startled to note that the unnerving sounds were getting closer. The few women and children who were present began to cover their ears and huddle together in fear and confusion. The attendant guards moved to the edges of the square, searching for whatever was causing the incessant drumming.

"The future of our people is no longer your concern," Barthilas said coldly. "I rule Hearthglen now, Tirion. And as long as I do, I swear that there will never be peace with the orcs! On my parents' departed souls, I swear that every last orc in Lordaeron will burn for what they've done!"

Tirion was shocked by Barthilas' words. There was no reasoning with the young Paladin. He had given over completely to his rage and grief.

The mighty drums thundered all around the panicked square as Barthilas ordered his troops to strike.

"Kill the orc now! Kill them both!" he yelled in fury. His roar was cut short as a crude, razor-sharp spear tore through his chest. Barthilas' blood splattered across the gallows as a legion of shadowy shapes leapt down into the square from the surrounding rooftops. Furious, high-pitched war cries filled the air as the savage orcs waded into the unsuspecting defenders of Stratholme. The mighty war-drums thundered through the panic-gripped square.

Tirion sat stunned as Barthilas slumped to the ground in a heap. Instinctively, he reached out to help the young Paladin, but Barthilas spat at him and waved him off.

"You've brought this down upon us," the young Paladin said shakily as blood poured from his mouth. His wild, hate-filled eyes locked on Tirion. "I always knew you'd betray . . ." was all he managed before he fell facedown on the blood-soaked scaffolding. The crude orcish spear stuck up from his back like a ship's mast.

Tirion immediately snapped to attention. He threw down the sledgehammer and hauled Eitrigg up on his feet. Leaning the heavy orc on his shoulder, Tirion led Eitrigg away from the gallows. Tirion couldn't imagine how the orcish force had bypassed the city's outer defenses. Typically, the orcs had always assaulted their targets head-on. Yet, as he watched the battle unfold around him, he saw that the stealthy orcs were using the rooftops and surrounding catwalks to their advantage.

Knights and footmen ran forward to meet the orcish onslaught as all hell erupted in the public square. Tirion kept his head down and headed for the side street he had used earlier. The sounds of clashing steel and the combatants' furious shouts of rage and pain mixed, creating a maddening din above Stratholme. Tirion tried to shut out the noise and concentrate on staying alive. All around him was a killing ground. Mighty orc warriors hacked at their enemies with great war axes while others hurled long, wicked spears with startling precision. A few orcs, garbed in what looked like wolf furs, charged forward and lifted their hands to the heavens. Before Tirion knew what they were doing, lightning arced down from the darkened sky and struck the front ranks of the human force. Charred human bodies and large chunks of stone flew through the air and rained down upon the chaotic battlefield. Stunned by the savage elemental attack, the remaining human ranks were forced to pull back before the orcs' awesome wrath.

Tirion was surprised to see that the orcs were working in unison to outmaneuver and flank the frayed human defenders. To his memory, orcs had never been so singularly united in battle. Despite their apparent cunning and skill, the orcs' numbers were few. Tirion wondered what the orcs were after, recklessly attacking a defended human city with such an insubstantial force. Soon every soldier in Stratholme would be bearing down on the square. *The outnumbered orcs wouldn't stand a chance against a fully armored garrison,* he thought.

Despite the chaos around him, Tirion managed to reach the edge of the square and escape down a small alley. Hefting Eitrigg's deadweight up once more, Tirion turned to take a last look at the ensuing carnage. He caught sight of an enormous orc, dressed in a full suit of black plate armor. The orc carried a mighty warhammer that resembled those used by the Paladins—except for the fact that the orc's hammer seemed to be ignited by living lightning. The dark orc waded his way through the ardent human defenders as if they were harmless children. It smashed and battered everyone that came near it with a calm lethality—all the while shouting sharp commands to its warriors. For a moment, Tirion could only watch in amazement and horror. The mighty orc leader was unlike any he had witnessed before. Tirion snapped out of his daze and hurriedly made his way out of the beleaguered city with Eitrigg in his arms.

With a supreme effort, Tirion succeeded in hauling Eitrigg out of the city and into the surrounding woods. Looking back, he could see that a number of fires had been started in various parts of the city. He could hear screams and clashing weapons even from this distance. Apparently the cunning orcs were attempting to distract and divide the human forces. Tirion noted that whoever the orcs' leader was, he was far more clever than any chieftain he'd ever heard of.

Wearily, Tirion laid Eitrigg down on the leafy ground and crouched next to him. He tried to calm himself and think clearly about the situation. He couldn't account for the orcs' unprecedented attack on the city, and wondered if the creatures had come to free Eitrigg, just as he had. Whatever the case, he was glad that they'd come. He was genuinely sorry to see so many of his brethren fall before the orcs, but at least he'd accomplished what he'd set out to do. Eitrigg was alive. And, as frayed and thin as it was, Tirion's precious honor was still intact.

Eitrigg lay silently on the matted forest floor. Tirion bent down to check the orc's pulse. Hopefully the orc was just exhausted from his trying ordeal, he mused. Gasping in panic, Tirion realized that Eitrigg's heart had stopped. The beating the humans had given the orc had obviously done serious internal damage. If he didn't do something quickly, he knew that Eitrigg would die. Instinctively, he placed his hands on Eitrigg's chest and prayed for the healing powers of the Light to wash over the battered orc. *Surely he was still strong enough to heal even these grievous wounds?*

Slowly, a feeling of dread spread through Tirion's heart. Nothing was happening. He bowed his head in defeat, remembering that he had been excommunicated from the Light. *This can't be happening*, he thought miserably. He could almost sense Eitrigg's life ebbing away into nothingness.

"No!" Tirion growled in hopelessness. "You will not die, Eitrigg! Do you hear me? You will not die on me!" he yelled at the comatose orc. Once again he slapped his hands on the orc's chest and concentrated with all of his will. *"By the grace of the Light, may your brethren be healed."* The phrase wafted through his mind repeatedly as he reached deep for the power that lurked somewhere within his spirit. *"In its grace he will be made anew."*

The Light could not be taken from him, he insisted. Men could strip him of his armor and titles, they could take away his home and his wealth—but the Light would always be within him. *It had to be.*

Slowly, Tirion felt a searing heat rising within his body. It filled his center with strength and light that snaked out toward his limbs. He almost cried out in joy as the familiar energies raced through his hands and engulfed the orc's ravaged body. Tirion felt as if he were floating on air. The strength and purity of the Light flooded his being and cascaded out through his body like a halo of holy fire. Awed and humbled by the reawakened power, Tirion opened his eyes and saw that a warm, golden glow had enveloped Eitrigg. He watched in amazement as the bruises on the orc's body healed before his very eyes. Even the infected laceration on the orc's leg sealed up as if it had never been.

The soothing energies subsided and Tirion dropped to the ground in exhaustion. He lay there for a few moments panting, attempting to keep his head from spinning. With a snort, Eitrigg sat up and looked around frantically. The old orc was pale and obviously weak, but his eyes were bright and alert. Eitrigg quickly sprung up in a defensive crouch and sniffed the air. He scanned the immediate tree line for any signs of danger and seemed to find none. Eitrigg looked down and saw Tirion lying near him. He shifted back on his haunches doubtfully and stared at the exhausted human with surprise.

"Human?" Eitrigg asked. "What's happened? How did we get here?" Tirion got to his knees and patted the orc reassuringly on the shoulder.

"We're outside the city, Eitrigg," Tirion said evenly. "You're safe for the time being. If we're both very lucky, there'll be no more hangings in our immediate future." Eitrigg grunted and looked at Tirion doubtfully. He glanced down at his big green hands and traced his fingers over where his wounds had been.

"This power you have, human," the orc began, "did it heal my wounds?"

Tirion nodded. "Yes. You told me before that pain is a good teacher. Well, you were about to have your final lesson. It would have been a rough one, I think," Tirion said jokingly.

Eitrigg grinned and slapped Tirion on the back. "Perhaps I've studied enough, after all," the orc replied wryly. The old orc coughed a few times and eased himself back down to a sitting position. The strain of the past few days proved to be too much for his tired old body, and he passed out in a heap. Although he was healed, Tirion knew from experience that the orc would be weak for days.

He was surprised to hear a sudden rustling in the dense branches and undergrowth all around him. Looking around frantically, he braced himself for danger. Slowly—ominously—the shadows of the trees began to move and shift in every direction. Huge, dark shapes took form and moved forward, encircling the sleeping orc and the nervous human.

Twelve in all, the creatures wore loose armor plates and tattered leathers that covered only the most vital areas of their muscular, green-skinned bodies. Feathers, multiple tribal trinkets and bone necklaces adorned the mighty orcish warriors who emerged with catlike grace from the shadowy tree line. Their bulging arms and bestial, tusked faces were marked by jagged, primitive tattoos that augmented their already feral appearance. They carried broad-bladed axes and heavy warblades with such practiced ease that the weapons appeared to be natural extensions of their bodies. Tirion was overwhelmed by the orcs' savage presence. He was most disconcerted to see the change in their beady eyes—no longer were the orcs' eyes ablaze with depravity and hate; they were cool and alert, showing an intelligence and wit that he could scarcely credit to them.

Tirion held his breath and made sure not to make any sudden moves. For all he knew, the orcs might think that he had attacked Eitrigg somehow. The orcs simply stood, staring at the two on the ground as if waiting for a command. Panic grated across Tirion's nerves. After all he had tried to do, he'd be damned if he just let himself be hacked to bits in the wilds. Yet no matter what he tried, he knew that he'd last less than a minute against such fierce warriors.

Suddenly, a larger form emerged from behind the warriors. A number of the orcs stepped aside silently as their leader made his way forward. Tirion gasped. It was the orc chieftain he had seen during the battle. Being this close, Tirion could see that the gargantuan orc's black plate armor was trimmed with bronze runic inscriptions. Never before had Tirion ever seen an orc in full armor. The sight was both impressive and chilling. The orc's mighty stone warhammer seemed to be as old as the world itself. The creature's black hair was tied into long braids that hung down over its armored torso. Its green face was somewhat less bestial than the other orcs', and its fierce, intelligent eyes were a striking blue. Tirion knew that this was no ordinary orc.

The mighty creature stepped forward and kneeled down beside Eitrigg. Tirion tensed. He remembered that Eitrigg had abandoned his duties as an orcish warrior. *Perhaps these orcs had come to punish him?*

Fighting back his fear, Tirion inched forward, intending to defend Eitrigg if necessary. The large orc gave Tirion a fierce, threatening glare—warning the human to stay put and remain silent. Surrounded as he was by the chieftain's guards, Tirion was forced to comply with the orc's silent command. Seeing that he would be obeyed, the mysterious orc placed his large hand on Eitrigg's head and closed his eyes, concentrating. Eitrigg's eyes fluttered open and focused on the dark orc looming over him. The mysterious orc's features softened slightly.

"You are Eitrigg of the Blackrock clan, are you not?" the orc asked in the human tongue. Tirion raised his eyebrows in surprise. *Did all of the orcs speak so clearly?* he wondered.

Shakily, Eitrigg looked around at the other orcs and nodded his weary head. "I am he," he said in a low tone.

The larger orc nodded and straightened. "I thought so. It's taken me a long time to track you down, old one," he said evenly.

Eitrigg sat up and looked upon the larger orc intently. "Your face is familiar to me, warrior. But you are far too young to be . . ." Eitrigg studied the orc's strong features for a moment and said, "Who are you?"

The orc nodded slightly and stood up to his full height. The gathered orcs seemed to straighten and lift their chins high as their leader spoke. "I am known as Thrall, old one. I am Warchief of the Horde," he said proudly. Eitrigg's jaw dropped wide open. Tirion stared in awe. This, obviously, was the upstart Warchief of which Dathrohan had spoken.

"I have heard of you," Tirion said, his voice heavy with contempt. He saw the surrounding orc guards stiffen and ready their weapons. Apparently they didn't take well to their leader being insulted. The orc turned to stare at the former Paladin in surprise. "And what exactly have you heard, human?"

Tirion held the orc's fierce gaze. "I have heard that you plan to rebuild the Horde and renew your war against my people," he said coolly.

"You are partially correct," Thrall began, with mild amusement evident in his tone. "I *am* rebuilding the Horde. You can be sure that my people will not remain in chains for long. However, I have no interest in making war for war's sake. Those dark days are over."

"Those days are over?" Tirion asked skeptically. "I just watched as you and your warriors hacked your way through Stratholme."

Thrall met the human's accusing stare levelly. "You presume much, human. We only attacked the city to reclaim one of our own. Times have changed. Your kingdoms and your people mean nothing to me. I seek only to finish my father's work and find a new homeland for my people," Thrall replied evenly.

Eitrigg's eyes were wide with sudden recognition. "Your father's work?" he sputtered excitedly. "I knew I recognized your face, warrior! You are the son of Durotan!" Thrall merely nodded once, never taking his piercing eyes off Tirion. Eitrigg was beside himself with joy.

"Could it be, after all these years?" he asked, flabbergasted. He looked around at the orcs' faces, searching for further confirmation. Their proud, stone-like faces revealed nothing.

Thrall turned his back on Tirion and knelt beside Eitrigg. "I have come to bring you home, old one," he said warmly. "I'm sorry it took us so long to find you, but we've been somewhat busy these past months. I have already freed a number of clans, but I need wise veterans like you to help me teach them of the old ways. Your people have need of you again, brave Eitrigg."

The old orc shook his head in shocked disbelief. He stared into Thrall's sharp blue eyes and found hope within their shining depths. After years of dispirited isolation, his heart was filled with pride again. Slowly, Eitrigg began to believe that there could be a future for his people after all.

"I will follow you, son of Durotan," Eitrigg said proudly. "I will help heal our people in any way that I can." Thrall nodded once and placed his hand on the old orc's shoulder.

Casting a sidelong glance at the surrounding guards, Tirion cautiously stood up and faced Thrall. "Eitrigg told me of your father—and of his fate. He must have been a great hero to elicit such devotion from his son."

Thrall's face was expressionless as he replied, "My people have always held that it is a son's duty to finish his father's work." Tirion nodded sadly. He wondered if Taelan would ever share that sentiment. *Probably not*, he concluded. *What boy would ever be proud of having a disgraced exile as a father? More than likely, Taelan would only revile me for what I've done.*

Thrall motioned toward Eitrigg and shouted a number of short guttural commands in the orcish tongue. Tirion looked around as the guards moved forward, unsure as to what to expect. *Would the orcs kill him? Would they let him go?* A number of warriors knelt down beside Eitrigg and hooked their arms under his shoulders. Tirion looked back at Thrall, questioningly.

The young Warchief smirked knowingly and said, "You risked your life to save our brother, human. We have no quarrel with you. You are free to go, so long as you do not follow us."

Tirion exhaled in relief and watched as the orc warriors gently gathered Eitrigg up. Thrall gave Tirion an orcish salute and, without a second glance, turned to leave. Many of the orcs had already disappeared back into the densely shadowed woods. Tirion shook his head as if in a daze. A strong hand grabbed hold of his arm. He looked down and saw that it was Eitrigg. The old orc had a look of peace and fulfillment upon his gnarled face.

"We are both bound by blood and honor, *brother*. I will not forget you," Eitrigg said.

Tirion smiled and raised his hand to his heart as the orcs led Eitrigg away. He stood for a moment, watching them go. The sounds of battle still echoed from within Stratholme's walls. He decided that he had better make himself scarce before the human troops arrived.

With a silent prayer to the Light, Tirion Fordring turned his back on Stratholme and set out to find solace within the perilous, uncharted wildlands of Lordaeron.

EIGHT
A Perfect Circle

Sunlight cascaded down through the open skylight in the cathedral's vaulted ceiling. Twenty-year-old Taelan Fordring stood upon an ornately carved dais and basked in the warmth and splendor of the holy Light. Large silver plates of armor adorned his broad shoulders. Beneath the plates, a carefully embroidered dark blue stole hung from his neck and streamed down his chest. He held a mighty, two-handed silver warhammer in his hands which, he was told, had once belonged to his father.

Taelan was a strong, handsome young man. Bathed in the Light as he was, he seemed almost transcendent. An aged Archbishop stood before Taelan holding a large, leather-bound tome. The old man had the light of joy in his eyes as he addressed Taelan.

"Do you, Taelan Fordring, vow to uphold the honor and codes of the Order of the Silver Hand?" he asked.

"I do," Taelan replied sincerely.

"Do you vow to walk in the grace of the Light and spread its wisdom to your fellow man?"

"I do," Taelan said shakily. He was overcome with a thousand different emotions at once and had to fight to get a grip on himself. This was the moment he had waited for as long as he could remember. He glanced around quickly and saw his mother standing proudly in attendance.

Though years of hardship and loneliness had streaked her soft, golden hair with silver strands, Karandra was as beautiful and radiant as she had ever been. She marveled at seeing Taelan being anointed as a Paladin. She wished that Tirion could have been present to see his son follow in his footsteps.

"Do you vow to vanquish evil wherever it be found, and protect the weak and innocent with your very life?" the Archbishop asked Taelan in a ritualistic tone.

Taelan swallowed hard and nodded while saying, "By my honor, I do."

The Archbishop continued to speak to the assembly but, overcome as he was, Taelan could not hear his words. Oblivious to the ceremony proceeding around him, he reached into the pocket of his ceremonial cassock and took hold of the rolled, tattered parchment that he always carried with him. It was the note his father had left him before he was exiled from the kingdom. Taelan couldn't count how many times he had read the tattered letter over the years, but he had memorized every line, every subtle stroke of the quill. He recalled one of the last passages in his mind.

My dear Taelan,

By the time you're old enough to read this, I will have been gone a long time. I can't adequately express how painful it is to have to leave you and your mother behind, but I suppose that sometimes life forces you to make difficult decisions. I fear that you'll no doubt hear many bad things about me as you grow older—that people will look upon my actions and condemn them as evil. I fear that others will look down upon you for the decisions I have made.

I won't try to explain everything that's happened in this note, but I need you to know that what I did, I did for honor's sake. Honor is an important part of what makes us men, Taelan. Our words and our deeds must count for something in this world. I know it's asking a great deal, but I hope that you will understand that someday.

I want you to know that I love you dearly and that I'll always carry you close to my heart.

Your life and your deeds will be my redemption, son. You are my pride and my hope. Be a good man. Be a hero.

Goodbye.

Taelan came out of his reverie just in time to hear the Archbishop say:

"Then arise, Taelan Fordring—Paladin defender of Lordaeron. Welcome to the Order of the Silver Hand."

Just as it had in his boyhood dreams, the entire assembly erupted in cheers. The joyous din echoed throughout the vast cathedral, drowning out every other noise. His friends and comrades clapped and hollered in congratulations. Almost everyone gathered in the cathedral was on their feet joining in the revelry.

Beaming with pride, Taelan turned and smiled warmly at his mother and his old friend, Arden, who stood a few paces behind her. The aged guardsman, who had watched over and protected Taelan for nearly fifteen years, smiled back proudly. Arden marveled at how much Taelan resembled his father. He knew that Tirion would have been proud.

The crowd surged up to congratulate Taelan and welcome him to the Order.

Arden had turned to make his way toward the exit, when, out of the corner of his eye, he saw a familiar figure moving through the crowd. The tall, nondescript figure wore a green, hooded travel-cloak and weather-stained leathers. But Arden would have recognized the gray-haired man's piercing green eyes anywhere. For a brief second, he locked eyes with the aged stranger.

"Tirion," Arden whispered under his breath.

The stranger smiled knowingly at Arden and raised a stiff hand to his brow in salute. He then pulled his hood low over his face and promptly slipped out the back of the cathedral.

Looking back at Taelan, Arden said, "Like father, like son."